Such
Devoted
Sisters

VIKING

Such & Devoted Sisters

Eileen Goudge

VIKING
Published by the Penguin Group
Viking Penguin, a division of Penguin Books USA Inc.,
375 Hudson Street, New York, New York 10014, U.S.A.
Penguin Books Ltd, 27 Wrights Lane,
London W8 5TZ, England
Penguin Books Australia Ltd, Ringwood,
Victoria, Australia
Penguin Books Canada Ltd, 10 Alcorn Avenue, Suite 300,
Toronto, Ontario, Canada M4V 3B2
Penguin Books (N.Z.) Ltd, 182–190 Wairau Road,
Auckland 10, New Zealand

Penguin Books Ltd, Registered Offices:
Harmondsworth, Middlesex, England

First published in 1992 by Viking Penguin,
a division of Penguin Books USA Inc.

1 2 3 4 5 6 7 8 9 10

Grateful acknowledgment is made for permission to reprint
excerpts from the following copyrighted works:
"Love the One You're With," words and music by Stephen Stills.
© 1970 by Gold Hill Music.
Sesame Street theme song, by permission of Children's
Television Workshop.

LIBRARY OF CONGRESS CATALOGING IN PUBLICATION DATA
Goudge, Eileen.
Such devoted sisters / Eileen Goudge.
p. cm.
ISBN 0-670-83954-X
I. Title.
PS3557.O838S8   1992
813'.54—dc20   91-29103

Printed in the United States of America
Set in Fournier
Designed by Ann Gold

To my dear agent and even dearer husband,
Albert Zuckerman, who gave this book its legs . . .
and me the heart to write it.

And to my own devoted sister, Patty Goudge.

ACKNOWLEDGMENTS

What could be more fun than researching chocolate? Not all of the data I collected ended up on these pages. Some of it, I confess, was eaten. But for what you see, I wish to thank the following people:

Robert Linxe of La Maison du Chocolat, both for his time and his divine truffles. The afternoon spent in the basement kitchen of his rue du Faubourg St-Honoré shop was truly a celestial experience.

Beverly Levine of Le Chocolatier Manon, who was so generous, and gave me an insider's view of chocolate retailing . . . and a good reason not to diet.

Martha Saucier of Li-Lac Chocolates, for showing me around her Village shop with its kitchen in back, which has been turning out delicious chocolates and other treats for more than half a century.

Bernard Bloom of Teuscher Chocolates, which makes the world's best champagne truffle.

Deborah Marsicek, my fellow chocophile, who generously provided me with reams of information about chocolate that she has collected over the years.

Lora Brody, chocolate consultant and intrepid soul, for whom turning out hundreds of chocolate tortes and touring cacao plantations in 110-degree heat is, of course, a piece of cake. Thanks to her for vetting this book, and for introducing me to the best flourless chocolate cake I've ever tasted.

Rabbi Ralph Shain, for his help with the Hebrew terminology.

John Robinson, former U.S. Customs agent, and Nancy McTiernan, Deputy Director, Office of Commercial Fraud, for their assistance in giving me a clear picture of the pitfalls of importing confectionary goods.

Victoria Skurnik and Susan Ginsburg, for their time, expertise, and moral support.

Catherine Jacobes, my loyal assistant, whose energy, enthusiasm, good humor, and adeptness at keeping distractions at bay made it possible for me to finish this book in two years instead of five.

Pamela Dorman, my editor at Viking, for her clear eye in both editing and following through on every level, from outline to publication.

And, last but not least, I'd like to thank Dale Stine, my gorgeous and merciless trainer, who flogged me into working off all those calories!

Prologue

And every woe a tear can claim
Except an erring sister's shame.
—Lord Byron

Dolly Drake got off the bus at Sunset and Vine. In the heat-shimmery air, the sidewalk seemed to heave as she stepped down onto it in an almost seesawing motion, as if she were standing on the deck of a ship at sea. Her stomach pitched and her head throbbed. Before her, the great curved flank of the NBC building reflected the sun back at her in a blast of white light that struck her eyes like hot needles.

Must be coming down with something, she thought. *A touch of flu . . . or maybe the curse.*

But, no, she wasn't sick, she realized with a pang. This was no flu bug . . . it was a whole lot worse. She felt sick in her soul. Up all night with her own tired brain running 'round in circles like a moon-crazed hound, not daring to decide which way to turn.

Dolly thought of the letter in her purse. Looking down at the shiny patent-leather bag looped over her arm, squiggles of thread sticking up from its frayed strap, she saw the letter as clearly as if she'd had Superman's X-ray vision—the long white business envelope, folded in half, then again for good measure.

Inside was a single mimeographed sheet, minutes of a meeting of the Common Man Society. The date at the top was June 16, 1944. Ten years ago.

So what? she thought. A pissant fellow-traveller club that broke up years ago, with a bunch of members nobody ever heard of. Except for one. A faded, but still legible scrawl on the bottom line. A name almost as familiar to millions of good Americans as their own. A name Senator Joe McCarthy back in Washington, D.C., would surely want to pounce on. The bottom line read:

3

Respectfully submitted,
Eveline Dearfield
1233 La Brea Blvd.
Los Angeles, Cal.
Recording Secretary

But that, of course, was long before Eveline got shortened to Eve and moved from La Brea to Bel Air. Before she won her Oscar and married hotshot director Dewey Cobb. Before she stopped giving two hoots about her sister, Dolly.

Dolly sucked her breath in, a lungful of air that tasted like melting tar. She thought of the air-conditioned Cadillac Eve rode around in these days, white as a virgin bride with cherry-red seats and a roof that folded down. Dolly imagined what it would feel like to be in that Caddy now, gliding up Sunset Boulevard with her hair blowing in the warm breeze. People rubbernecking to gape in admiration and envy and wonder to themselves, *Who is she? Somebody famous, I bet.*

A car horn blared, and the image was bumped rudely away. Then a group of would-be actresses—too young and blond and doe-eyed to be anything else—jostled her as they walked past, gossiping in low tones, sunlight skimming along their silk-stockinged legs. One of them wore a pair that was slightly mismatched, the result of careful scrimping, no doubt. Dolly smiled grimly, and thought of the can of Campbell's chicken noodle that awaited her back at her Westwood bungalow. Mixed with two cans of water instead of one, along with a good dollop of catsup and a handful of saltines, a can of soup filled you up right fine. Well . . . almost. And maybe she'd even treat herself to a Hershey bar for dessert. Chocolate was the one thing that almost always lifted her spirits.

But right now the thought of food was making her stomach knot up. Give Eve the slap in the face she deserved? Could she? But how could she deliberately hurt—maybe ruin—her own little sister?

In her mind, travelling back through the dusty miles and years to Clemscott, Dolly could still hear Preacher Daggett thundering from the pulpit, *Put on the armor of God that ye may stand against the devil. . . .*

Yeah, right, Dolly thought. And who was standing up for me while little Evie was out snatching up every decent role I went after?

And my guy too . . . a town full of men, and she had to get her hooks into mine.

Tears started in the back of her throat. Hard tears that burned like acid. She gave the corner of each eye a swipe with the heel of her hand and sniffed deeply. Damned if she'd get caught bawling in public, showing up at Syd's with her eyes all red and puffy. If Mama-Jo had taught her one thing in this life, it was to keep your dirty linen in your own hamper.

Dolly crossed the street and headed north up Vine. The hot air seemed to drag at her; she felt as if she were not so much walking but *plowing* her way through something solid and viscous. Would she *ever* get there? Shading her eyes against the sun as she was passing Castle's Cameras, she glanced up at the Gruen clock atop the ABC building, and saw that it was nearly two-fifteen. Her appointment with Syd had been for two. Late again, she thought. Well, that was the story of her life, wasn't it? Always missing one boat or another.

She stepped up her pace, her open-toed pumps flogging the hot pavement, her head pulsing like a marching band's drum. Syd got mad when she was late; he hated to be kept waiting. Then she thought: *To hell with Syd, that's what I pay him for.* Except, when you got right down to it, an agent's ten percent of nothing was . . . well, nothing. Her last picture, *Dames at Large,* hadn't even gone into general release, and since then there had been only a couple of walk-ons and one TV commercial.

That's the ticket, all right. Dolly Drake winds up with zero, while little Evie has a brass star and handprints in the sidewalk outside Grauman's.

And now Val, too.

Dolly had reached the Century Plaza Hotel, its windows turned to mirrors by the sun. Briefly, she saw herself reflected, a pretty woman in her late twenties—she'd be thirty next May—bottle-blond hair unravelling from the combs that held it up in back. A bit on the plump side maybe, wearing a flowery-pink rayon dress, her best. The sun winked off the safety pin fastened to the underside of her hem. She winced. It shows, she thought. No matter how hard you try to hide it, down-and-out always shows.

She thought again of the envelope in her purse, and felt her stomach turn. She'd received it in yesterday's mail, along with a note from Syd. *Thought you'd be interested. An old "friend" of your sister's sent me this. Call me.* First time she'd ever heard from him through the mail. His whole life was on the phone. But this was different. Syd had a real ax of his own to grind. Six years ago, Eve had dumped him—and not only as her agent, but a week before they were to be married. Syd had gone on a bender for two weeks, not seeing anyone, not even answering his phone, which for him was like cutting out his tongue. Since then, there had been a new, sour edge to him.

Dolly knew for a fact that the last thing in the world Eve wanted was to overthrow the U.S. government. *She's about as Red as Mamie Eisenhower,* she thought. Probably some casting director or assistant producer took her to the meeting on a date and then asked her to take some notes. By the next day, she must have forgotten all about it. Otherwise, wouldn't she have at least mentioned it to Dolly?

But things were so different from the war years. That wonderful sense of people reaching out to each other, working together to win, was gone. Now you didn't know who to trust. Anyone might stab you in the back, especially here in Hollywood. Anybody who had been the slightest shade of pink, or who was just plain accused of it, even big-time directors and producers, was getting fired and blacklisted. No work anywhere in town. Like a silent death. But dying had to be better. At least at funerals people said nice things about you.

And now, if she went along with this, one of those poor blotted-out souls could be Eve.

One thing about McCarthy, he loved his headlines. And the bigger the name he savaged, the more press he got. Eve was big, all right. And the bigger they were, the harder they fell.

Dolly felt a flash of hot bitterness. *Serve her right, wouldn't it just? Show her what it's like down on the dirty pavement with the rest of us. And then what would Val Carrera think of her?*

Dolly clutched her purse, as if afraid the damning document it contained might fly right out of her hands. All night she had wrestled over what to do, and now she knew why. She hadn't wanted to face the truth, but there it was. *Did Eve think twice before sticking a knife in my back?*

Dolly, her mouth set in a grim line, turned west onto Hollywood Boulevard and into the cool marble lobby of the office building on the corner. Well, she wouldn't definitely make up her mind until she'd talked it over with Syd. When she called him yesterday, he'd said he had something to tell her, something really big. But, Lord in heaven, what could be bigger than this?

"It'd be like . . . murder," Dolly said.

Seated on the low Scandinavian couch opposite Syd's kidney-shaped desk, her sweat drying in the tepid airstream blowing from the fan on the windowsill, she fingered the envelope she had taken from her purse, regarding it the way she would a nasty little dog that's quite capable of nipping you. Here, for some reason, it seemed more real . . . and more unthinkable . . . than it had on the way over. Her heart was beating fast, as if she'd climbed the four flights instead of taking the elevator.

She looked about Syd's compact office, marvelling at its lack of clutter—no messy shelves piled with scripts, no overflowing trays of unanswered mail, no ashtrays full of butts. Just pale-green walls, every inch of them taken up with framed photos—mostly of Eve Dearfield. Eve, hand on hip, posing in front of Sleeping Beauty's castle at the just-opened Disneyland. Eve, crouched down in front of Grauman's, hands planted in wet cement. Eve, flashing an Ipana smile, at the wheel of the brand-new Bel Air convertible presented to her by Universal.

A goddamn museum, she thought. Eve might have walked out on Syd, but he sure hadn't let go of her.

Dolly stared at him. The kind of handsome Mama-Jo would've called "slick as snake oil" . . . except he was starting to dry up a little around the edges, gray at the temples, a row of tiny pleats along his upper lip. Right now, with his feet propped on an open desk drawer, long legs clothed in gray tropical-weight serge, his brown eyes boring into her, Dolly felt as if she were staring down the twin barrels of Daddy's twelve-gauge Winchester. Syd's eyes, set alongside a jutting Roman nose, seemed almost gleeful.

Definitely a grade B agent, maybe not even that, but still she couldn't in all fairness blame him for the lousy turn her career had taken—the halfway decent box office of *Dames in Chains* notwith-standing. Judging him as a man, she'd as soon sleep with a side-winder.

But her feeling toward him at this particular moment was much stronger than mere distaste. Clutching the horrid document he'd placed in her care, Dolly hated the son of a bitch across from her —grinning like an egg-suck dog in a henhouse—for knowing her heart the way a local boy knows the hidden back roads of his hometown. And for giving her a choice she never should've had.

Why didn't she just stand up and walk out?

But he'd said he had something important to tell her. She'd come this far; might as well stick around to hear the rest.

"Why me?" she pressed. "Why send that thing to *me* when you could've been the big patriot and presented it personally to Senator McCarthy . . . if you hate Eve that bad?"

"You got it all wrong, this is business, *your* business, nothing personal on my end," he said evenly, betrayed only by a cold flicker of his eyes. "Now you're ready to talk, am I right? Are we having a conversation here?"

She leaned forward, trembling a little, bracing her elbows against her knees. Her stomach was rolling again.

"Okay, but don't you forget she's my *sister,* for God's sake!" Dolly thought of her niece, too, Eve's little Annie. Both of them her flesh and blood.

"First, hear me out," he said, his tone reasonable, soothing even, "then you make up your own mind." He waited until she'd settled back against the spongy sofa. "That's better. Dolly sweetheart, you know what's wrong with you? You're nice. And in this business, nice is just another word for stupid. Nice and a nickel will buy you a phone call. What it *won't* get you is the lead in *Devil May Care.*"

Dolly saw his mouth move, heard the words, but there was an infinite lapse before she made the connection. Then it hit her like a double bourbon straight up. *Devil May Care:* Maggie Dumont, the part every star in town was angling for. But Eve had it sewed up.

Anger flashed through her. The bastard! Where did he get off dangling this in front of her? How dare he suggest even for *one second* that a plum like that could possibly be within her reach?

Then she saw that he actually looked serious.

"What are you saying?" she asked.

"I'm saying that if you want it, I'm eighty-eight percent certain I could get it for you."

Dolly felt something snap like a sprung garter inside her, an

almost dead hope kicking to life. Then it came to her—*Devil* was
Preminger's. And last year it was Eve starring in his picture that had
gotten him that Best Director Oscar.

"Even if Eve got knocked out of the running, what makes you
think Preminger would consider me?" she demanded. "I was up for
Storm Alley too, remember? You were even negotiating terms. And
Eve somehow got it, and for probably a hundred times what they
would have paid me."

"Exactly my point. Preminger, he'd turn handstands for Eve
Dearfield. He's crazy about her. In his mind, she *is* Maggie Dumont.
Think, Dolly, sweetie. Put yourself in Otto's shoes. If he can't have
Eve, what's the next best thing?"

Could that be true, Dolly wondered? No question, she and Eve
did look alike. But if she could pin her downfall on any one thing,
that would be it. Only sixteen months apart, practically twins, except
that Eve was beautiful, and she was . . . well, okay, pretty. In the
framed photo above Syd's head, she saw Eve's hair, naturally blond,
almost platinum. Hers, under its honey-colored dye job, was just
plain dishwater. And where Eve's eyes were a deep, startling indigo,
Dolly's were the washed-out blue of faded denim. It was as if an
artist had done a rough sketch, then seeing where he could improve,
had painted an exquisite portrait. *I'd have been better off ugly . . . that
way there'd have been no comparing.* The only thing she had over Eve
was her tits—a perfect 38D. Until senior year at Clemscott High,
she was the one who had all the boys chasing after her like goats
in rut.

No, she thought. No way would Preminger cast a B-movie
lookalike when he could have the real thing. But if Eve were out of
the way . . .

Suppose Syd was right. He wouldn't be sitting here without
taking two dozen phone calls if he hadn't put out some feelers and
gotten some solid feedback. Why else would he be spending his
valuable time with *her?* He might not be loaded with hot properties,
but he had clients working all over radio and TV. Even so, a deal
like this, in addition to the cash, would put them both on the front
page of the trades; and it could just turn out to be her big break.
Syd had a decent enough client list, he had moxie to spare, but what
he didn't have was a star.

So, yeah, sure, Syd was looking to make a buck, make a

splash . . . but he also had to be remembering how Eve had dumped him like a load of cowshit off the back of a pickup.

"I could pretend I never saw this." She swallowed hard, and tapped the envelope against her stockinged knee. The tadpole in her stomach had become a bullfrog, huge and feisty. "What's it to me if Eve joined some pinko club way back when? She probably thought she was helping save the world—settin' around some smoky back room listening to a bunch of wet-eared wingers. She'd have gotten tired of *that* real fast." Dolly felt a thin layer of frost form over her heart. "Eve's for Eve, and you can take *that* to the bank."

She thought of Val, surprised by the keenness of the ache she felt. It had happened almost a year ago, and she hadn't known him more than a few weeks to begin with . . . certainly not long enough to go around moaning about a broken heart.

It was *Eve* who had hurt her, she realized. Not Val's double-crossing.

"You could do nothing," Syd answered, as if coolly thinking it all over. His swivel chair gave a little squeal as he leaned back even farther, hooking his long hands behind a head of hair so lush and springy it looked as if he must fertilize it with manure . . . which, considering how full of it he was, wouldn't be too hard. "You *could,* but I don't think you will."

Dolly felt a tightening in her gut. "I still don't get it. Why go to all this bother? Why don't you just send your thirty pieces of silver to Washington yourself? You don't need me."

"You're right, baby doll. I don't need you. It's *you* who needs me."

She found herself standing up, the envelope fluttering from her lap onto the beige carpet. To hell with him; for all the good he was doing her, she might as well be on her own.

"I need you, Syd, like I need two assholes."

The grin was back, but this time cold enough to make her shiver. He hunched forward, palms flat against the desktop, fingers splayed. Heat from his fingertips fogged the spotless glass.

"Dolly, sweetie. You still don't get it, do you?" He spoke softly, but each word hit her like a drop from a melting icicle. "All this time, you thought it was Eve, didn't you? That Eve was better-looking and more talented? But that's not it, baby. What Eve has that you don't is fangs. She'd *kill* to get a part, any part. You, Dolly, you're too soft. In this business, you've gotta think like a barracuda. Take it where you can get it. Shit, you don't think Jane Russell was fucking Howard Hughes for his *dick*, do you?" He paused, waiting for her to absorb all this; then he got up and walked around to where she'd dropped the letter. He picked it up and handed it back to her. He wore a gold signet ring on his pinkie, she saw; in the golden, dusty light that slanted through the venetian blinds, it seemed to be winking at her. "Show me how much you want this, baby. Show me you'd do *anything*, and you'll be halfway there. Then"—he smiled—"if something should happen to Eve, like she gets sick all of a sudden, or runs off to Acapulco with that stud of hers . . . or, say she just happens to get blacklisted—well then, what do you think Otto's gonna say when you walk into his office looking damn near enough like Eve to be her twin?"

Dolly only half heard him. Her mind suddenly was elsewhere. Clear as a Technicolor movie, she was seeing two bleary-eyed, scrawny girls stepping off a Greyhound bus—Doris and Evie Burdock, come all the way from Clemscott, Kentucky—lugging a single battered cardboard suitcase between them, giggling, punch-drunk with exhaustion and high spirits. She could hear Eve's high sweet voice ringing across the years: *It's just you and me from now on, Dorrie, like Mutt and Jeff. We'll always have each other . . . nothing will ever come between us. . . .*

Though they didn't have a hundred bucks between them, things were different back then. Better, in a way she couldn't have explained. Dolly thought of the stuffy one-room apartment they'd shared, overlooking the tarpits, which smelled all summer like the flatulent back end of a bus. No phone even; they'd had to use the super's.

And then, when they'd finally scraped together enough for a deposit on their own phone, the first time it rang, who was it but Syd calling to tell Eve she'd landed a small part in a low-budget picture called *Mrs. Melrose*. Eve, so excited she was practically jumping out of her skin, had splurged on two bottles of pink champagne, and they'd sat up all night, hugging each other, talking, spinning tipsy fantasies about how in just a couple more years they'd both be big movie stars, their names a foot high on marquees all over the country.

And even when times weren't so great, they'd struggled through them together, one week pooling the piddling change she earned waitressing with Eve's salary as a salesclerk in Newberry's to buy one good dress for the two of them for the really important auditions.

Except, come to think of it, wasn't it Eve who always ended up wearing that damn dress?

She squeezed her eyes shut, a pulse throbbing over one eye.

Yeah, she thought, Eve could be fun and sweet . . . and even generous at times. The trouble was, however much she gave, she needed to *get* double. And the things that were out of reach were what she wanted most of all. Eve could no more resist a challenge than the tides could resist a full moon.

Dolly opened her eyes, and saw that Syd was eyeing her with something close to sympathy. That, she decided, was worse than him ranting at her. She stood up.

"I'll think about it," she said.

"You think too much. Anyway, it doesn't have to be the end of the world, you know," he urged, lazily unfolding his lanky frame from the swivel chair, clasping her hand in a moist handshake that made her itch to wipe her palm on her skirt. "This whole McCarthy scare'll probably blow over in a month or two. She might lose out on a few pictures, but knowing Eve, she'll be back on her feet before you can say 'That's a wrap.' "

Maybe he was right, Dolly thought . . . but what if he wasn't? How would she feel knowing she'd ruined Eve's career, and maybe her whole life? No, let him find someone else to take Eve's place, to stick the knife in her back.

Not until she was outside, and halfway to Sunset, did Dolly realize she was still clutching the letter. She thought about tearing it up, and tossing it in a trash can. But she didn't see one, so she shoved it back into her purse and kept walking.

"Aunt Dolly, how did that crack get there?" Annie sat on a high stool in the kitchen of Dolly's Westwood bungalow, swinging her little feet back and forth between its rust-speckled chrome legs.

Dolly, stirring a saucepan at the stove, looked over at her three-and-a-half-year-old niece, then up at where Annie was pointing, at the dark jaggedy spine of a plastered-over crack that bisected the ceiling. In the middle of it was a single bare light bulb that cast an uneven glare over the cramped kitchen nook.

"That? Why, honey, that's what you call history. This old place is a map of every earthquake to hit Los Angeles County since the walls of Jericho came tumbling down."

Eyes glued to the ceiling, Annie licked her lips, a pink sliver of tongue neat as a cat's. "Is it gonna fall down on us?"

"Just don't breathe too hard," Dolly told her with a little laugh, turning her attention back to the stove. But when she looked around again, she saw that Annie's small face wore a look of pinched concern.

Dolly went over and hugged her. "I didn't mean that, honey. 'Course it's not gonna fall down. It's stayed put this long, it oughta hold us at least through dinner."

Looking at Annie now, Dolly saw, not a child, but a grown-up in a three-year-old's body, a somber little lady with her mother's indigo eyes and her father's olive skin and dark, straight hair. She was dressed in a polka-dot pinafore with a white Peter Pan collar ironed stiff as cardboard, and ruffled white socks that clashed oddly with the heavy black orthopedic shoes she wore to correct pigeon toes. *Poor thing, she's had enough fall down on her head to know to duck.* Her father getting killed in that plane crash last year, and Eve taking off for Mexico to film *Bandido* before the flowers on Dewey's grave had hardly wilted. Annie had been raised mostly by nannies—six, or was it seven? Dolly had lost count—the last one had eloped just two days ago with an assistant cameraman going off to Rio on location. Eve had phoned her in a panic. Would she baby-sit tonight? Unless she needed something, Eve hardly ever called her anymore.

Dolly had been on the point of saying no, but then she thought of Annie alone in that big house in Bel Air with some strange baby-sitter, and she'd relented. She adored Annie, and it just clean broke her heart to think of the loneliness the kid had to put up with.

"When's Dearie coming back?" Annie wanted to know. That funny nickname, "Dearie," never "Mama" or "Mommy."

"She didn't say, hon."

"Where did she go?"

"A party, she said." Seeing Annie's expression sadden, she added, "A big star like your mama has to go to a lot of parties. It's like . . . well, sort of like part of the job."

"Is Val part of the job, too?" Annie stopped swinging her legs, and stared at Dolly with enormous ink-blue eyes.

Dolly's heart caught high in her throat. Lord, help us. Out of the mouths of babes.

"Not exactly," she ventured.

"I don't like Val." Annie's face became very tight and small. There was something implacable in her expression.

Dolly remembered how once—Annie couldn't have been much more than a year old—at the Santa Monica pier, where Dolly had taken her for a stroll, a strange man had bent over the carriage and stuck his face right up close to hers. Most babies would've cried and shrunk away. Not Annie. Putting her dimpled baby hands on either side of his face, she'd pushed him emphatically away from her, piping in her clear, even then grownup-sounding voice, "Go 'way!"

"Oh, sugar, Val doesn't mean no harm . . . he's just not your daddy," Dolly soothed, hoping to jolly her out of it, but knowing it wouldn't help much even as she did so. She sighed. "I remember when my own daddy first brought Mama-Jo home, after my real mama died. You know what I did? I bit her."

That brought a tentative smile to Annie's lips. A tiny giggle escaped her. "On the shin, just like Toto?"

"On the cheek, when she tried to kiss me. Just like taking a bite out of an apple."

"She musta been real mad."

"Oh, sure . . . and Daddy whupped me good. But you know something, I wasn't sorry I bit her. After she and Daddy got married, Mama-Jo took away all my dolls and gave me a Bible, saying that idle hands were the devil's tools." She shook her head. "Lord, why am I telling you all this? Come on now, help me set the table. Soup's on. You like butter on your saltines?"

"Nuh-uh," Annie said, sliding off the stool. She headed for the low shelf where the dishes were kept, which was curtained off by a length of faded gingham thumbtacked to the counter above.

"That's good, 'cause there isn't any."

Later, when they'd eaten and the dishes were washed and stacked in the drainer, she tucked Annie into bed in the tiny bedroom, and made up the sleep sofa in the living room for herself. She ought to catch a nap while she could; God knew when Eve would roll in, maybe not until morning.

Dolly changed into an old silk kimono and curled up in the

sagging club chair by the half-open front window, hoping for a breeze as evening cooled into night. Suddenly she felt so heavy and tired. Her eyes drifted shut. Minutes later, she was asleep.

The slamming of a car door awakened her. Swimming up through gritty layers of sleep, she squinted at the glowing face of the clock atop the battered footlocker that served as a coffee table. Five after six. Lord! Her neck felt cramped from being scrunched against the backrest, and her legs tingled as she stretched them.

Pushing aside the frayed nylon curtain, she peered out.

Eve had arrived. She was weaving her way up the cracked concrete pathway with the elaborate caution of someone who's drunk too much. In the milky predawn light, her strapless blue-satin evening dress appeared almost liquid, and her platinum hair gleamed like polished silver. Reaching the front door of Dolly's bungalow, she swayed against the peeling door frame, leaning a pale shoulder against it for support.

"You'll never guess, never, never, never," she burbled excitedly. Her breath smelled sweet and somehow effervescent, like orchids and champagne. Shadowed by the narrow porch overhang, her eyes were enormous dark puddles. "I got married!"

"What?"

"It was Val's idea. At the Preminger party, he just got the notion into his head right after we got there, and I said, 'Oh hell, why not?' and we both jumped in the car." She giggled, sounding more than drunk . . . almost, well, hectic.

Dolly just stood there, stunned, listening to the crazed ticking of a moth beating itself to death against the dim yellow porch light, her face burning in the cool night air as if she'd been slapped.

Eve wiggled her hand in front of Dolly, and Dolly saw that the finger that had once worn Dewey Cobb's antique gold band now sported a glittering pear-shaped diamond.

Eve swayed in the doorway, a shimmer of blue and silver, her skin pale as buttermilk in the moonlight. "Did you know that in Vegas the jewelry stores stay open all night? Can you just imagine what Mama-Jo would have to say about that? Probably that it was the devil luring sinners down the path to hell." She giggled, then hiccoughed. "Bet she doesn't know I found that path all on my own. Me and Tommy Bliss, back of the henhouse when I was fourteen."

Dolly formed an image of Eve, spread-eagled on her back in the oat grass, torn dress rucked up. Only in her mind, it wasn't Tommy kneeling over Eve, but Val. She felt sick.

"Mama-Jo is dead," she reminded Eve. It was all she could think to say.

"I *know* that, silly. Didn't I send a truckload of lilies to the funeral? I figured the old cow had it coming, after a lifetime of looking forward to her Great Reward."

At the curb, the horn of Eve's white Cadillac honked once, impatiently. Then Val stuck his head out the driver's side, and called, "Come on, baby. You gotta be at the studio in two hours."

Dolly thought of the first time she'd seen Val. She'd been making her way across the RKO lot to the soundstage where they were filming *Dames at Large*. Crossing a Western street, she'd caught a sudden movement out of the corner of her eye, and had looked up just as a large man in cowhide chaps leaped off the roof of a false-front saloon. While Dolly watched, hands clutching her breast (exactly, she realized later, like the heart-struck heroine of a B Western), the stuntman landed precisely in the center of a hay-filled prop cart.

Catching her eye, he rose gracefully and made his way toward her, stepping around cameras and booms, and over the thick cables that snaked across his path. Tall and muscular, he wore dusty jeans, a checkered Western-style shirt, scuffed cowboy boots, and a sweat-stained Stetson. His hair, flowing from under the hat, was white as snow. It was the oddest thing. He was a young man, not more than thirty, and swarthy, almost foreign-looking. His eyes, she saw as he drew near, were black. Not dark brown or deep gray. But black as midnight.

Val Carrera was the most beautiful man she'd ever laid eyes on. She watched him repeat the stunt through two more takes; then, when the director dismissed him, Val asked her if she'd join him for a cup of coffee at the commissary.

Dolly didn't hesitate for a second, even though she knew it would make her late for her shoot.

After coffee, and then later that day, drinks and dinner, they'd gone back to his apartment in Burbank. And stayed in bed for an entire weekend. When Dolly finally got up, she'd felt as if someone had whacked her behind the knees with a baseball bat. She could hardly walk from the bed to the bathroom. She didn't know for sure if this was love, but it sure felt like *something*. Val must have thought so too, because he was with her nearly every day for a month, and the whole time he could never keep his hands off her.

Until he met Eve.

Dolly, watching her sister yawn and stretch languidly like a Siamese cat that's just finished off a bowl of cream, felt an odd weakness spread through her limbs. Speechless, trembling, she stared, unable to move. *Does she think I have no feelings? That her happiness counts more than mine?* Maybe that was it. Maybe Dolly was supposed to have felt sorry for Eve, and step aside gracefully, poor kid, because she'd lost Dewey . . . or maybe simply because she was Eve Dearfield, a star, *somebody.*

The memory of the night she'd walked in on them at Val's apartment came crashing back, Dolly screaming at her, telling her she was a rotten, selfish bitch. Eve, weeping and saying how sorry she was, that she hadn't meant for anything to happen between her and Val, it just *had.* Making it sound like some inevitable force of nature—a hurricane or an earthquake. And somehow, despite her rage and hurt, Dolly had ended up forgiving and even consoling her sister.

Now it all flooded through her again, all the pain and bitterness and resentment. Eve hadn't really cared one bit about her feelings, not then, and certainly not now. *Look at her, all lit up like a Christmas tree, never mind that I might be jealous or hurt.*

"We drove straight through, Vegas and back." Eve flung her arms about Dolly's neck, and planted a damp kiss on her cheek. "Be happy for me, Dorrie, please be happy for me." When she pulled away, Dolly saw that her cheeks were wet and her eyes shiny. "Is Annie awake? I can't wait to tell her!"

"It's six in the morning," Dolly replied dully.

"I'll get her." Eve darted past her, and returned a minute later holding the sleepy-eyed little girl by the hand.

Annie blinked up at her mother owlishly, then corked her thumb securely in her mouth. Her dark hair was mashed up on one side, and her cheek flushed where it had lain against the pillow.

Dolly watched them walk side by side down the path amid the sprinklers' stuttering spray, a gleaming blue blade of a woman and a stalwart little girl dressed in a cotton nightie and clunky orthopedic shoes, clutching her clothes in a bundle under one arm. Dolly felt her heart rip open, letting in a searing-hot pain. A red mist swarmed inside her head.

Then Eve stopped, half-turning, switching on her brightest smile, the one she reserved mostly for reporters and fans.

"Oh, did I forget to mention . . . ? Otto's promised me Maggie in *Devil May Care*. But there's a small part he hasn't cast yet, Maggie's kid sister. I told him you'd be perfect for it. Tell Syd to give him a call."

Dolly felt something inside her—the last thread of loyalty—give way.

She waited until the Cadillac's taillights disappeared into the gloom, then she ran inside and threw up in the kitchen sink.

Afterwards, moving like a sleepwalker, she went into her tiny bedroom, still fragrant with Annie's sweet baby smell, and rummaged in her dresser until she found an envelope. She addressed and stamped it, and carried it back into the living room, where she retrieved the mimeographed sheet folded inside her purse.

Outside, birds chittered in the cool air, and from the bungalow next to hers came the smell of coffee perking, the muffled thud of a door, and an old woman's voice calling, "Don't you use up all the hot water, hear?"

Still in her kimono and slippers, clutching the sealed letter, Dolly walked to the mailbox on the corner and slipped it inside.

The envelope was addressed to Senator Joseph McCarthy, Capitol Hill, Washington, D.C.

It wasn't until the box clanged shut that Dolly came to her senses as suddenly as if she'd been slapped. She sagged against its cool metal side, the red mist in her head receding, all the blood in her body seeming to drain right down into the soles of her slippers.

"Oh, Lord Jesus," she cried in a strangled whisper. "What have I done? What in God's name have I *done?*"

Part One

1966

*Each carried a flashlight but were
afraid to turn them on for fear of
being discovered. There was moonlight,
although it was obscured at times by
clouds.*

*About halfway to the cave-in,
Nancy suddenly stopped and
whispered, "Someone's behind us."*

       from *Nancy Drew Mysteries:*
       The Clue in the Old Stagecoach

CHAPTER 1

Annie lay in bed, staring at the dragon on her wall.

It wasn't a real dragon, only the shadow of one. Each of the tall posts on her Chinese bed was carved in the shape of a dragon, its tail starting at the mattress and twisting up, seeming to *writhe* almost, and ending at the top in a great snarling head with a forked tongue. She remembered when her mother had sent her the bed, for her fifth birthday, all the way from Hong Kong, where Dearie had been filming *Slow Boat to China*. She was sure it had never occurred to Dearie that such a scary-looking thing might give a little girl nightmares. But Annie hadn't been scared. The moment she saw it taken from its shipping crate and unwrapped amid a crackling burst of packing straw, she loved it. Dragons weren't afraid of anyone or anything . . . and that's how she wanted to be.

But right now, peering wide-eyed into the darkness, Annie didn't feel quite so brave. She felt closer to seven than seventeen—a small, scared kid crouched under the covers like a rabbit in its burrow, afraid that something bad was about to happen.

Lying very still, she listened. All she could hear was the rapid thumping of her heart. Then the usual creaks of Bel Jardin settling into itself. Now it came to her, the sound that a moment ago she had thought, no, *hoped* she was only imagining: the low growl of Val's Alfa Romeo Spider as it sped up Chantilly Road. The sound of the sports car's engine grew louder, pausing, then there was a faint hiccough as it switched to low gear. Now rumbling up the curving crushed-shell drive.

Earlier tonight, when she was getting ready for bed, she'd heard her stepfather go out, and had felt light-headed with relief. She'd prayed he would stay out a long time, maybe all night. But now he was back. A cold fist of dread squeezed her stomach into a tight ball.

She sat up in bed, holding her pillow scrunched against her

chest, nibbling on a thumbnail that was already bitten down to the quick. She'd always felt so safe here, in this room, and now somehow it was more like a cage . . . or a baby's barred playpen. She looked about her, at the walls stenciled with Mother Goose characters, the dressing table with its ruffled chintz skirt, and the dollhouse that was an exact replica of Bel Jardin in miniature. Except for her dragon bed, a little girl's room, full of things she'd long ago outgrown. Had Dearie stopped noticing she'd grown up . . . or was it just that when she drank, she hadn't cared?

Annie stared at the pale-blue bookcase—in the moonlight it looked white—filled with all her favorite childhood books. How she'd envied their heroines! Fearless Eloise and resourceful Madeline. Swashbuckling Pippi Longstocking. Laura Ingalls, girl pioneer. And her idol, Nancy Drew.

Nancy Drew would've figured out what to do, Annie thought. If Val tried to mess with her, she'd hit him over the head, get him arrested. Or she'd climb into her roadster and roar away off into the night.

Except Nancy Drew didn't have an eleven-year-old sister. A sister Annie had done everything for since she was in diapers, and whom Annie loved more than anyone or anything. The thought of leaving Laurel here alone with Val made her stomach ache even more, and caused her to chew her thumbnail harder. She tasted blood, warm and briny.

To calm herself, she went over the plan she had been mapping out in her head. Next time Val went out on a date or a job interview, she would pack two suitcases, one for her and one for Laurel. Then the two of them would run away. She'd gotten her license last year, and Dearie's stately old Lincoln was still parked in the garage. And she had the pearl necklace and diamond ear clips Dearie had given her, which she'd carefully hidden from Val. She could sell them, and use the money for food and gas.

But gas to go where? And what would they do once they got there? Who would hide them from Val? The only relative Annie had ever heard of—besides Uncle Rudy, who didn't count because he was Val's brother, and an even slimier creep besides—was Aunt Dolly, whom she hadn't seen or spoken to in ten or twelve years. Annie had a hazy memory of being at a sunny beach, Santa Monica or maybe Pacific Palisades, of a smiling lady with lemon-colored hair and shiny red lips helping her dig a hole to China.

Aunt Dolly.

What had become of her? Long, long ago, Annie remembered overhearing Dearie tell Val, a bitter, almost nasty note in her voice, that her sister, Doris, had gotten herself a rich husband and moved to the big apple, and good riddance. Annie had pictured her aunt as a worm burrowing into a gigantic apple. It wasn't until sixth or seventh grade that Annie found out the Big Apple was New York City. But was Aunt Dolly still in New York? Would she want to see her nieces? Probably not. For Dearie to have been so mad at her, there had to have been a good reason.

And even if they had a place to go, what about Val? Sure, she didn't belong to him; he wasn't her father. Her real father had died in a plane crash, so long ago she couldn't even remember what he looked like. No, Val wouldn't chase after her if she took off—they'd never gotten along. They didn't even like each other. But with Laurel, it would be different. Laurel was his flesh and blood. Not that he'd ever paid her much attention. She was like a toy to him, to be played with for ten minutes or so until he got bored, then handed over to someone else. Weeks went by when he hardly noticed her, then suddenly he'd scoop her onto his lap and tickle her until she cried, or feed her ice cream until she was sick. Still, he was her legal father. Annie's running away was one thing, but if she took Laurel, Annie knew Val would call it kidnapping.

Val might even try to have her arrested and thrown in jail. Annie felt her heart lurch in panic at the thought.

But what else could she do? She loved this great old house, with its Spanish-tiled roof and curlicued wrought iron, its pale-yellow stucco walls festooned in bougainvillea. In Spanish, Bel Jardin meant "beautiful garden," and even inside with all the windows shut, you could smell the honeysuckle and jasmine, and the fragrant, star-shaped blossoms of the lemon tree outside her window.

It made her ache to think of leaving, not just Bel Jardin, but her good friends Naomi Jenkins and Mallory Gaylord, too. And not being able to start college next week like she'd planned. Since kindergarten, she'd knocked herself out in school, getting so far ahead of her classmates that her fourth-grade teacher, in the middle of the

year, had moved her up to fifth. The thought of college, and life beyond that—away from Dearie and Val—had kept her going all these years, like some fabulous mirage shimmering at the edge of an endless desert. At seventeen, she'd been the youngest in her graduating class at Green Oaks. She'd been accepted at Stanford . . . but had turned it down in favor of UCLA. Partly because there wasn't enough money, she knew, for a college with an Ivy League tuition; but mostly so she could stay close to Laurel.

But to live here with Val? God, no, she'd rather die.

She remembered last night, and hugged herself tighter, shivering. Val following her upstairs and sitting on the end of her bed, saying he wanted to talk. She had gotten the creeps just looking at him, seated there like a great hulking polar bear. He didn't belong in her room; he filled up too much space, and seemed to take up all the air.

"Look," he'd launched right in, "I'm not gonna beat around the bush, you're not a kid anymore." His large hand shot out and closed over her wrist; then, to her horror, he drew her onto the bed beside him. "The thing is, we're broke."

Annie, shocked, had sat there as if frozen. He was so close, she could smell him. Under his perfumy aftershave, he smelled hot and sweaty, like after he lifted his weights. And the way he was looking at her made her feel as if her skin had shrunk two sizes.

"I had to let Bonita go," he went on. "Actually, she quit. I haven't paid her in three months."

Annie grew suddenly hot, burning with anger. "You *spent* everything we had?"

His eyes slid away from hers. "It wasn't like that. It didn't happen overnight. And it wasn't like we had money coming in. Your mother . . . she hadn't made a picture in twelve years. And when the school folded . . ." He shrugged. "You know how it is."

Val, who had a black belt, had started a karate school a couple of years ago, but like everything he did—being a real-estate broker, and then a foreign-car salesman—he'd screwed it up somehow.

"What's going to happen?" Annie made herself ask. She hated feeling so powerless, having to depend on him for things, food and money. If only she was old enough to be in charge!

He shrugged. "Sell the house, I guess. Rudy says we should

be able to get a pretty good price for it, but we owe a lot too, so there won't be much left over."

Val's brother, Rudy, was a couple of years older than Val, short and ugly, but a lot smarter—a hotshot divorce lawyer. Val was always quoting Rudy, and wouldn't make a move without asking his brother's advice . . . but Dearie had never liked or trusted Rudy, and thank goodness she'd been savvy enough to let someone else handle the trust money she'd years ago set aside for Annie and Laurel, fifty thousand each. The only bad thing was, Annie couldn't touch hers until her twenty-fifth birthday. Right now, that seemed eons away.

"We can look for something smaller," Val was saying. "Something closer to downtown . . . where you can catch a bus to work."

"I'll be in school," Annie reminded him, struggling to keep her voice even. "I thought I'd pick up a part-time job on campus. Maybe in the cafeteria, or one of the bookstores."

"Yeah, well, here's the thing. Rudy is pretty sure he can set you up with something in his law office. Full-time. You can type, can't you?"

Suddenly, she understood. Now that he'd run through all their money, he wanted *her* to take Dearie's place. She would go to work, forget about college, support all three of them. And he was so obvious about it! She wanted to hit him, smash her fists into his smug face. But she could only sit there, trembling, speechless.

Val, mistaking her helpless rage for sorrow, put his arms around her, patting her clumsily as if he wanted to comfort her. "Yeah, I miss her, too," he murmured.

She tried to pull away, but he only squeezed tighter. Now the embrace became something more . . . he was stroking the small of her back, her hip, his rough cheek pressed against hers, his breath warm and quick against her ear.

She felt sick.

Steeling herself, Annie gave him a hard push and jumped to her feet. A sweetish-sour taste filled her mouth. She really thought she might throw up.

"Excuse me, I have to brush my teeth." She said the first thing that popped into her head. Then she rushed into the bathroom and locked the door. She ran a hot bath and stayed in it for an hour, until her toes shrivelled into pale raisins.

When she got back to her room, Val was gone.

Today, all day, she had managed to avoid him. But now he was back, and if he felt like coming into her room again there was no lock on the door to stop him.

As if it were echoing her thoughts, Annie heard the front door slam downstairs, then the soft clacking of shoes against the tiled foyer. She sucked her breath in and held it until red spots swarmed before her eyes.

She could hear him climbing the stairs now, his footsteps heavy, measured, but muffled by the Oriental runner. Just beyond her door, the footsteps slowed . . . then stopped. Her heart was pounding so hard, she was sure he would hear it.

Then, after what seemed to her like an eternity, she heard Val move on, the whisper of his shoes against the carpet growing fainter as he made his way toward the master suite at the far end of the corridor.

Annie let her breath out in a dizzying rush. She felt flushed and weak, as if she had a fever. And sticky with sweat. A swim, that's what she needed. And the pool would be perfect, cool and still.

Annie forced herself to wait until she was absolutely certain Val had to have gone to bed. Then she slipped out. In her nightgown, she tiptoed out into the hallway and made her way along the thick carpet toward the narrow servants' staircase that would take her down through the kitchen and sun porch, then out onto the patio.

Reaching the half-open door to Laurel's room, Annie paused, then slipped inside. Looking at her sister, asleep on her back, her small hands folded neatly across the blanket that covered her, Annie thought of the print her art teacher, Mr. Honeick, had shown in class last year. A famous painting, by an artist named Millais—of drowned Ophelia floating face-up in the water, her long golden hair drifting like seaweed about her still, white face. Annie's heart caught in her throat, and before she could stop herself, she was leaning forward, listening for Laurel's breathing.

There it was, but so soft it could have been a breeze blowing through the open window. Annie relaxed a little. *Don't worry, Laurey. I won't let you down. I'll take care of you.*

That time when Laurel had had scarlet fever, when she was two, came back to her in a hot rush, that morning she'd never forget, looking into her baby sister's crib, and finding Laurel gasping for air, her face purple, her tiny arms thrashing. Annie, only eight and scared out of her mind, snatched Laurel up and ran through the house, screaming for Dearie. She could feel Laurel's frail chest hitching desperately, making a horrible honking sound. Despite how little Laurel was, she was still too heavy for Annie, and kept slithering from her grasp.

She finally found Dearie, passed out on the living-room sofa, an empty brandy bottle on the coffee table in front of her, exhausted, probably, from being up all night with Laurel. Annie, sobbing, more scared than she'd ever been, had hit her, pushed her, shouted in her ear, trying to make her wake up. But Dearie wouldn't budge. There was no one else; it was Bonita's day off, and Val was gone. Annie, terrified, had thought, *I'm just a kid, I can't do this, I can't save Laurey.*

Then a voice inside her head commanded: *Think.*

She remembered a long time ago, when she herself had had a bad cough and stuffy chest, and Dearie had put her in a steamy bathtub, and how it had made her breathe easier.

Annie lugged Laurel into Dearie's big bathroom and cranked on the tub's hot-water tap. Then, sitting on the toilet with Laurel facedown across her knees, she began to pound on her back, praying that whatever was choking her would somehow pop out. Nothing so dramatic happened, but as steam billowed and stuck Laurel's hair to her scalp in wet clumps, her breath gradually began returning, and the awful purple color faded.

Then with a tremendous whoop, Laurel began to cry. She was going to be all right. Annie's face felt wet—from the steam, she thought; then she realized she was crying.

And she had realized something else, that she was Laurel's real mother, that God had meant for her to look after and protect her sister, always.

Now, she leaned over and lightly kissed her sister's dry, cool forehead. A weird thing about Laurel, she never sweated, not even on the hottest days. She always had that fresh, baby-powdery scent, like the little bundles of dried flowers wrapped in cheesecloth that Bonita tucked among the sheets in the linen closet.

Annie sweated like a pig. In phys ed, playing basketball, it embarrassed her, the way her T-shirt always stuck to her back only two minutes into the game. When she was taking a test, especially in math, her palms dripped, and the insides of her shoes turned to swamps. Even her *hair* sweated, for God's sake. Once, in the fourth grade, on Parents' Night, when they all had to clasp hands while singing "America the Beautiful," Joyce Leonardi had dropped Annie's in disgust, and wailed, "It's *getting* on me!"

Even now, her palms were sweating. Annie pushed her fingers through her hair, still a little shocked by its shortness. She'd hacked it off only last week, with Dearie's sewing scissors, and hadn't quite gotten used to the idea of not having long hair. Still, she wasn't sorry. For some reason, it had made her feel better, seeing all that dark hair clumped at her feet . . . as if she were shedding an old skin, and making way for a new Annie, strong, shining, brave.

Downstairs, in the sun room that opened onto the patio, the moon shone through the palmettos in their huge terra-cotta tubs by the French doors, casting stiletto-shaped shadows over the Spanish-tiled floor. Stepping outside into the husk-dry September coolness, Annie could see the pool gleaming darkly, its glassy surface twinkling with sparks of orange light reflected by the electric tiki torches.

She peeled off her nightgown and dove in.

The cool water slicing along her naked body felt wonderful. She stayed under for half a length before she broke the surface, gulping in the night air, fragrant with the scent of honeysuckle and the faint smokiness of a brush fire burning way off in the canyons. She felt a breeze, and could hear the rustling of the hibiscus hedge surrounding the patio, where the lawn swelled up to meet a row of petticoat palms. Below them, the grass was matted with dry brown fronds. It had been a long time since anyone had raked them up. Hector, the gardener, had quit a while back, and Val never lifted a finger. He had some scheme cooking, and was trying to get together a group of investors so he could open his own health spa. It would fail . . . just like all his other schemes.

Her stomach tightened. Clinging to the edge of the pool, she pedalled water. She had to do something . . . and soon. Or she'd stay stuck with Val, cramped in a tiny house with no place to hide from him, and roped to a desk typing stupid letters for that troll Rudy.

She remembered, too, how Rudy always seemed to be staring at Laurel. His bulgy eyes fixed on her like a toad's on an iridescent-winged dragonfly. Seldom approaching her, but those eyes—always there, watching. A shiver coursed through Annie. What did Rudy want from Laurel? The same thing Annie suspected Val wanted from *her?*

No, that was too gross . . . too unthinkable.

Even so, she had to get *out*.

Then, in her mind, Annie heard her mother—the clear-voiced Dearie she remembered from when she was a little girl—drawl: *The good Lord is fine for praying, kiddo, but when the going gets rough you'd best be off your knees and on your feet.*

Annie now felt angry. *Oh yeah?* she thought. *Then how come you killed yourself?*

Annie pushed off against the slippery tiles with her feet and began furiously stroking her way across the pool. Swimming was her best sport. It was something you could do alone, where you didn't have to depend on a team member not to screw up. And if you sweated, nobody would notice.

Gradually, Annie felt her anger dissolve into sorrow. If only Dearie had talked to her before she took those pills. Let her say good-bye at least. Now, as Annie climbed out of the pool and pulled on her nightgown (why hadn't she thought to bring a towel?), it hit her like a slap that she really *was* on her own.

If only she could get her hands on that trust money! Maybe she could talk to Mr. Melcher at Hibernia, explain how important it was. Tomorrow she would call, make an appointment to see him.

Shivering with cold and dripping her way across the sun porch, Annie caught a sudden flicker of movement out of the corner of her eye. She froze, and looked up. Val stood framed in the archway leading from the living room down a short flight of steps onto the sun porch. The shadows around her went from black to gray, and for an instant she thought she might pass out. There was no sound other than the soft ticking of water as it dripped from her wet hair onto the tiled floor.

Moving with oiled grace, he glided down the four steps and crossed over to where she stood. In the orange glow of the tiki torches filtering in through the wide French doors, his wide tanned face, striped with shadows, reminded her of a tiger's. He was wearing a pair of navy satin pajamas monogrammed in white with his initials: VC.

"You oughta put something on," he said. "You'll catch cold."

"I was just going in."

The sound of her own voice in her ears had the effect of a sprung catch, somehow unlocking her. She began walking quickly toward the archway. *God, let him leave me alone.* She felt his eyes on her, and realized that with her wet nightgown clinging to her she might as well be naked. She felt herself grow hot with embarrassment.

In the cavernous living room, Annie was crossing the rug in front of the fireplace—a blackened cave big enough to roast a buffalo—when she felt Val's hand, shockingly warm and dry against her wet shoulder. Her heart seemed to stop. She spun away, banging her knee against a massive carved chair with a tooled leather seat. A bolt of pain shot up her leg, shocking her heart into sudden jarring motion. Blood rushed into her face, making it thump.

Then she saw that he was only offering her his pajama top, which he'd slipped off when her back was turned. She felt flustered, not knowing how to react. In his own crude way, he was trying to be nice . . . but that only made her loathe him more. Why didn't he just leave her alone?

Annie stood there, staring at Val's outstretched hand until it fell away. The pajama top slid in a little heap to the rug. His black eyes narrowed. The expression on his broad, planed face was a mixture of sullenness and fury.

She tried to step past Val, but he caught her roughly. Holding her pressed against him, he cupped the back of her head, stroking it roughly. "Give me a break, kid. It hasn't been easy for me either."

On his breath, she caught an all-too-familiar whiff of booze. That made her even more scared. Val wasn't a drunk like Dearie, but he liked his double scotches . . . and when he'd had two or three he sometimes turned mean and a little crazy.

Annie's gaze fixed on an old steamer trunk that Dearie had picked up years ago at some antiques barn. Huge and bulky, with rusty metal straps binding its leather hide, it smelled richly of age and dark cargo holds. She remembered how once, when she was little, she'd climbed inside the chest to see what it felt like, and the lid had accidentally banged down, plunging her into horrible, smelly darkness. She'd screamed and screamed, and finally Dearie had flung open the lid and scooped her up.

At this moment, Annie felt she was in that trunk again, trapped, suffocated. And she knew with a horrible lurch of her stomach that no Dearie was going to rescue her now.

Then anger took hold, and she tore away. Hugging herself, shivering so hard she had to clench her jaw to keep her teeth from chattering, Annie hissed: "It's all your fault! You never loved her! You only married her because she was famous and rich. And then when she . . . she couldn't work anymore, you treated her like . . . she wasn't even there."

"She was a drunk," he snarled, a righteous gleam in his blood-shot eyes. "Way the hell before I met her. You know the saying: Once a drunk always a drunk."

Over Val's shoulder, on the fireplace mantel, light winked off a shiny metal surface: Dearie's Oscar, the Best Actress she'd won for *Storm Alley*. Annie remembered how proud she'd felt that long-ago night, staying up late to watch her mother on TV, seeing Gregory Peck tear open the envelope and call out Dearie's name, then Dearie herself, floating up onto the stage, starry in sequins, thanking everyone, hoisting the glowing statuette in triumph.

Tears pricked at Annie's eyes, but she bit them back. She wouldn't cry in front of Val. She would not give him the satisfaction.

"If my mother drank, it was your fault." Maybe it wasn't entirely true, but she wasn't a bit sorry she'd said it.

"You little bitch." Val grabbed her, his fingers digging into her upper arms, pinching her. "You never even gave me a chance. Spoiled brat with your nose in the air, trotting off to that fancy school learning which fork to use, and how to ride a horse like an English pansy. You had it in for me since day one, little Princess Annie looking down at me like I was nothing but dirt."

His eyes glittered in the darkness, black prisms reflecting a whole spectrum of ancient hurts.

Annie felt shaken. She'd never seen Val this mad, not even that time he'd hit Dearie. She sensed danger, like static faintly crackling in the still, scented air. "I'm going up now," she said, shivering, biting her lip to keep her teeth from chattering. "I'm really cold."

His lips stretching in a cold grin, Val leaned down and with one meaty finger hooked his pajama top from the rug. He tossed it at her. "Put it on." It wasn't an offer.

Annie looked at the bundle of cloth as if it were a snake. She dropped it onto the floor and quickly stepped back.

With a low moan, Val fell on her.

At first she thought he was going to hit her. It *felt* as if he *had* hit her, a bruising blow to her mouth. It was so dark, and her head was spinning. She felt a sting of pain, and tasted blood where her teeth had cut the inside of her lip. Then she realized what it was: He was kissing her.

She tried to scream, to pull away, but he held her tightly. The sweet smell of his aftershave, mingled with the stale scotch on his breath, was suddenly overpowering, gagging her. Into her head popped that jingle, *There's something about an Aqua Velva man....*

Hysterical laughter bubbled up her throat.

This isn't happening. God, please, make this not be happening.

"I wanted you to like me," he said in a little boy's petulant voice. "I tried, but you . . . you wouldn't let me. I would have been a good father. I . . . would have loved you."

Annie, terrified, struggled to free herself. "Please . . . let me go." She thought of something else. "Laurey might wake up."

"She used me." He went on as if he hadn't heard. "She wanted me because I was her sister's . . . Christ, I *should* have married Dolly. Do you think *I* wanted it to end like this? You don't know what it was like for me . . ."

"Val," Annie pleaded, truly scared.

With one arm, he held her tight, while with the other he began touching her. Cupping a breast, stroking her with a strange, unbearable tenderness. Annie felt as if she were dying.

"I only wanted you to like me," he repeated sadly.

Summoning all her strength and twisting violently, Annie somehow managed to rip herself free of him. Ducking past Val, she felt strangely light, a comet spinning across a galaxy, her arms seeming to stretch on and on forever, until finally her fingers closed about something cold and hard—Dearie's Oscar. For a crazy second, she saw her mother once again, up on the stage at the Pantages.

. . . and most of all I want to thank my little girl, who stayed up past her bedtime to watch me . . .

Blindly, as she whirled about, Annie swung the heavy goldplated statuette like a club. Out of the corner of her eye, she saw Val feint to one side. Annie realized later that if he hadn't moved, she would have missed him, he was so agile and her swing so lousy.

But she connected. The impact slammed through her arm like an electric jolt, and she felt as shocked as Val looked.

Blood streamed from a cut over his right eyebrow. He froze, his face the color of cottage cheese. Slowly, as if in a dream, he touched his fingertips gingerly to his forehead. "Oh," he said in soft surprise, seeing his hand come away red. He sank down abruptly on the wide leather sofa. His arms and legs seemed to jerk at queer angles like a marionette whose strings have suddenly become tangled. A moment later he toppled onto his side and grew still. Frighteningly still.

I've killed him, Annie thought.

Terror was waiting for her somewhere in the back of her mind. But right now the only thing she felt was numb, as if she'd been shot full of Novocain. Staring down at Val's bloody, crumpled form, she thought, calmly, sensibly, *I won't pack much. A change of clothes, underwear, toothbrush. And Dearie's jewelry. I'll take the small overnight bag, it won't be so heavy.* She couldn't take the car; that had been a dumb idea in the first place. If Val wasn't dead, only hurt, he would have the highway patrol after them like a shot.

Packing was easy. It was waking Laurel that was the hard part. She slept like the dead. And when Annie finally got her up, she wore a glassy look, as if she wasn't quite sure whether she was awake or dreaming. She stared uncomprehendingly at Annie's face, then at the jeans and sweatshirt Annie had thrown on.

"Come on," Annie told her. "We don't have much time."

Laurel blinked, looking at that moment exactly like a doll, the kind you tilt back to make its eyes close. A pink-cheeked, blue-eyed baby doll who didn't have the slightest idea what Annie was talking about.

"I have to go away," she told her sister, more gently. "I won't be coming back. Do you want to come with me?"

The glassy expression was gone; Laurel's face crumpled in dismay.

"Where are we going?"

Annie was encouraged by the "we."

She tried to think, but couldn't come up with an answer. Maybe that had been her trouble before, trying to plan it out so carefully, when the best way might be just to make it up as they went along.

"On a bus," was the best she could come up with. "You'd better hurry and get dressed before . . . before he wakes up."

Then, because Laurel looked so worried and scared, Annie hugged her.

"It's going to be all right," she said. "In fact, it'll be fun. A real adventure." To her own ears, it sounded about as much fun as going over Niagara Falls in a barrel.

But first, they'd have to get to the bus depot. She wasn't even sure where that was, or which bus they should take. Well, she'd figure it out somehow.

"Won't we need money?" Laurel was on her feet, pulling her nightgown over her head. "I mean, for the tickets."

Annie hadn't thought of that. She wouldn't be able to pawn the necklace and earrings until tomorrow morning, when shops would be open. And by then she wanted to be miles and miles from Bel Jardin.

Then Laurel piped, "I have money, Annie. Almost a hundred dollars. Remember after Dearie's Christmas party when Mr. Oliver thought he lost his wallet with all that money in it? Well, I found it under the sofa . . . a week later." She blushed. "I know I should have told you before, but . . ." Her voice trailed off.

"Laurey! You didn't *keep* it, did you?"

Color flared in Laurel's pale cheeks. "Of course I didn't! I just didn't tell you about the reward he gave me. I . . . I was saving it to buy you something for your birthday. Then Dearie . . ." She stopped in the middle of buttoning her blouse. "Annie, you're not mad, are you?"

Annie hugged her again, relief rinsing through her. "Laurey, you dope. Come on, get dressed or we'll never get out of here."

Laurel gave her a long look that seemed burdened with far more than any eleven-year-old should have to carry. "It's because of . . . of Val, isn't it?" she whispered. "Something he did?" Not "Daddy" or "Dad"; since she could talk, she'd called him Val.

Annie nodded, her throat suddenly tight.

"Annie," Laurel whispered sheepishly as they were leaving. "Can I take Boo?" Boo was her old baby blanket, nubby and tattered from a thousand washings. She didn't like to admit she still slept with it, at her age, but Annie knew how much Boo meant.

" 'Course," she said.

At the front door, Annie paused, remembering another keep-sake: Dearie's Oscar. She couldn't bear the thought of leaving it behind, but she was scared of going back in there. What if Val was up, and tried to come after her again? Still, she couldn't just walk away without the one thing that had meant the most to her mother.

"Wait here," she whispered.

Her heart slamming against her ribs, Annie slipped back into the living room, and snatched up the Oscar from the rug where she'd dropped it, quickly averting her eyes from the still form sprawled on the couch. Reaching Laurel's side, she saw a horrified look dawn on her sister's face. Annie looked down at the statuette in her hand, and in the dim glow of the porch light she saw the blood smearing its bright surface. *Oh God.*

Then, wordlessly, her eyes as big and dark as holes punched in her chalk-white face, Laurel took it from Annie, using her precious Boo to wipe it clean. She handed it back to Annie, who quickly stuffed it into the bulging overnight bag. Looking into Laurel's trust-ing eyes, she found the strength to push open the door.

Minutes later, as they made their way in darkness down the long, curving drive toward the wrought-iron gates at the bottom, Annie turned for one last look at Bel Jardin. In the faint glow of a sickle-shaped moon, it seemed to rise like a huge, pale cliff from a wavy sea of honeysuckle, oleander, and hibiscus. Above the palms that lined the drive, she saw the first milky light of dawn touch the top of the tiled roof, and she turned away, quickening her step.

At that moment, clutching the heavy overnight bag, the bulge that was Dearie's Oscar banging against her leg, Annie's courage seemed to wither again. Where on earth was she going? And what was she going to do when she got there? And what if the phone booth at the Gulf station out on Sunset wasn't working and she couldn't even call a taxi?

Then, strangely, she felt an invisible hand against the small of her back, giving her a gentle push. Inside her head, a sweet, throaty voice drawled, *Once you've made up your mind to go someplace, don't waste all your time fiddling with your shoelaces. . . .*

Annie straightened suddenly, hitching the heavy suitcase a little higher so she could walk faster. She reached for Laurel's hand, which felt cool and dry in her sweaty grasp. Her heart was thundering in her ears—she had never felt so scared and unsure—but the main thing was to fool Laurel into thinking that she knew exactly where she was headed, and that she wasn't a bit afraid. Suddenly, that seemed like the most important thing in the world.

"I hope you wore socks." She spoke briskly to her sister, who trudged listlessly alongside her, hugging a tattered baby blanket smeared with her father's blood, a pale golden-haired stalk of a girl dressed in pink pedal pushers and a puff-sleeved blouse. "You know how you get blisters when you don't wear socks. And we have a long way to go."

CHAPTER 2

Laurel pushed the sausage to one side of her plate. Maybe if she hid it under her toast, Annie wouldn't notice. She felt too sick to eat another bite, but the last thing Laurel wanted was for Annie to start in again about her being too skinny.

Anyway, look who was talking! Annie looked awful, the way her green cashmere sweater hung on her. With her cheekbones sticking out, and those brown smudges under her eyes, she could have passed for Morticia Addams.

Why hadn't Annie ordered something besides toast? She looked hungry enough to gobble up every stale donut in this diner.

But, no, they had to watch every penny, Annie kept saying; they had to save for when they found an apartment. But when would that be? A whole two weeks in New York, and they were still stuck in that smelly, dark room at the Allerton. Laurel still believed that somehow Annie was going to make everything okay. But what if she just couldn't? Or what if something happened to her, like getting really sick or hurt?

Thinking of all the awful things that might happen, Laurel felt as if she were on a roller coaster, inching up that first big hill, when you don't know if you're going to pee your pants or throw up, or maybe both. In her whole life, she'd never felt so scared.

In the beginning, the $970 they'd gotten for Dearie's jewelry had seemed like a king's treasure . . . but now it was almost all gone. Everything cost so much! Annie hadn't told her they were almost broke, but Laurel had seen the worried look on her sister's face last night when she carefully counted out this week's money for Mr. Mancusi at the front desk. She saw it now, too, in the way Annie nibbled her toast, trying to make it last, carefully sipping her tea between each bite.

And dragging back in every night, trying to act cheerful even

37

though no one would give her a job. How much longer could Annie go on like that? Living in Bel Air and going to Green Oaks School wasn't exactly ideal for being a hotel maid or a waitress. But Annie was smarter than anyone. Hadn't she talked Mancusi into letting them have their room for five dollars a week less in exchange for her sweeping out the entry hall and reception area each day?

Annie would find something. She'd always taken care of everything, even when Dearie was alive. Like that time at Palisades Park, when Dearie had too many beers and, just as they were getting ready to go home, passed out at the wheel. Annie had somehow pulled her into the back seat, and driven them all safely home. Now, remembering it, Laurel realized that Annie had been only fourteen, not old enough to drive. How had she known what to do?

Laurel wished she could be strong like Annie.

If only I was older. Then I could get a job too, and Annie wouldn't have to do everything herself.

But who would ever hire an eleven-year-old kid, when Annie, who looked older than seventeen, was having a hard time?

Laurel watched Annie break open another plastic container of grape jelly, and begin spreading it thickly on her last wedge of toast. She felt a surge of love for her sister. At least she had Annie. What if she were alone? The thought made her stomach dip crazily, and the room seemed to tilt.

Holding tightly to the edge of her seat, as if she might otherwise be catapulted off, she glanced around at the other booths, mostly empty. Weekdays it was usually pretty crowded, but this was Sunday. Across the aisle, a man wearing khakis and work boots was drinking coffee and smoking a cigarette. At the counter, a baggy-eyed lady in a tight miniskirt sat hunched over a Danish, the spike heels of her black patent-leather boots hooked over the rung of her stool. The food wasn't very good, but it was cheap and nobody here seemed to mind that everything smelled and tasted like fried bacon—the air, her napkin when she wiped her mouth, even her milk.

Annie looked up, and said, "I have a feeling this is our lucky day." She sounded so cheerful and determined that Laurel believed her and began feeling a little better. Then she remembered, Annie said the same thing *every* day.

Laurel pushed her milk glass across the Formica tabletop. "Here, you finish it."

Annie frowned and pushed it back. "You need it more than I do. Anyway, I'm full."

It was a lie. Laurel wanted to shout at her sister, plead with her to please, please stop being so nice. Like ordering these eggs and sausages for her after she'd said all she wanted was cornflakes. Annie meant well, but she wished Annie would stop treating her like a two-year-old.

If only Annie would let me, I bet I'd be good at helping out.

But all Laurel said was, "Can I see the paper?"

One thing they had to buy every day was *The New York Times*. Sunday's fat edition, with today's date at the top, October 9, lay folded next to Annie's plate; she hadn't looked at it yet. Usually, she began circling ads the minute they got it—so did this mean she was losing hope? Laurel felt her stomach do a lazy somersault.

Some of the apartments they'd looked at were nice but way too expensive. Or they were so awful, in neighborhoods where the sidewalks were lined with overflowing garbage cans, and you had to watch so you didn't step on the broken glass. And inside, dark halls and pee smells, like the Allerton. In one, when the super switched on the light, a whole parade of cockroaches began scurrying over the kitchen counter, trying to escape while he muttered under his breath, smacking them with a rolled-up newspaper.

It was such an enormous city. Maybe Annie hadn't been looking in the right places. What about Brooklyn, for instance? That was where Val and Uncle Rudy had grown up. On the map, it looked close, connected to Manhattan by the colored lines that stood for different subway lines.

But where Laurel really wanted to be at this moment was back home, at Bel Jardin.

She badly missed her room, with its sunny window seat crammed with stuffed animals. And her best friend, Bonnie Pell, who knew every Beatles song by heart, and always picked Laurel first when they were choosing up teams.

In a weird way, even though when she *had* been there he'd hardly ever paid attention to her, she even missed her father.

She imagined Val asleep in the king-sized bed he'd once shared with Dearie. Hector was cutting the grass, and Bonita was flipping flapjacks at the stove while singing Spanish songs in her high, warbly voice . . .

Then the image dissolved, and all she could see in her mind was blood. Val's blood. And the darkness that had followed her and Annie all the way down Chantilly and Tarcuto, past the golf course, to Sunset, where in the yellow glow of street lamps, she'd seen the smears of dried blood on Boo. She remembered dropping her old blanket in the first garbage can they came to, yet feeling as if somehow *she* was the one being left behind. As if the girl she had been back then was a friend who had moved away, someone she barely remembered anymore.

If only Annie would tell her what Val had done that night to get her mad enough to hit him. Imagining Val dead, lying on the floor in a pool of blood, she felt gripped by an icy chill.

No, she told herself, that couldn't be. Val *couldn't* be dead. She didn't want him to be dead.

But if he was alive, then he might be out looking for them. Annie had said they had to be careful not to get caught, or Val would take her away from Annie. And maybe even get Annie arrested for kidnapping.

Annie in jail? Laurel couldn't bear the thought. Nor could she imagine being separated from her sister. So she had to be very careful, and not tell anyone too much about herself.

But clinging to Annie like a little kid in diapers, that wasn't how she wanted to be, either. As scared and sick as she felt, she didn't want to drag Annie down. Wouldn't it be great if they could somehow be partners? If Annie could lean on *her* once in a while?

I have to show her somehow . . . make her SEE that I'm old enough to be a big help.

Laurel, forcing herself to ignore the topsy-turvy feeling inside her, grabbed the paper, flipping through until she found the real-estate section. Moving her finger down columns for unfurnished studios, she pored over tiny advertisements. Two weeks ago, she hadn't understood any of those abbreviations, but now she knew right away that "A/C" meant air-conditioned and that EIK meant eat-in kitchen. Finally she spotted one for $300, which was the most Annie said they could afford, except when she showed it to Annie, her sister pointed out that East 116th Street was in Harlem, which was overrun by muggers and junkies.

Laurel felt discouraged, stupid somehow, like the time, playing softball, with all the bases loaded, when she fumbled the easiest fly ball in the world.

Annie, meanwhile, was buried in the "Help Wanted" section.

"Look at this," she said, reading aloud, " 'Gal Friday. Hat company seeks energetic young person for busy office.' You see? Didn't I tell you? I'll bet I'd be perfect for it."

"What about typing? Don't you need to type?"

"I can type . . . only not very fast."

"But if they give you a test—"

Annie cut her off, smiling forcefully. "Last time, I was nervous. The next time, I'll do better. I know I will." She looked down at Laurel's plate, and Laurel saw a worried look on her face. "You didn't finish your breakfast. Are you feeling okay?"

"I ate as much as I could. Why don't you have the rest?"

Annie looked up sharply, her eyes narrowing, as if she thought Laurel might just be pretending not to want it for her sake. But if anyone was pretending, Laurel thought, it was Annie. She acted so positive that everything would turn out okay, but look how bitten-down her nails were, worse than before, all red and puffy, and dotted with dried blood in spots.

Annie stared at her a moment longer; then hunger won out. Grabbing her fork, she gobbled up the rest of the scrambled eggs and sausage. Then with her last piece of toast, she scoured the plate clean. Watching her, Laurel felt the ache in her own stomach ease.

She noticed the waitress heading toward their table, a skinny girl with dark hair clipped back from her pimply face. She looked about Annie's age. Her red nail polish was chipped away almost to nothing, and there was a spot on the front of her powder-blue uniform that looked like strawberry jam.

"Will that be all?" She said it so quickly it sounded like one word, *wuthabyall.* Not waiting for an answer, she slapped the bill down on the table and stomped off.

Annie leaned across the table and whispered, "She's mad because I didn't leave her a tip last time."

Then Annie, as if suddenly in a great hurry, scrambled to her feet, and strode, the hem of her denim skirt swishing purposefully, along the row of booths toward the waitress in the back. Laurel saw Annie put some coins into the girl's hand; then they stood talking.

Annie was grinning when she returned. "You remember the sign in the window when we came in, 'EXPERIENCED WAITRESS WANTED'? Well, I have an interview with the boss at five." Her ink-blue eyes shone, and her cheeks were slightly flushed.

"But, Annie, you don't know *anything* about being a waitress," Laurel burst out. "Bonita waited on *us*." Then, seeing the smile leave Annie's face, Laurel immediately wanted to kick herself.

"Then I'll just have to learn, won't I?" Annie said, looking as determined as ever . . . but not quite as cheerful anymore. "How hard could it be, anyway, just bringing people what they order?"

Laurel felt tempted to remind Annie that she was the one who always lost when they played Concentration, but she didn't. For Annie it wasn't the details, but the "big picture," that counted most—like taking really hard classes in school and getting B's, instead of A's in the easy stuff. And trying out for the best teams even if you weren't as good as the other players.

But just for right now, Laurel thought, it might be better to be able to keep a BLT straight from a burger than to know Latin or hit a home run.

"I guess you're right," she said uncertainly.

But Annie was gazing out the steamy window, a faraway look on her face, as if she were an explorer scouting some distant mountain range. "We'll find a real place to live, too," she said, looking back at Laurel, a new sparkle in her eye. "I bet there'll be something in the *Village Voice*." She grabbed her purse, and slid off her seat. "Come on, Mr. Singh at the corner lets me look without paying."

On their way out, passing the quick-serve counter, Laurel caught sight of a folded newspaper left on one of the stools. Too small to be the *Times*. Laurel snatched it up, and tucked it under her arm.

Outside, pausing on the sidewalk at the corner of Eighth and Twenty-third while Annie went into the candy store to look at the *Voice*, Laurel unfolded the paper, and saw that it was the *Jewish Press*. Would there be apartments in here? Well, no harm in looking, was there? She turned five or six pages, and then she saw: "Apts. Unfurn." The very first one seemed to jump out at her.

*Midwd. 1 bdrm. Top of 2-fmly hse w/grdn quiet neighborhood, $290.
Shomer Shabbat. 252–1789.*

Her heart bumped into her throat. But where was Midwood?
At that price, it had to be in Brooklyn. But even so, it sounded
perfect.

A funny name, she thought—Shomer Shabbat. But just about
everyone in New York had strange names. Like the night clerk at
the Allerton, Mr. Tang Bo.

This could be her chance to show Annie she wasn't the only
one with nerve. But the first thing, she knew, was to make sure an
apartment wasn't already taken. Most times when Annie called, they
were already snapped up.

"What's that you've got there?" Annie asked, coming out of
the candy store. To make herself seem older, she'd worn her good
pumps, but the way she wobbled in them anyone could see she
wasn't used to walking around in high heels. Then Annie bent down,
feeling inside her shoe to make sure the Band-Aid on her heel hadn't
come off.

Laurel took advantage of the moment to stuff the paper back
under her arm. "Nothing," she said. "Uh . . . I just remembered . . . something I left at the table. Wait here, I'll run and
get it."

In the diner, there was a pay phone by the front door, next to
a coatrack. She dug a dime from the pocket of her jeans (Annie made
her keep one, just in case she ever got lost), and dialed the number
she'd memorized from the paper. After one ring, it was picked up.

"So don't keep me waiting in suspense," a lady's voice chimed
right in, before Laurel could even open her mouth. "Did you buy
it or not? New refrigerators, I'll bet you he said, don't grow on trees."

Bewildered and thrown off balance, Laurel felt shy and embarrassed, but she managed to stammer, "H-hello?"

There was a short silence, then the lady laughed—but a nice,
jolly laugh that made Laurel think of plump Mrs. Potter, the nurse
at Green Oaks, who kept a ready supply of Tootsie Roll Pops in
her medicine cabinet.

"You're not Faigie, are you? Who is this?"

Laurel felt like quickly hanging up, but the voice at the other
end sounded so nice, she forced herself to speak.

"This is Laurel . . . uh, Davis." Or was it Davidson? She'd

heard Annie tell so many lies to the landlords and supers who had interviewed them, Laurel couldn't keep them straight anymore. She began to feel panicky. What if she accidentally said something that made this lady suspicious? "Your apartment," she blurted. "The one you advertised in the paper . . . Could I . . . I mean, we . . . my sister and I, that is . . . It's not taken, is it?"

"How old are you, darling?"

"Twelve." She could get away with one extra year, but no one in her right mind would believe it if she said she was nineteen or twenty. "But my sister's twenty-one," she added quickly.

"Married?"

"Um, well, no . . . but she's a straight-A student except for math, and she can type." Had she said too much? Or all the wrong things?

"She's got a job, then?"

"Oh, well, yeah . . . she does . . . in a hat company. In the office. See, we're from . . . uh, Arizona . . . and we really, really need an apartment, especially one with a garden."

On nice days, I could sit outside with my sketch pad and paint box, she thought. And then maybe she wouldn't feel so very far from Bel Jardin.

"It's mostly weeds, you know. And the grass is up to here."

"Oh, I wouldn't mind that. I could even cut it for you, if you like. Hec— I mean, my dad showed me all kinds of stuff, like fertilizing, and how to put roses to sleep for the winter."

Laurel closed her eyes, and held tight for an instant to the image of Hector's leathery brown hands carefully scooping out soil around a rosebush, and filling the hole with the coffee grounds Bonita had been saving for weeks.

"Roses! I should be so lucky!" The lady—Mrs. Shabbat?— laughed her rich, bubbly laugh.

Laurel's heart was pounding. Had she gone too far in her lies? Well, at least the part about taking care of the garden was true. She *could.* Just like Mary and Colin in *The Secret Garden,* she'd make it beautiful, and plant lots of flowers—peonies, and black-eyed Susans, and snapdragons.

"Couldn't we just look at it to start with?" she asked meekly.

"Listen, darling, you and your sister, you got money for a deposit?"

"Oh, sure." Then she remembered to add what Annie always said, "Cash!"

There was a long pause in which Laurel's heart seemed to climb right up onto the roof of her mouth.

Then Mrs. Shabbat sighed and said, "To be one hundred percent honest, I don't know if you're exactly the right tenants for me, but you sound like a nice girl. I suppose it wouldn't hurt for you to have a look. So you want to come over now, or what?"

Laurel felt light with relief, like a balloon, so light that if she weren't holding onto the receiver, she'd float right up to the ceiling.

"That would be great," she said, trying to hold her excitement in. How long would it take to go by subway to that part of Brooklyn? She took a wild guess. "How about in an hour? Will you be home then?"

"Where else? I'm in my ninth month, Laurel Davis. Only God bless him, this baby is in no hurry to come out. So on your way over, say a little prayer for me that I shouldn't have to wait three weeks past my time like with my last one."

Laurel hadn't even met this Mrs. Shabbat, but she couldn't remember when she'd liked anyone so much right off the bat. Quickly, she got the address and directions, hung up, and rushed outside to find Annie.

"What took you so long?"

"I think I found us an apartment!"

Laurel, hugging herself to keep from floating away, told her about the phone call. A cold wind was now blowing, but Laurel felt hot with excitement.

Annie hugged her tightly. "Laurey, that's great! Let's keep our fingers crossed."

Laurel had never felt so proud. She'd showed Annie she was grown-up, responsible. Everything was going to work out all right, she was sure of it.

Laurel and Annie got off the subway at the Avenue J station. They hadn't walked more than two blocks when Laurel began to feel as if they didn't belong, as if they'd been whisked here by a cyclone like Dorothy and Toto into the land of Oz.

She couldn't help but gape at a group of boys her age and older huddled under a produce-market awning, jabbering in what sounded like a foreign language. They all wore black hats and oversized black suits with tassels hanging from their belts. And on either side of each boy's head, a long curl hung down.

Now she and Annie were passing a dark-skinned lady draped in what looked like a shiny sky-blue bedsheet, both her wrists circled with thin silver bracelets almost to her elbows, a red dot marking the center of her forehead. She was holding the hand of a little pigtailed girl in a ruffled pink dress and white patent-leather shoes.

Laurel was so busy staring, she almost bumped into a line of black preschoolers herded by a plump lady who shouted, "Hey, Rufus . . . yeah, I'm talking to YOU . . . get your young butt back in that line 'fore I whack it good!"

Laurel, in her almost-new Levi's and an old pink cardigan of Annie's embroidered with tiny pink flowers, her long blond hair brushed back in a ponytail, felt like an alien from Mars.

She glanced over at her sister. Annie—with her big dark eyes and jutting cheekbones, her olive skin and chopped-off dark hair—looked more exotic, like she could fit in here. Then Laurel saw her peer back over her shoulder.

Laurel's stomach jumped, and she thought of Val. What if he were following them? And if he found them, and had Annie put in jail, it'd be partly her fault, wouldn't it? Because secretly she'd been wishing she could call Val or at least send him a postcard, just to let him know she was okay.

But then Laurel saw that Annie was only peering at a street sign, and she relaxed a little.

"Are you sure we're in the right place?"

"East Fourteenth, that's what she told me. Fifth house on the left."

They passed a bakery with a mouth-watering display of fruit tarts, and a Buster Brown shoe store, then a delicatessen with melon-shaped cheeses and salamis big as baseball bats hanging in the window. At the corner, turning onto Fourteenth, another store, Lana's Fashion Shoppe, had a sign on the door that read: "NO BABY CARRIAGES." The sidewalks, Laurel saw, were crowded with them. Every woman, it seemed, was pushing a carriage, some of them double carriages, as well as holding the hand of at least one other child.

Laurel was getting the funny feeling in her stomach again. From the moment she'd arrived in the big, dirty bus station near Times Square, she had felt as if she'd swallowed a fish that kept flopping around inside her. On the bus, she'd been too busy looking out the window at everything, the license plates zipping past them, going from blue to green to yellow as they crossed state lines, passing cornfields and cows, forests, distant mountains like cupcakes with snow frosting their peaks, and the Woolworth stores and A & P's on a hundred small-town Main Streets. She'd even kind of liked all those tuna-fish sandwiches washed down by Cokes, and stretching out on the seat to sleep with the engine humming beneath her like a lullaby. Or maybe she hadn't believed it was really happening. As if that night, leaving Bel Jardin, the bus trip, were all part of some long, crazy dream—and when she woke up she'd be back in her bed at Bel Jardin.

Then, finally, Annie was pointing out the Manhattan skyline. They went down into a tunnel, under the Hudson River, and Laurel imagined the tunnel springing a leak, water pouring in, and drowning them before they even got to New York. She had gripped Annie's hand, her heart hammering, the fish in her stomach flopping like crazy.

Now, after two weeks, her stomach was still a mess. Sometimes, like now, she wondered if they'd done the right thing, running away. But then what if Annie had gone without her? That would awful too . . . worse than this.

Val. Suppose she'd had to stay behind with him? He wasn't mean to her, but he was hardly ever around. Without Annie, she'd be all alone. She'd be miserable.

"I think this is it." Annie's voice jerked her back to the present.

Laurel stopped, and stared at where her sister was pointing: a two-story wooden house, painted gray, with a little front porch and a tiny lawn surrounded by a neat hedge. A bunch of leaves had been raked into a pile near the sidewalk, under a big tree. It wasn't Bel Jardin, but it looked nice . . . and well, homey. She noticed a tricycle overturned on the front walk, and up on the porch, a cozy jumble of chairs. A sign nailed over the door read: "THE GRUBERMANS." Laurel's heart lifted. A real family lived here.

But wait. The name was supposed to be Shabbat, not Gruberman. Could this be the wrong house? Or maybe the sign was left over from another owner.

"Don't get your hopes up," Annie warned, but Laurel could see that she was excited herself. "It'll probably be like that last man. They'll say I'm too young, and we need references."

Even so, Laurel squeezed her eyes shut, and prayed, *Please, God, let Mrs. Shabbat take us.*

She felt Annie tug on her hand, pulling her up the path. "Well, here goes nothing." She pressed the doorbell.

"Coming, coming, I'm coming!" someone yelled to them from inside.

After a long minute, the front door swung open. A woman stood before them. A checkered apron was tied about her enormous belly and a flowered scarf knotted around her head. A round face with crinkly brown eyes smiled at them.

"Miss Davis?"

"Yes," Annie answered at once.

"Huh? . . . Um, yeah," muttered Laurel at the same time. She flushed, and quickly shut her mouth, realizing she better let Annie take over now.

"I'm Annie . . . and this is my sister, Laurel. She's the one who called you."

"And I'm Rivka Gruberman." She smiled at Laurel. "And you talk lovely on the phone, darling, but I've never seen such young girls as you two looking for an apartment. You understand, I can't have someone who's going to move in, and then bim-boom-bam, they move right back to Mama."

"We don't have a mother," Annie answered quietly. "She died."

"Oh," said Rivka, nodding several times, then opening the door wider. "Well, you better look at it."

Rivka gave them a sharp look as she ushered them into a dim vestibule smelling of cooked carrots, but said nothing more as, huffing and puffing, she led them up the narrow stairs. Laurel breathed a sigh of relief. *I don't think she believes Annie's twenty-one, but she's not going to make a big fuss about it.*

The apartment was small: a tiny kitchen with yellow cabinets, a living room with a faded green carpet, and a bedroom not much bigger than her closet at Bel Jardin. But the place was clean, and all the walls had fresh light-blue paint. A delicious smell of baking bread drew Laurel to an open window. She peered out to see where it was coming from. Across a weed-grown lot, she saw a huge exhaust fan whirring on the roof of a small building.

"Is that a bakery?" she asked.

"Bagels," Rivka explained. "All day long, and all night, twenty-four hours they don't stop with the bagels. And as if we don't get enough of it, what does my husband bring me every day on his way back from *shul?*" She chortled and threw up her hands.

Laurel wanted to ask what a bagel was, but Annie shot her a warning look, and Laurel bit back her question.

"It's a very nice apartment," Annie said. "We'll take it." She sounded firm and grown-up, but then a trace of unsureness crept in. "That is . . . if . . . if it's okay with you."

"I don't know from Arizona," said Rivka, eyeing them carefully. "But before you make up your mind, you would like to see our *shul,* no?"

Something was wrong; Laurel could feel it. Her stomach began to flop. And she could see from the way Annie was nibbling at her thumbnail that she felt it, too.

Annie, her face reddening, echoed, "Your *shul?*"

Rivka gave them a long look, and said gently, "Come, *shainenkes,* come downstairs with me. Manhattan's a long trip, and you could use some hot tea, and maybe a piece of babka, yeah?"

Downstairs, the Grubermans' apartment was a madhouse. Children everywhere—a cluster of older boys on the sofa, reading aloud to each other in that same foreign language she'd heard on the street. Two little ones with toy trucks, scooting about the cabbage-rose carpet. A baby sitting up in a playpen, banging a set of plastic keys against its bars.

The noise was incredible.

"*Sha,* everyone! We've got company!" Rivka yelled as she sailed through, stepping over dolls and stuffed animals, but no one paid any attention.

In the big cheerful kitchen, a dark-haired, pink-cheeked girl about Annie's age was rolling out dough on the counter.

"My oldest," Rivka said, "my Sarah," waving a hand in her direction. The girl nodded shyly and went back to her rolling pin.

This house, this woman, reminded Laurel of the old woman who lived in a shoe, who had so many children she didn't know what to do. Except Mrs. Gruberman seemed so happy. And nice.

Laurel and Annie sat down at a long table covered with a yellow-checked oilcloth. Looking around, Laurel noticed something odd: everything was in twos. Two sinks, two sets of cupboards, even two refrigerators.

"I see you looking at my refrigerators," Rivka observed. "You know why I have two?"

"I guess it's because you have such a big family," Laurel ventured, feeling shy, and scared because she could feel that Mrs. Gruberman was somehow working up to telling them no.

"No, darling, it's because we're kosher. Everything that's meat, and everything that's milk, we keep strictly separate."

Laurel wanted to ask why, but it didn't somehow seem like a good idea.

"I know about kosher," Annie said. "My mother once took me to Fairfax Avenue for hot dogs. She said they were the best ones."

Rivka chuckled as she bustled about the stove, putting the kettle on and lighting the fire under it. Then she turned to face them, hands folded over her fat belly. "So, what shall I do with the two of you? You don't even know what *Shomer Shabbat* means. Am I right?"

Laurel's heart sank. Shomer Shabbat plainly was not the name of Rivka's husband. And worse, Rivka Gruberman was not going to rent them the apartment.

"We're not Jewish," Annie confessed.

Rivka sighed, and then ruefully nodded. "Darlings, this I saw the second I laid eyes on you. We don't let our girls live alone, without a father or a husband." The laughter left her face as suddenly as a cloud passing in front of the sun. "I'm sorry. *Shomer Shabbat* means Sabbath observers only."

"We won't make one bit of noise on the Sabbath," Annie pleaded. "My sister and I, we don't have a TV, or even a radio."

Rivka shook her head, even while plunking mugs of steaming tea in front of them. "You seem like nice girls. Please, don't take it personal." She set out a plate of yeasty cake laden with raisins and nuts, which smelled as if it had just come out of the oven.

Laurel's mouth watered. Her eyes were watering, too. Feeling hungry and miserable, she helped herself to a big piece.

"I have money. I could pay you the deposit right this minute," Annie pressed, desperation in her voice. "Cash."

"Please, it's not the money," Rivka replied sorrowfully. "It's how we live."

"But . . ." Annie started to plead, then suddenly her mouth clamped shut, and she sat up very straight, shoulders squared, as if there was an invisible needle poking her in the back. Laurel knew that look . . . it was Annie's stubborn look. She wouldn't beg, no matter how desperate she was. "It's okay," she said briskly. "I understand."

Laurel took a swallow of hot tea, scalding her tongue. Tears welled in her eyes. Why didn't Annie tell her that they'd looked everywhere and they were too exhausted to look any more? Why couldn't she admit she was hungry? Laurel saw Annie eyeing the plate of cake, but, no, she was too proud to take any.

Laurel's stomach churned up into her throat, and for a second she thought she might be sick.

Then she had an idea.

"I could babysit for you," she said softly. "I wouldn't even charge for it."

Shaking her head pityingly, Rivka turned back to her stove, picking up where she must have left off when they'd arrived, flouring chicken drumsticks and dropping them into a hot, sputtering skillet.

Annie stood up. "Thank you anyway for showing us the place. Laurey, I think we'd better be go—"

She was interrupted by a loud wail from the other room. The older girl, Sarah, shot her mother a pleading look, and said, "Please, Ma, I just gave Shainey her bottle. And I have to finish this before Rachel gets here. She's coming special to help me with my algebra."

"And I"—Rivka threw up her floury hands—"have four hands all of a sudden?"

Laurel, guided by instinct, rushed into the next room and scooped the crying baby from her playpen. The infant kicked and squirmed, letting out a loud screech, her round face bunching up, as Laurel, feeling awkward, tried as best she could to comfort her. Laurel wished she knew more about babies—she'd only helped Bonnie babysit her baby brother that one time, and little Jimmy had screamed too until they got his diaper changed. Maybe that's what this one needed.

While the boys on the sofa looked on in fascination, Laurel peeled off the baby's plastic pants. Underneath, her diaper was soaking wet. Then Laurel saw why she'd been crying—one of the diaper pins had popped open, and was sticking her in the side.

She had just gotten the pin out and the diaper off when Rivka rushed in, drying her hands on a dish towel. "Oy, what now? My little *shainenke*!" She hoisted the baby onto her big belly, cradling its bare bottom with the dish towel. She smiled at Laurel.

"So? You know about babies? You're just a baby yourself!"

"I know a lot about babies," Laurel lied, careful not to meet Annie's eyes.

"A pin was sticking Shainey!" cried a dark-haired boy wearing a round skullcap that had slipped to one side of his head, giving him a cockeyed look. "The girl pulled it out."

Rivka covered the baby with kisses, then said, "By my husband, it's enough already I have the older girls to help out." She sighed. "But believe me, with Sarah and Chava and Leah in yeshiva all day and this new one coming any minute, I could use a little more help."

Laurel looked up into Rivka's kind face, and saw an uncertainty that hadn't been there a few minutes ago. She felt a surge of hope. Was there still a chance? Had Rivka changed her mind?

She took a deep breath and thought, *We'd be safe here.* Safe from muggers and mean landlords and cockroaches. Safe from policemen and from Val.

"Stay," Rivka said softly. "Stay and meet my husband, Ezra. He'll be home soon. Maybe he meets you and then he'll change his mind."

Laurel let her breath out, feeling a rush of happy relief. And pride, too. Because she was the one who had made this all happen. She grinned at Annie, who grinned back.

Somehow, Laurel felt sure it was going to be okay. For right now, at least. She didn't want to think about tomorrow, or the day after that. She didn't want to think about going to school in this weird neighborhood, or whether or not Annie would find a job before they went broke.

Later, if Rivka's husband said they could have the apartment, she'd ask her about the bearded men with the round fur hats and curls. And the ladies with the red dots on their foreheads.

She could see she had lots and lots to learn.

CHAPTER 3

Annie reached for the fat man's empty plate. The stack of dirty dishes balanced against her other arm chattered and swayed, and for a dreadful second, she was sure the whole mess was going to crash to the floor. But she managed somehow to right it.

"Excuse me," she said, trying to sound calm and polite, scooping up knives and forks and side-order plates from the Formica table where the fat man and his even fatter wife were finishing their lunch.

"Excuse *me*," the fat man's wife snarled as Annie accidentally brushed her shoulder.

Annie noted that Mrs. Fat had just packed away a double cheese-burger with side orders of onion rings and coleslaw, and strawberry cheesecake for dessert. *Probably miserable with heartburn from all that,* Annie guessed, then remembered, no, the old cow had snapped at her even before she'd started packing it in, back when Annie mixed up her order, and brought lettuce and tomato instead of coleslaw.

Annie felt an angry flush ride up her neck. Sweat popped out on her forehead, and it frustrated her that she couldn't just stop and wipe it away. But then she thought, *It's my fault. I'm just no good at this,* and her anger cooled.

A full week at the Parthenon now, and she still hadn't gotten the hang of it. Worse, she felt she never would. How did the others manage it? Loretta, for instance. Only a little older than Annie, she made it look so easy . . . as easy as walking and chewing gum at the same time.

What was it Loretta had said to her that first day?

"Honey, I was bawn with flat feet." Looking Annie up and down, sucking in her pimply cheeks, she'd added, "What I can't figure is what *yaw* doin' here."

Right now, Annie wondered the same thing. But she knew that

without this job she couldn't buy groceries or set aside money to pay next month's rent.

No, she had to start getting better at this, or she and Laurel would be sleeping on the subway. And eventually they'd be picked up, and then Val—if he wasn't dead—would surely find them.

A chill sliced through her. He could be out looking for them right now, this very minute. Suppose he'd gone to the Los Angeles Greyhound terminal and found out somehow that they'd bought tickets to New York?

". . . so I told him, 'If you can't come up with a better excuse than that, young man, you can just march yourself up those stairs, and . . .'"

The fat lady's whiny voice grated like fingernails on chalkboard. Annie felt all sweaty. Hardly noon, and already she was dripping under each armpit. She'd have to wash her uniform again tonight, and hang it to dry in front of the oven. And, God, would she ever get rid of this rancid-grease smell? Her hair, her fingers, even her pantyhose smelled like yesterday's hamburgers. One of these days some hungry dog would probably charge up and take a bite out of her.

The table cleared, she turned to go, clumsily bumping her hip against its corner. The coffee cup at the top of her leaning tower tottered, then slid. Annie, her heart lurching, grabbed for it, but the cup shot from her sweaty grasp. While she watched in horror, time seemed to wind down, as if this were some slow-motion movie—the thick white cup tumbling over and over, the smudgy pink imprint of the fat woman's lip against the rim almost grinning up at her. It hit the table with a spray of milky dregs, then suddenly, like a billiard ball shooting into a side pocket, the cup skidded over and dumped itself, along with the little bit of coffee still left in it, smack in the fat woman's bulging lap.

Mrs. Fat let out a yowl and began mopping frantically at the stain covering the front of her lime-green polyester pants suit. "You stupid thing! Just look what you did! I'll just bet it's ruined for good."

"I'm sorry," Annie said. Flustered, she grabbed a crumpled napkin, dabbing at the wet spot, but only succeeded in adding a new catsup stain.

Mrs. Fat swatted her hand away. "I want the manager! Get me

the manager!" She glared at her husband. "Don't just sit there, Hank. *Do* something."

Annie felt as if the whole scene were taking place underwater. She watched the woman's rubbery lips opening and closing, like a fat carp's, and now her husband lumbering heavily to his feet. A noise like rushing water filled her ears, and the light filtering in through the steamy plate-glass window seemed to ripple strangely.

Then Nick Dimitriou, the boss, was scurrying over, and everybody was staring, forks poised in midair at tables all around her. Annie wanted to be swallowed up by the floor. Her heart thumped, and now she could feel the sweat rolling down her neck and back.

But she stood her ground. She'd show them. She wasn't just some knock-kneed kid who was going to fall apart at the drop of a hat. But, oh God, Nick did look pissed, his thick brows scrunched together, his dark eyes glowering.

"Go on, go," he hissed at her. "Wait in kitchen. I take care of these people. Then we talk."

Annie, her cheeks burning, carried the dirty plates back and lowered them into the big rubber bin by the dishwasher. She felt tears pressing against the backs of her eyes, but she wouldn't let herself cry. Not with Loretta and J.J. and Spiro watching. She fixed a squinty gaze on the cloud of steam rising from the sink, where shaggy-haired J.J. was scrubbing out one of the huge stockpots. From the other end of the kitchen, the sizzle of something abruptly dunked into the industrial-sized fryer hit her ears like a muffled blast from a machine gun.

Then Loretta was touching her arm, and Annie realized she must have seen the whole thing. "Don't worry," she said, her faded blue eyes full of sympathy. "Nick can fly off the handle for a minute, but he's okay. It wasn't your fault anyway. Coulda happened to anyone."

But Annie knew that wasn't true. Loretta wouldn't have dropped that cup. And mixed up all those orders—yesterday alone, at table five, split-pea soup instead of minestrone, and a steak well-done instead of rare. All of which had to be scrapped, and replaced.

No, Loretta might never have studied French or trigonometry, but when it came to waitressing she was a genius compared to Annie.

Annie had a sudden vision of herself seated at the long, Spanish-style dining table at Bel Jardin, helping herself from the platter of roast beef Bonita was holding out. Plump Bonita, in her black-and-white uniform, her brown face shining, as if she were offering Annie some wonderful gift. *And I just took it for granted . . . I never appreciated how hard she worked.*

She felt a sharp pang of loss; she missed Bel Jardin so. The tears she had been holding back now sprang to her eyes. She wanted so much to bury her face in a dish towel and just let herself sob. But she knew she couldn't. Laurel would be waiting for her back in their empty apartment. No food in the refrigerator, except a carton of milk and a half-eaten can of tuna fish—hardly enough to feed a cat. If the tips weren't good today, she'd been planning to ask Nick for an advance on her paycheck, then pick up some groceries on the way home.

But now, as she watched her boss shoulder in through the swinging doors, Annie felt herself shrivel inside. How stupid she'd been, how smug, thinking that this job would be a cinch.

But even though she felt like running out the back door, she forced herself to stay put and hold herself tall. *I need this job,* she thought.

She walked over to the boss, a wiry Greek man with a livid pink scar extending from the corner of his right eye down to his jaw. He'd worked as a stevedore while saving up to start his own business, Loretta had told her, and one day a piece of baling wire had snapped, springing up to slice open the right side of his face. Now, where the scar pulled down the corner of his mouth, it gave him the look of a permanent scowl.

Annie, her heart hammering, made herself look him square in the eye. *No whining, no lame excuses,* she commanded herself. Dearie, with all her bad luck and sickness, never let anyone get away with whining, herself included.

"I'm sorry for what happened back there," Annie said. "I'm trying my best, Mr. Dimitriou."

Some of the sternness left his face, and he shook his head. "This I know . . . but, listen, I have business to run. I can afford one mistake, maybe two. But you, Annie . . . maybe you try *too* hard. You make yourself trouble that way. You make me trouble. Lady in there, she's a regular customer, and she wants I should pay for cleaning dress. I smile and say, 'Nicholas Dimitriou always make good,' but what way is that to make money? No, sorry, you got to go." He turned, and started to walk away.

"Wait!" Annie called after him. She couldn't beg . . . and yet she couldn't let him fire her. A trapped sob quivered in her chest, making her voice come out high and shaky. "I'll pay for my mistakes. Take it out of my paycheck. Mr. Dimitriou, I really n-need this job. Please . . . give me another chance." For a terrible instant, everything went wavy and hot, and she was afraid she was going to be an idiot and burst into tears.

Nick's ruined mouth screwed downward in a sad smile. "I give you good advice, Annie. This no place for girl like you." Annie watched, stunned, as he turned, and disappeared through the swinging doors.

Loretta came up, and put her arm around Annie. "You don't want to hear it right now, I know, but he's right," she said. "You're too good for this dump. I bet you're an actress or a model, waitin' for the big break, right?" Loretta's watery blue eyes grew wistful. The worst part of this job, she'd once confided to Annie, was that she had to miss watching *Days of Our Lives.*

Annie, who purposely had avoided talking about herself, couldn't help feeling flattered. She was grateful to Loretta, too, for distracting her. But the black thoughts at the edge of her mind couldn't be kept out. How was she going to get another job, pay next month's rent, feed herself and Laurel?

In her locker in the back there was exactly forty-two dollars and seventy-two cents—tips she'd earned so far, plus the last of her jewelry money. That, with the week's pay she had coming, ought to be just enough to last them until the end of the month . . . if she was really, really careful. But after that . . .

Oh God, what am I going to do?

Feeling shaken, like that time at Bel Jardin when she'd accidentally walked into the sliding glass door of the pool house, Annie collected her pay envelope from Mr. Dimitriou and left.

On Eighth Avenue, passing a greengrocer with bushels of lettuce, tomatoes, and apples sitting out on the curb, she thought of that scene in *Gone With the Wind,* where Scarlett upchucks the radish, then shakes her fist at the sky and vows, "I'll never go hungry again."

Thinking just how much like a movie her own predicament was, Annie gave a harsh laugh. "Now what?" she said under her breath.

But she'd think of something. She *would*.

"*Baruch ata adonai, elohenu melech ha-olam . . .*"

Annie closed her eyes and let the sound of Rivka's voice, as she chanted the blessing over the candles, flow through her. She felt herself relaxing, this afternoon's ordeal at the Parthenon fading from her thoughts.

Adding a little prayer of her own, Annie muttered, "Please, God, let me find another job." *Something I'd be good at . . . a place where I'd fit in.*

Now, opening her eyes, Annie watched Rivka, in her neatly coiffed brown *shaitel* and long-sleeved flowered dress, take her place at the crowded dining-room table opposite her husband, between Laurel and Sarah. There was more chanting in Hebrew, this time led by Mr. Gruberman, with the others joining in, their voices overlapping—the sweet high tones of Sarah and Leah and their four younger brothers mingling with the wavery, self-conscious contralto of thirteen-year-old Moishe. Beside her, Annie could hear Laurel softly chiming in, just a phrase here and there. Annie looked over at her sister in her blue-and-white checked jumper and navy cardigan, feeling a little jolt of surprise. When had Laurel learned that?

Rivka must have noticed, too, because now she was smiling at Laurel. "That's good, *shainenke*. Now you will help me say the blessing over the bread, *nu?*"

Laurel nodded shyly as Rivka handed her the sterling bread knife, in which Annie could see reflected the dancing flames of the Shabbat candles in their silver holders atop the sideboard.

"*Baruch ata adonai . . .*" Rivka and Laurel began together; then Rivka stopped and nodded to Laurel, beckoning for her to continue. Laurel faltered, her pale cheeks blooming with color. She looked up, casting a furtive glance about the table, then when she saw that no one was snickering at her, she pulled in a deep breath, and finished haltingly, ". . . *elohenu . . . melech . . . ha-olam . . . hamotzi . . . le-chem min ha-oretz.*"

Beaming, Laurel pulled off the snowy linen cloth covering the challah, and waited while Rivka sliced off one end of the large braided loaf. Following Rivka's lead, she tore off a small piece from the chunk Rivka handed her, and popped it into her mouth, passing the rest to Annie. The chunk of challah went around the table that way, everybody tearing off a shred until it was all gone.

This was the second time Rivka had asked them down for Shabbat dinner. Last Friday night it had been the same, Annie recalled, the lighting of the candles, then the blessings over the wine and the bread. But then, Laurel had just sat quietly, looking down at her plate throughout the chanting. Now she was joining in, *and in Hebrew.*

Annie had known her sister was quick at picking up new things—card games especially, and after only a couple of weeks of tagging after Rivka she was becoming a pretty good cook, too— but she couldn't help being impressed. What would Laurel come up with next?

Now, with Rivka and Sarah and Leah getting up and ferrying in from the kitchen steaming platters of roast chicken, potatoes, broccoli, and noodle kugel, and the boys chattering to one another in Yiddish, Laurel nudged Annie and asked, "Do you like the challah? I made it."

"*You* did?"

"Well, mostly I just helped, but Rivka let me knead the dough for this one, and then braid it. What makes it shiny on top is you brush it with egg whites."

"Egg whites," Annie repeated. She was staring at her sister, noticing how much more poised and grown-up she seemed than even a few weeks ago. Even her hair—she'd stopped wearing it in braids and pigtails, and now it was clasped loosely at the nape of her neck. Her eyes, too, had a new sparkle in them.

Annie thought of how last night, arriving home from the Parthenon, reeking with grease and sweat, hungry, and so tired she could hardly stand up, she'd found Laurel in their tiny kitchen with dinner all prepared—meatloaf and scalloped potatoes she'd made herself, along with a slightly wilted salad. The meatloaf was a little burned around the edges, and the potatoes were on the watery side, but Annie had gobbled them up, and hadn't lied when she told Laurel it was the most delicious meal she could remember.

She'd hadn't yet told Laurel that she'd been fired. She hadn't had the courage. And Rivka? What was Rivka supposed to do if next month Annie failed to come up with the rent money—keep them on as charity cases? No, the Grubermans, with all these kids, were having a hard time, Annie knew, just making ends meet. They needed the money from the upstairs apartment.

No, she *had* to find something . . . and quick.

But meanwhile . . . oh, how wonderful just to sit here, soaking in the good, savory smells rising from the laden platters and bowls being passed around the table, and feel the bounty of warmth and togetherness filling this room. Even the squabbling between the younger Grubermans didn't break the spell.

"Ma, Chaim is kicking me under the table, make him stop!"

"Chaim, stop," Rivka ordered calmly, and without even looking up from cutting chicken into tiny pieces for Shainey, perched in her high chair just behind Rivka, she added, "And, Yonkie, your broccoli—it belongs in your mouth, not in your napkin."

Annie watched five-year-old Yonkel, his yarmulke askew on his close-cropped curls, his chubby cheeks growing pink, sheepishly unfold his napkin and shake the smashed-looking broccoli inside it back on his plate.

"I'm not eating mine," announced pole-thin Moishe, who looked far younger than his thirteen years, except for the peach fuzz sprouting on his chin. Steam from the potatoes he was shovelling onto his plate misted his thick square eyeglasses. "How do I know there's not a bug in it?"

"Bugs?" Rivka looked up sharply.

"Well, I haven't ever actually *seen* one . . . but if I eat one by mistake, they're *treyf*."

"Says who?"

"Rabbi Mandelbaum."

"Listen, if Rabbi Mandelbaum wants to eat at my table, then he can come over first and personally wash every bit of broccoli himself. Until then, I cook, and you eat." Rivka sounded indignant, but her eyes sparkled with amusement.

"Look, Yonkie, *I'm* eating it," Laurel said encouragingly, spearing a huge chunk, and popping it into her mouth. "It's really good!"

Everyone at the table except Laurel and Annie burst out laughing.

"*You* can eat anything you want," giggled Leah. The dark-eyed fifteen-year-old, with her rosy cheeks and smooth brown pageboy, was a smaller, livelier version of her older sister, Sarah. "You're not Jewish."

"Moishe's not leaving it because he's Jewish," Laurel replied matter-of-factly. "He just doesn't like broccoli."

More laughter around the table.

Rivka smiled, and beamed at Laurel. "Smart girl."

Annie felt a new respect for Laurel. Here she was, plunked in the middle of a strange city that might just as well be Hungary, with people she hadn't the slightest thing in common with, and somehow she was fitting in, making the best of it . . . even learning new things. And maybe, at the same time, teaching these people something, too.

The burden of taking care of Laurel, of worrying about her and about how they would survive, now seemed suddenly lighter than it had even this afternoon. Maybe it wasn't Laurel who was depending completely on her . . . maybe, in some small ways, *she* was coming to depend on Laurel, too.

CHAPTER 4

Dolly slammed down the phone.

She felt mad enough to spit. Four whole days, she thought. Those Customs peckerwoods at JFK had been sitting on her shipment for almost as long as it took Moses to free the Israelites. And the inspectors she'd spoken to either didn't know what the hold-up was all about, or were too lazy to find out, or both. Damn them!

She picked up the receiver again, and started dialling. She'd call back and read them the riot act. And this time she wouldn't waste her time with the I & C boys, she'd go straight to the top, to McIntyre himself. He was the import specialist. He was supposed to have a handle on things. What the devil did he expect her to do with two thousand dollars' worth of highly perishable chocolates going gray and soft in some customs shed? And Thanksgiving only two weeks away!

All at once, Dolly thought better of it, took a deep breath, and put down the phone.

That's not what's really needling you, is it? You're just using this to let off steam. . . .

Remembering that phone call from Ned Oliver a few weeks ago—dear swishy Ned, so distraught, telling her that Evie's girls had run away from home—Dolly felt a stitch in her gut pull tight. Ned, her old friend, and Eve's too, who over the years had secretly kept Dolly up to date on Annie and Laurel, sending snapshots, and also managing to pass off as his own the little gifts and small amounts of cash Dolly sent for them. If she could have, she would have given them more, but that might've made Eve suspicious.

Those poor girls! It had to be Val's fault somehow. She'd called him, immediately after talking to Ned. Swallowing her dislike, she'd begged him to tell her everything he knew, which wasn't much. Ever since, she hadn't been able to shake the feeling that he was keeping something from her. Maybe he didn't know where the girls had gone, but she'd bet her bottom dollar he had a pretty damn good idea of *why* they might have charged off in the middle of the night.

But why blame Val? When you got right down to it, wasn't *she* the one to blame? If it hadn't been for her knifing Eve in the back, probably none of this would ever have happened.

Dolly began to get that familiar downward-spiraling feeling, and she quickly caught herself short. What was the use of beating on herself over and over? Better if she could *do* something . . .

She had to find her nieces somehow.

She thought of the private investigator out in L.A. she'd hired. If only she could *do* something besides sitting around waiting for O'Brien to call with some news.

Itching with impatience, Dolly grabbed the phone and dialed the long-distance number.

"O'Brien," he answered, his smooth, pleasant voice making her think of an insurance salesman or a young bank executive, not hard-boiled enough to be a P.I. But she knew he'd been with the L.A.P.D. for ten years.

"Dolly Drake here," she told him. "You turned up anything on my nieces yet?" She felt out of breath, as if she'd been talking for hours instead of just asking one simple question. The other times she'd called, he'd merely told her to be patient, that he'd get back to her as soon as he had anything. Why should today be any different?

But now, dear Lord, he was saying something that made a bubble of hope start rising up in her.

"Funny you should call, I've been trying to reach you, but your phone's been busy. Look, don't get too excited, but I think I know where they are . . . at least the general vicinity. I talked to a Grey-hound driver who recognized the photos." He paused, and she could hear him shuffling papers. "He says they were headed for New York City. But . . ."

New York? *Here!* Dolly's heart lurched.

". . . the chances of finding a couple of runaways in such a big city, I have to tell you, could be a million to one. These kids just get swallowed up somehow. Believe me, I know."

"Does this mean you're giving up?" She felt frantic, her heart beating like a trapped bird in her throat.

"Look, it's your dime. But if you want my opinion, you're best off sitting tight. Sooner or later, they get desperate enough, and then they call home."

Fat chance, Dolly thought. Some home. He didn't know Val Carrera.

No, she told O'Brien, you keep looking. To herself she added, damn the expense. She had to keep on hoping. But as she hung up, she felt suddenly leaden.

She could not count on O'Brien. It was going to be up to her. She would have to think of something. One way or another, she herself would have to find them. . . .

Get busy, she told herself, *keep moving, and maybe an idea will come to you.*

In the tiny office above her shop, Dolly squeezed out from behind her desk, and walked over to the refrigerated case containing her overstock. Through its clear glass panels, she could see the boxes lining the wire shelves. Fifty-eight degrees, not enough to cause condensation—but exactly the right temperature to keep her precious chocolates from melting, or from turning gray with bloom. Fine chocolates, she had learned, were like fragile flowers, orchids or gardenias; they needed to be coddled, babied. But what good were all her precautions here when her next two weeks' inventory was going stale in some shed at the airport that was probably either overheated or freezing?

She scanned the reorder list that was taped to the front of the case. Damn, they were just about out of the Bouchons—and those dark chocolate buttercreams flavored with cognac were Mrs. Van Dyne's favorites. Every Thursday, rain or shine, that forever-smiling Filipino driver of hers came in the huge antique Packard to pick up a pound. She'd heard that the old lady existed on Girod's chocolate and champagne. What would she tell that wonderfully obsequious driver tomorrow? Would he take bourbon creams instead?

And the Petits Coeurs, heart-shaped shells of bitter chocolate filled with coconut and *crème fraîche*—her best-selling bonbon, and not just on Valentine's Day, either. She was supposed to supply eight dozen for a wedding party at the Carlyle this coming Saturday, and right now she didn't have one full box.

She was short on everything—praline Gianduja, Noix Caraque, and those lovely little snail shells of Escargot Noir filled with dark coffee cream. And that appointment tomorrow that had taken the better part of a year to set up, how in heaven's name could she romance the Plaza's food buyer without a single one of Girod's signature Framboise truffles?

Dolly felt the beginning of a headache—as if there were an invisible thumb pressing just above the bridge of her nose. Then she remembered something else, something good: Henri was coming today. His plane was due in at JFK around five. She should've asked him to pack an extra suitcase full of chocolates while he was at it. In his shop in Paris, the original La Maison de Girod—shortened here to Girod's—they were made fresh every day.

Then it occurred to her—two birds with one stone, why not? She could personally try to sweet-talk McIntyre into releasing her shipment, and then afterwards meet Henri's plane.

Oh, it would be so good to see him, to have him here again. And maybe Henri would come up with a good idea about how to find Annie and Laurel.

Her spirits rose, and her headache seemed to fade. Wouldn't Henri be surprised, and pleased? Usually, she waited for him at her apartment, with champagne on ice and wearing nothing but black silk-chiffon. Well, the champagne she could manage—she'd have Felipe pick up a bottle of Cristal. But the black nightie? For now he'd have to settle for the black silk panties and bra she was wearing under her dress.

Dolly caught her reflection in the refrigerator's glass door. Black was fine for lingerie, she thought, but she wouldn't be caught dead in it. *Bury me in fuchsia,* she thought, *Or orange, or kelly-green . . . anything but black.* Her dress from Bloomie's was a brilliant tomato-red with a navy polka-dot panel over her bosom that, for a dressier evening look, she could unsnap to reveal more of her deep cleavage. In her ears, she wore the ruby-and-diamond earrings Dale had given her for their fifth—and last—anniversary. About her wrists, a wide hammered-gold bracelet and two smaller ones. Her long nails a defiant fire-engine red.

Dolly believed in bright colors the way some people swore by lucky charms and rabbits' feet. Somewhere she'd read that in mental hospitals they painted the walls a soft, cool blue, and that was supposed to keep depressed people from jumping out of windows. But what kept Dolly from the low-downs were brights that leaped out at you—crimson and yellow, orange, pink, deep purple. She loved stuff that glittered and twinkled—rhinestone buttons, shiny patent-leather shoes, oversized jewelry. Dale had once joked that the inside of her closet at home looked like Carmen Miranda's turban. The way Dolly looked at it, the world was already gray enough without adding to its misery.

Dolly straightened the mother-of-pearl combs in her upswept honey-blond hair (twice a week, Michael took care of the wisps of gray that had begun showing up lately), and applied a fresh coat of Fever Red to her lips. Oh, she knew how the blue-rinse dowagers in her Park Avenue building gossiped about her, and their holier-than-thou butlers and housekeepers too. *Loud, vulgar, cheap,* she could almost hear them whispering. *Her late husband was some oil wildcatter. She was waiting tables when he married her. Lavished a fortune on her . . . as if it did any good. She still looks right out of a five-and-dime.* Well, what did she care? Those antique snoots with their dreary clothes and tasteful pearls, what could they offer her that was better than what she already had with Henri?

Henri.

Dolly felt herself grow warm. Just thinking about him made her feel as if she was coming in from the cold and stretching out in front of a blazing fireplace. Starting at her toes, a rosy glow spreading up all through her, soothing and sexy. And it had been so long, almost three months. Oh, she couldn't wait.

But at the same time, she felt uneasy. Tonight she was supposed to give him her answer. She had promised she would.

And if I say yes? If I agree to move to Paris? Dolly let herself imagine the two of them together, nights in Henri's arms, weekends roaming the galleries on the Left Bank, or going off for a picnic in Chaville. An elegant flat near the Trocadéro, and fresh croissants every morning.

But, dammit, Henri was still married. *You can look at a mule ten different ways, but it's never gonna be a horse,* Mama-Jo always used to say. And, well, yeah, no matter how you sliced it, she'd only be what she was now—Henri's mistress.

And what about Girod's? Gloria could probably keep things going here, but that wasn't the point.

She loved having her own business, knowing each time she unlocked the iron grate at 870 Madison that the shop was hers, that it couldn't fire her, or simply fade away like one more dead-end screen test. Dale might not have understood (*Why, honey,* she could hear him say, *you can* own *most anything your heart desires, but whyever would you want to stand behind a counter when you could* hire *somebody for that?*). But Dolly knew somehow that her well-being, if not her livelihood, was grounded somehow in this store.

She needed Girod's, the chit-chat with the customers, with the UPS boys and the mailman, the figuring and ordering, the satisfaction of selling, the fun of arranging windows. And, of course, all those heavenly chocolates.

Dolly thought back to when she first decided to open a chocolate shop. One rainy spring day, some months after Dale had died, when the thought of spending the rest of her life alone had almost sent her reeling back to bed, on the spur of the moment, she'd packed a suitcase, grabbed her Baedeker and a battered French phrase book and escaped . . . to Paris.

On the rue du Faubourg St-Honoré, poking among the elegant shops, she'd happened upon La Maison de Girod. Stopping at an antique shop where she was admiring a Cupid garden ornament in the window, she'd spied a young mother across the street with her little boy in tow, emerging from an old-fashioned-looking shop with windowpanes set in gleaming dark wood. The boy was clutching something in his free hand, his fat cheeks smeared with chocolate, wearing an expression of ecstasy.

Intrigued, Dolly had crossed the street and pushed her way inside with a tinkle of the brass bell over the door.

Within the hour—having sweet-talked her way into a tour of the chocolatier's basement kitchen, inhaling aromas that made her almost dizzy with pleasure, and sampling flavors that tasted too delicious to have been created on this earth, she'd learned that Monsieur Baptiste was indeed eager to franchise a Girod's outlet in New York. Dolly suddenly knew exactly what she wanted to do when she returned home.

And now, after five years, her little Madison Avenue shop felt more like home than the cavernous Park Avenue apartment. Could she just go off and turn her back on it? Did she love Henri enough to give up what she'd worked so hard to build for herself?

Stop torturing yourself . . . you can make up your mind when you see him.

Impatient now to get to the airport, Dolly dialled her apartment.

Louella answered and summoned Felipe. She told her driver to get over to Girod's as soon as he could, with a bottle of Cristal on ice.

Now, she had to come up with some charming way to unbend Import Specialist Julio McIntyre—couldn't be a bribe, exactly, but some kind of *incentive*. He *had* to release that shipment.

Dolly plunged into the closet-sized storeroom catty-corner to the office. She'd bring McIntyre some chocolates, she decided. What else could she offer that wouldn't be out-and-out bribery? But first she'd need a box . . . something really special. Her gaze scanned over the stacks of flat cardboard yet to be folded into boxes, embossed with Girod's gold imprint, which lay in cartons on the floor. Above, lining the shelves, were the special containers, ones she'd collected herself: antique cookie tins and Art Deco canisters, gaily painted Mexican boxes, baskets studded with seashells, a quilted-satin jewelry chest. Gloria called this room her magpie's nest. And that's kind of how it had started, something catching Dolly's eye one day while browsing through the Twenty-sixth Street flea market—a bright cloth-covered Indian box stitched with tiny round mirrors. On a whim, she'd lined it with gold foil and filled it with chocolates, then stuck a stiff price tag on it and placed it atop the pine washstand in the front of the shop. Within an hour, it had sold.

Now, rummaging through her magpie treasures, Dolly wondered what in the world would impress a seen-it-all Customs agent.

Then she spotted it. Perfect—a cookie jar in the shape of an apple. She would fill it with Rhum Caramels and champagne truffles . . . and play Eve to McIntyre's Adam. It had worked in the Good Book. Why not now?

With the cookie jar tucked under her arm, Dolly made her way down the world's narrowest staircase—it had to have been built with a midget in mind, she thought, ducking to avoid hitting her head against the landing. Definitely not for a size fourteen on five-inch spike heels.

Downstairs, she found Gloria bent over the counter, folding boxes. She straightened and looked up at Dolly, her enormous brass earrings swaying and tinkling like wind chimes.

"You manage to kick some ass up at Customs?"

"Better." Dolly held up the apple jar and grinned wickedly. "I'm mounting a personal attack. Death by chocolate."

"Amen to that," Gloria laughed.

Dolly had never known anyone like Gloria. In Clemscott, blacks were called colored, and you never saw them except cleaning the mansions along Shady Hill Avenue, or working down at the car wash on Main. But Gloria didn't look down when spoken to, and she saw no reason to straighten her hair, which rose in an untamed cloud about her head. Gloria's wardrobe reflected her outspoken style as well—a dress made out of sewn-together scarves one day, a man's crewneck sweater over miniskirt and tights the next. Today, it was a fuzzy pink boat-necked sweater, black toreador slacks, and ballet flats. She sort of added to Girod's exotic flavor. But it would be a blessing, Dolly thought, if Gloria didn't get quite so darn many personal calls here at the shop. She had as many boyfriends as Zsa Zsa Gabor had husbands.

Dolly was just finishing filling the cookie jar when she spotted Felipe illegally pulling into the bus stop across the avenue. She grabbed a shopping bag, and threw on her coat with the Cacharel scarf stuffed in a pocket—Henri had given it to her last time, a silk replica of a stained-glass window from the Sainte Chapelle. Dashing out into the street with barely a glance in either direction, she reached Felipe—but not before a taxi, seeming to whip out of nowhere, missed hitting her by a hair.

"You don' watch out, you gonna get youself killed one a these days!" scolded her feisty Guatemalan driver as she slid into the back seat. She could see his broad face with its queerly flattened nose scowling affectionately at her in the rear-view mirror.

Dolly shrugged. Henri, too, was always after her for her supposedly reckless jaywalking, but in this city how else were you supposed to get around?

The Lincoln was inching its way along the Long Island Expressway, the world's longest parking lot, when it started to rain, a torrent of fat droplets that sounded as if the car was being pelted with eggs. Dolly sighed, and slipped off her shoes, tucking her feet under her. It was going to be a long ride.

Her thoughts returned to Annie and Laurel . . . out there somewhere. Did they have any money? A place to sleep? Enough to eat?

For ages she'd so yearned to be a part of their lives. But she'd had to settle for mere scraps—fuzzy snapshots Ned Oliver had taken, and his well-meaning, but scattered remembrances.

Lord, what it must have been like for them—those last years,

Eve's drinking more and more out of control, then the drying-out spells, when she'd be gone for months at a time. No money coming in, having to cut back until there was almost nothing left.

Dolly had so wanted to do things to help her sister. And there wasn't a day when she didn't regret having sent that damn letter. But every time she had called, some Spanish maid at Eve's house would pick up and say, "Missa Dearfield no home." Eve never returned a single one of her calls. And at Briarwood too, Eve's instructions had been strict—no visitors.

Once, Dolly had managed to slip past the reception desk and into Eve's room. Eve had been sitting on the end of the bed, smoking a cigarette and staring out the window. Her back, exposed by the flimsy robe she wore, made Dolly want to cry—it was so thin, every bump and ridge of her backbone clearly visible—and Dolly had seen that her hair, once bright as a gold locket, was now a dull ropey yellow, the color of straw.

But what shocked Dolly most was how fast her sister had deteriorated. It had been only a few months since her stone-faced refusal to give McCarthy one single name. Hollywood was still buzzing about Preminger snagging Grace Kelly in place of Eve. Syd had been way off about Dolly's prospects, as it turned out, but that now seemed like ancient history. What she cared about now was making Eve understand how sorry she was. Whatever Eve had done to her, however thoughtless or selfish she'd been, she hadn't deserved this.

Then Eve turned, and saw her. Her blue eyes, in that first instant dull and flat as carbon paper, turned suddenly bright. She smiled, but it was a horrible smile that made Dolly shiver. Cigarette smoke swam up, and eddied about her head.

"So you found me," she said, her voice flat. "Well, you've seen me. Now you can go. It's closing time at the zoo." Eve stubbed out her cigarette in the ashtray by her bed.

"I'm sorry," Dolly told her. The words seemed as inconsequential as pebbles tossed into a vast ocean. But what else could she say? What else mattered? "Oh, honey, do you think you could ever find it in your heart to forgive me? I never thought . . ."

Eve fixed her with a gimlet gaze, freezing her. "Is that what you want to hear?" she replied in that same toneless voice. "Will that make you go away? Okay, then, I forgive you."

Inside Dolly, something snapped, and she started to cry. Then she realized that stupidly, she hadn't brought a handkerchief, or even a tissue. Eve didn't offer her one, either. Dolly's nose started to run, and she wiped at it with the sleeve of her jacket.

"How did you find out it was me?" Dolly managed to croak.

"You mean you don't *know*? About Syd?" Eve coughed out a harsh laugh. "God, that's rich . . . that's really rich. I'll bet he promised you the whole pie in the sky for sticking it to me. And all the while, it was *you* he was screwing over. Well, both of us, really. For a minute or two he actually convinced me that it was your idea, that he'd done the pitch of his life to talk you out of it. Big hero. Undying loyalty no matter how bad I'd treated him. Fade to sunset, our disgraced heroine melts gratefully into his arms, now promising to become his good little wife. Only he didn't know I'd just married Val. He figured there was still a chance, and then when everybody else in town had kicked me in the face, when I was nice and humble, he'd pick me up and dust off my career somehow. What a laugh, huh?"

Dolly stood there, feeling as if she'd been punched in the stomach.

And then, as if the fragile string that had been holding her sister upright had been abruptly severed, Eve slumped, her hands falling limply to her sides.

"You want to hear the best part?" Her voice was a thin rasp. "I'm pregnant. That whole bit about Val itching to marry me, it was all a big lie. Vegas was my idea. At heart, I guess I'm just an old-fashioned girl." With a small crooked smile, Eve turned toward her, enough so that Dolly could see the swell of her stomach under her loosely tied robe. Then the smile was gone, and in a reedy whisper Eve pleaded, "*Now* will you go away and leave me alone?"

Twelve years. It had taken Eve that long to die, but all the time that's what she'd been doing. Dying.

Now, staring out the window of her car at the rain-slashed grayness of the Long Island Expressway, remembering that scene, Dolly thought, *I helped kill her. It was me, not the booze and the pills, that did her in.*

And now, because of what Dolly had done, Eve's girls were out there somewhere, maybe in this pouring rain, probably scared to death. . . .

Dolly covered her face with her hands, and wept. She didn't deserve anything good. She didn't deserve Henri . . . nor had she deserved that dear man she'd married—huge-hearted Dale, who had picked her up when she was waiting tables at Ciro's, lavished her with affection and every ridiculous luxury, and died leaving her so wonderfully well provided for.

Then came the trickle of cool reason. Her tears were, she realized, like filling a bucket with a hole in the bottom—no earthly good at all. They weren't going to help her or her nieces the least bit. No, she would have to come up with something—something that both Val and O'Brien had missed, some hint, some small clue that might lead her to the girls. . . .

She closed her eyes and combed her brain. Could there be a friend in New York Annie might have gone to? Dolly had already called everybody she could think of who'd known Eve . . . but most of them said they hadn't seen Eve in years, and had seemed downright astonished to hear from Dolly. The teachers at Annie's school weren't helpful, either. One old sourpuss snapped that she'd already told the police everything she knew.

Dolly allowed herself to imagine being reunited with her nieces. They'd live with her, of course. But what if they were staying with someone else, a friend? Or what if Eve had told them about her betrayal, and the girls blamed her, hated her even? Well, she'd find ways to make it up to them. Short visits at first, while they got to know each other, then maybe they could all go on a nice long trip somewhere. Paris. They'd stay at the Lancaster. They'd love the little garden, the *boiserie* on the walls, the pillowy croissants at breakfast. She pictured the three of them, under the vast glass dome of the Galeries Lafayette, trying on shoes and chic dresses, picking out smart silk scarves.

Dolly felt her heart lift. Lord knew, she couldn't replace Eve . . . but she *could* be sort of like a mother to those girls, couldn't she? She'd longed for children of her own, but after a whole year of trying, the tests had shown that Dale's sperm count was impossibly low (*The dick of a bull, and the nuts of a gelding,* he used to joke, though it pained him plenty). No babies ever . . .

But wouldn't this be almost as good, in a way? If she could be a mother to her nieces, wouldn't it, in some small way, help make up for what she'd done to Eve?

The traffic was clearing now, and the green approach signs for JFK could be seen through the rain up ahead. Minutes later, they were pulling up in front of the gray concrete cube of Cargo Building 80, and Dolly was dashing across the rain-slick tarmac, shopping bag tucked up under her arm.

Inside, the place looked even more dreary than it had outside: pea-soup walls, scuffed linoleum floor, furniture that looked as if it belonged in the Bates Motel. At the reception counter, she asked for Mr. McIntyre, and a bored-looking blob of a woman pointed the way down a corridor without even asking if she had an appointment.

She found his office easily enough; McIntyre's plastic name tag was in a slot by the door. It was open, and he was at his desk, shuffling through an immense sheaf of papers. A middle-aged man with sallow, pitted skin, almond-shaped brown eyes, and red hair shot with gray, the color of rusty iron.

Dolly waited while he wrote something down. When he put down his pen, she knocked softly against the open door.

He lifted his eyes without raising his head. Then, seeing an attractive woman, someone he didn't know, he sat up and looked at her. Appreciatively, she thought.

Though they'd spoken to one another a number of times over the phone, they'd never actually met.

"Dolly Drake," she introduced herself, and at his sheepish wince she grinned. "Guess you know why I'm here. Looks like your fellows are sitting on something that belongs to me, and I was sort of hoping you could help me out."

She asked, trying not to overdo the flirty lowering of her lashes, if he wouldn't mind taking a minute from his busy schedule to look into it for her. Now he was standing up, looking as if he really wanted to help her, and she noted also the generous slab of gut hanging over his belt. *A man with a healthy appetite. That's good.*

While McIntyre went across the hall to hunt up the paperwork, she slipped the apple-shaped cookie jar from her shopping bag and placed it on his desk.

After a few minutes that felt like an hour, he came back holding some papers. He looked weary, not as if those papers spelled good news.

She put on her knock-the-producer-dead smile, and drawled,

"I brought you something." She pointed to the cookie jar. "Cute, isn't it? And wait'll you see what's inside."

McIntyre's own smile faded. "Hey, come on. You know I can't take that. You don't want to get me in trouble, do you?"

She suddenly felt hot, ashamed, as if she'd been caught by her favorite teacher cheating on a test. But what good would it do to back down? *Show him your stuff,* she told herself. *You're an actress, aren't you?* She forced a brilliant smile, exclaiming, "Why, Mr. McIntyre, what a thought!"

"Because the plain fact is, Dolly"—he held up the papers— "I'm afraid you've come all the way out here for nothing. Approval on your shipment is being held up until the lab results come back."

"Lab results?"

"Standard procedure. We do a random check every so often to make sure the alcohol level doesn't exceed point zero zero five per chocolate. Any more than that, and you're against regulations."

Dolly felt her neck muscles knot with frustration. Hell's bells, what did he think she was, some know-nothing moron? *She* knew the law, and so did Henri. Why, there wasn't enough liquor in Girod's chocolates to inebriate a kitten!

What now? It was McIntyre's rubber stamp and his alone that would release her shipment. And she needed that *now* . . . not a week from now.

Dolly felt sick; she was going to fail. And if she couldn't pull off even a simple little thing like this, what hope could she have of finding her nieces?

Then it struck her. Why wait around for lab results? Why couldn't they have the damn test right here and now?

"Julio, I'm going to ask you to do yourself and me a small and perfectly legal favor. Try one," she said, pointing to the jar on his desk. "Go ahead, one itty-bitty one, just to taste. No one in the history of the United States ever lost their job for eating one chocolate bonbon."

"Now, come on, Dolly, I run a serious operation here."

"I'm serious too. I want your honest opinion. It's this new flavor we cooked up." She lifted the cookie jar's apple-stem lid, and gently extracted one of the dark Rhum Caramels. "Taste it, and tell me what you think."

As the weary official was opening his mouth to protest, she popped the bonbon in.

A look of annoyance creased his face. But he was chewing it, not swallowing it in a hurry or spitting it into the ashtray. She was on pins and needles, like watching a producer's face at an audition. But he kept on chewing, his eyes drifting shut, his face smoothing, as contented as a cow with its cud. And now—praise the Lord!—he was smiling.

McIntyre swallowed, and then reached for another.

"No alcohol in these," he said, grinning. "But, damn, they ought to be outlawed."

Dolly felt a rush of triumph that left her a little dizzy.

Five minutes later, clutching a duly stamped CF 7501 form, she was back in the Lincoln, heading out to Air France cargo to pick up her shipment.

After that, Henri.

Then, remembering her nieces, the heady anticipation she'd felt abruptly dissolved. Back there, with McIntyre, she'd felt so strong and smart. By hook or by crook, she was somebody who could get things done. But it would take more than a little brass to find Annie and Laurel.

She'd need some kind of miracle.

"Dolly?" Henri called softly in the darkness.

Dolly looked up from the television she'd been staring at, but not really watching. One of those old Lana Turner tearjerkers, the kind that makes you wonder, *Were they always this bad or is it just the mood I'm in?*

Henri stood at the entrance to the den, a stocky figure wrapped in a silk dressing gown, his thick pewter-colored hair mussed with sleep. A present from her, she recalled, that robe—a rich burgundy satin, with quilted lapels and a tasselled belt, a little fancy for Henri, who was more the plain terry type. Still, he wore it to please her. He kept it here along with a spare razor and toothbrush and a few shirts. When he was three thousand miles away, which was most of the time, Dolly would wear it to remind her of him, with its faint acrid smell of the bedtime Gauloises he smoked.

"I couldn't sleep," Dolly told him. She'd been worrying about Laurel and Annie.

But now she had to think what to do about Henri.

On the way from the airport, Henri had told her as matter-of-factly as he could that he had come across the most charming flat, with a garden view, near Place des Ternes, a stone's throw from Girod's, perfect for her, and the price was more than reasonable. Henri had even left a deposit to hold it for a week. Of course, she didn't have to take it, he'd hastened to add. But he'd thought perhaps if she came over and looked at it . . .

What should I tell him? The thought of being with Henri, and not just here and there, squeezed in between transatlantic appointments, shimmered in her head like a green oasis in a desert.

But the truth was that things had changed since she'd promised him she'd think about moving to Paris. How could she leave now? She couldn't. Not until Annie and Laurel had been found. And even after that, there were still, let's face it, Henri's wife and children . . .

Whichever way she turned, she'd still wind up short-sheeted.

Henri sank down beside her on the deep sofa, tucking an arm about her. He kissed her shoulder, the ends of his mustache pleasantly scratchy. Oh, was that nice! After Dale, she'd thought she would never again know that sweet tug a woman feels in her belly when her man kisses her.

"What are *you* doing up?" she asked him.

"I dreamed about you," he murmured, nibbling her earlobe, "a marvelous dream. Then I woke up, and you were gone. Can it be that you are tired of me so soon?"

Dolly smiled, remembering their first time together, two years ago in Paris. Afterwards, as soon as she got back to New York, she'd gone to the lingerie department at Bergdorf's, and startled the elderly saleslady by blurting: "Show me everything you've got in shameless." She'd bought at least a thousand dollars' worth, including a high-toned tart's get-up—a luscious Harlow-esque satin nightgown the color of a White Russian with matching marabou-trimmed slippers she wore only with Henri—which was not often enough.

Dolly looked around her. If she moved to Paris, she wouldn't miss this place, with its rooms the size of roller rinks. Park Avenue had been Dale's idea; she'd have been happier with one of those

cozy row houses in the West Village. But once he made up his mind
to buy Matson Shipping (*There's more money to be made in shipping
than in drilling, Dolly-pop*), and move to New York, where Matson
was headquartered, it was a penthouse on Park Avenue or nothing.
She remembered how dark and stuffy it had seemed at first, with its
walnut wainscoting, yellowing wallpaper, and floors that hadn't been
refinished since before World War Two. The former owners had
been old money . . . and real old money downplayed itself, she'd
learned. But what was the point of even *having* money, she wondered,
unless you spent it?

It was Dale's idea, hiring that satyr-faced decorator, Aldo, who
had bleached the dreary wainscoting the color of driftwood and
covered the walls in nubby beige linen. Wall-to-wall taupe carpeting
went down over every inch of the parquet, and modern cone-shaped
light fixtures replaced the old haunted-castle chandeliers.

Her gaze now fell on the free-standing sculpture atop the hi-fi
cabinet, which Dale had paid a fortune for, but which looked to
Dolly exactly like a bent coat hanger stuck in a block of cement.

"A fairy decorator's wet dream," Dale had jokingly dubbed the
penthouse when it was finally finished. But he'd been so proud of
it. For Dale, it had meant being able to show his business buddies
and Cadwalader, Wickersham & Taft lawyers that despite his eighth-
grade education and his Red Man chewing tobacco, he was somebody
who could distinguish high-class art from a twisted coat hanger any
day of the week.

In some ways, Henri was a lot like Dale—he had that same
restless energy. Henri wouldn't abide sitting still when he could be
doing something; and he never settled for second best.

She thought of the first time she'd laid eyes on him, in the
basement confectioner's kitchen of his shop, bent over a steaming
copper cauldron, holding a wooden spoon to his lips. Dolly, surrounded for the first time in her life by chocolate—ten-pound blocks
of couverture wrapped in silicone paper, sheets of chocolate cooling
on racks, tray after tray of bite-sized dollops of ganache, the truffle's
soft chocolate center, en route to the enrober—felt as if she'd died
and gone to heaven. And incredibly, here was this man shaking his
head, scowling, wagging a fist at the ceiling as he growled in French,
and then gallantly translating for her: "Who do those fools think
they are dealing with, sending me cream from underfed cows?"

Now, snuggled against her, Henri whispered, "Without you, the bed is cold. And I miss your snoring."

"Like hell I snore!"

Henri grinned. *"Exactement."*

"My grandpa used to say, 'You can dress a frog in silk drawers but that don't stop him from croakin'.'" She elbowed him lightly in the ribs. "Hey, you ever been west of the Mississippi?"

"When I was very young, my parents took me to Yellowstone Park to see—how do you say, Old Reliable?"

She giggled. "Old Reliable? Sounds like the stuff Mama-Jo used to swallow before bedtime, to keep her bowels moving. You mean Old Faithful, don't you?"

He rolled his eyes, and chuckled.

"You know what I love about you, *ma poupée?*" he said. "You make me laugh. It is rare in a woman, the ability to make a man laugh. Also," he kissed her nose, "I adore you because you are adorable and sweet with the big heart . . . and you have the breasts which are *formidable.*"

Dolly laughed. "Know what Dale called them? 'The Knockers That Ate Cleveland.'"

"Well, then, I shall have to visit Cleveland one day . . . very soon, I think." Through the thin fabric of her nightgown, she could feel the warmth of his hand cupping her breast.

Dolly wriggled closer, and they kissed. She felt an almost electric sensation shoot from her lips to her lower belly. She heard herself groan. This would be the third time tonight. Already she was a little sore down there. By morning, she'd feel as if she'd ridden bareback over the Rockies.

"No," she murmured, pulling away. "Henri, we need to talk."

His slate-colored eyes regarded her from beneath his bushy brows with—could that be fear? "But of course," he said, nodding gravely.

It came straight to her then, the decision she'd been holding at arm's length all evening. And she realized that all along she must have known it would be this way. What surprised her was the pain she felt, the sharpness of the ache gripping her chest.

Dolly took a breath. "I'm not moving to Paris," she told him. "Not now, anyway. It wouldn't be right, not with . . . with the way things are. Your wife . . ." She gulped, feeling the tickle of tears in her throat. Henri started to speak, and she held up her hand to stop him. "Oh, I know you don't love Francine. And I know all your reasons for not divorcing her—your children, your religion, Francine's father . . ."

Henri's face sagged; his skin looked gray as his hair. He seemed suddenly a decade older than forty-seven. "What you don't know," he finally said, "is how she despises me. If not for her father, she says, I would still be an assistant chef at Fouquet's. It is not true, of course, but . . ." He gave a Gallic shrug. "But the fact is, until the old goat takes his retirement, I remain, as you say, under his thumb."

Once, while in Paris on business, Dolly had met Henri's wife, a grim woman who looked as if she'd devoted her forty-odd years to mastering the art of smiling without moving her lips. A lift of a brow, a flicker of an eyelid, seemed as close as she got. No denying she was good-looking—or had been, at some point, with her blade-thin figure and chic clothes, her perfect skin the color of vichyssoise, and the heavy dark hair she wore up in a twist, skewered in place with four tortoiseshell hairpins (Dolly had counted). But now, twenty years into their marriage, Francine was like some spindly chair in a museum on which one wouldn't dare sit.

Dolly felt a toad of resentment growing in her belly, a great, nasty thumping thing all covered with warts. *How can he stay with Francine when it's me he loves?* Why didn't he just go and ahead and divorce his wife, Papa Girod and the pope be damned?

But Dolly knew full well it wasn't that simple. If Henri walked away from Francine, he'd have to leave Girod's. And Girod's was more than a business to him; it was his whole life. His son was pretty much grown, already at the Sorbonne, but he absolutely doted on his eleven-year-old Gabrielle. And of course, they were Catholic. Francine, he'd told her, never missed a Sunday or First Friday mass, and often attended vespers as well. Once a month like clockwork, she confessed her sins to Father Bonard; she'd no doubt prefer being widowed over the sacrilege of a divorce.

Okay, maybe not a divorce, not right away. If they could just stop all this cloak-and-dagger stuff, stop sneaking around and be together right out in the open.

But no point in beating a dead horse. For months, they'd been over and over it.

"It's not just your . . . situation," Dolly said. Quickly, she told him about Annie and Laurel. Dolly gripped Henri's arm. "So you see, I *have* to stay here. They're out there somewhere, and they *need* me. Other than Val, I guess I'm their only living relative. I've got to find them. You see that, don't you?"

Henri frowned, as if fighting back his own selfish need to persuade her to come to Paris. His face seemed to sag with the effort, but then at last he gained control of himself.

"Of course I do. And you will, *ma poupée,*" he conceded sadly. Then after a moment, he ventured, "But instead of looking everywhere and not finding them, could you not perhaps bring them to you instead?"

"What do you mean?"

"I was thinking . . . perhaps an advertisement in the newspaper?"

Dolly thought for a moment, feeling herself growing excited. The personals? Yeah, it could just work. If Annie knew she was in New York and wanted to reach her, this way, since Dolly's home phone was unlisted, she'd know where to find her.

She hugged Henri, feeling a surge of hope. Tomorrow, first thing, she'd see about placing an ad.

"You're a genius. How am I ever gonna get along without you?" She felt a desperate urge to be wrapped up in him, engulfed by his body. "Come on, let's go back to bed."

In Dolly's oversized bed (custom-built to accommodate Dale's six-foot-six frame), Henri carefully untied each of the three flimsy ribbons holding the front of her gown together. Reverently, he palmed the straps off her shoulders, smoothing them down her arms to her elbows. Dolly felt her breasts sag free of the tight bodice. The cold air, and Henri's hot touch, made her nipples stiffen with an almost painful suddenness. Reflexively, she crossed her arms over her chest.

Henri pried her arms away gently, and kissed first one breast, then the other.

"Cleveland from here looks very nice," he murmured.

She glanced down his torso, and smiled. "Right now," she told him, "Old Faithful looks even better."

Moments later, he was inside her, and Dolly forgot everything but how wonderful she felt, all that heat wrapping itself around her, flowing through her, like sinking into a hot bath on the coldest of days. She kissed him, opening her mouth to take in as much of him as possible, loving even the roughness of his tongue and the coarse prickling of his mustache. What could be sweeter than this? A man who loved her. Who thought she was beautiful. Why, she could die this very minute, and she wouldn't feel she'd missed out.

Dolly came with a falling-through-space sensation. It was wonderful, but a little frightening too, as if in a way she really *had* died. As if she might soar on and on forever without coming back down to earth. And dear Henri, she could feel him holding back, reining himself in until the moment she began to descend, before he let go with a heave of pleasure.

Afterward, in his embrace, listening to Henri's breathing as it deepened into its sleeping rumble, she felt sublimely content.

"I love you, Henri," she whispered into his unhearing ear.

But she'd been around the track enough to know that the odds were not so great on love conquering all. That only happened in movies, and then all you got was the fade-out—so who knew?

"Looks pretty foxy," Gloria said.

"If it works." Dolly held up crossed fingers.

She had the *Times* open atop the display case and was staring at the half-page ad. A selection of chocolates was featured at the top, plus the usual copy about Girod's seventy-five years of international awards, including this year's top prize at *Gourmand* magazine's annual chocolate fair. And smack in the center, a cut-out from an old glossy of Dolly from her Hollywood days, heavy lipstick, ice-cream-cone tits, tight sweater and all, the weirdest chocolate ad in history. But she was hoping—grasping at straws really—that Annie might see it, and recognize her. Her name below it, read big as you please: DOLLY DRAKE, proprietor.

For a whole week now, she'd run personals in the *Times,* the *Post,* the *News,* the *Voice.* But no reply.

The idea for this big display ad had come to her on her way back from seeing Henri off at the airport. Hugging him, she'd promised him saucily that The Knockers That Ate Cleveland would still be waiting for him next time he could get to New York. And that made her remember that old publicity photo. Thinking of her nieces, she wondered, why not a big spread that included her photo? That way, even if Annie only leafed through the *Times,* she couldn't miss it.

The important thing now was to get to them before anything happened to them. She shivered, tugging on the arms of the pink sweater draped over her shoulders.

"If it doesn't work, you'll come up with something else," Gloria piped up, breaking into her thoughts. "And, lady, if you can figure out what to do with all those Easter eggs we got sent by mistake, then what's a little problem like finding two missing girls?" She winked at Dolly, then sallied over to greet a woman in a fur coat who had just walked in, holding a fidgety Yorkshire terrier tucked under one arm.

Easter eggs? Good Lord, she'd almost forgotten them. Yeah, she'd better think of something. Quick.

Descending on the front window, she began tearing down last month's display. Out came the Amish half-bushel baskets overflowing with red and gold maple leaves, and the old cider press painted to match the window's hunter-green trim. Next, the flowered Victorian washbasin heaped with gilded walnuts and marzipan apples, and its matching pitcher, overturned, spilling a cornucopia of truffles—bittersweet brandy-ginger, café au lait, cognac and hazelnuts, white chocolate flecked with Sicilian pistachios, caramel-centered ones rolled in crushed pralines.

It felt good to be clearing out the old, making way for the new . . . though she hadn't the slightest idea yet what the new would be. She felt oddly reassured by her own ghostly reflection mirrored surrealistically in the small square windowpanes, swimming in and out, arms flashing, hands flitting like minnows.

Scooping out armloads of dry, sweet-smelling grass, she suddenly realized how to use those fancy chocolate eggs they had sent her instead of the chocolate turkeys she'd ordered. Here in the window, she would display the *real* Fabergé egg Dale had given her as a wedding present, and surround it with the chocolate ones; and in those wonderful Russian lacquer frames she'd bought at Gump's on her last visit to San Francisco, she'd put photos of the Czar and his family against the backdrop of an antique embroidered shawl. Maybe she'd throw in a samovar while she was at it, like the ones at the Russian Tea Room. In her mind, she could see it perfectly. Her customers would be intrigued. They would ask about it. *And I'll tell them that any woman who spends all day cooking and washing dishes, or busting her buns at work, deserves something more than turkey leftovers.* . . .

Well, okay, it was a little off base . . . but then, the best ideas usually were. And how Henri would love it when she told him! Dolly felt her spirits rise.

With the window-well bare, she stopped and looked about her, at all that she had accomplished over the past two years. Why, the space alone was a marvel—a former apothecary that had somehow escaped the twentieth century, with a massive, ornately carved built-in breakfront meant for displaying pharmaceuticals. She'd left the green-and-blue tiled floor alone, installed reproduction oak display cases parallel to the breakfront, now gleaming under a fresh coat of varnish, its brass pulls and handles polished to mirror brightness. Along its shelves, and in its crannies, tucked among Girod's gift-wrapped boxes and confitures from the Girod orchards, was a hodge-podge of knick-knacks—a fluted carnival-glass bowl, a pair of pewter candlesticks, an old shaving mirror, an antique bisque doll wearing a leghorn hat trimmed with a faded ostrich feather. Eons ago, in leaner times, Dolly had disguised grungy furnished apartments with her flea-market spoils, and even now she loved poking around in flea markets, searching for buried treasure.

But even as she sketched out the new display in her mind, Dolly couldn't stop worrying about Annie and Laurel. The radio had said it might snow today. She imagined them shivering on the sidewalk somewhere, crouched over a steam vent. . . .

Dolly's heart twisted in her chest. Good Lord, ad or no ad, what was she doing here when she could be out *looking?* Impulsively, she darted into the small room behind the counter, and reached for her coat, which hung on a peg inside the door.

By the time her cab reached Grand Central, snow was coming down in earnest. Thick fat flakes danced in the updrafts created by the jammed traffic along Lexington Avenue, and swirled dizzily before catching on Dolly's coat sleeves and in her hair. She pushed her way inside, relieved to be out of the numbing cold.

This was a hub of the city, but New York had so many. As she made her way across the vast domed chamber, crowded with commuters hurrying in all directions for their trains, she wondered why she had come here. What did she expect to find? All these people, focused on only one thing—getting home—how could any of them help her? Then she noticed that some weren't in any hurry. Near the entrance to one of the tracks, she saw a man and a woman in scruffy clothes, squatting, each holding a paper cup, begging.

Dolly felt someone tugging at her sleeve, and she turned to find a teenage girl in a navy pea coat and filthy jeans gazing at her beseechingly. Her heart flipped over. So young . . . just a kid . . . could it be . . . ?

"Annie?" she whispered.

"Yeah," the girl muttered, her youthful face hardening, seeming to age ten years in the blink of an eye. For a terrible instant, Dolly felt her joints loosen and her head grow light, and thought she was going to faint. "Annie, Frannie, Jannie, you got a quarter, you can call me anything you like." She stuck out a grimy hand.

Dolly, trembling, dug into her purse, and fished out a bill. The girl snatched it from her hand, and darted off, the torn heels of her sneakers slapping the tiled floor.

Dolly had an urge to run home. This was nuts. Even if she saw Annie, she probably wouldn't recognize her from those fuzzy snapshots of Ned's. But next thing she knew, Dolly was down on the lower level, still searching, looking everywhere for two girls together, going from track to track, through tunnels where the clacking of her high heels echoed back at her like some crazed pursuer, and then up to the waiting room again, going from bench to bench. Scared that she wouldn't find them . . . and scared that she would.

This is crazy, she told herself, after scanning a thousand strange faces. *I'm going crazy just like my sister.*

From Grand Central, she took a cab to the Port Authority Bus Terminal. It was newer, more brightly lit, but even more dreary. She took an escalator up to the platforms where the buses let their passengers off. She caught sight of a black man in an ankle-length fur coat, a jeweled ring on almost every finger . . . a pimp on the prowl for fresh talent. The thought of innocent girls falling into his diamond-encrusted hands made her stomach turn over. But he wouldn't bite. And what if he *did* know something?

She went up to him, and tapped him on the shoulder. "Excuse me . . . I'm looking for my nieces." She pulled a dog-eared photo

from her purse—more than a year old, but the best she could do—
and thrust it at him. "Have you by any chance seen them? It would've
been about three weeks ago."

The pimp glanced at it, then shook his head and quickly moved
off, as if he thought she might be an undercover cop trying to pin
something on him.

Dolly watched him go, feeling both relieved and despairing.

She returned to the shop late, worn out, shivering, her feet
numb inside her suede boots. All she wanted to do was go home,
soak in a hot tub, then help herself to a stiff brandy, maybe two.

Gloria, who should have closed up and gone home an hour
ago, looked up from the package she was wrapping. "No luck? Well,
look at it this way . . . least you got it out of your system."

Dolly shrugged, almost too disheartened to speak. "Thanks for
waiting. But you go on home now."

Tomorrow, she told herself. She'd try Penn Station, and then
start checking YMCAs. And she'd keep on looking, even if it was a
wild-goose chase.

Two days later, the snow along the curb had melted to filthy
slush. Dolly, depressed by the weather, had almost given up hope
of ever finding the two girls. She was checking over the day's receipts
when the old-fashioned bell over the door tinkled. Looking up, she
watched a tall, angular young woman hesitate a moment on the
threshold, then, with a deep breath, enter the shop. The girl wore a
thin coat, and loafers that looked soaked. Her dark shoulder-length
hair wasn't covered, not even a scarf.

Dolly was about to turn away, leave this one to Gloria, but
something about the girl held her. That long neck and those high
cheekbones, those startling indigo eyes.

The girl looked straight at Dolly, and Dolly felt her heart tip
sideways in her chest, seeming to tumble over and over as if down
an endlessly steep slope.

"Annie," she whispered. "Honey, is that you?"

"Aunt Dolly?"

She thought: *If this was the Bible, a bolt of lightning could come right
down out of the sky and strike me dead.*

But there was no lightning. Only this silence, which hung in
the air between them like the smell of ozone before a storm.

A scrap of memory surfaced. That day she had taken Annie to

the beach—Annie couldn't have been more than three—and they'd stopped at a clam house for a bite to eat. And when the waiter came around to their booth, little Annie, sitting up straight, dressed in a checked pinafore and white shoes with little ruffled socks, had piped clearly: "I'd like a hamburger. And french fries, please, but don't put the catsup on top. I like it on the plate."

Even way back then, Dolly had seen the mark on her—the smart, headstrong woman she would someday grow up to be.

And here she was . . . practically grown up. And beautiful, as Dolly had known she would be. A bit too thin, maybe, but she'd soon fix that.

Then all at once, it struck her: *She's really here.*

"Jesus in the manger," Dolly whispered. She started to cry. "Oh, sugar, I was afraid . . . Well, don't just stand there, come over here and let me give you a hug." Dolly gathered the tall, angular girl into her arms.

Annie remained stiff at first; then, tentatively, her hands came up and circled Dolly's back, and with a sigh, she brought her head to rest against Dolly's shoulder, like a weary traveller easing a heavy burden.

"I saw your picture in the paper." Annie drew away, a thin smile touching her lips. "Well, actually . . . it was Laurey who saw it. But I recognized you."

A thousand questions bubbled to Dolly's lips, all at once. But she asked only the most important one: "You okay, sugar?"

"Sure."

Annie stiffened, glancing fearfully about the shop, as if she half expected someone to spring out from behind a door and clap a pair of handcuffs on her.

"I don't bite," Gloria called out, moving out from behind the counter. She stuck out a hand, and shook Annie's. "Hi. I'm Gloria. I guess you two have a whole lot of catching up to do, so why don't I close up and let you go at it."

Dolly led Annie up to her office, and plugged in the space heater next to her desk for extra warmth.

"Now slip out of those wet shoes," she told her niece, "and I'll make you a cup of tea. You like chocolate?"

Annie nodded, looking around her, that suspicious look still firmly in place.

"Good, because that's one thing I have lots of. And you look as if you could do with a bit of fattening up. Been pretty rough for you, huh?"

"Please . . . don't tell Val," Annie pleaded softly. Her clear, deep-blue eyes fixed upon Dolly with a scared, desperate look . . . but Dolly saw something hard there, too, a glint of steel.

She didn't know how to answer. She didn't want to make a promise she couldn't keep, but at the same time she sensed that a wrong word now would send Annie bolting like a panicked deer. All along she'd had that niggling feeling down deep that everything was far from kosher where Val was concerned. Why else, after she'd learned the girls were probably in New York, had she held back from calling to tell him?

"Why don't you tell me all about it," Dolly said, "and let me decide. Fair enough?"

Annie was silent for a long moment, then she said, "I guess that'd be okay."

Dolly boiled water on the hot plate in the storeroom, and made tea, which she brought to Annie in a thick ceramic mug. Annie held the mug balanced against her knee, not drinking from it, merely cupping her fingers about it—they were blue with cold, Dolly saw—and began to talk.

Haltingly, at first, then with gathering passion, she told Dolly about Eve, how she'd died, the hurried funeral to which only a few people had come. And then Val, in the weeks that followed, acting so strange . . . and finally, *that* night, the night they ran away . . .

"I couldn't stay," Annie said, leaning forward, her eyes bright and her cheeks a little flushed. "He would have . . . Well, I didn't stop to think it through all the way. I just grabbed Laurey, and . . ."

"He's saying you kidnapped her."

The color drained from her niece's face, except for those feverish splashes on her cheeks. "It's not true! Laurey wanted to be with me!" Annie regarded her with a coolness that sent a ripple of unease through Dolly. "And I wouldn't have come to you. Even if I had known how to find you. Not unless I was really desperate. I . . . I didn't think you'd want us."

Dolly felt the bare honesty of her words sock home, a dull blow in the pit of her stomach. *Why, of course, you're practically a stranger to her. And why should she trust you, after the awful things Eve probably told her?*

"Did your . . ." She licked her lips. Her heart was doing a crazy riff against her rib cage. "Did your mama ever talk about me?"

"You had some kind of fight, didn't you? She never said what it was about."

Dolly felt her body sag with relief. *Thanks to heaven, she doesn't know the whole story.*

"Sometimes, people say . . . or do . . . something hurtful that they're sorry for later. And the more you love that person who let you down, the worse it hurts." She sighed, the old pain surfacing.

Annie was staring at her, her dark blue eyes seeming to say, *I'll let you keep your secrets, if you agree to keep mine.*

But *could* she make that promise? Even after what Annie had told her—and yes, she believed her—the plain fact remained that Val was Laurel's father. Was it right, to keep a father from his daughter? After all, she hadn't heard Val's side. . . .

Then she looked into Annie's blue eyes—so much like Eve's it nearly broke her heart—and found herself saying briskly, "Val doesn't have to know. Just leave everything to me. Now, drink your tea before it gets cold, and let's see what we can do about straightening out this mess before it gets any worse."

"**A**nnie, *why* can't we spend Christmas with Aunt Dolly?" Laurel stopped in the middle of the sidewalk, looking up at her sister.

Annie felt a bead of annoyance form in her stomach. *How many times do I have to go over this with her? Why can't she just trust me?*

But she bit back the harsh words. No, it wasn't Laurel's fault. Why should she want to stay in a bare, empty apartment when she could have a tree and piles of presents at Dolly's?

Annie reached for her sister's mittened hand and squeezed it. "Look, Laurey, we can't go to her apartment because it wouldn't be safe," she explained gently. "People would see us, and it might get back to Val."

What if right now, this very moment, Val was on a plane, on his way to New York? He didn't really care much about Laurel, Annie was sure, but he'd take her away in a minute, just to spite Annie.

Laurel, dropping her gaze, said nothing. Annie wondered if she was wishing she were at Bel Jardin, with Val, instead of here. Her insides suddenly felt as chilled as her chapped, cold-reddened hands. Should she tell Laurel everything that had happened that night with Val—the real reason she'd had to run away?

No, it was too awful to talk about. Annie just wanted to push it out of her mind.

God, how can I tell her how scared I am? She's just a kid.

"But you're *working* for Aunt Dolly," Laurel reasoned. "And what's so safe about that?"

"At the shop, nobody but Gloria knows she's my aunt," Annie explained. "But her apartment has doormen, janitors, nosy neighbors. If we started hanging out there, pretty soon everybody would *know.*"

She gave her sister a little nudge. "Now come *on,* or you'll be late for school."

Most days, Laurel walked to school with a classmate, Rupa Bahdreesh, who lived on their block, but today Rupa was home sick with the flu. Certainly, Laurel was old enough to go by herself, but Annie liked keeping her company. Except now she was beginning to wish she'd gone straight to work instead.

Laurel glared at Annie. "I don't care! I hate it here! It's cold and yukky . . . and . . . and . . ." Her voice wobbled. ". . . we'll be all alone on Christmas!"

"What about the Grubermans?"

"The Grubermans don't celebrate Christmas." Laurel's wide blue eyes glittered with unshed tears.

Annie, not wanting Laurel to see the tears starting in her own eyes, looked away as they walked, concentrating on the sidewalk with its row of parked cars, grimy and salt-streaked from last week's snowstorm, and the dirty snow pocked with yellow holes where dogs had peed on it.

"Well, of course they don't believe in Christmas," she said, keeping her voice even. "They're Jewish." Her words puffed out on tiny clouds of frozen vapor.

"They're not allowed even to *speak* the word!" Laurel burst out. "Sarah told me. It's because it has 'Christ' in it." She kicked a crumpled paper cup, sending it spinning out over the curb. "We might as well be Jewish if we're not even going to have a tree."

Annie couldn't think of anything to say. She wanted a tree, too, and not just for Laurel. Should she have taken the money Dolly offered? She thought back to that first day at Dolly's shop, Dolly pressing several folded twenties into her hand and pleading with her to take them. But Annie just couldn't somehow. Not even when Dolly said it could be a loan. When would she ever be able to pay Dolly back? And if she accepted Dolly's charity, wouldn't she somehow be betraying Dearie? Once her mother had referred to Dolly as a "two-faced snake in the grass." Did that mean that Dolly, no matter how nice she acted, couldn't be trusted?

She'd settled instead for agreeing to work for her aunt, and accepted a small cash advance against her salary. But now it had been three weeks, and she still hadn't saved enough to buy half the things they needed. The list seemed endless—long underwear, warm clothes, heavy boots. Dishes, sheets, towels.

She glanced over at Laurel, wearing a Salvation Army duffel coat that didn't quite reach her wrists. Laurel's bright hair spilled like sunshine from under the red knit cap squashed over her head, but her lips and the tip of her nose were tinged with blue.

"Are you warm enough?" Annie shivered inside her own coat, a man's gabardine that flapped at her ankles.

"I'm okay," Laurel said. "I've got a sweater on under this. Rivka gave me one of Chava's that didn't fit her any more."

More likely Rivka had seen that Laurel needed one, and had hunted one up that would fit her. But Rivka had been so nice, practically adopting her and Laurel into her big, noisy family, that Annie couldn't help being grateful for the cast-off clothes and extra blankets, the fresh-baked *kugel* and loaves of challah she sent up to them.

"That's nice," she said as they turned onto Avenue K, which was wider and lined with red-brick apartment buildings.

"Guess what? After school today Rivka's gonna show me how to sew, and when I get good enough I'll even make *you* something. . . ." Laurel's voice trailed off, and she peeped up at Annie from under her red cap with a sheepish expression. "Annie, I'm sorry I got mad at you. But it *would* be nice to have a little tree, or maybe just some holly branches."

"Yeah . . . it would," Annie forced herself to sound cheery, but inside she felt terrible.

Laurel's outburst oddly had been easier to take than her sweet acceptance. Annie longed to give her little sister a nice Christmas. But the fir trees they trucked into the city from upstate were so much more expensive than Annie had imagined. Ornaments cost a fortune, too. No, it was out of the question.

Last year at this time, she recalled, they'd had Christmas at Bel Jardin with Dearie. Her mother was in pretty good shape, for a change. They had such a wonderful time decorating their tree, Dearie singing "Rudolph the Red-Nosed Reindeer" and then Laurel chiming in with silly made-up verses of her own. Stringing colored lights, hanging ornaments, setting up the crèche with Mary and Joseph, the three Wise Men, a donkey, some sheep, and Baby Jesus, of course.

Except one of Baby Jesus' plaster feet had broken off, so Dearie got out a tube of glue and said, "We've gotta get you fixed up so you can walk on water someday, my little man. Why, you've got a whole *truckload* of miracles to perform."

Annie wished a miracle would happen now, like a tree suddenly dropping out of the sky.

At K and Sixteenth, they cut across the corner lawn of a neat red-brick house with a cut-out of Santa perched tipsily in the crook of its chimney. The frosty grass crunched like broken glass under Annie's loafers. Halfway up the block, across the street, Annie caught sight of P.S. 99, a massive, grim-looking brick building surrounded by a high chain-link fence. So different from Green Oaks, with its lawns, playing fields, and tennis courts. Here just a concrete yard and a crossing guard. Sort of like a prison. She hated Laurel's having to come here every morning.

Annie remembered coming to enroll Laurel. She'd been so nervous, saying that she was Laurel's guardian, and that her school records had been lost in a fire. But the school secretary hadn't even seemed suspicious, just bored. Now Annie knew it was because a lot of the kids here were illegal, with parents from places like Haiti and Nicaragua who didn't even have green cards.

Annie felt Laurel hanging back a little, her footsteps slowing, as if she'd hit a patch of ice that she needed to pick her way across. *She must hate it there,* Annie thought, feeling again as if she were going to cry, the thickness in her chest pressing the air from her lungs.

"Our class Christmas play is this Friday night," Laurel said when they'd reached the concrete steps leading up to a row of graffiti-sprayed doors. "I'm in charge of the scenery. It's going to be really neat."

"I can't wait to see it."

Laurel was so artistic. Annie remembered the wonderful cards she used to draw for Dearie in the hospital—amazingly lifelike dogs, monkeys, squirrels. And she had such an eye for color, too, like the other day, rescuing that old paisley shawl Rivka was throwing out, seeing how perfect it would be to dress up their own shabby couch.

"Do you think Dolly would come, too?"

"Why don't I ask her? I bet she'd like that." With forced brightness, Annie added, "Look, Laurey, about Christmas . . . Why don't we invite Dolly over to *our* place? We'll get some holly, and hang some mistletoe. And we'll sing all the carols."

"The Grubermans will hear us." Annie could see the tiniest smile was prying at the corners of her mouth.

"Let them," she said, feeling her spirits rise. "So what if everyone in Brooklyn hears us!"

"No, darling, you see how it's crooked? Here, let me show you."

Rivka pulled up a chair next to Laurel, sitting hunched before the old Singer in the corner of her crowded living room, the fabric swatches Rivka had given her to practice on spread across the girl's lap. She showed Laurel how to measure the seam and mark it with pins, and then how to hold it steady under the needle while she pressed on the foot pedal that powered the machine.

Laurel nodded, and tried again, her fingers white with the strain of pressing the fabric flat while she stitched, so that no wrinkles would appear.

Poor little shainenke, Rivka thought, noting the child's spindly arms sticking out from her too-big T-shirt, as thin and straight as the pins holding the pieces of fabric she was sewing. *She tries so hard. Such a little wife!*

The way Sarah had been at this age, hovering over Rivka in the kitchen, pinching off handfuls of dough to roll out, eager to crack eggs, dredge chicken wings, even to peel potatoes for *kugel*. And Laurel's questions, they never stopped!

"Rivka, how come you threw away that egg?"

"Darling, it had blood on the yolk, that means it's not kosher."

And just yesterday:

"Rivka, how come your matzoh balls are so fluffy and mine came out like golf balls?"

"A little secret. With the batter, instead of water, I mix in seltzer. Then the balls, you must shape each one gently, gently, like you would pick up a newborn baby."

Now it was sewing Laurel was determined to learn, and she would, too—of that, Rivka was sure. She had a good strong backbone, this one. Not strong like her big sister, not like a soldier marching off to war. Sure, Laurel was the quiet one, but she was clever, too. Look how she'd managed to coax tongue-tied Shmueli out of his shell, simply by asking him if he would teach her how to read Hebrew. Laurel had seen what nobody else had, that nine-year-old Shmueli, in the middle between bossy Chaim and noisy Yakov, needed to have his say, to be listened to and looked up to.

Now Laurel was holding up her redone seam for Rivka's approval. "There, is that better?"

Rivka nodded. "Perfect. Tomorrow, I will show you how to cut from a pattern." She turned to scoop up Shainey, crawling at her feet. "What's that you've got in your mouth?" she clucked, pulling out a spit-shiny jack the baby was sucking on, then calling across the room, "Yakov! How many times do I have to remind you not to leave your games lying around?"

Laurel was now holding out her arms to take Shainey, who'd begun to fuss. "Do you want me to put her down for her nap?"

"You're such a doll. You read my mind, maybe?" Rivka, thinking of the *cholent* she still had to make for tomorrow, and the ton of latkes she'd have to get started for Hanukkah, gratefully handed the baby over to Laurel.

Rivka, watching Laurel carry off Shainey, now happily snuggled in her arms, felt a surge of affection for the girl. Who would have thought that in just a few short weeks this little *shikseleh* could fit in almost like a part of the family?

A short while later, as Rivka was chopping onions in the kitchen, Laurel walked in carrying something under her arm—a sketch pad, it looked like.

"The *cholent*," Rivka explained to Laurel, who was now peering over her shoulder, "has to bake in a very slow oven overnight, so on Shabbat, when we don't do any cooking, there it is, all ready, hot and delicious."

"Will you show me how to make it? Then maybe I could surprise Annie. She really liked the stuffed cabbage." Lowering her voice, she added confidentially, "I hate to say this, but Annie is a terrible cook. She burns everything. If I didn't do the cooking, we'd both starve."

Seeing the glint in Laurel's eye, Rivka chuckled. Nothing about this blue-eyed, fair-haired *bordekeh* failed to surprise her.

Now Laurel was flipping open her sketch pad and sitting down at the kitchen table.

"Rivka, you've been so nice," she began shyly, pulling a pencil from the sketch pad's spiral binding. "I . . . I'd like to do something for you. Um, can I draw you? Sort of like a portrait?"

Rivka threw up her hands. "Draw me? When do I ever sit still long enough even to have my picture taken, I would like to know?"

"Oh, you wouldn't have to sit still. Just pretend I'm not here."

In the next room, Rivka could hear the boys squabbling, and Chava shrieking at them to stop, *please,* she was trying to do her homework. She sighed, thinking how not since she was an eighteen-year-old bride posing in her stiff white gown for the photographer had anyone thought of her as more than a pair of hands, a warm lap, a shoulder to cry on. And here was this little girl wanting to draw her portrait!

Nearly an hour later, the onions and tomatoes simmering, the beans soaking, Rivka washed her hands and dried them on her apron. At the table, Laurel was still hunched over her pad, pencil flying, so absorbed in her drawing that she didn't see Rivka creep up alongside her.

Then Rivka saw what she'd done, and her hand flew to her mouth. "*Vey iz mir!*" she cried softly.

Right there on that piece of paper, Laurel had captured her exactly. Not like the Mona Lisa, God forbid . . . but something even better. She'd caught her expression exactly, harried and flushed, with those little hairs curling out from under her scarf—even a smear of flour on her cheek!—and look how the woman in the drawing actually seemed to be *moving.*

Rivka, feeling both touched and full of awe, absently brushed the flour from her cheek. Then she leaned over and kissed the top of Laurel's shining head.

"Does that mean you like it?" Laurel's big blue eyes searched her face.

"I like it."

"I'm going to be an artist someday," she said. "I'm going to sell my paintings, and make enough money so Annie won't have to work."

"A regular Picasso." Rivka smiled.

"You think I could?"

"Darling, anything you set your mind to I know you could do."

"I should be so lucky," Laurel quipped, borrowing one of Rivka's expressions.

"Just watch out you don't become a *yenta* like me." Rivka laughed, remembering when she'd wondered how Annie and Laurel, such young girls, would ever manage without a mother and a father. But they would, she could see now. The two of them, *baruch Hashem,* they would do just fine.

Annie checked the order form against the merchandise.

> *2 doz. praline turtles*
> *1 doz. dark chocolate hazelnut-rums*
> *1 doz. white chocolate espressos*
> *4 doz. champagne truffles*
> *3 lbs. bitter-chocolate almond bark*
> *1 Coquille St. Jacques*

All there, cradled in molded Styrofoam trays, in the big brown-and-gold Girod's box on the counter in front of her. All except the Coquille St. Jacques—that was packed separately, in a smaller box.

She pulled it from the shelf below. She'd never seen a Coquille St. Jacques—a Girod's specialty—except for the picture in the catalogue, and she was bursting with curiosity. Carefully, she lifted the top. A wonderful toasty aroma—a blend of chocolate, vanilla, coffee, nuts—drifted up. Gently she removed the inner cover of corrugated paper.

It was exquisite.

"Oh!" she cried softly.

A shell of milk chocolate molded in the shape of a giant scallop, and filled with smaller shells. Bittersweet snails. Whorled clamshells. Chocolate-chip-sized periwinkles. Speckled cowries. Milk-chocolate sea horses. And—like something right out of Ali Baba—a pearl necklace fashioned from beads of white chocolate.

If only Laurel could see this! Annie hoped the guy she was delivering it to, whoever he was, would appreciate it half as much as she knew her sister would.

She glanced at the invoice—Joe Daugherty. The address was a restaurant, Joe's Place, on Morton Street.

Just her luck. All the way down to the Village. And it was snowing like crazy out there. Oh well, at least she'd be in a warm cab. And maybe, since it was almost four, Dolly would tell her to go on home after she'd delivered her package.

She went to the narrow storage area below the stairs for her coat, and was pulling it on when she heard Dolly call out, "Lord, you'll catch your death!"

Then Dolly was bustling over, snatching the coat off her before Annie could button it.

"Honey, you can't go around in weather like this in a coat as flimsy as a handkerchief," Dolly scolded. "But if you won't let me buy you a new one, leastways let me lend you mine. I'm not going anywhere, not unless I have to."

Annie, following her gaze, saw that the sidewalk and street beyond it looked like a sheet cake after a four-year-old's birthday party, all the beautiful whiteness smashed and trampled.

Dolly reached for her own coat, hung casually over a peg on the wall—a gorgeous full-length Russian sable that had to have cost a fortune. Annie's heart sank. She'd feel like a fool in it, like a beggar girl masquerading as a duchess.

"No thanks . . . I'd better not. I'd probably wreck it."

"Nonsense." Dolly held out the coat. "If I worried about every speck of dirt that got on my clothes, I'd be running around naked. I'm a lot more concerned with your staying healthy. Now, here, put it on."

Annie knew her aunt was just being nice, but she felt a bit smothered. She wished Dolly would stop giving her stuff, like that scarf last week—sure, she'd needed it, but did it have to be cashmere? Plain wool would have been fine.

But what would it hurt just to borrow it? *It won't kill me, and Dolly will be so pleased.*

Annie, nevertheless, found herself turning away, pretending to be suddenly preoccupied with the order form stapled to the shopping bag in which the chocolates were now stowed.

"Maybe you'd better check this over before I go," she said. "I took the order over the phone, but there was so much noise in the background I'm not sure I got everything. Does this look right?"

Dolly laughed. "Sounded like inside a car wash? That'd be his kitchen. I don't believe Joe Daugherty has set foot outside of it since he took over that beat-up old place."

"You sound as if you know him pretty well," Annie commented, glad to get her aunt off the subject of her coat.

"Mostly through his father, Marcus Daugherty. He and Dale did some business—Dale bought a chunk of an office building he syndicated. A stuffy, stiff-necked type—he took it real hard when his only son quit law school to start this restaurant. Nice boy, he's really made a go of it." Dolly's eyes sparkled. "Say! I bet you two would get along real well. Joe's not much older than you, three or four years maybe." She winked at Annie. "Not half-bad looking, either."

Annie rolled her eyes. Sure, that's just what she needed right now, Prince Charming in a white chef's hat. Between this store, looking after Laurel, and worrying about Val, did she even have a free half-hour once a week?

A boyfriend? She couldn't afford one, not now at any rate.

"Well, I guess I'd better get going," she said, hoping to slip out before Dolly could press the fur coat on her a second time. "I—

A blast of cold air startled Annie, as a man in a Santa Claus suit staggered in, his fake beard drooping like an old billy goat's, his boots clotted with snow.

"HO! HO! HO! Meeerrrfuckinchrishmass!"

He stumbled over to the counter and sagged against it. His sour reek caused Annie to draw back sharply, engulfed by memories of her mother. But it was Gloria, busy tying tartan bows on a newly arrived shipment of chocolate Scotties, he focused on.

"Whassamatter? You don' like Chrishmash?" Santa's bloodshot eyes fixed her with a baleful glare.

Gloria dropped her roll of ribbon and slapped her palms down so hard on the marble counter on either side of him that his head jerked like a puppet's. "Okay, Santa. You want the naughty first, or the nice? 'Cause this is as nice as it gets, and you're gonna see me get real naughty in about two seconds if you don't haul your ass right outa here."

His face sagged, and he cast her a reproachful look. "I jus' wan t'wish ever'body a mer' Chrishmash."

"You get any merrier, buster, and they gonna lock you up."

He straightened, attempting to strike an indignant stance, but he swayed on his feet, lurching forward as he stabbed a finger at the ceiling. "Now jus' a fuckin' minute!"

Then Dolly, in her crimson bolero jacket and black stiletto heels, was hurrying over, and Annie imagined her aunt grabbing Santa by the collar and tossing him out into the snow.

But Dolly was sliding an arm around his shoulders and drawling, "Hey, Bill. Remember me? It's Dolly. Dolly Drake. Listen, you tell the brass at Macy's that I think you're doing a helluva job. It must be tough, hour after hour, listening to a bunch of kids whining about G.I. Joe and Barbie."

Annie was shocked. Why was her aunt being so nice to that old drunk?

"Li'l bugger bit me! I ask him wha' he wants from ol' Santa, and he takes a bite outa me." Bill drew his crimson sleeve back to show a ring of purple teeth marks on his puffy forearm. "Bad enough I gotta wear this shitty costume." His bloodshot eyes shimmered with tears.

"You want me to call you a taxi?" Dolly asked in a conspiratorial whisper.

The Santa shook his head, his elasticized beard snagging on a button, and stretching down to expose a gray-stubbled chin. A tear trickled down his cheek. "All I wan' is a drink. It's col' out there. Fuckin' snow ever'where . . . in my boots, in my eyes."

Dolly paused a moment, deliberating. Then she patted his shoulder, and said, "Hold on there, Bill, I've got just the thing."

Dolly ducked into the back room, appearing a moment later with a gift-wrapped bottle of Cherry Heering a customer had given her yesterday.

"Merry Christmas, Bill," she said as she handed it to him. "And next time an elf bites you, you just bite 'em back." She winked.

Annie watched him give Dolly a long, sober-seeming look filled with gratitude, then stagger to the door. With a jingle of the overhead bell, he disappeared into a swirl of snow. She turned to Dolly.

"Do you really *know* him?" she asked.

Dolly shrugged. "I see him around the neighborhood, bumming quarters when he's not working, which is most of the time. Nice guy, just drinks more than he should."

"Why did you give him that bottle, then?"

Dolly shot her a sad smile. "Like the man says, it's cold out there." Her eyes turned suddenly bright, and for a moment Annie thought she was going to cry. Then she brought her hand, dry and soft as a powder puff, to Annie's cheek. "There's all kinds of sins in this world, sugar . . . but wanting to stay warm isn't one of them. If he ever comes around to licking this, it'll be in his own time, not when I tell him to."

Annie felt ashamed, was suddenly filled with a new respect for her aunt. How could Dearie have disliked her so? What could Dolly have done that was so awful?

Annie walked over, and retrieved Dolly's sable coat, which her aunt had tossed over the back of a chair.

Dolly clapped her hands with pleasure, light winking off the rings crowding her fingers. "Well, look at you . . . just like a movie st—" She caught herself and finished weakly, "Like a fashion model."

Could she be right, Annie wondered—do I look like Dearie?

But before she could start thinking about how much she missed her mother, Dolly was hugging her and saying brightly, "Go on now, scoot. And tell that Joe I said hi."

Annie didn't look down as she was getting out of the taxi, and by the time she did it was too late. Her foot was sliding out from under her on the icy curb, and she was falling backwards. She landed on her bottom with a hard smack that jolted her badly and sent the shopping bag of chocolates flying.

Picking herself up, and retrieving her thick gold shopping bag, she prayed that none of the chocolates were broken. God, she felt like enough of a klutz without having to go through a bunch of explanations and apologies.

Joe's Place turned out to be one of those aged Federal-style brick houses common to the Village, narrow as a chimney, with a few stairs leading up to a panelled door set with an oval of bevelled glass. Below the snow-covered window box, Annie could just make out a sign pointing to another flight of steps going down to the basement service entrance.

Buzzed in through a wrought-iron gate and the door beyond, Annie immediately smelled baking bread as she entered a narrow vestibule. To the rear, down a dimly lit hallway, she could see into the kitchen, stainless steel and copper skillets hung in a row above a hulking black range. She heard voices, the clatter of pots, the hiss of steam.

Then, a smashing sound, crockery crashing against a tiled floor. *"Goddamn it!"* a voice roared. *"Asshole! Idiot!"*

Annie jumped.

The voice coming from the kitchen seemed to reverberate, as if directed exclusively at her. Annie shrank back, reminded of Oz bellowing at Dorothy—*Who are* you *to question the great and terrible Oz!*

A figure appeared, a long shadow dancing on the propped-open door to the kitchen, followed by its owner—a lanky man in his early twenties, his rangy height making even five-foot-nine Annie feel short. He wore a stained apron over blue jeans, and a faded chambray shirt with its sleeves rolled up over his elbows. His longish hair was pushed back from a sweaty forehead, and his eyes swam murkily behind steam-fogged eyeglasses. Not the great and terrible Oz, after all.

Annie felt herself relax a little, though he wasn't smiling. His face was flushed; a line of red was drawn along each sharp, angled cheekbone as if with a crayon.

"Yeah, what do you want?" he barked.

"I . . ." For an awful moment, her mind went blank.

Before she could get the words out, he blurted, "Look, I'm really busy. I've got a party of twenty-four arriving in a couple of hours, one of the ovens just fritzed out on me, two of my waiters are out sick, and the floor in there looks like a bomb went off, so whatever it is you want, for Chrissakes, spit it out."

Something in Annie snapped. "I don't *want* anything," she said in her haughtiest voice, thrusting her shopping bag at him. "If you're Joe Daugherty just sign the stupid invoice, and I'll get out of your way."

He stared at her, the condensed steam on his lenses beginning to evaporate, revealing eyes that looked gentle, wide and brown, with a thick fringe of lashes any girl would have envied. The angry flush left his cheeks, and now he looked chagrined.

"Oh, Christ. I'm sorry. Look, can we start over?" He pushed long fingers through his streaky brown hair, and turned a sheepish grin on her. "I *am* Joe Daugherty, and I've been having a day you wouldn't believe. I guess I just sort of came unglued."

Annie thought of the poor guy—some dishwasher, no doubt, struggling to live on fifty cents an hour—that he'd yelled at back there. Even Mr. Dimitriou, at the Parthenon, wouldn't have called her an asshole. And if he had . . . well, she'd have given it right back to him in spades. So she wasn't buying this jerk's Mr. Nice Guy act.

"Right." With a crisp gesture, she handed him the invoice slip. "Sign here." Then she remembered that the chocolates might be damaged. She swallowed hard, and said, "Wait. You'd better check to see if they're okay. I . . . I sort of slipped and fell on the ice on my way over, and some of them might be, uh, broken."

Annie waited for the other shoe to drop, for this guy to explode again, but after a tense moment, he surprised her by laughing. A low, easy laugh that made her want to smile in spite of herself.

"I guess this isn't your day, either," he observed mildly. "Sorry about your fall . . . and you can stop looking at me like I'm going to cut you up and serve you for dinner. I really *am* sorry I snapped at you. You may not believe this, but I'm actually a pretty mellow guy. I have a long fuse, but when I blow, I *really* blow."

"Great. But what about that poor guy in there who you dumped on?"

Daugherty looked puzzled, then he began to chuckle, and in a minute was roaring with laughter. Shoulders shaking, he leaned into the wall for support, pushing up his glasses to wipe the tears from his eyes. "*I* was the one who dropped those dishes. I was cursing myself out." He shook his head, still laughing weakly. "Pardon my French, but I didn't know you were out here."

Annie felt like a perfect fool. She didn't know what to say. Then she began to laugh, too.

"Why don't we step down the corridor into my executive boardroom, and assess what damage has been done," Joe suggested with a wry arch of his brow, leading the way down the dim hall to another door, which opened into a tiny, grungy office. "Look at it this way, you couldn't have made a worse mess than I just did."

He lowered the shopping bag onto a desk heaped with papers, and gestured for Annie to sit in a chair wedged between a file cabinet and an empty fish tank filled with glass ashtrays. "By the way," he said. "I'm Joe Daugherty. But I've already said that, haven't I?"

"I know."

"And you're—" He looked at her, questioningly.

"Annie," she blurted without thinking, though at Girod's she'd been using only her middle name, May. Now why had she let that out?

"You must be new with Dolly," he said.

"I just started last week."

"Funny, I would've pegged you for the college type. Vassar, or Sarah Lawrence maybe."

Annie shrugged. "Well, you'd be wrong then," she answered evenly. College, which she had once yearned for, couldn't seem further away.

"Hey, I'm one to talk. I deep-sixed law school to open this place. And the crazy part is," he grinned, "in spite of all the hassles, I love it. My old man is figuring this is temporary insanity. He's even saving a space for my name plate on the door to his old office. Poth, Van Gelder, Daugherty and Prodigal Son."

"Your father's a lawyer?" From what Dolly had told her, she'd imagined Joe's father to be some kind of real-estate mogul.

"Used to be. Now he's a judge. The Honorable Marcus Daugherty." He took his glasses off, and began polishing them with his apron. "There you have it. My life story on the half-shell. So you see, you're not the only one who's running away."

Annie now felt herself turn to ice. How did he know? Could Dolly have told him?

She forced a smile. "Who said anything about running away?" Her face felt as if it were cracking under the strain.

Joe shrugged, hooking a leg up onto the seat of the swivel chair in front of his desk. "One way or another, aren't we all running to get away from someone or someplace? I mean, isn't that what this town is all about?" With his glasses off, she saw that his eyes weren't really brown, they were sort of a cross between green and brown, a shifting, mossy hazel.

He just missed being handsome—not ordinary handsome, but really knockout handsome, like a movie star. Only none of his features seemed to fit exactly right. One cheekbone slanted slightly higher than the other, and his nose crooked a little to the left (had it been broken?). His smile, too, was faintly skewed—as if he couldn't quite make up his mind if he was smiling or not. No, not a movie star, she thought, more like a rock idol. Mick Jagger, or George Harrison, or Peter Noonan. Some of them, she thought, were downright ugly in fact, but they had a kind of . . . well, an energy. A brash, jangly, almost *rude* energy that drove girls right out of their seats.

Annie realized she was staring, and jerked her gaze away.

"Sure. I guess so." She felt relieved—he hadn't really been talking about her personally. "Coming here is a little like joining the circus, isn't it?"

Joe laughed. "Yeah, a high-wire act. One false move and you're flat on your ass." He snatched the invoice from her hand, and signed it with a flourish. "Stuff the chocolates," he said. "Even if a few of them are smashed, it's too ugly out there for you to make a second trip."

"I'd feel better if you would at least check," she said, not wanting to feel *too* grateful, in case there had been no harm done after all. "Then I could tell Dolly to take it off your bill."

Joe shrugged, and reached for the shopping bag. "If you insist . . ."

The first box was okay; only a few pieces of almond bark were broken. But when Joe opened the box containing the Coquille St. Jacques, Annie nearly cried. All those beautiful, delicate shells, completely smashed, the necklace of white-chocolate pearls broken and scattered.

Joe stared at the ruins for a long moment, then he shrugged. "*In arena aedificas.* That's Latin for 'If you build your house on sand be prepared for a whole lot of shakin' going on.' Anyway, it won't go to waste. My staff will eat anything that doesn't crawl."

Seeing how hard he was trying to make up for how he'd acted before, Annie actually found herself smiling.

"You haven't been in New York very long, have you?" he asked. It was more a statement than a question.

"Why . . . does it show?"

"Your smile, it's definitely west of the Mississippi." So he *had* noticed.

"How do New Yorkers smile?"

"They don't."

She giggled. "Does it ever get any easier here?"

"Nope. Only it sort of grows on you after a while. You'll see."

Annie stood up. "I'd better go. I have to get home." At the door, she stopped and looked back. "Uh . . . well, thanks."

She was making her way out down the hallway when he called out, "Wait!"

What now?

Joe loped past her, and up a flight of stairs to her left, which presumably led up to the dining area. Minutes later, he reappeared holding a large plastic carton. He presented it to Annie as if it held the crown jewels.

"To make up for acting like such a jerk," he said. "Merry Christmas."

Annie heard a faint, scratching sound, and peeked inside. A big lobster, its claws bound with rubber bands, scuttled feebly about in some seaweed and a bit of water. She was so startled she nearly dropped the container.

She looked up at Joe, at his handsome, broken face and greenish-brown eyes so obviously full of good intentions. No, it wasn't a joke.

But what on earth was she going to do with a . . . a *lobster,* for God's sake? She didn't even have a pot to cook it in. She thought of some of the things she so badly needed and wanted . . . but *this* . . . well, it was so far off the list it was almost funny.

"Uh, thanks," she managed, reddening a little. "I'm sure it'll be . . . uh . . . delicious."

"With a little butter and lemon."

"Well . . . thanks."

"Don't mention it. And, hey, drop by any time."

Trudging through the falling snow to the subway at West Fourth, wondering how she was going to explain to Laurel—who suffered pangs if anyone accidentally stepped on an ant—that they'd have to *boil* this creature alive, Annie spotted a man selling Christmas trees out of the back of his truck. Her heart sank.

If only she could afford one. And the irony of it was, this lobster, if she'd bought it in a store, would have cost a lot. With that money, she might have been able to buy a small tree.

Then it hit her.

She walked over to the truck. The man was burly, bearded, wearing a red plaid lumberjack shirt, and he was nailing a cross of two-by-fours to the trunk of a bushy fir on his tailgate. He waved his hammer in greeting.

"Can I do for you, miss?"

Just come right out with it, she told herself.

"Uh . . . I was just wondering . . . would you be interested in trading one of your trees for . . . for . . ."

"Whatcha got there?" He tossed his hammer down.

Annie opened her box, and held it up so he could see inside.

The man looked at her as if she'd just offered him a slice of green cheese from the moon. But after he'd poked the lobster to see if it was still kicking, and she had agreed to accept his skinniest, spindliest tree—one he probably couldn't have gotten much for anyway—she had a deal.

At West Fourth, as she made her way down the slushy steps to the IND, awkwardly dragging the tree behind her, Annie thought of how pleased Laurel would be, and how they would decorate it with paper chains, popcorn, and tinfoil stars.

Maybe it would turn out to be an okay Christmas after all.

CHAPTER 6

E ven in L.A., Val thought, December was a bitch.

As he churned his way across the pool, he tried not to feel how cold the water was, or how his head was throbbing, or to think about the real-estate broker and her shit-don't-stink clients, who right now were tramping around inside his house, peering into closets and pointing out cracks in the plaster.

Instead, Val thought about Annie.

The rotten little bitch.

She had done this to him.

Why? Had he hurt her in any way?

Okay, so I had a couple of drinks that night . . . you can't crucify a man for that. As to what he might have said or done, it couldn't have been much. And if he raised a hand to her, she sure as hell must have deserved it. No matter what the hell it was, she'd had no right to clobber him like that. Fifteen stitches. Christ!

The little bitch was nuttier than her old lady, accusing him of killing Eve. So how was it *his* fault that she'd swallowed all those pills?

If anything it was Eve who'd done *him* wrong—leaving him in the lurch like this, with two nagging kids to look after. If only he weren't so broke! Not enough bread even for a plane ticket to New York to check out Dolly, see if she was being straight with him. He remembered the last time he'd spoken with her on the phone, the way Dolly had gushed on and on like he was her long-lost brother instead of the creep who'd dumped her for her sister. *Had* she heard from the girls? Val wondered. Did she maybe know where they were?

He didn't care about finding Annie—she could go where she wanted. Ten minutes, that's all he'd want with her. Ten minutes and the flat of his hand to show her she couldn't get away with treating him like this.

But Laurel, that was different. If he could just get his daughter back, there ought to be some way of getting a hold of that trust money of hers. He'd mentioned it to a lawyer at the karate club, who told him that, with things being so tight and all, he could file some kind of petition.

Val let himself imagine a nice house, nothing as grand as this maybe, but classy, Westwood Village or Pacific Palisades. And he knew a guy who had an inside at the track . . . a way he could double, maybe even triple his money.

But first, he'd have to find Laurel. Without her, he wouldn't have a chance in hell of breaking into that trust.

And then, when he had her back, he'd make damn sure Annie Cobb never saw her again. Yeah, wouldn't that be a great way of teaching her to mess with him?

Fifty laps. Val grabbed hold of the ladder, and hoisted himself out of the pool. He was breathing hard now, heart pounding, blood pistoning through his veins.

"Jesus, how can you swim in that muck?" A gravelly voice penetrated the red tide surging in his ears. "You oughta get it cleaned."

Val focused his bleary, chlorine-stung eyes on the stubby figure sprawled on a nearby chaise. As always, he felt a tiny prick of incredulity. No one in a million years would guess that Rudy was his brother. A full foot shorter, squat, balding, and ugly—uglier than Val, even in his worst nightmares, could imagine being.

In his Hawaiian shirt and Pepto-Bismol-pink shorts, his round face and stubby legs pinkening under a glistening coat of tanning oil, Rudy reminded him of a roast pig at a luau.

"With what?" Val grabbed a towel and flung himself into the nearest deck chair. "You think the old lady fixed it so I'd be left with anything?" He gestured at the weed-grown expanse of lawn below the patio. "The Alfa and the Lincoln, you think I got more than peanuts for them? Even this house is a fucking joke. By the time I get through paying off what's left of the mortgage, plus the bills and back taxes on this mausoleum, I won't have a pot to piss in. If I still had Laurel, things might be different, but—" Val's words were cut off by the sight of Rudy jumping up, and strutting over to where Val lay stretched out.

"Forget about that money," Rudy snapped. "Even if you could get your hands on it—which I'm not so sure you could—how far do you think it would go? If you'd had any sense, you'd have sewed things up for yourself *before* Eve kicked off."

In his brother's wraparound sunglasses, Val saw himself reflected, twin images no bigger than two flies.

"And just how was I supposed to do that?"

"There's ways. There's always ways. A pitcher of martinis, and it's, 'Honey, how about signing this little bitty paper?' Boom! You've got power of attorney."

"Eve was a drunk. But no one ever said she was stupid."

"So? You never heard of salting away?" He looked pointedly at the diamond signet ring flashing on Val's pinkie. "Yeah, I see you have. Jesus Christ, is that all you've got to show for twelve whole years—a fucking ring, and a bunch of suits a pimp would cream over? You're pathetic, you know that?" His voice had dropped to a growl that sounded oddly tender, and he gently kneaded Val's shoulder. "I don't know why I bother with you sometimes."

Val jerked his shoulder free. "Yeah, neither do I. So why don't you just take a hike?" It hurt, what Rudy was saying, but in a funny way he had a sense it was doing him some good—like iodine on a wound.

"Relax," Rudy told him. "In another week or two, the girls'll run out of money, get tired of Big Macs, and you'll find them right on your doorstep scratching to be let in. How far do you think a couple of spoiled Bel Air brats are gonna get?"

"I don't know." Val fingered the scar over his eyebrow. It still felt tender, and under the puckered scar was a hard ridge. "If they had somebody to go to, maybe they wouldn't be in such a big hurry."

"Like who?"

"Dolly, maybe."

"What makes you think the girls would go to *her*, knowing the way Eve felt about her?"

"Just a hunch." Val shrugged. "The way she was acting over the phone—nice as pie, like my shit don't stink. I can't put my finger on it, but I got a funny feeling she might know something she's not telling." With his fist, he smacked his open palm. "Jesus, if only I had the money, then I'd fly out there and see for myself." He thought about asking Rudy to spot him a few hundred, but then he remembered he was already in the hole with him for almost a grand. And Rudy had made it clear: no more, not another penny.

Rudy's grin seemed to slip a notch, as if he knew what Val was thinking, and a hard gleam stole into his beady black eyes. But then he was kneading Val's shoulder again.

"What you need is a drink," he said. "How about I fix us a couple of Bloody Marys?"

Later, sipping their drinks under the magnolia at the outdoor bar, Rudy said, "Sorry about giving you a hard time. Guess I've been pretty keyed up lately."

Rudy? With his fancy law practice and all his money, what the hell did *he* have to worry about?

"It's this case I'm on," Rudy went on. "Haven't come up for air in months." He looked off into the distance, rubbing his chin. "Diaper pins. Who ever thinks about the guy who invented diaper pins? He turns baby shit into a hundred-million-dollar empire. Three ex-wives, no less, and eight kids, then he goes and dumps my client, wife number four, for a twenty-year-old bimbo. Now she's really out to stick him good, you'll pardon the pun. You should see the filings and motions. Eight months, and they can't even agree on a court date." He ran his finger around the inside of his collar. "Jesus, even on a cloudy day this sun can really get to you." He eyed Val's nearly empty glass. "How about another one?"

"No thanks. After this, I want to get in a few more laps."

After staring at an algae-covered birdbath for several minutes, Rudy said, "She's just your type."

"Who?"

"My client. Soon-to-be-ex number four. Nice-looking lady. Knockers the size of watermelons. I'm telling you, she's hot." He took a long swallow of his drink, and fixed his gaze on Val. "*And she's loaded.* At least she will be when we settle."

"What the fuck you think I am, the kind of guy who'd sleep with somebody just for money?"

Rudy just kept on giving him that unnerving stare.

Finally, he shrugged and said, "If the shoe fits."

Val, reminded of the looks people had been giving him down

at the club, the whispered conversations that often stopped the minute he walked into the steam room—*I know what they're saying, that I used Eve, bled her dry*—felt something inside him snap. He grabbed his brother's shirt and hoisted him off the bar stool. It felt like lifting a kid having a tantrum. Rudy thrashed and wriggled, lashing out with his fists and his feet. His face flushed a furious, boiled-looking red.

"Take it back!" Val demanded.

"Put me down! I wasn't trying to insult you, for Christ's sake!"

Val let go of Rudy, plopping him so suddenly down onto his stool that he nearly toppled over. Rudy's elbow caught the remains of his Bloody Mary and sent the glass spinning over the edge of the bar, spewing tomato juice down the front of his shirt before smashing on the root-heaved patio bricks. Val felt the tiny shards fly against his ankles like sparks, and was absurdly reminded of a TV commercial: *How about a nice Hawaiian punch?*

The anger ebbed, and he began feeling bad that he'd roughed Rudy up. In his own weird way, Rudy might actually have been trying to help.

Christ, if it hadn't been for Rudy, he could still be cruising some crummy Times Square sidewalk doing back-flips and walking on his hands for nickels and dimes. A stuntman in Hollywood, all Rudy's idea. And it was Rudy again, after they'd hitched clear across the country, who somehow fast-talked his way past the guard at the Universal lot, and two hours later, into a job for Val. Boy, could he *talk*. Except when it came to women.

Their mother, God rest her maggoty soul, had never done half as much for Val. Christ, he could just picture Shirley up there somewhere, looking down at him; he could hear her raspy whiskey voice, telling anyone who would listen, *You see? I always said he'd amount to no good. . . .*

Rudy had brains, a head like a goddamn encyclopedia. He knew about flowers and trees, and how atom bombs were made, and all the fifteen-syllable words that lawyers slung around. Partner in a classy firm, a house in Brentwood, a Mercedes, a weekend place in Malibu. Rudy's only problem, as Val saw it, was women.

Val guessed that the only times Rudy had gotten laid were when he'd paid for it. Probably thought he was too short and too ugly for any woman to go for him. But what he really lacked was confidence.

Rudy mopped at his shirt with a napkin. "Jesus, you don't have to go apeshit!" He tossed down the napkin, now drenched with what looked like blood. "Look at this. Brand-new shirt. I'll never get this out."

"Soak it in milk."

"Now how would you know a thing like that?" Rudy stared at him in amazement.

"Looks like the fake blood they dumped all over me when I was doing stunts—a real bitch to get out once it sets. I learned that milk trick from Heloise. You know, in the newspaper."

Rudy sputtered as if he were choking. He sounded like an outboard motor having trouble getting started. It was a moment before Val realized he was laughing.

Rudy slapped his shoulder.

"You know, little brother, sometimes you amaze me. You really do. I think you and Roberta will get along just fine."

"Roberta?"

"Look, think of it as charity. You'd be doing her a favor. That husband of hers, she probably hasn't been properly fucked since the flood. And if in return she decides to show you her gratitude, well, what are friends for? You scratch my back, I'll scratch yours. It's the American way."

"Charity, huh?" Val, looking at Rudy's lumpy face, sort of a cross between Baby Huey and Mr. Magoo, felt himself getting a little excited. Maybe for a change something good would start happening. "So what do you get out of it? Why all of a sudden are you so fucking concerned with my getting laid?"

Rudy tried to look innocent, but his brother knew him better than almost anyone.

"Okay, the truth is, Roberta's thinking of backing out."

"What do you mean?"

"I mean, he's got her so brainwashed into thinking he's king of the universe, she's this close to signing whatever bullshit agreement he wants her to sign, and maybe kissing off millions."

"And there goes your fat fee, right?"

He shrugged. "Yeah, well, I got a big overhead."

There was more to it, Val sensed, seeing a queer, hard glint in his brother's eye that said this went beyond him just pulling down his fee. Maybe he had the hots for Roberta himself, and figured if

he couldn't fuck her, the next best thing was having his brother do
it. And this way, with Val the muscle man stroking her real good,
she wouldn't be so quick to sign away a fortune.

Val, flexing his hand, admiring the wink of the diamond on his
little finger, thought that for such a little runt his brother sure did
have a big pair of balls.

"I'll think about it," he said. "That's all I'm promising." But
he was beginning to feel tempted. He could use the money, no doubt
about that. And what else did he have going for himself right now?

"You could meet her for a drink while you're thinking it over,"
Rudy urged. "No strings."

"Shit, Rudy." Val felt himself getting pissed again. "I hope
you're not forgetting I got a few other things on my mind."

"Yeah . . . well." His eyes narrowed, nearly disappearing into
the folds of puffy flesh surrounding them. "You really think Dolly
might know something?"

"Like I said, it's just a hunch."

"Hey, tell you what," Rudy said in a soft, almost sinuous voice.
"Day after tomorrow, I'm flying out to New York to see this client
of mine, and collect some depositions. Custody case—my guy's ex-
wife is trying to keep him from seeing his kid, on account of he's a
faggot. I gotta prove to the court somehow that even wearing ladies'
undies, he's still Father Knows Best. It shouldn't take long, though.
Afterwards, I could drop in on Dolly, check out her story."

Val sat up straighter. "Would you? Hey, that'd be great." How
could he have doubted Rudy? When push came to shove, didn't
Rudy always come through? Gruffly, he added, "Thanks."

Rudy shrugged. "Hey, no sweat. What are brothers for?"

Two days later, an hour after checking in at the Pierre, Rudy was
in a cab bouncing over the potholes up Madison on his way to
Dolly's shop. Could Val be right? Did Dolly maybe know where
Annie and Laurel were? He felt excited, hopeful, almost squirming
in his seat . . . but his stomach was in knots.

What if Dolly *wasn't* hiding anything?

What if he came away with nothing more than what she'd
already told Val?

Val. In spite of his jumpiness, Rudy found himself smiling at the memory of how he'd conned his brother. Making him think that old Rudy was doing him such a big favor, first setting him up with Roberta—who'd keep Val so busy, in bed and out, he wouldn't know which end was up—then oh-so-casually offering to follow up on Dolly. It never even occurred to his totally self-involved brother that Rudy was doing this, not for him, but for Laurel.

Rudy, in his mind, saw his niece standing in the doorway at Bel Jardin, hovering just beyond his reach—her sweet face and those big, blue eyes. She was spooked by him, he knew. But who could blame her? What kid wouldn't be?

If only he could somehow let her know he wouldn't hurt her for the world. He felt so clumsy, so stupid around her. Like that time he'd given her a doll—the most expensive one in Bullock's, made of porcelain, with a frilly silk dress—not realizing it was far too fragile for a child. He remembered Laurel, only six, accidentally dropping it on the sun porch's tiled floor, watching in horror as it shattered into a million tiny pieces, then bursting into tears.

He'd wanted to hug her, wipe her tears away, buy her a hundred more dolls, the right kind this time. But he knew if he got too close, that would probably make her cry even harder. And then, too, there was Val, always looking over his shoulder, feeling sorry for him probably. Poor, pathetic Rudy, who couldn't even scare up a date for Saturday night, much less ever hope for a wife and kids of his own.

So he'd just let her cry. And after that, he'd held back . . . watching her from a safe distance . . .

And now everything had changed.

Rudy, remembering Val's frantic call several months ago, his brother babbling something about "the little bitch" clobbering him, felt the knot in his stomach tighten. Even while calming Val down, and taking him to Emergency for stitches, Rudy had felt a slow rage building inside him. He had known that this was Val's fault somehow. The self-centered prick. From day one, he'd never cared about those girls, not even Laurel, his own daughter. And though Val insisted he hadn't done anything to make Annie fly off the handle, Rudy suspected he had—and that it must have been bad, *real* bad, to make a pampered teenaged girl run off in the middle of the night to God knows where, and take her little sister with her.

Now, staring out at the antique shops and clothing boutiques whipping past, Rudy thought, *He doesn't deserve Laurel.*

If he could somehow track down his niece, things would be different. Never mind about Annie—with her fierce eyes and sharp gestures, she'd always made him want to keep his distance. No, *that* one could do as she pleased. Sweet Laurel was all he cared about. And if he found her, he'd figure out a way of keeping her to himself, away from Val and his money-grubbing.

But what about Laurel? Will she be glad to see me? Or will she look at me with those big eyes like I'm some kind of monster?

They were practically stalled now, the cab lurching its way through the heavy traffic cramming Madison Avenue—horns bleating, drivers yelling out their windows, the hiss of hydraulic brakes. But Rudy was far away from it all, remembering something that had happened in high school, eons ago, yet was etched in his mind like initials carved into a table.

Marlene Kirkland. Pretty, blond, popular. How could he ever have thought he had a chance with her? Marlene, who always seemed to have half a dozen guys hanging around her locker—guys with crewcuts and suede bucks and letter sweaters. Marlene, who wore a tiny gold chain about her lovely ankle, and whose charm bracelet, jingling softly in the quiet of a classroom, could bring a lump to your throat.

And yet somehow, with Val prodding him, and even coaching him on what to say, Rudy had gotten up the nerve to ask Marlene to the junior prom. Scared shitless, he'd pretended to be cool, even tough, swaggering over to Marlene's table in the cafeteria, all five feet four inches of him quaking in his Cuban heels.

"I hear you ain't got a date for the prom," he'd blurted, forgetting all the suave lines Val had taught him. "So how's about going with me?"

Rudy would never forget the shock on Marlene's pretty cheerleader's face. Her girlfriends, clustered around her, began to giggle. Rudy had felt his face begin to burn, a scorching heat spreading up to the roots of his Brylcreemed pompadour. He watched her cast a sharp look at Val, standing nearby, and then her eyes narrowed, and Rudy realized—too late to save himself—that she must think this was some kind of joke.

Marlene, looking straight at Rudy, had said, "I'd rather eat dogshit."

Each word, even in memory, was like a hole punched through his heart.

Had Val set him up? Rudy would never know, not for sure.

But one thing he was damn certain of was that he didn't ever want to see that kind of scorn in Laurel's eyes.

Rudy felt the cab jerk to a stop. Madison and Seventy-second —Dolly's shop was just down the block. He paid the driver, and got out, hunching his shoulders against the light rain spattering his face and coat. Though it was midafternoon, the street looked gloomy as a cave. He'd forgotten how dark the city got when it was overcast, all those tall buildings blocking the light, making him feel like a bug in a jar. Passing the fancy shops, stuffed with expensive dresses, hats, antiques, jewelry, he wondered briefly if he was wasting his time. If this wasn't just one more wild-goose chase, like in L.A., when for two whole days he'd helped Val look for the girls.

Finally, between a swank jeweler and a tweedy men's clothing store, he spotted Girod's. Its sign hung outside in fancy gold script against a hunter-green background. There was a window box, of all things, but no flowers, nothing but a clump of dirty snow left over from the last storm. A miniature Christmas tree lit with tiny white lights and tied with gilt-wrapped bonbons twinkled in the front window. It reminded him, perversely, of the Christmas he'd have waiting for him back home—alone, sleeping off the too-many whis-key sours he'd have drunk at the office Christmas party the night before.

Rudy's heart twisted in his chest. Why should Val have every-thing, and he have nothing? Val, so obsessed with himself and with money, he didn't even realize he'd let the greatest treasure of all slip between his fingers.

If Laurel were my daughter, he told himself, *everything would be different.*

But, dammit, he was getting ahead of himself. First, he'd have to see if Dolly knew anything. Right now, everything depended on her. Was she telling Val the truth? Or was it just Val's paranoia making him suspicious?

And what if she *did* know something? She sure as hell wouldn't come right out and tell him her secret. In her mind, no doubt, that'd be the same as telling Val.

Well, if she was lying, he'd see right through her. One thing he was good at was reading people. When a client wasn't being straight with him, he could tell just by his expression. Like when Roberta Silver swore to him she'd been faithful during her marriage, absolutely one hundred percent, he'd believed her like he believed in the tooth fairy.

Yeah, he'd know. And then he'd have Dolly tailed, and sooner or later she'd lead him to Laurel.

Feeling cheered again, Rudy pushed his way in through the bevelled-glass door.

CHAPTER 7

Laurel peered through the slit where the stage curtain met the wall. From where she stood, at a darkened end of the stage, she could see the whole auditorium. Every folding chair looked filled, and people were hovering in the back, leaning against the walls.

She scanned row after row, but Annie and Aunt Dolly still hadn't arrived. Where could they be? It was almost six-thirty, and the play was half over! Could something have happened to them? On the news yesterday, she'd heard about this horrible car wreck on Ocean Parkway, six people killed. Could they be hurt, lying by the side of the road, bleeding, or—

No. That was too horrible. She'd better stop right now. She was making herself sick. Her stomach felt jiggly as a bowl of Jell-O. What if she got so sick she had to throw up?

"Group four," she heard Miss Rodriguez whisper. "Kitty, Laurel, Jesús . . . you're on next. Line up over there when I give the signal."

Laurel looked around at her red-cheeked teacher, who was herding everybody together. Reluctantly, Laurel joined the others, edging in next to Jesús.

"Phutt! Phuuuuut!" Jesús had a hand tucked under one armpit, and was pumping his elbow, making it sound as if he were farting.

Laurel felt like jabbing him with her papier-mâché scepter, but she didn't dare. Yesterday, during Spelling Bee, on his first turn, he got "constitution" wrong, and when she won, he'd tried to trip her on her way back to her seat. The day before, he stole her milk money, and threatened to beat the crap out of her if she told.

The teacher scowled in their direction and pointed her finger at Jesús. "Can it, Jesús. If I need sound effects, I'll call on you."

Miss Rodriguez, with her thick body and long face, her big soft eyes that bugged out a little, reminded Laurel of a pony. But she

could be really nice. Laurel remembered her first day, she'd been
so scared, she threw up on the bathroom floor. And Miss R. kept
everyone out until it'd been cleaned up, so the other kids wouldn't
tease her.

"I want each and every one of you," Miss Rodriguez went on
in a low, I-mean-business voice, "to remember that your mothers
and fathers are sitting out there right now, and they're expecting
you to try your very best. And I know you'll want to make them
as proud of you as I am . . ."

While Miss Rodriguez was giving her pep talk, Laurel slipped
over to peek through the curtain again.

Nothing but a blurry sea of faces. In the semidarkness, they
seemed to float like bubbles, bobbing and dipping. Then Laurel could
make out separate people, mothers with babies squirming on their
laps, fathers still in their work clothes, old-country grandmas in black
dresses and kerchiefs. But no Annie. And no brightly clothed Aunt
Dolly, either.

She began to feel really scared, a hot, fluttery feeling, as if
something inside her was pushing to get out, beating against her
ribs.

What if something did *happen? What if they got hurt? Or what if Val
found Annie and . . . and this time Annie couldn't get away?*

Then she remembered Uncle Rudy, how he always used to *look*
at her, almost as if he wanted to gobble her up. Laurel shivered.
Could Uncle Rudy be looking for her, too?

The thought was so awful, she began to feel dizzy, her head
seeming to float up like a balloon attached to a string.

"My ma ain't here." Jesús spoke softly behind her, causing
Laurel to whirl about. "She home."

"Well, maybe she's just late," Miss Rodriguez offered, then
turned to hiss, "Laurel, what are you *doing* over there? Take your
place."

Laurel turned away from the curtain, her eyes swimming. She
felt miserable. The thought of Jesús making fun of her was the only
thing that kept her from crying.

"Nah, she's a-sleepin'," Jesús replied with elaborate noncha-
lance. "She tole me not to bother her."

"That's cause she knows you're gonna 'barrass her," Rupa
Bahdreesh whispered loudly. She poked Jesús with her crutch. Rupa

was playing the part of Tiny Tim; she wore a baggy blouse and knee pants, her long dark braids stuffed under a knitted cap.

"Hush now, all of you!" Miss Rodriguez clapped her hands softly. "Pedro, straighten your crown. It's practically falling off."

"Ah, Miss R. . . . it don't look cool that way."

"Spirits aren't supposed to look cool, Pedro. You're Christmas Past, not Elvis Presley. And it's '*doesn't,*' not 'don't.' "

Looking past the folding screen that separated her group from the brightly lit stage, Laurel could see Andy McAllister, who was playing Scrooge, dressed in a nightshirt and striped cap, swaggering about the stage just like he did around the schoolyard during recess.

"Yaw nuttin' but a blob a gravy! A . . . a . . . dab a muhstaaad!" he bellowed in his nasal Brooklyn voice, making Laurel want to giggle suddenly in spite of herself.

She bit her lip. It'd be her turn to go on in just a minute.

Laurel was the Spirit of Christmas Present. She was wearing a red chenille robe that was so long it dragged on the ground, and a crown made out of plastic holly leaves. She had to speak sixteen whole lines. But if she was thinking about her sister and her aunt the whole time, how would she be able to remember them?

And the set—she'd worked so hard on it! It had been her idea to make Scrooge's door knocker—a lion's head with a ring through its mouth—out of tinfoil, which she'd glued onto a refrigerator carton (donated by Marta Saucedo's father, who worked in a furniture store) painted to look like a door. For the Spirit of Christmas Present's cornucopia, she'd collected a bunch of apples, oranges, grapes, even a pumpkin, sprayed them with gold paint, and heaped them in the enormous glass punch bowl the school used on Open House Night. And the costumes, too—Scrooge's tall black hat she'd borrowed from Mr. Gruberman, and Belle's dress she'd made from a flouncy slip Chava had helped her dye pink.

Laurel remembered when Miss Rodriguez had first suggested that she design the set, how unsure she'd felt. But Miss R. liked her art-class drawings, and had assured her she'd be good at it. Now Laurel had to admit her teacher had been right. And she'd been so excited, thinking how surprised Annie would be when she got here and saw what a great job she'd done.

But Annie wasn't here.

And she wouldn't, *couldn't,* have forgotten something this important, unless . . .

Something had to be wrong, Laurel was sure of it.

She felt a dull coldness in the pit of her stomach, like when she ate ice cream too fast.

"Who was you lookin' for, Beanie?" a sly voice whispered in her ear. Jesús—ugh! The first day of school, he'd named her "String Bean," then shortened it to "Beanie." "The *Prez*-i-dent maybe?"

"N-nobody," Laurel stammered, feeling her cheeks flood with heat. She hated Jesús. Why wouldn't he leave her alone?

He pressed closer. He smelled a little sour, like he hadn't taken a bath in a while. "Your mother ain't coming neither, huh?" His voice dropped to a conspiratorial whisper. For once, he sounded almost . . . well, *nice.*

"My mother's dead." Laurel was somehow shocked into admitting the truth.

"Yeah, so's mine. She always tellin' me that, so me and my brother'll leave her alone. She tired all the time."

"Why's that?"

"Workin'. Sal's Pizza in the daytime, and after that she do the cleanin' up at Sunnyview—you know, on Coney Island Avenue where all them old people sit around like mummies? It's 'cause my father's a son of a bitch."

"What's he got to do with it?"

Jesús' dark eyes flashed with scorn. "For someone who ain't got a *mami* or a *popi,* you sure don't know shit, Beanie."

Laurel stiffened, and glared at him. What a dope she'd been to think Jesús could be friendly.

"Oh, just go away."

Jesús shrugged, stuffing his hands into his pockets. "Yeah, that's what *she* tole him. Now he's gone. And he ain't never comin' back." He stared at the floor, chin tucked against his chest, his thick black bangs fanning away from his forehead.

Laurel stared at him. Suddenly, she realized he wasn't faking. All that other stuff, the mean things he did, that was the act. But this was the truth.

She touched his arm. "Hey, you okay?"

Jesús jerked as if she'd stuck him with a pin. His head whipped up. A clown spot of red burned on each cheek, and his dark eyes glittered.

"I'm glad he's gone," he hissed. "I hate the son of a bitch."

Laurel thought of her own father. She remembered once, in kindergarten, she'd made him a Valentine's Day present—a cigar box she'd covered in construction paper and crusted with glitter and macaroni. She'd spent hours cutting and pasting and decorating. She wanted it to be beautiful. So Val would love it, and then love her, too.

He seemed so glad when she gave it, kissing her and telling her how much he liked it.

Then one day, she found it in the back of his closet, half-crushed under some shoe boxes. She remembered taking the box outside and throwing it in the trash can. Her hurt was so deep, she hadn't even been able to cry. She never told Val about it, and he never once asked.

Yeah, she kind of understood Jesús. But he'd probably be embarrassed if she told him that.

She gave him a little push. "Why don't you go jump in a lake?"

"Eat shit." He grinned.

"Shhh." Miss Rodriguez frowned at them, raising a finger to her lips. Center stage, Dickie Dumbrowski was droning through the narration.

" 'A strange voice called him by his name, and bade him to enter . . .' "

Miss Rodriguez flapped a hand at Laurel. "You're on!"

Laurel could feel her face going rubbery, her eyes hot. Any second now she would be crying. With everyone staring at her. Oh God.

"Behold, the Ghost of Christmas Present . . ." Dickie Dumbrowski trumpeted in his froggy bellow.

"Be-hold my dick," Jesús muttered as Laurel slipped past, shocking her into a giggle. The urge to cry faded.

Gliding onto the stage, Laurel felt almost grateful.

Rudy's voice drifted up the stairs. Where she was crouched, down in the narrow space between the desk and the wall in Dolly's office, Annie couldn't hear his words, only his flat growl, like grinding machinery. Any minute now, she'd hear him creaking up these tiny stairs. And no matter how small she made herself, or how far she wriggled in behind the desk, he'd find her. And then he'd rush to tell Val . . . and Val would come and take Laurel away.

A memory drifted up—she was sitting in Mrs. Pomerantz' English class, staring out at the sun twinkling on the dew-soaked lawn, and listening to the record her teacher was playing, some dippy-sounding British actor reading Poe's "The Tell-Tale Heart." She could hear Susie Bell giggling a little at the really creepy parts, which had sounded pretty dumb in the bright classroom with the smell of new-mown grass drifting in the open window.

But here, three thousand miles from Bel Air, crouched with her spine pressed uncomfortably against the wall and her knees aching, Annie felt like the man in that story, listening to the loud beating of that heart . . . only it was *her* heart that was booming. It seemed to rattle the desk and vibrate the floorboards under her feet. And, oh, God, Rudy had to be hearing it too.

But maybe he wouldn't find her. Thank God, she'd been up here when he'd come in. She'd been on her way down, in fact, when she'd heard the bell over the front door tinkle, then his familiar, grating voice calling out, "Hello, Dolly!" A low chuckle. "Hey, isn't that a song? No kidding, it's great to see you. You're looking good, *real* good. Bet you're surprised to see me, huh?"

Annie had shot back up the stairs, and dived into this hiding spot beside Dolly's big desk.

How long had she been here? It seemed like hours, but it had probably been fifteen minutes or so. She had to pee, desperately, but didn't dare budge. God, what could he and Dolly be *talking* about all this time? Did Rudy *know* anything? Is that why Val had sent him?

In some ways, Annie was more afraid of Rudy than she was of Val. Because Rudy was so much smarter, and Val always listened to him and went along with him. Like the time when Dearie's drinking got so bad, and Rudy convinced Val to commit her to Briarwood, even arranging for all the legal papers. She was there for three months that time, and when she got out, she was like a zombie; she'd sit for hours and hours in one place, just staring out at nothing. Six weeks later, Annie had found her mother on her bathroom floor, cold as ice, not breathing, an empty Darvon bottle on the sink above her. They buried her two days later.

And the way Rudy looked at Laurel, it was so creepy. Not talking to her much, or even trying to play up to her . . . just staring at her all the time, like a fat carp eyeing a minnow.

Rudy would be a lot harder to fool than Val, Annie thought. Could Dolly pull it off? She wished Gloria hadn't left early; she, at least, would have kept Annie posted on what was going on down there.

A new thought made Annie break out in goose bumps. What if Dolly couldn't hold back, and told him *everything*? She seemed so good and kind; but Annie still remembered Dearie saying her sister couldn't be trusted.

Annie began to shake, her teeth actually chattering as if she were freezing cold. But she was burning up, sweat dripping off her, running down her forehead and into her eyes, salty, stinging her. Her shirt was stuck to her back, and underneath, her bra and slip felt horribly clammy, as if she'd put clothes on over a wet bathing suit.

Any second now . . . yes, she was sure of it . . . Rudy would come creeping up the stairs, his fat, shiny head, with those sparse black hairs pasted across it, poking up above the landing.

He'd try to make her tell him where Laurel was, but she wouldn't, not ever. Not even if he threatened to have her locked up. Because if Rudy told Val, then Val would take Laurel away.

Please, God, not now . . . just when things are starting to go right.

She liked working at Girod's, a lot more than she'd thought she would at first. And Laurel, she finally seemed to be settling in at school. All week, she'd talked about nothing but her Christmas play. . . .

God, the play! If they didn't leave now, this second, they'd be late. They might even miss it. But she couldn't exactly waltz downstairs now and remind Dolly of that.

What would Laurel think? She'd be so disappointed . . . and probably worried to death.

I've got to let her know I'm okay. . . .

If she *was* going to be okay.

Rivka. Maybe she could call Rivka and ask her to rush over to the school and tell Laurel she'd be late. Annie felt awkward about asking, but Rivka was always so nice. And it was an emergency, so Annie felt sure she wouldn't mind.

Then Annie remembered, no, it was Friday evening, Shabbat. It was forbidden for Rivka even to switch on a light. Rivka never, ever went anywhere on Shabbat, except to synagogue. Annie wouldn't even be able to get through to her. At sundown, Rivka took her phone off the hook.

Annie found her thoughts drifting back to last Friday night, when she and Laurel had sat at Rivka's table having Shabbat dinner. In her mind, she saw Rivka lighting the candles—two of them in heavy old silver candlesticks—and covering her eyes with her hands and chanting a prayer in Hebrew. Annie hadn't understood one word, but it had sounded holy, ancient and soothing, like the rush of a brook that has been flowing for hundreds of years and will go on for hundreds more.

Annie closed her eyes now, to try to recapture that good, calm feeling she'd had at Rivka's table, her hands folded against the snowy linen, seeing the faces of Rivka's children all around her, shining like polished spoons in the candlelight, their lips moving in prayer.

And now, Annie, too, was praying.

Scared as she felt, she was glad that no one could see her like this, huddled like a frightened mouse. What if Laurel knew that this was how she often felt? Would her little sister still have faith in her if she knew that sometimes in the middle of the night, even for no reason, Annie woke up sweaty, heart racing, terrified that something awful was going to happen?

Annie noticed now that Rudy had stopped talking.

Then Dolly's voice came, low and lilting, with a hint of the Smoky Mountains in it, like bluegrass music. Strangely, at this moment, it reminded her of Rivka praying over the candles, soothing her somehow. Annie felt the cramp in her belly ease.

She made herself stand up, slowly. Her joints and muscles, cramped in one position for so long, tingled at first with numbness, then began to ache. Still shaky, she reached for the phone on the desk, and tiptoed with it into the tiny toilet, where Dolly always took it when Henri called from Paris—as if she and Gloria didn't already know about them.

There *was* someone she could call besides Gloria or Rivka. She didn't know him well . . . no, the truth was she hardly knew him at *all.* But she had a feeling somehow that it might be all right.

She remembered Joe Daugherty's warm smile when he'd stopped in yesterday to say hello. He was on his way uptown to meet a supplier, he'd explained, but he hadn't seemed in any particular hurry. Annie remembered feeling a little tense, waiting for him to mention the smashed chocolates to Dolly, but he didn't bring it up. And then his asking her to lunch, was he just being nice? Maybe, but at the little deli around the corner where they'd stuffed themselves on pastrami on rye, and talked and laughed for more than an hour, she'd begun to think that she'd made a friend.

Was it so crazy to think he'd want to help her out now?

Then she remembered how he'd snapped at her the first time they'd met. What if he got really annoyed at her for bothering him now—just before the dinner hour? And why should he want to do her any favors? He didn't owe her a thing.

But still . . .

Annie got the number from Dolly's Rolodex, and dialled it quickly, before she could change her mind.

At the other end, it began ringing, over and over. Suppose he wasn't even there?

Then a harried-sounding female voice piped, "Joe's Place." She could hear noise in the background, people talking, glasses clinking.

Keeping her own voice as calm and controlled as she could, Annie asked, "Is Joe there? Joe Daugherty?"

"Hold on."

A minute passed, stretching into what felt like an hour. Annie's heart, which had settled down, began pounding again.

Then Joe's voice came on, sounding out of breath, as if he'd run up a flight of stairs, which he probably had. " 'Lo. Joe here." He didn't sound mad, just rushed.

"This is Annie. Annie Cobb," she blurted. "Joe . . . I know this is going to sound funny, but . . . but I need your help."

She took a breath, and blurted out enough of the story for him to understand why she felt so desperate. It gave her an awful upsy-daisy feeling—like having the floor snatched out from under her—

opening herself to him, trusting him with her secret, but then, she didn't have much choice, did she?

There was a long silence, and Annie suddenly was scared he was going to tell her he was too busy. Or worse, advise her to talk to Rudy, explain things to him so he'd understand. Oh, God, *why* didn't he say something? Anything?

Annie felt the receiver sliding from her sweaty grasp, and the black silence seemed to expand, to swallow her almost.

Then Joe said crisply into the phone: "You're in luck. My whole crew showed up tonight, and we've got our preparation nailed down. I can be at your sister's school in half an hour if the traffic doesn't kill me. I'll take her back to your apartment, and wait with her until you get there."

He got directions from her, then hung up.

Annie started to sob, pulling her sweater up over her face so Rudy wouldn't hear. Okay, they weren't really safe yet, but just knowing Joe was out there, and that he was willing to help, made her feel she'd come to the end of a long road.

Laurel took her bow with the others, ducking her head low so that her long hair fell in front of her face. That way, nobody could see she was crying.

The play had been pretty awful, but the clapping was loud and long. No one seemed to mind that Jesús had forgotten most of his lines, or that Mary Driscoll had dropped the papier-mâché Christmas goose and it rolled off the stage into somebody's lap in the first row. All those mothers and fathers and sisters and grandmothers, they'd loved it.

With her head bent low and tears blurring her vision, Laurel couldn't see one single person in the audience, but she just *knew* Annie wasn't out there.

Jesús, not waiting for the applause to end, gave a wild hoot and scampered offstage. He had to be feeling pretty crummy, too. But a tough guy like him would rather throw up in front of everyone than cry. Laurel wanted to chase after him, and tell him she knew how he felt . . . but she didn't think he'd want that, either.

Now all the mothers and fathers and grandmothers were getting out their cameras and snapping pictures, flashbulbs going off, making everything gray and swimmy.

Laurel crept away, stumbling down the steps that led to the auditorium floor. The other sixth-graders were streaming down to join their families, the room echoing with cries of congratulations, but no one was pushing through to hug her or take her picture. Laurel saw Mary's parents, both almost as short and fat as coffee-colored Mary, swoop down on her, hugging her so tightly Laurel thought Mary's eyes would pop right out of her head.

Laurel wiped her wet eyes and runny nose with the drooping sleeve of her robe. She was slinking out into the corridor, hoping to make it to the girls' bathroom before anyone saw how miserable she looked, when suddenly a large hand gripped her shoulder.

Laurel turned, looking up at a tall man in faded jeans and a blue jersey that had been washed so many times it was almost white. He wore glasses like the principal, Mr. Moss—square black frames with thick lenses that slid down his nose. Only Mr. Moss was old and mean . . . and this man was young. Through the light flashing off his lenses she could see that his eyes were smiling.

"Laurel?" he asked.

Laurel nodded, wary. Was he a teacher, is that how he knew her? Maybe. But even dumb little kindergartners knew you weren't supposed to talk to strangers.

She started to back away; the man didn't try to stop her.

He smiled. "I'm Joe. Your sister said to look for the prettiest girl up on that stage, and I guess you're it."

What a lie! She looked awful, she *knew* she did. Still he seemed nice; he was probably saying it to make her feel better. He must have noticed that she was crying. She sniffed loudly.

"Here," he said, pulling a folded handkerchief from his back pocket and handing it to her.

"Thank you," she said, blowing her nose into it.

"Hey, you think we could find a chair and sit down? Annie sent me over here to tell you she's okay, and Dolly too. She'll explain everything when she gets here."

No, this man didn't feel like a stranger. Just looking at him, she could tell he wasn't bad.

Then something clicked in her head: Joe . . . the lobster man? It had to be him, those glasses and his wavy, blond-brown hair that looked as if he'd been too busy to do more than rake his fingers through it. He was just the way Annie had described him.

The cold spot in her stomach eased. All of a sudden, Laurel felt very tired. "Annie's really okay?" she asked. "And Aunt Dolly?" She had to fight to keep from yawning.

"Sure, they are. They just got . . . held up. Nothing to worry about, Annie said she'll be home before you know it. So why don't I take you back, and we'll wait for her. How does that sound?"

"Okay." Laurel yawned. "Then you can see our Christmas tree. The one you gave us."

"Tree . . . what tree?"

"The one Annie traded the lobster for."

Joe stared at her for a moment, then started to laugh. "Shep did that?" He shook his head. "Your sister is really something." He squatted down so that she could see into his eyes, and he placed his hands on her shoulders. "She told me about . . . well, your leaving home and coming here. I think both of you are pretty brave."

Laurel felt cold again. He *knew*? Annie had *told* him? Nobody but Aunt Dolly was supposed to know.

"Are you going to tell?" she whispered.

Joe just kept looking at her, his eyes steady and serious, like the look Miss Rodriguez got when she stood up in front of the class to say the Pledge of Allegiance.

"No," he said. "I'm not going to tell."

And she believed him.

Now he was rocking back on his heels, and rising, up and up, becoming even taller than before, it seemed. Looking up at him, Laurel felt dizzy. He held out his hand, and she took it without hesitating. Big and warm and dry, his fingers curled about her hand, making her feel safe.

She thought about Santa Claus, a fat elf in a red suit with a bushy white beard, who she used to think was a real person. Now it occurred to her that if Santa was real he might not look like that. Not old and short and white-haired. He might be a tall man, and young—not much older than Annie—wearing faded jeans and a blue polo shirt washed so many times it was almost white, with glasses that slipped down his nose, and eyes that crinkled up at the corners when he smiled.

Watching Rudy go out the door, Dolly wondered, *Did he believe me?*

Feeling light-headed, she sagged against the counter, torn between relief and worry. Had she overplayed it? Acted too helpful? After she'd told him she hadn't the slightest idea where her nieces were, did she have to go on and on about all the places where they *might* have gone? And her acting so friendly, practically falling all over him, had that made his antennae go up? Lord knows, she'd never liked Rudy . . . and in the old days, she hadn't tried too hard to hide it.

A memory came to her. She'd been dating Val, and they'd gone to a big Beverly Hills lawn party. When Val introduced this ugly sawed-off gnome as his brother, she was sure it had to be some kind of joke. The two didn't look the least bit related. Then later, Rudy had cornered her in the gazebo, where she'd been taking a breather from all the guys coming on to her. He'd had too much to drink, but even so, she'd seen the sly intent in his piggy eyes as he blurted, "You're wasting your time with Val . . . he's in love with somebody else."

She had felt her face flush, and before she could stop herself, she asked, "Who?"

Rudy grinned, and tossed back the rest of his drink. "Himself. Who else? And, believe me, you can't compete. Nobody could."

Now, standing in her shop, hugging herself to keep from trembling, Dolly thought, *He's crude . . . but definitely not stupid. Isn't that why Val sent him?* Sure, Rudy the bigshot lawyer, she'd heard Val say he was a whiz at cross-examining witnesses in court, trying to get them to trip up and admit stuff they wouldn't have otherwise.

Had she let something slip without realizing it? Or maybe he'd caught her glancing toward the stairs, on which she'd been half terrified Annie might appear at any moment?

No, she told herself, *I was careful. I was an actress, wasn't I?* And even a failed B-movie flop like herself could pull off something as easy as pretending not to know where a couple of teenage girls she supposedly hadn't seen in years might have gone off to.

Still, Rudy's last words as he was leaving kept buzzing inside her head like a fly against a windowpane: "You'll let me know when you hear from them?"

Sure, she'd said. You betcha.

Now, as she straightened, and started for the stairs to get Annie, it struck Dolly: Rudy hadn't said *if* you hear from them. . . .

He'd said *when*.

A slip of the tongue? Or did it mean something?

Either way, she thought, the day that little bigshot Rudy and his stuck-on-himself brother heard from her would be the day she'd have a snowball fight in hell.

CHAPTER 8

Joe stared into the saucepan at the curdled mornay, and had to clench his jaw to keep from really losing it this time. Holt had left the sauce to boil, *again,* and now it was ruined—history.

Jesus, where had the kid *been* his two years at the Culinary Institute—in the toilet, where he was now?

If only Rafael were here. But his sous-chef had had to run off to Puerto Rico to look after a sick dog. A stud pit bull, no less. Joe didn't know what Rafy and his brothers did with those dogs besides breed them. But when it came to whipping up a perfect sabayon, béarnaise, or beurre blanc, one thing he did know was that Rafael had the touch of an angel.

But now he needed more than Rafy; he needed a double dose of Irish luck. Because upstairs, at about this very moment, Nan Weatherby had to be dipping her spoon into her Navajo sweet potato soup.

He'd spotted the food critic when he'd dashed upstairs to help Marla set up for a party of eight that had wandered in without a reservation. No one was supposed to recognize *Metropolitan* magazine's arbiter of the food scene; but that braying laugh of hers, and those thin penciled lines drawn where her eyebrows should have been, he'd remembered them from years ago. She must've been a stringer back then, interviewing his father for a piece on New York State Appellate Division judges. She'd even snapped his picture, along with his father's. Though, of course, she'd never remember him—he had been twelve or so at the time.

And now, with one sentence, she could ruin him. And his father's oft-repeated warnings would all come true.

Joe's belly felt as if it had an iron bore in it, twisting up and up, filling his mouth with a bitter taste.

Christ, just cool it, will you? I'm a good chef. Not great, maybe . . .

but pretty damn good. If things could start going right for a change—
if Holt got with it, and if Burke and Marla between them could
handle the tables upstairs without Nunzio, who was out sick. If,
if, if . . .

Well, maybe . . . just maybe . . . he could pull it off.

Hell, he had to.

First, the mornay. La Weatherby had ordered salmon as a main
course. No choice but to start a new batch.

Joe grabbed for the pan with the ruined sauce, jerking it off its
burner. Pain from the over-heated handle shot through his hand.
Jesus! Forcing himself not to drop it, Joe swung the saucepan over
and thunked it onto the stainless counter. Then he ran cold water
over his throbbing palm.

At the refrigerated locker that spanned the kitchen's far end,
Joe reached in and grabbed a cardboard tray of eggs, which he carried
over to the center work station. As he cracked and separated, he
found himself thinking of Cloetta, his family's cook since Creation
—a somehow ageless figure bent over their kitchen's old-fashioned
tiled counter. He saw her large, rough, mahogany-colored hands
cracking eggs into a yellow bowl, then guiding his own small ones,
pale and clumsy, trying to do the same.

Yes, Cloetta had believed in him, no matter how many times
he messed up. And then with time, he had learned. All the magic
those big, dark hands brought forth from the kitchen she ruled. Rich,
savory Virginia-style gumbo. Beaten biscuits light as a feather. Spicy,
clove-perfumed duck with honey-marmalade glaze. Sausage stew
flavored with fennel and cumin, covered in a crackling corn-bread
crust.

And never any recipes—she couldn't read or write. So what
she'd passed on to Joe was all the more precious. No written words,
just a certain lightness of touch, how to measure with your eyes,
and how to know the exact moment a sauce was peaking.

As he whisked egg yolks, Joe willed himself to imagine a glorious future.

Three stars from Nan Weatherby, or even two (let's not be
greedy) would bring him all the bookings he could handle. He'd
seen it. The Belgravia, L'Assiette, Purple Broccoli. So why not Joe's
Place?

Four thousand in rent due in thirteen days, and he might do

more than just barely scrape by. He might actually wind up with a few thousand to spare.

He began to feel excited, but only for a minute. Nan Weatherby, he remembered with a pang, gave mostly scathing reviews. Acid, that's what she'd dumped on Le Marais: *The lighting was funereal, which, considering the sadly wilted salad and sorry excuse for a béarnaise blanketing the decomposed trout, was probably a mercy. . . .*

Le Marais, one of the best, went out of business eight weeks later.

His father's voice, dry and measured, droned in his head: *I can't stop you, Joseph. Your grandmother left that money in your name, and it's yours to do with as you wish. But let me say one thing: You'll fail. Inside a year, you'll be out of business. I'm not simply guessing . . . it's a fact. You'll fail us, and yourself, the way you failed that poor girl at Yale, and so needlessly.*

Caryn.

All day, her memory had been pushing at him with an odd insistence, and then it struck him: *Today would have been Caryn's birthday, her twenty-fourth. . . .*

Joe squeezed his eyes shut. He felt the throbbing of his burned hand spread up into his chest.

No, he mustn't think about Caryn. Not now. No time.

He snatched a clean saucepan from its hook, and poured in clarified butter into which he whisked a few tablespoons of flour. Next, he added hot fish stock from the huge cast-aluminum kettle on the back burner. When the mixture was simmering, he added several more cups of stock. Now came the hard part—hurry up and wait.

While he stirred, waiting for the sauce to thicken, Joe looked about the kitchen. Long and narrow, like a railway car, with old brick walls the color of sun-dried tomatoes, black-and-white floor tiles worn to a smooth depression in the center, a flaky pressed-tin ceiling. He remembered Dad seeing it for the first time and declaring, *What this place needs is a wrecking ball.* Joe had cringed inside, but only for a minute. He already was in love with its deep enamel sinks, its hulking eight-burner Vulcan range, and the enormous brick hearth that dominated one end.

You're wrong, Dad, he thought, *I'm not going to fail. But if I do, it's on my head. You can be damn sure I'll never come begging to you.*

In his mind, he was seeing Annie Cobb, remembering her calling him that night—was it only a week ago?—the stiff-necked, even dignified way she'd asked his help. With one oven out and the place fully booked, why had he dropped everything just because a girl he barely knew asked him to?

He couldn't explain it, not even to himself. But something in Annie had touched him. With those big eyes of hers, she made him think of a half-starved alley cat—tough, independent, but also a bit lost.

Now Annie and her little sister thought he was some big hero. What a laugh. He'd be lucky if he could keep his own head above water.

Joe was nudged back to reality by the sight of hulking, ginger-haired Holt shambling into the kitchen, wiping his hands on his apron. In spite of his annoyance with the clod, Joe felt a twinge of pity. Holt Stetson. Jesus, a movie cowboy's name with the face and body of Bullwinkle the Moose, he had to be the butt of a million jokes.

"Holt!" He was trying not to yell. He pointed at the ruined mornay. "What do you expect me to do with this . . . hang wallpaper? Christ, man, I've got ten minutes to deliver a miracle to Nan Weatherby and you're off scratching your ass!"

Holt reddened. "I'm sorry, Joe, I—"

"Here." Joe thrust the whisk at him. "Take over while I grill the salmon. And don't forget the lemon juice."

"Ay, Joe! The dishwasher ees makin' that funny noise again!" shouted Julio from the small room in back, drowning out Holt. "You choor the man fix the hose like ee say?"

God, yes, he *could* hear it, a faint clunkety-clunkety-clunk amid the hiss of hot water and rattle of china. Shit.

But before he could take a look, Marla came flying through the double doors like a kite snapped loose in a high wind.

"That's it! I quit!"

She slung the plate she was carrying, the food on it untouched, onto the butcher-block island, and shook a fist up at the ceiling, middle finger extended.

"The bastard! Copping a feel every time I turn around, and now this. He orders his steak well done, and now he tells me he wanted it rare. Someone ought to make his face into a steak!" Her

thin face was flushed, and her bleached hair stood out in an electro-
cuted frazzle.

Christ, this was the last thing he needed right now. Joe wanted
to shake her—with her Betty Boop chest, and her little ass, shrink-
wrapped in black jersey—until she rattled.

Then he caught himself.

"Whoa . . . time out." He *did* grab her shoulders, but gently.
"You want me to beat the guy to a bloody pulp, is that it? Throw
him the famous Daugherty oarlock? At Yale, there were guys who'd
run if I stuck out my hand in a friendly handshake."

Marla's eyes widened. "*You* were a wrestler?"

"Crew." He grinned. "Nineteen sixty-three, we won the Henley
regatta."

"Huh!" She tossed him a disgusted look.

"Look, I mean it. Find me an oar, and I'll work the guy over.
Better yet, lash him to the mast and give him fifty with my cat-o'-
nine-tails."

He almost had her now. He could see a smile struggling to
surface.

Then she pulled away, muttering, "College boys, jeez." But it
was going to be okay. He could see the high pink fading from her
pointy cheekbones.

Exhaling slowly, Joe went to the refrigerator and grabbed a
salmon filet marinating in lime and garlic. The fire in the big brick
hearth was down to a rosy ash, and heat rolled from it in shimmering
waves. He found a corner of the grate where it wouldn't be too hot,
just enough to char the outside lightly while leaving the center moist
and pink.

"What's he drinking, the guy giving you such a hard time?"
he tossed over his shoulder at Marla as he slapped on a fresh
T-bone.

"Manhattans. He's on his third, and practically falling out of
his chair."

"Bring him another. On the house. If we're lucky, by the time
his steak is ready he'll be so out of it he won't know it from a rat's
ass. Oh, and Marla? Make a note of his name when he pays his bill.
And then if he ever calls for a reservation, tell him we're booked
solid for the next ten years."

Marla grinned. "Gotcha." She whirled out of the kitchen, sling-
ing her jersey-clad ass.

Minutes later, Joe slid the salmon gently onto a heated plate
and ladled the newly made mornay sauce in a little moat around it,
adding a side of garlic-fried fiddleheads and crusty Santa Fe pudding
made of finely ground white cornmeal with bits of mildly hot peppers
and cheddar cheese. Nan's companion had ordered the venison stew,
which he ladled into a pottery dish atop another plate, and garnished
with baby ginger carrots and bite-sized corn dodgers.

Looking around, he saw no trace of either Marla or Burke.
Great. By time these plates reached Nan Weatherby, the food would
be lukewarm. Damn.

But *he* could carry them up, couldn't he? Why the hell not? And
then he might be able to catch the look on Weatherby's face when
she took her first bite—and maybe get some hint as to whether he
was going to live or die.

In seconds, Joe was upstairs, weaving his way among the closely
packed tables. He'd done the dining room in what he liked to call
Early Quaker—plain scrubbed-pine flooring, natural wood tables,
and high-backed benches padded with bright calico. Over the res-
ervations desk hung a slightly faded antique wedding-ring quilt he'd
found at a country auction. Framed samplers and a child's dented
sled hung from the whitewashed brick walls on both sides. And
instead of candles, on each table he had placed an old oil lamp.
Simple, clean—the way he wished life could be.

He spotted La Weatherby's honey-blond coif—a shellacked
helmet of hair that looked impenetrable enough to ward off a nuclear
attack. Across from her sat a paunchy middle-aged man who looked
sallow and dyspeptic, as if he'd just eaten something that disagreed
with him. Joe's own stomach flipped over.

Forcing himself to look relaxed, smiling even, he set the plates
on the hand-loomed mats in front of the dragon lady and her
companion.

Stepping back, his gaze swept over the other tables, zeroing in
on each false note, a dropped fork lying unnoticed on the floor, a
faulty bulb flickering in the punched-tin arts and crafts chandelier,
a spot of what looked like tomato sauce on Marla's white blouse.
Then his eyes were drawn back to Weatherby, and he watched as
she raised a forkful of salmon to her lips.

Never had he wanted anything as badly as he now wanted to see Nan Weatherby smile as she tasted what he'd cooked for her.

Nan's fork hovered, then disappeared between her lips.

Joe held his breath, hoping. His blood thundered in his ears.

Shit. She wasn't smiling. She wasn't reacting at *all*, for God's sake.

He felt himself gritting his teeth, despair welling up in him.

Then he remembered how Cloetta used to say, *Ain't nothing in this life black and white 'cept the color of our skins, Joey.*

Okay, so it wasn't all black. She was eating it, wasn't she? At least she wasn't sending it back. Maybe he'd just have to lower his sights. One star—pleasant and good value—might not be the kiss of death. He could squeak through, and then continue building through word of mouth. So far it'd worked. Most nights he could count on filling half the tables, anyway.

At any rate, in a couple of weeks he'd know. Either way, he'd be out of his misery. So get back to the kitchen now, he told himself, and forget about it.

Making his way down the steep service stairs, Joe found himself thinking of Annie Cobb, and the tree she'd exchanged for a lobster. Christmas was the day after tomorrow—would she and Laurel spend it out there in Brooklyn . . . alone? That'd be tough. Especially for Laurel. It didn't look as if Old Santa would be making more than a pit stop there this year, if that.

He recalled the hour he'd spent with her in that tiny, scantily furnished apartment on Fourteenth Street in Brooklyn, waiting for her big sister to show up. Laurel at first had seemed pinch-faced and withdrawn. But then gradually she'd relaxed and began chattering as if they were old friends. After a while, she'd even gotten out a dog-eared deck of cards and coaxed him into a game of gin rummy. And damned if that frail-looking, angel-faced kid hadn't beaten the pants off him.

Tomorrow, Christmas Eve, he'd be closed. Maybe he could take Laurel somewhere, say, to look at the windows at Saks. Except for a funny rattling in the transmission, the old Dodge was running okay, so picking her up would be no problem. She would probably love that. Or he could just drop by for a visit, if they were going to be around. Yeah, he'd like that. And maybe playing big brother would be good for him, help him get Caryn out of his head.

But the memory he kept trying to lock away came rushing in. At the bottom of the stairs, Joe leaned against the wall, that hellish night replaying itself again in his head. He heard Caryn's toneless voice over the phone, then he was sprinting down York Street, past the colleges, past Yale Drama, past Art and Architecture, his heart pounding. Finally, crossing College Street, he got to the building where she had a little studio and vaulted up three flights.

He found her on the floor, curled up, her body not cold yet, but white, bluish even, and blood . . . blood everywhere, staining the bedspread and the rug, matted in her long black hair, still oozing from her slashed wrists.

Then the ambulance and police cars, dome lights pulsing, their red glare spilling like more blood over the darkened street and the shocked white faces of Caryn's neighbors. And all the while, her last words over the phone, like a stuck record that wouldn't shut off, playing over and over in his mind, *I've taken care of it. You don't have to worry, Joe.*

An abortion. Christ, what else could he have thought? What else could any sane person have thought? They'd talked and talked about it, and yeah, true, she hadn't been exactly keen on the idea, but he'd thought . . . well, that with a little time she'd come around.

She came around all right, you asshole, all the way around the bend.

He'd been so scared. But why? Of what? Why couldn't he have *listened* to her? She was so funny and smart and sexy. He'd loved her, dammit, he *had.* But marriage, kids, a house in the 'burbs, at twenty. It had seemed too crazy even to think about.

Joe now saw her in his mind, sinking down on a stone bench outside Sterling Library just after she'd first told him she was pregnant, her crow-black hair shining in the May sunshine. She'd been crying, her eyes puffy, her milk-white cheeks marbled with red.

"Oh, God, Joe . . . what are we going to *do?*"

And what *had* he done?

Like a jerk, he'd smiled.

Seeing her there, looking so little-girlish in her navy Ship 'n Shore culottes and crisp white blouse, it somehow didn't register. How could she be pregnant? Even a little bit. It had to be some sort of crazy mistake.

Then it hit him. Serious. She was serious. He'd felt his knees wobble, like somebody had pulled the linchpins that held them together. He'd wanted to sink down beside her, but he'd stopped himself.

Looking back on it, Joe realized that right then, unconsciously, he must have been distancing himself . . . removing himself from her . . . from *this*. But at the time, he'd been so stunned, he didn't know what the hell he was doing or thinking.

Only when she began to weep had he lowered himself onto the bench next to her. "We'll take care of it somehow," he'd tried feebly to reassure her. But she had to have seen right through him, known that he was nowhere near up to handling this.

"Is that all you can say?" She fixed him with a hot, accusing glare.

"Look, I'm not going to ditch out on you if that's what you're thinking."

"Ditch out?" She repeated the words as if they were a new vocabulary she hadn't yet learned. "No . . . I never thought that. I thought . . . Oh, never mind."

"What do you want to do?" he asked gently.

"Do I have a choice?"

He could feel that she was waiting for him to say something, offer something. But what could he possibly offer? "Are you . . . you're not thinking of having it?" He thought of diapers, a baby squalling all through the night while he was struggling to finish a term paper. Jesus.

Caryn had looked off into the distance, cupping a hand over her eyes to shield them from the sun. But he could see the tears on her cheeks, and wanted to put his arms around her. At the same time, he felt hemmed in, trapped, the sun pressing down on his shoulders like a heavy hand.

"I don't think . . . at least, under these circumstances . . ." Hearing his father's pompous tone creeping into his voice, he'd felt shocked, ashamed, and immediately started over. ". . . I mean, I was thinking maybe someday we'd get married . . . but not like *this*. Jesus, Caryn, I don't even know what I'm going to do with *my* life after I graduate, much less yours and a . . . a baby's." There. It was out. He'd said it.

Caryn stood up, smoothing her culottes with short, jerky strokes. Over and over, until it seemed as if she must have rubbed most of the skin from her palms. Then she straightened, looking tall as a statue, her hair hanging in front of her face, partially shading it from his view.

"Caryn . . ." He put out his hand, but she jerked away as if he'd tried to hit her.

"You think I should kill it, don't you?"

Now, too shaken to lie, or even think of a gentler way of putting it, Joe blurted: "Yes . . . I do."

It was as if a rope connecting them had just snapped in two, one half containing all the love they'd once felt . . . and the other, only bitterness and blame.

For a whole week after that, he'd tried calling her, at all hours, knocking at her door, trying to track her down at her classes. But no answer. No Caryn. No one had even seen her. Joe had even called her parents in Plainview.

Where she'd hid out that week, or how she'd managed to slip back up to her room without anyone noticing, he'd never know. There had just been that call: *I've taken care of it.*

Yes, he'd later learned from Caryn's shattered parents that she'd been seeing a psychiatrist, and that in high school she'd been hospitalized for a nervous breakdown. He supposed he could've stacked up all the excuses high enough to let himself climb off the hook . . . but, deep down, he knew that if he'd handled things differently, Caryn would not be dead.

Joe, standing in the stairwell of his restaurant, passed a shaky hand over his eyes, as if to shield them from a piercing light that, had he looked into it, would have blinded him. Then, taking a deep breath and grabbing hold of himself, he plunged back into the kitchen.

"Hey, buddy, what's cooking?" Wayne chuckled at his own joke.

Joe grinned, phone receiver tucked between shoulder and ear, the cord stretching all the way over to the workstation, where he was kneading bread dough. A nice surprise, hearing from his old friend. They hadn't gotten together in a while, but Wayne, a copy editor at *Metropolitan,* had to know the agony Joe was going through. He'd probably seen more than his share of hopefuls cut down by Weatherby's ax. Was Joe's Place going to be next? It'd been more than two weeks; if the review was going to appear at all, it had to be in this week's issue. Could that be why Wayne was calling, to offer his condolences?

"Not much," he said, keeping his voice light despite the sudden tightness in his chest. "I'm saving the carcass for the buzzards."

"Feast or famine, huh?"

"Something like that."

"Listen, that's why I'm calling. Weatherby reviewed your place. This week's issue, they just shipped out. Should be hitting the stands today or tomorrow."

"Was it . . ." he tried to ask, but the pressure in his chest was pushing up into his throat, closing it off.

"A hatchet job? Geez, I sure hope not. I haven't seen it yet . . . just heard it was in. I figured I'd let you have what I hope will be the fun of seeing for yourself."

"Thanks," he forced out.

"Next time, maybe they'll let me review you. I'll say that you never poisoned me." Another chuckle, but this time Joe didn't smile.

"Yeah, well . . . thanks again."

"Don't mention it. What are friends for?"

Even as he hung up, Joe's mind was racing ahead. He'd check with Mr. Shamik at the newsstand three doors down, find out when his delivery would arrive. If it was late today, he'd ask Annie to grab a copy on her way over from work to pick up Laurel, whom he'd hired for the holidays to letter menus for him.

With his sourdough bread rising, Joe called to Rafy—just back from Puerto Rico—to keep an eye on things; then he ducked outside, dashing half a block in the freezing rain only to be told by Mr. Shamik, who was kind enough to put in a call to his distributor, that he wouldn't be getting his *Metropolitan* delivery until some time after four. Hours away! How could he wait that long?

Well, he'd just have to, that's all. And maybe once he read it, he'd wish he hadn't.

Back inside, Joe headed up to the dining room, to Laurel. He found her at a booth in back, exactly where he'd left her several hours ago. She sat hunched over the table. A stack of completed menus was piled at one elbow. At a glance, Joe saw that she'd done something extraordinary. He'd only intended for her to neatly write in the appetizers, entrées, and desserts, and their prices. But this . . .

Picking up a finished menu from the pile, he saw that every corner and blank space was filled with delicate, exquisite ink drawings. Morning-glory vines twisting around the borders. A bird's nest with tiny speckled eggs. A crested spoon, with a top-hatted mouse sipping from it. Joe felt a tremor of delight travel through him.

Years ago, backpacking through Mexico with his college roommate, in a dusty roadside dive, he and Neal sipping their Cuervo Golds and slapping at flies, he'd come across a crippled boy with a guitar—kid couldn't have been more than twelve, and was blind as well. As Joe and Neal sat down, the boy had begun playing, the sweetest music Joe had ever heard—"La Malagueña," Villa-Lobos, even some Vivaldi—and the dust, heat, and flies somehow had ceased to exist. Joe had never forgotten that boy, and sometimes he could hear the boy's sublime music in his head.

He was hearing it now.

Leafing through one menu after another, he was so awed that he all but forgot about the *Metropolitan* review. My God, Laurel had done this? She was just a *kid*. These looked like the work of a Tenniel or a Beatrix Potter. Each menu was unique—a basket of wildflowers, ladybugs having a picnic, koala bears peeking impishly from behind a screen of eucalyptus leaves, a ring of winged fairies dancing atop a sunflower, tiny monkeys contorted to form various letters in the alphabet, a polar bear carrying an Eskimo family on its back.

Did she have any idea how talented she was?

Her pictures made him think of Christmas. First, at Mom and Dad's for their annual holiday get-together, it had been the usual, Mom in her diva caftan holding up a brittle, cheery front while Dad told endless inane jokes to so-called friends, neighbors, a second cousin he hardly knew, opening every gift except the Van Gogh art book Joe had brought him. And then Joe had noticed Sammy, their driver, wearing the shirt Joe had given Dad *last* Christmas, and before Joe could say or do something he'd regret, he'd mumbled an excuse and slipped away, taking his wrapped gift with him. Dad never even noticed him leaving.

Joe, catching the BMT at Bloomingdale's, had headed for Brooklyn, planning to surprise Annie and Laurel. But the surprise was on him. Walking into that shabby living room he'd felt so good, instantly enveloped in warmth and Christmas spirit. Dolly had gotten there ahead of him, armed with a mountain of presents. But the way Laurel had looked at him when he handed her the shopping bag of gifts he'd brought, it was as if he'd presented her the moon on a silver platter. He'd forgotten about the art book, which he'd thrown in the bag along with the perfume for Annie and the Monopoly game for Laurel, but when she tore off its wrapping paper, Laurel could hardly contain her delight. Wide-eyed, she'd turned the pages, stopping to gaze rapturously at "Starry Night," his own favorite.

"This one," she said in the tone of voice she'd have used if she were shopping, picking out a new coat or a pair of shoes.

Then Joe's eyes had met Annie's, and in hers he'd seen something altogether different. Gratitude, yes. But a kind of amused weariness as well. As if to ask why, if he was going to spend that kind of money, hadn't he given her something more practical? And looking around the painfully bare room, with its threadbare sofa and single derelict chair, brightened only by the spindly Christmas tree decorated with construction-paper chains, popcorn strings, and tinfoil stars, Joe had felt sheepish. What good was Van Gogh when you needed winter gloves, thick blankets, sheets and towels?

But then, looking back at Laurel, caught in Van Gogh's spell, he'd known that this somehow was more important to her than any of those things.

Now, gazing down at her as she sat motionless, except for the scratching of her fountain pen, Joe was struck by her loveliness. A patch of sunshine had found its way down the airshaft and through the high transom window above the table at which she sat, casting a silvery light that made Laurel's skin look almost transparent.

"Laurey," he called softly, Annie's nickname for her. She looked up at him and blinked, her blue eyes over-bright and her cheeks flushed, as if he'd abruptly awakened her from a deep sleep. Joe held up a menu. "These are really something. I mean it. Who taught you how to do this?"

Laurel blushed, but he could see how pleased she was. "Nobody," she said. "I learned how myself. Mostly, I just draw what's in my head."

"That's quite an imagination you have."

Her color deepened. "Annie says I daydream too much, that if I spent half as much time studying, I'd probably get straight A's."

Joe considered this, then said, "Maybe . . . but I happen to think daydreaming is pretty important too. Van Gogh, when he painted

'Starry Night,' couldn't have been thinking about how many times six goes into eighty-seven."

"Well, drawing isn't the only thing I can do," she was quick to inform him. "I'm learning how to sew. I made this." Proudly, she smoothed the front of the plaid shift she was wearing.

He whistled. "I'm impressed. Your sister show you how to do that?"

"Annie?" Laurel laughed, and rolled her eyes. "The only time she ever tried to sew anything, she stuck her finger and it bled all over everything. She says she doesn't have the patience."

Joe thought of how restless Annie always seemed—even sitting in one place, she couldn't quite keep still, hands gesturing, legs crossing and uncrossing, foot bobbing. And those alley-cat eyes of hers . . .

"Somehow"—he smiled—"that doesn't surprise me. But you . . ." He tapped the stack of finished menus. "These should be in a book, or hanging on someone's wall. They're too good for this."

Laurel looked down. Her long lashes cast honest-to-God shadows over her cheeks—she had the longest lashes he'd ever seen. Jesus, in just a few more years, she was going to be a knockout.

"Thank you for saying so, it's very nice of you," she said primly, as if she'd picked up her manners from some etiquette book. Her voice dropped to a hush. "But it's just for fun, really. Just doodling. When Miss Rodriguez catches me during class, she really yells at me. She thinks I'm not paying attention. But you know what . . ." She looked up at him again, her eyes wide and blue. ". . . I *think* better when I'm drawing. Know what I mean, Joe?"

"Sure, I do. I feel that way when I'm making an omelette."

"Huh?"

"Not just any omelette, mind you. I'm talking about Omelette à la mode de Joe. Come on down to the kitchen with me, and I'll show you. You hungry, kiddo?"

Laurel hesitated. "Annie said I shouldn't get in your way."

"Hey, we're not just talking empty stomachs here—knowing how to make an omelette is important. Because what if you ever get stranded on a desert island?"

Laurel giggled. "You're silly."

Joe put on a serious face, drawing the corners of his mouth down and straightening his eyeglasses. "You mean you've never eaten seagull eggs? And, hey, did you know a single ostrich egg would make an omelette big enough to feed ten people?"

Her smile was radiant, warming him.

Downstairs, in the warm brick-walled kitchen, Joe showed her how to crack eggs one-handed, without letting any bits of shell fall in the bowl. While Rafy and Holt were shelling Maryland crabs for she-crab soup, Joe stood at the butcher-block island, watching Laurel expertly whisk the eggs.

Seeing the glow on her face, he could almost—*almost,* but not quite, dammit—forget that his career as a restaurateur might soon be demolished.

The buzzing of the service door cut through the clattering of the wire whisk.

Joe went to answer the door, and a tall figure bundled in a dripping coat rushed in, nearly colliding with him. Annie. What was she doing off work so early?

"Joe, you'll never believe it! It's incredible! Oh . . . I'm all out of breath. It's pouring cats and dogs. And I ran six blocks without stopping." She shook her wet hair, spraying his face with icy droplets.

He waited while she caught her breath, his own heart wildly knocking with impatience, his lungs sucking in air, as if he were the one who had just run six blocks. Good news? It had to be . . . she wouldn't look this happy otherwise.

Annie's face was flushed and sweaty. She tore at the buttons of her shabby, sopping coat. Underneath, she wore a skirt and blouse, loafers, knee socks that were bunched down around her ankles. Her legs were chafed raw by the icy rain blowing outside. He spotted the magazine rolled up under her arm, and he felt his heart lurch.

He wanted to wrench it from her, but he waited.

"Three stars!" she cried at last, throwing her arms around him. He caught a whiff of damp wool mingled with the perfumy scent of chocolate. "Oh, Joe, I'm so happy for you! Isn't it wonderful?" She drew back, flipping open the magazine. "And just listen to this: 'As soon as you walk through the door, you feel as if you're in a cozy country inn, with deliciously hearty food to match . . . the Oysters Rockefeller, if a bit of a cliché, were perfectly cooked, the grilled salmon and spicy venison stew worthy examples of regional cuisines elevated to the level of *haute* . . .' "

Joe couldn't speak or move. Then in a dizzying rush, it came

to him, what this would mean: the rent, the payroll, and his overdue
wine bills. He'd be able to pay them all. And one day, maybe even
take another floor . . .

A sound like wildly chiming bells careened in Joe's head.

"Joe!" Annie was pulling at his arm to get his attention. "Your
phone. It's ringing!"

Joe rushed into his office, and snatched up the receiver. Probably
his first reservation from the review. Jesus, the word travels fast.

"Joseph? Is that you?" No one but his mother called him Joseph.

Joe felt himself tense, drawing in on himself the way a sea
anemone curls up when poked.

"Darling!" She rushed ahead without waiting for him to speak.
"Dad and I just saw it. It's marvelous, isn't it? Hugs and kisses and
all that. And can you guess who just called me . . . just this very
minute? Frank Shellburne. You know Frank, always looking for a
tax dodge. Well, when he read that review, he wanted to know
immediately if you'd consider selling out. I told him I'd have a word
with you, and maybe you two could set up a meeting. Joseph . . .
are you there?"

"I'm here, Mother." But his excitement was gone. He felt like
Wile E. Coyote, flattened by a boulder while the Road Runner on
a cliff stood above him, cackling with mad glee. "I'm here," he
repeated dully.

"Promise you'll at least *consider* it," she said. "Daddy says it's
not too late to squeeze you in next semester at Yale. He'll have a
word with—"

"Mother, I have to go," Joe cut her off, struggling to remain
civil.

It came back to him, the ugly scene after Caryn died, when he
told them he was dropping out of Yale. Dad reading him the riot
act, and Mom sobbing, *How can you, after all we've done for you?* Center
stage, just like always, everything he did somehow having to revolve
around them. And all the years of holding himself in, going along
with their demands, like that time—he'd been ten or eleven—Mom
forced him to return the necklace he'd planned on giving Cloetta for
her birthday, a tiny gold crucifix that he'd saved his allowance for
months to buy, saying it was much too extravagant, it would only
embarrass Cloetta. But this time, he'd shouted at them, accused Dad
of only wanting a son he could show off like a trophy to his Appellate

Division cronies. And rushing to get the hell out, he accidentally knocked over and shattered Mom's favorite Staffordshire lion.

Now, he made himself speak evenly, even politely. "Look, do you want me to put you and Dad down for one night this week? If you ate here once, you might be surprised. Hell, you might even *like* it."

"Joseph, there's no need to swear." He could just see her, her red lips rolling in against her teeth, a disapproving crease appearing between the perfect arches of her eyebrows.

Joe fought down the dry laugh rattling up his throat. "I'll say a rosary as penance," he told her. "And an extra 'Hail Mary' for good measure. That ought to satisfy the big guy upstairs. Anyway, just to be sure, you put in a good word for me next time you've got him on the line."

"Joseph! If your father could hear you. It pains him, you know, this flippancy of yours. And there is absolutely no use in your pretending you don't go out of your *way* to needle him." He could hear the tears in her voice, crouching, nearly ready to spring. "I should think you would want to keep in mind Dad's heart condition, but I suppose you're far too busy with this little venture of yours to give him, or me, even the slightest consideration. You know, you can be very selfish at times."

"I know," he said softly. "Mother, I really do have to go. Good-bye."

Slowly, carefully, he lowered the receiver. Standing in his tiny, cluttered office, he gazed out the tiny iron-barred window that was eye-level with the sidewalk outside, watching a woman in spike heels totter past.

Oddly, he was remembering Caryn, and wondering what would have happened if Caryn had lived, if she'd had the baby. He—if it'd been a boy—would be almost five by now, old enough to understand things. Old enough, maybe, to have discovered that mothers and fathers could be real shits sometimes. Christ. What an awful thought.

He felt something brush up against him, and jumped a little, startled. It was Laurel. She slipped her hand into his, and gazed up at him as if she knew exactly how he was feeling. But how could she know? Was he that transparent?

Joe felt touched . . . as well as a bit panicked. He had a strong urge to get away, to run as fast and far as he could from those trusting blue eyes and the slim, delicate fingers wound about his. He could hear Annie in the kitchen, greeting Rafy and Holt, her strong voice ringing out, and he wanted to plunge into Annie's bracing presence as if into a cool shower.

He had invited Laurel into his life. He'd coaxed her into warming to him. But now, Joe was suddenly gripped with cold fear. Would he only end up disappointing her? Maybe not today or tomorrow, but . . . someday? Would she know then what Caryn had known—that Joe Daugherty couldn't be counted on?

CHAPTER 9

"Eight dozen . . . nine . . . ten . . ." Annie stopped counting and looked up from the trays of chocolates stacked atop the counter in Dolly's cramped storage room. "Dolly, how are we ever going to have these ready in time?"

She picked up a bonbon—milk chocolate with a toffee-cream center, specially ordered for David Levy's bar mitzvah, each one meant to go inside its own little silver-foil-covered box. Except the printer had screwed up, and instead of "Mazel Tov, David!" he'd sent over two hundred eighty-two unfolded two-by-two-inch boxes with "Forever, Jan and Jeff." And here it was, Friday afternoon, too late for new ones to be printed—the bar mitzvah was tomorrow!

"We'll have to find *something* to put them in," Dolly said. "Oh, dear, how could this have happened?" She fiddled with the fuchsia chiffon scarf knotted about her neck. In the two months she'd been working at Girod's, this was the first time Annie had seen her aunt looking so rattled. "Let's see . . . wrap each one in tissue paper, and tie it with a bow? Uh-uh, too ordinary. And the Levys will have a cow. I promised them something really special."

"What about silver foil?"

"They'll look like Hershey's kisses. No, no, it has to be something . . . well, that'll make people sit up and take notice. Remember those little red-wrapped chocolate hearts we hung on silver cords for Nancy Everson's wedding?"

"They had the bride and groom's picture pasted on the back. How could I forget?"

"The point is, people *remembered*. Since then, four of those guests have called me, and want us to do *their* parties." Dolly glanced through the open door at the front of the shop, where Gloria was waiting on a gray-haired woman in a tan raincoat. "The walk-in trade is nice, and important . . . but it's the parties and hotel contracts where you make the real money."

"Like records," Annie mused aloud.

"Huh?"

"I was just thinking, you could sing the same song over and over . . . but you wouldn't get rich off it unless you made a record and sold lots and lots of copies."

"You get the picture. But that still doesn't solve our problem." Dolly swept her arm out over the trays of chocolates that Annie had just unpacked from their shipping carton, her silver bracelets jingling. Annie saw that her long fingernails were painted a bright magenta.

Annie, now staring at Dolly's bright zigzag-patterned dress, was remembering something. That wonderful birthday party Dearie had thrown for her when she was maybe seven or eight—little sandwiches with the crusts cut off, a cake in the shape of a clown's face, a man in a braided jacket with a pet monkey on a little red leash . . .

And a piñata—a bright-colored donkey made of papier-mâché, filled with wrapped candies and hung from the living room's ceiling beam. She remembered being blindfolded, and swinging at the piñata with a long stick, missing it again and again, until finally she hit it with a hard *thwock* and felt it break open. Then tearing off her blindfold and watching the candies shower down, kids hooting and screeching as they dove to retrieve them. She'd felt so excited, like she'd made something magical happen, given her friends this wonderful gift.

"I have an idea," Annie said, feeling herself grow excited as she spoke. "We could wrap these in foil or paper or whatever . . . and put them inside three or four piñatas. Let the kids break them open . . . and the adults have the fun of watching them."

As soon as the words were out, Annie wondered if maybe she should have given her idea more thought before opening her mouth. Mexican piñatas at a bar mitzvah? But a couple of weeks ago, her aunt *had* liked what she'd come up with for that March of Dimes fund-raising banquet: scallop shells—which she'd picked up for nothing at the fishermen's market, and sprayed with nontoxic gold paint—each with an exotic Lapsang Souchong truffle nestled inside, wrapped in iridescent cellophane and tied with a thin gold cord.

But now, clearly, her aunt wasn't convinced. Dolly was frowning slightly, and tapping her forefinger against her chin. Was she trying to think of a polite way of saying what a stupid idea it was?

"Piñatas," Dolly repeated, as if musing aloud. She began to chuckle, and then her chuckling rose into a full-bodied laugh that seemed to roll up from her middle, unhampered by the wide belt cinching her waist.

Annie felt her face heating. Okay, so it *was* stupid. She should have kept her mouth shut.

Only now Dolly was wiping the corners of her eyes, and crowing, "I love it! It's brilliant!" She frowned slightly. "But where the heck are we gonna get piñatas at practically the very last minute?"

Annie's mind raced ahead. "I'll bet Laurey could make them. She made a papier-mâché mask once of a lion's head. But we could have any animal we wanted."

"Wonderful! But I'd better call Mrs. Levy first, and check it out with her." Dolly raced up to her office, where she kept her fat, dog-eared Rolodex.

When she returned, Dolly was bubbling over. "She was a little skeptical at first . . . but when I told her how talented you are, and what a big hit your March of Dimes scallops were, she started to see how cute piñatas would be. How on God's green earth did you ever think of such a thing?"

Annie levelled her gaze at Dolly. "It was Dearie who made me think of it. When I was little, she gave me a birthday party with piñatas." She swallowed hard, memories now tumbling over and over inside her head. She was a tiny girl again, holding tightly to a hand glittering with cheap rings and bracelets, looking up into her Aunt Dolly's smiling red-mouthed face. "Dolly," she blurted out, "what happened between you and my mother?"

Dolly's sigh was more than a sigh—it sounded like the air being slowly let out of a tire, or a balloon. At the same time, she herself appeared to deflate, her face seeming to fold in on itself, full of creases that hadn't been there before, her shoulders sagging, her jingling bracelets silent.

Annie watched her aunt bring a magenta-tipped finger to her temple, pressing lightly as if inside her skull there was a button that would shut off the awful memory that she seemed to be reliving.

"Lord . . . it was all so long ago." She tried to smile, but her smile collapsed before it even got off the ground. "Your mama and me . . . well, we had sort of a disagreement."

"I *know* that. But what was it about?"

"It started with Val, I guess you'd have to say. Though, looking back, I believe your mama did me a big favor, marrying him out from under me."

"Val?" Annie stared at Dolly, shock rippling through her. "You and *Val?*"

"Oh, well . . ." Her hand fluttered to rest on her full bosom, and this time she managed a weak smile. "Like I said, it was all such a long time ago. I don't honestly remember *what*-all I felt for him." She straightened, pulling herself together with what appeared to be a great effort. "Now, what about those piñatas—why don't you give your sister a call, and see if she's up to the job?"

Annie had the feeling there was more to Dolly's falling-out with her mother than just Val—the way Dolly was acting, there *had* to be—but she didn't press her. This wasn't the time. Besides, she was just getting to really know Dolly. Did she want to risk hearing something that might make her dislike her aunt?

Annie glanced at her wristwatch: half past three. Laurel would be home from school by now. Annie called her from the storeroom wall phone, and asked if she'd be willing to make the piñatas. Laurel thought it sounded great, and said she'd be thrilled to do it. She gave Annie a list of materials to pick up on her way home.

Annie grabbed her coat, and was heading for the door when she stopped and turned back to give Dolly a quick hug. Looking up, she saw there were tears in Dolly's eyes.

"Thanks," Annie mumbled.

"What for?" Dolly seemed genuinely not to know what Annie might say next.

"For . . ." She was about to say, *For being there, for giving me this job, for being so nice to Laurey and me,* but all she said was ". . . for everything."

Someone was following her.

Annie had first noticed him as she was leaving the shop at six to go home, a thickset man in a rumpled khaki raincoat loitering by the mailbox. And now, glancing over her shoulder as she finished crossing Lexington on her way to the IRT at Seventy-seventh, she saw that he too was starting to cross the avenue—which meant he'd been following her for blocks. Why? What could he want?

Annie felt a pocket of cold form about her heart.

You're being ridiculous, she told herself. Dozens of people, thronging the sidewalk, headed this way for the subway—why should she imagine this man was after her? And even if he was, probably he was harmless, the kind of pervert who just liked to follow girls.

He'd get tired of tailing her soon enough. And if he didn't, she could easily dodge him.

But deep down, she knew that she was kidding herself. Over one eye, a pulse fluttered, and her legs felt rubbery. *I'm going crazy,* she thought, *just like Dearie.* Annie had been like this since that night Rudy had shown up—jumping at noises, glancing over her shoulder all the time. But that was stupid, she told herself. Val was thousands of miles away, and by now so was Rudy. And Dolly seemed pretty sure she'd managed to convince them both that, as far as she was concerned, they were barking up the wrong tree.

But what if she was wrong?

Annie saw a variety store up ahead, and ducked into it. Roaming the aisles, taking her time, she collected some of the items on Laurel's list—balloons, crepe paper, poster paints. Annie would buy the starch and flour her sister would need to make the papier-mâché paste at the grocery store on Avenue J.

As she stood in line at the checkout counter, Annie tried to forget about the man in the khaki raincoat. Anyway, he'd have disappeared by the time she finished in here. It'd be as if he never existed. How could she have been so paranoid? Under the glare of the fluorescent ceiling strips, looking at the shelves of candy bars and greeting cards and camera film—ordinary things, stuff that everybody bought, nice normal people like postmen and school-teachers—she felt pretty stupid, imagining she was being followed by some shady character out of a private-eye TV show.

No reason for Val or Rudy to be after her now. It had been three months since she and Laurel had come to New York, and more than a month since Rudy's visit.

And since then Dolly hadn't heard a word from either of them, not even a phone call.

Still, Annie took her time, even as she was checking out, count-ing her money out slowly, giving the clerk exact change in nickels and pennies.

Outside the store, Annie saw no sign of him. Then, out of the corner of her eye, she caught a glimpse of him, idling at a newsstand not far away, pretending to peruse the headlines. It was pretty dark, and the brim of his fedora was tipped over his forehead, so she couldn't see his face. But she recognized the raincoat. He was def-initely watching her.

Annie felt blood rush into her head, pressing like hot fingers against the inside of her skull. Her knees buckled a little, and she nearly collided with a woman carrying a briefcase.

As she passed the newsstand, Annie didn't dare look over her shoulder; she was afraid she wouldn't be able to go on if she did. But he was there. She *knew* it. The skin along her arms and neck felt tight, as if it had suddenly shrunk three sizes.

Starting down the steps to the IRT, she grabbed hold of the iron railing to keep from stumbling. From the waist up, she felt strangely light, as if her upper body had melted down into her legs, now heavy and clumsy with extra weight.

He had to be connected to Val or Rudy. A private detective, maybe. Or else why would he be following her?

Her thoughts flew ahead to Laurel, alone back at the apartment. What if he followed her all the way there? Then they'd have to leave, right away, before Val and Rudy caught up with them and took Laurel away.

At the prospect of leaving Dolly and Joe and Rivka, Annie's throat tightened. And then having to start all over, stay in some grubby hotel while she searched for another apartment . . .

Annie felt her knees buckle as she reached the bottom step. She had to gather up all her strength just to keep moving.

The station, she saw, was crowded. Maybe she could lose him. Rush-hour commuters streaming down the steps were jammed up against the turnstiles and pushing their way through onto the platform. A train had just pulled in. If she could somehow fly in there before the doors shut, then maybe she could leave him behind.

Glancing over her shoulder, she spotted him at the foot of the stairs, surrounded by commuters. But there were people in front of her, too. She wouldn't make it unless the train waited, which they almost never did, or unless . . .

On an impulse, Annie darted forward. Clutching her package and purse under one arm, she vaulted over the waist-high railing to the right of the turnstiles. Her skirt caught on something; she could feel it ripping, and thought, *Damn, it'll be ruined.* But the energy from every nerve ending kept her racing toward the train before its doors shut.

"Hey! Hey, you . . . stop!" she heard a man yell. God, he was yelling at *her*. Out of the corner of her eye, she caught a glimpse of navy blue against the grimy white-tiled wall: a transit cop, his badge glittering with reflected light.

She froze. You were supposed to respect the police. She remembered her fifth-grade class trip to the Beverly Hills Police Department. A grandfatherly white-haired officer in a crisp blue uniform had given them each a sucker after their tour.

No! Annie thought. *If he catches me, I'll miss the train. And maybe he'd find out who I was, and arrest me . . . and . . . and . . . oh God . . .*

Annie, freeing herself, darted forward, reaching the train just as the doors banged shut. She wanted to scream and hammer at it with her fists. No, it wasn't fair!

Looking back, she saw that the cop was rushing toward her from the other end of the platform, weaving his way through the crush. And behind her, the man in khaki was just now pushing through the turnstile. She was trapped. It was only a matter of which one would get to her first. She felt herself grow faint.

Then a miracle happened.

The doors of the train jerked open, and she heard the conductor bawl, "Stay inside! Don't block the doors! This train won't move until everybody's inside!" In that split second, Annie threw herself in, flattening herself against the almost solid wall of people already jammed inside. The doors banged shut.

She felt the train shudder, then jerk forward, picking up speed as it moved into the tunnel. With her shoulder wedged against the door's glass panel, she watched the platform roll away from her like a bad dream. The man in khaki was standing at the edge; he'd missed her by a hair. She caught a glimpse of his face below the brim of his fedora—light-blue eyes, a reddish mustache, thin, sagging lips.

Then he was gone, and they were racing through the tunnel, black as a coal mine, except the white glare inside the car, which felt like a magic shield of light. A sob rose in her throat, and was choked off by the deep breath she sucked in at the same time.

Annie leaned her forehead against the steamy glass and closed her eyes. She was almost glad for the press of bodies all around her, a tide of damp-smelling wool, scarves, hats, packages, briefcases, which surged against her with every lurch of the train, seeming to hold her up, keep her afloat somehow.

Of all things, she found herself thinking about Joe, wishing he were here with her right now. He'd know how to make her feel better.

Like last weekend, when he'd taken Laurel and her skating at Rockefeller Center. She'd watched him with Laurel, patiently teaching her, one arm firmly about her waist as he guided her slowly across the ice. And Annie, not much of a skater herself, and with no one to help her, kept falling down and having to pick herself up. One spill had been really nasty, knocking the breath out of her and bruising her hip, and then she couldn't seem to get up—her legs scissoring, her skates flying out from under her. But she hadn't yelled for help. She'd have died before humiliating herself. And just then, like the hand of God swooping out of nowhere, she'd felt herself lifted up off the ice, onto her feet, and suddenly she was sailing like a kite, Joe with his arm around her, holding her tight, his wool scarf fluttering against her cheek. For the first time since Dearie's dying, Annie had felt wonderfully protected, like a child. And a little scared, too, because being a child also meant not being able to make your own decisions, not being in charge.

But being alone was even harder. She had Laurel, of course, but that only made it worse in some ways, because Laurel depended on her so much, and when you got right down to it, Laurel was the whole *reason* for all this secrecy and hiding away and getting chased after.

Not that she resented her sister. No, not even the tiniest bit. But sometimes . . . like right now . . . Annie couldn't help imagining how much less worrisome life would be without her.

She immediately felt a pang of guilt. God, what had she been thinking? Without Laurel, she'd be miserable, lonely. Who would she love? Who would love her?

Then she remembered Dolly and Rivka . . . and Joe. Maybe it wasn't the same with them, but they cared about her.

Joe's face swam up in her mind, his beautiful, uneven face. Those muddy hazel eyes. There was pain in him, too. She'd sensed it more than once. With Joe, she sometimes felt the way she had with Dearie; behind the jokes, the almost-callous offhandedness, her mother, she knew, had been struggling with herself. But unlike Dearie, Joe, she suspected, would come out okay.

Maybe that was what drew her to him, the sense that they were somehow muddling through this together, Nancy Drew and Ned Nickerson creeping about the graveyard in the dark, flashlights bobbing bravely. Except whatever was plaguing Joe had nothing to do with shady characters skulking about, or policemen chasing after him.

Annie opened her eyes, and noticed the graffiti scratched into the metal: DOLORES CRISTO LOVES RAMON DE VEGA, 1964. Almost like an epitaph, she thought. Where were they now, those two? Had Dolores and Ramon married young, had a baby or two already? Or did they now pass each other at school, or on the street, and look the other way? For some reason, Annie found herself hoping they were still together. It made her sad to think that maybe the only trace left of their love was this faint scratching on a train's wall.

When I fall in love, it'll be for keeps, she thought.

Then Annie caught herself. How ridiculous, after being pursued by a strange man, and nearly arrested by a cop, to be mooning about *love,* for God's sake. Leave that to Nancy and Ned.

But as the train roared through the tunnel, Annie again found herself thinking of Joe, imagining her name scratched on the train wall alongside his.

"Oh, I'm glad you're home, Annie. *Such* good news, just wait until you hear!" Rivka beamed at Annie from the open door to her apartment.

Annie glanced about the small, cluttered living room, and saw that something *was* different. Sarah, who had just turned eighteen, was standing in the middle of the braided rug, all dressed up, in a below-the-knee pleated flannel skirt and high-necked, long-sleeved pink sweater, even though it was only a Thursday night, and not any Jewish holiday that Annie knew of. Sarah was also blushing wildly, and covering her red face with her hands. On one finger twinkled a small diamond.

"Sarah is getting married!" Rivka crowed, slipping an arm about Sarah's shoulders. "Just today, it was agreed. Can you imagine? Our little Sarah, she's going to be a bride! Such a wonderful thing, no?"

Annie stared at Sarah, amazed. Why, Sarah was hardly older than she was! A teenager! And who was the boy? No one had ever mentioned a word about him. Modest, quiet Sarah, before you knew it, she'd have a house full of kids. She and Rivka both looked so happy, but still, to Annie, it came as a shock.

She forced herself to try and look happy, too. And maybe she would feel happy in a little while, when she got used to the idea. Right now, she was still too tense.

Annie stepped forward, and hugged Sarah, thinking how much easier it was to be affectionate around Rivka's daughters than her sons. Boys weren't allowed to touch a woman, not even to shake hands. Rivka had explained that it was because the woman might be menstruating, and therefore ritually unclean. Annie remembered learning the hard way, that first day, sticking out her hand to shake Mr. Gruberman's, and having him shrink back as if she had leprosy.

"Hey, that's great!" she congratulated Sarah. "Who is he? I don't think I've seen him around here."

Sarah giggled shyly, and Rivka replied, "They only met a few weeks ago. But they hit it off right away, and Yitzak is going to Israel next month to study Talmud under a famous rabbi . . . so they didn't want to wait."

"You mean . . . just like that. You met, and . . . and now you're getting married?"

"We've been seeing each other for almost a whole month," Sarah said, as if that was enough for anybody to make up their mind. "And Yitzak is a real *masmid*! He's into *pilpul*, and his *rebbeim* say he's something special." Nothing about how cute he might be, or that he'd brought her flowers, or even how romantic he was when he proposed.

Rivka shrugged, and bent to pick up Shainey, who was struggling to climb out of her playpen. "It didn't happen so fast, not the way it sounds. First, there were two others."

"Two others?" Annie's mind whirled, trying to digest all this.

The idea of plain, shy, soft-spoken Sarah dating a gaggle of men . . . it just didn't seem possible.

"Come, sit down, I'll make tea and I'll tell you how it was." Rivka motioned her into the kitchen, in which Annie probably had spent more time these past few months than in her own tiny one upstairs.

"I'll get the cups," Sarah offered.

Laurel, who'd been at Rivka's when Annie arrived, stayed in the living room to watch Shainey and to help five-year-old Yonkel spin the dreidels he'd gotten on Hanukkah. On the sewing table in the corner was a pattern pinned to a length of plum-colored fabric, a dress Rivka was helping Laurel sew.

"Here, do it this way, it'll go faster." Annie heard Laurel's sweet voice raised above the babble of younger ones, patient and good, as she always was with Rivka's children. *She'll make a good mother someday,* Annie found herself thinking.

Even now, Laurel did most of the work around the apartment. Not only doing most of the cooking, but every Saturday lugging their clothes down to the laundromat on the corner of J and Sixteenth. Upstairs, she already had a pile of strips torn from newspapers, which she would dip into a mixture of flour and starch and water, then paste over the balloons Annie had bought, layering them until the piñatas were the right thickness.

While Rivka bustled about, filling the kettle, setting out a plate of homemade *rugelach,* Sarah laid out cups and plates. She moved precisely, deftly, as if newly sure of herself, already thinking of herself as a wife rather than a teenaged daughter. Annie watched her closely, hoping to see something in her face, or in her movements, that would set her apart from other girls their age. But there was nothing, really—she could have been any middle-class girl getting ready for her first prom, or going off to college. Or—

She could be me. I could be her.

The thought rattled Annie so that she almost spilled the tea Rivka had just poured into her cup. I sure don't want to get married, she thought. Certainly not now. Maybe not even ten years from now. Or ever.

"The first two, and Yitzak as well, came to us through the *shatchan,*" Rivka explained, sinking heavily into the chair opposite Annie's, while Sarah scurried off to check on the new baby, now squalling in one of the bedrooms down the hall. Rivka grinned. "I can see you never heard about a *shatchan*."

Tonight, Rivka was wearing a flowered shirtwaist that showed off her newly slim figure, and instead of a scarf to cover her hair, she was wearing her *shaitel,* a short brown wig styled in a neat bouffant. An Orthodox girl, Rivka had explained, covered her hair with a wig once she got married, which she took off only when she was alone with her husband. So only he would see her at her loveliest. But how beautiful would your hair look, Annie had often wondered, after it had been squashed under a wig all day?

"A matchmaker," Rivka elaborated. "Esther Greenbaum, she arranges these things, shows pictures, makes introductions. Such a fuss Sarah made over having her picture taken! You'd think she was auditioning for Miss America! As if any boy could turn down such a face, no matter how bad the picture!"

Annie couldn't help but smile. "So what happened? She didn't like the first two boys?"

"The first one, she took one look at his picture and burst into tears. You should have seen him—teeth out to here. Esther swore up and down that he would make a wonderful husband for any girl, but Sarah wouldn't even look at him again. And I don't blame her! I should have a grandson with a face like a donkey?" Rivka leaned forward for emphasis, wagging a finger in front of her face. "The other one, he wasn't so bad-looking. But he never said two words to Sarah when they met. And Sarah is no big talker, either. With those two, I thought to myself, ha! I'll be in the ground before I live to see my first grandchild!"

"What about . . . ?" Annie hesitated, struggling to remember his name.

"Yitzak," Sarah put in softly.

Rivka sat back abruptly, a grin spreading across her face. "Yitzak will make Sarah a good husband. Solid and steady, and a *masmid* like she says, very studious. But he has a twinkle in his eye too. He'll bring her out of herself. And you couldn't ask for anyone more observant. His father is a rabbi, you should know. A very learned man."

Annie wanted to ask Sarah what she'd thought when she saw his picture, but it might seem rude. Fortunately, Rivka volunteered it for her.

Leaning forward again, she whispered, "And between you and me . . . Yitzak, he's not bad-looking, either. A real catch. But then, my Sarah is nothing to sneeze at either." Rivka popped a *rugeleh* in her mouth, and sat back, casting a proud look at Sarah, who now stood in the doorway, holding the blanket-wrapped bundle that was Rivka's youngest child. When she'd stopped chewing, she asked, "What about you, Annie? You ought to be thinking of getting married, too. It's no good, a girl running around with no family, no husband."

Annie laughed. "Without a matchmaker, I don't think I'd find anyone so fast. And, besides, I'm not ready to get married."

"What about that young man? The one who comes by to see you and Laurel? What is he, chopped liver?"

"Joe?" Annie's voice squeaked a little as she said it, betraying her. She felt herself blushing. "Oh, he's just a . . . a friend, sort of. He comes around mostly to see Laurey. Sort of like a big brother."

Rivka was looking at her, head tilted back. Rivka might lead a narrow existence, but she knew about the world of men and women, and she knew that Annie's words didn't tell the whole story.

Once Annie realized she could trust Rivka, she'd confided in her about Val, so that if he ever showed up here, Rivka would be able to cover for her. Now Annie found herself longing to tell Rivka what had happened tonight, on her way home from work. About the man in the raincoat. But she didn't want to scare Laurel, or cast a shadow over Rivka's happiness. Better if she kept it to herself for now.

"Listen to me," Rivka laughed. "Sticking my nose in like a regular *yenta*. You want more tea? I'll pour you another cup. Here, have one of these, I just took them out of the oven."

Then Annie heard Mr. Gruberman, back from *shul*, letting himself in the front door. Rivka rushed off to greet him. Annie, sipping her tea in Rivka's big warm kitchen, listening to the excited voices in the next room, felt safe and warm.

Probably the man in khaki had only been hurrying to catch the train, and the disappointment she'd seen in his face was only because he'd missed it. She probably imagined the whole thing, she told herself.

And she believed it too.

Almost.

Sitting in the darkened East Village revival theatre, Dolly felt
her stomach knot with tension. Her hands were clenched so
tightly her nails were digging into her palms.

She peered at her watch. It was getting close to midnight, the
movie almost over.

Was he sitting somewhere nearby, she wondered, or up in one
of the front rows? She had failed to spot him when she came in, but
he'd probably slipped in after the movie started.

Meet him afterwards, in the lobby, he'd said. Weird, his wanting
to meet her here of all places. What was he on, some kind of nostalgia
kick?

Craning her neck, she saw that the theatre wasn't crowded.
Dolly, not wanting to be recognized as the now-aging star of the
picture up on the screen, had chosen a seat in the back row near the
exit, where she wouldn't be noticed. But why was she so antsy?
The kids here, most of them had been in diapers when she was
making *Dames in Chains*. And the way she looked now, she could
pass for the mama of that cute wide-eyed thing up on the screen.

Hell of a thing, to call a picture a cult classic. Meant it was so
bad that with time it became sort of a joke. At first, Dolly had felt
the joke was on *her,* listening to them all laughing at the lines that
she'd poured her heart into all those years ago. But, after a while,
she'd begun to see the humor in it, and even found herself chuckling
every now and then. Some of those clinkers *were* pretty funny.

Right now she was watching a tightly corseted ten-foot image
of herself lean over, practically spilling her tits into her lawyer's lap,
and sob, "How did I get myself *into* this?"

She was laughing, and it felt good. Hell, she had about as much
in common with that woman up on the screen as a green tomato to

a grackle. Sure, her acting might be a joke, but she'd come a long way since then.

Her thoughts flew to the work that lay ahead—Valentine's Day coming up, and next month alone, two weddings and that Metropolitan Museum fund-raiser. And just yesterday, a cousin of Mrs. Levy who had been at the Levy boy's bar mitzvah last week—some kind of big-time Long Island caterer—had called. He was so impressed by Laurel's piñatas, he'd given Dolly the go-ahead to supply the chocolates for all his functions.

Now the credits were rolling, the lights coming on. People were shuffling to their feet, stuffing their arms into coats, filing toward the exit.

Dolly didn't budge. She was afraid, worried stiff about the man who supposedly was waiting to meet her in the lobby.

Rudy Carrera.

What could he want? Hadn't she already told him she didn't know anything, that she hadn't heard from Eve or her girls in years? Why the third degree now? She shivered at the memory of his call last night. There had been something in his voice . . . something she couldn't place . . . no, not *something,* but something *missing.* He hadn't seemed desperately curious, or terribly eager, or any of that. It was as if . . .

. . . he already knew.

Dolly felt her heart start pounding with dread.

At first, she'd tried to worm her way out of meeting him. But he'd persisted, a real dog with a bone. And in the end she'd felt she owed it to her nieces to find out what, if anything, Rudy knew. Suppose it was nothing? Then at least they could relax a little.

Gathering her coat and rising to her feet, feeling stiff, Dolly wondered how the hell she'd managed to sit through two features. *Storm Alley.* She hadn't watched it in years. What a sweet thrill it had been, and a shock, too, to see Eve up on the screen, bright and sassy and full of beans, shining like the star she was. Nothing like the poor wasted creature she had been at the end.

And that bit where Eve's tart-with-a-heart-of-gold, Maxie Maguire, gets back at Gino, telling him she's dying of cancer, and then tricking him into plugging her so he'll wind up with a murder rap. Lord, what a tearjerker. Who but Eve could've pulled it off, making it all seem so natural? At the end, Dolly had heard quite a few of those around her sniffling and honking quietly into their Kleenexes. And she'd been one of them. But maybe she had another reason for getting choked up.

Dolly peered around at the theatre—tatty plush chairs, thread-bare curtains, and flaking Egyptian-Deco gilt. Eve—the *old* Eve—would've gotten a kick out of all this, seeing her star mellowed to golden-oldie status.

She remembered first seeing this retrospective advertised in the *Times*: "Sisters of the Silver Screen." Six double billings, films starring famous (or, in her case, not-so-famous) Hollywood sisters. Olivia de Havilland in *Hold Back the Dawn*, along with Joan Fontaine in *Suspicion*. Two real oldies with Lillian and Dorothy Gish. Then *her* name alongside Eve's.

An omen. A *bad* omen, she had thought.

And then, out of the blue, Rudy Carrera.

It *had* to be money. Why else would he have called her? Because if he already knew how to get to Annie and Laurel, then what did he need her for?

Now, slowly rising to her feet, Dolly saw that she wasn't alone. A man hunched way down in the first row seemed to be in no hurry, either. And now he was getting up, too, making his way up the aisle, his head tucked low so she couldn't see his face. But there was something about his troll-like body, that strutting cock-of-the-walk gait, that made her feel cold all over.

"Rudy." She almost choked saying it.

He stopped, and tilted his head up at her. "Hey, Dolly, nice seein' you again."

He was grinning. He had the look of an egg-suck dog fresh from raiding the henhouse. On a taller man, his clothes might have looked stylish: light-colored trousers, two-toned shoes, and a paisley print challis sports shirt unbuttoned at the top. He carried a coat over one arm. But Rudy was so stubby—even in his stacked heels, the top of his head came maybe as high as her chin—that his dapper clothes looked comical. He made her think of Mickey Rooney swag-gering around like he was seven feet tall.

Except that nothing about Rudy Carrera was cute. Dolly felt a glimmer of pity for the picked-on little boy he once had to have been. It must've been tough, growing up alongside his handsome younger brother.

"You know, I never saw *Dames in Chains* when it first came out," he said, eyeing her calmly, with amusement.

"Not many people did."

"Too bad. You were terrific in it."

"Thanks. Is that why you're here? So you could see what I used to look like?"

"Not exactly. But, you see, that's sort of my point." He reached into the front pocket of his shirt, and fished out a stick of Juicy Fruit, which he unwrapped, then folded in half before popping it into his mouth. "You *were* an actress," he went on, working his jaw in a grinding circular motion. "A pretty good one, too. A point my brother, I think, failed to take into account when he spoke with you over the phone." Despite a coating of lawyerly polish, his gutter intonation still came through.

Dolly felt trapped. She had to take the offensive, and fast.

"Cut the crap," she snapped. "What is it you want?"

Rudy glanced around. An usher stood by the door, pointedly staring, wanting them to leave so he could lock up. It was nearly midnight. "Let's get out of here," Rudy said. "You know a place around here where we can talk?"

Up the avenue, at an all-night deli, Rudy ordered coffee and a pastrami on rye. Waiting for his sandwich, he lit a cigarette, leaned back, and squinted at her through the drifting smoke.

"I found them," he said.

Dolly felt as if she'd stuck her finger in a light socket. It took all her training to maintain her bland expression, to keep from ducking Rudy's cool gaze. She pressed her palms up against the underside of the table to still her trembling.

"What are you talking about?" she hedged.

"Look, let's not dick around. I know you were lying to me before, and so do you. I had an investigator friend follow Annie home the other day. Smart kid, she managed to ditch him the first time. After that he was just a little more careful." Rudy patted his breast pocket. "I have the address right here. East Fourteenth. Midwood section of Brooklyn. Not a bad little setup for a couple of runaways, my man says."

Dolly had an urge to smack that smug look right off his face. She felt blood rushing into her head, her scalp prickling. Okay, hardball. No use in her playing innocent; she'd toss it right back at him.

"What do you want?" she snapped.

Before he could respond, the waitress arrived with their coffee and an obscenely thick pastrami sandwich. He bit into it with relish, tearing off a huge chunk, which he chewed for what seemed like an hour. Finally, he swallowed, tore a paper napkin from the dispenser, and dragged it across his mouth.

He stared at her, his piggy eyes boring into her.

"I don't want anything," he said. "*Nada,* not a thing."

Was he for real? What kind of bargaining ploy was this? She'd pay him anything she could, but better not tell him that straight out.

"Look," she persisted. "Tell me what you want . . . anything within reason. If I can swing it, it's yours." He had to be pulling down a good income of his own, but maybe he had gambling debts, or had made some bad investments.

Rudy grinned, dabbing at a spot of mustard in the corner of his mouth. "Yeah, I heard you married oil. Smart move. But then, I always did think you were a smart babe. Smart enough not to marry my brother, at least."

"You didn't call me just to butter me up," Dolly said, narrowing her eyes. "What *do* you want?"

"And that business with your sister," Rudy continued, almost as if she hadn't spoken. "How you stuck it to her . . . Boy, that took balls. I gotta give it to you, Dolly. A woman like that, I said to myself at the time, you'd sure as hell want her on *your* side."

Dolly felt an urge to cram that sandwich of his down his throat until he choked.

"How . . . how do you know about that?" She had to push the words past the tightness in her throat, as if *she* were the one being choked to death.

"Val got the lowdown from your sister. Yeah, he was real pissed about it, but Eve made him keep his mouth shut. She didn't want everybody knowing it was her own dear sister that turned her in. Ashamed, I guess. She must've been afraid people would think she was a real bad person if her own flesh would do something like that." He paused long enough for his punch to hit home. "Val came to me right after Eve died, figuring there might still be some way of turning the whole thing around to his advantage. Like maybe suing you, and getting you to pay him off with some big settlement. But I told him it wouldn't work. He'd waited too long. There's a statute of limitations on these things."

Dolly was trembling so hard, she didn't dare even pick up her coffee cup. "Okay, Rudy, spit it out. What are you getting at? What do you want from me?"

"What do I want from you?" He tipped his chin back, eyes narrowing in concentration. "Just a little cooperation, is all. Set up a meeting with Val's daughter—Laurel. I don't want to scare her by popping up outa the blue."

Dolly felt herself breathing too quickly, her chest squeezed tight, as if she'd been stuffed back into that too-tight corset in *Dames in Chains*. He was really scaring her now. It took a minute to control her breathing before she could say, "Why should I?"

"Because I know you care about her, want what's best for her, that's why." He dropped his head, and was staring at her in a way that made her itch all over as if she were breaking out in poison ivy. "Because from the way you're acting I'd guess you feel guilty as hell about what you did to Eve. You want to make it up to her kids, right? You want to make it nice for them . . . and for yourself?" He blew out smoke with a slow hissing sound. "Am I right?"

Dolly felt as if he'd somehow stripped off all her clothes, as if she were stark naked. She wanted to get out of here, fast, leave this creep in the dust and never see him ever again. But she forced herself to sit perfectly still. She knew she had to. This was for Annie and Laurel, not for herself.

"What about Val?" she asked. "How come he's not here?"

"This isn't about Val." Ignoring the ashtray at his elbow, he ground his cigarette out in the saucer of his coffee cup.

A shiver rippled up Dolly's spine. Just what the hell was he up to? Could it be something . . . well, *dirty?* Like back in Clemscott, when Pop Farraday got caught in his drugstore's back room trying to diddle little Nancy Underwood? She had a violent urge to leap up and wrap her hands around his fat pink neck.

"Listen, buster, you better not have any perverted ideas about—"

"Hey, hey there." From the pouches of flesh on either side of his squashed-looking nose, his small eyes peered reproachfully. "You think I'm one of *those* creeps, get it out of your head. I just want to see the kid. Talk to her, get to know her a little. She's my niece, too, you know."

"Why now? I never heard about you bothering with her or Annie before."

"Before." He digested this. "There was a lot of things different before. And, anyway, this is now."

He squinted, staring dreamily off toward the quick-serve counter up front, where a girl in a pink uniform was cutting a wedge of lemon meringue pie.

"What about Val?" Dolly asked.

Rudy's eyes snapped back from whatever dark place he'd been peering into. "Forget about Val . . . this doesn't have a thing to do with him. He doesn't know about this. And I intend to keep it that way."

"I don't get it. And I sure as hell don't see why *I* should help you."

"Look, let's get one thing straight." He levelled his gaze at her. "I don't need you. I'm only doing this for *her* sake. I figured you could make it easier for the kid, explain the situation so she doesn't have a fit when she sees me."

"How do you know I won't warn them? By this time tomorrow, they could be in another city, or even out of the country."

He smiled. "I know you won't let that happen. Because you want what I want. Because you and I, underneath, we're not so different."

Dolly shivered. Yet deep down, she couldn't deny it. Yes, she was selfish. She wanted to be near Annie and Laurel. Be a sort of mother to them. Was that so terrible?

Okay, then, maybe what Rudy wanted wasn't so terrible, either. Even so, thinking of Laurel off somewhere with him, even just walking in the park, gave her the creeps.

I have to make him go back to L.A., forget about her.

But Rudy, she realized, wasn't like Val. He couldn't be gotten rid of just by hanging up the phone. Better shoot straight from the hip.

"Name your price," she told him. "Come on. I know you're

not doing this for the money. But for what I'll pay, you could set yourself up with a nice, classy lady who'll give great head and tell you twice a day how you remind her of Paul Newman."

Rudy's face darkened, his hands curling into fists, and for a second she thought he might hit her. Then he pulled himself up and grinned. "The deal I have in mind is a little different. Your silence for mine. Even Steven."

"Wh—What?" she stammered.

"When I *do* talk to Laurel, you wouldn't want it to leak out just *who* it was that handed her mother in to Senator McCarthy, now would you? And in exchange, I'll trust you not to say a word to Annie of our little . . . arrangement."

Dolly felt as if every drop of blood had been drained from her body.

"You . . . bastard." It was an effort just to make her lips move. "You're doing this to get back at Val. That's it, isn't it?"

"No, you've got it wrong. It's not that at all." He leaned forward slightly, color rising in his pasty cheeks, a gritty undercurrent of passion in his voice. "I don't want to get *back* at Val. I just want something of his."

"What about Annie? How do you plan on keeping this from her?"

"Leave that to me. I have an idea."

Dolly knew then that she had lost. And that once again, she would be dragged into deceit and betrayal. She'd have to lie to Annie, set up Rudy's meeting Laurel behind Annie's back. Because if Annie ever found out, she'd bolt. She'd grab Laurel and run away all over again. Dolly wanted to rest her head on the table and weep.

No, she couldn't tell Annie the truth. With Henri in Paris, with no hope of his ever getting a divorce, she couldn't bear the thought of being without her nieces as well.

I betrayed my sister, Dolly thought, her heart feeling as if it were being ripped apart, *and now I'll be betraying my sister's child.*

"Why does it have to be a secret?"

Laurel peered at Uncle Rudy in the swimmy gloom. The aquarium at Coney Island seemed like a funny place for her to be meeting him. But Aunt Dolly, who often took her places on Saturdays, said it wouldn't be any different than going to the zoo or the park with her. On the way over here in her chauffeured Town Car, Laurel's aunt had explained that Uncle Rudy wasn't going to hurt her or tell on her—he just wanted to see her and make sure she was okay. But if that was all, then why had her aunt's face looked all puffy and red, as if she'd been crying? And why was Uncle Rudy now making her promise to keep this a secret, even from Annie?

Laurel wished Dolly was with her now. But her aunt had stayed in the car, saying she'd be back in an hour to pick her up. Laurel had been so scared at first, but Uncle Rudy had been nice, leading her through the shimmery-green walkways lined with huge tanks, and pointing out the different kinds of fish. He'd asked her all about school, and Brooklyn, and the Grubermans. He hadn't tried to hug her, or even hold her hand—she would've *hated* that. And he hadn't said one word about her and Annie running away . . . until now.

"Trust me," he told her. "It's better this way."

"But if Aunt Dolly knows, then shouldn't Annie know, too?" she asked, whispering even though this early in the morning there was nobody around to hear.

"Your sister . . . she wouldn't understand," he said, his eyes sliding away from hers. He had that look grown-ups got when they were holding back from telling you something they thought maybe you were too young to hear.

Starting to feel a little scared now, she stared at him, his rubbery face with its bulging forehead making her think of the shapeless manatees swimming behind the thick glass in front of her. Until now, she'd never really thought about her uncle one way or the other. He was just this funny-looking little man who came to see Val, and had hardly paid any attention to her except that he stared at her a lot, which gave her the creeps. Only now he *was* talking to her, and he really seemed interested in her, so maybe he wasn't so bad after all.

"If I told her . . . if I explained that you—"

"Look," he cut her off, "you're a big girl so I'm gonna be straight with you." He leaned close—they were almost the same height—his fat neck jutting from the collar of his wrinkled raincoat, his eyes small and black. "Val . . . your dad . . . that night you ran away . . . well, he was in pretty bad shape. By the time I got him to the hospital, he was out of it. Whatever Annie hit him with, it messed up something in his brain. The doctors did everything they could for him, but he . . ." Now Rudy was looking away, squinting at the manatee twisting in lazy circles behind the greenish glass. "He didn't make it."

Dead? My father dead? Laurel felt suddenly hot and dizzy, the hot dog he'd bought her at Nathan's on the way over backing up her throat, seeming to swell into something huge and liver-tasting. Then she remembered—Aunt Dolly had said she'd spoken with Val on the phone. So how could he be dead?

"It's not true!" she cried. "He *isn't* dead! Aunt Dolly would've told me."

"Your Aunt Dolly, she's a good lady. And she's looking out for you and your sister . . . just like I am. She knows what'd happen if something like this got out. If the police knew it was Annie that . . ." His voice trailed off.

Laurel shuddered, remembering the blood on Dearie's Oscar and on her blanket. "Annie didn't mean to. I know she didn't!" She was almost sobbing now, her breath coming in dry, hot gasps.

"Sure, *I* know that." Now he was clumsily patting her shoulder. "That's just what I told the doctors, and the police who came nosing around . . . that it was an accident, that he must've slipped and fallen and hit his head on a table or something."

"You didn't tell them about . . ."

"Annie? Of course not. Listen, kiddo, that's what I'm trying to tell you. I'm on your side. From now on, I'm gonna be looking out for you. Whenever I'm in New York, I'll visit you, and if you ever need anything . . . any little thing . . . all you have to do is just pick up the phone and call me. Collect. But it's gotta be our little secret. *Capisce?*"

Laurel gulped back her tears. The dim walkway with its weird, ripply light made her feel as if she were underwater, gulping for air, drowning almost.

"But why . . . why can't Annie know?" she choked.

"You want her to know she's a murderer? How do you think she'd feel? Look, I know Val wasn't the easiest guy to live with, but not even your sister would've wanted . . . well, what happened."

"But . . ."

"You love your sister, don'tcha?" His voice was a gravelly whisper. She could feel his breath against her face, warm and smelling of Juicy Fruit and cigarettes. "You don't want to upset her, do you?

A thing like that, it could really eat away at a person . . . and maybe wind up pushing them right over the edge."

Like Dearie. He means she could feel so bad about what she did, that maybe she'd . . .

No, she thought, *no,* Annie wasn't like that. She'd never kill herself.

But she might worry so much that she'd make herself sick.

Laurel could feel tears running down her cheeks. The manatee swimming close to the glass seemed to be staring out at her, its eyes big and sad and eerily human.

She remembered how she'd wished that there could be something big she could do to really help—something besides cooking and doing the laundry. And now she had found something, but she didn't want it . . . she didn't want to have to keep this horrible secret.

But if she told her about Val, then Annie would really feel terrible. And maybe she'd forget it was an accident and start believing she'd meant to . . . to hurt him. And then . . . well, maybe Rudy was right: Maybe it'd eat away at her until she . . . she ended up like Dearie.

She thought of Annie's fingernails, chewed down to the bloody quick. And how sometimes, waking up in the middle of the night, she'd see Annie sitting up in bed, just staring out at nothing.

"I won't tell," she said, her voice a thready whisper.

She didn't feel so dizzy any more, and the watery dimness of the walkway had settled enough so she could finally breathe. She actually began to feel a tiny bit pleased with herself.

Even if Annie didn't know, Laurel told herself, *she* would. She'd know that she was doing something important, that she wasn't just some dopey little kid dragging her sister down.

She'd know that in a kind of a way she was taking care of Annie, just like Annie had always taken care of her.

Part Two

1972

The Queen was terrified, and offered the little man all the wealth of the kingdom if he would let her keep her child. But the little man said, "No, I would rather have some living thing than all the treasures of the world."

from "Rumpelstiltskin"

CHAPTER 11

"I'm going to fall flat on my face."

Annie looked at the girl beside her in the back seat of the limousine. In the strobe flash of passing headlights, she looked younger than nineteen, and scared.

"No, you won't," Annie told her. "You told me you've sung that aria a hundred times. Anyway, you don't have to sing it all the way through, just enough to give Mr. Donato the idea."

"I don't mean *that.*" The girl—Suzanne, wasn't it?—rolled her eyes. "I mean this *dress* . . . it's a mile long. I just know I'm going to trip over it. God, how did women ever get around in these things?" She plucked at the heavy wine-colored velvet puddled about her feet.

Trip? More likely it'd be something a lot worse. Annie's eyes travelled up to the gown's bodice—a hand's width of fabric stretched across the Juilliard student's chest; above the fabric, her breasts swelled alarmingly—and had a sudden, frightening image of Suzanne taking a deep breath to launch into her aria, and those big boobs of hers popping right out.

God, what a scene; Donato and the other men at the party would be gaping, and the women blushing, scandalized—and these people were the food industry's top wholesalers and distributors. If that happened, and Donato found out who sneaked this over-developed singer in, Girod's wouldn't stand a chance.

No, she had to make this work. Donato's, a branch of the renowned Donato's of Milan, with its marble floors and frescoed ceilings, would be the most elite food store on the East Side, in the whole city even, when it opened this fall on Madison in the Sixties. And Annie wanted Girod's to be among the select number of choco-latiers whose confections were sold there. She was determined that they would be.

Sure, she could've gone the usual route, sent samples over to

Donato's buyer and then followed up with a phone call or two, but every supplier in town was doing that. So why sit back and just be just one of the crowd?

No, better to take a chance . . . try something that might capture Donato's attention. If she *could* pull this off, then the food magnate might well remember Girod's to his dying day.

It's the squeaky wheel that gets the grease. Isn't that what Dolly was always telling her? And in the six years she'd been working at Girod's, hadn't she proved that over and over? Annie found herself thinking about burly, bearded Nate Christiansen, food and beverage buyer for the Carlyle, how for months she'd chased after him, calling him, sending letters, even taking him to lunch. And Nate, jovial, friendly, flirtatious even, laughing boisterously at all her jokes . . . always hinting, but, dammit, never *allowing* himself to be backed into any kind of commitment. What he *had* let slip was that he was a G. K. Chesterton fan. And wasn't it lucky that, after combing secondhand bookstores, she'd unearthed an autographed first edition of a Father Brown mystery? Wrapping the book in heavy floral paper, she had then sent it over to Christiansen with a pound of Girod's assorted truffles. A week later, she was *his* guest for lunch, and they were hammering out an agreement for Girod's to supply the hotel's complimentary bedtime chocolates.

So why shouldn't this work, too? The girl, Suzanne McBride, a student at Juilliard, had the voice of an angel. She even *looked* angelic, with her peaches-and-champagne coloring and Pre-Raphaelite red hair. And Donato, she'd learned, while he was in New York getting this store on its feet, had not just one, but *two* season subscriptions to the Metropolitan Opera. What better way to grab his attention than by having a lovely young woman show up unexpectedly and serenade him with the balcony aria from *Roméo et Juliette?*

"Don't worry." Annie patted the girl's hand, which felt moist and cool. "You'll be fine. Just remember to pick up your hem."

The costume *was* too long for her, but there hadn't been time for alterations, and anyway, it was only on loan. A friend of Gloria's who worked in a theatrical-rental store on Broadway had found it for them, and Annie had promised to have it back by tomorrow.

Now the limousine—Dolly's Lincoln—was turning off Fifty-

seventh Street onto Sutton Place, and gliding to a stop in front of a
charming brick townhouse festooned in English ivy. Annie slid out,
and helped Suzanne onto the curb, holding the hem of her gown up
in back so it wouldn't drag as she climbed the few steps to the front
door. In her other hand, Annie carried a silver Girod's shopping bag.

Ignoring the ornate brass knocker in the center of the heavy
door, she rang the bell instead.

Shivering in the cool evening, waiting for the door to be answered, Annie could feel a pulse throbbing in one temple. She nibbled
at a fingernail. What if, after all this, she was turned away? Or what
if Suzanne, in front of a bunch of strangers, got stage fright and
froze? Annie took a deep breath, and smoothed the front of her dress,
a simple black jersey sheath, elegant enough for this party, but one
she knew wouldn't compete with her hired soprano's eye-popping
costume.

*I'm the one who's going to fall on my face . . . and then I can just
kiss good-bye any chance of my getting to Paris.*

For one tantalizing moment, Annie allowed herself to think
about Dolly's promise to speak to Henri about the apprenticeship.
Three whole months in Paris, learning how to actually make
chocolates—God, if only she could! Working for Dolly was never
boring, but she'd already learned practically everything there was to
know about managing a store, setting up displays, packaging, ro-
mancing buyers. Now what she'd been dreaming about was to open
her own shop. And what better way to learn how to make her own
chocolates than under Henri's Swiss-trained M. Pompeau, who had
been turning out mouth-watering confections for Girod's for over
fifty years?

So, yes, this just *had* to work. If Donato liked her little surprise,
and gave Girod's the go-ahead, then Henri couldn't fail to be
impressed—an account like Donato's might as much as double Girod's U.S. sales. Being Dolly's niece wouldn't count for much, he'd
once told her. Apprenticeship applicants were chosen based solely
on their merit.

Annie's thoughts were interrupted by the door opening in front
of her. A young man in a dark suit and striped silk tie stood before
her. Too suave-looking to be a butler, and with those dark eyes he
had to be—

"Hello," he greeted her. "I'm Roberto . . . Roberto Donato." His gaze flickered over Suzanne's dress, and one heavy eyebrow arched in amusement.

"I'm Annie," she said. She hesitated before stepping inside, scared that he would want to see their invitations, or worse, ask why Suzanne was wearing that absurd dress. Then, quickly, before he could say anything, she added, "We're a little late."

But the young man, who probably had been pressed into service by his parents and looked bored out of his skull, merely nodded and allowed them to pass. "They're all upstairs," he said. "You missed my father's big speech."

"That's okay." Annie tossed him a grin. "We're here for the encore."

Then, holding tightly to Suzanne's clammy hand, she tugged her through the marble vestibule into a circular room dominated by a life-sized bronze nude standing at the foot of a spiral staircase. She heard voices, laughter, music drifting down from the floor above. She glanced at Suzanne, who looked even paler than she had on the way over, her thin face the color of library paste. Annie tightened her grip on the girl's hand. *Don't you dare flake out on me . . . Don't you dare. . . .*

At the top of the stairs, a pair of tall panelled doors stood open at the entrance to a large room filled with elegantly dressed men and women, their mingled voices rising above the tinkling of a piano. Annie could feel Suzanne holding back.

"I wasn't expecting . . . God, look at all those people . . ." The girl's voice dropped to a panicked whisper. "I mean, at school I sing in front of people, but this is different. I had no idea . . ."

Annie, dropping Suzanne's hand and taking firm hold of her elbow, whispered, "You'll do fine. Just remember what I told you . . . Donato is that tall gray-haired man over there, the one with the bushy mustache." She pointed him out, recognizing him from a photo she'd seen on the business page of the *Times*. He was standing by the black marble fireplace, talking to a group of men, one of whom Annie recognized as Stanley Zabar, whose world-famous upper-Broadway store she regularly supplied with truffles and tiny marzipan fruits.

She found it odd, how calm her voice sounded . . . much calmer than she felt. Though she'd skipped dinner, she felt slightly queasy, as if she'd eaten too many cheesy canapés. But then she forced herself to think how pleased Dolly and Henri would be if she could snag this account.

Annie, placing her hand in the small of Suzanne's back, gave the girl a gentle push. At the same time, she somehow thought of Laurel, who would be eighteen in just three days, almost the same age as this girl. Laurel was shy, too, but she could be surprisingly tenacious as well. Annie remembered Laurel, at seven, learning to roller-skate, falling so many times that her legs were a mass of bruises, but always she'd pick herself up, make herself keep going. Laurel, in this girl's place, would never let Annie down.

But now, thank God, Suzanne, staggering a bit under the weight of her cumbersome velvet costume, was moving forward. As she crossed the room, people stopped talking and stared, stepping back to make a path for her as she made her way toward Donato. A hum of whispers rose, people asking each other who this creature decked out like a Renaissance princess could possibly be.

Stopping a few feet from Donato, the young soprano opened her mouth. At first, no sound came out, and Annie felt her heart lurch. Then the girl's soprano voice, sweet, lovely, incredibly pure, began to flow forth.

"Ah, tu sais que la nuit te cache mon visage . . ."

Donato stared at her, his mouth—small and pink under that enormous bushy mustache—dropping open in astonishment.

Annie felt her heart begin beating again. It might work—Suzanne was good. But after this moment of surprise, would the man be charmed . . . or merely annoyed at the intrusion?

As Suzanne sang her final plaintive notes, a huge empty silence seemed to fill the room. Annie felt herself drifting, weightless. The floor seemed to tilt beneath her, and the beautiful room with its egg-and-dart ceiling, watered-silk walls, and antique tables and chairs the color of fine port rocked gently from side to side. Donato, she saw, still wasn't smiling; he hadn't moved a muscle.

Then came the applause, the muted cries of delight . . . and now Donato was clapping, too, the ends of his mustache lifting in a wide smile. Annie felt the room right itself, and she could once more feel her feet on the ground. Taking a deep breath, she stepped forward and briskly made her way toward Donato.

It's going to be all right . . . everything is going to be all right. . . .

From her shopping bag, she pulled a lovely old Wedgwood soup tureen—one of Dolly's flea-market treasures—which she'd filled with truffles and bonbons.

Smiling, she handed it to Donato along with her card. "Compliments of Girod's."

Then quickly, with as much regal poise as she could muster, she did an about-face and swept out of the room with Suzanne in tow.

Annie, curled in the deep, sway-backed easy chair in Joe's living room, watched Laurel unwrap the birthday gift she'd given her—a beautiful lacquer box containing watercolor paints and a set of delicate brushes.

"It's Japanese," Annie told her. She remembered the hole-in-the-wall Oriental art store down on Barrow Street where she'd found it, and the elderly Chinese man who had waited on her. When she'd told him it was for her sister, who was turning eighteen, he'd given her a sheaf of handmade rice paper to go with it.

"Oh!" Laurel gasped, staring down at the box, tracing with her fingertip the mother-of-pearl rose on its lid. "It's . . . oh, Annie . . . I love it."

She was sitting cross-legged on the floor near the couch where Joe sat, her shoulder almost grazing his knee. Now she was twisting around so she was nearly facing him, holding the box up for him to see as if this gift from Annie were something she was offering to *him* instead. "Joe, look, isn't it beautiful?"

"Beautiful," Joe agreed. And then Annie saw that he was looking not at the box, but at Laurel.

Barefoot, in her faded jeans and embroidered Mexican peasant blouse, her bright hair shining about her shoulders, Laurel looked so radiant, so completely, unaffectedly lovely, that Annie felt a stab of envy.

Then it hit her: *She's in love with him.*

The room went suddenly bright—the Mission oak sofa and chairs, the Navajo rug and wrought-iron candlesticks atop the low redwood burl table—all of it magnified somehow as if she were peering through a telescope. Dolly, in a swirly-patterned kelly-green dress and silver lamé heels, like a bright parrot perched on the edge of the chair by the radiator. Rivka, seated beside Joe on the sofa, smiling serenely, wearing a new ash-blond *shaitel*, and looking impossibly young to be the mother of nine. Joe, in a navy pullover and light-blue cords washed so many times they were almost white, grinning down at Laurel and leaning forward with his elbows propped against his knees.

"I thought you could use it," Annie said, then cleared her throat and added, "I'm glad you like it." She quickly looked down, concentrating very hard on the rug, on a black thunderbolt—or what looked like one—that seemed to be zigzagging out from under one leg of her chair. She knew that if she looked at her sister again, she wouldn't be strong enough to stop the black thoughts from rising up again.

"*Like* it? I love it!" Laurel beamed at Annie. "You always pick the perfect thing . . . and it's something I can really use."

"That's what sisters are for," Dolly piped. "It's up to aunts to give you wonderful *useless* things you'd never in a million years buy for yourself. Here." She thrust a small robin's-egg-blue box tied with a matching blue satin ribbon at Laurel—from Tiffany's, Annie could see at a glance. "Happy eighteenth."

Annie smiled, thinking of the little blue boxes like that one stacked inside her own dresser drawer, six of them—each containing a little silver pin or bracelet, a pendant, a pair of earrings—one for every birthday since she'd come to New York. She watched Laurel untie the ribbon and open the box. Inside, in a blue flannel drawstring pouch, was a gold heart locket with a tiny diamond in its center. Pretty, Annie thought, but too sweet somehow, too little-girlish.

Laurel must have thought so too, because even though the smile never left her face, some of her radiance seemed to dim. "You're absolutely right"—she laughed—"I never would have bought it—I couldn't have afforded it. But I love it. And I love *you* for thinking of it."

Annie, watching her sister get up and hug Dolly, thought how good Laurel was at pretending—Dolly would never guess she didn't absolutely adore it. *If only I could be more like Laurel that way,* Annie thought. Less blunt and more gracious . . . and more generous when it came to showing affection. And with Dolly, especially, Annie still couldn't quite let herself go a hundred percent—there was always that tiny kernel of suspicion, way down deep, the feeling that Dolly hadn't told her *everything* that had happened between her and Dearie. And somehow that made all the wonderful things she'd done for them seem, well, tarnished.

"My Sarah, she has such a locket," Rivka said, "With a picture of her husband, Yitzak." She cast a meaningful glance at Laurel. If Laurel were Rivka's daughter, Annie thought, she wouldn't be going back upstate to finish her second semester at Syracuse . . . she'd be getting married, settling down. Annie, on the other hand, at twenty-four, was an old maid already.

As if she'd read Annie's thoughts, Rivka sighed and said, "I still can't get used to it, you girls living so far away."

Annie laughed. "You make Manhattan sound like it's another continent."

"For you, maybe it's not. For me, I should have to ride the subway an hour to see my two California *shainenkes?*"

Annie missed Rivka, too. They still saw each other, but nothing like when she and Laurel had been living in Brooklyn. For the past five years, they'd been renting an apartment in this building, a tiny one-bedroom two flights up from Joe's.

"Next time, I'll come to you," she promised.

"And next time I come to Manhattan," Rivka teased, shaking her finger at Annie, "it will be to dance at your wedding."

Annie felt herself blush, and fought the urge to glance over at Joe.

She watched as Rivka rose from the sofa, brushing invisible lint from her high-necked white blouse and smoothing her stylish, below-the-knee houndstooth skirt. "Now . . . who wants cake?" She had made it herself, kosher, of course, carrying it all the way here on the D train from Avenue J in a hatbox.

"Do I get to blow out the candles first?" Laurel asked.

"Not until you open my present," Joe said. He got up and went into the bedroom, reappearing a moment later holding a small, square package clumsily wrapped in tissue paper and tied with a piece of fat red yarn.

Laurel unwrapped it slowly, revealing a small, hand-painted wooden box. Inside was a braided silver band.

"The Indians of Mexico make them," Joe explained. "They're called friendship rings."

Laurel was silent as she stared at it, rolling it between her thumb and forefinger, seemingly mesmerized by the light flashing across its surface. With her head down and her hair curtaining her face, Annie couldn't see her expression.

Then Laurel looked up, a quick glance before looking down again, and Annie saw why she wasn't jumping up to hug Joe, or even going out of her way to tell him how much she liked it: her eyes were bright with tears and her cheeks stained a deep red. She looked as if she were about to cry.

After what seemed like an eternity, Annie watched Laurel get up, rising awkwardly, with quick, jerky movements, and walk over to Joe. Leaning down, she kissed him, not on the cheek, but on the mouth, carefully, deliberately, lingering a split second longer than was merely polite.

"Thank you, Joe," she murmured.

Joe looked pleased, Annie saw, but also a bit embarrassed. Had she only imagined that he'd seemed to be returning Laurel's kiss?

Now the thoughts she'd been trying to shut out—not just to-night, but for months, since long before Laurel went away to college—rose up in her mind.

Images flashed through her head. Laurel, a skinny twelve-year-old, running along the sidewalk to catch up with Joe. Laurel in the kitchen at Joe's Place, kneading bread dough alongside him. Laurel, nestled up against Joe on this couch, watching *Invasion of the Body Snatchers* on TV, burying her face in his shoulder during the scary parts.

Then she was seeing her sister—thirteen, with legs up to here and absolutely no coordination—slip in some mud in Prospect Park and open an awful gash in her knee. Blood everywhere, soaking her stocking, her shoe, the grass around her. Joe had scooped her up, and he and Annie had run to the street. And then they had to stand and wait, while Annie waved frantically for a taxi. But when the driver saw all that blood, he started to put his car in gear and pull away. Joe, in a sort of reflex action, reached in and grabbed the cabbie by his shirt, hauling him partway out the window.

"She's thirteen. She's hurt." He spoke in a soft, level voice. "You're taking us to Kings County. Now. I'll pay whatever you need for the cleanup. Do you have a problem with that, sir?"

The grizzled cabbie, his face the color of cottage cheese, had shaken his head. Then, without a word, he had driven like lightning to the entrance of Kings County Emergency, where Laurel, fiercely blinking away her tears, had had eight stitches put in her knee.

But what Annie remembered most about that awful day wasn't the blood or the stitches . . . it was the way Laurel, afterwards, had looked at Joe—as if he'd slain a hundred dragons and scaled a tower as tall as the Empire State to rescue her.

She's in love with him. The thought repeated itself in Annie's mind, over and over, like some annoying advertising jingle she couldn't get out of her head. She'd always known it, hadn't she? The difference now was that Laurel was no longer a knock-kneed kid . . . and Annie could no longer pretend this was just some adolescent crush.

But that wasn't what was bothering her now, she realized. What was making her heart bump up into her throat was that it had suddenly, jarringly, occurred to her that Joe might be falling in love with Laurel.

Why not?

At eighteen, Laurel seemed older than most girls her age. Still a little dreamy at times, but so poised and gracious, and adept at doing things, like her artwork and sewing all her own clothes. *Sure, I looked after her, but she's had to fend for herself a lot of the time.* "My little wife," Rivka used to call her. And so what if Joe was thirty-one? Lots of guys went for younger women. And lately Joe had been talking more and more about finding a wife and settling down, joking that he'd like at least half a dozen kids. What would be so—

Stop it, she told herself, you're being ridiculous. Sure, Joe loves Laurel, but not the way you think. He loves her the way he'd love a little sister.

The way he loves you.

Annie felt a sharp pain in her chest, like a muscle cramping. *Did* Joe look at her that way, as just a good friend, a sister, sort of?

She remembered the day, the exact moment, when she first realized she was in love with Joe. Four months ago, walking home with Steve Hogan after a movie, this madman on a bicycle had careened out of nowhere, knocking her down as she stepped off a curb ahead of Steve. Thrown to the pavement, she banged her head and bruised her knees. But the worst of it wasn't her pain, or the idiot on the bike not even bothering to stop. No, it was that she couldn't stop laughing.

Joe would've held her tight, she'd thought, kept her warm, gotten help. Like with Laurel, when she'd cut her knee. He would've known she was in shock, semi-hysterical. But Steve, cute, top of his class, NYU Law School, whom she'd been seeing for almost a year and had even thought about marrying, had just hunkered down on the pavement beside her, patting her back as if he was halfheartedly trying to burp a baby. She'd known then—as if the bike hitting her had somehow knocked the realization loose—that the only man she wanted, right then, and always, was Joe.

But she hadn't had the guts to tell him, not yet. There was still time. Maybe in a few days, after Easter vacation, when Laurel went back to school . . .

"Happy birthday to you! Happy birthday to you!" Dolly's robust contralto broke into her thoughts. And now Joe was joining in. And Rivka, too, in a wavery soprano, her round face shining in the glow of the flickering candles foresting the cake she was carrying in from the kitchen. "Happy *birth-day,* dear Lau-rey. Happy birthday to yooooouuuu!"

Annie watched Laurel take a deep breath, and with her eyes fixed on Joe, blow out the candles on the cake.

I don't need a crystal ball to know what she's wishing. Annie felt guilty for wishing the same thing for herself, but dammit, why should Laurel have any more of a right to Joe than she did? And, anyway, Laurel would get over him. At Syracuse, there had to be dozens of guys her own age chasing after her; in no time at all, she'd be mooning over one of them, and Joe would go back to being no more than a big brother.

While Rivka was cutting the rich coconut cake and Laurel was passing out slices, Annie went over and sat down next to Joe. "How did it go last night?" she asked. "You know, with your party?"

Joe's Place had just branched into catering, and she knew they hadn't yet ironed out all the kinks. The restaurant, though, was almost running itself now, and was fully booked almost every night. In the past six years, it had become a Village institution.

"Not bad," he told her. "Except the lady's oven fritzed out, and Rafy had to sweet-talk the next-door neighbor into letting us use hers. Other than having this ditzy neighbor crash my client's black-tie party in her sweatpants and running shoes like she and her oven were some kind of package deal, it went okay."

Annie smiled, and rolled her eyes. "Believe me, I know."

"You too?"

"Yesterday, I'm offering a sample to this buyer who warns me he's allergic to nuts. I tell him not to worry, I know for an absolute fact that this Framboise truffle has no nuts. Then he takes one bite, and turns absolutely white, and has to rush for the toilet."

"Oops." Joe winced. "Guess you had it wrong."

"Nope. I was right about the Framboise, but I'd given him the wrong truffle. I gave him a rhum praline by mistake."

Annie remembered how embarrassed and apologetic she'd been at the time, but now, with Joe, she could laugh. Telling him about things that had upset her at work always made them seem better.

"You still so dead set on opening your own shop?" His eyes, behind the round, steel-rimmed glasses that had replaced his old, square ones, were mildly challenging.

"I'd like to . . . if I ever get it together. You know, little details like knowing how to make chocolates, and having enough money." She shrugged, keeping her voice light, not wanting him, or anyone, to know how desperately she wanted this. What if Henri—even after her triumph with Donato (who just this afternoon had called to set up a meeting with her)—didn't come through with the apprenticeship? And even if she did get it, what if the money she'd been counting on from Dearie's trust—the money she'd have to have to start her own business—had somehow vanished, stolen by Val, whose silence all these years worried her almost as much as his lechery once had?

"I'm not worried about you," Joe said. "Anything you really want, you'll find a way of getting it."

Looking into Joe's eyes, those green-brown eyes flashing with quiet amusement, she felt a good, steady warmth spreading through her. She longed to wrap her arms around him, to bury her head in his raglan sweater and listen for his heartbeat, see if it was racing the way hers was right now. *Oh, Joe, if you knew what I was wishing for now, would you still be so sure I'd get it?*

She *had* to tell him how she felt, and stop all this babyish mooning. Even if he didn't feel the same way, at least then she'd know. And she'd deal with it somehow.

I will *tell him,* she thought, *the day after tomorrow, when Laurel is gone, when I have him all to myself again.*

And if he does want me . . . well, Laurel will just have to understand.

She's a big girl; she'll get over it. Haven't I always given her everything? Just this once, don't I deserve to come first?

"What are you guys whispering about?" Annie looked up and saw Laurel standing over them, a plate of cake in each hand. She was smiling, but her eyes, Annie observed, had narrowed the tiniest bit.

"You, of course," Joe teased. "I was wondering—now that you're eighteen and all—if you're finally going to introduce us to your mystery boyfriend."

"What boyfriend?" She glared at him as she handed them their plates.

"The one you're always sneaking off to be with."

"I don't know what you're talking about!" Laurel was trying to laugh, but the color in her cheeks was giving her away.

It was nothing new, this secretiveness of hers, but Annie wondered now, as she had a hundred times before, *What is she hiding?* All those evenings, getting home from work to find Laurel not home, and not at Rivka's, either. Laurel would always say that she'd been doing homework at a friend's house, or had stayed late at the library, but she'd cut her eyes away when she said it, and her cheeks would color.

Dolly, when Annie told her about it, had said maybe it was Laurel's way of showing her independence. Probably she *was* at a friend's house, Dolly reasoned, but she wanted to let Annie know she was too grown up to have to check in like a little kid.

And years ago, Joe had begun teasing Laurel about her "mystery boyfriend." Laurel always pretended not to know what he was talking about, but Annie thought she was probably secretly pleased that Joe cared enough to be intrigued.

"Then how come you're blushing?" Joe ribbed her now, his eyes twinkling.

"I'm not!" Laurel's hands flew to her reddening cheeks. But now her smile looked strained, and she cast an odd, furtive glance at Annie.

What is she hiding?

Joe, probably sensing he'd gone too far, was now trying to smooth things over. "Okay, okay. Forget I said anything." He wiggled his eyebrows, adding in a low, mock-seductive voice, "Maybe I'm just jealous. Maybe I want you all for myself."

Annie felt herself grow hot, burning hot—then, all at once, very cold. But why was she getting so upset? Joe was just kidding around, same as he'd been doing with Laurel forever . . . Why should now be any different?

You *know, even if Joe refuses to see it.*

Enough. She had to tell him how she felt, before Laurel ended up getting hurt.

Tonight. As soon as Laurel went upstairs. She wouldn't even wait until her sister had gone back to school.

Now she looked over at Dolly, who was standing up, reaching for her purse. "I'd like to make a little announcement," she said, looking straight at Annie, smiling, her face pink with anticipation, like a kid about to blurt some wonderful secret. "I know this is Laurey's big day, but honey, I have something for you too." Reaching into her large lizard-skin purse, she pulled out an envelope and handed it to Annie. "Go on," she urged, "open it."

Inside the envelope, Annie saw, was an airline ticket—to Paris. She stared at it, numb with shock.

"I talked to Henri," Dolly gushed. "It's all arranged. You'll be working under Monsieur Pompeau. He's an old goat, let me warn you, but what he knows about chocolate would fill a dozen volumes."

Now Annie was seeing the date on the ticket—a week from today!

"It's . . . so soon," she managed to get past her frozen lips.

"Sorry I couldn't give you more notice, but the other apprentice you'll be working with starts next week, and Pompeau wants you both at the same time."

Now the numbness was beginning to fade, and feeling crept back in. She felt a burst of sudden joy—Paris! She was finally going to be a *real* chocolatier, not just an assistant manager in a shop.

Then her joy wilted. Three and a half months without Joe. It'd seem like forever.

Now it didn't matter if she told him how she felt. Either way, they'd be apart. And Laurel . . . well, Syracuse was a lot closer than Paris. She'd see Joe on long weekends and on holidays. . . . And maybe with Annie out of the way, he and Laurel would—

"Well, *say* something, for heaven's sake!" Dolly threw up her arms. "If I have to lose the best manager I've ever had, the least you can do is be happy about it."

"I . . . I . . . don't know what to say . . . It's just so . . ." Annie stood up and hugged her aunt. "I don't know how to thank you."

And Annie *did* feel grateful, but at the same time she couldn't help thinking that Dolly had picked absolutely the worst moment to play fairy godmother.

Annie, getting her boarding pass at the Air France check-in desk, heard her flight being announced. She turned to Joe. "I'd better go." She bent down to grab her carry-on bag, but Joe got to it first, hefting it easily.

"I'll walk you to the gate," he said.

"You don't have to."

She felt so awkward, standing here with Joe in the middle of the international-departures corridor, people rushing by in both directions, the two of them acting more like strangers on a blind date than best friends. She felt a sudden urge to grab him, right here in front of everyone, and shout, *I love you, dammit! Why can't you see that?*

But, of course, she wouldn't. Instead, she just trudged alongside Joe, sneaking sidelong glances at him every so often. He was more dressed up than usual, wearing pressed flannel slacks and a button-down shirt under his scuffed leather bomber jacket. His hair was neat, as if he'd just combed it; under the overhead fluorescents she could see the damp tracks left by his comb. His glasses, though, were slightly askew, one wire earpiece not quite resting on his ear.

Her heart felt hollow, a husk that had been dried out by the heat of her longing. Why didn't *he* say something, *anything,* to let her know how he felt, if he was going to miss her?

He didn't speak until they reached her gate. Putting her suitcase down on one of the plastic chairs bolted to the floor in long rows, Joe reached up to touch her cheek, his fingers cool and light. "I'm not going to promise to write, because I'd only end up disappointing you. I'm lousy with letters."

"Well, I'll probably be too busy to write back, anyway." She looked down, so he wouldn't see the disappointment she was feeling.

"Annie." He hooked a finger under her chin, and tilted her head back so she was looking at him. She felt herself growing warm, her skin prickling under her cowl-necked sweater and the new tweed skirt Laurel had made for her. "That doesn't mean I'm not going to miss you."

"Are you?" *God, what a dumb thing to say.*

"Who else is going to wake me up Sunday mornings by banging on the door, and yelling, 'Extra! Extra! Read all about it'?"

"If I didn't get you your *Times,* Mr. Abdullah would be all out by the time you rolled out of bed."

"I think you just like seeing me stagger to the door in my skivvies."

She laughed, feeling herself relax a bit as they slipped into their old, familiar banter. "Don't flatter yourself. I've seen better-looking bodies on Wheaties boxes."

"Annie, I *am* going to miss you." His crooked smile was fading now, his eyes serious.

"Joe, I . . ." She felt a high, throbbing ache in her throat, as if a thumb was pressing into her Adam's apple.

Over the PA, the final boarding call was being announced. The lounge, she saw, was nearly empty now.

". . . I'd better go," she finished weakly.

She was about to turn when he caught her in his arms, and pulled her close—so close she could almost taste him, a sharp sensation at the back of her throat, like biting into a green apple, tart and sweet at the same time, flooding her mouth with saliva and filling her eyes with tears.

He kissed her. Full on the mouth, a deep kiss that pierced her heart. His lips were soft, and she could feel the tip of his tongue, and just the edge of his teeth. She breathed in the good, rich smell of him—a smell that reminded her of cuddling up inside one of those baggy sweaters of his she was always borrowing. His arms tensed, drawing her even closer, his lean frame pressing hard against her.

Oh God, dear God, was this really happening?

A happy, stunned heat flooded through her, making her feel heavy, and the tips of her fingers prickled. Light-headed, too. A word popped into her head: *swoon.* Like a heroine in a Victorian novel, she was swooning.

Annie, pulling back and looking into Joe's eyes, those green-brown eyes so quiet and still behind the lenses of his steel-rimmed glasses, sensed that Joe, under that calm surface, felt as shaken as she did.

Say it, she willed. *Say you love me. You want me.*

But all he said was, "So long, kiddo."

Annie, moving away from him, toward the ramp to the plane, half hated him for that, for kissing her, for letting her go off to Paris, where she knew she would dream about that kiss for weeks and weeks, not knowing exactly what it meant.

CHAPTER 12

Laurel stared at the naked man lying in front of her.

Dark hair down to his shoulders, a bandana knotted about his forehead, his lean muscled torso just a shade lighter than the burnt-sienna pastel crayon she was using to sketch him with. And . . . down below . . . his . . . well, she'd never seen a man who was so . . . but then, what did she know? How many naked men had she ever examined up close? Male models like this one, sure, but the last one they'd had in Life Drawing had been on the skinny side, and pale, his pinkish-grey penis nestled like a toadstool in the downy moss between his legs.

This guy—he looked about her age—there was something about him . . . an edge . . . a humming tautness . . . like a wire cable stretched too tight. She sketched furiously, using bold, sweeping strokes. There. She was getting it now. A little more definition here . . . and just a suggestion of shadow there . . .

Laurel found herself thinking of Joe, imagining it was Joe she was drawing, the shadowed curve of his rib cage she was now smudging with her thumb. In less than an hour, as soon as this class was over and she could catch a ride into town, she'd be on a bus heading home. And with Annie in Paris, Laurel, for the first time, would have the apartment . . . and Joe . . . all to herself. When she'd called last night to let him know she was coming, he hadn't answered—probably working late—and now she prayed that tonight, when she got there, he'd be home.

She felt heat gather at the base of her throat.

Would things be different between them now? Could he begin to see her in a new light?

I'll make him see. I'll show him how much I love him, how I'd be so right for him.

Thinking of just *how* that might be accomplished, Laurel felt the heat in her collarbone begin to spread upward, fanning into her cheeks. She forced herself to concentrate on the drawing clipped to her easel, and on the model. Stretched languidly on his side on a sheet-covered bench in the center of the classroom, his head supported on one elbow and one knee hiked up with his foot resting on the bench, he made her think of Tarzan, sunning himself on a rock. Or Tonto . . .

Hi-ho, Silver!

Laurel, suppressing a giggle, pressed too hard against the paper and felt her crayon break apart with a loud snap. In the intense silence of the classroom, several of her fellow students glanced up from their easels. Laurel felt herself blushing, and when she looked back at the model, she saw that he was staring at her, his tea-colored Apache eyes boring into her.

He looked familiar somehow, but she couldn't quite place him. *Those eyes.* Was he a student? He wasn't in any of her classes, but she might have seen him around campus.

Then she remembered, yes, she *had* seen him . . . last week in front of the student center, passing out flyers for an antiwar rally. But if he was a student, what was he doing modelling for Life Drawing? Maybe it was like the twice-a-week tutoring she did at the local high school, something to earn pocket money.

After class, as she was putting away her pencils and pastel crayons in her box, the boy sauntered over.

"Not bad." Flicking his hair off his shoulders, he stared at the sketch she'd done of him.

"Thanks." Laurel was relieved to see he'd put on some clothes—patched jeans and a dark blue T-shirt. Even so, having him so close, chatting with her . . . after she'd been staring for forty-five minutes at his . . . well, *all* of him . . . it made her feel weird somehow. And she still couldn't shake the feeling that she knew him from somewhere, and not just from having seen him that one time in front of Schine.

"You're trying to remember where you know me from, but you haven't figured it out yet, have you?"

Laurel started and looked up. He was staring at her with the same bold expression as before. How had he known?

"I'll give you two guesses . . . Beanie." His full lips flattened in a smile, and he tilted his head back so that all she could see of his slitted black eyes was a teasing glint.

"Beanie" . . . her old nickname from grade school. It hit her then: The little boy in Miss Rodriguez' sixth-grade class who'd made her life so miserable. "Jesús!" she cried. "God, no wonder I didn't recognize you. Last time I saw you, you were about five feet tall, and . . . and . . ."

"And I was wearing clothes." His smile widened into a grin that seemed to mock her. As if he knew his frank, insouciant nakedness had made her uncomfortable.

Laurel could feel the heat in her face seeping up into her hairline. Was it that obvious? Could guys tell just by looking at her that she was inexperienced . . . a virgin? Was that why Joe treated her like a kid?

She stared at Jesús, remembering the Christmas play, and how afterwards they'd become friends . . . sort of. More like a truce, actually. Jesús hardly speaking to her, but not hassling her anymore . . . and even going out of his way to stop other boys who did. But then his mother had died, and he'd moved away. To a foster home, somebody had said.

"How . . . ?"

"It's Jess now, not Jesús," he answered before she could ask. "Jess Gordon."

"I heard you'd gone to a foster home."

"You heard right—my foster parents, the Gordons, they wound up adopting me. Beats me how come . . . I was murder in those days. Pissed off at the whole planet and everybody on it."

"Yeah, I know."

"You had it good, Beanie. I *liked* you." He laughed, an easy, rich laugh. "Man, what a kick, running into you like this."

"Well, I'm glad things worked out for you."

"Me, too. My dad . . . you'd like him. He's retired now, but he used to teach English in this little high school in Newburgh where we lived. He really pounded it into me, all that stuff, spelling, too —remember how you used to beat me in every spelling bee?"

"It wasn't hard," she recalled. "You'd have been the first one down if you hadn't told the other kids you'd beat them up if they didn't purposely spell every word wrong."

"*You* weren't scared of me."

She shrugged, and waved to a friend, petite frizzy-haired Shari McAuliffe, who was on her way out the door, a huge black portfolio almost as big as she was tucked under one matchstick arm. Laurel glanced at her watch. Ten to four—she'd better get moving if she was going to get down to the Greyhound station in time to catch the next bus to Manhattan. But Jess, with his tea-colored eyes and mocking smile, was holding her somehow.

"I guess I had bigger things to worry about back then," she told him.

She thought of Uncle Rudy . . . and of the secret she'd kept from Annie all these years. It had started with Val . . . but now Uncle Rudy had become a sort of secret himself . . . her "mystery boyfriend."

All through that first year, then junior high, and Music and Art, Rudy, the three or four times a year he was in New York, would just show up at her school, and take her for a ride in a chauffeured limousine. He asked about every one of her teachers, who her good friends were and who she hated, what rock groups she liked and even her favorite TV shows. On a nice day, they'd go to Riverside Park near the boat basin, and sit on a bench tossing bread crumbs to the pigeons and peanuts to the squirrels. Uncle Rudy never talked about himself. He was kind of weird that way . . . he only wanted to know about her. And sometimes . . . well, she'd catch him looking at her so hard, the way you'd look at a blackboard if you were trying to memorize a homework assignment on it. Then she'd feel creepy inside. But he never touched her, not a hug, not even to hold her hand. It was always, "Hiya, kid," and then he'd push the car door open wide enough for her to climb in.

This year, for her birthday, he'd given her a beautiful Madonna figurine carved out of ivory. It was old, and probably cost a lot. How strange for Uncle Rudy, who seemed so rough, to have picked out something so exquisite. Maybe he was secretly religious, or thought she was. Either way, she'd felt touched. But when she'd given him that peck on the cheek, Rudy had looked at her as if *she* had given him something priceless.

"You were a tough little thing, I remember that."

Jess' words made her drop the heavy drawing paper she was rolling up. It fell to the scuffed linoleum floor, unfurling with a little snap. She retrieved it, and looked up at him, bewildered, thinking he must be talking about someone else.

"Me? I was absolutely terrified all the time!"

"Yeah, well, there's all kinds of tough," he said.

"I guess so." He made her think about Annie, how her sister had held things together for them, working so late every night at Aunt Dolly's shop, budgeting their money so carefully (what Laurel earned baby-sitting could hardly be counted, but Annie always referred to it as "our" money), always somehow finding enough for her—for the clothes she didn't sew, for shoes, for art supplies, even for movies with her friends.

Laurel was swept with a sudden tenderness for her sister, who was so good and so tough . . . tougher than she could ever be.

"Listen," Jess was saying, "me and some others, we're organizing this antiwar rally for next week—maybe you heard about it?"

"I saw a poster, I think."

"You interested?"

"Maybe."

She was against the war, sure, but all she really cared about right now was getting home to Joe. Thank God Joe's nearsightedness had kept *him* from getting drafted.

Jess stood with one hip thrust slightly forward, his thumb hooked in a frayed belt loop, his eyes flicking over her, sizing her up. "You got a minute? We could grab a cup of coffee and, you know, talk about it."

"I'd like to, Jesú . . . uh, Jess. But I'm in kind of a hurry right now." She saw that the classroom was almost empty, only a couple of stragglers still packing up their supplies and their drawings. Their teacher, Mr. Hanson, was standing by the door in his paint-spattered chinos and wrinkled chambray shirt, talking with Amy Lee, a shy soft-spoken Chinese girl whose drawings and canvases, with their jarring, vivid splashes of color, always seemed so unlike her.

She supposed she must be like Amy that way—one thing on the outside, and another on the inside. If only Joe could see that, too.

Laurel's mind darted ahead: She was imagining Joe, the surprised look on his face when she showed up. She'd play it cool, tell him she'd come down for the Pre-Raphaelite exhibit at the Met. Wednesday, she knew, was his day off, so she'd suggest he go to the exhibit with her . . . and then afterwards maybe dinner, a movie, and . . .

Laurel saw that Jess was staring at her, his dark eyes hooded. She took in his jutting cheekbones, his oily black hair with that faded red bandana twisted about his forehead. She shuddered, feeling suddenly scared.

Of Jess?

Maybe it wasn't Jess who scared her; maybe it was Joe, the thought of what he might do or say when she . . . when she . . .

God, *could* she? Could she really make it happen? Could she make Joe love her *that* way?

Now Jess was shrugging, reaching behind him and pulling a tattered knapsack from behind a chair. "No problem," he said, tipping her a sly wink, as if he could read her thoughts. "Anytime. You come see me anytime, Beanie. I'll be around."

"Laurey! What are you doing here?"

Joe stared at her. She was wearing some kind of Indian smock made of crinkly raspberry-colored cotton. Tiny round mirrors were sewn into the smocked bodice, and they glittered in the harsh light of the bulb over the landing.

"Joe!" She hugged him and kissed his cheek, so lightly, so quickly, his senses barely had time to record it. "Surprised?"

"Let's just say I wasn't expecting you."

"Does that mean you aren't going to invite me in?"

"Actually, I was just on my way out." Seeing her look of disappointment, he explained, "My mother. I promised her I'd catch this opening down in SoHo, some artist friend of hers who's having his first show. You want to come along?"

"I'd love to." He saw her eyes light up, and felt a short, sharp tug inside his chest.

He knew that look; he had, in fact, been avoiding it for a very long time. For months, years even, he'd pretended it wasn't what he thought it was, holding back from any kind of real acknowledgment of what it meant . . . of what he was going to have to do about it. And now she was here, and truthfully, was it such a surprise? She hadn't told him she was coming down on this Tuesday evening of all times, but hadn't he known, deep down, that she *would* come—

if not this time, then some other? That he'd have to face this, sooner rather than later?

Coward, he accused himself. *You're ducking this, just the way you ducked Caryn.*

Only Laurel wasn't Caryn, not by a long shot. Soft-spoken, a little dreamy sometimes . . . but she could hold her own. Not as fiery as Annie, but in her own low-key way Laurel could be just as determined as her sister.

He knew she wouldn't let go of this . . . this idea . . . not until . . .

. . . you do something about it.

But what the hell was he supposed to do? What could he say that wouldn't break her heart, make her hate him?

But he didn't want that. He couldn't bear the idea of Laurel hating him.

"I thought you and your parents weren't getting along," Laurel said as they were strolling across on Twenty-second toward Seventh Avenue, where they'd be able to catch a cab headed downtown. A light rain was misting his glasses, making everything look soft and unfocused, wreathing the streetlamps in fairy rings. He was acutely aware of Laurel, who had thrown on an old corduroy jacket of his over her dress, tucking her arm into his. "It shows something, your mother wanting you to come to this."

"Let's not make this into too big a deal," he countered. "We're not talking *Make Room for Daddy* here. But, yeah, I guess things are loosening up a little. Get this—last week my mother and the great Marcus Daugherty finally deigned to eat in my restaurant. I'm thinking of having a brass plaque inscribed and put over the table where they sat."

"Don't make fun, Joe. I think it's nice that they came."

Oddly, she sounded a little like Rivka now. He and Annie had always laughed at how Laurel liked to scold him and mother him, as if he weren't eleven years older than she was. *Eleven. Count them, buddy-boy.* But he wasn't laughing now. These days, he had to keep reminding himself of the gap in their ages.

"So do I, actually." He *was* glad . . . or maybe just relieved. This tug of war between him and his parents had been going on so long, he didn't feel the least bit smug about the fact that he'd won . . . if that's what he'd done. He was just glad that it was over.

His father, he sensed, had felt the same way. Following his coffee
and a couple of Armagnacs, Marcus had seemed almost . . . jovial.
Maybe he *was* mellowing. Maybe the old man and he both were.
"It's just that I would've liked it a lot better if he'd remembered to
leave a tip. I had to make it up to Marla out of my own pocket."

"He probably just forgot."

"My father? Never. That was just his way of saying, 'Don't
think, young man, that just because I'm here I'm letting you off the
hook.' I suppose he's reminding me, too, that corporate lawyers
make a helluva lot more money than restaurateurs."

Laurel laughed. "I like your father. He's got . . . character."

"We Daughertys have never been short on character."

As they reached the corner, he watched the corpulent but nimble
Mr. De Martini unpacking a box of oranges onto his sidewalk display.
They looked bright and luscious.

Remembering that Laurel, if she'd come straight from the Port
Authority, might be hungry, Joe asked, "Have you eaten? There may
be some wine at this art show, but not much in the way of edibles."

"It's okay," she said. "I had a sandwich on the bus. I'm not all
that hungry."

"Come on, that long ride, you've got to be starved. It's almost
seven."

"No, really. Joe, I—"

Leaving her on the sidewalk, he ducked into De Martini's, and
grabbed a bunch of red grapes and a handful of the tiny, mouth-
puckeringly tart kumquats he knew she loved. On impulse, he
snatched a yellow rose from a bucket half full of them, on the floor
by the register. Returning to Laurel, and handing her the bag of fruit
and the rose, he saw her eyes widen in delight.

Watching her bite into a kumquat, her mouth puckering at its
tartness, he thought, *Christ, she's beautiful.* Those blue eyes of hers,
with their thick, dark lashes. Her perfect, straight nose with a narrow
plane on either side of the bridge that made it appear almost bevelled.

And those lips . . .

He realized he wanted to kiss her. Very much.

I must be losing my mind.

"Why didn't you call and let me know you were coming?" he
asked, needing to keep on pretending that this visit of hers was one
of those spur-of-the-moment things.

"I tried. Last night. You weren't home."

Joe remembered. Yeah, it was slow, and he'd taken a night off. An old Exeter friend, Curtis French, had dropped by, and they'd gone over to St. Mark's Place to catch a revival double feature, both movies starring Eve Dearfield.

Somewhere between the ticket booth and the popcorn line, it had hit him, *I must have come here because of Annie.* In Eve Dearfield, her face, her voice, would he recognize Annie? He'd seen all those oldies on TV when he was a kid, but not since he'd known Eve's daughters. And these days, by the time he got home from the restaurant, he was too bushed even to turn on the TV.

And the thing was, he had felt as if he *were* seeing Annie. It was uncanny, eerie. Not a mirrorlike physical resemblance, but in movements, gestures, like the jaunty way Eve tipped her head back when she spoke, and dropped one shoulder slightly when she meant business. The way a corner of her mouth hooked down when she cried, as if a part of her stood back from her misery, mocking her. And that wonderful moment, when she told Stewart Granger to go to hell, then put out her cigarette in his champagne. That was so much like Annie, something she might have done.

Annie. He loved her . . . he missed her . . . and, dammit, yes, he wanted her. All of her, even her brashness, her sharp corners that were forever prodding him like a shirt with too much starch in the collar. For months, years even, he'd put off telling her how he felt. It was too soon, he told himself. He wasn't ready to get serious. Things were just taking off at the restaurant, and he was working his tail off to make ends meet. But gradually, as his life began to settle into comfortable grooves, when the prospect of a wife, kids, no longer seemed part of some nebulous future, he began looking at Annie with new eyes, wondering how she'd react. Did she love him? Maybe. But he knew that with Annie there was no such thing as going halfway—and was she really ready for a husband, house, kids on top of opening her own business? No—she was on fire, needing to *prove* herself somehow . . . as if she hadn't already. Wait, he'd told himself, wait until she's ready . . . until she wants this, *really* wants this, as much as you do.

But why, if he loved Annie, was it Laurel he felt drawn to now? What was it about her that made him want to hold her, lie down beside her, sink into her as he would into cool, still water?

Get a grip on yourself, for God's sake.

This isn't a movie, he told himself. This is real. Somebody could get hurt. Hurt real bad.

But it wasn't until a couple of hours later, back from the opening—which had turned out to be so crowded and noisy that he suspected his mother, despite her distracted wave in his direction, had hardly noticed he was there—that Joe realized one of the people who got hurt could be him.

He'd intended to wind up the evening with a quick goodnight peck and the promise of doing something together tomorrow. But as he was letting himself into his apartment, Laurel clung to him and whispered, "Let me stay with you tonight, Joe." Her voice was quiet, controlled, but he could hear the slight tremor in it. He knew her so well; he knew it was when she was scared that she acted the most nonchalant. In that way, she and Annie truly were sisters.

Joe felt as if he'd been sucker-punched. Christ. Had he heard right?

"Laurey, I . . ." His voice choked up on him. He cleared his throat, and took her hand, which felt powder-dry. Annie's hand was always slightly moist when he held it. "Look, I have a feeling that no matter what I say it's not going to come out right, and I . . ."

I'm in love with your sister. Is that what he meant to say?

But was it even true? How could he be in love with Annie if he felt this attracted to Laurel?

". . . I don't want to hurt you," he finished, feeling weak, cowardly. Hearing footsteps ascending the stairs below, he gently pulled her inside, into his narrow vestibule, and shut the door. It was dark, but he didn't reach for the light switch.

"You don't love me," she said, and made a sound that was halfway between a sob and a laugh. She tilted her head back, and in the thin light that trickled in under the door, he could see the glint of tears. "Oh, I know that."

"I . . ."

"You love me, but you're not *in* love with me. Is that it?"

She was putting on such a show of being brave and worldly that he felt even more torn; if she had melted into tears, or gushed like a teenager, it would be so much easier to soothe her. To pat her on the back, and tell her how honored he was, and that she'd get over him someday. But Laurel, somehow, when his back was turned, had grown up.

"I could tell you that things might be different," he spoke softly, with great care, "if this were ten years from now, and I was meeting you for the first time." He smiled. "But then I'd be middle-aged, with a receding hairline or maybe completely bald, and"—he thought of his father—"I'd smoke cigars and read the *Wall Street Journal* religiously. And you . . . well, you probably wouldn't even want to know me."

"You'll never read the *Journal* religiously." She laughed shakily, then with a fierceness that seemed to leap out of nowhere, she said, "Joe, this isn't some crush. I love you. I always have." Her eyes, in the shadowy dimness of the vestibule, cast a fine, gray light.

Before he could stop her, or stop himself, she was slipping her arms around his neck, drawing him to her. He felt her flesh against his, cool and silken, and her lips, tasting of the kumquats she'd finished off on the way home, their citrusy tartness stinging him lightly. Now her lips were growing softer, sweeter. *Jesus.* He wanted to tear himself away, stop this . . . stop her from pulling him in the wrong direction . . . but, Jesus . . . oh, Jesus, her mouth . . . her sweet mouth . . .

She's just a baby, he tried to tell himself.

But he knew it wasn't true. Laurel was no baby, and never had been. Not since he'd known her. Sometimes laughing, sometimes serious, but always this little woman. It was Laurel who, in the summer, remembered to put little cloth bags of cedar shavings in with her and Annie's wool sweaters. And who, in the winter, put seed out on the windowsill for the birds. Ordinary things . . . but she somehow wasn't ordinary. Not with that imagination of hers, and the wild, wonderful, fanciful things that seemed to spring from her head onto paper when she drew.

But he had to stop this. Stop it *now*. Before it was too late. Before he'd taken a path that would lead him forever away from Annie.

Joe drew away, a button on his sleeve snagging against one of the little mirrors on her dress, tearing it away with a small, popping sound. He felt himself trembling, on the verge of doing something he'd surely regret. He had to stop himself. Now. Quickly.

"Laurey, this isn't . . . us. It's just, well, things are different now . . ."

"Annie, you mean." Her voice was shaking now; he could hear the tears close to the surface. "You think this has to do with Annie being gone. That I'm somehow . . . that us being on our own . . . that I'm just *overreacting.*"

"No. This has nothing to do with Annie." He could tell from the way she was looking at him that she didn't believe him.

"Okay then." She pulled in a deep breath, and reached for the door knob, twisting it sharply. "Okay." Forcing a smile that appeared almost ghastly, she said, "Well, goodnight."

She opened the door and walked out, out into the hallway, her shoes clicking against the stairs with hard, rapid strokes, and Joe, watching her go, ached. He ached to call her back. To take her into his bed, wrap himself around her, make love to her. But if he did that, wouldn't he be hurting her even more?

CHAPTER 13

Annie watched as tiny white-maned Monsieur Pompeau peered into the pot of couverture she had been stirring. With the backs of his fingers—more sensitive than the tips, he'd told her—the elderly chocolatier briefly touched the melted chocolate, testing its temperature.

She held her breath, her heart racing. Was it all right? Such a simple thing, but after two weeks at Girod's, she still had trouble melting chocolate without somehow scorching the bottom or causing the cocoa butter to separate from the solids into curdled-looking clumps.

Was the water in the bottom of the double boiler too hot? It should be no more than eighty-nine degrees, Pompeau had said. But gauging the temperature, that was the tricky part. He did not believe in thermometers; he claimed they were not accurate enough.

So far the chocolate—or couverture, as it was called—looked okay, dark brown and satiny. Still, she felt herself tense as Pompeau dipped a long-handled stainless spoon into the pot and raised it to his lips. The taste would be only the first test, before she added the hot cream that would turn this into ganache—the truffle's soft center. But it was really *she* who was being tested. And this afternoon, when Henri Baptiste arrived back from Marseilles, Pompeau, she knew, was bound to give a report on her—whether she had any promise as a chocolatier . . . or not.

And would *she* too be shown the door, like the two before her Thierry had told her about, that absent-minded Italian who was always spacing out, like putting chestnut paste instead of almond in the massepain crèmes, and Cointreau instead of cognac in the Escargots Noirs; and the French girl with ten thumbs who was always dropping things? Apprenticeships at Girod's were precious, the waiting list endless. After a week or two, if one didn't show both a willingness to work hard and a deft touch, one was replaced. And if Pompeau gave her a bad report, Henri would feel he had to dismiss her. Even being Dolly's niece probably wouldn't cut her any slack.

Annie nibbled a fingernail. *God, please.* She *needed* to stay, to learn. Otherwise, the whole brilliant career she'd dreamed of for herself would be derailed. Then how could she face Joe? She'd have failed before she even started. And soon he'd come to realize she wasn't smart enough or talented enough for him.

But if she could make this work, she'd be able to open her own shop—and soon, make her own handmade chocolates. In a little more than a year, she'd come into the money Dearie had left her. Enough to rent a vacant store, install a small kitchen, somewhere with a low rent. But, first, so much depended on—

Pompeau's wizened face puckered, concentrating as he ceremoniously tasted the couverture. Annie felt herself daring to hope. *Such a simple thing—how could it go wrong?*

A hundred ways, she reminded herself. A thousand. Each day, Pompeau watched her like a hawk, criticizing her every move. Nothing was ever quite good enough. The ganache was not bad, but not precisely as it should be—too much liqueur, not enough cream. Or the couverture—which, when tempered, became the truffle's dense outer coating—not firm enough. For the *marrons glacés,* she had to mash the chestnuts more finely. For the leaf-shaped chocolate-cream *feuille,* she had used the wrong molds. Yesterday, as she was ladling hot ganache onto a stainless cooling tray, he had shrieked at her, *What do you think, thees ees cement you are pouring?*

Again and again, she had stifled the impulse to snap back that she was trying her best. But what if her best just wasn't good enough? There surely were other places where she could learn . . . but none of them could turn a sow's ear into a silk purse.

No, she told herself, somehow she had to make *this* work.

Henri Baptiste, whom she hadn't seen since she'd arrived in Paris two weeks ago, was finally due in today, returning from a month at the Girod factory in Marseilles, where the cacao beans from the family's Antillean plantations were roasted, then ground and conched, and the finished blocks of couverture—except for what was needed here at Girod's—shipped to a wholesaler in Holland. Henri had been down there overseeing the building of a new storehouse, she'd been told.

Annie was eager to see him. She remembered Henri from his visits to New York as warm and outgoing, always gesturing, and laughing that great booming laugh of his. But how would he treat her if he was told she'd turned out to be, well, not good enough? From stories she'd heard around Girod's kitchen, she knew how exacting he could be. Dolly had told her once how Henri had tossed out an apprentice for having dirty fingernails—the boy, he'd declared, had no more chance of becoming a master chocolatier than did a coal miner of becoming a Cartier.

Oh God, what if he were to fire *her* as well?

Annie watched Pompeau's tongue flick, catlike, to catch a drop of melted chocolate from the end of his spoon.

"No, no, *c'est gatée!*" he pronounced sadly. "The bouquet, he has gone away."

She felt numb. A cold, humming emptiness in her head. And then she was flying back in time, standing in the kitchen of that greasy Greek diner being fired all over again by Mr. Dimitriou. As if all the years she'd worked for Dolly had never happened.

Looking around the large kitchen, she half expected to see that everyone was as frozen as she was—that the entire world had stopped turning. But no, all about her figures in starched whites were bustling about, their reflections rippling along the shiny, blue-tiled walls. The clatter of pots, the hum of the enrober as it conveyed nuggets of ganache along its conveyor belt to be drizzled in couverture, voices calling to one another in French. Light sparkled off the copper cauldrons, the marble counters, the stainless-steel refrigerator doors.

"You permitted it to make the vapor, you see that? And now, he has become like mud. *Regardez cela!*"

Annie had no choice but to peer into the oversized double boiler on the cooktop in front of her. Instantly, she saw he was right. Droplets of moisture were now dribbling down the inside, and the lake of silky dark-brown chocolate that began halfway from the rim had begun separating into grainy lumps.

"I'm sorry," she said, struggling against the urge to cry. "I thought I was doing it the way you—"

Pompeau cut her off with a wave of his hand.

"No, no! The words I tell to you, the words in a book, they

are only words. The *chocolat,* you must *know* when it is right, *here.*"
He tapped his breast. "And here." He touched a finger to his fluffy
white temple. In his pink gibbon's face, his blue eyes flashed.

"Let me start over. I'll get it right this time. I—"

Again, he cut her off, this time with a flap of his white apron
—already smeared with chocolate, she noticed, though it was still
early in the morning. He was shooing her away as if she were a
stray alley cat that had wandered in and was getting under his feet.

Annie felt a pulse jump in her temple. Her cheeks burned. At
the other end of the long cooktop, Emmett caught her eye and gave
her an encouraging thumbs-up. Thank God for Emmett. Always
there with a wink or a smile. His coppery hair bright amid the cold
steel and tile. Relaxed, confident, always rambling in his Texas drawl
about the glories of Paris—the intoxicating Monet water lilies at
the *Orangerie*; a street violinist at Les Halles, who'd played Mozart
like an angel; a tiny shop on the passage des Princes that sold nothing but meerschaum pipes, carved into the faces of the world's
great men.

She watched him as he lifted a coffeepot from the counter and
poured *filtre* into two thick white china cups. Coffee break. At nine-
thirty, Pompeau allowed them a luxurious ten minutes. Now she
caught Emmett signalling to her. But could it be that late, nine-thirty
already? She'd started work at six A.M., and it seemed as if hardly
an hour had passed. Suddenly, Annie felt weary, as if invisible sandbags were pulling down on her wrists and ankles. She glanced at
the brass ship's clock over the doorway leading upstairs. They'd
have to move fast, before the nougat syrup bubbling on the stove
peaked.

Annie followed Emmett into a small storage area to the right
of the wall of stainless refrigerators. He walked with a jaunty stride,
broken by a slight limp that hardly slowed him. A cup in each of
his square brown hands, held aloft, a thick finger curled about each
handle—a dainty touch that made her smile. He wore a red Henley
jersey stretched across a chest as thick and solid as a hickory stump,
faded jeans, and snub-nosed cowboy boots that clacked on the tile
floor, like an impromptu tap dance. If he hadn't told her about his
crippled foot, she might never have guessed it was more than a
slightly twisted ankle. Ask him about it, though, and he'd give her

that big smile, wide as Texas, and drawl, "Only handicap I got is these here freckles. Damnedest thing. Must've stood in front of a screen door too long with the sun shining through."

Annie liked Emmett's freckles. She liked everything about Emmett, even the way he talked—his faint Texas twang, which he purposely exaggerated when he was kidding around, and all his homegrown expressions that reminded her of Dearie, and of Dolly too. Though for all his openness, he was in some ways a mystery.

When she'd first asked him where he was from, he'd told her, "A little bit of everywhere." With time, she'd learned that he'd grown up mostly in Texas, where his mother had settled with her second husband after his father died, when Emmett was a little boy. But since leaving home he'd been all over, working on a beef ranch in El Paso, as an oil field roustabout in Oklahoma, and in Louisiana as a shrimper, a boat builder, a cook aboard a merchant ship. The way he talked, he seemed to have lived enough to be fifty, instead of only twenty-nine. But when she asked if he'd fought in 'Nam, if that was how he'd hurt his foot, Emmett had just smiled and said, "Ever heard the rumor that alligators don't bite, only crocodiles do? Well, don't believe it."

She never could be sure when he was or wasn't giving her the runaround. They'd worked side by side since she got here, two weeks ago . . . and even with all the stories he'd told about himself, she couldn't help feeling there was something he was holding back. Unlike Joe, who was a smooth deep river with an occasional raging current, Emmett was like a three-ring circus where you could keep your eyes on only one ring at a time, so you couldn't know what was going on in the other two. Like how had *he* managed to snag this apprenticeship,which dozens of applicants—some with degrees from culinary institutes and experience working in three-star restaurants—had lost out on. He'd told her everything about lobstering, from building the trap, to baiting it, to tying up their claws, but he hadn't told her that.

They settled into a pair of rickety folding chairs set near a narrow wooden table that looked as if it had been around since the storming of the Bastille. Modern, adjustable metal shelving lined the walls, the shelves stacked with ten-pound slabs of couverture—extra bitter, caraque, dark lactée, cocoa pâté, white, gianduja—next to cast-iron molds, sacks of unshelled nuts, vanilla beans, coffee, and gallon jugs of liqueur, orange-flower water, whole chestnuts in syrup.

Emmett hiked his bad leg onto one of the extra chairs and winced slightly. She could see it hurt him, though he'd never let on.

"You look like a mile of bad road," he told her. "Take a load off, Cobb. Old Pompeau, believe me, he's not so mean . . . he just looks that way. I'll bet he drinks hot milk before bed and sleeps with a night light. A regular old pussycat."

"An old concentration-camp guard is more like it."

Emmett laughed. "Pompeau, he's not the problem. It's *you*. My guess is, whatever's eating you, he's twice as tall as that old fart, and ten times better-looking. Boyfriend back home, right?" He pronounced it "raht."

"Are you always this nosy?"

" 'Fraid so." He grinned.

"Well, then, I guess you won't mind if I get a little nosy with you."

"Fire away."

"You never did tell me how you ended up here. I mean— chocolate?"

He shrugged. "Beats hauling shrimp nets."

"You're doing it again," she sighed. "You're purposely not telling me anything."

Emmett cocked an eyebrow. "Me? Hell, some've said I could talk the other ear off Van Gogh."

"I don't mean *that*." She smiled, and sipped her coffee, which was heavenly, better than any back home. "You talk, but you haven't *told* me anything about yourself."

"If you want to start at the beginning, I was born in North Carolina. Fort Bragg. Army brat. Moved to Osaka after the war, when I was still in diapers."

"Seriously?"

"Colonel Cameron had the honor, I believe, of being the last American officer to die at Japanese hands. Stabbed to death in a brawl at a teahouse, more commonly known as a brothel."

"Oh . . . I'm sorry."

"Don't be. My mother, God bless her, has succeeded, over the years, in canonizing the poor bastard. If he came back now, she'd have him dipped in fluorescent paint and stuck to her dashboard. According to Rydell, he died a hero, defending truth, justice, and the American way."

"Rydell?"

"Born in Atlanta, named after her great-great-granddaddy, a big Confederate hero."

"You still haven't told me how you got here."

"Oh . . . that." He shrugged. "Not much to it. I was working as an assistant pastry chef at Commander's Palace . . . you heard of it?"

"New Orleans. It's famous, isn't it?" She remembered Joe mentioning it.

"You could say that. Anyway, turns out Prudhomme and Baptiste are old friends. A few months ago, Baptiste flies over for the ACF convention—that's the American Culinary Federation—and old Paul puts in a word, and boom, next thing I know they got me singing the Marseillaise and munching on croissants."

"Might be hard to manage both at the same time."

He laughed. "A crip like me? I can chew gum, chug boilermakers, *and* walk a straight line. All at the same time. Like those commercials, we're number two, we try harder."

"Emmett, I . . . I didn't mean . . ."

"Folks, when they say they don't mean something, usually that's exactly what they *do* mean."

"Well, *I* wasn't talking about your foot. But since you brought it up, how *did* it happen?"

"Ever heard that saying, Let sleeping dogs lie?"

"I wasn't prying," she explained. "I'm just interested . . . in you." As soon as she heard herself, Annie felt heat crawl up her neck. She hadn't meant it *that* way. God, why was she always saying the wrong thing?

Emmett's eyelids drooped, his lips curled up in a sardonic little smile, one that seemed to say, *I know what you meant, but I'm gonna give you a hard time anyway.*

But then all he said was, "Let's just say I tried teaching a lesson to someone who needed it." His grin faded, and she watched his blue eyes grow dark. "Thick-headed son of a bitch. I'd have taught him, too . . . except he had something a lot tougher than me. Winchester pump-action. Blew a goodish chunk out of my foot."

Annie looked at Emmett, and thought, *Whatever it was, I'll bet you'd go do it all over again.*

Just a feeling. Emmett Cameron, for all his joking, was not a guy to be taken lightly.

"Your mother must have been pretty upset . . . after what happened to your father."

His eyes slid away from her, again that odd dark look. She found herself staring at him. Somehow, she'd always thought of freckles as a flaw, like a weak chin or jug ears, but on Emmett they . . . well, they suited him. Made him even more rugged-looking. Sort of a cross between Huck Finn and James Dean. With his blue-denim eyes and square features, she could imagine him leaning against a split-rail fence, squinting off into the distance, the mud-caked heel of one cowboy boot hooked over the bottom rail.

"In a manner of speaking," he said, throwing his head back and gulping the rest of his coffee. His throat was tanned too, she saw, with freckles spilling down it. Adam's apple the size of a child's fist. The harsh overhead light burned on the top of his head, making the wiry ends of his rusty hair glow like electric filaments.

"Yeah . . . she was." Again, that faraway look. "Upset I got it blown off 'fore some Viet Cong could get to me. My kid brother, Dean, he went over in '69. Squeaky-clean-eighteen. Shades of the old man, 'cept Dean died of dysentery. Way Rydell tells it, though, you'd think he'd bought it storming Hamburger Hill instead of the goddamn crapper 'round back behind the barracks." Emmett's eyes grew bright, and he unashamedly dragged his knuckles across them. "Poor Dean."

A tense silence filled the small room, and Annie became aware of all the sounds she'd learned to blot out—the gentle grinding of the electric enrober in the next room, the hum of the refrigerators, the rattling of a tiered metal cooling rack being wheeled across the tile floor.

"I still don't quite get it," she said.

"Get what?"

"Seems like you could have gone in any one of a dozen directions. Why this? Why here?"

Emmett shrugged, and smiled. "Like you, I was figuring on having my own business one of these days."

"You sound like maybe you're having second thoughts."

"Could be. I know two weeks doesn't sound like I've given it much of a chance, but I'm beginning to think this is gonna be just one more dead end for me."

"Why don't you leave, then?"

"It suits me fine . . . for now."

"And after that?"

He brought his lopsided boot heel clopping to the floor, and leaned so close she could feel his warm breath, smelling of bitter grounds. Holding her gaze, spreading callused hands as broad as spades, he spoke with an intensity that startled her, punching the air with words. "Land. Property. Buildings. My old man, he owned zip, and was proud of it. The army suited him that way. Soon as he and Rydell'd get settled in somewhere it'd be time to move on. With my stepdad, it was a different story, same ending. Newt owned the house in El Paso, or at least we thought he did . . . until he died, and the tax collector took it away." His eyes took on a feverish light. "When I do settle down, and one day I will, I mean to sink my roots so deep they'll be pulling them up in China."

"But owning things, that's not a living, not something you *do* every day," Annie persisted. At the same time, she thought of Bel Jardin, and felt a longing for her childhood home that brought a hot ache to her belly, as if she'd gulped her coffee too quickly.

"Owning," Emmett echoed, turning the word over like a jeweler scrutinizing a diamond for flaws. "Way I look at it, more you own, the more it'll keep your livelihood from owning you."

Annie understood. Security. That was something she'd never known, not even as a child. She'd always felt as if she had to be in charge. As if even Dearie's love couldn't be counted on. Maybe that's what made it so hard for her to believe that Joe could love her. That love was something anyone could have, something you could just reach out for, like picking an apple off a tree.

Then she remembered Joe kissing her, how wonderful it had felt, and the heat in her belly spread up through her chest.

Well, yes, she thought, maybe in some ways loving *is* that easy. It's *trusting* that's so hard. Maybe people weren't quite telling the truth when they said they trusted each other. Maybe deep down everyone felt as scared as she did of needing someone else too much.

Annie abruptly felt her rosy warmth turn sweaty-cold. What if

Joe met someone else while she was away? Or what if she'd read more into his kiss than he'd intended? What if it turned out he didn't want her at all?

Annie realized Emmett had fallen silent, and was staring at her.

"So what about you? What are you doing here?"

Before she could answer, they were interrupted by Pompeau's shrill voice crying, "Nougat! Nougat!"

Annie rushed in, with Emmett close behind, just as Pompeau was pouring the kettle of hot caramel and nuts onto the table, a long marble slab on stout metal legs, in the center of the kitchen.

"*Allons!*" shouted Pompeau, flourishing his spoon like a baton, signalling for the men to hurry. His gaze flicked over Annie, as if not seeing her; this was *man's* work.

You old phony, she thought. *I could do twice what you do with one hand tied behind my back.*

Still, Annie had to step aside as Emmett rushed to the table along with the two full-time helpers, skinny, pony-tailed Thierry, and Maurice, who always looked half asleep (and no wonder: Each morning Maurice had to get up before dawn and shop for the produce they would need that day—today, fresh-picked cherries and rasp-berries, wild strawberries sweet as gumdrops). The men descended on the pond of hot nougat with metal paddles, beating at it deter-minedly to flatten it before it cooled and then became too brittle to work with, a sound like oars slapping water. The air, smelling of nuts and caramel, brought back to Annie nice memories of carnivals and Cracker Jacks.

She watched Emmett now begin cutting the warm, flattened nougat into even squares with the "guitar"—a tool with metal strings that looked like an oversized egg slicer.

Suddenly, she became aware that Pompeau was staring at her, his small blue eyes hard as bullets beneath a hedge of shaggy gray eyebrows. The despair she'd felt earlier came rushing back, making her stomach tighten.

Why couldn't she be more like Laurel, to whom things like cooking and baking seemed to come as naturally as water from a spigot? Annie wanted to tear off her apron and run from the kitchen, run away from those disapproving eyes that mirrored her own self-disgust. But then something inside her stiffened. She straightened her shoulders and moved toward the old man, telling herself, *It's not all his fault. I have to get him to change his mind somehow. I have to convince him . . . and myself . . . that I can do this, that I could be good at it.*

"Show me," she said in a firm voice, keeping her eyes fixed on him. "Please. One more time. I want to learn."

Pompeau, she was half surprised to see, did not turn away. He merely shrugged, eyebrows lifting, the corners of his mouth stretching downward—an expression she had come to recognize as very French.

"*C'est facile,*" he said mildly. "Come, again I will demonstrate for you. Sometimes one needs the failure before one can arrive at the understanding."

She winced at that, but followed him over to the cooktop—a single long row of gas burners under a gleaming stainless-steel hood. While Pompeau worked, dropping brick-sized chunks of chocolate into the top of the big double boiler, he explained how it was required that it be heated gently, as gently as you would bathe an infant. And if even a drop of steam from below touched it, the cocoa butter would separate from the solids, causing it to seize into curdled lumps.

Now came the cream—always from Alsace, he insisted, chosen to provide a smoother texture because it had slightly less fat. He poured the cream into a separate pan, and heated it. When it was almost hot enough to boil, he strained it through a wire colander into the melted chocolate. And now, he said, slicing a chunk of butter from a square slab he had removed from the refrigerator, the sweet *beurre des Charentes,* just a little, more for the flavor than for the richness.

Gently stirring the ganache until it was smooth and mocha-colored, the old man hefted the weighty copper pan from the slightly larger pot of simmering water it was nestled atop, as easily as he would a loaf of bread. He carried it over to the wooden doors that were laid out horizontally, resting on metal shelving with several inches of space between each one, at one end of the kitchen.

"Monsieur Henri, this is his discovery." Pompeau beamed. "Clever, no? We could not find the trays large enough, so we find the old doors rescued from the demolished buildings."

Annie, listening, pretended that she'd had no past failures. She was starting from scratch. She pictured a deserted beach, and saw herself walking there, her footprints stamping into smooth, blank wet sand. She already knew everything Pompeau was showing her, but that didn't count. Today was today, and she was making believe she was learning it for the first time.

Pompeau now was pouring the ganache in a dark, silky river onto the uppermost door, which was covered in silicone-treated paper. With a broad spatula, he smoothed it, coaxing it outward to meet the edges of the paper.

Then he stepped back. "*Voilà*. You see? No grains, no lumps. *Parfait*. It will cool, and then we shall do the enrobing."

On the other doors, different flavors of ganache stood cooling; they would form the centers of Girod's world-famous truffles—bittersweet chocolate with soft mocha-champagne centers; Grand Marnier and dark chocolate, flecked with candied orange peel; a purée of fresh raspberries and a dash of Framboise in a smooth milk-chocolate ganache; bourbon and bittersweet, laced with sweet almonds from Provence; white chocolate and fresh-grated coconut dusted with ground pistachios from Sicily. Her own favorite was bittersweet and *crème fraîche* flavored with an infusion of smoky Lapsang Souchong tea.

But by herself, on her own, could she do this? Would she ever be able to create such wonders?

An idea came to her, at least the beginnings of one, a way she might be able to redeem herself. But before she could think it through, the old man was clutching her arm, propelling her over to a corner where the tempering machine stood like a huge Rube Goldberg Mixmaster.

"Now we temper the couverture," Pompeau lectured. "The part of the greatest importance. Without the coat who is perfect, the truffle, she is but a poor, ugly girl with a heart of gold. And who will marry her?"

Annie smiled at his little joke, pretending she thought it was funny, though she'd heard it a dozen times. And she felt herself relaxing a little. This would be easier, because the temperer did all the work for you. In stainless tubs, pure caraque chocolate would be melted—without cream, butter, or liqueur—and subjected to a series of machine-controlled temperature changes.

"You see, it is required that the couverture, she be cooled first, to twenty-nine degrees—centigrade, that is—then very slow warm up again to thirty-three, so the proper crystals, they will form. That is crucial. If the crystals do not form, the truffles will develop white streaks . . . *catastrophique*." His voice trembled slightly, and he looked stricken at the thought of any truffle of his being blighted with what was known as bloom.

The tempering process, he explained further, would ensure each truffle its glistening dark color, and also keep it from melting at room temperature. The tempered couverture would then be taken to the enrober to be mechanically drizzled over nuggets of ganache borne along a conveyor belt.

Watching as electrically driven oar-sized metal paddles stirred the tubs of couverture, Annie remembered the glimmer of an idea she'd had a minute ago. *What if I created a whole new flavor, one Pompeau never even thought of? And did it so perfectly that even Henri would be impressed?*

She turned it over and over in her mind, like a silver dollar picked up off the sidewalk you couldn't quite believe was real.

It might work. It might also backfire. And what then? She'd look like an even bigger fool. And Henri might be even more likely to send her packing.

But, hey, she'd taken a lot bigger chances than this, hadn't she? And then in the back of her mind, she could hear Dearie's voice, faint and scratchy like one of her old 78-rpm records, chuckle dryly, *Best foot forward, hell. You gotta jump in with both feet up to your fanny or it ain't worth the bother.*

Annie concentrated hard. Then she remembered the little bistro on the rue de Buci where she and Emmett had eaten the other night. Pears. After their cassoulet, the waiter had brought a basket of pears—the best she'd ever tasted. Full as she was, she had eaten two, not even bothering to stop the juice from running down her chin, as if she were a kid.

Chocolate and pears, would they go together? Maybe. But what if instead of fresh pears, she combined the chocolate with Poire William? She'd seen a bottle of the liqueur once, with a whole pear inside. They were grown that way, she'd learned, the bottle positioned over the branch while the fruit was still a tiny green nub. A miracle, in its own way. As this would be, too, if she could ever pull it off.

Of course, she'd have to ask Pompeau. But how? *Doesn't matter. Just do it. Do it now, or you never will.* Her throat seemed to tighten, too small an opening for her voice to squeeze through, then somehow she was telling him. She was sure he'd turn her down, or worse, laugh at her. But after a long moment he began tapping his forefinger against his lower lip and peering at her as if she were a racehorse on which he was considering the odds. Then he nodded.

"*Bien,*" he said. "To create a new flavor, it is more difficult than you imagine. But this way, perhaps, you will understand."

Yes, that I won't ever be any good at this. He's hoping I'll fail. She saw it in his eyes, fleetingly, like a bird flushed from its cover: pity. He didn't want to have to dismiss her. Better if on her own she came to the realization that she was no good.

And maybe that was the truth.

Annie loosened her apron's ties, and pulled them even tighter, knotting them so that they cut into her waist, making her stand up straighter and somehow reminding her of who she was.

I'm Annie May Cobb. I may not be a genius, but God gave me a brain and a backbone. And if I don't use them, what's the point of even going on?

Feeling a little better, despite the panic in her cinched-in stomach, she went into the storeroom to get the chocolate she would need.

Emmett, hoisting a tub of warm couverture from its seat on the tempering machine, watched Annie sail across the kitchen like a galleon setting out to discover the New World. *Good for you, Annie Cobb,* he said to himself.

She'll make it, he thought. Mule-headed woman doesn't quite believe it, but she's got what it takes. And she wants it so. The way Lindbergh wanted to be first to fly the Atlantic. The way I want to own something—a house with some land, maybe even a skyscraper. And why not? Why shouldn't we both get what we want?

Then he was remembering Atlanta, all those black people marching for what they wanted, trying to storm the Georgia State Capitol, chanting, "Julian Bond! Julian Bond!" Some politicos had railroaded Bond out of the legislature, and they were demanding he be restored. People pushing, yelling, with rage-twisted faces. And air that clung like hot, wet rags, and smelled of gas fumes and gunpowder and hatred. Steaming off the pavement, off the hoods of the cars parked around the Capitol. Making him long for the bone-dry heat of El Paso.

There were lots of white people too. Old, young, men, women, teenagers, *children* for Chrissakes, all heaving against the blue police barricades. Screaming obscenities, hurling rocks, bottles, anything they could get their hands on. *Niggers! Filthy coons! Go back where you belong! Cain't write your own goddamn names and you want to take over the WORLD!*

And those grim black faces, and a few white ones, too, holding up with pride despite their fear.

He remembered wanting to close his eyes, turn his back, ram his hands against his ears to shut out the ferocious chanting and obscenities. He wanted no part of it. He didn't even *live* in Atlanta, for the love of Jesus. This was his mother's town, her birthplace, where she'd moved back to after Newt died. He hadn't lived with her since he left at fifteen to work in an oil field, hauling equipment almost as heavy as he'd been at the time. He'd had soft hands then, but that day—he'd been twenty-four—they were hard as canvas tarp left out in the salt air.

And inside him there were things he wanted to close his eyes to as well. All his life, Rydell had fed him the family dogma, speaking in a hushed, reverent voice about his father's heroism, about his rich, God-Bless-America heritage. And Dean, in his grave at Arlington, ostensibly because of dysentery, but really because of Rydell—she'd sucked the truth right out of his bones and filled him with lies.

This visit, she'd been trying the same with him. Hounding him about his duty to our flag, to the good boys over in Vietnam, to the memory of his father and brother. Not enough she'd sacrificed one son; she wanted *his* blood too. Two graves, side by side, like trophies, or the sets of bronzed baby shoes on the mantel.

The time had come, he knew, to tell her that she had some other son in mind, a boy who looked and talked like him, but who wasn't *him*. And here, today, he felt no allegiance to either group, white or black. He just wanted to go his own way, find his own place, and eventually sink roots in real soil, not the cow shit Rydell had been shovelling out so long she couldn't even smell it.

But just then, with people screaming, sirens wailing, bottles smashing against the pavement, Emmett couldn't make believe he was somewhere else.

Rydell, five feet eleven inches in her silk-stockinged feet and built like a steamroller, clung to his arm as if she were a frail invalid. Had she been alone, he was convinced, she would have stridden tall, wielding her enormous handbag like a brickbat. Her coiffed red hair gleamed in the sun like a knight's helmet, her soft moth-white face turned to his, her mouth against his ear, spouting in honeyed outrage.

There's no call for this, no call 'tall. White trash, that's what these people are. Redneck white trash. Quality folk know how to treat coloreds, always did, even 'fore the war. Treat them decent, Daddy always said, and they won't go actin' up. We always did, you know. Why, Clovis was prac'ly a member of our family! And Ruby—you remember Ruby, don't you, son?—she cried at Grandpa's funeral. Cried like it was her very own kin nailed inside that coffin. . . .

Then he saw something that shut out his mother and made his stomach tip like an overfull bucket. A black kid, no more than twelve or thirteen, pinned to the pavement by a slab-armed man twice his size who was beating him with the butt end of a shotgun. And two policemen standing not six feet away, studiously looking in the other direction.

Until Emmett felt his mother's grip on his arm turn from rose petals to iron, intent on holding him back, he had not been aware that he was straining in that direction. *It's not your fight, son. You just stay away, hear. None of this is any of our business.*

Christ, in her view, his whole life had been none of his business.

It all clicked into place, why he didn't give a shit for any of this. He'd been running away, not wanting to face what was eating him: that he hated his mother. What she stood for, what she'd been cramming down his throat all his life. And mostly for speeding his brother off to get killed.

No, he would not be like her. And he wasn't going to stand here listening to her shit while some kid got beaten to a pulp.

He tore away, pushed his way into the fracas.

Blood. He remembered being hit first in the mouth and tasting his own blood, hot, salty, oddly metallic. Then hands, white hands all around him, disembodied somehow, tearing at his shirt, fingernails clawing him, leaving fiery trails down his back, his arms. The man with the shotgun wasn't a man at all . . . a Brahma bull . . . broad face, bulging eyes, no neck . . . just a head spliced onto a pair of meaty shoulders.

And the kid. Not real either, more like a doll that had been discarded or accidentally dropped. A pair of dust-streaked jeans. A small face the dull, dirty gray of old asphalt. Except for the blood.

Blood on his Monkees T-shirt, trickling down his arm. Almighty Jesus. What kind of a man would do this? This wasn't about race, or color, or busing, but a man kicking the shit out of a defenseless little kid.

"Son of a *bitch*!" Emmett heard himself roar as he dove at the Brahma bull, plowed his fist into unyielding meat. His blows seemed to do nothing, as if he were hitting a brick wall, bruising only himself. Then he felt his head in an iron vise. He was being crushed.

He saw sun reflecting brightly off case-hardened steel. An ear-shattering blast. A sudden, shocking numbness in his foot. He heard a woman scream, a high-pitched whine like a mosquito buzzing at his ear. His mother? Everything else faded except that whine; it kept building until it sounded like a DC-10 using his head as a runway.

He must have passed out, because the next thing he remembered was lying in a hospital bed, his mother's face hovering over him like an Arctic moon, coral lipstick freshly and flawlessly applied. A single crevice between her brows, as if drawn by a ruler, bisecting her otherwise smooth forehead into two neat halves.

. . . *sheared off half your ankle bone. And three toes. Some muscles and nerves too . . . but don't worry, the doctors say you'll walk again.* Spoken like it was nothing worse than a sprained ankle. *But you can just forget about the army. They'll never take you now.* Eyes rolling back, hands clasped in prayer. *Lord, what have I done to deserve this? I've tried to be a good mother to my boys, to hold up their father as an example, but seems like whatever I say, this one does the opposite . . . and now look what it's come to . . .*

Emmett was jerked from his reverie by a hand on his arm, firm but gentle. He turned and saw Annie. Thin face, saved from mere prettiness by strong bones that made him think of delicate but powerful alloyed steel. Huge eyes the color of blue ink. No makeup, but then she didn't need any. Skinny as a rail. Wearing pegged jeans and a black turtleneck, like some throwback from the Fifties. No bell-bottoms or miniskirts for Annie.

"Let me give you a hand with that," she said, reaching for a handle of the heavy tub he was hefting.

Pity? Give the cripple a break? Emmett felt resentment kindle in him. Then he caught himself. No, she couldn't have meant it that way.

He smiled. "Thanks, but I can manage. Just don't offer me your foot . . . I might take you up on it."

"Not funny." But a corner of her wide mouth curved down in a small don't-make-me-laugh smile.

She didn't move away. She was standing so close, he could smell her perfume, something musky and Oriental, overriding even the pervasive aroma of chocolate. There was a smear of chocolate on one cheek. He thought about licking it off.

Jesus.

Emmett felt panicky. What had come over him? He wasn't some horny teenager. He didn't need her. He'd had plenty of women . . . before and since getting his foot shot. He thought of the married lady he'd been seeing in Neuilly, who really got off on his being a cripple. Like it was some sexy new kink. But she was just a diversion, and that was all he was to her.

Suddenly, Emmett knew why he was panicky. He felt a mild tremor go all through him. If he took so much as a step in her direction, he could fall in love with Annie.

And, with Annie, he suspected that if he fell, it would be a long, hard fall. She was hungering for something too . . . but not for a half-crippled drifter. Whatever she was looking for right now, it was more than any one man could supply. She was travelling the blue highways of her soul, and there was no map or guide for that.

He saw her follow him to the enrobing machine in the next room, watching while he slowly poured the fresh couverture into a stainless trough that fed a silken, dark-brown drizzle over the slow-moving slotted conveyor belt. A little farther down the line, nuggets of glistening newly coated ganache passed under the infrared lamp and blow-dryer, where Thierry stood ready to transfer the finished truffles onto wide plastic sheets.

"Dinner tonight?" she asked in a low voice. "I found this little café off rue de Seine. The most amazing omelette, made with potatoes. Cheap, too. And if you're really poor and musical, someone told me they let you play for your supper. Oh, say yes, Em . . . it'd be so much fun!"

Her eyes shone, but he sensed it was not for him. She was excited over her discovery, and the new idea he'd heard her discussing with Pompeau, eager to share it with someone.

Don't let her see. Don't let her know you're not the joker you pretend to be.

"Sure thing," he said, forcing a hundred-watt grin. "I'll even bring my harmonica."

Annie stared at the small metal box she was holding. Inside was a single truffle, its glossy black coating of couverture dusted with toasted bitter almonds crushed to a fine powder.

Was it any good? Thinking back over the week, Annie counted fourteen batches of her pear ganache, and everyone around here who'd tasted her Poire William truffle had said they loved it. But Emmett and Thierry and Maurice, they were probably only saying it was great instead of just ordinary, because they were her buddies.

She loved it, but she'd sampled so many batches, how in God's name could she be sure this was the perfect one? Emmett, when he'd tasted this latest effort, had grinned and rolled his eyes in ecstasy, but when she pressed him, he'd admitted he could hardly tell the difference between this batch and the last. So thank heaven Pompeau had agreed to hold off reporting on her progress until Henri, who knew nothing of her attempt, had tasted it. He would be the judge . . . the only one who counted.

Annie mounted the narrow staircase leading up from the kitchen to the shop, which faced out onto the fashionable Rue du Faubourg St-Honoré. She carried the chilled metal box that held her Poire William truffle. Her hands shook a bit, but she forced herself to ascend briskly, one foot after the next, stepping squarely in the middle of each stair. The rumble of Henri Baptiste's deep voice carried down to her, blending with the rush of blood in her ears.

What if he doesn't like it? What if it really is nothing special?

The thought heightened her panic. No, not that, please . . . Total thumbs-down failure, that she could handle. That would just convince her he was way off-base or having a bad day. Because it *was* good. But if he said *ordinary,* that could be true.

Even so, she mustn't let it destroy her. She *mustn't.*

At the top of the stairs, she turned left, entering the packing room where squat, ruddy-cheeked Marie-Claire, in a spotless white apron, gauze cap, and white gloves, hovered over the finished chocolates that had been brought up in chilled metal boxes like the one Annie was carrying. Her nimble fingers were a blur, moving quickly as she transferred the truffles into Girod's signature brown-and-gold boxes, placing each in its own pleated paper cup. Above Marie-Claire's head, deep shelves were crammed with yet-to-be-folded boxes, yards of satin ribbon in every color, fat rolls of gilt gift-wrapping paper, sheets of gold stickers stamped with Girod's dark-brown lettering, and plain brown cardboard shipping cartons. Annie nodded to Marie-Claire as she brushed past. The Frenchwoman smiled and nodded back, her fingers not missing a beat.

Annie passed through a narrow door, and into the shop itself. As always, she paused on the threshold, a bit dazzled. Girod's was like no other chocolate shop—not even Dolly's could compare. It looked more like a reproduced nineteenth-century room in a museum. An Oriental carpet, soft under her feet after the hard tile of the kitchen, muted gold-flecked wallpaper above walnut wainscoting; on one wall, glass shelves on which artisans' works were displayed—a carved alabaster vase, a pair of Lalique mermaid candlesticks, an ancient jade horse from China, a nineteenth-century Sèvres platter commemorating Napoleon's coronation.

Above the display cases, the shelves were laden with hand-painted wooden boxes. Henri had commissioned an artist to decorate each lid with a different scene: bouquets of flowers, clusters of fruit, rambling grapevines, birds, children playing. Annie's favorite was a village scene, a woman shooing geese from the stoop of a thatched cottage festooned with tea roses. For a thousand francs, Marie-Claire had told her, customers could have their chocolates packed in one of these unique boxes, and tied with a satin ribbon dyed especially to match.

But what Annie loved best of all were the chocolates themselves. On all sides, displayed on silver trays like precious jewels, in antique wicker baskets, and in fluted crystal dishes. In the bow-front window sat a multitiered silver epergne, like great leaves on an ornate silver bough, each tier adorned with truffles, and with bonbons from antique molds in the shapes of horses, grape clusters, leaves, cherubs. Surrounding the epergne were the small cakes Monsieur Pompeau baked himself. They reminded Annie of exquisite jewel boxes, decorated with candied violets, miniature silver bells, and curls of gold leaf.

But right now Annie knew it was Henri to whom she needed to devote all her attention. He stood talking to Cécile, a tall, slim woman whose neck seemed too slender to support the heavy coil of graying hair at its nape. When Henri wasn't around, she managed the shop. Soft-spoken and discreet, and impeccably dressed in a soft gray wool jersey adorned only by a heavy gold chain, Cécile looked as if she could just as easily have been the doyenne of a haute couture house on the avenue Montaigne. It was she who had created the rule: Never, *ever,* ask if a box of chocolates was a gift; *every* purchase of Girod's was a gift . . . if only to oneself.

Henri, in comparison, looked rumpled, more like a shaggy philosopher than the director of this chic establishment, his bespoke chalk-stripe suit badly creased, hair mussed and cheeks flushed, as if he'd ridden a bicycle here. Not handsome—his strong broad features made Annie think of a Van Gogh potato farmer. And from what Dolly had told her, she knew Henri wouldn't hesitate to roll up his sleeves and dig in, no matter how dirty or menial the job. But yes, she could see why Dolly had fallen for him, married or not.

Henri caught sight of her and grinned, his mustache twitching up at the corners, his broad face creasing.

"Ah, how does it go, Annie!" he called, then looking beyond her he added, "And Bernard, how is it that you do us the honor of climbing the stairs in the middle of the day?"

Annie realized with a jolt that Pompeau had followed her, coming up behind her so quietly she hadn't heard him. Of course, the old fussbudget couldn't resist seeing her make a fool of herself. Her cheeks burned, but she fought the urge to turn around; she wouldn't give him the satisfaction of seeing how nervous she was. She made herself focus on Cécile, who had returned to her station behind the display case, where she was rearranging one of the baskets. The bell tinkled as a customer pushed her way in through the door, a heavyset woman who looked about timidly as if she didn't dare step farther into so fancy a store. Cécile beckoned to her reassuringly.

Behind her, Annie heard Pompeau give a low, raspy chuckle. "I may be of a certain age, but I still feel strong as a Turk. And in a few weeks, when I take the baths at Baden-Baden, I will be made young again. And you?"

Henri sighed and something dark, like a cloud shutting out the sun, flitted across his face. Looking closely, Annie could see how tired he appeared to be. More than just a little run-down . . . he seemed . . . well, shrunken somehow, much older than she remembered him.

He misses Dolly, she realized. She knew, because she'd so often seen the same sad expression of longing on Dolly's face. They only saw each other about every other month, and even the letters and phone calls in between were clearly not enough to bridge the gap.

But if Henri was sad, he seemed determined not to let it show. As Pompeau stepped past Annie, Henri strode over and clapped the old man's stooped shoulder. Then he kissed both Annie's cheeks, greeting her as if he had not seen her in years, instead of just months.

"Monsieur Henri," Pompeau asked, "did all go well in Marseilles?"

"In Marseilles, yes." Sighing, he added, "But I have just learned of problems in Grenada, at the plantation."

"Not serious, I hope."

"Broken windows, a fire in one warehouse. Agitators, I am told. We have reports that they are controlled by the Communists. And the government, such as it is, also wishes only to make trouble. It appears that I must go there to see for myself the extent of the damage, and whether the political situation is as bad as they say. Monsieur Girod, he believes we must sell. Sell!" Henri shook his head, and pressed a thick finger against the bottom button of his jacket, as if to soothe some indigestion.

He seemed lost in himself; then he appeared to shrug off his gloom, and cast a bright, curious gaze upon Annie. "Forgive me, I have not even asked about you. Is there something you wish to speak with me about? Monsieur Pompeau here . . . he has not terrorized you, I hope, into losing your voice, hmmm?"

His gray eyes shone with kindness and good humor. Annie felt the knot of dread in her stomach loosen. Henri was no Pompeau. Even if he felt he had to let her go, he wouldn't be cruel.

No, Henri would let her down easily. But would that be any better? Oh, she couldn't bear it, having him feel sorry for her!

And to top it off, he obviously wasn't feeling well. How could he enjoy *any* truffle now, even a good one?

"Monsieur Henri, I don't wish to impose on your time any further," Pompeau began, without looking at Annie. "But, Mademoiselle Cobb . . ."

"It's a new flavor we came up with," Annie abruptly interrupted. "We'd like your opinion." If Henri hated it, she'd take the full blame, but until then . . . she didn't want him to be prejudiced by her inexperience.

A crease formed between Henri's heavy brows, and Annie's heart sank. Suddenly, she was seeing herself through Henri's eyes —wearing jeans and a turtleneck (why hadn't she thought to put on a dress?), her hair damp and dishevelled from a morning spent over a hot stove, no makeup, not even lipstick. Why should he take her seriously?

She handed him the box, her heart pounding. Henri peered at the lone truffle for a long time, examining it the way a doctor might study a wart. Annie felt a cool thread of perspiration trickle between her breasts.

Emmett had said it was good . . . but he might have been exaggerating to be nice. And Pompeau had refused even a small taste, protesting that he wanted Henri's opinion to be unclouded by his own.

Now Henri was nibbling at the firm outer shell of couverture with its pale dusting of bitter almond. Should she have used a different kind of nut, hazelnut or pecan? No, she had tried them . . . and they were both good with the Poire, but the bitter almond was better.

She watched, her every nerve strung taut, as Henri popped the truffle into his mouth, and chewed thoughtfully.

Just as she thought she couldn't bear the suspense a moment longer, Henri smiled.

"*Formidable!*" he pronounced. "It has a marvelous texture, and the taste . . . sublime. Bernard, I compliment you. This is an achievement. And will do well with our customers, I am certain."

Pompeau! He thought the old man had done it! She felt sick. What should she do now? How could it ever have turned out like *this?*

"I . . . you see . . . it was . . ." She watched Pompeau flush a brick red, and begin to sputter. She breathed a little easier. A bullying martinet he was, but not a cheat; he would tell Henri the truth.

Then something occurred to Annie. Maybe letting him take the credit could help her even more than if she took it for herself.

There's more than one way to skin a cat, she could almost hear Dearie saying.

"Monsieur Pompeau has a gift like no one else," she put in quickly. Not a lie exactly. "It's such a privilege for me to be able to work with him."

Shovelling it on pretty thick, aren't you?

Had she gone too far? Then she saw how the old man was puffing up with pride. The glance he shot in her direction was one of pure delight. Good, she'd made the right choice. If she had pointed out that the truffle was her creation—after Henri had mistaken it for Pompeau's—the old man would have been embarrassed, and would probably have held it against her. It was to Pompeau that she had to answer each day, not Henri. And if Pompeau decided to like her, to take her under his wing, she could really *learn* from him, everything he knew, not walk away with just this one little feather in her cap.

And when this was over, she'd have something.

Annie felt a surge of happiness that seemed to fill her with bright light. An orange sun shimmering just below her breastbone, warming her insides, radiating from her fingertips, flying from her hair in sparks. She was magic. Nothing could stop her.

And, yes, there was more than one way to skin a cat.

CHAPTER 14

"You're not enjoying this," Emmett whispered in the darkness.

Annie felt a stab of guilt. Their big evening out, a chamber music concert at the Sainte Chapelle, and she was ruining it for Emmett. Above her, and surrounding her on all sides, the Gothic chapel's famous stained glass shone in the murky light like a crown of dark rubies. And under the spotlight, in front of the double rows of folding chairs, the cellist was playing Mozart, the music resounding in this soaring space with a clarity she'd never before heard. But she couldn't concentrate, couldn't keep her mind off Joe. . . .

Two months, Annie thought. Two months and eleven days, to be exact—it had taken him that long to answer her letter and post-cards. Not even a phone call. And then finally, among this morning's mail, which her landlady, Madame Begbeder, had left in a little pile on the rickety hall table by the front door, between letters from Laurel and Dolly, she'd spied it: a thin blue airmail envelope addressed to her in Joe's bold scrawl.

Annie recalled how in her eagerness to open the envelope she'd ripped off one corner of the letter inside. And how her pulse had thumped as she'd scanned the page. He was happy she was getting along so well at Girod's, he wrote, and that she was learning so much. Wasn't Paris beautiful in May? Had she visited the Jeu de Paume yet? Had she seen the produce stalls at Les Halles?

Nothing about him missing her, or not being able to wait until she got back. Nothing about him at all, except how busy he was with the restaurant, and his catering. And, oh yes—how poor Rafael had been badly bitten by one of his dogs.

Annie had felt so disappointed, she'd wanted to cry.

Even now, with Emmett, who was so much fun, and who usually kept her from being homesick, she felt a loneliness so deep it ached in the pit of her stomach. It had to be partly this place, too, this heavenly music—too much loveliness, Annie thought, could break your heart as well as too little. Especially feeling as miserable as she did.

"It shows?" she whispered to Emmett.

"We don't have to stay."

"But . . ."

Before she could remind him how much he'd spent for the tickets, she felt him tugging her to her feet. Together, they slipped down the narrow aisle alongside their row of chairs. In the dim light, Annie stumbled on the ancient, uneven stone flooring, and would have tripped if Emmett hadn't caught her. She felt his arm, solid and sturdy under hers, and was both steadied and reassured. Even his smell—a smell she associated with campfires and crackling autumn leaves and old leather worn smooth as glass—comforted her somehow.

Outside, in the stone courtyard abutting the entrance, Annie turned to him and said, "Em, there's absolutely no reason for you to miss the concert because of me. I can make it home on my own."

"Listen, Cobb, I've got an even better idea." He winked at her, hooking an arm about her shoulders. "I know a café not far from here. When you're feeling low, a Pernod and a shoulder to cry on beats Mozart any day."

"Stop being so nice! You're making me feel even more guilty."

"In that case, I'll let you pay for the drinks."

"Okay." She laughed. "It's a deal."

As they strolled in the mild summer evening past the thick stone walls surrounding the Palais de Justice, Annie began to feel not only selfish, but slightly ridiculous. She was probably making a big deal out of nothing. Did it really matter what Joe had written? The important thing was, he'd *written*. And it wasn't as if her letter to him had been so gushy either.

Annie glanced over at Emmett. He was wearing gray dress slacks, and a tan blazer over a white button-down shirt. She couldn't help thinking how handsome he looked; he could have passed for a young lawyer or stockbroker—except for his boots. Annie had never seen him without those old cowboy boots, tanned leather rubbed smooth as driftwood, their toes scuffed almost white, heels rounded with wear. They gave him not only a quirkiness she liked, but a faint air of detachment—with those boots, he seemed to be saying, "I'm a travelling man, so don't you get too attached."

She felt a surge of gratitude toward Emmett, for being a friend . . . and at the same time not putting even the slightest romantic pressure on her. After all their weeks of working together so closely, and the meals they'd shared in smoky bistros, he'd never even kissed her good night. Was he even attracted to her? At times, she felt something between them . . . a kind of energy . . . a heat . . . and other times she couldn't be sure how he felt about her, other than that he liked being with her.

Crossing the Seine at Pont St-Michel, where an old man peddling postcards blew her a kiss, Annie wondered what it would be like if Emmett were to kiss her. She felt suddenly, acutely conscious of the warm weight of his arm draped about her shoulders.

God, what's wrong with me? I thought this was about Joe, not Emmett.

The sidewalk café was only a pleasant walk from the bridge, on the place St-Michel, tables and chairs pushed up against one another under a scalloped green-and-pink awning, people all crowded together, chattering and gesturing, as if this was some wonderful, noisy party to which everyone was invited. Annie and Emmett waited a few minutes until they spotted a couple leaving, and then quickly slid into their still-warm seats.

"Feeling any better?" Emmett asked.

"Much," she told him, realizing as she spoke that it was the truth.

"You want to talk about it?"

"Not really," she said.

"That bad?"

"No, it's . . . well, it's silly. There's really nothing to tell."

"Let me guess—tall, dark, and handsome?"

Annie, despite a slight chill in the air, felt her face flush with warmth.

She nodded, her gaze wandering over to the couple across from her, the man leaning across their table to light the woman's cigarette, their gazes locking. The woman put out her hand to steady his as he extended the match.

"Only two things harder than pig iron—a woman's will, and a man's heart," Emmett quipped, affecting the Will Rogers drawl he used when he was trying to kid her out of a bad mood.

Annie looked at him, and saw that he was wearing a languid smile, his blue eyes flicking over her as if trying to read her. But she sensed the empathy behind that smile, and she found herself leaning toward him, drawing into his warmth as she would to a campfire's on a cold night.

"There's no reason . . . absolutely no reason at all for him to get all sentimental just because I'm here and he's there," she blurted, speaking in a firm voice, more to convince herself than Emmett. "I mean, we're just friends, good friends. Why should he suddenly start writing me love letters when he's not even in love with me?"

"But you're in love with him." Again, not a question, but a statement. Emmett's gaze fixed on her, mildly challenging.

"No! I mean . . . well, maybe. God, Emmett, I don't know anymore. How long can you stay in love with someone who doesn't feel the same as you?"

His eyes narrowed, the tiny squint lines at their corners spreading outward, as if he were gazing into bright sunlight. "A long time, I reckon."

Annie knew he wasn't just talking about her, but before she could probe further, a harried-looking young waiter appeared, and Emmett ordered their drinks.

Annie listened to him, marvelling, as always, at his fairly fluent French. He hadn't studied it in any classroom, he'd told her, but had picked it up here and there, mostly among the Cajuns he'd hung out with in New Orleans. While she, with her four years of private-school French, could barely order a croissant without tripping over her tongue.

But Emmett was like that, she'd noticed, picking up things and people as easily and naturally as a roaming hound picks up burrs. Like the pigeon lady they'd met in the Tuileries the other day— within minutes, Emmett had learned her whole history, her husband who'd been in the Resistance during the war and had died of tetanus poisoning; the three sons she'd outlived; her rheumatism that ached on cold nights; the pigeons she fed every morning, her favorites among them named after France's great generals. Annie remembered how the old lady in her black shawl, touched by Emmett's attention, had then pointed out an unusual-looking pigeon with feathers the dull red of terra-cotta, and chirped, "*Pour vous,*" meaning she would name it after him.

On their way back, Emmett had laughed and said, "I can think of worse things than being a pigeon."

Now, feeling light-headed from the Pernod, Annie said suddenly, "I lied before, when I told you I wasn't sure if I loved Joe. I do. Why is that so hard to admit? Why do I feel as if I'm confessing to some horrible crime?"

She felt the tears she'd almost (but not quite) talked herself out of pressing close to the surface again.

"Because you're afraid of making a fool of yourself," he said. "You're not alone, Cobb. Most folks'd rather be hit by a bus than be made a fool of. 'Specially in love."

"If only I *knew* how he felt . . . then I could . . ." She shrugged, and felt her mouth form a small, crooked smile. "Well, then *you* wouldn't have to sit here listening to me make a fool of myself."

"You sure it's *him* holding back? Or could it be that it's you?" He tipped his head to one side, eyeing her with some amusement while he stroked the stem of his glass with his square, callused thumb. His crinkly hair, in the amber glow of the old-fashioned street lamp overhead, was the color of old pennies worn smooth by countless exchanges.

Annie, feeling his words hit home, looked down, staring into her empty glass—its rim a circle that seemed to grow wider, swimming up at her like the mouth of an approaching tunnel. She realized with a tiny ripple of unease that she was a bit drunk. God, was she now going to make an even bigger fool of herself?

"I think I'd better be getting back," she said. "I don't know about you, but getting up at five every morning means that by ten o'clock at night I'm ready to turn into a pumpkin."

He laughed. "Now that you mention it . . . yeah, you are looking a little orange around the gills."

Minutes later, recrossing the river on the Pont au Change, it struck Annie that in just a few weeks she'd be back in New York, and Emmett . . . well, who knew where he'd be? Maybe they would never see each other after that. She felt a pang, and quickly pushed the thought away. Right now, he was here, and she was grateful for him. For his friendship, for having so patiently listened to her carry on like a moonstruck teenager.

As they stopped to watch a barge decked in fairy lights glide under the bridge, Annie impulsively leaned over and kissed Emmett lightly on the lips.

Then, unexpectedly, Emmett was kissing her back. Not tentatively, or half-heartedly, but full and hard, bruising her almost, his mouth sharp and sweet with the anise taste of the Pernod. One arm circling her waist, holding her so tight she couldn't have gotten away if she'd wanted to, which somehow she didn't—*God, oh dear God, what am I getting myself into here?*—at the same time cupping the back of her neck, the tips of his fingers lightly pressing into the curve of her skull, as gently, as tenderly, as if he were cradling a newborn.

Annie felt a sharp tug low in her belly. The blood seemed to drain from her head; sparks of light danced on the insides of her eyelids. She felt heat rising in her, collecting in the hollow space where moments before her stomach had been. God . . . how could she be . . . how could it feel this good when it was Joe she wanted, not Emmett?

And Emmett, did he really want *her?* Or was there someone waiting for him back home . . . someone he hadn't told her about?

Emmett, drawing away, seemed to stagger a bit, and she wondered if maybe he was a little tipsy as well. And whether, if they'd been perfectly sober, this would have happened at all. She stared at him, his face inches from hers, his breath quick and warm against her cheek, and it suddenly occurred to her that probably she had wanted this, *needed* this, for a very long time. Was it reassurance she was looking for . . . the reassurance Joe wasn't giving her? Proof that she was lovable, desirable, even?

"Jesus," he muttered, staring at her and rubbing his jaw. "Where do we go from here?"

"Not my place." She gave a short, breathless laugh. "Madame Begbeder would throw us out," she said, feeling overtaken by a kind of reckless momentum. *What are you suggesting?*

"That kind of whittles it down, doesn't it?" He stepped back and grabbed her hand, squeezing it hard.

Before she could think it over, they were in a taxi, rocketing along the boulevard St-Germain on the way to the place Victor Hugo, where Emmett was subletting. Annie felt both exhilarated and oddly resigned . . . as if she'd climbed aboard a roller coaster and now had to see it through to the very end.

Then there was a massive wooden door with a button that automatically buzzed them into a courtyard, and then into a vestibule smelling of fresh laundry. Climbing the winding stairs, Emmett thumbed a button on the wall at each landing, and light flooded the stairs above. But by the time they reached the next landing, the light had gone off.

"Timers," he explained, knowing that the private home in which she rented a small room had none. "That way, no one can forget and leave them on. Smart, huh? It's only us ugly Americans who act like electricity and oil and gas are gonna be around forever, like the air we breathe."

How could he be so calm? With her legs wobbling, her heart thundering, she could barely climb the stairs. *I shouldn't be here. I should turn around right now . . . this very instant . . .*

But somehow her feet kept moving, and then they were past the tall, brass-handled door, and inside the narrow but high-ceilinged salon. The woman who owned the place would have smiled, Annie thought, to see Emmett, broad and rugged, clumping in his cowboy boots amid the plump, satin-covered sofas and spindly Empire chairs, the tiny round table covered in a fringed shawl and crowded with Sèvres figurines and silver-framed family photos.

But even with his limp, Emmett was surprisingly graceful as he moved about the room switching on lamps, not the least hindered by all this clutter. Watching him right a picture frame that had tilted to one side, she thought of the pigeon lady in the park, and how gentle he'd been when he helped the old woman up from the bench.

Still, she wondered, *What am I doing here? I don't love him.*

At the same time, she felt drawn to him, the tug in her belly when she kissed him on the bridge now a low throb of wanting. She let herself imagine how it would be—Emmett taking her clothes off, kissing her all over, his hands rough and hot against her skin. No, she didn't love him . . . but, dammit, she *wanted* him. She wanted him, now, at this moment—regardless of reason or possible repercussions—the way a hungry person needs to eat.

But could she?

Emmett, who seemed to sense her confusion, came to her and, with his arms loosely about her shoulders, kissed her forehead. When she pulled away, she saw that he was smiling, almost as if he found her amusing . . . possibly childish.

Annie felt embarrassed, annoyed even, at herself and at Emmett. "Emmett, I shouldn't have come. This is . . . crazy. I don't love you. And you don't love me."

"And you . . . you're not the kind of girl who'd go to bed with a man just for the fun of it, right?" He was mocking her now; she was almost sure of it.

"Not if I wanted us to stay friends afterwards."

"Is it *us* you're worried about, or this fellow of yours back home?"

"Joe." Like a shield, she held Joe's name out in front of her, letting it fill the silence that was broken only by the measured ticking of a clock somewhere. "No," she lied, "it has nothing do with Joe."

He shrugged and stepped back with a low, easy chuckle. "Hell, Cobb, you could walk right out of here, right this very minute, and I promise you there won't be a speck of hard feeling."

"Em . . ."

"On the other hand," he added soberly, placing a work-roughened fingertip under her chin, "if you stay, I can promise you something a lot better."

When he kissed her this time, Annie felt it flash through her like summer lightning. In the heat that followed, she thought, *Joe,* and felt a small, mean triumph. *I don't need him.*

Then Emmett was leading her into the bedroom. A massive headboard decorated with ormolu like the icing on a wedding cake seemed to dominate the tiny space. As if in a dream, Annie lay down on it, and let Emmett undress her. His callused fingers were rough . . . but at the same time, surprisingly tender and adept. No fumbling with buttons or hooks—he seemed to know exactly how to go about this, where to touch her. Kissing her lips, her temple, throat, and now—as he removed her bra—each of her breasts, causing her to shiver and goose bumps to break out. She'd been undressed before—by Steve, and by Craig Henry back in high school—but never had it been so arousing as this. Annie felt her heart racing, as if she were skimming close to the edge of some kind of illness.

Now, watching Emmett sit down on the bed and begin prying off his boots, she wondered how seeing his crippled foot would make her feel.

When she did—its purple, puckered flesh and oddly bent

shape—she felt a welling of tenderness. She touched it lightly. "Does it hurt?"

"Only when I'm walking in places I shouldn't," he said with a wry, cockeyed smile.

"Like now?"

He shrugged. "Yeah, okay, I'm a little scared, too. Mind if we leave the lights on?"

He drew a finger across her belly, tiny spurs of rough skin scratching her lightly. She shivered, and then he was bending down, his tongue warm against her skin, and then moving lower—*God, he shouldn't do this, no one ever has . . . but, oh, it feels so good*—the wiry ends of his hair, so soft, softer than she could ever have imagined, brushing the insides of her thighs. And now his tongue, quick, feather-light . . .

She was burning up. She would die of this heat. She would die of wanting him. *Please, oh please . . . I can't bear it. I'll go out of my mind.*

Then Emmett was getting up, taking off his shirt and trousers, not seeming impatient, though she could see he was aroused. *He's had a lot of practice at this.* She was surprised at the hair on his chest and down below, not red but dark brown. Muscles broad and thick as beams, a scattering of freckles across his belly. He looked as if he'd spent a lot of time outdoors, his forearms a shade darker than the rest of him. But what struck her most was how utterly unselfconscious he seemed, as if this were an everyday thing, their being naked together like this.

But when he lay down beside her, she could feel the tightness of him, of his wanting her; his whole body clenched, almost quivering.

He went on tasting her, teasing her, exploring even places she hadn't known could feel so exquisitely sensitive—the half moon of flesh under each breast, the backs of her knees, and between her fingers. She was hot, but she was shivering, too, wanting to draw her knees into her chest, protect herself from this agony of wanting. But Emmett now was slowly stroking her, soothing her, and she could feel herself opening to him, arching to take him into her. *Yes . . . oh yes . . .*

Then there was only his solid weight pressing down on her, into her. Over his shoulder, a pane of moonlight glimmered on the wall, and seemed to grow brighter, expanding until it appeared to encompass the whole wall, until she became part of the light, *inside* it, its white heat consuming her. . . .

"God!" Hardly aware of what she was doing, Annie bit into Emmett's shoulder. A sharp, briny taste, and then she heard him cry out, too, and push high up into her, several short, fierce thrusts.

Afterwards, she clung to him until the mingled sweat of their bodies began to dry. Emmett, his face buried in the hollow of her neck, murmured, "Annie."

Annie. Since the very first day at Girod's, he'd never called her anything but Cobb. Just now he'd called her Annie. What did it mean? What did he want from her?

Annie shivered, feeling out of control, as if the roller coaster she'd been on, instead of stopping, had dropped off the edge of the world. And what about Joe? Why, if she owed him nothing, did she feel as if she'd betrayed him?

Now it was her turn to murmur, "God, Em, where *now?* Where do we go from here?"

Stroking her hair, and her neck where it still burned from the roughness of his stubbled jaw, he said gently, "We don't have to go anywhere, Annie. We're already there."

CHAPTER 15

Dolly felt the plane begin to bank. Looking down, she caught her first glimpse of the island. So green! No roads or buildings that she could see . . . as if not a soul lived there. Not at all like Bermuda, where Dale had taken her for their honeymoon. She remembered Bermuda as a sort of tropical English countryside, neat drystone walls, manicured golf courses, clipped lawns, and trimmed hedges of colorful hibiscus. Nowhere near as lush and primeval-looking as this.

She wondered if the Garden of Eden had been anything like Grenada. Stretching in her seat, she thought of Henri—*four whole days in paradise!*—and felt a languid bliss seep through her. Then she remembered this could well be their last time together, and felt a hollow thump inside her, as if the plane had suddenly dropped several thousand feet.

I have to tell him. No more. I can't do this anymore—sneaking around behind his wife's back, seeing him only five or six weeks out of the year. I love him too much.

Dolly shut out the awful prospect of breaking the news to Henri. Instead, she imagined his surprise when she showed up at the plantation. How delighted he'd be. And, okay, maybe a little bit annoyed with her, too. Hadn't he warned her not to come? Dolly replayed their phone conversation last week, Henri telling her he had to fly to Grenada to sort things out at the plantation. She had jumped at the chance of having a long weekend in the tropics, just the two of them. But Henri, though she could tell he was sorely tempted, had been adamant in his refusal. The Grenadian government was in chaos, and there were leftist gangs stirring up trouble. It might be dangerous.

Physical danger? No, that wasn't why Dolly's heart was racing now, or why her hands felt cold as ice. She didn't give a hoot about

Communists or gangs . . . what was scaring her was the prospect of losing Henri. How could she? How could she bear to be without him?

But how could she *not* tell him? How could they go on this way, rattling along like a three-wheeled cart?

Dolly heard something snap, and looked down at the empty plastic glass in her hand. She'd squeezed it so hard, it had cracked apart. Cold droplets from the melting ice cubes inside dribbled onto her lap, soaking into her lemon-colored skirt.

You don't have to tell him right away, she reminded herself, clinging to the thought of the blissful days that lay ahead and concentrating on the green paradise looming below her.

Grenada . . . an island . . . another world . . . where they could be together without Girod's, or her nieces, or Francine, or Henri's children. A safe place, maybe a magical one, where for a few days they could forget everyone else in the world. And where she could postpone, for just a little while longer, the terrible pronouncement that lay ahead.

She glanced at her watch. Four after two. They'd be landing in minutes. It felt like a hundred years since she'd last seen him. Three and a half months since the Montreal Confectioners' Exposition, and then it had been only one night—a few hours snatched between visiting booths, meeting with customers and prospective buyers, discussing new products.

Over the phone at the shop, it was always the same with him: talk about which items were selling best, currency fluctuations, new hotel contracts, the merits and drawbacks of this or that shipper . . . never about how much they missed each other. Even when he called her at home, usually late at night, she felt like she was doing some elaborate old-time minuet, telling him how much she missed him, loved him, but dancing around the thing that was really eating at her: that after eight years Henri still wasn't any closer to getting a divorce than he had been in the beginning . . .

. . . and *she* certainly wasn't getting any younger.

As the plane circled in to land, Dolly spotted buildings, roads, runways, and then the corrugated roofs of shanties, a massive pile of rubbish spewing down a hillside. Welcome to paradise, she thought ruefully.

Minutes after a bumpy landing, she stepped down onto the

tarmac in a pouring rain. Then she was inside the stuffy Quonset shed that served as a terminal, soaked to the skin, showing her passport to a scrawny black official who scrutinized it suspiciously for what seemed like an hour before finally stamping it. Inside the sleepy terminal, she rounded up a porter, who collected her luggage and trundled it out to the curb, where several taxis were parked. She chose the one with the fewest dents.

"L'Anse aux Epines," she told the driver, hoping she'd gotten the pronunciation right. "Spice Cove."

Then they were splashing off into the driving rain to her hotel, careening over roads so narrow and rutted Dolly was certain they'd be catapulted into a ditch. Wiping a circle in the condensation fogging her window, she glimpsed dense foliage, palm trees like telephone poles topped with green petticoats, pink and yellow stucco houses alongside outhouse-sized shanties. And dotted here and there, thatched-roof roadside lean-tos heaped with unhulled coconuts and sheaves of green bananas, where dark-skinned vendors huddled, waiting for the rain to let up.

Soon she'd be with Henri. In an hour, Bartholomew, Henri's overseer, was picking her up at the hotel. She'd called ahead, and told him that she planned on surprising Henri, but she didn't want to risk getting lost in the jungle trying to find her way to the plantation. Bartholomew had agreed to take her there, and also to keep her secret.

An hour, she thought. Enough time to get out of these wet clothes, take a cool shower, make herself beautiful for Henri.

Dolly could feel her heart pounding. How was it that after all these years, and all the thousands of miles that had separated them, just the thought of Henri made her giddy?

And if she felt this excited now, before she'd even seen him, then how on God's green earth was she going to have the strength to look Henri in the eye and tell him it was over?

Dolly felt the Jeep lurch to a stop. Prying her fingers away from her eyes, which she'd kept covered to avoid having to see the frightening mountainous hairpin turns, she saw that they were stopped on the crest of a steep ridge. Below, the junglelike growth gave way to acres of cleared land, in which row after row of banana trees stretched on, seemingly forever.

"Here we be, Miss." The grandfatherly Grenadian overseer who'd driven her here sounded cheerful and relaxed, as if barrelling willy-nilly up a narrow, twisty road bumpy as a washboard, with trucks and minivans hurtling at you from the opposite direction, was not a bit scarier than a ride on a merry-go-round.

She turned her gaze back to the banana trees, slipping on her sunglasses—great owlish lenses set in a tortoiseshell frame studded with rhinestones—to shade her eyes against the raindrop-reflected dazzle of the sun that had switched on like a klieg light almost the moment the rain ended.

She could see wisps of steam rising from the muddy red soil. The air smelled wonderfully fragrant—like a cup of hot mulled cider. It was the spices they grew, Old Bartholomew had told her. In every village they'd passed, wherever they braked for dogs or chickens or goats, there was an old woman or a gaggle of youngsters pressing up against the Jeep, eager to sell them spices—brown hands thrusting at them homemade baskets filled with bags of shiny brown nutmeg, bay leaves, orange flowerets of dried mace, cinnamon sticks, cloves, balls of pressed cocoa.

But here she could see only bananas.

"Where are the cacao trees?" She pronounced it "ka-*cow*," the way Henri had taught her.

Bartholomew grinned, his seamed black face rearranging itself into new patterns of fissures and folds. White-haired, thin and crinkled as a hairpin, wearing saggy shorts and a faded yellow shirt-jac that hung on him like a pup tent, he looked almost as old as the jungle itself. A real crackerjack, though. Henri had once told her that without Bartholomew, there would *be* no plantation. The old overseer supposedly knew every gully and track of this jungle; he could get shipments through when the main road was impassable, and when workers quit or didn't show up, Bartholomew seemed to have endless cousins, nephews, and grandsons to fill in. Coming here, in this battered Willys, Bartholomew had told her proudly that he'd outlived five wives, and had eighteen children and forty-two grandchildren.

Snow on the roof maybe, but still plenty of coal in the furnace, she thought.

"Bananas, dey shade de cacao trees," he explained with a sage nod.

Dolly looked again, and there, yes, she could see them, machetes flashing among the green, the winking of sun on steel. This was the season for harvesting the pods, Henri had told her.

Henri. So close now!

Dolly, climbing from the Jeep to get a better look, felt her knees give a little. Her stomach pitched queerly, and speckles of gray swam before her eyes. The heat felt thick as foam, dense, clinging to her, making her polka-dot cotton sundress drag about her calves, heavy and damp as laundry hung out to dry. The air here smelled of freshly turned earth and rotting leaves. She adjusted the brim of her hat, a navy straw cartwheel with a wide polka-dot ribbon that hung down to tickle her shoulder blades. The heat, though oppressive, was also having a pleasurable effect on her—she felt heavy and swollen with desire, eager to be alone with Henri.

Closing her eyes against the brightness that stung them even through her sunglasses, she thought again, *Lord, how can I ever give him up?*

Bartholomew touched her arm. "Okay now, Miss? We go down."

And then she was hoisting herself back into the Jeep, and they were rattling along a muddy, rutted track that veered off from the main road and down through a tangle of weeds and vines that bordered the neat rows of banana trees. A lone breadfruit tree—she recognized it from one Bartholomew had pointed out earlier—marked the spot where the road ended and a smaller footpath led off into the rows of cacaos and bananas just beyond. A perfumy fragrance rose from the hacked-away brush surrounding it.

"De flower, she smell sweet." Bartholomew braked to a stop, pointing a bony finger at a daub of brightness amid the flattened greenery.

"I don't think I've ever smelled anything so pretty," Dolly said. "What's it called?"

"Jump-up-and-kiss-me." The old man grinned slyly, his gold-crowned teeth twinkling in the sun.

Dolly flushed, then winked to let him him know she appreciated his keeping her visit a secret.

Then she saw that Bartholomew was pointing down at her feet, his wizened teak-brown face furrowed with disapproval. Shaking his head, struggling not to smile. Of course! Her shoes. All wrong. She stared down at her flimsy canvas espadrilles, their rope soles already caked with mud. Why in heaven's name hadn't she worn something more practical?

Stepping out of the Willys, she could feel the mud sucking at her feet. Trying to follow Bartholomew as he headed down the footpath, she almost slipped, and quickly caught herself before she fell and made an even bigger fool of herself.

The grooved path ended, panning into flat cultivated rows of banana trees, their broad fringed leaves rising in glossy plumes from squat, serrated trunks, clusters of green bananas suspended from their branches like chandeliers. Shaded from the sun's withering heat by the banana trees, the cacaos were set in red dirt rows; some were no taller than she was, others twice or three times the height of a man. They looked unexceptional, except for the purplish, football-sized pods sprouting from their branches and even directly from their trunks.

Dolly stopped to watch one of the workers, a shirtless islander in shorts and thongs, hacking at the pods he could reach with his machete, and piling them into a hand cart at his side.

Pointing at a pod, she asked, "Do the beans come out of that?"

In reply, Bartholomew went over, picked up one from the bucket, and in rapid patois, directed the worker to cut it open with his machete. He turned to Dolly, holding out the split halves, one in each hand. Around each pulpy, whitish center was a ring of pale seeds. A flowery fragrance rose from it. The old man scooped a seed out with his finger, and held it up for her to see.

"Take many, many seeds to make little bit chocolate," he said, dropping the pod back into the bucket. "Wait. I show you."

He led the way along a seemingly endless furrow, sprinkled with workers harvesting pods, some with machetes, others using long, blade-topped wooden poles to reach the highest branches. There was the rustle of leaves, the twinkle of steel amid the lush, dripping green. Voices calling to one another in Grenadian patois —a combination, she'd been told, of English, French, and some African languages—blending in a tatterdemalion chorus.

While they walked, Bartholomew explained in his quaintly truncated English that each tree produced only about five pounds of chocolate a year. And these, she knew, were the *criollo* variety—originally from Venezuela—which produced a lower yield than the hardier *alemondo*. But the quality was better, and that was one of the reasons Girod's chocolate was world-renowned.

Up ahead, she caught sight of the drying and fermenting sheds—long barnlike buildings made of aluminum siding with corrugated plastic roofs, set on a slight rise on the other side of a rickety wooden bridge built across an irrigation ditch. Henri would be in one of the sheds, Bartholomew had told her.

Dolly felt the sting of tears, and she adjusted her sunglasses, glad that Henri's first glimpse of her wouldn't be a pair of swollen red eyes.

She didn't even know why she was crying. It wasn't as if her breaking up with Henri would end something that wasn't already pretty much over—at least as far as any hope of him marrying her went.

And not that she was without prospects. There was Reese Hathaway, a sweet, funny man—a Columbia librarian, of all things—whom she'd been going out with on a purely friendly basis—dinners, and sometimes he just happened to have an extra ticket to a concert or a play. And she sensed that if she were to give him even the slightest encouragement, he'd be over the moon.

And Curt Prager, the balding attorney she often ran into in her building's elevator, who was always inviting her up to his place for a drink. And never one bit shy about making his intentions known. The memory of her last encounter with him caused her to smile. She'd been wearing a cream-colored angora sweater, and kissing her, he'd gotten little white hairs all over the jacket of his tailor-made charcoal suit.

The trouble was, neither one—nor anyone else—made her feel the way Henri did. And pretty soon, she wouldn't have him.

How could she not cry?

Dolly followed the old man across the narrow plank bridge, the sun beating down once more on her shoulders. A hundred yards or so, and she would be there. Her gaze fixed on the nearest shed, about the size of the merry-go-round pavilion in Central Park, where one long-ago morning she'd talked Henri into riding on the painted horses. Because it was so early, they had been the only ones, their laughter ringing through the deserted pavilion. Why, the ticket taker must have thought they were a couple of loonies!

Dolly remembered the joy she'd felt, the cool kiss of the brass ring against her fingertips as it slipped from her grasp, again and again, and the sight of Henri in front of her, like a Bourbon knight astride his gilded charger, his curly graying head thrown back in boisterous delight.

But now she found herself thinking, *I didn't catch the brass ring that day. Not once. Not all the times I tried.*

"He maybe inside," Bartholomew spoke, jolting her back to the present. The old man stepped back to let her in first through the wide entrance.

Inside, as her eyes struggled to adjust to the darkness, she was struck mainly by the smell. A high, cloyingly sweet smell. Bushels of pods were stacked near the entrance, and along the walls. Workers, local men and women, stood before long trestle tables, hacking open pods with long knives, scooping out the pulp with their hands, and deftly picking out the seeds, which were piled in sticky clumps atop banana leaves. Next, Bartholomew explained, the seeds would be placed in shallow wooden trays, which were covered with burlap and left to ferment for a week or so, until they turned brown. After that, they were dried, sorted, and placed in hundred-pound burlap sacks, which were then shipped off to Marseilles.

Last year's harvest had been a good one, he told her proudly, more than twenty tons. This year's would be smaller, due to a rainy spell that had hurt some of the trees, and damage caused by "bad men," which came out sounding like "bad mons." The old man pointed at the far end of the shed, where the metal siding was newer and shinier, and black soot grimed the wooden ceiling rafters.

"Them boys," he said angrily. "They crazy bad. Tink dey gonna fix de world by settin' dis place on fire. We los' one lotta of cacao."

Dolly's gaze swept the shed, but no Henri. Her heart lurched a little, then steadied. Surely he would be in the one next door.

Bartholomew introduced her to a gangly young man, seventeen or so, all spindles and shanks, his skin a soft milky brown. "My son, he name Desmond," he said proudly, though it didn't seem possible that anyone as old as he was could have a teenaged son. Still, all those wives.

"Pleased to meetcha," Dolly said.

But the boy hung back, cupping a hand over his mouth as he smiled. She saw in an instant why he was embarrassed—he was missing several front teeth. What a shame. With some dental work, and a little meat on his bones, he'd be right handsome.

When they were outside again, she said to Bartholomew, "Nice-looking kid. But he should see a dentist." She knew that might sound rude, but she wanted to see what Bartholomew's reaction would be.

The old man shrugged, patting the pockets of his baggy shorts.

Just what she'd thought. Well, heck, how much could a dentist cost down here? And even if it meant offending the old man . . . well, she'd been wondering about how to tip him without making him uncomfortable . . . but this seemed like a better idea, and it just might do some real good.

She reached into her straw bag, and fished out one of her business cards. "Look, you may think I'm being awful pushy, and you can say no, if you like. But here's my address. You take that boy to a good dentist, and just send me the bill. I'll take care of it. You've been real nice to me, and I'd like to return the favor."

Bartholomew just grinned, and tucked the card into the front pocket of his shirt-jac. Good, he wasn't going to get all prickly. For him, it was a wonderful gift. For her, no more than a large tip.

"Bartholomew!" a deep, French-accented voice boomed from somewhere behind Dolly. "What has been taking you so long a time? And who is this person you have brought back with you?"

She knew that voice. Her heart leaped. Henri!

Dolly whirled, and a gust of wind scooped her hat from her head and carried it off. She felt her hair, which had been tucked up inside, spill down over her shoulders. She was momentarily blinded by the sun backfiring off the corrugated aluminum siding. Through the glare, she could make out a sturdy figure striding toward her, limned in a red corona, as if he were walking through fire. Somehow, she found she couldn't move. Her feet were glued to the earth.

She blinked, and suddenly he was there. Henri. Standing before her, a shocked expression on his face. High color rode up his cheekbones, already ruddy with tan. His silver mustache, she saw, was bushier than when she'd last seen him. He wore khaki trousers, and a white short-sleeved shirt open at the collar. As he lifted one arm to shade his eyes, she could see the veins that marbled the paler slab of muscle along the underside of his bicep.

"Henri," she whispered, finding her voice.

He didn't respond. His eyes fixed on her as if he didn't quite believe it *was* her, not flickering, not creasing with happiness. His face still as stone.

He's angry that I came.

Was he just being overprotective, or did he somehow sense the terrible thing she had to tell him?

At the thought of losing Henri, Dolly felt a shaft of pain in her chest. Her heart spun, down and down, like a wingshot bird.

Then, while old Bartholomew looked on in amusement, while Dolly stood dying in the West Indian sun, Henri stepped forward with a startled cry, and took her firmly in his arms, burying his face in the hair that tumbled loosely about her shoulders, and murmuring her name, over and over, as if by saying it he might somehow hang onto her forever.

"Henri, we've got to talk."

Dolly moved away from Henri in the big bed facing the sunlit terrace of her hotel cottage in L'Anse aux Epines. Through the sliding glass door that overlooked a sloping green hillside, she could see splashes of crimson hibiscus and pink oleander, and the deeper greens of calabash and lemon trees. Farther down, past the pool with its palm-thatched cabana, a crescent of freshly raked white sand gleamed against clear sparkling water. An early swimmer was stroking away from the dock, etching a thin trail of froth.

The scent of lemon blossoms floated in on a gust from the sea. The only sound was the soft whirring of the ceiling fan overhead, cooling her naked body as she lay beside Henri, the bedsheet tangled about her ankles. But instead of feeling peaceful, Dolly's stomach was in knots. The past seventy-eight hours had been paradise, she thought, but in just a little while she'd be leaving.

She *had* to tell him.

"Would you prefer that we talk or that I make love to you once more?" Henri teased.

Dolly closed her eyes, and felt hot tears squeeze out from under her eyelids. "I mean it, Henri. I . . ."

But Henri, no doubt thinking she was just getting herself all worked up over the two- or three-month separation that lay ahead, silenced her with a kiss, the ends of his mustache tickling her upper lip, his mouth soft and tasting faintly of rum. The memory of last night swooped up from her belly in a rush. All those punches they'd drunk . . . Lord, what had been in them besides rum? Some kind of aphrodisiac—crushed dragonfly wings and tiger's teeth? She'd lost track of how many times they'd made love . . . two, three, five? Like dreams, but hot, sweaty, clutching, one tumbling into the next, from which only a little while ago she had awakened in a bloom of sweetly aching tenderness.

Now, he wanted her again, and her own not exactly youthful body astonished her. She couldn't remember ever having so limitless an appetite. A drowsy heat fanned through her lower belly, and she became acutely aware of the slippery swollenness between her thighs.

Yesterday, she'd tried to tell him, again and again, and each time he'd kiss her, and she'd be lost. Now she'd run out of time . . . and excuses.

A band of pain tightened about her chest, and she felt as if the breeze drifting in had turned suddenly chilly. She would never again lie next to Henri like this. Never make love to him again. And who would love her?

Her nieces?

She thought of letters Annie had written from Paris, bubbling over with enthusiasm and warmth. But was Dolly kidding herself about Annie the way she had for so many years about Henri? Lord knew she loved that girl. She'd cut off a finger for her. But Annie, she'd never really let down her guard, not all the way. She wasn't as distant as she once had been but she still held back a little when Dolly tried to get too near. Behind the smiles and hugs, there was an unspoken wariness.

And Laurel, such a dear, but now that she was away at school and so wrapped up in her art, Dolly hardly ever got to see her anymore.

Dolly had so wanted to make them into her daughters. But they were, and they would always be, Eve's girls. A dart of jealousy nicked at her heart.

The story of my life, she thought. Second place. With Henri, too. He'd never divorce Francine. Never leave his children, though Jean-

Paul was off on his own, and Gabrielle married with a baby on the way.

And it wasn't just Henri. *She* had changed . . . she was no longer the young, insecure widow who had wandered into his basement kitchen that long-ago day in Paris. Now she had a family of sorts, a business. She was on the board of the New York Film Society, as well as those of two corporations. She was a person of substance, a woman people looked up to, and she'd realized that what she had with Henri was far from being enough. And her caring for him was probably keeping her from finding a man with whom she *could* share everything.

So it had come down to this—a last moment stolen from the real lives they led, where they each belonged. A long and lovely good-bye, which was now almost at an end.

Dolly felt a hollowness inside—could a heart be broken so many times that finally there's nothing left?

"I can't." Drawing away from him as he tried to snuggle against her, she sat up. Looking down at his dear face, gazing up at her with veiled amusement from his pillow, she almost couldn't get the words out, but then she was telling him, "Henri, there's something I've been meaning to say, and it's got to be said."

"What is that, *ma poupée?*" He rolled onto his side, supporting himself on one elbow, his smile so sunny and innocent she nearly lost her nerve.

Just come right out with it.

"You're never going to divorce Francine." It was a declaration, but she needed an answer.

Henri's gray eyes clouded, but he did not look away—he would never lie to her, or be evasive. She could count on that, at least.

No, he seemed to consider her statement, to ponder it even, his face seeming to age before her eyes, to sag with jowls and wrinkles that hadn't been there minutes before.

"It is not so simple as a divorce," he told her. "If I leave, I lose everything, the work of my life. The business is the property of Augustin, though, of course, I direct it. He has the power . . . the right according to the law . . . to take . . ." He broke off, rubbing his face with his fingertips. When he looked at her, his gray eyes were bright. "But, you see, it's not the rights of the law Girod is concerned with but the right *moral.* I know he respects me, even loves me. But his moral obligation—and Augustin takes such things seriously, believe me—is to concern himself first with his daughter."

She had heard all this before . . . but she needed to hear it again. So she could be sure there was no hope, that she was doing the right thing.

If only she didn't ache for him so! But how could she not cherish such a man? His way of remembering each little anniversary . . . roses for the day they met, and for the April night they first made love, a silk nightgown or a pair of lacy panties. And how in the morning he always got up before her, bringing her coffee in bed, milk and no sugar, just the way she liked it. Yes, she adored him, she loved him. More than any man . . . even Dale.

Seized with a new, desperate longing, she blurted, "We could start over, couldn't we? Our own business! We'd keep the shop on Madison, only change the name. We'd find another supplier. Or make the chocolates ourselves. We'd—"

Henri was shaking his head, slowly, sadly.

"Dolly, the house of Girod is my life. And even if I could find the heart to give it up, how would we live? To build a business like Girod's, that costs money, lots of money. And Francine is exact. If I go, I am fortunate if I have the clothes on my back. Dolly, my angel, *think*. Think what it is you love about me." He managed a wan smile. "Without my independence, my pride, I would not be this man who you love."

But, dammit, what about *her* pride? Didn't that count for something, too?

Once before, out of despair, she had wavered making a choice . . . and ended up killing her sister and killing a part of herself. No, this time she would do the right thing. . . .

"I *do* love you, and in a funny way I even understand," she told him, nearly choking on her words. "But, Henri, I . . . I just can't go on like this. It's . . . killing me."

Henri got up out of bed and reached for his robe, which was draped over the rattan footboard. *He wants to run away from what's coming, but he can't, not this time.* Dolly shivered, sitting bolt upright, holding her pillow tight to her chest, as if it were a life raft without which she might just float away.

"If you would consider again moving to Paris . . ." he began.

She shook her head, her tears now spilling down her cheeks. "It wouldn't work, and you know it. Even if I saw more of you, I'd keep on wanting something you could never give me. Don't you see, Henri? If I can't marry you, or at least live with you . . . then I . . . I'm better off without you."

Henri, standing before her in his terry robe, raking a hand through his tousled silver hair, his eyes flat with disbelief, appeared too stunned to argue. He just stared at her, swaying slightly on his feet, making her think of a boxer who had just been given a knockout blow that hasn't quite caught up with him.

"You have my love," he said, his voice thin and raw-sounding.

"Yeah, I know . . . and that's what's killing me."

"Dolly, I realize I have not been able to give you what we both wish for, but is it not possible to find some way to—"

She cut him off with a firm shake of her head. "No. I'd feel like . . . well, you ever see somebody with an old dog just barely alive that they can't bear to have put down?"

"I don't see what—"

"It'd be kinder, don't you see? A whole lot kinder just to put the poor creature out of its misery. But people don't think that way, do they? They're always figuring what's best is to keep going no matter what. But that's not always true. Sometimes it's better to have nothing than even a little piece of something you love that's hurtin'."

"I cannot imagine how I could ever love any other woman as I love you."

Dolly closed her eyes, and let his words seep in slowly, slowly, so she could savor them. She wanted to remember them, so she could replay them again and again in the lonely days to come.

And it wasn't Dolly Drake he loved, but Doris Burdock—the woman underneath the platinum hair and bangles. The woman who in her heart was still a little girl from Clemscott, sitting on a dusty stoop, poring over the Sears catalogue . . . dreaming of the fine house she would someday own, and the wonderful, handsome man who would live in it with her.

Only Henri, she reminded herself, was not going to share this with her. She remembered when she was a kid, entering one of those contests where you copy a cartoon off the back of a matchbook. And then, six weeks later, she got a letter saying she'd won this art scholarship. She'd been so excited, she nearly jumped out of her shoes. Running around telling everyone, "I won! I won!" And then her stepmother had spoiled it.

Dolly could still see her, clearly etched against the sun streaming in the kitchen window. Mama-Jo was standing by the sink, ironing, her hair done up in pink curlers, wearing a flowered smock with rickrack sewn around the neck and pockets. The Philco on top of the icebox was lit up, and she was humming along with Maybelle Carter singing, "May the Circle Be Unbroken." Tomorrow was the church's annual jumble sale, and she wanted to get over there tonight so she could help Preacher Daggett set up. And then she'd turned her gimlet eye on Dolly, hopping about in glee, and said with a little smirk, "Oh, everybody knows that's a lot of hooey. They'd give one of those so-called scholarships to a one-legged chicken if they thought the silly thing would put up good money for the rest of the tuition."

And now, once again, Dolly felt as if she were losing something precious that it turned out she'd never really had in the first place.

But then she thought, *It's not over yet. Not until I step on that plane.*

"No more talking," she told him. "I'm tired of talking. Come on over here instead." Smiling through her tears, her heart aching, she held out her arms to him. "My plane isn't for another three hours, and I've got this whole bed just goin' to waste."

Annie looked around Dolly's living room, filled with party guests. Nothing much had changed in the months she'd been away. The white leather sofa that had always reminded her of a giant squashed marshmallow faced the fireplace just as it always had. Behind it, forming an L-shaped wedge alongside the entrance to the dining room, the wet bar with its buttoned-down leather base, a relic of the early sixties, made her smile—she could imagine Rock Hudson in a tuxedo leaning an elbow against the lacquered surface, sipping a martini, dry, with an olive. Even the bent coat hanger wedded to a lump of concrete atop the stereo cabinet—the ugliest so-called sculpture she'd ever seen—made her feel nostalgic.

But something has changed. I have.

She felt the way she once had revisiting her old elementary school after she'd graduated. Part of her had belonged, and part of her had been a stranger. Had it been only three and a half months? Looking at Dolly, elegant in a low-cut ruby velvet caftan studded with tiny rhinestones, darting and swooping among her guests like some exotic parrot, Annie felt as if she were watching it all through a window.

She looked about, peering at the faces eddying around her, searching for just one, the only one who would make her feel as if she had truly come home.

Joe.

Where was he? Yesterday, by the time she arrived home, she'd been too exhausted to see anyone until she'd had some sleep. Then late this afternoon, she'd been jolted out of a dream by Dolly telephoning to say that her driver would be picking her up in exactly one hour, and she was to put on her sexiest dress. Her aunt, it seemed, was making her a little homecoming party—the last thing

Annie needed or wanted, but with everything already all arranged, how could she refuse? She owed Dolly so much.

And how on earth could Dolly have been expected to know it was Joe she wanted, not all these people—some of whom she didn't even recognize? She longed to be off with him somewhere quiet, just the two of them, where she could . . .

One step at a time, she cautioned herself. What if he wasn't eager to share her dream? Or what if he'd taken up with someone while she was away?

She felt a stab of jealousy, then thought of Emmett. A dormant warmth stirred to life low in her abdomen, below the lacy hem of her ivory satin camisole, a gift from him. *Who am I to talk?*

The difference was . . . well, she didn't *love* Emmett . . . at least not the way she loved Joe, with all her heart and soul.

Annie glanced at her watch. Almost nine-thirty. Dammit, where *was* he? If one more person asked how she'd liked Paris, she'd scream. The doorbell announcing each new cluster of guests had stopped chiming a while ago. And the prettily garnished platters of shrimp toast, crab cakes, and stuffed mushrooms that two tuxedoed waiters were passing about the crowded living room had grown sparse.

Annie caught a glimmery reflection of herself in the huge window that looked over Madison and Fifth and then Central Park. Had she overdone it with this dress? What would Joe think?

Not her style, really, but it was chic, *très Parisienne*—this black crepe sheath that skimmed her thighs well above the knee, adorned only by a loop of faux opera-length pearls knotted just below her plunging neckline. She'd worn this on her last night in Paris with Emmett. Remembering the obscenely expensive dinner at Taillevent he had insisted on, the *grand cru* wine they'd drunk too much of, and afterwards, going back to Emmett's apartment. . . . God, had she really *done* that thing with the ice cube? Emmett had showed her how, but she had gone along with it—even now, she could feel the ice cube numbing her fingers, the fierce spasm that jerked through Emmett as she pressed it into the seam of flesh below his scrotum, just as he was about to come. . . .

Annie, suddenly aware that she had begun to tremble, and that her face was on fire, quickly slammed her mind shut against the memory.

Emmett. He'd made her feel things, do things . . . things she'd never even known existed. Again, and again, he'd pushed her to the edge of losing control . . . and that had excited her, and frightened her, too. Mornings, drifting up from sleep, feeling bruised by and half ashamed of the things they'd done the night before, half terrified of the things they still *hadn't* done, she would nevertheless find herself stealing over to him, wrapping herself around him, needing to feel him *in* her.

But would she ever see him again? He'd talked about maybe coming to New York, but he didn't say when. And anyway, what difference would it make if he did come? Whatever they'd had in Paris wouldn't, *couldn't*, be a part of her life here in New York. Still, at the thought that she might not see him, Annie felt a pang of regret . . . along with a childish desire to relive the wickedly delicious sensations he'd introduced her to.

Okay, so you had great sex with Emmett. That doesn't take anything away from how you feel about Joe.

Pushing Emmett out of her mind, Annie crossed the room toward the bar. She could feel the faint whispering of her smoke-colored silk stockings—real ones, from Aux Trois Quartiers. Would Joe even recognize her at first? She'd gotten her hair cut, too, really short—Dolly had said she looked like Audrey Hepburn in *Sabrina*. And to complete her new look, she had bought a pair of these huge dangly earrings, intricately fashioned silver wire and glass beads, from a street vendor on the rue des Saints-Pères. But now, swinging from her ears, they felt as conspicuous as chandeliers. *He'll look at me and he'll wonder if I'm the same person. He—*

Annie was distracted by a bray of laughter. She glanced to her left and saw a woman who clearly was tipsy over sharing a joke over by the piano with Mike Dreiser, the buyer for the Pierre. He was a stout man with a gray mustache, who couldn't keep his eyes off Dolly, now perched on the glass coffee table a few feet from him, holding court with the handful of men seated on the couch. At the keyboard, the Bobby Short soundalike Dolly had hired was improvising some kind of jazz version of the Stones' hit "Ruby Tuesday."

Enough mooning, Annie told herself. Who should she go and talk to? That blade-thin woman in a cashmere dress the shade of clotted cream, wasn't that Bitsy Adler, who'd played in *Dames in Chains* with Dolly? She was chatting it up with a potbellied, droopy-

eyed man who looked vaguely familiar. Then she remembered—
Bill, the drunken Santa Claus from Macy's. Thanks to Dolly, he now
worked here in her building as a doorman. Certainly, no one could
ever accuse Dolly of snobbery. But Annie didn't feel up to making
small talk.

Threading her way through the cluster of people at the bar
(who *were* they all, anyway?), Annie accepted the dripping glass of
champagne the barman thrust at her. Then she spotted Laurel, at
the far end of the bar, sipping what also looked like champagne.
Laurel looked gloomy, and Annie felt a dart of unease. At the JFK
arrivals terminal, her sister had seemed so happy to see her, but in
the car driving back, she'd sort of clammed up.

Something's wrong with Laurey. She'd gotten so thin! Annie had
noticed it right away, but until now it hadn't fully sunk in. Her
thinness had a feverish brightness to it that bothered Annie, yet in
some uncanny way it seemed to make her more beautiful. With no
makeup or jewelry, wearing a simple, peach-colored halter dress
she'd probably made herself, and a silk orchid in her hair, she out-
shone every woman in this room.

There was only one other time she'd seen such high color in
Laurel, such sparkle—when she was six, and had had pneumonia.
Annie remembered, too, that Laurel hadn't wanted any breakfast this
morning.

Probably just a touch of flu, she told herself.

She hiked herself onto the bar stool beside her sister. "What's
up, Doc? You look a little down. I guess this isn't your kind of party.
No Grateful Dead . . . no black lights . . . no body paints."

Laurel shrugged, smiling a little to show that she knew Annie
was just teasing. "I guess I'm in the wrong place then."

"*Entre nous,*" Annie confided, "it's not my scene, either."

"Hey, you're the guest of honor."

"Listen, I'm sure Dolly meant well. She usually does. It *was*
sweet of her. But . . ."

"But," Laurel echoed.

"Remember the white stretch limousine she rented for your
junior prom?"

Laurel winced. "*Red* seats. The color of red licorice. I almost
died of embarrassment. And a *bar*. On the way to the restaurant,

Rick just sat there staring out the window like he had to go to the bathroom and couldn't wait. It was *awful*. If Joe hadn't . . ."

"Yeah, I remember," Annie finished with a laugh. "He showed up just in time to rescue you with his beat-up old Ford." She'd heard this story so many times she felt as if she'd been there—Laurel coming out of the restaurant and finding Joe, who, with a conspiratorial grin, had tossed Rick his car keys and then climbed into the limo idling at the curb. Hours later, Laurel had come back from the prom, Annie remembered, with roses in her cheeks and a sparkle in her eyes that she suspected had had very little to do with Rick Warner. "Hey, have you seen much of Joe this summer?" She tried to sound casual, but it came out sounding somehow false, pitched too high.

She wasn't prepared, either, for Laurel's reaction. Her sister flushed, and her eyes slid away. She put her drink down and began chasing bubbles with her index finger.

Panic crept into Annie's heart. Was Joe seeing someone? That would explain why Laurel seemed upset, wouldn't it? God, yes— *she's jealous.*

How stupid of her ever to have kidded herself into thinking that what Laurel felt for Joe was just some silly girlish crush. When had Laurel ever acted silly or giggly over a boy? In grade school, when all her friends were mooning over Paul McCartney and Mick Jagger, she had been this solemn-eyed woman in a little girl's body, more interested in Rivka's babies than in rock stars.

Still waters run deep—the phrase could have been coined just for Laurel.

"Joe?" Laurel muttered. "Not much. My job kept me pretty busy." Licking a drop of champagne from her finger, she managed a tiny smile. "Though no one ever told me that interning in the creative department of an ad agency means mostly sharpening pencils, emptying wastebaskets, and fetching people coffee."

"I guess Joe must be pretty busy too . . . with the restaurant, I mean."

"I guess so."

Annie waited for her to elaborate, but Laurel seemed far away somewhere, off in her own world.

"You wouldn't happen to know if . . ."

. . . he's been seeing anyone, would you? Come on, she couldn't say that. What would it sound like? Besides, Joe had never kept the women he'd dated a secret; if he was seeing someone, he'd tell her himself.

". . . he's still planning on showing up tonight?" she finished weakly. He'd told Dolly he was coming, but something—some crisis at the restaurant—could have cropped up at the last minute.

"I don't know." She looked up at Annie, tossing back the hair that had slid down over her cheek. Her eyes glittered against the fevered pinkness of her face. "I haven't talked to him in a while."

Annie shrugged. "I guess he must've gotten stuck."

"Sure. Probably."

Out of the corner of her eye, Annie caught sight of a familiar face. Gloria De Witt, Dolly's old assistant. She'd be hard to miss in a snowstorm, Annie thought. Wearing a hot-pink minidress and huge silver ear hoops, with an Afro that stuck out like a Christmas wreath, she waved enthusiastically to Annie from across the room. It had been what? . . . four years since Gloria had left Girod's for a job selling display ads for the *Voice.* By now she was probably running the place.

"I see someone I want to say hello to," she told Laurel. "Talk to you later." She slipped off her stool and made her way over to Gloria, who slung an arm casually about her shoulders as if it'd been hours, not years, since they had seen one another.

"How does it feel to be back? You leave your heart in Paris, like the song goes?"

"Wrong song . . . and no, I was too busy being a slave for that kind of thing," she told Gloria with a little laugh. Well, it was partly true . . . she *had* felt like a slave to Pompeau.

"I must've been thinking of the one that goes, 'They don't wear pants in the sunny south of France.' You mean to tell me it's not for real?"

Annie laughed, an image forming in her mind of Emmett, naked except for his cowboy boots, standing straddle-legged in front of the bed while she knelt in front of him, and—

God, is that all you can think about? Sex?

Annie, fighting to bank the rush of heat she felt climbing up her neck, forced herself to concentrate on Gloria.

But Gloria now was looking at something beyond Annie's shoulder. "Hey, will you look at who the cat just dragged in?"

Annie's heart gave a little slip-sliding thump, and she turned so suddenly she nearly spilled the flute of champagne gripped tightly in her hand.

"Joe," she said with a tiny gasp, but he was too far away to have heard.

He was just coming out of the glass-brick vestibule and stepping into the living room, smiling and greeting people. A tall, loose-limbed man who just missed being Gregory Peck–handsome, wearing faded but clean khakis, a crisp white shirt, with an old World War II aviator's jacket slung over one shoulder. The lenses of his round wire-rimmed glasses were flecked with September rain—rain that had also brought out the curl in his streaky brown hair. Light drizzle, the weatherman had promised, no storm expected. But she felt as if a hurricane had been let loose inside her.

Then his gaze caught hers, and she felt herself being pulled toward him . . . not as if she were actually moving, but as if the two ends of the room were being pushed together by powerful bookends. And suddenly he was close enough to touch, and to smell his good outdoors autumn-rain smell. But she didn't reach out to embrace him. She just stood there, an unbearable awkwardness clamped over her like a bell jar.

He doesn't want me. He never did.

Panic swarmed through her, stinging, making her acutely aware of every nerve ending.

She found herself saying the first stupid thing that popped into her head: "I didn't know if you were coming or not."

"I got held up," he said. "Traffic jam, water main broke on Park . . . it's really backed up. I ditched the cab and walked the last few blocks." He forked a hand through his damp curls, making them spring up in wild corkscrews. "So how does it feel to be back?" His words sounded as awkward as she felt.

She saw him glance over at Laurel, then he cut his gaze back to her. What was going on?

"Good," she told him. "Still a little tired. Sort of like the hangover you get after drinking too much *vin ordinaire.*"

"You look wonderful." He was staring at her.

She stared back. "You let your hair grow."

"You cut yours."

Her hand crept self-consciously up her neck. "Do you like it? I almost cried when I first saw it. Only the hairdresser didn't speak English. I was afraid she'd think I was having some kind of nervous breakdown."

"No. You look fantastic. I mean it."

"Can I get you some champagne?" She could feel herself running out of small talk. Her voice had a funny, overbright ring—like a young stewardess chirping, "Something to drink, sir?"

"What happens if I say no?" Joe seemed to have picked up on her nervousness and was trying to put her at ease. It worked . . . a little.

She smiled. "As soon as Dolly notices you don't have a glass in your hand, the waters of Babylon will flow."

"In that case," he said, seizing her hand, his long cool fingers wrapping about hers, "we'd better get out of here." He tugged her toward the dining room.

There were a few people standing around the dining-room table —a monumental slab of bevelled glass resting atop a single marble pedestal. The table seemed to float above the blue Chinese carpet like an ice floe on an Arctic sea. Here, the old walnut panelling had been left intact, but stained a sort of silvery white. A chandelier hung over the table, a great bouquet of electrified candle holders, each with a ring of dangling cut crystals that shimmered like dappled sunlight on water. Young waiters in crisp white shirts were briskly laying out platters of food for the buffet supper, and she saw one of them look at Joe and touch a hand to his forehead in a jokey little salute.

"I see you got the Belons," Joe addressed a short, pitted-faced young man with dark hair scraped back in a ponytail, pointing at a tray of half-shelled oysters on a bed of chipped ice. "Good. I wasn't sure they'd get delivered in time."

"Close call," the youth replied with a shrug, heading back into the kitchen.

"*You're* catering this?" Annie whispered. "Dolly didn't tell me."

"She wanted it to be part of the surprise."

"I'm impressed. It's wonderful . . . what I've tasted so far, that is." The truth was she'd been too nervous to do more than nibble at one crab cake.

"Things are really taking off with the catering. Only problem is the kitchen's too small to handle the extra volume, so I'm expanding."

"You've been talking about that for a while, but won't it cost a mint? You don't even own the building." Falling back into their familiar habit of talking shop was like slipping into an old pair of loafers. She felt herself relaxing. *This doesn't have to be hearts and flowers,* she reminded herself briskly. *Let's just be friends for now.*

"I was getting to that part."

"Joe! You didn't! You actually *own* it?"

"Well, mostly it's the bank that owns it, but the deed's in my name. I was pretty lucky. My landlord was in a hurry to unload it . . . he needed the cash for some other investment. I would've written to tell you, but I only closed last week. And I didn't want to say anything before that, in case it fell through."

Annie did some quick calculations in her head. "But even so, the mortgage payments will be a real stretch . . . plus building on . . ." She saw Joe's forehead start to crinkle in a frown, and she caught herself. She was doing it again, trying to run the whole world singlehandedly. "Well, I guess you know better than I would," she finished weakly.

"Believe me, it's time. We're bursting at the seams." He took off his glasses, which were still a little misty, wiping them with his handkerchief. Annie fought an absurd impulse to reach up and stroke the pink indentations on either side of his nose. "What about you —when are you going to strike out on your own?"

"As soon as I can get the bank out in L.A. to release my trust."

She'd had two letters from Wells Fargo out in Los Angeles, and it was still there, twenty-five thousand, plus the interest that had been piling up over the years. And since she was only months away from turning twenty-five, her trustee, Mr. Crawford, had agreed to release the money early, as soon as the paperwork had been completed.

He cast a glance at Dolly, who was flitting through on her way to the kitchen. "You wouldn't be moving in on anyone's territory?"

"Dolly's given me her blessing. She says the competition will keep her on her toes."

"Well, of course, you have *my* blessing. Though I doubt you'll need it. You could take on the national debt and come out ahead."

Annie felt a flicker of annoyance. What was that supposed to mean, that she was some Superwoman? Because she was determined and capable, did that mean she couldn't ever feel weak or scared? Didn't he know that she worried? She worried a lot. And she got scared sometimes . . . so scared that her stomach knotted up and she felt like staying in bed all day with the covers pulled over her head.

She was scared right now. Couldn't Joe tell? Couldn't he hear the way her heart was pounding?

Tears filled her eyes.

Then suddenly he was pulling her off to one side, through the swinging door into a narrow closet that once upon a time had been a butler's pantry. It was empty except for deep built-in cupboards, above and below, where in the old days dishes and tablecloths had probably been kept, but where Dolly now stored her woolens in the summertime. Except for the light filtering in through the thick-paned porthole window, it was dark. It smelled of mothballs and silver polish, but Annie scarcely noticed. In the close darkness, she felt overwhelmed by Joe's nearness, his crisp, outdoor smell and the heat of his body so close to hers.

He touched her cheek, and his touch was so tender that Annie had to fight to keep from breaking down into real tears.

"This isn't how I imagined it would be," he said softly. "I guess you can look forward to something so much and so hard that when you finally get it, you're too paralyzed to make a move."

"Oh, Joe." She tried to say more, but her throat clicked shut. She could feel tears pressing like hot nickels against the backs of her eyes. Finally, she tore loose with a ragged laugh. "Don't say you missed me or I'll cry. I really will. Buckets. You'll think you never came in out of the rain." Then she grabbed a crisp handful of his clean white shirt, and whispered with desperate urgency, "No, say it. If you don't say it, I'll cry when I get home . . . and I don't know which is worse. I'll even say it first. Joe, I missed you. I missed you so much I thought it'd eat a hole right through me."

He gripped her upper arms tightly, but he didn't kiss her. She was relieved, glad even, because she knew that if he did she wasn't going to want him to stop. She saw that there were tears in his eyes, too.

"Listen, I guess you know by now I wasn't making it up when I told you I was lousy at writing letters. If I'd told you how much

I was missing *you,* it would've come out sounding like I'd cribbed it from *Now, Voyager.*" He gave her that funny down-turned smile of his, adding softly, "I wanted to see you first, find out if you . . ."

She began to laugh, soundlessly, as she leaned against the wall behind her, weak with relief. "And all that time I was thinking—"

"What?"

"It's just . . . oh, it seems so silly now . . . but I thought . . . well, that maybe you'd met someone while I was away . . ."

His eyes cut away from hers. "What gave you that idea?"

"I don't know . . . just me, I guess."

"There's no one, Annie."

Was he telling the truth? There had been something in his voice just now . . . and in his eyes . . .

She felt a stab of jealousy, but told herself quickly, *Okay, so what if he went out with someone, maybe even went to bed with her? Who am I to judge, after Emmett?*

"I love you, Joe." There. It was out. She'd said it. Annie felt her face grow tight and hot, as if she'd crept in too close to a fire and had gotten burned.

Joe's grip loosened, and his hands slid down her arms, finally capturing her wrists, gently . . . so gently. She felt as if her heart might burst like a glass unable to withstand an exquisitely high note. He brought her hands up and held her palms to his cheeks. His face felt rough, as if he hadn't shaved in a while, and very warm . . . no, *hot* . . . as if he, too, were burning up.

She had fantasized about this moment for so long that even now it didn't seem quite real—as if she were in some kind of a dream. Then she became acutely aware of his body tensed against hers, his long fingers stroking her spine, that faintly spicy smell of Joe's Place he wore against his skin, like something good left warming in the oven. She felt a stirring in her lower belly that was becoming almost painful. She drew closer, pressing against him, fitting her hollows to his angles. Her need for him was so intense, she thought she might die if she couldn't have him.

"I thought a lot about how it would be when you got home," he said in a low, thick voice. "I thought about this." He brought her palm to his mouth and kissed it . . . and Annie thought, yes, it *was* possible to die from too much happiness all at once.

She wouldn't let herself think about Laurel, about how hurt her sister would be. Later. There would be time to deal with all that later. Here, now, she wanted this moment all to herself. It seemed essential that she grab hold of this before it slipped away from her . . . slipped away like all the good things she'd ever known.

"Annie?"

Annie was scrubbing the last of the Noxzema from her face when Laurel came into the tiny bathroom and perched on the edge of the tub. It was the kind with those old-fashioned claw feet that always made Annie think of some old geezer saying, "Yup . . . they don't make 'em like they used to." And it was true. It took a good fifteen minutes to fill it, but stretching out in that great iron-and-enamel boat was one of her greatest pleasures. Laurel had painted its feet red and gold, and added with tiny brushstrokes feathers and talons, so the feet looked like a medieval griffin's; on the side that faced out she'd painted a family of mallard ducks waddling along in an unbroken line—not just any mallards, though; these all wore rain slickers and bright red boots. Sitting on the tub's curled edge, wearing a man's T-shirt that came down almost to her knees, Laurel looked even droopier than she had coming home from the party an hour ago.

"Hmmm?" Annie answered, turning back to the wide oval pedestal sink where she stood. The medicine chest was partly open, and in its mirror she could see Laurel's reflection, her face a pale oval set above a pair of thin, sagging shoulders. Under the ceiling's fluorescent light-bar, the skin under her eyes looked bruised somehow.

"I'm pregnant." Laurel's soft voice dropped into the stillness like an explosion.

Annie felt a shock travel through her, like touching an exposed electric wire. She turned to face her sister, sagging against the sink, its cool porcelain pressing into the small of her back. The trickling of the faucet filled her ears, suddenly deafening, like the roar of a waterfall.

"Oh Laurey." She couldn't think what else to say. She stared at her sister, feeling a chill that seemed to rise out of her bones.

"You look worse than I do." Laurel managed a tiny smile that only succeeded in making her look more miserable. "Maybe you'd better sit down."

"I think maybe you're right."

In the tiny bedroom she had taken over when Laurel went away to college, Annie, going through the motions despite her shock, slipped into her pajamas, thrift-shop men's pajamas made of dark-blue satin with burgundy silk twist piping. Now, feeling her senses begin to clear a bit, she sat down on the bed facing Laurel, who was curled up in the flowered easy chair by the window, hugging her knees to her chest.

"How many weeks?" Annie asked, grimly determined to be sensible.

"Three *months*. Too far along for an abortion, if that's what you mean."

"Oh, Laurey, I wasn't . . . God, why didn't you tell me right away?"

"I only found out myself a couple of days ago. I know that sounds really stupid, but you know how irregular I've always been. I just kept thinking I'd missed a couple of periods."

"You're sure?"

"I saw a doctor."

"Okay . . ." Annie took a deep breath, feeling she could handle this if only she could lay all the facts out in front of her, and go through them one by one, like a census taker collecting statistics. "Do you want to tell me how it happened?"

Laurel gave a short, mirthless laugh. "The usual way, I guess. I mean how *do* these things happen?"

"You know what I mean."

"You want me to go all the way back to the very beginning? Okay, how about we start with 'Once upon a time there was a girl named Laurel who loved someone so much she thought she could make him love her back by . . .'" Laurel broke off, and all at once her taut face went slack. Tears welled in her huge eyes and dripped down her cheeks.

Laurel saw the puzzled look on Annie's white face and longed to cry out, *I only wanted Joe to love me. And maybe, deep down, I thought that somehow, by sleeping with Jess, I could make Joe see that I was mature enough for him.*

But for some reason she didn't quite understand, Laurel found herself holding back. . . .

Annie longed to go to her sister, to comfort her as she had when Laurel was a little girl. But there was something steely in Laurel's expression and in the set of her shoulders that warned Annie to keep her distance.

She looked about her room, at the tiny cracks in the plaster walls, at the Salvation Army bureau and nightstand. On the dresser in the corner stood Dearie's Oscar. She hadn't dusted it in a while, and now it seemed to glower at her, a dim cousin to the magical, twinkly little man she remembered from when she was child.

"Does he know?" she asked gently. "Have you told him?"

"You mean did I make a complete fool of myself?" She sounded angry, and that seemed to be helping her get herself under control. "Anyway, it's got nothing to do with him."

"What do you *mean?* Believe me, whoever he is, and whatever you think of him, he's in this with you, fifty-fifty."

Laurel shot her a hard look that cut Annie to the bone. "You don't know anything about it," she said. "*It's not Joe,*" she started to say. But again, Laurel held back.

"Well, of course I don't . . . you're not *telling* me anything. Like, for instance, who *is* this guy? And if you love him so much, why can't you tell him?"

Laurel just shook her head, staring down at the carpet.

Annie felt both hurt and exasperated. "Stop acting as if I'm out to get you. For God's sake, Laurey, I just want to *help* you."

"Well, then maybe *you* should talk to him." Laurel's eyes flashed.

"*Who?*"

Even before Laurel answered, Annie sensed she was about to hear something she didn't want to. In the space that stretched between her sister and her, Annie felt an invisible tunnel form, a tunnel down which Laurel's voice seemed to whistle toward her like the coldest of winds.

"Joe," she heard her sister say.

CHAPTER 17

Laurel couldn't face Annie. She stared down at the cabbage-rose carpet, faded in spots and worn away in others, so that it looked sadly frayed, a garden whose insects had nibbled away most of the roses and half the leaves too. In her mind, she could still see vividly Annie's shocked, horrified expression. But it wasn't shame that made her look away from her sister, it was something worse. She had a terrible mean urge to smile.

That was what was making her feel ashamed. What rotten part of her soul could it have come from? How could she *want* Annie to suffer? How could she have led Annie to believe that it was Joe who'd gotten her pregnant?

At first Laurel hadn't meant for Annie to think that . . . but then, once she realized what she was saying, what it was leading to, she hadn't pulled back or tried in any way to correct her sister's mistaken belief. Now she realized that in a way—a sick way—she even *liked* the idea. Well, suppose it had been true? It wasn't impossible. Suppose Joe *had* slept with her? Maybe he didn't love her, but he *had* wanted her . . . she'd felt it that night she'd kissed him, when he was kissing her back. And since then there had been times when she'd catch him looking at her a certain way. . . .

Dammit, why did he love Annie more than her? And why should Annie have any more right to him than she did?

I saw them at Dolly's party. I saw the way he was looking at Annie. . . .

After *she*, Laurel, that night after the gallery opening, had practically thrown herself at Joe. It was insulting, humiliating. She found herself reliving the awful moment when she'd followed them into the dining room, seeing them slip off into the butler's pantry—Annie's hand in Joe's, her dark eyes fixed on him like those of a drowning woman on her rescuer. And worse, the tender way Joe was looking at Annie. They hadn't noticed her standing nearby; they probably wouldn't have seen her if she'd been standing right in front of them. She had felt so small then, as if she'd shrunk to the size of a thimble. And so shocked—a letting-go feeling—all her muscles sagging like worn-out elastic.

He loves her. It's Annie he wants. Annie, Annie, Annie . . .

Come on, hadn't some part of her always known that? Way down where her worst thoughts were stored like dirty socks at the bottom of a hamper, sure, she had known about Joe and Annie. She just hadn't wanted to look. She *couldn't* look.

And now it was staring her right in the face.

She remembered once reading in the *Post* about a man who had eaten an automobile. So he could be listed in the *Guinness Book of World Records.* He'd done it a little at a time, of course . . . hubcaps for breakfast, over easy, and some ground-up tire on the side. But the hardest thing to imagine . . . what had made her throat squeeze shut and her stomach actually hurt . . . was the glass. All that *glass.* Even ground up really fine, what must it have felt like, all those sharp splinters inside you?

Well, now she knew.

I thought there was hope. I thought I could make Joe love me somehow . . . someday.

But now there was no hope. No hope at all.

It's not fair. Why is it always Annie who ends up first? The smartest and boldest. She says I'm the prettiest, but I see how men look at Annie, how they want her. Look at Joe . . . he wants her . . . he'd rather have her than me.

"Joe?" she heard her sister repeat, exhaling sharply, as if the air had been forced out by a hard punch to her stomach. *"Joe?"*

Laurel kept her eyes fixed on the carpet's balding swirls. She felt hot, wrapped in heat like steamy water up to her neck.

Should I tell her? The truth?

She felt rocked by a sudden swell of shame and love. How could she hurt Annie? She loved her sister. If it weren't for Annie . . .

. . . you'd be at Bel Jardin right now eating grapefruit still warm from the tree and looking out your window at green grass and trees instead of concrete and garbage.

No, not true, she told herself. Val had been planning to sell Bel

Jardin all along, her sister had told her. And anyway, Annie had just wanted to protect her from him.

Are you so sure? Or had Annie somehow known that Val was going to die, and that's why she'd been so anxious to get away?

Laurel glanced up at the shiny gold statuette atop a chest of drawers in the corner. Dearie's Oscar. She remembered wiping blood off it, getting her old blanket all bloody, then having to throw it away . . .

Did Annie know that Val was dead? Could she have found out, and been keeping it from her, just as Annie had kept her feelings for Joe a secret?

All these years, I thought I was helping her by keeping my promise to Uncle Rudy, not telling her about Val, but maybe I was just being stupid.

Even more stupid, now she'd gotten herself pregnant.

But how could *that* be Annie's fault?

No, she had to tell Annie about Jess.

Laurel let the memory come. She recalled exactly how it had happened, every tiny detail, even the dog with the red bandana and the morning glories growing up out of the trunk of the old Ford rusting in the backyard. She wanted to bring it all back so she could explain it to Annie. . . .

That first time, walking up the front path of the ramshackle house where Jess lived with five roommates, Laurel noticed its grayish-white paint peeling away in long flakes like dead skin, and the porch propped up at one end by an untidy stack of bricks like a boat listing to one side. A tangle of bikes was pushed up against an old ripped easy chair with the stuffing spilling out in big dirty tufts. And in front of the door, where the porch paint had been scuffed off in an area roughly the shape of continental Africa, panting in the heat of that June day, lay a big golden retriever with a dusty red bandana tied about its neck. The dog lifted his head as she mounted the sagging steps and thumped his tail in halfhearted greeting.

She wondered if Jess remembered he'd invited her over to talk about doing those posters for the Helping Hands project. With him, you never knew for sure—nailing him down was like trying to predict whether it was going to be raining on a certain day a month from now.

He was different . . . older-seeming than other guys his age Laurel hung out with on campus. He'd ridden freight trains, he'd told her. And picked peaches with fruit tramps. And last year he'd spent the whole summer out in California, helping organize migrant farmworkers. If he didn't get drafted first, he'd told her, he was going to join the Peace Corps.

Since that day in Life Drawing, they'd seen each other a few times. Once, she'd bumped into him in the student center and they'd sat and talked for a half hour or so. Another time, they'd had coffee, and when he heard about the tutoring she did in town, he invited her to join a group giving free tutoring to high school dropouts trying for their GEDs. No big deal. He'd never tried to kiss her or even hold her hand. With Jess, you were always just a part of the group.

In that sense, Jess was like Joe, not seeming to want anything from her. But Jess had an edge that made her blood pump faster. . . a hard edge like fingernails scraping on a blackboard or a police siren wailing up a dark street. He kept it pretty much under wraps . . . but it was there. In sixth grade he'd been throwing spitballs at the back of her head, but now he was organizing protest rallies and writing scathing editorials for the *Daily Orange*.

Laurel bent down to give the dog's head a pat before knocking on the door. She waited, but no one came. Funny, when she'd called only a little while ago the girl who answered had said Jess was "around somewhere." The door, thank goodness, had a thick glass pane through which she had a wavery view of a corner of the living room, where a bunch of people were sitting around. She didn't spot Jess, but at least *somebody* was here. She knocked again, harder this time.

Finally, a barefoot girl in long braids, wearing jeans and a skimpy midriff top that barely reached her navel, shuffled over to the door. She gave Laurel an odd look.

"Jeez, you'd think it was *locked* or something," she said. "Why didn't you just come in?"

"Sorry, I didn't know," Laurel said.

"Well, *nobody* here ever locks the door," the girl said, as if Laurel had committed a major social blunder. "We're not into that kind of thing."

"Uh . . . is Jess home?" Laurel asked, now feeling intimidated. And she hadn't gotten even one foot inside yet!

"Upstairs, I think," the girl said, waving her hand in the direction of the staircase. She was already drifting back into the living room.

On the way up the creaking, sagging stairs, Laurel wondered if maybe the reason Jess wasn't hanging out downstairs with his roommates was because he was busy . . . with a girl. She stopped halfway up, feeling suddenly awkward and unsure. But he *had* told her to come. And, anyway, if he was with someone, so what? She'd just leave.

At the top of the stairs, a shower was running. And then before she could go any farther, the water stopped and the bathroom door swung open. Jess emerged in a cloud of steam that caught the sunlight streaming in through a high window over the landing.

He was naked, except for a towel wrapped around his waist, his wet black hair flattened to his skull, from which rivulets dribbled down his chest and arms.

"Hi," he said casually, as if it were every day he found a girl standing outside his bathroom door.

"Hi," she said, not knowing what else to say.

The old line popped into her head: *What's a nice girl like you doing in a place like this?*

She started to giggle, then she remembered . . . the posters.

"You said I should come over so we could talk about the posters," she reminded him.

"Posters?"

"For the Helping Hands meeting."

"Oh . . . those. Sure. Wait here while I throw something on."

He disappeared into one of the bedrooms, but left the door partway open, wide enough for Laurel to watch a bare leg being scooted into a pair of worn Levi's. Then he called: "Come on in."

Jess' room was small, but neat, the bed made. A few posters were thumbtacked to the walls: Joan Baez, and one of Jerry Rubin wearing his American flag shirt, and a banner with the words FREE THE CHICAGO SEVEN. By the bed, a plastic milk crate served as both nightstand and bookcase, with a small Tensor lamp on top. Shelves along one wall, fashioned out of pine planks and cinderblocks, held books and his neatly folded clothes. Otherwise it was bare . . . almost monkish. The one lighthearted touch, probably a former tenant's, was a stained-glass decal stuck up on the window. The light hitting it gave the room a rosy and inviting glow. The window, she saw, looked out over a weed-choked yard and the rusted hulk of an old Ford. Its trunk was permanently open, and growing up through the car's rusted-out bottom was a riot of morning glories that trailed up over the roof and through the empty windows.

Jess, she then realized, was staring at her, his mouth quirked in amusement. He stepped over the wet towel that lay puddled at his feet, and slipped a cool, damp arm about her waist. Then he kissed her.

Laurel had a fleeting sensation of warmth and softness; then, as if she'd been stung, she drew back.

No! She wanted Joe, not Jess. But Joe, she remembered, didn't want *her*. He'd sent her away that night after they'd kissed. And hadn't he told her right to her face that they couldn't ever be anything more than friends? Friends! She felt the hurt all over again, hurt that made her hollow inside, a great burning shell. For weeks afterwards, she'd hardly been able to think of anything else. She'd be in class, or studying for an exam, or hunched over her easel, and suddenly, floating up into her consciousness like pieces of a wrecked ship, the memories would come—Joe's mouth on hers, one sharp corner of his eyeglasses lightly pressing into her cheekbone, the faint juniper taste of the gin and tonic he'd drunk at the gallery. Then the gentle firmness with which he pushed her away, the look of sheepish dismay on his face, as if he were saying, *Don't get any ideas from this . . . you just caught me off guard, is all.*

Laurel remembered how stricken she'd felt . . . and how she'd wanted to run away, as quick and as far as she could. She felt that way now.

But Jess didn't seem to mind that she wasn't fainting in ecstasy. His dark, tipped-up eyes regarded her with cool amusement, and once again she was struck by how different he was from boys she'd dated, with their mushy kisses and awkward, clutching embraces.

"It's not what you're used to, is it?" he said with a lazy chuckle. "You're used to frat rats and jocks who put a record on the stereo first, a little Creedence . . . or some Johnny Winter . . . and after that maybe smoke some good weed they bought outa the pocket money their folks send 'em." He shook his hair out in a rain of droplets that struck her hands and face like a fine mist. "Well, listen, Beanie, I ain't got no stereo . . . and I don't got no time or money for smokin' dope," he continued in an exaggerated Latino accent. His smile widened. "I got time for *you,* though. If you want it."

He was mocking her. Laurel started to feel upset, and a little angry.

"I think I'd better be going," she said stiffly.

He made no move to stop her, just stared at her, that languid smile never leaving his face. What was it about him? Why couldn't she move? She found herself fixated by a bead of moisture that clung stubbornly to the dusky hollow at the base of his throat.

"I'll bet you were the type of kid who ate all the Wheaties to get to the prize at the bottom of the box," he said. "Me, I never saw the point. Man, if you want something, why do it the hard way? Just reach down and *get* it."

Laurel felt her skin burn where his finger was now tracing a line down the side of her face. Then he was kissing her. And this time she didn't pull away.

To her surprise, she found she *liked* kissing Jess. His mouth was incredibly soft, but when she felt his teeth, she tensed a little. That hard, searching edge she'd sensed in him, it was there . . . pressing into the tender flesh of her underlip . . . pressing *hard,* but not cutting. She could feel his hands printing damp circles into the thin cotton of her blouse, and she shivered, not from the wetness of his touch . . . but from the *sureness* of it.

Laurel, not wanting to or intending to, began imagining it was Joe she was kissing . . . Joe, whose cool fingers skated along her sides as he pulled her blouse free from the waistband of her skirt.

Jess pushed the door shut with one swift kick. As it thunked into its frame, Laurel felt it in the pit of her stomach. She felt a sudden need to say something . . . *anything.*

"The girl downstairs says nobody around here locks doors."

"Not for keeping people *out,*" he laughed. "Just for keeping them *in.* Now," he said, his laughter dying as a spot of color rode up each of his high, Indian-looking cheekbones. "There's something I been wanting to know about you since we were in the sixth grade. Are you really that white *all over?*"

As if in a trance, Laurel began to undress. Her blouse lay

crumpled on the floor at her feet, and now it was joined by her flowered skirt and her sandals. Last, her bra and panties.

Finally, she stood before Jess, naked in the rose-colored light, goose bumps up and down her arms and legs. Somewhere downstairs she could hear a dog barking. And through the window, just beyond Jess' right shoulder, she could see the furled purple head of a morning glory nodding in the bright sun. But except for those small, comforting touches of everyday life, she knew this wasn't really happening . . . that it was all a dream . . . and that in a few minutes she would wake up and be back in her own room at Smith Hall.

Jess, for the first time ever, appeared to have lost his composure—lips parted, his eyes wide open, his face stamped with color that had formed ridges of red along his cheekbones.

"Holy Christ," he whispered, letting his breath out in a long, awed sigh. Then in a single, neat motion, he shucked off his jeans. She'd seen him naked before, that time in her drawing class . . . but this time was different . . . he was . . . well, *hard*.

Under Jess' intense scrutiny, Laurel's dreaminess ebbed and she began to feel panicky. Wouldn't it be better to just stop right now —tell Jess she'd never done this before? Not that she hadn't had plenty of chances, but let's face it, hadn't she known, somewhere in the back of her mind, that the real reason those guys always seemed to do something to turn her off at the crucial moment—whether it was their funny whimpering noises, or whispering "I love you!" in her ear loud enough to break her eardrum, or catching her slip in her zipper while they were trying to open it—was because of Joe. She had wanted her first time to be with Joe.

The hurt she felt over Joe's rejecting her was a solid thing, a thing she clung to, holding it in a tight ball against her the way she'd long ago held her old blanket, Boo. She knew it was childish, and wrong, but somehow she still couldn't make herself let go.

"I don't know if I like being compared to a box of Wheaties," she tossed back lightly, determined to hide her true feelings.

And the thing about cereal-box prizes, she recalled, was that they were mostly not what you'd expected from the picture on the back of the box.

Jess nuzzled a breast, nipping at it lightly with his teeth, sending a sharp, delicious shiver through her.

"Breakfast of champions," he said with a little laugh. "And, you, Beanie, you're the champion of them all. Only the trouble with champions, they don't hardly ever get to roll in the mud with the rest of us lowlifes."

He brought his hand down and cupped it between her thighs, a sudden gesture that shocked her. Not moving, or pressing . . . just holding it there . . . creating a pocket of warmth that built to a fine, maddening point and began to spread up through her belly.

"Hey, maybe rolling in the mud is what it's all about," he whispered in her ear, bringing the sharp edges of his teeth down against her earlobe hard enough to bring tears to her eyes.

Then, with surprising gentleness, he led her over to the bed.

Laurel, facing Annie's shocked, miserable gaze, realized something odd: The possibility of getting pregnant had never entered her mind. Not at the time. Unless, deep down, she'd known perfectly well what she was getting into and had secretly *wanted* something like this to happen . . . something cataclysmic and final.

But if so, then it had been a secret to her, too. Mostly she knew that she did not want to be pregnant. But now that she was, more than three *months,* she couldn't pretend it wasn't so.

She hadn't told Jess, and she didn't intend to. The baby seemed hardly connected to Jess, with whom she'd slept only a few times, and who hadn't written or called all summer. Since the start of the new school year a couple of weeks ago, she'd only seen him once. So somehow she'd begun thinking of it as Joe's baby . . . conceived out of her love for him.

Still, she would have to tell Annie how it had really happened . . . she couldn't go on just making believe.

"Does he . . ." Annie swallowed with what appeared to be an effort, her face a white circle above the navy silk pajamas she wore. "Does Joe know? Have you told him?"

"No."

"Why not?"

Because it's not his baby. The words were on the tip of her tongue.

She started to say them, but then something inside her stopped her.

"I haven't told *anyone,*" she said, horrified and amazed at her smooth cunning.

Not a lie. Not *exactly*. Then why did she feel so guilty? And why was her stomach heaving? She hadn't felt sick at all in the beginning—that was another reason she hadn't bothered going to the doctor—but now she felt like she might throw up.

"I don't believe it," Annie said. "Joe wouldn't—" Her words were choked off.

Laurel remained silent, her lips pressed together, her knees pulled tightly in against her chest.

"Have you . . . has this *affair* of yours been going on a while?" Annie seemed to be slowly falling apart, her voice looping strangely in and out of pitch, like a warped record. But the bitter note in it was clear.

"No," she said. "It was just a few times."

Annie seemed to be gulping for air. Finally, like a mountain climber gaining a tenuous foothold, she said, "Well then. You'll just have to tell him."

Cold sweat broke over Laurel. She wanted to run for the toilet, but she didn't. She forced herself to remain where she was. She *had* to tell her sister the truth. It wasn't fair to let Annie go on thinking it was Joe. And anyway, Annie would find out the truth the minute she talked to him.

But you could let her think what she wants for just a little while longer, couldn't you? It's not as if you actually lied . . . Annie just assumed *that was what you meant . . . and when you really got down to it, if she really, really trusted Joe, why would she have thought it at all?*

No! she snapped at herself. *It's wrong! It'll break Annie's heart!*

The way yours is broken, you mean?

Laurel saw it then . . . like the fork in Robert Frost's yellow wood: perfectly clear in her mind, the two choices before her. On the one hand, letting go . . . letting go of Joe and the dream of his ever loving her . . . letting go and letting the pain wash through her in a great, stinging, healing tide. She could tell Annie, not only about Jess, but that she understood about Joe and Annie loving each other. It would be hard. The hardest thing she'd ever done . . . and that was what Frost must have meant about that road being a lot less travelled than the other one. But she *could* do it. If she wanted to, she could.

A strange, wild exhilaration filled Laurel . . . and for the briefest moment she glimpsed the woman she could be . . . the woman she *would* be if she could just . . . just let go.

Then she was remembering watching them at Dolly's party, remembering how she'd felt. And how she had felt year after year, always following in Annie's firm footsteps. And now this—the only thing that she had ever *really* wanted, Annie had taken from her. All her longing and resentment came boiling to the surface.

"I can't think about it right now," she controlled herself enough to say. "I don't feel too good."

"But—" Annie began, then her mouth snapped shut.

"Can we talk about it in the morning? I really just want to go to bed." And as she spoke, Laurel realized how exhausted she was. The sick feeling had gone away . . . and now she felt so tired and heavy she could hardly stand. The room pitched drunkenly.

I'll tell her tomorrow, Laurel thought.

Annie, gripping the banister for support, slowly descended the stairs to Joe's floor. This hallway was usually a place she passed through and never noticed, but tonight it seemed dingy, the treads worn, the air sour. She felt weak and frail, as if in the last half hour she'd become an old woman. And why was it so dim? On the landings above and below, bulbs were lit, but she felt as if she were going down into some kind of cavern.

Joe's baby.

After the hours and hours they'd spent together, wouldn't she just once have seen that side of him—that he could be so devious? Wouldn't she have *known?*

Joe . . . kind, sweetly impulsive Joe . . . underneath the man she'd been so sure she loved, could there be a whole other person, a person capable of letting her think he loved her *after he'd slept with her sister?*

No. Not Joe. Not possible.

Only minutes ago she would have sworn to it, bet her life on it. But now . . .

She pictured Laurel, white as a sheet, looking both scared and defiant . . . almost as if she was protecting him. Why would she lie? Why would she have made up something as horrible as this?

Annie's knees buckled, and she sagged against the banister rail, covering her face as a sob broke loose. How could he have done this to her? To Laurel? *How?*

And Laurel, damn her, how could she? With him! And to have been so stupid, so naive? At eighteen, to get herself pregnant!

Annie lowered herself until she was sitting on a step, and found herself imagining how it might have happened: Laurel pouring her heart out to him, and Joe being kind, taking it all in, not wanting to hurt her feelings. But after that, he must've started to see her in a new light . . . not that first time, or even the second . . . but later, after a week, a month . . . noticing more and more how beautiful she'd become. How alluring. And then maybe a movie or dinner, like in the old days when it was the three of them, not intending that anything should happen, but then, well, it just had. . . .

Anger rose in her, engulfing her. She felt herself being pulled to her feet, not as if she was just standing up, but as if somehow she was propelled upward by some explosive heat.

Damn him, how dare he! *How dare he have made me think that he loved me . . . that we . . . oh, God!*

Or had he thought she wouldn't find out? That it would remain his and Laurel's little secret, a tiny slipup he'd take care not to repeat? And, actually, if Laurel hadn't gotten pregnant, she might *not* have found out.

One . . . two . . . three . . . four. Descending, she counted each step as if in doing so she might somehow arrive at a sum, an answer to how she was ever going to get through this.

Now she reached the door to Joe's apartment with its mottled brown paint, its round glass peephole staring back at her like a dead eye. She knocked. Then rang the bell, over and over, then knocked again. Pounding, she felt pain shoot up through her knuckles.

Joe appeared, so quietly she was only barely aware of the door swinging open. He was barefoot, holding a coffee mug, and still wearing the clothes he'd had on at the party—jeans, white shirt rolled up over his elbows. She felt as if she were seeing him from a great distance, but as if through a powerful telescope, every tiny hair of his beard stubble, even the specks of gold flecking his irises, magnified to an unreal clarity. Music was playing on the stereo. Jazz trumpet. Stanley Turentine. But how could she have known that? She hardly ever tuned in to Joe's jazz—she preferred rock and roll. It felt as if her senses had been honed to needle-sharp points.

"Annie!" Joe broke into a grin, which faded just as quickly. "Annie, what's wrong? Jesus, are you all right?"

She nodded, but somehow she couldn't speak.

"Is it Laurey? She looked really out of it at the party, like she was coming down with something."

It was as if he'd grabbed her, shaken her, sprung her voice free so that the words tumbled out.

"She came down with something all right." Annie shot him a cold look. "She's pregnant."

"Jesus Christ."

Joe took a step back, as if to let her in, but then he staggered a bit, off balance. He swung his arm out as if to steady himself, the mug in his hand throwing an arc of liquid that spattered onto the frayed hall mat at his feet and on the Miró print on the wall.

"Jesus," he said again.

Annie shouldered past him, forgetting, until she felt herself step into the coffee's wetness, that she hadn't even thought to put her slippers on. She still had on her pajamas too, under the coat she'd thrown on before stepping out her front door into the hallway. She probably looked awful. No makeup, her hair standing up in damp spikes where she'd scrubbed with a washcloth along her hairline. But what did that matter now? She wasn't going to make love to Joe, not now, not ever.

She moved out of the narrow vestibule into the living room, not bothering to take her coat off, or wipe off her wet feet before she stepped onto the zigzag-patterned rug. She heard the door click shut behind her, and glancing back, she saw Joe standing there, not following her. The trail of her footprints on the floor seemed somehow to be pointing at him, accusing him.

Then in three long strides he was beside her, reaching out to help her off with her coat. Annie jerked away, bumping her hip against the slatted arm of the couch. Everywhere around her, sharp angles—blocky Mission oak furniture, a low glass table on which stood a pair of wrought-iron arts-and-crafts candlesticks—all seeming to prod and poke at her. An old movie poster—Bogie in trench coat with a cigarette slanting from a corner of his downturned mouth—glowered at her from the wall.

"Don't," she said.

Joe's arms dropped to his sides. He looked startled. No, more than that, shocked . . . bewildered even. As if she'd pulled off a mask, and underneath was a face different from the one he'd always known. A stranger's face.

Then, all at once feeling wildly hopeful, Annie was wondering if this might be some kind of absurd mistake, or a bad dream. Could she have imagined Laurel telling her she was pregnant? Or maybe what she'd just imagined was Laurel saying Joe was the father . . .

"Annie, for Chrissakes, what is going on?" He managed to grab hold of her elbow, and she could feel his fingers squeezing, pressing into her, paralyzing her somehow. "Listen, you don't think I *knew*, do you? Is that why you're mad? You think Laurey told me, and I kept it from you?"

"Stop it," she hissed. She couldn't believe he was doing this, lying to her, pretending not to know anything.

"Stop what? I don't even know what the hell you're talking about."

"How can you just . . . stand there . . . acting as if . . . as if you didn't know? You *bastard*."

She saw color flare along the side of his neck, and his eyes grow hot and shiny, the look he got once in a blue moon when he was about to lose his temper. But then with visible effort, he dropped her arm, and brought himself under control, stepping back, holding his hands out as if to ward off an onrushing car. On the wall behind him, a print of a red-and-black Lichtenstein abstract seemed to jump out at her. Next to it was another, smaller work—a Joe's Place menu from years ago adorned with Laurel's graceful drawings, full of birds: a pair of mourning doves, a kingfisher, a peacock, a flock of tiny sparrows. He must have framed it and hung it while she was away. *God, suppose he really loves her.* She felt a hot shaft of pain, piercing her chest.

"Okay, I can see you're not in any kind of mood to sit down and talk about this rationally, but do you mind telling me what the hell you're so pissed about?" He spoke slowly, enunciating each word as if to calm himself. "I mean, if I'm going to be hanged, don't I at least first get to be accused?"

"Laurey told me. About you and . . . and everything."

There. That guilty flicker. In his eyes, just now. Unmistakable. So he *had* meant to keep this from her. Annie wanted to hit him, hurt him, make him suffer the way she was.

"What's 'everything'? What was there to tell?" His face, like a hand clenching, seemed to close, become unreadable. "I figured it would blow over. I figured that as soon as some good-looking, artistic-type guy took her by the hand, she'd fall in love and forget she'd ever felt that way about me, in fact, she'd be *embarrassed*. Look, I don't know what you're getting so upset about. It's between Laurel and me. It's got nothing to do with you."

Nothing to do with *her?* A huge pressure was building inside her head, making it feel as if her skull might split open.

"Now"—Joe was looking at her steadily, grimly—"let's start over. And let's take it slow this time. Laurel's pregnant?" He raked a hand through his hair. "Are you sure? I mean, hell, suppose she and some guy went just a little too far, and now her period's late, and she's ready to call out the marines—"

"Joe." Annie felt as if she was screaming, but somehow her voice was almost normal, even weirdly muted, the thud of a muffled clapper against a bell. "Joe, I can't believe you're doing this . . . trying to pretend it wasn't you. I *know,* dammit."

"You think I . . ." He stopped, cocking his head a little to one side, looking at her with the stunned disbelief of someone being arrested for a crime he didn't commit. He shook his head, tiny squares of light dancing across the surface of his glasses.

"I don't think. I *know.* And if you ever come near Laurey again, if you ever try to talk to her, or even phone her . . . if you ever so much as nod in her direction . . . I swear to God I'll find a way to have you locked up. I'll have Laurey say it was rape. I'll say you r-rape—Oh, God, Joe, how *could* you? How could you do this?" She was sobbing now, her whole body seeming to fold in on itself. She sidestepped, sagging against the wall to her right. "I trusted you! Laurey trusted you! *How could you do this to us!*"

"I didn't—"

"Stop it! Stop lying!"

"Damn it, will you just *listen!*"

Out of nowhere, with the shock of a meteor crashing into a cornfield, Joe's fist came looping at her, a rush of air kissing her cheek; then his hand was smashing the wall inches from her head. There was a crumping sound, followed by small chips that struck the side of her face in a stinging hail, and then in her nostrils the chalky smell of plaster dust. She could taste it, too, a slight grittiness on her tongue.

Annie was too stunned to move. She felt herself collapsing, but managed to lock her knees, brace herself against the wall. She was numb, trembling.

That blow was meant for me. He wanted to hit me.

Oh God, how had all the sweetness of just a few hours ago come to *this?*

Annie remembered once, years ago, being on a cable car in San Francisco that lost its brakes going down a steep hill. That horrible screeching sound, everybody petrified, screaming, one man leaping off. She wanting so badly to hide her face in Dearie's skirt, but knowing that that wouldn't stop it, so she forced herself to look, frozen with terror, watching the cars jerking out of the way to avoid them, the pavement that seemed to be roaring at her like a great ocean wave. And worst of all, the squeezing pain in her stomach, from knowing that there was no way of stopping the car, or of getting off.

By God's grace—or at least that's what Dearie said it was— they'd struck a double-parked delivery van that jarred and buffeted them to a stop. And miraculously, except for the man who'd jumped off, no one was hurt.

But now no miracle could stop this car. She and Joe were here in it, and it had lost its brakes. Jump off or stay on—either way, they could never be saved.

Two stairs. Three . . . five . . . seven . . . eight. She counted them as she climbed them. Now she was on her landing, fumbling with her key, which seemed to want to jump out of her hand, letting herself in her front door. When she snapped on the light, Laurel, asleep on the sofa bed in the living room, jerked upright, swollen-eyed and blinking.

"Annie!" she cried. "What happened? God, you look as if you've been mugged. Where have you been? What's wrong?"

It all came tumbling loose from wherever it had been anchored inside her. Annie staggered over and collapsed in the chair by the sofa, cupping her hands over her eyes to shield them from the light that suddenly seemed to be stabbing them.

"Joe . . . I told him." Her voice came in quick, gasping sobs. "But he . . . he said . . ." She stopped, remembering that look of wounded perplexity she'd seen on his face.

And then she knew this had to be a nightmare, because she heard Laurel, in a small, stricken voice, cry, "Oh, Annie! I didn't mean to make you think it was Joe, not really . . . not at first . . . it just came out that way. Joe . . . he didn't . . . he never . . ." Then an odd, defiant gleam stole into her eyes, her voice becoming stronger, more sure. "I wanted him, though. I wished it was him. I still do."

Annie couldn't believe what she was hearing. She looked up, trying to focus her stinging eyes on her sister. Slowly—so there could be absolutely no mistaking it this time—she asked, "Are you saying Joe is *not* the father of your baby? That you and he *aren't* lovers?"

"It was someone from school," Laurel said. "Jess Gordon. I knew him from Brooklyn. It was just . . . well, I'm not in love with him or anything."

"But you *are* in love with Joe."

Laurel held her gaze, tipping her chin a fraction higher, as if challenging her.

"Yes." No apology. No excuse.

"Why did you lie, then? Why did you tell me . . ." She started to choke, and clamped her lips shut before a sob could escape.

I didn't even give him a chance to explain. I didn't believe him. God, oh God, will he ever forgive me?

Gently, in a clear voice that held no regret, Laurel replied, "I didn't tell you he was the father, Annie. That's just what you *heard.*"

Anger flared in her—sharp, galvanizing. She stood up, jerking to her feet as if propelled by some unseen force. "Damn it, Laurey, don't you put this on me! Don't you dare! You may not have said the words, but you wanted me to believe it was Joe!"

"I didn't mean to. But when I realized that you'd misunderstood, well . . ." Now Laurel's voice caught, and her eyes narrowed. Annie could see that she was trembling. "You love him, don't you? You want him for yourself. It's not *me* you're upset about, the fact that I'm pregnant. It's just Joe. You're mad because you thought you'd lost him. Isn't that right? Well, *isn't* it?" Her voice rose to an alarming shrillness.

Annie, before she could stop herself, was lunging forward, grabbing Laurel's thin shoulders and shaking her. "How could you? *God, how could you?* Haven't I always watched out for you, done everything for you? How could you do this to me? *How?*"

Framed by the absolute whiteness of her face, Laurel's large, clear eyes seemed to cut right through Annie's, right through to the back of her skull. "You never asked," she said with a bitterness that seemed utterly unlike the Laurel she had always known. "You just assumed that wherever you went, I'd follow . . . but, Annie, *you never asked.* You've always done just exactly what *you* wanted. So maybe now it's my turn. Maybe for once I'd like to be first."

Annie stepped back, stunned by the force of the sudden hate she felt. How could she hate her own sister so? But right now, she did. She hated Laurel so fiercely she had to keep her arms locked at her sides to keep from striking her.

"Do what you want then," she snapped. "Just don't expect me to be there when you *do* need me."

CHAPTER 19

Annie stared at the empty store with the FOR LEASE sign in its boarded-up window. Definitely not a great neighborhood—Ninth Avenue between Fourteenth and Fifteenth—and it was stuck between a dreary-looking Hispanic barbershop and an appliance-repair store with a pair of old TV sets throwing a flickering bluish glow over the snowy sidewalk below.

Could this be the right place? Shivering as gusts of wind whipped around her, Annie glanced at the address Emmett had given her, which she'd scribbled on the back of a grocery receipt. This was it, all right. But, God, what a dump! She noted the empty half-pint bottles littered in front of the door, and her heart sank even further.

A former coffee shop, Emmett had said, and it supposedly had a very large kitchen in the back. Maybe it wasn't as bad as it looked. Maybe once he showed her the inside . . .

The last place she'd looked at, down on Hudson Street, had seemed almost ideal. It was a charming Village location, and it would have needed hardly any renovation. But it was also three times the rent.

Annie glanced at her watch. Quarter to twelve. Emmett would be here any minute. All of a sudden, she couldn't wait to see him. To hear his voice explaining how if this or that wall were ripped out, what a magnificent space this could become.

Annie marvelled, not for the first time in the past four months, how lucky it was that at what had to be the lowest point in her life, Emmett Cameron had showed up. She remembered him calling, a couple of weeks after that awful night with Joe. He was in New York, he told her; he'd gotten a job in a friend-of-a-friend's real-estate firm through some connection he'd made in France. Could she meet him for dinner that night at the Chelsea Hotel?

Seeing him waiting for her, beer in hand at El Quijote's massive old-fashioned bar, wearing that cowboy grin, she'd felt something in her let go, as if she were stepping off some shaky platform she'd been trying to hold her balance on. An hour, maybe two . . . she could escape for that long, couldn't she? And then Emmett was walking over, hugging her, so solid. She'd felt safe, grounded, and at the same time oddly charged, every circuit in her body suddenly alive and crackling.

Then they were in a booth with a pitcher of sangria, catching up on everything . . . Emmett's terrific deal on a furnished studio just down the street, opposite London Terrace, and this great chance he had to make a go of it in the real-estate business, where a lot of guys his age made six figures just from leasing office space. Not that he regretted his time at Girod's. Just the experience of living in Paris was well worth Pompeau's slave-driving. But chocolate making, he'd realized, was not ever going to be his thing.

She, in turn, had told him how excited *she* was about going into business for herself . . . and about her so far exhausting and fruitless search for an affordable location. Emmett didn't know if he could help, but he said he'd talk to the guy in his firm who specialized in retail.

Since then, she'd seen him a lot. And Emmett, thank goodness, was putting no pressure on her. He acted as if he'd pretty much put behind him those wild nights in Paris. That was a relief—because these days all she had in her to give him was some companionship. It was Joe she still wanted, needed . . . and, yes, missed. An ocean even wider than the Atlantic separated them now—an expanse of icy politeness she found herself drowning in each time she passed Joe on the stairs, or mumbled hello to him at the mailboxes.

She'd twice tried to apologize, but she knew her being sorry just wasn't good enough. Joe, she sensed, wasn't trying to be mean or to punish her. No, it was worse, deeper. She had broken something precious, something that—unlike the hole Joe had punched in his wall—probably could never be made solid again.

"Hey, there, early bird."

Annie turned to find Emmett walking toward her, his red hair flecked with snow, his breath streaming out in a long white plume. The collar of his overcoat was turned up, but otherwise he looked as if he could be strolling through a sunlit meadow. She felt warmed, too, just seeing him.

"I was afraid I'd be the one to keep *you* waiting." She laughed. "The story of my life."

"You've got that look on your face," he said.

"What look is that?"

"The same look you used to get with Pompeau . . . your I-don't-like-this-a-bit-but-I'm-doing-it-anyway look."

"Well . . ."

He placed a finger lightly against her lips, his touch surprisingly warm, despite the fact that he wasn't wearing gloves.

"Just don't say anything until you see the inside, okay?"

Emmett fished a ring of keys from his pocket and unlocked the metal accordion gate, then the front door.

"Don't look so gloomy, Cobb," Emmett told her when they were inside. "It's second-class, but it's not the South Bronx."

Annie eyed the empty circular holes in front of the counter where stools had been ripped out. Cigarette butts and cellophane wrappings littered the worn-down, warped vinyl tiles, and along the wall where the grease-coated grill stood like some ancient forge, she saw droppings—or maybe just bits of dirt—sprinkled about.

Her disappointment growing, she looked back at Emmett. "It's not exactly what I had in mind," she said gently, not wanting him to think she didn't appreciate his efforts.

"Look, it's a rathole. But don't you see, that's what makes it perfect," he assured her. "Leastways, it *could* be. Hell, a good cleaning crew and a few coats of paint and you'd be halfway there."

That might be true, she thought, but even with this place fixed up, it was a far cry from Madison Avenue. Or even Hudson Street. On the other hand, she reminded herself, nothing she could afford was going to be on Madison Avenue. And wherever she was, to start off, the business would have to be mostly wholesale. She'd already spoken with the department-store buyers and Murray Klein at Zabar's. Some had been nice, some hadn't had two seconds to spare her, but they'd all agreed to try her samples—if she ever got to make them.

And there was Emmett, looking so confident, as if one slap of a paintbrush would do it all. She could now see how he might have talked that syndicate of Westchester doctors into buying that Garment District loft building that Emmett's boss hadn't been able to sell. Already Emmett's commissions had to be substantial. Soon, she bet, he'd be buying property on his own.

No more funky clothes, either. He was wearing a rich-looking camel-hair coat over a finely tailored gray worsted suit that looked as if it had set him back a few paychecks—though, knowing Emmett, he'd probably gotten it for cost somewhere on lower Fifth Avenue. A lush red tie of heavy silk was knotted jauntily at his throat. The only memento of the old Emmett—out of keeping, and at the same time reassuring—was his cowboy boots, tanned and creased with age, their stitching worn off in a few spots, but saddle-soaped and newly heeled. Emmett was fond of saying he'd grown into them the way a philodendron grows into its pot. His bad foot wouldn't know what to do with a new shoe. He liked to claim he even slept in his boots . . . which she knew wasn't true.

Even so, her mind formed a picture of Emmett asleep, stretched out on a bed, with only his boots on, heels dimpling the mattress cover, squared-off toes pointing up at the ceiling. She felt herself growing warm. Stop it, she told herself. *That* part of their relationship was over.

"Compared to my studio apartment, this place is the size of Madison Square Garden," he continued, his breath puffing out in frozen clouds. "You should see it . . . maybe a hamster would feel at home there. They ran out of room in the john for the shower stall, so they put it in the kitchen instead. A real time-saver . . . I can wash dishes while I'm showering."

"Well, I'm glad you can see the bright side." Annie ran a finger along the counter, leaving a track in the dust and grime.

"Hey, when you've spent most of your life living out of a knapsack, you learn to appreciate those little homey touches."

"Oh, Em, I don't know . . . it's so . . ." She looked around again, this time zeroing in on the banquettes in back. Most of the seats were cracked or torn, with tufts of gray stuffing sprouting up here and there like some strange fungi. "Well, I just wonder—all that work and expense. And for what? Just so I could pick up and move somewhere better if the business ever gets going?"

"So it's the neighborhood, huh?"

Looking out through the cloudy side window, across the street, she watched a line of pathetic-looking people forming in front of a storefront mission that ran a soup kitchen.

"Look," he went on. "What if I told you there's talk of the whole block south of here being redeveloped, high-toned condos, John Portman–style designing . . . you know, lobbies with indoor waterfalls and maybe even those glass-walled elevators. It's a secret, since there's still a few crummy old buildings over there they haven't finished negotiating for. But they'll get them." Emmett's blue eyes sparkled. With his hair ruffled into a cowlick, his hands shoved deep in his pockets, he made her think of a mischievous Tom Sawyer trying to convince his pals that painting a fence was fun, not work. "I'll bet you a dollar for a dime, this whole neighborhood'll be coming up like rye grass out of cowshit before you can say boo."

Annie laughed. "Em, you *do* have a way of putting things. And, yeah, that does sort of put a new complexion on this. I'll definitely think about it. And I'll want to come down and look at it again with a contractor."

"While you're thinking about it, how about grabbing a bite with me? I know this great deli just a few blocks from here where they give you the pickles and sauerkraut right out of a barrel."

Annie was tempted. But she'd planned on dropping by Joe's restaurant to see the new addition, which had to be nearly finished by now. An excuse—really, she just wanted to see him. And at the restaurant, he couldn't duck away or ignore her.

She remembered the last time she'd cornered him in the lobby of their building. She'd pleaded with him to believe how sorry she was, begged him. Well, maybe *begged* was too strong. But he had to have seen how miserable she was, how she wanted so very much to make things right between them. He was late for an appointment, he'd told her, then had rushed off. Only his eyes, in the split second before he'd turned away, had spoken the truth—*What's the point,* they seemed to ask, *of hashing it out all over again?*

Her stomach, calm since Emmett had appeared, cut a slow, looping orbit. No, she had to go see Joe.

Still, she couldn't help feeling torn. She liked Emmett, liked him enormously. And in a way, she even loved him. Or at least she thought she *could* have loved him . . . if it hadn't been for Joe.

"Thanks, Em, but I've got another appointment." She cut her gaze away from his, suddenly unable to look him in the eye. "I'm supposed to meet this confectioner up in the East Eighties who's going out of business. He's selling his equipment, and I may be able to get a good deal on some of the stuff I need."

"I could check it out for you, if you'd like," he offered. "Make sure you don't get stuck with any lemons. I'm pretty good with machines, if you recall."

Annie didn't know what to say. Her appointment was hours away, not until four. But how could she tell Emmett that right now she had to see a man who didn't know she was coming and who probably would not want to see her when she got there?

"Thanks, I just may take you up on that. Let me see what it looks like first."

Emmett shrugged. Outside, as he was locking up, he asked, "By the way, how's your sister? Isn't she about due?"

"Not until the end of next month." Annie didn't want to talk about Laurel or the baby. Talking about her sister only reminded her of Joe . . . and of how Laurel had deceived her. Even so, she could feel the tiny spur of anger buried in heart begin to chafe and burn.

"Is she still thinking of . . ." Emmett stopped himself, seeming to hesitate about bringing up a sore subject.

"Giving the baby up for adoption?" Annie felt a pang that went even deeper than her sister's betrayal. "She's talked about it, but she hasn't made up her mind." Annie didn't realize how tightly clenched her hands were until she felt her nails—the chewed-down remains of them, anyway—digging into her palms.

Did she want Laurel to keep the baby? Could they take on the extra responsibility? Because in spite of Laurel's being so capable, it *would* place an extra burden on her as well. No . . . yes . . . no . . .

"Hey, Cobb. Relax, will ya?" She became aware of Emmett touching her arm. "No need for you to be taking on the whole world's problems, not until you're elected God, that is. Right now, shouldn't you just concentrate on getting this business of yours going?" He smiled. "If you're busy for lunch, how about dinner? My place? I'll bet you've never eaten broccoli steamed in a shower, have you?"

She shook her head. "I'd like to, but I'm going to a *bris*."

"A *what?*"

"My friend Rivka's daughter, Sarah, just had a baby. Her

third . . . a boy. A *mohel* does a circumcision, and there's a little party afterwards. You want to come?"

"Not me. I'm Catholic. Church of the Latter-Day Lapsed."

"What difference does that make?"

Emmett arched a brow, a corner of his wide mouth turning down. "Lapsed or not, the whole idea of somebody snipping away at the family jewels makes me a little nervous."

"I always close my eyes."

"Yeah, well, you can afford to."

Annie thought about Laurel's baby. Boy or a girl? She might never even *see* it, she realized. And that would probably be best . . . though she didn't know how Laurel was going to live with it.

Lately, a lot of things about Laurel had been bothering her. Like her asking Joe to be her Lamaze coach. With Joe there, Laurel said, she fit in with the other couples. *Married* couples.

And, Joe, dammit, had agreed. But Annie was keeping her mouth shut. Who was she to say it wasn't right? What claim did she have on Joe anymore?

Annie looked at her watch. "I'd better get going. Or I'll be late." She felt guilty about lying to Emmett. And wondered why she even bothered.

She waited in the outer doorway while Emmett finished locking up. Two Medeco deadbolts in the door, and a steel accordion over the whole façade. The neighborhood might be up and coming, but it hadn't come all that far yet.

Out on the sidewalk, Annie watched Emmett amble to the curb to hail a cab. When it pulled over, he held the door for her.

"Good luck," he said.

For a second, she thought he meant good luck with Joe, and she felt a stab of remorse. Then she realized he must have meant about getting that equipment from the Yorkville confectioner.

"Thanks," she said, thinking of Joe, her heart quickening. "I'll need it."

The framing for the walls looked complete. In some places, they were already Sheetrocked, and in others the studs stood bare, the electrical conduit and pipes coiled between them left exposed. Annie wandered about the largest of the three rooms, which when finished would open directly onto the kitchen. Carpenters were measuring, levelling, sawing wood, pounding nails. The sharp, sweet smell of sawdust filled her nostrils, bringing Annie a glad, hopeful feeling. Here, everything smelled of fresh starts.

"I can't believe it," she said, turning to Joe. "Last time I was here, this area was just a weed patch."

"One of Rafy's brothers is a contractor," he said, adding with a little laugh, "You'd be amazed how quickly things get done when you're in with the Puerto Rican mafia." He took her elbow, lightly, so lightly she hardly felt his touch, and steered her around a big coil of conduit and yet-to-be-installed outlet boxes. "We should be ready for taping in a week or so, and from there it's just plaster and paint." He paused. He seemed to be waiting for her to say something.

Annie nodded. She couldn't take her eyes off Joe. It was him . . . and yet it wasn't him. Except for glimpses caught in passing, she felt as if she hadn't seen him in years. It was strange, she thought, how easy it was to avoid running into a person even when you both live in the same building. And he wasn't exactly beating her door down, either. When Laurel saw him—which these days seemed to be pretty often, Lamaze sessions or no—she always went to his place.

He looked the same . . . so what was different? As he spoke, describing how things were going to look, she kept scrutinizing him. And then she got it: *He's keeping his distance.* Literally. Where once they had seemed to walk practically in each other's footsteps, Joe was now determinedly keeping a polite three or four feet between them. A minute ago, when he'd taken her arm, she'd thought . . . well, she didn't know *what* she'd thought. But then he'd stepped back, so easily, so *naturally,* even she at first had failed to notice how purposeful it had been.

He stood close to the wall, one hand braced against an exposed stud, leaning away from her, most of his weight settled on one long leg. He was wearing a pair of blue jeans, old and faded, an equally ancient navy corduroy shirt, and a pair of desert boots. His brown hair and the lenses of his glasses were flecked with sawdust. He caught her gaze, then looked away, unhooking his glasses and squinting at a point beyond her shoulder as he slowly wiped them on the clean handkerchief he pulled from his back pocket.

Annie was struck afresh by the odd beauty of his slightly skewed features—the way his nose seemed to knuckle in at the bridge, and the way his cheekbones seemed to slant at slightly different angles, giving one eye the appearance of being not quite level with the other. Under the thick fringe of his lashes, he seemed to be viewing everything with faintly amused suspicion.

She felt an odd, downward-slipping feeling in her chest. *You may take two giant steps and three baby ones.* She was somehow back in third grade, playing Mother-May-I out on the school's kickball court.

So whose permission did she need now to cross the distance that stretched between her and Joe? It wasn't as if she had far to go . . . only two or three steps. But Annie could not bring herself to make the move.

Then Joe hooked his glasses back over his ears, and said cheerily, "Listen, it's pretty noisy out here. Let's go inside where we can hear ourselves think. You feel like a cup of coffee?"

Annie nodded, afraid to trust her voice.

In the kitchen, Joe poured two ceramic mugs, and carried them upstairs to the dining room, which was deserted except for a couple of coffee-skinned waiters setting out tablecloths and napkins. Joe chose a booth under a Wyeth print of a pumpkin field at harvest time.

"Everything okay with Laurey?" he asked cautiously, sipping at his coffee like someone who doesn't really want it, but needs something to do with his hands.

I didn't come here to talk about Laurel, she felt like shouting.

"Laurey's fine," Annie said, regretting at once the hard edge in her voice. "And you?" she added quickly. "How have you been, Joe?"

"Fine. Just fine." His greenish-brown eyes regarded her with a puzzled look, as if to say, *Then why did you come?*

"And your father? I heard he was in the hospital."

Joe gave a dry laugh that didn't quite mask the concern he clearly felt. "Marcus? It'd take more than a heart attack to take the starch out of him. He'll be okay."

"Joe, I . . ." Annie set out to say how much she'd missed him, but the words wouldn't come. God, it had been easier when the thing separating them had been three thousand miles of ocean.

"How's the search for shop space going? Have you found any-thing yet?" he asked quickly . . . a little too quickly.

"I think I may have," she replied. "But I haven't made up my mind yet. It's a little grungy."

"You should've seen this building before I took over. It was a wreck," he told her. "Looked like the morning after a Hell's Angels New Year's Eve bash."

What Annie was seeing in her mind, though, was a hole punched in a living-room wall. A hole the exact size of Joe's fist, with bits of plaster clinging to its ragged edges and hairline cracks radiating out into the wall around it like tiny thunderbolts. Beside it, like a flash of light after an explosion, Joe's face seemed illuminated somehow, like the face of a prophet in a Renaissance painting. Some-thing in his expression, in that instant, drove a sharp splinter of doubt into her, and she'd wondered, back then, *God, could he have been telling the truth about Laurel?*

Now, three months and twenty-one days later, seated across from Joe in the afternoon light that slanted in through the curved front window and formed a pane of glaring brightness on the table between them, Annie thought: *Is it too late? Did we really ruin everything for us?*

"Judging from the places I've looked at so far, I can imagine," she said, pushing that painful memory aside. She pressed her hands together in her lap, feeling her fingertips sting where she'd bitten them. Her palms felt moist and itchy.

And then she became aware that Joe was leaning forward, frowning slightly.

"Annie . . . are you all right?"

"Yeah, sure . . ." She caught herself. "No . . . I'm not okay. Joe, I don't think I've been okay since September. You don't know how many times I've wanted . . . well, I *did* try to talk to you about it, to explain, but maybe it was too soon. Maybe . . ."

A strange expression crossed Joe's face, a look she couldn't quite read, but that scared her and made her stop.

"Look," he said, "if it means anything . . . I . . . I shouldn't have blown up the way I did."

"How could you *not* have?" she cried. "How could you . . . after the way I acted, the things I said?"

Now, in the clear light of reason, her accusations seemed even more unfair. After all, she hadn't told him about Emmett, had she? Even if Joe *had* made love to Laurel, would that have been so much worse than her sleeping with Emmett?

"You only said what you thought was true." He shrugged. "Come on, Annie, you've always been harder on yourself than on anyone else."

Annie felt oddly taken aback. How could he be so forgiving? Or was it just that he didn't care enough to be angry anymore . . . and he'd put the whole episode behind him and moved so far ahead of it, and of her, that there was no way she could ever catch up?

"Joe . . ." She felt her throat catch, and she had to stop and take a short, gulped swallow. "I didn't mean it. I didn't mean those terrible things I said. I don't blame you if you can't forgive me."

"But I have." He regarded her calmly, too calmly. "I forgave you a long time ago, Annie. That's not why you're here, is it? Because I think you know that already. It's never really been a question of forgiveness, has it?"

She could see now that she was wrong about Joe not feeling anything. His gaze, though steady and kind, seemed terribly strained.

"What I'm saying is that it doesn't change anything," he went on. "Forgiving isn't the same as forgetting, Annie. *I* know that better than anyone, believe me." For an instant, he stared off into space as if he were turning inward, trying to see something inside himself. Then, seeing her again, he curved his mouth down in a slow, sad smile. "Please, don't misunderstand me. I think maybe it happened for the best."

Annie felt like a brittle eggshell about to crack. Nothing she had ever faced had ever made her feel this helpless or abandoned. Not even when she was little, standing on the sidewalk in front of school, watching the shadows grow longer and longer, waiting for Dearie to pick her up, praying she hadn't forgotten, or wasn't too drunk.

"The best?" she croaked. "How can you say that? Joe, I *need* you."

"You don't need me, Annie . . . you don't need anyone, not really. I think that's partly why I fell in love with you, but maybe also why I couldn't admit it to myself for so long. Your strength, your determination . . . it's like this fire in you, and it makes you shine, makes everyone around you want to draw in close. But the thing is—you can't get *inside* a fire, not without getting burned." He gave her a look of infinite sadness. "Annie, it wouldn't have worked, you and me."

Tears flooded her eyes, but with a force of will she kept them from spilling over. She wanted to tell him, *insist* that he was wrong . . . dead wrong . . . that she *did* need him. That the only reason she was strong was because she'd *had* to be. Who else would've taken care of her, and of Laurel? But the look in his eyes said it was too late.

"I love you, Joe," she told him instead. "More than you know."

His face seemed to contort with pain . . . then he straightened himself, and shook his head.

"No, you *think* you do. But don't you see . . . love and trust, they come together in the same package, two for the price of one. And you can't separate them. If you try to . . . the whole thing comes apart."

It hurt, a pain in her chest, a fierce cramp in her belly. At the same time, she thought, *He's right.* That was the awful part. He was right, absolutely right . . . except for one thing. If she had never loved him as he seemed to be saying, then why did she now feel as if she were being stabbed in the heart?

"I think . . . we've both said enough for now," she told him. "I think I'd better be going." Annie slid off the bench, and rose heavily to her feet.

Joe didn't try to stop her.

"Tell Laurey I'll pick her up at seven tomorrow," he called after her.

Right. Tomorrow night was their Lamaze class. She felt a swift, unexpected thrust of resentment. It was all so cozy . . . just like a real, married couple. Anyone would think it *was* Joe's baby. Then it struck her: *Suppose Joe is falling in love with her?*

Why not? Laurel's beautiful, talented, lovable. Why shouldn't he?

Nevertheless, the idea sent a new wrench of pain through her chest.

Because if she were to lose Joe to Laurel, that would mean losing Laurel as well . . . the two people around whom her whole life revolved, the only two she really loved. And how could she keep going after that?

Annie watched the white-gowned *mohel*—a gentle-looking man of forty or so with a short, dark beard—squeeze the clamplike device over the baby's tiny penis, severing its foreskin with a single neat snip. Beside her, she heard Sarah, the baby's mother, let out a tiny mewing cry, and out of the corner of her eye saw Sarah hide her pale, drawn face against her husband's shoulder. Annie winced inwardly. She knew how Sarah had to be feeling . . . wishing she could take away her son's pain and make it hers.

She realized that was the way she felt about Laurel—or used to, anyway. Now, every time she looked at Laurel's big belly, the love and sympathy she started to feel was bitten off by a surge of anger. She still couldn't bring herself to forgive her sister. If it hadn't been for Laurel, then she, Annie, would still be with Joe. And Laurel, damn her, wasn't even sorry. Look at her, Annie thought, she's *glad* I've broken off with Joe. She doesn't care how much it hurts me.

And the way she acts, it might just as well be Joe's baby.

"See how brave he is! Hardly a peep," Rivka whispered to Annie. Her round face was beaming. "Forgive me if I'm *kvelling,* but from this boy we'll *shep naches,* he'll make us proud, I can feel it."

Then with a big intake of breath, baby Yusseleh began to shriek. Annie watched as the *mohel* calmly wrapped a bit of gauze about the newly circumcised penis and deftly pinned on a clean diaper. He handed the baby to his nervous-looking grandfather Ezra, and began intoning the blessings, rocking back and forth on the balls of his feet as he did.

Every eye in the group of twenty or so seemed to be on the little star of the show, but now what Annie was noticing was Laurel, standing off to one side, well away from the knot of people clustered about the cloth-draped table in the middle of Rivka's living room. Except for her big stomach, she looked haggard, morose. Was she thinking that she might never hold her own baby the way Sarah was beginning to cuddle and soothe little Yusseleh?

In spite of herself, Annie wanted to go to her sister. How awful she must feel! Annie wished somehow she could turn back the clock, and soothe Laurel as she had when her sister was a baby herself.

Then a wave of bitterness welled up in her. Why, she asked herself for the thousandth time, had Laurel wanted to hurt her by pretending her baby was Joe's?

Why?

Now Dolly was sidling over to Laurel, hooking an arm about her thin shoulders. Annie felt a pang of jealousy. Or was it resentment? It should be *her,* not Dolly, consoling Laurel. So why couldn't she do it? Why couldn't she forgive Laurel? Why couldn't she let herself believe—as Laurel had insisted over and over—that her sister *would* have told her the truth about Joe, if only Annie hadn't gone flying off the handle before she could?

Now she watched as Laurel turned her head into Dolly's shoulder, her long hair sliding forward, hiding her face from view. Was she crying? Annie felt as if, like Yusseleh, she'd been cut, except her cut was on her heart, a tiny nick. With a small, unsteady motion, she found herself threading her way across the small room crowded mostly with bearded men in dark-colored fedoras and *tsitsiss,* which looked like clumps of long threads hanging from beneath their black suit coats, and with women in long-sleeved, high-necked dresses and stylish *shaitels.* And crowded too with a churning sea of children, babies crawling at her feet, toddlers lurching and bumping into her knees, little boys and girls scooting trucks and tops across the floor.

Stupid to have brought Laurel here. Annie realized she should've known it would be too much, seeing all these happy kids, reminding her of what she stood to lose. Annie definitely should have talked Laurel out of coming. . . .

Now Laurel looked wretched, and Annie couldn't bring herself to comfort her. Why did Dolly have to butt in? And what was she doing here in the first place? Rivka and Dolly weren't at all close, just acquaintances. Probably it was Dolly who'd invited herself.

Annie stopped then, almost tripping over a fat blond baby in blue corduroy overalls trying to pull himself up on the leg of the coffee table. Dolly, she told herself, was only trying to be nice. And she'd been so terrific with Laurel, really, not a bit of reproach for her getting pregnant, and always ready to chauffeur her to the obstetrician, or to a fabric store for sewing supplies, or to Eastern Artists for more drawing paper, pencils, pastels.

If only Dolly were less *there.* Her very presence sometimes seemed overwhelming, and her generosity, too. Was it possible that someone's kindness could be just *too* much, the way too many sweet things can make you sick?

Yet some part of Annie yearned to be comforted by Dolly, too. How would it be, she wondered, to rest her cheek against Dolly's deep, soft bosom, feel her plump, beringed hand stroking her hair?

But by the time she reached their side of the room, Laurel and Dolly were off ahead of her, down the dim hall leading to the bedrooms. Annie hesitated, then followed them.

She found them in Shainey's room, perched on the edge of the bed atop a ruffled pink bedspread crowded with what looked like a whole zoo of stuffed animals. In the corner stood what had been Shainey's crib, which Rivka now kept for the times her grandchildren came visiting. Annie paused in the doorway, feeling awkward, as if she might be intruding. But how could that be? Didn't she know Laurel best? Hadn't *she*, more than anyone, been a mother to Laurel?

Dolly looked up at her with a bright, welcoming smile, making Annie feel guilty for feeling so critical. Laurel, in a pretty red maternity smock she'd made herself, didn't even glance up. Annie longed to sit down beside her, but something held her back.

"Why, it's enough to make *anybody* upset." Dolly plunged into the awkward silence. "That poor little thing lying there on that table, getting snipped at like a butterflied leg of lamb. You'd have to be made of stone not to feel plenty bad for him. I don't know how his mother—"

"That's not it." Laurel's head snapped up, flags of red standing out on her pale cheeks. Softly, she repeated, "That's not really it at all."

"Why don't you tell me, then?" Dolly asked gently, but firmly. "Maybe I can help."

"It's *my* baby." Laurel locked her hands over her stomach, as if it were a balloon she had to anchor or it might float away. "I don't want to give it up . . . but I'm afraid to keep it. I don't feel ready to be a mother." Her voice caught. "I don't know what to do."

Annie opened her mouth to speak. She wanted to tell her sister not to worry. But no words came out. She felt so torn, both irritated with Laurel and sorry for her. For months she'd been trying to talk to Laurel about the baby, but always she'd thought that when Laurel *did* let go and confide in her, it would be in private, just the two of them. Why couldn't Laurel have waited just a few hours longer until they were home?

"Oh, you poor, poor thing." Now Dolly was fluffing up like a mother hen, tucking Laurel under her wing, while Annie watched, feeling helpless and frustrated. And then her annoyance with her aunt faded . . . there were *tears* in Dolly's eyes. "I know I haven't let on, but I've been so worried about you. About this . . . this awful choice you're having to make. And I've been afraid, too . . . of giving you the wrong advice. Of . . . influencing you."

"What do *you* think I should do?" Laurel asked, so quietly Annie had to strain to hear her.

Dolly chewed her lip as if she were wrestling with herself, then she seemed to come to a decision. "The mess I've made of my life, I wouldn't dare tell another living soul what he or she ought to do. All I know is what *I* would do if I were in your shoes . . . how I'd feel if I were somehow blessed with the miracle of a baby. So maybe I am the wrong person to ask."

"You think I should keep it?"

Dolly blinked away the brightness in her eyes, and a tear rolled down her heavily rouged cheek. "Oh, sugar, if you *did* . . . and I'm not saying you *should* . . . it would be the most loved little baby in the whole universe. Between you and me and Annie . . . why, I can't think of a blessed thing it'd be wanting for."

Annie felt a sob rising in her. Somehow, with all her bumbling, Dolly had bigheartedly found exactly the right thing to say. She'd put into words what Annie felt in her heart . . . that in spite of Laurel having no husband—not even a boyfriend that anyone knew of— and of how it would interfere with Laurel's education, and how it would tie her down . . . it would be all wrong, terrible, to give this baby away.

"Dolly's right," she told her sister, managing to keep her voice clear and steady. Now she found herself walking over, sinking down beside Laurel. She reached for her hand, cool and still under her fingers. "We'll manage somehow. Haven't we always?"

Laurel shot her an odd, flat look. "You have. *You* always manage somehow, Annie." Her voice held a note of accusation, but only a faint one. Mostly, she sounded sad.

"Listen," Dolly put in, "I know it'd be hard . . . but that doesn't have to mean you dropping out of school. You could transfer to NYU, or Cooper Union, or better yet, Parsons. I could help . . . I could pay for a nanny." She shot Annie a quick, defensive look. "Now, I don't want to hear a word against it. You've done everything yourself, the hard way . . . just like you always said you would . . . and I admire you for it. Hell, I couldn't have done what you did, not all on my own. But this is different. You'd be shortchanging Laurel . . . and the baby . . . by saying no."

"It's not up to Annie." Laurel sat up straighter, and turned to Annie, giving her a look that cut through Annie like a sharp blade. "It's up to me." She stood up. "Excuse me, but I have to use the bathroom." She gave a tiny flicker of a smile. "Seems like with this baby I have to pee about every five minutes."

When she was gone, Annie stared at the crib in the corner. It had, Rivka had proudly told her, survived nine babies, and it showed. The headboard's eggshell enamel was scratched and chipped, the teddy-bear decal on its footboard so faded it was barely visible, and its slats were gouged in places where teething mouths had gnawed them. She felt . . . defeated somehow. Though she'd never meant for this to be a contest, a struggle. Weren't she and Laurel supposed to be on the same side?

She remembered when Laurel was a baby, and she just a kid herself, struggling with those stiff safety pins to change her diapers. One time she'd turned her back for a second . . . and Laurel was somehow tumbling off the changing table. Annie, terrified, lunged forward blindly, by some lucky stroke of fate grabbing hold of Laurel's ankle just before she hit the floor. A hard little jounce, like a yo-yo makes at the end of its string. Then seeing that her head—her sweet little head with those squashy spots on top—was dangling about a quarter of an inch from her hard-cornered wooden choo-choo toy. Hearing a loud cry, she'd thought it was Laurel . . . and then realized it was *she* who was crying . . .

Annie felt like crying now.

She became aware of Dolly touching her arm.

Annie turned to face her. "Why didn't you ever have kids?" she asked, suddenly curious. "I mean, you and your husband."

"We tried and tried. But Dale . . . well, his heart was in the right place . . . and he had all the right equipment . . . but I guess there must've been a cog loose somewhere. And then later, with

Henri, I thought maybe—" She broke off with a shrug, pressing a crimson-nailed finger against one eyebrow, as if talking about Henri was giving her a headache.

"You still love him, don't you?" Annie said softly. It wasn't a question, really. She knew how Dolly had to feel.

Dolly shrugged again, but Annie saw her lips tremble. "Oh, well, us Burdock gals, we don't give up so easy."

"Guess I'm pretty stubborn too," Annie said with a dry little laugh.

Dolly turned so that she was directly facing Annie, taking Annie's shoulders and holding them so tightly she could feel the tips of her aunt's sharp fingernails digging into her shoulders. Platinum wisps had come loose from Dolly's French bun, and in the orangey glow of the Donald Duck night-light plugged into the wall next to the crib, she looked almost wild. Dolly had never been beautiful, Annie thought. Pretty, yes. But never gorgeous like Dearie had been. Yet the loving feelings that flowed from her were more powerful even than beauty . . . and they drew people to her like magnets. Even Annie, who resisted her a lot of the time, now couldn't help feeling moved by the powerful thrust of Dolly's love.

If only she could let herself lean on Dolly now and then, allow herself to be comforted by her. She remembered Joe's words, *You don't need anyone,* and felt something inside her loosen just the tiniest bit. If she could do that, let her stiff self-sufficiency bend just a little, then maybe she could find a way to mend what was wrong between her and Joe.

Annie felt as if she were pushing at a huge invisible stone right next to her . . . pushing with all her might. She could feel her arms, legs, her whole body, her mind too, *straining* to move it away. But no matter how hard she strained, it wouldn't budge. Why, God, why? Could it be she was scared . . . scared that once she got the stone moving, she might lose control?

The stone was *there,* right in front of her . . . if she could *feel* it, then she could push it away, couldn't she?

Annie gave her aunt a clumsy hug. Briefly, she allowed herself to be pulled into her aunt's warm softness . . . but she somehow couldn't let go and give in to Dolly's loving embrace.

The chance, she realized with a sharp wrench of disappointment, had once again slipped away.

"You're thinking of Laurey, aren't you?" Dolly said. "It must be hard for you, taking the backseat this time when you're used to being up there at the wheel."

"Something like that."

Dolly surprised her by clutching her, hard, squeezing so tightly Annie could hardly breathe.

"I made a mistake once," Dolly said in a fierce, hoarse whisper. "And I'll never forget the lesson it taught me. The most important lesson of all. You and your sister. Don't let anything . . . or anyone . . . ever come between you, or you'll regret it for the rest of your life."

CHAPTER 20

Rudy stared at the bright mobile dangling over the empty crib. It was the most elaborate one in the store—an array of small gingham teddy bears, each one holding a tiny fishing pole with a nylon string attached to it from which another teddy bear dangled. At its base was a music box. He tugged its string, and listened as it began tinkling a tune that sounded like "Teddy Bears' Picnic."

Beside him, Laurel said softly, "I like to come here sometimes in the afternoon, when I'm too tired to do any more drawing. It makes me feel . . . I don't know, connected somehow. Like I'm really having this baby. Like I'm really going to be a mother."

Rudy felt his heart catch. So beautiful, even more beautiful than before, if such a thing was possible, her eyes the clear, unclouded blue of the baby-boy blankets and crib quilts draped and folded all around him . . . but faded somehow, like something that's been left too long in the sun. In her oversized man's workshirt and denim skirt, the despair behind her stalwart expression not quite hidden, she reminded him suddenly of her mother—how Eve had looked when she was pregnant with Laurel.

A mother? Jesus, could she be serious about maybe keeping the kid? Last time he'd spoken with her, just two weeks ago over the phone, she'd been pretty definite, couldn't see any way she'd be able to manage a baby.

Thinking of what he had to talk her into, why he'd rushed all the way to New York, leaving two big cases hanging on continuances, Rudy's heart began to pound. He'd asked that she meet him in some neighborhood spot, figuring she'd pick a coffee shop or maybe that Chink restaurant around the corner where they'd gotten together the last time. Meet her here, she'd said. A baby store? He'd been surprised. But what the hell, in a way it made sense. A pregnant lady in a baby store? Who would ever notice?

Now, if he could just get her to see how much sense this made . . . how it would be so much better for her . . .

But he'd have to be careful as hell how he put it to her. Because if she knew he wanted the kid for himself, she'd never buy it.

"Hey, what's with the long face?" He picked up a pink stuffed bunny rabbit from the crib and gently nudged her with it. "You're gonna make all these ladies here think I'm treatin' you bad or something." He glanced around at the handful of women browsing among the racks of tiny clothes nearby.

"Oh, Uncle Rudy." Laurel sighed. "It's not *you.*"

As if she needed to tell him. Christ, he *knew* he wasn't the biggest thing in her life. She liked him, was always glad to see him, but beyond that . . . hell, he was just like the genie in the bottle who pops up from time to time to grant wishes. Rudy remembered the time—she'd been sixteen, hadn't she?—he'd wangled two tickets for her and a friend to see the Rolling Stones at Madison Square Garden. Cost him a hundred bucks each, from a scalper, and worth every penny just to see the glow it had brought to her eyes.

He felt a sharp longing, like a stitch in his side from too much running. A child. His own kid. Now that'd be a different story. Somebody who'd look at him and see, not a fat little pygmy, or a genie out of bottle, just . . . good old Dad.

"You like to come here just to look, or what?" he asked, praying she wouldn't say she had already bought a bunch of this stuff and had it back at her apartment sitting there ready for the baby.

"Just looking." She fingered a fuzzy blue sleeper the size of a half-grown kitten that was draped over the crib's rail. "I mean, what's the point of buying stuff if . . ." She stopped, sucking her breath in sharply. In a low voice, she added, "A couple of weeks ago, I made an appointment with this lady at an adoption agency, but at the last minute I cancelled it. I started thinking—what if I kept it? The baby, I mean. I could still go to school part-time or something . . . and . . . and . . . oh, I know it'd probably be horribly selfish of me . . . I mean, a baby should have parents . . . a mother *and* a father, but, well . . . I can't help wanting it, can I?" Her blue eyes shimmered, and she caught her lower lip in her teeth as if to keep her tears from spilling over.

Rudy leaned close. Jesus, here was his opening, his chance. "Listen," he said. "I might be able to help."

"You? But how?"

"Can we talk? In here?"

"Sure, why not? Nobody here knows me."

"It's no secret . . . it's just . . ." He took a breath, rocking forward onto the balls of his feet to make himself as tall as his five feet three inches would allow, the way he sometimes did in court when he was trying to appear more imposing to a witness. "Laurel, I have someone who would be interested . . . *real* interested."

"You mean . . . in adopting?" Laurel's voice dropped to a whisper. Her eyes looked back at him, huge, scared-looking.

"Yeah, that's right."

"A family?"

Rudy felt himself beginning to sweat. Under his overcoat and wool scarf, he was as hot and itchy as if he'd been roasting too long on his Malibu sun deck.

Tell her it's you. Explain how you'd be the best dad any kid could have, that he . . . or she . . . would lack for nothing in this world, a house in a neighborhood with great schools, a cottage right on the beach, the best nanny, and when the time came, Little League, Boy Scouts, music lessons, you name it. Best of all, you'd love him like he was your own . . . not in spite of the fact that he was Laurel's, but because of it. . . .

"Well, see—"

"Because it'd have to be," she said. "Otherwise, I wouldn't even consider it. I mean, if my baby wasn't going to be part of a family . . . a real *family* . . . what would be the point?"

"What if I said it was me?" he tossed off, making it sound as if it were a joke. "That I wanted to adopt it?"

"You? Oh, Uncle Rudy!" Laurel's tense look dissolved, and she giggled, cupping her hand over her mouth.

She couldn't know he was serious, but still . . . it hurt. Behind her laughter just now, he'd caught just a hint of something he couldn't put his finger on . . . disgust? Disgust at the thought of her baby nestled in his arms? Rudy felt as though something were curdling inside him, and he tasted something sour on the back of his tongue.

Hell, even if he were to line up the perfect couple, she could still back off, say no way, and then what? He couldn't force her. Not that he would want to. He'd never hurt her. In this whole damn world, who else did he love?

Hey, you're a good lawyer, he reminded himself. *The best damned matrimonial man in L.A. County . . . and if nine out of ten you can usually swing a who-cares jury and a tight-ass judge, you sure as hell ought to be able to handle this one.*

Rudy took a deep breath. "What I'm saying is, they don't have any kids, so they're not a family *that* way . . . but the sweetest couple you'd ever want to meet," he began. "Husband's a real-estate developer, great big house, plenty of money, loves kids. He takes off Saturdays to spend the whole day with this spi—Mexican kid he's Big Brother for. He's even taught him to play chess. His wife raises dogs, out in their backyard. Cocker spaniels or something. Puppies running around everywhere. They've been trying for years and years to have a kid, but the doctors tell them it doesn't look too good. You shoulda seen the look on her face when she told me how bad she wanted a baby . . . it was enough to break your heart. Nice people. They'd be terrific parents."

"Did you tell them? About me?" She looked stricken.

"Hell, no. I wouldn't do that, not without talking to you first." She was so close, he could smell her . . . the smell of talcum powder and rosewater. A baby's smell. He felt a longing so fierce it ached, pushing inside his skull, making his blood sing in his ears. But he kept his voice even. "Don's one of our firm's big clients, mostly on real-estate deals. But since I handle the family law, he thought I might be able to help him out with, well, finding a child to adopt."

What he'd actually done was give the guy the number of a shyster in Pasadena who specialized in bringing babies in from Colombia and Brazil. Perfectly legit. He'd handled Don's problem . . . and, by providing Rudy with a convincing cover story, Don was inadvertently squaring things for him.

He could tell Laurel was struggling. Yeah, he'd done right to throw in Don and his wife, a real-life Ozzie and Harriet. She could relate to them more than to some anonymous listings on an adoption agency's waiting list. And maybe, by gilding the lily like he had, he was really doing her a favor, putting her mind at ease. Painting her a rosy picture of her baby crawling around some palace, with dewy-eyed Mom and Dad exclaiming over every dirty diaper like it was a precious gift, and dozens of cute puppies to roll in the grass with.

"I don't know . . ." Laurel's gaze drifted off in the direction of the teddy-bear mobile. She pushed at it gently, making the little bears break into a jiggling little dance. She was trying very hard, he could see, not to cry.

Now, he told himself, *now.* While she was still wrestling with this, he had to really pitch it, before she backed away. Like with that case he'd handled years ago. Rudy remembered looking at Judge Weaver, and seeing that despite all the motions, filings, depositions, hours of direct and cross, the man had still not yet come to a decision. And he, Rudy, knew that if he didn't say something, *do* something, Weaver could well retire to chambers and then eventually rule that, no, a fag shouldn't have any real rights as a daddy. Then the idea came to him, and he scribbled one word onto a scrap of paper: *cry.* He'd shoved it at his client. The poor guy stood never to see his daughter except in the presence of some court-appointed guardian, but always he kept the stiff upper lip like he'd been taught in those snob schools he'd gone to.

You'd have thought Ashgood was an actor instead of a *Mayflower* blueblood. One, two, three, bowing his head to his chest and letting loose a muffled sob, with tears that looked like the real McCoy, which they were. Got him six weeks of visitation a year, but unsupervised. Not the twelve they'd wanted . . . but more than Rudy had ever thought they would get.

"You'd be doing it for the baby, not for that couple," he told Laurel. "And for yourself. You're young. You'll have other kids . . . later, when you're married, with a house in Montclair or Scarsdale, lawn with fruit trees, nice shaggy dog, the works. Why go and mess up your life now when you're so young, make everything so hard for yourself, for your baby? These people are good people, Laurel. Think about it. I mean, *seriously.*"

"I *am.*" Whipping around to face him, she said sharply, "I think about it every day. I can't sleep sometimes for thinking about what it'd be like to give my baby away. And do you want to hear something really crazy? For the first time, I'm glad my father is dead. Maybe he wasn't the best father in the world, but I'm sure it would've hurt him to know I was somewhere out there where he couldn't reach me."

The prickling under Rudy's wool scarf now made him reach under it and begin rubbing his neck, kneading it, feeling his skin grow even more irritated. Val. Christ. Like the proverbial bad penny,

Val kept turning up. Last month, calling Rudy's office to beg money—on top of the five grand he already owed. Something about quitting his job—the dipshit who ran the health club where he worked was always on him, Val had said, always ragging his ass about some diddly-squat thing, so finally he'd thrown in the towel. He'd pay Rudy back soon as he'd lined up something else.

Yeah, the day I grow a square asshole and shit bricks, Rudy had wanted to say. Quit? More likely Val was fired, and the "diddly-squat" his boss was after him about was Val half the time not showing up for the classes he was supposed to teach . . . yeah, and maybe hitting on some of his female students.

This wasn't the first time. Over the years, it had happened so often Rudy wondered why his brother even bothered to make excuses. Still, he'd written him a check, hadn't he? Blood money, that's how he thought of it. Val didn't know it, but Rudy was the one who owed him. For Laurel, for the sweetness she'd brought to his life. Not that he was really taking anything away from his brother. Val had never wanted kids, couldn't handle being a father. The main reason, Rudy guessed, that he'd been so pissed off at Annie and Laurel's jumping ship was his stupid pride. Yeah, Val had been mad because he'd been dumped.

He wanted to tell Laurel that there was no need for her to mourn Val, but how could he, without admitting that he'd lied to her all those years ago?

"You wouldn't be giving it away," he told her instead. "Not like that, not like giving away something you didn't want. Hell, you'd be giving him something good, a great chance. A normal life. *Two* loving parents instead of just one."

"Why are you doing this? Why do you care so much?"

Now Laurel's eyes were narrowing suspiciously. He felt sweat pop out on his forehead. Christ, that's all he needed, to start sweating like a pig, so she might get suspicious, maybe guess he was trying to pull something, and not just doing her a favor like he'd said.

Easy, he told himself, *take it easy. Don't push or you'll blow this.*

Rudy shrugged, dropping the stuffed bunny back into the crib. "Hey, if it's a crime to care about somebody, and to want what's best for them," he said lightly, "then call me guilty."

She touched his arm. "Uncle Rudy, I didn't mean . . ."

"I know, I know." He smiled. "It must be tough, what you're going through. Jesus, when I think of the guy who—" He stopped himself, shoving his fists into the pockets of his cashmere overcoat. If he started in about the creep who'd knocked Laurel up, he'd end up blowing a gasket.

"Don't blame him," Laurel said quickly. "He doesn't even know about the baby. I never told him."

"Why not?"

"Oh . . . lots of reasons. But not what you probably think. He'd have wanted to help out. No, more than that . . . he'd have turned it into some kind of . . . of . . . crusade. Like I was some Head Start program to educate migrant farmworkers or something." She shivered, hugging herself. "I didn't want that. Believe me, it's better this way."

"Okay, never mind about him, then. What about *you?* What do you want? You tell me. Whatever it is, I'll help you any way I can. Tell me"—and here he was sticking his neck way out—"I'm on the wrong track here, and we'll forget the whole thing."

He watched her chew her lip, and felt a flicker of hope. He wanted to shout that *he* would be the baby's father, he would love it and take care of it like nobody else could.

But how could he expect her to understand how much he needed this . . . and how much he'd love her child?

"Can I think about it?" Laurel asked.

"Sure," Rudy told her. "This couple, they'll stay right where they are until you decide."

"Do you think maybe I could meet them?"

Rudy's stomach did a cartwheel, but he kept his expression neutral. "Yeah, that was my first thought, too. But then I said to myself, 'Hey, wait, I'm no expert at this kind of thing.' So I talked to a couple of people, a psychologist I know, and this lawyer friend who handles cases like this all the time, and they both read me the riot act. Said it'd be really nuts to let you meet them. Believe me, Laurel, they've been through a lot of this, and they know what's best. Best for everyone. Trust me on this."

"Well, I . . ."

"Can I help you?" A torpedo-chested, gray-bunned saleslady was now bustling toward them down the narrow aisle between two rows of cribs.

Shit, Rudy thought. *I had her. I just about had her.* He felt like kicking the old bat for interrupting them.

"No thanks," Laurel told her, flushing a little. "Maybe later."

"I saw you looking at cribs." The old lady wasn't backing off. She was standing there like Dick Butkus getting ready to block a tackle. "If I can be of any help, you just let me know. We're having a sale, you know. Twenty percent off on our floor models. Just until the end of the month, though."

"That's nice," Laurel said.

"Your first?" she asked, glancing at Laurel's big belly.

Laurel nodded, her cheeks growing pink.

"And you must be Grandpa." The old lady winked at Rudy. "I've got six of my own, and I wouldn't trade a single one for all the rice in China."

Grandpa? Rudy wanted to rip the blue-and-pink gingham quilt off the crib in front of him and stuff it down the old busybody's throat.

"When are you due, dear?"

"March," Laurel mumbled, her color deepening.

"The end of March, I hope. You know the old saying, 'March comes in like a lion, and goes out like a lamb.' You want a little lamb, don't you?" Twittering, she drifted off toward another customer, calling back over her shoulder. "Just holler if you need me."

"Come on," Laurel whispered to Rudy. "Let's get out of here."

Outside on Seventh Avenue, Rudy squinted against the sun just now burning its way through a milky grayish haze. Laurel, beside him, wrapped in a hooded woolen cape the same heathery-blue shade as her eyes, was blowing on her fingers to keep them warm. "Buy you a cup of coffee?" he asked.

"Thanks, but I'd better be getting back," she told him, not looking at him. "Did I tell you? About those drawings my art teacher sent to a publisher friend of hers? Well, it turns out she—this publisher—wants me to illustrate a book . . . a children's book. I have a meeting with her in an hour to show her some sketches, and I want to get my stuff organized."

"Hey, that's terrific. I mean it." Rudy was happy for her—and God knows, with her talent, she deserved it—but he suspected her real reason for being in such a rush to get home just now was so she could be alone. "Listen, I'll drop you off."

Even though her building was only a couple of blocks away, Rudy hailed a cab. Maybe she wouldn't have coffee with him, but she couldn't very well say no to a ride.

Minutes later, they were pulling up in front of her building's soot-blackened brick façade.

"I'll give you a call sometime tomorrow," he told her. "Think about what I said."

"I will," she told him, again looking as if she might cry. "I really will, Uncle Rudy." Now she was looking directly at him, her eyes full of pain, and he knew she was telling the truth . . . that she would think about it. And think hard. He'd made it this far, at least.

Rudy paid the cabbie, and walked back to the baby store. The teddy-bear mobile was still there, bobbing gently above the crib. Thinking of the son or daughter who might soon be his, and feeling ready to burst wide open—fear or happiness? He wasn't sure which—Rudy approached the gray-haired saleslady and, pointing at the mobile, said calmly, "I'll take that."

"These are good, Laurel. Really good." Liz Cannawill looked up from the sheaf of drawings spread across her desk. "I think you're definitely on the right track here."

Liz, whose graying page boy didn't match her youthful face and slim figure, slid out from behind her desk. In Liz's tiny office overlooking lower Broadway, with its shelves and tables stacked with rubber-banded manuscripts and galleys, its walls covered in C-prints and cover sketches and dust jackets, Laurel felt oddly at home. Not like her own apartment, where more and more she'd begun feeling like a guest who'd overstayed her welcome, divided by an invisible wall—the Berlin Wall of unspoken accusations that lay between Annie and her. This was only her second visit to Fairway Press, but here she felt she could relax, and be Laurel the artist instead of poor *pregnant* Laurel.

"Of course, I'll have to show these to our art department, and I'm sure they'll have some suggestions for layout," Liz was saying, "but I don't see a problem in giving you the go-ahead. Laurel, it's been ages since I've seen work as good as yours. Especially coming from someone of your"—she paused, smiling—"shall we say, relative inexperience?"

Laurel could feel herself beginning to blush, but she was determined not to let her awkwardness show. What would Liz think if she knew that, aside from the program covers she'd done for the theatre department at school, this was her first real illustrating job? Standing up, Laurel smoothed her skirt. She'd worn her most businesslike maternity dress, one she'd sewn herself, a long-sleeved charcoal jersey with starched white piqué cuffs. The bright silk scarf knotted loosely about her neck would draw attention from her big belly, she hoped, and with her long hair pulled back with a gold barrette, maybe she could pass for twenty or twenty-one.

"I'm glad you like them," she said. "Of course, they're just preliminary sketches. The final ones will be more fleshed out . . . and I thought maybe one or two colors? What do you think?"

"Well . . ." Liz was tapping the eraser end of her pencil against the eyepiece of her square tortoiseshell glasses, her mouth pursed in contemplation. "We're working on a pretty tight budget with this one—a retelling of a fairy tale isn't going to go out with a huge first printing, I'll be honest with you. And colors . . . that would make it quite a bit more expensive. But I'll do an estimate. In the meantime, why don't you give me one of these with colors so I can compare them."

"No problem," Laurel said.

"End of the week?"

"First thing Monday morning," she promised. "And I should have the final drawings ready in about . . . oh, eight weeks. Will that be okay?"

"Don't rush. We haven't even set a pub date. Probably it won't go into production until summer, in time for the Christmas season." She stopped, glancing at Laurel's belly, her lip-glossed mouth turning up slightly. "But it looks like *you'll* be going to press before then."

Now the blush Laurel had fought earlier came over her full force—her face burned as if Liz had just switched on a bank of klieg lights in front of her. Inside, she felt hot, too—like one of those balloons with a flame making it expand and lift off the ground. In spite of her big stomach and swollen breasts and lumpy ankles, she felt hollow and light, as if she could just float away . . . right up through the roof and out over the avenue below with its colorful galleries and display windows. God, why did everyone have to keep reminding her? Why did she have to get beat over the head with it every time she went out somewhere?

"You know, I've always wondered how you mothers do it," Liz went on. "I mean, working at home with a baby at your feet. It's going to be quite a change."

"Oh . . . I'll manage."

She felt a little dizzy and light-headed, Fourth of July sparklers dancing at the corners of her vision. *A baby at my feet? If only she knew . . .*

"I'll bet." Liz, in her trim ocher-and-black suit, with her head cocked to one side, made Laurel think of a bird, a curious finch. She meant well, Laurel knew. And she probably had no children of her own, so she couldn't possibly know what she, Laurel, was going through. "On the other hand, children . . . I imagine they give you all kinds of wonderful insights. Valuable, if you're going to be illustrating children's books."

"Yes, I'm sure." Laurel, desperate to steer the conversation away from her impending motherhood, quickly put in, "What do you think about my making the bear a bit more menacing?" She pointed at the uppermost drawing on Liz's desk.

An old story, a retelling of "East of the Sun and West of the Moon," but one of Laurel's favorite fairy tales. She wanted to capture exactly the right mood, but not make it so realistic that it might scare the youngest readers.

"I think you've got it just right," Liz said after peering carefully at it for several long seconds. "Authentic, natural, with just a touch of Walt Disney. Maybe a bit less teeth in this one—we don't want it to look as if our bride is in danger of being eaten. But otherwise, I'd stick with what you've got here." Liz glanced at her watch. "Oops. I hate to cut this short, but I'm late for another meeting."

Liz started to walk out with her, but Laurel waved her back. "Please, don't bother. I know the way out."

"Okay. See you Monday, then."

"Monday."

Liz laughed lightly. "Deadlines . . . don't you just love them?"

On her way down in the elevator, Laurel thought, *Deadlines*. It wasn't Monday's deadline that was tugging at her now, but tomorrow's. She'd have to have an answer for Rudy by then. Stepping out into the polished marble lobby, panic clutched at her.

How can I do it? Give my own baby away?

You have to, a voice urged. *It's the only sensible thing to do.*

But if that was so, then why didn't it *feel* that way? Why did it feel about as sensible as cutting out her own heart?

Maybe she *should* have told Jess. But, no, what good would that have done? And besides, she *had* tried, that one time.

Laurel, as she made her way toward the subway through the crowds thronging the sidewalk, found herself remembering that day. She'd been sitting on the grass in front of Hind's Hall, with Jess standing over her like a fiery Old Testament prophet, so furious he was punching the air. The My Lai mass murderer was acquitted. The government was shit. And he personally wanted to blow up the whole of Washington, D.C.

"Jess . . ." She'd plucked at the tail of his T-shirt, which had come untucked from his faded chinos. The shirt was black, with cut-off sleeves that showed the knotted muscles in his dusky arms.

"The guy's a butcher, a fucking animal!" Jess ranted on, not hearing her. "Yeah, sure, it wasn't him personally, but Medina was the commanding officer, the buck stopped with *him.* Calley's guilty as hell, too, but he's just the scapegoat. Man, I can't *believe* this."

"Jess," she said, "the whole war doesn't make sense. So why should this? Please, don't let it get to you so much."

He'd stared down at her, his arms falling to his sides as abruptly as if she'd yanked on them. "We can't just stand around and do *nothing.*"

"Of course not. But, Jess, some of the time we have to think of ourselves, too. I mean, when was the last time we talked about anything but, well, changing the system?"

He shot her a burning look that seemed to say, *What else matters?*

Then, as if realizing she might be right, he dropped down on the grass opposite her, forking his long legs so that they formed a V about hers. He smiled at her, that heavy-lidded lazy smile that had once melted her defenses but now had little effect on her. A summer apart from Jess had given her a new perspective on him— he seemed more childish than she'd thought at first, like a kid rebelling just for the hell of it. And what about the fact that for three whole months he hadn't once written or called?

"Hey, Beanie," he said, reaching out to wind a strand of her hair about his long, brown finger. "Maybe you're right . . . maybe I ought to kick back once in a while. Let's go back to my place . . . and afterwards we can talk about anything you like."

That was the moment. He was next to her, sitting quietly, and she was going to tell him. But then a group of his buddies, spilling out of Carnegie Library, came over, waving and hooting. Jess asked if they'd heard about Medina, then they were shouting, each one cursing Nixon louder than the next. Laurel slipped away, and she felt sure nobody even noticed.

Since she'd dropped out of school, Jess had called her once to say he was going to be in the city and could he drop by. But she'd put him off. What was the use? There was nothing he could do. Nothing she wanted from him. And she certainly didn't want to marry him.

God, why couldn't it have been Joe? If he were the father of this baby, she wouldn't care if he didn't love her. Because if he was willing to give her even half a chance, she could *make* him love her. And maybe it wasn't so farfetched. Lately, she'd been catching this look in his eyes—as if he were seeing her in a new light, and maybe imagining how it might be, the two of them. Each time she'd seen that expression on his face, it was like another stitch in the gossamer fabric of hope she was secretly weaving.

Reaching the Broadway-Lafayette station, Laurel reminded herself harshly that this *wasn't* Joe's baby. And she had only until tomorrow to decide what to do about it.

Don't think about it, she told herself. *There's still time. You don't have to make up your mind this very moment.*

When she arrived home, Laurel was surprised to see Annie at the kitchen table, bent over what looked like a stack of contractors' estimates—one bony elbow propped next to a coffee mug, her short hair rucked up on one side where she'd been leaning into her cupped palm. She was wearing a ribbed orange sweater, its sleeves pushed up to her elbows, and a pair of wide-wale tan corduroys. She blinked up at Laurel, then straightened, her thoughtful expression shifting, tightening somehow—the change so quick and subtle that only Laurel, who knew her sister better than anyone, would have noticed. Seeing that look, she felt something inside herself close off as well.

She still hasn't forgiven me. And why should she?

Annie, she knew, was still as much in love with Joe as ever. So how could Annie forgive Laurel for what she'd done?

But what was she supposed to do about it? And, really, was she responsible for what had happened? She *would* have told Annie about Jess . . . but Annie, with her usual bulldozer approach, just had to run right downstairs and confront Joe, not giving her . . . or even him . . . a chance to explain. Okay, she felt bad about it, guilty too, but was it her fault Joe and Annie were hardly speaking *now*, more than three months later?

Maybe it was meant to be this way, she thought. Even if she hadn't gotten pregnant, maybe it never would have worked out with Joe and Annie.

And . . . well, when you got right down to it, why should Annie have any more claim on him than she did? Laurel remembered his kiss, still as fresh in her mind as if it had happened moments ago, rather than months—that first startled stiffening of his mouth, then the delicious feel of him yielding . . . opening to her . . . wanting her in spite of his telling himself he didn't, he mustn't. God, if only she could have that again . . . if only she could make him *see* that it wasn't wrong to want her.

Not that he'd been unfriendly since then. No, he acted the same as always—kidding around with her, not holding back on the occasional brotherly hug. And hadn't he agreed to be her Lamaze coach? Still, Laurel sensed the strain between them, the unspoken gap between what she wanted from him and what he was willing to give her. If only . . .

"Hi," Annie said.

"Hi." Laurel threw her coat and empty portfolio over one of the cane-back dinette chairs. "What are you doing home so early? I thought you'd be out quarterbacking with contractors."

Annie groaned. "I was." She riffled through the papers in front of her. "Would you believe it? Eleven estimates, and the lowest one is still about twice what I figured on."

"What about doing it yourself?" Laurel suggested.

"You mean knocking out walls, installing electrical cables, plumbing, that kind of thing? If I could, I probably would." She laughed. But Laurel hadn't been joking.

"I don't mean that. I meant, why pay a general contractor? You could hire the subcontractors yourself, couldn't you? It'd mean overseeing everything yourself, but I can't imagine you *not* hanging over everyone's shoulder anyway. And that way you could cut your expenses by about fifteen or twenty percent."

Annie's mouth dropped open in amazement, then she recovered with a little snort of laughter. "I have to admit I'm impressed. What do you know about building and contractors?" As soon as the words were out, her smile vanished, and the room's temperature seemed to drop ten degrees. She had to have guessed the reason: Joe.

Laurel thought, *She knows I've been spending time with him, not just the Lamaze classes, but at the restaurant . . . watching his addition go up, listening to him deal with plumbers, electricians, carpenters. . . .*

Laurel shrugged. "You think I spend all my time doodling? I know a thing or two."

"I'm sure you do." With a sharp look, Annie gathered up her papers, and rose, the scraping of her chair against the linoleum sounding harsh and somehow dismissive. "Well, I guess I'd better start dinner."

"It's in the oven," Laurel told her. "Eggplant parmesan. I made it this morning, before Ru—" She caught herself. "Before I finished getting my portfolio together."

"How did the meeting go?"

"Good. She liked my drawings."

"Well, I'd be surprised if she didn't. They're really fantastic." Annie's stony expression softened, and in her indigo eyes, Laurel caught a hint of pride. Laurel felt a pang, wishing she could bridge this awful gulf between them.

Then she remembered Joe—she was meeting him downstairs in less than an hour. Their Lamaze class was at eight. Laurel wished things between Annie and her weren't so strained. But how could she be sorry that this falling-out between Annie and Joe had brought her closer to Joe?

"You could set the table while I get dinner on," Laurel suggested mildly. "Just let me get out of these shoes." She sat down and pried off her low-heeled pumps. Rubbing a swollen foot, she added, "At the rate I'm going, my feet will look like scuba fins by the time this is over."

"Good. Then maybe you'll stop borrowing my shoes. It's a curse, having a younger sister with the same size feet."

Neither one mentioned the baby, but Laurel felt the tension

between them ease a bit. As Annie came around and stood beside her, she found herself, out of old habit, leaning into her sister's side, the sharp angularity of Annie's hip as comforting somehow as a mother's plump belly. Now she could feel Annie's fingers, cool and competent, kneading the tired muscles in her neck, and Laurel allowed herself to slip backwards in time, remembering when it had been just the two of them—two survivors in the same boat, paddling toward shore.

How had the horizon become so blurred? How could they have drifted so far apart? In spite of Annie's touch, or maybe because of it, Laurel felt the pinch of tears beginning in the bridge of her nose. This little moment wouldn't last, she knew. Why kid herself?

She felt the baby move inside her, a gentle twisting sensation that somehow stabbed her more deeply than if a knife had been plunged into her. *I can't keep this baby,* she realized. *It'd be wrong. Selfish.* And now she wouldn't even have her sister to console or comfort her. Annie wanted to help her, she sensed, but something was holding her back. Resentment? Or was it her feeling that if she gave in, she'd somehow be letting go of Joe for good?

Laurel felt her sister draw away from her, watched her move toward the row of bright yellow cupboards that Laurel, years ago, had painted with Dali-like designs of plates, cups, knives, baskets of bread and fruit. Noting the square angle of Annie's shoulders as she began taking down plates and glasses, the sharp knot of bone sticking up from the scooped neck of her sweater, Laurel felt the tears in her nose rush up into her eyes, and wondered why, when she needed Annie's strength the most, were they holding one another at arm's length?

CHAPTER 21

Annie watched Emmett stamp on the doormat as he came in, small rivulets of water cascading off his boots. She waved to him from behind the display case where she was waiting on a customer, holding up a finger to say she'd be with him in a moment.

"I'll have one of those. Just one." The plump woman in a raccoon coat pointed a gloved finger at a tray of dark, lumpy chocolates. Not dainty like Girod's truffles—these were the size of golf balls. A mistake Annie had made with her very first batch, which strangely, wonderfully, had turned out to be a success. The woman gave a nervous laugh. "I'm supposed to be dieting."

"Why is it," she heard Emmett drawl, "that the women who're so worried about their weight are usually the ones who don't need to be?"

Annie glanced up, and saw him now leaning up against the old marble-top shaving stand on which sat the cash register, one water-stained boot crossed casually over the other. He caught Annie's eye and winked. Annie felt a rush of heat in her cheeks, and quickly looked away, busying herself with wrapping the single bourbon truffle in filmy crimson tissue, and placing it in a small bag—also crimson, with the name she'd given her shop embossed in gold script: Tout de Suite.

She handed it to the woman, who was now blushing and smiling delightedly. Annie felt both irritated with Emmett and happy to see him.

She'd agreed to meet him for dinner, but at Paolo's, not here. It was only a quarter to six, and she wouldn't even be closing for another fifteen minutes. And after that, she'd still have to tally the day's receipts, take inventory of what was left in the display cases and in the refrigerator in back to see how many of each item she'd need for tomorrow, and she also needed to check to see if Doug had really fixed the tempering machine.

Emmett, damn him, knew perfectly well that she couldn't stop and chat with him right now. So why was he giving her that impish smile, as if . . . as if he possessed some delicious secret that he'd reveal only if she begged him. As if she didn't already know!

Warmth crept into Annie's cheeks as she remembered Emmett, earlier this week, quietly, almost offhandedly, inviting her to go away with him for the weekend. She'd told him no, but he'd merely shrugged, as if he felt confident it was only a matter of time before she would cave in. After all, what was holding her back? They'd been lovers once, so why not now?

Annie couldn't have explained it to him. She wasn't even sure she understood herself what was holding her back. When she was with Emmett, she felt it, sure . . . this urge, a compulsion almost, to touch him, to feel the span of his broad hand covering hers; to stroke the underside of his jaw, where the roughness of his beard stubble gave way to skin soft as chamois. And yes, dammit, she thought about him in bed, his hard shanks pressed against the insides of her calves, his broad brown chest hoisted above her like a bulwark. And him inside her . . . thrusting . . . high . . . each stroke bringing her closer to the edge of delicious frenzy . . .

God, she had to stop this . . . this sophomoric fantasizing. It wasn't love, what she felt for Emmett—it couldn't be—because how then could she still feel so strongly about Joe?

Sex, she thought. It's like the tides or the sun rising, you can't control it, but you sure can count on it. In her case, she could count on it messing up a perfectly good friendship, and distracting her with memories and feelings she'd have been better off leaving behind in Paris.

But with Emmett, there was more to it than just sex. Though —let's face it—sex was a big part of it; Emmett was an incredible lover. But he was also a wonderful friend. Not the way Joe had been, unfailingly kind, a kind of big brother—Emmett teased and needled her, he challenged and coerced her. He . . . well, he got under her skin somehow . . . and sometimes it wasn't all that comfortable.

Emmett, she sensed, knew things about her that she didn't want him—or anyone—to know, and that made her nervous. Like now.

How, when she hadn't given him the slightest encouragement, could Emmett *know* that he was starting to get to her?

The heat in her cheeks had moved up to her hairline, making her scalp feel tight, itchy. Part of her wished Emmett would just go away . . . stop making her feel things she didn't want to feel . . . and part of her was glad he was here, glad he was so persistent. If it weren't for Emmett, she knew she'd never do anything in the evenings but drag herself home and crawl into bed. After getting up at five each morning to pick out fresh fruit at the wholesale market on Ninth Avenue, then coming here, setting up in the kitchen, constantly checking that her two eager assistants, Doug and Louise, didn't burn anything or fall asleep stirring the huge pots of ganache, then racing through the rest of the day waiting on retail customers or hailing cabs to get to a meeting with some hotel or department-store buyer, by this time of day Annie was usually ready to drop. Yet Emmett's popping in was like a cool breeze on a hot day. It revived her somehow.

"You're early," she told him when the plump woman had left.

"I was showing a loft in Tribeca, and I thought I'd drop in, see if you needed a hand with anything." He looked over at waiflike Louise, a Twiggy lookalike with her cropped hair and miniskirt, busy refilling one of the white wicker display baskets. Louise caught his glance, and lowered her eyes, blushing deeply. "Looks like you've got everything under control out here, but how about that tempering melter you said was cutting out on you?"

"Doug supposedly fixed it before he left."

"Mind if I take a look?"

"In those clothes?" As he was shrugging off his overcoat, she took in his muted cashmere blazer, button-down shirt and silk tie, perfectly pressed gray slacks. In her plain black skirt and ivory silk blouse, she felt underdressed by comparison. "You know you're going to get chocolate all over you."

But Emmett's blazer was already off, and he was rolling up his sleeves. "Good. I'll taste irresistible then. Make it twice as hard for you to say no to this weekend." He winked at her again. "And even if you do, I may shanghai you. For your own good. Before you work yourself to death. Besides, with or without me, you owe it to yourself to visit Cape May. It's like going back in time."

"I thought it was a summer resort." Annie closed the sliding glass panel to the refrigerated display case.

"You're changing the subject. But yeah, it is. Only didn't anyone ever tell you the best time to visit a summer place is in the winter?"

"Why is that?"

Emmett came around to her side, and hooked an arm about her shoulders. "Because when it's cold and blowing like hell outside, you get to go inside where it's warm. And because we'd be just about the only visitors around. Sort of like having the whole playground all to ourselves."

He was so close, she could see the faint sprinkling of freckles on his jaw, and the layers of blue, like a river's shifting depths, that his eyes were made of. Imagining the two of them snuggled under a quilt in an antique brass bed, the wind howling about the eaves of some seaside inn, she felt something low in her belly give way.

She drew away from him. This was crazy! She was just lonesome. For Joe. She'd be using Emmett . . . the way (*oh, come on, admit it*) she'd used him in Paris. And Emmett . . . wasn't he using her in a way, too? He was new in town, probably lonely, so why not fall back on the good times they'd shared?

"Em . . ." she started to say.

He held a finger to her lips, and she could smell him, a nice leathery broken-in smell. "Later. You don't have to decide right now. We'll talk about it over dinner." He stepped back with a smile as slow and sure as a sunrise. "Now, I'll let you start closing up the joint while I go check on that melter."

Watching him amble through the doorway that led into the kitchen, Annie asked herself, *Sure, and what're you going to tell him tonight? "Em, I shouldn't, I'm not in love with you, but you see, the thing is I'd dearly love to get laid"?*

But there was more to it than needing to put a lid on her raging libido. Dammit, she had a business that was just starting to get off the ground. It needed every ounce of her strength, and every minute of her time, or it would slip away and go under—like most start-up enterprises.

Grabbing her clipboard with order forms for bulk supplies from the shelf under the old-fashioned nickel-plated register, Annie was seized by a sudden exhilaration. She looked about the place, at all she'd accomplished. Tout de Suite had happened so fast, was *still* happening so fast, that even when she slept she dreamed she was working.

She remembered her revulsion the first time she'd seen the place, with its grease-coated backsplash and hood, its grime-encrusted vinyl floor tiles. Now, seeing the walls with their gay, strawberry-trellis paper and the floorboards painted country white and covered with colorful hooked rugs, she felt a rush of satisfaction. Across the front display window, on café rods, she'd hung white eyelet-lace curtains and a ruffled valance. And fixed to the walls, antique gaslight sconces, no two alike, which she'd scrounged up in a Nyack second-hand shop up the Hudson. Along the top of the display case, she'd placed white wicker baskets filled with finger-sized slivers of almond bark and tiny chunks of pecan brittle for customers to nibble on while they waited. Louise Bertram, the temp she'd hired for Valentine's Day, who had stayed on when the orders continued to flood in, had just finished filling one basket and was starting on another.

Annie remembered how she'd feared that no one who could afford to buy fancy chocolates would ever venture into this grungy neighborhood, even if the word ever got out about how good her stuff was. And on the three wholesale accounts she'd managed to land, the profit margin was so low at first she thought she'd never keep afloat. But since opening up six weeks ago, her retail trade, at first almost nonexistent, had grown steadily, and now paid almost enough to cover Louise's salary.

She looked up at the huge gilt mirror behind the register, over which hung a discreet hand-painted sign, black on Chinese red, bordered in gold: TOUT DE SUITE. HANDMADE CHOCOLATES FOR THE CARRIAGE TRADE, SINCE 1973. People appreciated a sense of humor, Annie had discovered. Especially those not sticking to their diets.

Thinking back on those first weeks was like remembering a long illness, a delirium from which only moments survived with any clarity. She remembered how she'd worried. The money Dearie had left her—would it be enough for the designer, the contractors, the permits, the equipment, the decorating, the chocolate supplies, the two years of fourteen hundred dollars a month rent? What if the renovating went over budget? She wouldn't have anything left to run the shop, and she'd be dead broke.

She'd decided to cut corners, as Laurel had suggested, by acting as her own contractor, but even then, when the carpenters, plumbers, and electricians came in with their bids, even the lowest ones were so much more than she'd estimated. She'd almost backed out right then and there. If Emmett hadn't dug up a contractor one of his clients had recommended, who was supposedly both good and cheap, she might well have.

Andrzej Paderewski *did* seem honest, and his references checked out. But no one had warned her that not one of his carpenters, plumbers, or electricians spoke or understood a word of English. How to tell them they were supposed to be hanging a swinging door, and not one with ordinary hinges? Paderewski himself was nowhere to be reached, and how to convey to two seemingly deaf and mute Poles that they were installing a radiator where her cooling cabinet was supposed to go? She'd tried shouting at them, then cajoling, finally trying to get her message across through miming and hand signals. But aside from exchanging puzzled glances, and giving her sympathetic looks as if she were some kind of crazy lady, the men resolutely, even cheerfully, continued hooking up the radiator, which later on they just as cheerfully moved across the room.

And then of course when the Sheetrock men came to close in the wall, the wiring wasn't completed, so they disappeared for a whole week. Then the wall couldn't be closed because the building inspector first had to check out the venting, which it became clear he would never do without a bribe of a hundred dollars or so. So that when the job actually got finished, pretty much the way she wanted it, only two weeks behind schedule, it felt like a miracle. Most of the decorating, thank goodness, she'd managed somehow to do on her own, with Emmett pitching in—painting, refinishing the antique display case she'd picked up on Atlantic Avenue in Brooklyn, persuading Doug, who'd been a painter's assistant before going to chef's school, to hang wallpaper.

And then two days before she was scheduled to open, with the new stove and refrigerator fully installed, the cabinets hung and stocked, the butcher-block workstation in place, the cooling cabinets, tempering melter, prebottomer—the machine that formed the chocolate shells for filled bonbons—and enrober ready to go, and the bulk couverture and condiments stored in back, Mr. New York City Health Inspector marched in and wrote up a violation prohibiting any sales of edibles or any food preparation on account of rats. She could see him in her mind now, his narrow pocked face and pointy nose, looking like a rat himself as he crouched in a corner of the supply room, scraping the offending "droppings" into a vial while in pure Brooklynese he lectured her about possibly lethal diseases, poisons, exterminators. She'd been ready to scream. There *were* no rats; she was positive. And then it hit Annie. Of course—that shipment of couverture she'd gotten in the other day; there had been loose chocolate shavings in the bottom of the box that must have fallen on the floor. Scooping up a handful, she'd tried to convince Mr. Rat he was way off base, but no, he wouldn't listen . . . he'd only disgustedly wrinkled his nose. And then, desperate, knowing that it might be days, weeks, before the test results on the "droppings" came back, she'd taken the only way out she could see— she'd popped the chocolate shavings into her mouth. And however unsanitary, it had been worth it . . . just to see the goggle-eyed, horrified look on his pointy face. He'd sickly shaken his head and then scurried out of there, clipboard tucked under his arm, as if *he* were about to be exterminated. But she'd heard no more about the violation.

The morning she began making her first batch of ganache, Annie, both weary and exhilarated, had felt as if at last she'd succeeded in climbing an enormous mountain and was planting her flag at the top. But then she realized she'd been vastly overoptimistic. The mountain turned out to be a mere foothill, and ahead of her rose the real Mount Everest. By six A.M., three whole batches of ganache had come out stiff and tasting slightly grainy, and she'd thrown them out. Could the couverture she'd bought from Van Leer in New Jersey, she'd wondered, be so different from what she'd worked with at Girod's? Then she'd discovered that easily half the fresh raspberries she sent Doug out to buy were moldy. On top of that, most of the decorations—hazelnut *crocants* and *violettes*—lay crushed in their boxes, and to make her misery complete, the old enrober had clunked to a standstill. For the time being, all she could do was dip the truffles by hand, and she'd ended up with gross things that resembled chocolate-covered golf balls, only lumpier. And poor Doug—she could see him now in her mind, his thick glasses with their Coke-bottle lenses slipping down his beaked nose as he peered underneath the enrober's conveyor belt—after dashing around on a million errands, scrubbing the pots, chopping the nuts, struggling valiantly to get the enrober going, then standing and helping her dip dozens upon dozens of truffles by hand, she'd insisted he eat six of those monstrous truffles, each with a different filling, to be absolutely sure they tasted all right. He'd gobbled them up, pronouncing them delicious . . . but then had gotten so nauseated, she'd had to send him home, and she'd been left all alone, working and worrying herself crazy.

What would happen, she'd agonized, if none of the buyers with whom she had appointments liked her ugly truffles? With not quite ten thousand left in the bank, barely enough to cover her costs for three months, she'd have to start selling these chocolates practically this minute, or this whole house of cards would come tumbling down around her ears.

At her first appointment that afternoon, with the buyer from Bloomingdale's, she'd actually been laughed out of their uptown office. At the memory, Annie's stomach knotted even now.

"Horse apples," the haughty, gray-haired woman had pronounced. "They look exactly like horse apples." She wouldn't even taste one, saying that her customers clearly would be put off by the way they looked.

But then her old friend from Dolly's shop, Russ Kearney, the Plaza Hotel's bearded young buyer, though plainly apprehensive, had been kind enough to take a nibble. And then another, and another, finishing the whole truffle and licking his chocolate-smeared fingertips. Though too large and ungainly to be offered as an on-the-pillow-at-night freebie, Russ had ordered six dozen for a Palm Court luncheon he was organizing—making her want to cry with relief. Annie, luckily, had had the bright idea of wrapping each of the truffles in iridescent cellophane, tied with silver ribbon, onto which she pasted a postage-stamp-sized "Tout de Suite" sticker. And just that little bit of advertising had brought her several retail customers and a small gourmet shop on Amsterdam Avenue.

Annie also managed to get tiny orders from Zabar's and Macy's Cellar. Modest reorders at first, and at prices below what she figured it was costing her to make the chocolates. But she had no choice. She had to swallow the loss in the hope that people would like them and come back for more. And gradually, very gradually they did. Then, as Tout de Suite began to catch on, the orders began coming for eight, nine, twelve dozen. She dared to raise her prices, just enough to leave her a tiny profit. But even priced at a dollar apiece, her unique homely truffles were being snatched up. And for Valentine's Day, she'd thought of packaging each one individually in a tiny box, decorated by Laurel with trimmings she'd bought from a milliner who was going out of business—silk flowers, bits of ribbon, tufts of netting, tiny faux cherries, strawberries, apples. She'd sold every one, and had orders for dozens more. With Doug and her both working every night, she'd also hired Louise, a Culinary Institute dropout who turned out to be inspired when it came to chocolate.

Even now, getting up while it was still dark, each day was an uphill climb. Riding the nearly deserted subway, which made her more uptight than at rush hour. Then here, plunging in up to her elbows, a batch of ganache on the stove, one on the tempering melter, another in the enrober, by the time most people just were pouring their first cup of coffee. Sweaty, her feet aching, her hands chapped, by the time she opened her door for business, she felt ready to drop.

Hard to believe it was a little more than a month; and now people were sending their drivers, from as far away as Sutton Place.

"I'm having a dinner party next week . . ."

Annie became aware that someone was speaking to her, a woman in a shamrock-green cashmere cape and stylish wide-brimmed hat that hid most of her face. Annie hadn't seen her walk in.

"Oh, Mrs. Birnbaum, it's you." Annie started, then laughed. "You caught me daydreaming. I was just about to lock up. What can I do for you?" Felicia Birnbaum had been her first customer that scary opening day—her *only* "real" one, aside from Emmett and Dolly and Laurel.

"It's a party for my husband's biggest clients and their wives," Felicia Birnbaum went on, tugging fretfully at her gloves. "And I'd like to do something they'll *really* remember."

Now Annie brought her into focus, and thought for a moment. "Marzipan," she said. "Little braided marzipan baskets. I'll fill them with twists of candied ginger and miniature truffles." Her mind raced ahead, and she thought, *Marzipan? God, I've only worked with it once before, with Pompeau watching my every move. Suppose I can't do it. . . .*

Annie felt her coolly competent expression slipping, and she concentrated on fixing her smile in place.

Felicia Birnbaum frowned in contemplation, and brought a gloved hand to rest against one fashionably sunken cheek. *She* certainly wouldn't indulge in anything as caloric as marzipan, but then a lot of Annie's clientele was like that. They bought chocolates for their aged mothers, their clients, their husbands' secretaries, sometimes even their lovers.

"Oh," Mrs. Birnbaum said, "Well, I never thought . . . but that *would* be lovely, wouldn't it? Do you have a sample . . . or a picture at least?"

"Only in my head." Annie prayed she wouldn't ask for details. "I'd do it as a special favor, Mrs. Birnbaum. Just for you. That way, no one else will have anything like it."

The woman looked relieved, and she relaxed against the refrigerated display case crowded with wicker baskets like the ones on top, each heaped with truffles Annie had created herself: Drambuie, with flecks of orange peel; chocolate lemon custard; dark, smoky espresso, with a crunchy roasted coffee bean at its center; coconut, dark rum, and crème-fraîche confections wrapped in milk chocolate.

"Oh," she said. "That would be . . ."

Annie smiled. "Trust me."

". . . perfect."

"How many guests will you be having?" she asked, pulling a slip of notepaper from a drawer under the register.

"Twenty-eight, give or take a few, but the party's next Monday, only a week from today. Are you sure you'll have enough time?"

"Absolutely," Annie assured her with a confident flick of her pencil, while in her mind she was picturing herself working frantically through the weekend. "Twenty-eight did you say? Let's make it an even thirty then. Believe me, Mrs. Birnbaum, you won't have any leftovers."

Minutes later, Mrs. Birnbaum was dashing through the rain, ducking into the bright red MG parked illegally at the curb, leaving behind a faint slipstream of Chanel No. 5 and a check for three hundred dollars. Annie slipped the check into the register, then went over and locked the front door, and put up the "CLOSED" sign. Returning to the counter, she noted that Louise had gone into the kitchen, probably to clean up, or maybe to give Emmett a hand—the way poor Louise blushed whenever Emmett was around, she might as well be wearing a neon sign. And why not? Wouldn't any unattached woman in her right mind be attracted to Emmett?

Annie, suddenly too tired to stand, sank down on the old piano stool that stood between the wall and a second-hand sewing stand crowded with jars of candied grapefruit and orange peels dipped in chocolate. From the kitchen came the dreadful, broken-sounding clattering of the melter starting up. Obviously, Doug hadn't fixed it properly. But would Emmett have better luck? Maybe it couldn't be fixed, and she'd need a new one. Not that she had money to buy one, with every cent being funnelled back into supplies, rent, salaries, phone, electric, you name it.

She sighed, wondering how, with the melter down, she'd ever be able to have Mrs. Birnbaum's baskets ready on time, when just keeping up with the Zabar's order and two other parties she'd booked was already more than she could handle. *When it rains it pours,* she thought, glad for the business . . . but a little scared too. What on earth had she gotten herself into?

With Emmett, too. Was it fair to risk letting this thing between them get out of hand when she didn't know if she'd ever be able to give him more?

I miss Joe. The thought gripped her with sudden force, leaving her weak and breathless.

Since that day at the restaurant they'd hardly spoken. He was busy with Joe's Place and who knew what else, and she with Tout de Suite. They smiled, and nodded to one another in the hallway. Once in a while, he'd chat for a moment about Laurel, who was due any day now.

And these days Joe saw more of Laurel than she did. One night a week, he took her to her Lamaze class, and on other nights, when he wasn't too tired, he'd phone and she'd go down and practice her breathing exercises at his apartment.

Laurel had grown secretive. She hardly talked to Annie about anything other than the book she was illustrating, or Tout de Suite. Never about Joe. It was almost as if the two of them had formed some kind of . . . well, an unspoken pact.

Oh, Laurel was courteous . . . and she listened with a look of rapt concentration whenever Annie spoke about the shop. But it was like talking to a doll . . . that silly doll that Dearie had once given Laurel that chirped, when you pulled the string in its back, "Hi! My name is Chatty Cathy! What's yours?"

Six months ago, Annie could not have imagined she'd ever be

jealous of her sister . . . but now, weirdly, she was. That Laurel was in love with Joe, well, she could handle that. But he, could *he* be falling in love with her? It seemed impossible. It *felt* impossible. But then, why not? Laurel was lovely and sweet-natured . . . and she needed him. . . .

So what right have I to be jealous of Laurel? Especially now. At least I have Tout de Suite . . . but what does she have really? A make-believe husband, a baby she's about to lose?

Once or twice, she had come upon Laurel sitting quietly with her hands placed almost protectively over her enormous belly, and an expression on her face that to Annie looked like agony. Not physical pain . . . but something inside that was maybe even worse. Now that she'd decided to give the baby up, could she be regretting it?

But this time Annie knew she had better keep her mouth shut. She'd already done more than enough interfering in Laurel's life. Hadn't Laurel made that plain enough? Besides, deep down, Annie hadn't entirely forgiven her sister for coming between Joe and her.

In the kitchen, Annie could hear the melter's clattering smooth to a steady hum. Relief swept through her. Well, at least she wouldn't have *that* to worry about, not for the time being. Emmett, bless him, had once again pulled a rabbit out of his hat.

Paolo's, on Mulberry Street, was a Little Italy institution, its old tongue-and-groove wainscoting scarred from years of chairs scraping against it, every inch of wall space covered with autographed eight-by-ten glossies of celebrities who'd dined there. Frank Sinatra. Dean Martin. Fiorello La Guardia. Tony Bennett. An etched-glass panel separated the long oak bar from the dining area. At a table against the rear wall, Annie spotted a swarthy barrel-chested man in a fully-buttoned double-breasted suit, a napkin tucked in his collar, wolfing down a big bowl of spaghetti while a couple of younger men, clearly his thuggish bodyguards, occupied a smaller table near the entrance, their eyes roaming the packed dining area.

"Are they for real?" she whispered jokingly to Emmett. She couldn't help thinking these guys were just actors the management had hired, sort of like a floor show, to make this place look more authentic.

Moments later, seated at the table only a few feet away, Emmett leaned across and whispered, "That's Cesare Tagliosi. He's right up there in the Bonnano family. I met him through this deal my boss and I are putting together on a couple of warehouses in Red Hook. Tagliosi and Ed Bight, the guy who's selling the warehouses, are supposedly business partners. But my guess is it's the kind of business where Tagliosi does the talking, and Ed listens . . . if you get my drift."

Annie glanced over her shoulder at the man behind them devouring his spaghetti.

"You mean it really happens that way, like in the movies?" she whispered to Emmett. "God, I'd die." She caught herself, and frowned. "No, I wouldn't. I'd tell him where he could shove it."

Emmett stared at her for a moment, then shook his head, smiling. "Sure, and the next day they'd be fishing you out of the East River. Face it, Annie, there are some things you just *can't* fight."

"I haven't come across one yet." She thought of Joe. If only this distance between them were just an obstacle, a fence she could somehow climb over.

"Yes, you have." He paused, watching as their waiter poured into his glass a small amount of the wine he'd ordered. Sipping it, he nodded to him. Then Emmett looked at Annie and said, "Me. You can't fight me."

The easy smile had dropped from his face, and Annie could see now how much she meant to him. How could she have missed it before? Wasn't this exactly how she felt about Joe?

He gazed at her, his blue eyes a little somber, his pale lashes tipped with silver from the street light that seeped above the café-curtained windows.

"Look, Em . . . I'm sorry if . . ." How was she going to say this? How could she make it come out right? She liked him so much. If it weren't for Joe, she might even have loved him.

His hand closed over hers, firmly, shutting off her words.

"No," he said. "No more excuses. Look, I'm not stupid . . . and I'm not so crazy about you I can't see straight." A corner of his mouth curled up slightly. "Not yet, anyway. I'll say it just this once, Cobb . . . and if you don't want to hear it, I won't say it again." He paused, and picked up his wineglass, not by the stem, but by the bowl, gripping it so tightly Annie had a sudden, disturbing vision of it shattering, blood and crimson wine spraying everywhere. "Damn it, *yes,* I'm in love with you. I know you're not in love with me. I *know* that. But if you think there's a chance you *might* be someday, even a *slim* chance, then for God's sake, take it. I'm not asking for any promises . . . just a gamble. Your chips on the table across from mine."

Annie felt so uncomfortable she wanted to disappear, vanish. She was imagining that everyone in the restaurant had stopped talking, and they were all listening to her, *waiting* for her reply. Even the Mafia boss.

"Emmett, what are you asking?" Annie forced herself to meet his steady gaze. "What exactly do you want me to say?"

"Say you'll go away for the weekend with me. Just that. I'm not asking for the moon, Annie Cobb."

"Just the sun and the stars," she replied lightly, suddenly too exhausted to argue.

He smiled faintly. "Yep. That's about the size of it."

Annie stared at his sturdy hands, at his knuckles big as knotholes in fence posts. She remembered the freckles on his back, and belly, and on his—

A memory pushed its way into her head—Emmett, on the night train to Marseilles, lowering the shades of their old-fashioned compartment and then slipping his hand under her skirt and tugging her panties down over her knees. Then he was unbuckling his belt, undoing his zipper, and pulling her onto his lap, and . . .

Heat. Quick, pumping, desperate heat that was making her glow, not just down there, but her whole body.

They'll see us, she'd whispered, somebody will see us. Somebody will come in. . . .

But she wasn't stopping, and neither was he.

She sat facing him, her knees straddling him on either side of his straining hips. She could feel the seams of his jeans pressing into the soft flesh along the insides of her thighs, and with her face buried in the crook of his sturdy shoulder, her senses were flooded with him, the quiet, economical power with which he moved, and his smell, steaming up at her, a pungent animal smell, bringing images of Emmett on horseback, dust in the creases of his jeans and his shirt plastered to him with sweat.

He was coming, but she couldn't, too scared of their being caught, or maybe the angle was wrong. Then, Emmett was pushing her down so that she was lying on her back on the hard vinyl seat, knees hiked up, and she was closing her eyes, half hypnotized by the rackety sway of the train beneath her, the rhythmic clinking of his belt buckle as it struck the metal edge of the seat. She felt slippery between her legs, and a kind of delicious throbbing ache, then his mouth on her, his tongue inside her, and . . . God . . . oh God . . .

Stop, she told herself now, feeling herself grow warm. She had to stop this. Back then with Emmett it had been just . . . well, not just sex; she'd been lonely, too. And maybe a little drunk with Paris.

Then she thought: *So why is it so terrible to want him even though you don't love him? It's been so long . . . and what am I saving myself for, anyway? Not Joe, that's for sure.*

At the thought of Joe, her heart seemed to bump. *You're a fool, Annie Cobb,* a small, sharp voice spoke inside her head. *If you don't take Emmett, you might end up with nothing.*

The refrain from a Stephen Stills song popped into her head: *If you can't be with the one you love . . . love the one you're with.*

Then she remembered: Felicia Birnbaum's marzipan baskets. She'd promised to have them by Monday. And that'd mean working straight through the weekend.

Annie looked down, at the faint red stain their wine bottle had left on the white tablecloth. She could feel Emmett's gaze on her.

"I'm sorry, Em. I can't. Not this weekend."

"Don't shit me, Cobb," he said mildly. "If you don't want to, now or ever, just say so."

"Em . . . I'm afraid," she told him, leaning forward on her elbows. "And a little confused. I don't know what to tell you."

"How about the truth?" he said, sipping his wine. His blue eyes peered at her over the rim of his glass, bright and sharp as sunlight on barbed wire.

"Okay," she told him. "The truth is, I have a big order to fill by Monday so I really can't get away. But I"—even before the words were out, she wondered, *Am I making a mistake?*—"I wouldn't mind having you ask me another time."

I could still say no, she told herself. *If he asks me again, I could tell him it would never work.* But something kept her from telling him no. She was seeing herself ten years from now, how the business could swallow her up if she let it. And then one day she'd be like Dolly, lonely and middle-aged, pining for a man who could never be hers.

"Maybe I'll do that," he replied evenly and without a trace of rancor.

Their pasta arrived, steaming noodles piled with tomato, mushrooms, peppers, olives, all in a fragrant red sauce. Annie realized that she was starving.

After he'd eaten half of what was on his plate, Emmett leaned forward and said, "You know what 'puttanesca' means, don't you? 'Like a whore.' That means everything goes into it but the kitchen sink. Hell, maybe that too." Emmett was once again his old self, cocky, impudent, making her smile. "Hey, Cesare," he called over to the big man in the rubout suit, his tone polite, deferential even. Only Annie could see the twinkle in his eye, and the tiny smirk lurking behind his smile. "How was your puttanesca? Good, eh?"

The man frowned at him; then recognition dawned, and he gave Emmett the barest of nods, wiping his greasy chin. If he thought Emmett was being flippant with him, he gave no indication of it.

Annie ducked her head, hiding her face in her napkin to muffle her laughter. She felt a little shocked, too, by Emmett's boldness. But then, why should it surprise her? Since she'd known him, when had Emmett Cameron ever been afraid of anything or anybody?

When they'd finished their dinner, both of them groaning about the amount of pasta they'd eaten, Emmett suggested they walk a little ways before hailing a cab. Strolling west on Grand Street with Annie, Emmett felt a sudden terror grip him, a sensation not unlike being grappled about the middle by a two-hundred-pound running back.

Jesus Christ in a handcart . . . how did I manage to get myself poleaxed by this girl? Annie was tough on the outside, but there was something inside her, a softness, a deep-down neediness, that touched him and made him want to reach out to her.

Once, Emmett remembered, on the shrimp boat he'd worked on, an egret had somehow gotten caught in one of the nets. One of its legs was clearly broken, but it valiantly struggled on, wildly flapping its wings and croaking frantically. By the time he was able to free the bedraggled creature, he wondered if the kindest thing would be just to put it out of its misery. Instead, he'd bundled it up and taken it home with him, and cleaned out an old dog crate left rusting in the backyard of the house he was renting. Even so, when-ever he tended the little bugger, its leg splinted and bound up in adhesive tape, one wing hanging limp as a torn sail, it never missed a try at taking a chunk out of his finger. He could still remember its eyes, like flat black marbles, and its hoarse croaking cry. Never did take to him . . . and weeks later when he finally let it go, its leg and wing healed, it took off without a backward glance. But some-how . . . that damned bird had touched him. He'd admired it, not just for hanging in there, but also for the way it had seemed to be sizing him up each time the door to its cage squealed open on its rusty hinges. *Nobody told you to care about me*, it seemed to say, *so don't look for any reward.*

Maybe that was the lesson he'd learned from that damned bird, and what Annie was teaching him now—that it doesn't always make a whole lot of sense who you care about, or why. And caring doesn't always mean you'll get it back in spades.

He looked at her now, striding alongside him, her hands stuffed in the pockets of her thick tweed coat, shoulders scrunched and head slanted low as if she were squaring off to do battle. But against whom? Or what?

The wind had lifted her short hair, forming a little crest above her forehead. Damn, she was pretty. Not like those models on the cover of *Cosmopolitan*, with their tits pushed out at you like a sales-man's calling card. No, her prettiness was the kind you couldn't always put your finger on—like how he loved the ocean at five o'clock in the morning with a light fog squatting atop its waves, or the sound a cornfield makes in August with the wind rushing through its drying stalks. He loved the way sunlight brought out the ocher in her skin, and the way at certain angles her dark blue eyes looked black, and how the mink-colored hairs on her forearms stood up when she was aroused. He loved how she sucked her cheeks in when she was thinking real hard, and how she always blushed when he caught her biting her nails, as if he'd walked in on her on sitting on the john.

He loved the way she looked now, each street lamp they passed under bestowing a brief, glittering halo on her dark crown, and the way the cold had formed slashes of red on her high cheekbones. He wanted more than anything to kiss her, and then make love to her . . . and that's what scared him. Because, dammit, there was nothing worse than making love to a woman who's got one man between her legs and another between her ears.

Still, Emmett knew that if he *didn't* kiss her, he was bound to spend the rest of the night regretting it. There was an image in his mind that wouldn't let go—Annie, sprawled naked on the Victorian couch of his Parisian sublet, imitating Manet's "Olympia," which they'd seen that day in the Louvre, her head thrown back so that she seemed to be half asleep, eyeing him through lowered lids, a thin black ribbon tied about her neck and one golden arm curled about an armrest, her thighs insouciantly, invitingly parted. He remembered how he'd stood in the middle of the living room, knocked for a loop, feeling a sudden hot rush of blood to his groin. And how Annie had laughed nervously, jumping up and throwing on a robe as if she suddenly couldn't bear to have him see her that way, even in jest.

"Listen, Cobb, I've got an idea . . . let's go back to my place," he spoke casually now as they strolled up Broadway, his gut clenching in anticipation of her reply.

"Em." She stopped near a sidewalk grate sending billows of steam up into the frozen night air, and gave him a warning look. "You know perfectly well what would happen if we did that."

"Matter of fact, I was counting on it." He grinned his cowboy grin that concealed so much.

"I'm not ready."

"That's funny. I'd have sworn that naked lady in Paris was you."

She laughed, and he could see the red along her cheekbones spread down into her cheeks. "Emmett, stop. Stop teasing me."

He kissed her then. Leaning forward, one hand resting lightly on her shoulder, the other holding the nape of her neck, her cropped hair pushing up between his fingers, cool and springy as new grass, it was so easy, so natural, like breathing. She must have felt the same as he, because she didn't pull away. She opened her mouth, and he tasted her sweetness—she tasted of the warm zabaglione that had been whipped up at their table for dessert, Marsala and foamy egg whites. He could feel steam from the vent nearby seeping into his coat, forming beads of moisture on his cheeks and forehead.

"Oh, shit," she said softly as she drew away. Around them,

pedestrians bundled in their coats hurried past, and cars and taxis formed a blinking river of headlights along the busy street. A man squatted in front of a bicycle shop, seemingly oblivious to the cold, a tattered blanket lined with earrings and belt buckles on the sidewalk in front of him. With a quick, nervous laugh, she joked, "It must be the puttanesca."

Emmett spotted a taxi, and stuck out his hand.

The heater in their cab was broken, and one of the back windows was stuck partway open, so by the time they reached his apartment, across the street from London Terrace, they were both half frozen. The shower stall off the kitchen, for a change, was right where he wanted it to be—in plain view, just beyond the closet where he hung their coats. Without any hesitation, Emmett stripped off all his clothes, and after clamping his frozen fingers under his armpits to warm them, he began removing Annie's. She didn't protest.

When they were both naked, he reached into the old rust-streaked tin shower stall and cranked on the water. Pushing the vinyl curtain aside, he stepped inside. "Ever taken a shower in a kitchen?" he asked, drawing her with him under the stinging spray. He felt her initial stiffness begin to yield as he slowly, lovingly, began soaping her arms, now her breasts, his hands sliding down over her flat belly.

"No," Annie said. "It feels different somehow."

"Walk into a kitchen and what do you instantly think of? Food, right?"

"So?" She arched, and he felt a spasm in his groin at the sight of her small breasts with their dark, almost purplish nipples pointing up at him.

"So"—he bent and touched the tip of his tongue to a soap bubble shimmering on the tip of her breast—"I'm feeling hungry all of a sudden."

"But we just—" Her words were cut off as Emmett suddenly squatted before her and drew his tongue along the wet silk of her inner thigh. He heard her groan softly as he moved higher. He felt the shower's warm spray rolling off his back, and her fingers in his hair, tugging, almost painful, but immensely exciting too. Yet he could feel her holding back just a little, quivering like a high-tension wire. Jesus. She was so . . . so damn passionate. Why couldn't she just let go all the way? What did this other guy have that was so goddamn wonderful it blotted out everything else? As far as Emmett knew, she hadn't even *slept* with Joe.

Then he was tasting her, inside her, all her warm slipperiness, salty and sweet at the same time, and he was lost. Lost to reason, and to thoughts of the future. He wanted her. He had to have her. Now. Like the drumming of the water against the tin walls of the shower stall, he could feel his blood pounding in his head, and in his groin, and one word repeating itself over and over inside his brain: *Annie . . . Annie . . . Annie . . .*

He rose, flattening her against the wall, his hands squeezed about her buttocks. Annie, moaning, her head thrown back, hair sleek as an otter's coat, water streaming down her throat, arched against him, both arms gripping him about his neck, hoisting herself up so that her legs were wrapped about his thighs.

She cried out as he entered her, a sharp high yelp that was swallowed by the pounding of the water and the hollow, rhythmic thump of tin.

Emmett revelled in her, the sweet weight of her against his arms, the smooth wetness of her limbs coiled about him, the flick of her wet hair as she buried her face into his neck, biting him, her cries muffled by his shoulder.

He came with a burning, almost painful, rush just as the water turned cold. Jesus. Oh, Jesus Christ. He could feel her coming, too, and the cold water sluicing down, making his skin shrivel and his balls climb up into his belly . . . all his senses heightened, slapped alive, his pleasure so intense it was damn near excruciating.

"Cold," Annie shrieked. "G-God, it's freezing!"

As he lowered her and reached to shut off the water, he could hear the soft sucking of their wet skin as they peeled away from one another. He looked at her, shivering, her arms wrapped about her chest, her skin ridged with goose bumps, and they both began to laugh.

Emmett caught her in his arms, threw his head back, and let out a great hoot of laughter. He didn't even know why he was laughing, except that it felt good. In a rusting shower stall in the cramped kitchen of his rented apartment in the sooty heart of a city that swallowed him up each morning and spat him out at night, Emmett Cameron felt as if he'd at last come home.

CHAPTER 22

Laurel was soaking in the bathtub when she felt the tightness in her belly again.

It didn't hurt much—she couldn't call it a pain. Definitely not a *labor* pain. Actually, she'd been having them all morning, but she was pretty sure it was no big deal. Sally Munroe from her Lamaze class, who was pregnant with her second child, had once told Laurel that having a baby felt like shitting a watermelon. This little pang wouldn't be enough even for a watermelon *seed.*

She stared down at her huge belly, rising above the water like the hump of a whale. She watched the taut muscles ripple slightly, and felt them drawing inward. She thought of Scarlett O'Hara being laced into an impossibly tight corset. *That* would hurt. Now, aside from the tightness, what she felt was a sort of coldness in the small of her back, as if the water temperature in that one spot had dropped sharply.

Movie images of birthings floated into her mind: stoic pioneer women biting down on rawhide straps to keep from screaming. Anxious fathers in hospital waiting rooms pacing back and forth. Wild-eyed women strapped to gurneys, moaning and thrashing.

But *this* wasn't near anything like that, certainly not labor . . . it *couldn't* be.

She remembered her Lamaze teacher saying that false labor was common . . . contractions that didn't hurt much and came at irregular intervals. How irregular were these? Earlier, she'd timed a few, but they were jumping all over the place: ten minutes, then six, then ten again. She was too tense, that was it. She'd decided that a bath would relax her.

But now, just to be on the safe side, maybe she should call Dr. Epstein.

Laurel started to pull herself up . . . and quite abruptly the

343

tightness eased. She let herself sink back into the water's warmth, feeling a guarded relief steal through her.

Why bother the doctor when it's probably still a long way off, she told herself. He'll just tell me get over to the hospital, and if it *is* labor, they'll start sticking me with needles, and poking fingers up me. Then, when the baby comes—

No, don't think about it. It was as if an alarm had jangled in her brain, warning her to back off, keep all thoughts of the baby out of her head. She grabbed a washcloth, wringing it hard enough to send droplets spattering out over the rim of the old cast-iron tub.

They'll take it away . . . I won't even get to hold it.

Laurel felt a sharp pain, but this time it was in her chest. It came to her then, not just the *thought,* but the full weight of it, slamming into her: *It won't be* mine *anymore.*

Some other woman would come to the hospital to claim her baby and take it away. This woman and her husband, nice people, would see that her son (somehow she felt sure it was a boy) would always be fed, changed, rocked to sleep. And when he got bigger they would take him to the beach, and to baseball games, and Disneyland. They would make him honey-lemon tea when he was sick, listen to him practice the piano or the saxophone, help him with his math homework. They would love him.

She touched the shining mound of her belly, and whispered, "You won't know me, will you? You'll forget you ever belonged to me."

Her head tipped back, tears slipped sideways down her temples, pooling in her ears, a hot tickly sensation. She imagined her baby curled inside her, looking like a tiny sleeping kitten, with its downy hair, its tiny pink fingers and toes.

"Please . . ." she whispered, not knowing quite what she was pleading for.

My choice, she reminded herself. No one had forced her to give up her baby. Rudy had merely persuaded her that it was for the best.

She remembered his phoning her the day after they'd met in the baby store, how relieved he'd sounded that she'd come to this decision. Over and over, he'd assured her she was doing the best thing . . . best for the baby as well as for her. And all along, she'd kept on telling herself he was right, but now she wasn't so sure. . . .

Again, she found herself thinking, *If only this were Joe's baby . . .*

Maybe he did love her after all . . . just a little. And maybe he'd love her more—a lot more—if it weren't for Annie.

Annie. It all came back to Annie. Laurel couldn't help feeling that if she ever did end up with Joe she'd be cheating her sister. Lying in the cooling water of the claw-footed tub, Laurel wondered, *Why is this so hard? Why should I have to choose between two people I love?*

Tears filled her eyes, and she pressed her hands to her belly, fingers spread like starfish.

For one sweet interlude, which she knew she shouldn't allow herself, she imagined how it would be if she changed her mind and kept the baby. Uncle Rudy's nice couple would be disappointed, sure, but they'd get over it. Before long they'd find some other kid to adopt, maybe one that needed their good home even more. And then *she* would take her baby home. She'd buy that homemade-looking oak cradle she'd spotted in the window of the Salvation Army store on Eighth Avenue, and put it right by her bed. Whenever he cried she'd pick him up. And when he was older, she'd point out the evening star the way Annie had once pointed it out to her, so every night he could wish on it.

A wonderful, warm sensation filled her, as if the water had suddenly grown more buoyant and was lifting her up, letting her float as easily as a leaf.

I could get a job, maybe work for Aunt Dolly—something to pay the bills in between illustrating jobs—then finish college later, when he's in school. Then when I've saved up enough, I'll find us a studio apartment somewhere . . . or maybe Annie will move out and let us keep this one. Then I'd still be near Joe.

But even if Annie did move out, Laurel thought, how could I afford the rent?

In four years of high school, why hadn't she done something *practical?* Yeah, she could draw pretty well, and she could cook and sew, but so could ten thousand other people. Laurel suddenly envied her friend, Hillary Ambrosini. Laurel remembered how dumb and tedious she'd thought it was to give up your summer typing for a law firm. But now Hillary could get herself a well-paying job if she ever needed one.

Laurel remembered years ago bringing up the subject of maybe getting a part-time job to help out with their finances, which had always been close to desperate. And Annie would get this *stretched* look, her skin pulling back at the temples, making her eyes look huge and the bones in her face stick out. She'd stare at Laurel, and say, "If you have all this extra time, wouldn't it be nice for you to join one of those school clubs? I hear the art history club takes all kinds of great museum trips . . . you'd get so much more out of that, wouldn't you?"

And so she had. And a lot of good traipsing around the Frick and the Cooper-Hewitt did her now!

Sure, there was last summer's internship at Blustein and Warwick, but what creative work had she done in those two and a half months except rushing stuff to the color labs and fetching coffee?

The book for Fairway Press she'd illustrated, *that* was what she wanted to do, what she was good at. And the twenty-five hundred they were paying her was wonderful, fantastic, unreal. But she couldn't count on a windfall like that happening very often. Well, not unless she really hustled—the way Annie did, every minute of every day.

Laurel yanked out the rubber tub stopper. She watched the scummy water swirling down the drain, then she heaved herself to her feet, and stepped out onto the fluffy pink rug by the tub. Reaching for a towel, she felt that tight sensation across her middle again. She stood still, gripping the towel rack until it had passed. Was she imagining it, or had this one lasted longer than the last?

She knew she ought to time them to see if they'd gotten any more regular. Dr. Epstein always said that first labors usually took ages. So even if this was for real, it'd be silly of her to rush.

A cup of tea was what she needed, something to relax her. Then she'd sit and finish that last drawing for "East of the Sun and West of the Moon." The others had been turned in, but this was one with which neither she nor Liz Cannawill had been completely satisfied, so she'd promised to redraw it.

Laurel towelled herself off, and slipped into her old chenille robe, which not too many months ago had fit her like an elephant skin. Now it barely met across the front. But the hugeness of her stomach, by now, had come to seem sort of normal. What seemed unreal was her breasts. They'd grown from sunny-side-up eggs to cantaloupes. Life wasn't fair, she thought, a rueful smile tugging at her mouth. For the first time ever she had cleavage . . . and no one to show it off to.

With a steaming mug of chamomile, she curled up on the big red corduroy hassock by the window. The sun, streaming in through the tall iron-barred windows, cast a grid of shadows on the dhurrie carpet. She loved this room, with its warm daylight and hanging plants, fat cushions and scruffy furniture. With Annie frantically making chocolates night and day, Laurel had the place almost all to herself, which was a blessing. No interruptions, hassles, hardly any dishes to wash up; she could spend all the time she wanted drawing.

Clumsily, she knelt and pulled her sketch pad from the bottom shelf of the old oak glass-front bookcase. She flipped through the pages, filled with rough sketches of bears. Weeks ago, she'd ridden a jammed subway car, standing up most of the way, to the Bronx Zoo, and sat on a bench opposite the polar-bear island, capturing the great beasts in various positions until her fingers had turned numb with the cold.

In the drawing she was working on, the bear was rearing up on his hind paws in fury, having just found out that his bride has unwittingly betrayed him. The drawing was mostly good . . . even *she* had to admit it was good. She'd gotten the bear's enraged expression just right. But the bride, the way she just lay there, crouching in terror, she seemed all wrong. Wouldn't she have jumped to her feet to beg his forgiveness and declare her love? Even her face was wrong, bland, vapid, abject. All in all, she was . . . oh, face it, a *wimp*.

Suddenly it came to Laurel how the bride should be. She grabbed an eraser and with a few swipes rubbed out an arm, a leg, half a face. Then she began to sketch. Her pencil flew. Her mind filled with visions of a frightened, but determined woman . . . determined to get her prince back.

She lost all track of time, and was only dimly aware of the contractions that came and went, rolling through her like mild ocean waves.

She tasted the tea, on the floor beside her, and found that it had turned cold.

The grid of sunlight crept to the edge of the carpet, then dissolved into shadow.

Laurel, concentrating on the bride, was seeing her vision take shape, a maiden who was . . . well, *worthy* of a prince. Or else how could any reader be expected to believe she would spend years searching the world for him? Laurel knew she was getting it now. Oh, yes! The terror in her eyes . . . the stubborn tilt of her chin. Already she was calculating how she would get back the man she loved. And when she did—

A hard contraction, harder than any of the others, gripped Laurel so fiercely that she dropped her pencil. Shuddering from the pain, she realized she hadn't just dropped the pencil. Somehow she had sent it flying into the wall opposite her, its lead point shattering, leaving a black squiggle on the baseboard. She hunched forward, clutching her belly. God, it hurt. This one really *hurt.*

She'd better call Dr. Epstein. No more fooling around.

She waited for the contraction to pass. It felt like an excruciating eternity. But when she tried to stand up, her legs collapsed underneath her like warm butter.

How long had she been sitting here? Long enough for her legs to have gone numb, she realized. She saw that the late morning's sunshine had dimmed into afternoon shadows. She began to feel panicky. Now something was happening. *Definitely.*

The circulation in her legs gradually came back, but Laurel was still too shaky to stand up. She managed to get onto her knees, and began crawling toward the phone. She felt herself lumbering like a polar bear. No, heavier than a polar bear. Her bare toes caught at the carpet, dragging it up into little hillocks.

She could feel another contraction coming on, this one more racking than the last. *Dear God . . . please no.* It felt as if a rope was wrenched about her middle. Sweat was pouring down her face, and she *never* sweated.

She was scared. Wild thoughts of blood pouring out of her, of the baby somehow strangled by its cord, overwhelmed her. Help. She had to have help.

Annie? Would Annie be at the shop?

She was almost to the old school desk where the phone sat. She pulled herself up, and clutching the phone receiver in one hand, she paused to catch her breath. The desk's surface, she saw, was gouged with decades of schoolroom graffiti, initials with lopsided hearts drawn around them, arithmetic sums, an outline of what might have been a penis or Washington's monument.

As she began to dial, another contraction seized her. She crumpled in agony, and the phone pitched to the floor with a crazed jingling.

"Oh!" she cried, clutching herself and rocking back on her tailbone. Knives. It felt like knives in her back, and deep down in her groin.

Something had to be wrong, she thought. It was not supposed to hurt this much, not this soon.

The pain finally ebbed, but by then, Laurel was no longer thinking about calling Dr. Epstein. Or Annie. There was one person, only one, she wanted now. *Needed.* She dialed a number that she knew by heart, and waited in sweaty panic while it rang and rang and rang.

Please, God, let him be there. Oh, please.

"Joe's Place," announced a harried-sounding voice, *his* voice.

She felt a sob rising in her, then remembered the pathetic bride in her drawing, and held it in. She squeezed her eyes shut, and forced herself to take a slow, even breath. When she spoke finally, she made her herself sound no more desperate than if she'd been calling from a phone booth with only a minute or two before she had to catch a train.

"Joe? It's me, Laurey," she said. "Listen, I think I'm just about to have this baby."

The front door, Joe saw, was unlocked and slightly ajar. With a swift, backhand stroke, he knocked it wide open. "Laurey!"

No answer. His heart dropped in his chest. He was suddenly imagining that he'd come too late. It felt so much like that hellish night he'd raced to Caryn's. In his dreams, every time he ran to her, he almost made it, but then just as he got there, the razor would slice down, and the blood begin to spill from her pale wrists. Christ.

"Laurey!" he called again. This time he thought he heard a muffled reply.

He shot glances about the shadowed living room, and his gaze fell on the sketch pad lying open on the carpet. The detailed drawing caught his eye: a great white bear rearing up on its hind legs, looking as if it were on the verge of devouring the girl who faced him defiantly, arms wide, the full sleeves of her flowing gown falling back to her elbows. It was good . . . and incredibly lifelike as well. But what struck him was the girl's uncanny resemblance to Laurel herself. Was that how she saw herself—about to be eaten alive?

For a moment, the drawing had him mesmerized. Then it hit him again why he'd come . . . why, when he couldn't find a cab in the rush-hour chaos, he'd raced here on foot through a drizzling rain, almost a mile, then up four flights without stopping. Now he stood dripping on the rug in an old army-green canvas anorak soaked through from the inside with his sweat. He was breathing so hard his ribs hurt, and steam clouded his glasses, making the room seem wreathed in ominous fog.

Christ, what was he doing? Why, before he headed out like a chicken with its head cut off, hadn't he called an ambulance? Suppose she was really in trouble?

"Joe?" From other the end of the small apartment came her faint, but distinct reply.

Joe had always thought the bedroom had the look of marking time, as if the people who occupied it were here only until something better came along—two travellers caught overnight in the same Greyhound terminal, with two different destinations in mind. Looking around at Annie's and Laurel's things, it struck him then how different these two sisters were . . . and how unaccountable it was that he should love them both.

Laurel lay curled on her side on the bed. She was wearing an old chenille robe that had somehow gotten all twisted and bunched up underneath her. Her long hair hung in damp tatters over the edge of the mattress. Her face was very white. It looked *polished* somehow. Then he realized with a jolt it was because she was sweating. He'd never seen Laurel sweat before. She made him think of a Raphael Madonna in the throes of some morbid ecstasy.

Joe crouched at her side. He felt his heart lumbering in his chest.

"Laurey, I'm here. It's going to be okay." He struggled to clear away the panic that cobwebbed his mind, and to remember all the training in their Lamaze classes. "When did it start? How far apart are the pains?"

Laurel shook her head, forcing her words through gritted teeth. "All . . . together."

No intervals at all between the pains. That meant she was in the final stage of her labor. Christ. Why hadn't she called him sooner?

Joe felt a low swell of resentment. Why the hell did she have to call him at *all*? How had he gotten into this? Why, when she asked him to be her Lamaze coach, hadn't he turned her down? Or at the very least, couldn't he have had the guts to admit that the main reason he'd ever agreed to it was to hurt Annie?

Hey, it wasn't Laurel who got you into this. All right, he had been concerned about Laurel. He still was. But mostly he was so pissed off at himself he could barely concentrate.

And when you got right down to it, what right did he have to be mad at Annie for accusing him when—*Go on, admit it, asshole*—it *could* so easily have been his baby? He thought back to that night when Laurel had kissed him, and how part of him had wanted to carry her off to bed right then and there. And since then, watching her bloom with pregnancy, hadn't he felt it again and again—that deep-down tug? His admiration for her had grown, too. The way she'd handled all this, not whining or trying to shove the responsibility onto anyone else, just quietly accepting it. Even the decision to give up the baby, she'd made it on her own, no moaning or crying on anyone's shoulder.

Ashamed now of wanting to run away, Joe frantically shucked off his anorak, then reached out to place a hand on Laurel's round belly. He could feel it moving, the muscles actually *heaving* beneath his palm, and was startled. He thought of an earthquake, primal, uncontrollable. He felt as helpless as if it *were* an earthquake. What could he do? He was no doctor, dammit.

Where the hell was Epstein, anyway . . . had Laurel called him?

Something was pinching his arm, a claw biting into his flesh. He looked over and saw Laurel gripping his forearm with all her might, her fingers looking bloodless, almost transparent, as if an X ray were revealing the fine bones underneath.

"Joe . . . I'm scared," she gasped.

Me too, kiddo. I'm scared shitless.

"What did the doctor say?" he asked.

"I . . . I haven't talked to him. After I called you . . . I had to . . . to lie down. Oh God, it hurts so much!" She hugged herself tighter, her face crumpling into an agonized grimace.

"Where's his number?"

"In . . . the . . . the little blue book inside the desk . . . under the phone."

"I'll be right back. Hang on, Laurey."

He found the blue address book just where Laurel had said it would be, in the slot under the desk where school kids had once kept their *Dick and Jane* readers and peanut-butter-and-jelly sandwiches. He looked up Dr. Epstein's number, but his hand was shaking so badly he misdialed twice before he finally got it. A bored-sounding woman at the answering service asked if he would like to leave a message, or was this an emergency?

"Shit, yes, it's an emergency!" he barked.

A minute later, the doctor called back and told him what he already knew: get Laurel to St. Vincent's, pronto. Epstein said he'd phoned for an ambulance—it shouldn't be more than five minutes. Next, Joe tried the number at Annie's shop. A girl who sounded young enough to be selling Girl Scout cookies informed him that Annie was out. He left a message saying that he was on his way to the hospital with Laurel, and the girl breathlessly promised to do her best to reach Annie.

Waiting for the ambulance to arrive, Joe remembered a bet with his best friend in grammar school. Teddy Plowright's betting him a dollar that he couldn't stand on his head for five minutes; and know-it-all Joey taking him up on it, thinking, hey, no big deal. Five minutes? Hell, he'd do *ten*, that'd show dinkweed Teddy. But then, feet up high, his blood slugging into his head like a truckload of sand, his ears roaring, eyes bulging, he'd found out that five minutes could seem longer than a year.

Which was how he felt now, as if for five interminable minutes he'd been standing on his head . . . and he still had five more to go.

He found Laurel on her back, clutching a knee in each hand, the great white moon of her belly rising from the twisted folds of her robe. He stood at the foot of the bed, feeling suddenly as if he didn't belong here . . . as if Laurel were engaged in some atavistic ritual prohibited to men.

Everything was still, as if the earth somehow had stopped turning, and was simply suspended in space. Feeling hot, and realizing he was still wearing his sweatshirt, Joe shucked it off, half expecting to see it float above the carpet as if gravity had taken a vacation.

"The ambulance'll be here any minute," he told her. "And Dr. Epstein will be waiting for you at the hospital."

"I . . . don't think . . . I can . . . oh *God*!"

Joe strained to remember the breathing exercises they'd practiced in Lamaze. Fine coach he was turning out to be.

"Pant," he urged, leaning close so that their mouths were almost touching. He could almost taste her breath, sweet, with a trace of metallic panic. "Shallow breaths. That's it. Go with the pain. *Roll* with it. Great, that's *great*. You're doing great."

Laurel kept up the panting for another minute or so, then fell back, clutching at his shirtfront like someone drowning. He glanced down and saw the red and blue flannel of his shirt blooming from each of her fists like some surreal bouquet.

"No!" she screamed. "I can't do this . . . oh God . . . *please don't make me do this!*"

Joe felt as if he'd touched a fallen power line, a huge jolt cracking through him like a bullwhip. Even though he was sitting down, he could feel himself stagger a little. Then he pulled himself together and instinctively gathered Laurel into his arms.

"You *can*," he told Laurel. "You can do it."

"Joe." He was close enough to feel her lips move under his, an almost delicious rippling sensation that caused his heart to rock. "I never . . . stopped. Loving you. Please . . . I'm sorry. I . . . I didn't mean to lie to Annie. It's just that . . . I . . . wanted it to be yours . . . *our* baby. Do you hate me?"

"No, Laurey, I could never hate you." He stroked her hair, which felt damp and hot. What *did* he feel?

He didn't know, couldn't sort out all the emotions Laurel summoned up in him. *In* love with her? No. But what he did feel was certainly more than brotherly affection.

"I didn't love him," she panted. "Jess. He was just . . . somebody." She moaned. "He doesn't know . . . about the baby. I . . . didn't tell him."

"Were you afraid he'd let you down?" Joe remembered that morning on the library steps with Caryn, and felt a coldness about his heart. He touched Laurel's cheek, freeing a strand of hair stuck to her mouth.

"No. He . . ." She broke off, pulling at his shirt. "He's . . . not like that. He would have helped. I just . . . wanted . . ." She gasped, and her mouth dragged down in a horrible grimace. "It's coming! Joe! I can feel it!"

"The ambulance . . ." he started to say, as if this birth were something she could put on hold. But it was going to happen, he realized, whether the ambulance was here or not.

Jesus. They hadn't covered *this* in Lamaze. What should he do? In the movies, the doctor or midwife always told the man to boil water. But what were you supposed to do with the water once it boiled?

Sweat poured from him in rivulets, running into his collar, misting into half-moons on his eyeglass lenses. He'd felt this way once, in high school, before the qualifying heat for the four-hundred-yard dash in the tri-state finals. He remembered toeing up at the mark, his heart jackhammering, sweat pooling inside his running shoes, making his toes slimy and his soles itch.

But now, he couldn't remember how fast he'd run that day, or even if he'd made it to the finals. All he remembered was that endless agony before the starting gun went off.

Where is that ambulance? It should be here by now. Goddamn it, what do they think this is, a sprained ankle here?

But glancing at his watch Joe saw that only four minutes had elapsed since he'd spoken to Dr. Epstein.

Laurel screamed. Blood had rushed up into her face, turning it a dark crimson. He realized that now she had to be pushing . . .

Christ, what if the baby was turned around or something? What if she started to bleed?

Inside his skull he felt pressure building up. A sound like crashing surf roared in his ears. He ran into the bathroom, and snatched a clean towel from the rack. Returning to Laurel's side, he placed it under her hips. He didn't know what else to do.

"It's okay," he heard a calm stranger speak. "Push if you have to."

"GOD!"

With the first push, water gushed from between her legs. He'd heard that this was supposed to happen; but actually seeing it came as a big shock. In the midst of kneeling at the foot of the bed in order to see what was happening, he froze.

The bed was soaked, along with the towel. But there was no time now to boil water or hunt for a fresh towel or even to sneeze. Between Laurel's hiked knees, he spied a dark wet circle . . . the baby's head. He grew dizzy, momentarily disoriented, as if a part of him was standing at a distance from all this, high up, watching himself watch this unfolding miracle. Could God have observed the creation of the world this way? The dark circle widened. He could hear Laurel grunting as she pushed again . . . then again . . . another mighty push. He saw his arms stretch out, as if from a universe away, hands cupped to receive the infant's head as it slowly burrowed into the world, slick and dark and pointed. But something was wrong . . . the baby seemed stuck, its shoulders jammed somehow. Now he could see blood oozing onto the folded towel beneath Laurel. Jesus.

Joe's panic mounted. Suppose the cord was wrapped the wrong way and was holding it back? What if Laurel was hemorrhaging? He dimly remembered something in a film they'd seen in Lamaze class about the baby needing at this point to be rotated a bit. Carefully, as carefully as if this child were a butterfly cupped in his palms, Joe turned the baby until he felt its shoulders loosen and finally slide free. Now came a long soapy torso, a pair of rumpled red legs. Joe let his breath out with a whistling rush.

With one hand supporting the infant's head, Joe cradled the Lilliputian knobs of its buttocks, and cried: "A boy . . . and, look, he's peeing!"

A stream of urine arched from a penis not even as wide as Joe's little finger. The baby gave a choked, startled cry . . . then began to wail, thrashing his arms and legs like a beginning swimmer dropped into the deep end of the pool by mistake. Blood streaked his face and torso. Joe, looking down at Laurel, saw that the blood that had so panicked him a moment ago was from a tear the baby must have made pushing his way out. He felt relief sweep through him. She'd need a few stitches, but it didn't look as if she was in any danger of bleeding to death.

Joe felt the weirdly distorted dimension he'd been in shrink back to normal. Suddenly, he was back in the real world. With Laurel lying there, panting, exhausted . . . and he, holding this brand-new human being who, when he was just a bulge under Laurel's loose-fitting shirts, Joe hadn't really thought of as a person, an actual baby. Now, feeling the infant's tiny wet body squirm in his hands, the little boy he somehow managed to bring unharmed into this world, he was so thrilled that he started to laugh. Then, seemingly for no reason, he began to cry. He saw that Laurel, too, was laughing, and had tears streaming down her face.

Joe looked down at the baby boy in his arms, tied to Laurel by its ropey cord—a startling turquoise that wasn't at all ugly or repulsive, as he'd imagined these things were—and for maybe the first time in all his thirty-two years, he felt connected to something larger than himself. To God? The mysteries of the universe? No, smaller than that . . . a heartbeat, a new life, a measure of grace.

Best of all, he'd been given this chance to prove to himself that he would have been there for Caryn, too, if she'd lived. Where he would go from here he didn't exactly know. All he knew was this: *Joe Daugherty is the kind of man who can be counted on.*

The baby had stopped crying. A pair of indigo eyes stared fixedly into his, and a tiny, mottled hand locked about his finger. Joe felt a rush of unexpected joy that nearly knocked him over.

Before he was even aware he'd thought of it, Joe found himself saying, "Adam. His name is Adam."

CHAPTER 23

Val stood in the lobby of St. Vincent's Hospital, and asked the bullet-eyed black lady behind the reception desk which room Laurel Carrera was in.

While she riffled through her alphabetized index cards, he glanced around, taking in the blacks and spicks waiting around on the benches, the green vinyl floor tiles scuffed by countless pairs of shoes. Jesus, what a dump. What was he even doing here? His little girl, all grown up, a mother herself now, and he was probably the last person she'd want to see. Hadn't she made it clear how she felt about him all those years ago when she took off into the night without so much as a kiss-my-foot?

No Laurel Carrera listed, Big Mama behind the desk told him. "Sorry, mister."

Shit. He rubbed his chin, feeling its scratchiness and remembering he hadn't shaved. Could she be listed under a married name?

So what if she is? Any way you slice it, she won't want to see you, so why don't you just turn around right now and get the hell out? In seven years, not one letter or phone call, not even a frigging postcard. If he hadn't seen that article in the *L.A. Times* magazine on Annie's chocolate shop, he wouldn't have known either of them were still alive.

But he'd come all this way, blowing his last hundred on a low-fare red-eye to New York. Dammit, he *couldn't* just walk away.

"What about Laurel *Cobb?*" A long shot, but worth a try.

Big Mama thumbed her card index and then looked up at him quizzically. "Third floor. Room 322."

Val tried to swallow, but his mouth felt dry as an old sock . . . and tasted just about as bad as one, from all the coffees he'd drunk. It was close to noon, but he'd been up practically the whole night, and the night before that—five hours from LAX, plus one more circling La Guardia in heavy fog before the plane could land. And the whole time, he hadn't shut his eyes once. Thinking about Laurel. Wondering what she'd look like, if she'd be glad to see him.

The taxi in from Queens had taken forever, crawling through the fog and bumper-to-bumper traffic. The driver was an Arab . . . goddamn Mohammed-something, weird screechy music on the radio, and the guy couldn't even speak English. Val had had to repeat the address of Annie's shop three times. And when he finally got there, he'd had to wait around outside in the cold all day and well into the evening, until Annie finally emerged. Seeing her in her stylish coat and paisley scarf, he'd wanted to confront her, smash his fists into her, but he'd held himself back, knowing that if he did that she'd make it twice as hard for him to get to Laurel. Trailing half a block behind, he'd followed her down into the subway, where she'd taken a train to Twenty-third and Seventh. A couple of blocks away, she turned into the lobby of a brick apartment building. Did she live here, or was she just visiting someone? After a few minutes, he'd gone inside to check the intercom directory. Finding her name— A. COBB—he'd felt a surge of triumph. Finally, finally, things were starting to go his way.

He'd pressed the buzzer marked "SUPERINTENDENT." A baggy-cheeked middle-aged lady with a wet mop slung over her shoulder, probably the super's wife, opened the vestibule door. When he asked about Laurel, if she lived here with her sister, the lady's tired eyes lit up.

"Oh, you missed all the excitement," she told him. "Yesterday, it was, around suppertime. They carried her down on a stretcher . . . white as a sheet, she was, the baby lying on her belly, cord still attached and everything. Well, it was something."

Val had started, feeling as shocked as if he'd walked into a pane of glass he hadn't known was there. *Baby?* Christ, Laurel couldn't be much more than a baby herself.

The super's wife directed him to St. Vincent's, on Seventh Avenue and Twelfth Street. On the way over, Val had a chance to let the idea of Laurel's being a mother sink in. But it still didn't feel right. They'd left him out of everything. It was as if he'd been cheated somehow.

Now, riding the elevator up to the third floor, Val was hit by it—he *had* been swindled. If Laurel hadn't run away, the past seven years might've been so different. He'd have had a kid to look up to him, make him feel like he was somebody. And with Laurel to buy food and clothes for and keep a roof over her head, he was sure he could've wangled that trust money out of the bank. And instead of having to take shit from know-nothing bosses and stand in line to collect unemployment checks, he'd have been on easy street.

If it hadn't been for Rudy . . . well, Val didn't like to think where he'd be without his brother, old Rudy spotting him whenever he got really desperate, which lately seemed to be happening more and more.

Three-twenty-two turned out to be at the end of the corridor, last one on the right. The door was propped open. There were two beds inside, but one was empty. In the other, a slender woman sat propped up with pillows, her long blond hair tied back in a loose ponytail. She was staring out the window and didn't see him, so he had time for a good long look at her.

Laurel? That grown-up young woman, his little girl?

His heart seemed to stop, and the air around him felt heavy, still as fog. He remembered he still had on the slacks and raw-silk blazer he'd worn on the plane, which were now messy and wrinkled. Jesus, she was going to think he was some kind of a bum.

She was wearing one of those hospital gowns that tied in back, and her face was clean of any makeup. Even so, he thought she looked like a movie star. No, more like one of those folk singers, girls with long hair and long fingers and voices that rippled like cool water. Not all of them were beautiful, but *she* was . . . the most beautiful woman he'd ever seen. The way the light hit the curve of her cheek, he could've sworn it was shining from within her. And those eyes . . . *Eve's eyes* . . . God, a man could be blinded by those eyes.

"Laurel? Baby?" He managed a thready whisper, and took a step inside.

She turned, and even in the movement of her head as it swivelled on her long neck, he could see how graceful she was, like a ballet dancer. *She's mine. I made her.* He felt stronger, more confident. She was his, a part of his flesh, his blood, like his arm or his leg. How could she reject him?

She stared at him, her eyes huge and uncomprehending. Then recognition dawned, and the blood drained from her face. Her mouth dropped open.

"Val?" she croaked. "God, it *is* you." She clapped both hands over her mouth, and spoke through white fingers that dragged at her cheeks. "But you . . . you're . . . I thought you were . . . *dead*."

Now Val felt himself reel. "Dead? Jesus. Where did you hear that?" He'd played a million scenarios in his head, but never *this* one.

"Uncle Rudy t-told me you that you'd d-died that night we r-ran away. That Annie—" She gulped. She was shivering as if he'd thrown open a window and let in a blast of freezing air. "H-he m-made me p-promise not to t-tell anyone."

Rudy? *Rudy* had told her that? Val felt as if he'd had the wind knocked out of him, a dull ache spreading through him. But why? Why would Rudy do a thing like that?

It made no sense. No sense at all. Like a rat let loose from its cage, his mind raced, but seemed to be going nowhere in particular.

"How . . . how did you find me?"

He could see that she, too, was struggling to somehow make sense of all this. He watched her drop her hands, and on her white face he could see the red marks left by her fingers. "I read about your sister in the paper." He kept his voice even, while his thoughts continued to tumble. It hadn't occurred to him when he was reading that article, but now he was seeing that from the very beginning Rudy had to have known where Laurel and Annie were living.

"*Annie* told you I was here?" Laurel's voice was hollow with disbelief.

"Not exactly. I, uh, followed her home from her store. Your super's wife told me where to find you."

"Oh."

Was she glad to see him? He couldn't tell. Maybe once her shock wore off . . .

"You're looking good," he told her. "I hear you had a kid."

"That's right." Her eyes welled with tears, and for a second he thought she was going to start crying. Had he said something wrong?

He tried to remember what Eve had been like when Laurel was born . . . but all he could recall of that night was passing out a lot of cigars, first at the hospital, and then down at the Rusty Nail on

Sunset, where he'd ended up shooting pool and getting blasted out of his skull with a bunch of the guys.

"Boy or girl?" he remembered to ask.

"Boy." She didn't sound too happy about it. Had she had her heart set on a girl?

Val grinned. "Hey, that makes me a grandfather. What do you know?" He paused, his grin fading. "It's been a long time. I thought you'd forgotten about me."

"I would've written, but . . ." Her voice trailed off. Her forehead knotted, as if it suddenly occurred to her that *she'd* been lied to by Rudy as well.

Rage rose in him, and pounded at his temples. The room seemed washed in a honeycomb of red. Rudy. That little cocksucker. Val wished his brother was here now. He'd smash his face in . . . and that was just for starters. Had Rudy and Annie been in this together? Yeah, Val could see it. Rudy giving her money, maybe helping her find a place to live. What an idiot he'd been to fall for Rudy's big-brother routine.

Val felt his hands knotting into fists, and made a herculean effort to relax them. He'd better not let Laurel see how pissed he was. He'd only scare her off.

"Hey," he said, "the important thing is, I'm here now."

"I . . . I don't know what to say."

"How about giving your old man a hug? It's been a long time."

Val went over to her and perched on the edge of the bed. Feeling awkward and somewhat self-conscious, he pulled her into his arms. She seemed to resist a bit, but then he felt her sag against him, the tension going out of her. He wondered if it was too late to try being a father to her. And for a fleeting instant—which made him feel a little ashamed—it crossed his mind that maybe it still wasn't too late to get his hands on some of that trust money.

Laurel drew back, using the back of her hand to wipe her nose, the way she had as a child.

"Uncle Rudy is handling the adoption," she said, sniffing. "He . . . he found the couple. They're very nice, he says." She paused to take a deep breath. "That's why they put me here, in this room . . . instead of in the maternity wing. I'm not supposed to be around the other mothers. I guess maybe they think if I see the mothers with their babies I'll jump out a window or something, and they don't want to be responsible."

So, no husband. The kid was a bastard. Figures. Just like him and Rudy.

Rudy.

I'll kill him, I'll squeeze the life out of that fucking prick.

"What's with you and Rudy?" Val asked, more harshly than he'd intended.

"He's been good to me," she replied, a little defensively. She plucked at the sheet covering her, twisting it around and around until it began to resemble a large strand of taffy. "It was my idea about the baby. I mean, he didn't say I should give it up or anything. He j-just . . . oh c-crap . . ."

Her chin wobbled helplessly, and a tear spilled over, sliding down her flawless cheek.

It all tumbled into place. The baby . . . the one Rudy had said he was adopting. Val had thought it was pretty weird when his brother mentioned it, anyone letting a middle-aged loner like Rudy adopt their kid . . . but he'd figured that Rudy, being such a hotshot lawyer, had to have all kinds of connections. But all the time it was Laurel's kid he'd been yakking about. *His* grandchild.

Yeah, he'd been swindled all right. Twice. But compared to Rudy, what Annie had done was just small-time. Annie, at least, had never come on with a ton of bullshit, pretending to be on his side. Val felt like grabbing the heavy chair next to the bed and throwing it. He hated having to admit it, but deep down hadn't he known all along what a shit Rudy was?

Val squeezed his eyes shut. He was fourteen again, and back in that booze-and-cigarette-smelling apartment where he'd grown up. He was seeing himself standing there, looking down at Shirley, passed out on her bed. Her face a funny bluish color . . . and, Jesus, the blood, it was all over her pillow. He remembered how he'd felt as if he might throw up. And he'd been so scared. Plenty of times she'd been crocked, and had thrown up on her bed, or on the floor, but never *blood.* He'd felt himself panicking. But Rudy was with him; Rudy would know what to do. *Shouldn't we get somebody,* Val had asked him, *some help?* But Rudy was shaking his head, saying, naw, if they got her dragged to the hospital and it turned out there was nothing much wrong with her, they'd just come out looking like a couple of stupid crybabies . . . and when Shirley came to, she'd give them something to be *real* sorry about. *But the blood,* Val said, starting to blubber, *what about the blood?* He was remembering how sick Shirley had seemed lately, hardly eating, bitching all the time about her stomach hurting. But Rudy, he'd just laughed. Go ahead, he'd taunted, *you* call a doctor, a fucking ambulance, but just where d'you think you're gonna get the money to pay for it all?

Val, feeling scared, but also sort of dumb for not seeing what to Rudy was so obvious, had followed his brother out of the room. He'd left Shirley just lying there.

By the time he *did* call, hours later, and the ambulance got there, Shirley was dead.

Now it hit Val, *Rudy, he had to have known all along that Shirley was dying. He wanted her to die.*

Val felt shaken. Sure, she'd been no great shakes as a mother, but to let her die? Jesus. If only he'd known . . .

But Rudy *had* known.

Just like he'd known about Laurel.

All this time, he knew where Laurel was . . . and he kept it from me.

Val's hands closed about the bed's metal side rail, hard enough to cut off his circulation. His fingers turned white and bracelets of cold formed about his wrists. He imagined it was Rudy's neck he was squeezing, and he could almost hear the separate crunch of each vertebra . . . the sound a big cockroach makes when you smash it under your heel.

Then he realized something important: Laurel didn't know Rudy was planning on keeping her baby for himself.

When he finally spoke, Val was amazed at the steadiness of his voice.

"Let me tell you a few things about good old Uncle Rudy," he began.

Waiting for his suitcase to drop onto the carousel in the Pan Am baggage-claim area, Rudy couldn't stop himself from whistling. What a day, what a great day! He'd thought of bringing Alicia, the Mexican baby-nurse he'd hired, along with him for backup. But then he'd realized he didn't want anyone else around. Just him and little Nick—that's what he was going to name him, Nicholas Carrera. He wanted his son to get to know his daddy without some nanny butting in . . . for Nick to know who came first in his life.

But what about the baby things? Did he have everything? He wasn't going to waste time buying a bunch of stuff in New York, so he'd brought it all with him. He ran through a mental checklist. A zip-up papoose thing, the cutest damn baby clothes, Pampers, blankets, bottles, nipples, cans of formula. Oh, and of course, Dr. Spock. He'd fallen asleep twice on the plane trying to read the thing. But still, come hell or high water, he was going to get through it. He and the nanny both were going to do everything right.

Watching his brass-cornered Louis Vuitton bag trundle on to the carousel, it struck him: In less than an hour he'd be holding little Nick. His son.

Excitement swelled in him, lifting his spirits up so high that he felt as if he had to look down at his feet to make sure his shoes were still touching the ground.

But a minute later, strapping his bag to the little fold-up wagon he carried, he started feeling anxious again.

Maybe he ought to give Laurel a call at the hospital. She'd had a tough time, poor kid . . . giving birth at home like that. Damn shame she couldn't have made it to the hospital delivery room. That way, they'd have whisked little Nick away before she even got a good look at him. And maybe giving him up wouldn't be so hard.

Rudy wished to Christ that he *could* tell her the truth . . . but if he did, she'd probably back out. And why not? Who would want a lonely old bachelor to raise their kid when they had been promised Ozzie and Harriet? And besides, she'd know then that he'd lied to her. No, he couldn't take that chance. Getting Nick, that's what counted. There was nothing more important than that.

Soon—maybe in a year or so—when the adoption was final, he'd find a way to tell her the truth . . . and by then she'd see that she'd made the right decision. That her son was in the best possible hands, with a daddy who loved him more than anything.

Rudy found a pay phone over by the Avis desk, and fished in his pocket for change. His hand was trembling as he dropped the coins in the slot. Jesus, why was he so nervous? Everything was all set, wasn't it? All he had to do was—

The phone was ringing.

"St. Vincent's Hospital," the operator spoke in a nasal whine.

"Room 322, please."

"Just a minute . . . I'll see if I can put you through."

There was a click on the line, then he could hear it ringing again. It rang and rang . . . and just when he thought Laurel must be in the john or something—just when his heart seemed like it was going to drop out of his chest—it got picked up.

"Hello?" Laurel's voice, but it sounded different . . . all stuffed up, as if she had a bad cold . . . or had been crying.

Something was wrong. He could feel it, a crackling in his brain, a burnt smell in his nostrils.

"It's me, Uncle Rudy," he said.

Silence. It was as if she'd hung up . . . except he could hear the stopped-up sound of her breathing.

"I know," she said finally, her voice cold as frost on a windowpane.

"Hey, what is this . . ." he started to say, but then his lungs seemed to fold over on themselves like an accordion that's wheezed to a stop, or a tire that had been slashed. He felt as if he were breathing underwater.

She spoke again, her voice breaking.

"I know everything. You lied. You . . . you said he was a real estate developer and she was . . . she raised dogs . . . and they'd been trying for years to have a baby. You told me all about their great house that was near a beach. And *lots* of other things . . . Oh, Uncle Rudy, how *could* you? How could you have done that?"

"Laurel, honey, you don't understand. If you'd just listen to me . . ."

"No. I don't want to listen." She was sobbing in earnest now. "You lied. You just used me so you could take my baby. Val told me everything."

Val? Jesus, what did Val have to do with this? How had he found her?

"Laurel, please listen to me. I was going to tell you—"

"Like you told me about my father?"

"That was—"

"Don't," she said abruptly. "I don't want to hear it. There can't be any excuse for lying about a thing like *that*. God, I was *eleven*. Can you imagine how I felt, thinking my father was dead? That my own sister had killed him?"

"I wasn't trying to hurt you. I . . ." He swallowed against the huge knot in his throat. Rudy couldn't remember when the last time was that he'd cried, but he was close to tears now. ". . . love you."

He'd never said those words, not to anyone, not in his whole life. Would they mean anything to her . . . anything at all?

"Good-bye," she said.

There was a click, and the line went dead.

Rudy leaned against the wall of the phone booth. The floor seemed to be heaving beneath him, and people rushing by with their suitcases were blurring into one another. He felt a pain in his chest, so bad he didn't think he could move. And there was a funny prickly feeling in his arms. Was he having a heart attack? Christ. Oh, Christ.

After a few minutes, the pain subsided . . . but his anguish was so great he felt weighed down, as if he were carrying his heavy suitcases himself. I lost it all, he thought. Nicky, Laurel. Everything he'd ever wanted, cared about, loved.

And because of Val . . . all because of Val.

That muscle-head didn't care about Laurel, not really. It was just an ego thing with him. Like his daughter was some kind of a prize he could stick up on a mantel. Why couldn't he have made her understand that she was better off without Val. That he, Rudy, was only trying to protect her?

Rudy lowered himself shakily onto the kidney-shaped bench inside the booth. Slowly, his breath returned, and his head began to clear. A single thought formed in his mind, and trembled there like a bead of poison on the tip of a scorpion's tail.

Someday, somehow, he'd find a way to get rid of Val . . . and when he did, this time it'd be for good.

"**B**ring me my baby."
          Laurel heard the words reverberate out loud, and felt as if she were almost shouting. But the nurse didn't even look up from the thermometer she was squinting at in the dim light of the small bedside lamp. Laurel cleared her throat, determined to be polite but emphatic.

"I want to see my baby, please."

This time, the nurse looked up. She peered at Laurel with about as much warmth and interest as she had at the thermometer, and said, "Well, now, I don't think that's such a good idea. Why don't we try and get some sleep? You'll feel better in the morning."

"It *is* morning." Laurel hated the nurse now, hated her saccharine voice, her officiousness.

The broad-hipped young woman, who had pale reddish-blond hair and a blue plastic I.D. tag pinned to the front of her uniform that read "KAREN KOPLOWITZ," glanced at her wristwatch and said brightly, "Well, so it is!"

According to Laurel's Timex, it was five-thirty. She'd been lying here in the semidarkness, staring up since lights-out at ten, listening to the faint sounds of traffic in the street below. Her eyes felt swollen and scratchy. And now this nurse had come bustling in to take her blood pressure and temperature, not even asking if she was awake, or if she minded. As if she were a cantaloupe in a supermarket being squeezed to see if it was ripe.

But worse than this nurse, worse even than the stinging discomfort between her legs and the squishy tenderness of her stomach, was the awful *emptiness* inside her.

Uncle Rudy. How could he have done something like this to her? Not just trying to take Adam for himself, but before that, making her believe her father was dead.

367

She recalled her shock at seeing Val walk in here yesterday. In her confusion, she hadn't known what to feel . . . for so many years she'd thought of him as dead. They'd sat and talked for close to an hour, and every so often she'd found herself staring at him, noticing how much older he looked, his perennially tanned skin webbed with fine creases, his white hair not as thick and luxuriant as she remembered—now the dull, yellowish color of old piano keys. Still a sharp dresser, with his expensive silk jacket, off-white slacks and Gucci loafers, but the jacket had to have been at least ten years old, and the cuffs of his shirt, she'd noticed, were beginning to fray. And he hadn't once mentioned any kind of a job, or what kind of house or apartment he was living in.

What he *had* talked about, besides Uncle Rudy, was the night she and Annie had run away. He'd told her how upset Annie had been about Dearie, and how when he tried to calm her down, she'd gotten furious at him, hysterical almost, accusing him of killing her mother. Val even showed the faint pink scar on his forehead where Annie had clubbed him with Dearie's Oscar. He'd seemed upset about it, tears welling up in his eyes. All he'd wanted, he'd said, was for them to be a family, to stick together.

Now, thinking it over, Laurel realized that apart from being glad to see him, and glad that he was alive, she felt sorry for Val . . . and guilty, too, as if she were partly responsible for the way his life had obviously gone downhill. Even so, she was sure that there had to be another side to his story. Annie would have a different explanation, she felt certain. But why in heaven's name *hadn't* Annie ever told her her side of things?

Maybe if they'd stayed in Los Angeles, and Annie had worked things out with Val, then she wouldn't be here in this hospital ward and *none* of this would have happened.

I trusted them, she thought, *I trusted Annie . . . Uncle Rudy too. . . and look where it got me.*

But another voice in her responded, *What did Val ever do for you? And look at all Annie has done. If you want the* real *story about that night, ask Annie.*

But what did any of that matter now? All she knew, all she cared about was that, through some dreadful series of wrong turns, her baby had been taken from her.

Laurel began to get a tight feeling in her chest. She knew she mustn't panic. She was pretty sure she hadn't signed any papers or anything, so maybe it wasn't too late . . . she could still change her mind. Or she could find a *real* couple to adopt Adam. Every adoption agency probably had hundreds, *thousands,* of really nice people desperate to adopt a healthy baby.

But she had to see him again first . . . until she'd actually held him in her arms, she didn't want to make up her mind. She couldn't. It wouldn't be fair. Adam's birth had happened so quickly. When she tried to remember it, it seemed mostly a blur. She remembered Joe . . . his white face hovering over her, steadying her like a bright beacon on a dark night. There had been pain, excruciating pain . . . she'd felt as if she were being pulled apart. Then something that felt like a fish had slithered between her legs . . . and a tiny wet body was held up to the light, its limbs flailing.

Then when Joe laid him against her stomach, she had felt the baby go still. She had felt his mouth moving against her skin, soft as a moth's wings. Her breasts had prickled in response, and a corner of her heart had chipped away.

At St. Vincent's, an intern who looked about sixteen—he had acne, she remembered, and peach fuzz on his upper lip—cut the cord; then a brisk nurse whisked Adam upstairs to the nursery. She hadn't seen him since then. Two whole days. Now her milk was coming in. Her breasts had turned hard. They felt weird, like a Barbie doll's molded plastic cones, and when she tried to lie on her stomach, they hurt. But that was a small hurt compared to the ferocious, aching need she felt. She could no longer bear it, not a minute more. She *had* to see Adam, to hold him.

"I don't care what time it is," she told the nurse, surprised by the sharpness she heard in her voice. "I want to see my baby. Get him for me, or I'll go get him myself."

In the past, trying to get her way, no matter what words she used, they always seemed to come out sounding wishy-washy. She was always so terrified of offending people, even perfect strangers who couldn't have cared less about offending *her.* Or afraid of causing a scene, having people *stare* at her.

But not now, not anymore. It was as if, in giving birth to Adam, she'd given birth to a new Laurel as well. The small, closed place whose boundaries had always pressed in on her was somehow gone. She felt as if she'd stepped out into a great openness where anything was possible, anything at all, terrible or wonderful.

"I want my baby," she repeated.

The nurse frowned. "Well, honestly, I don't . . ."

Laurel swung her legs out of bed. She was trembling, and her body felt like a giant boiled pudding. The abrupt exertion caused a sudden warm gush between her legs. She'd been bleeding, and Dr. Epstein had warned her against getting up, except to go to the bathroom. But right now she didn't care. The baby, her baby—the only thing she cared about was him.

"Get out of my way," Laurel commanded.

"Let's not get carried away here." Koplowitz took a step back, as if she thought Laurel might actually strike her.

And I will, Laurel thought, *if she doesn't move.*

"Why don't you wait here while I see what I can do?" The nurse bustled out, the door catching her on the hip before it bumped shut.

Laurel waited a minute; then she followed the nurse out into the corridor. Bright fluorescents stabbed at her eyes, and the floor tipped to one side like a banking airplane. There was something wrong with her balance. She had to walk with one palm scooting along the wall to keep from falling into it. She could feel her hospital gown gaping open in back. Cold air flapped against her rear end, and with each shuffling step, the hard plastic buckle of her sanitary belt dug into her tailbone.

She noticed an orderly staring at her as he wheeled a laundry cart past, and realized what she must look like—a crazy woman, that's what. Her hair hung in damp, oily strings about her face. And she stank. The rich smell of sweat and sickness and gooey dark blood rose up around her. Once, hiking in the woods with Annie and Dearie during a vacation at Lake Arrowhead, she had poked her head into an empty fox den, and the smell had been so thick it seemed to have fur and teeth. That's how she felt now. If she'd had fur, she'd be a bristling mother fox, and her fangs would be bared.

She reached an elevator door, and felt a burst of elation. Just another minute or two, and she'd be there. But which button to push, up or down?

Then the door slid open, and a harried-looking man in a white doctor's coat with a stethoscope peeking out of its front pocket was stepping out. "Excuse me"—she snatched at his starchy sleeve— "which floor is the nursery on? Where the babies are?"

He gave her a curious look, but appeared to be in too much of a hurry to give her bedraggled appearance any thought. "Eight," he said, jabbing a finger upward as he brushed past her.

Laurel dove into the elevator just as it was closing. It was empty, she saw, and it was going up. Thank God. She pressed the button for the eighth floor, then sagged against the elevator wall, closing her eyes.

Seconds later, she was stumbling into a bustling corridor, residents, nurses, orderlies scurrying past. So many people! How could it be only five-thirty? Even some patients were up and about. A wraithlike woman in a terry robe shuffled by her, pushing a wheeled pole on which was suspended an IV that was attached to her wrist. On the walls around Laurel were fat colored arrows that seemed to be pointing the way to different wings. But which was to the nursery?

She began to feel even more light-headed.

"Get a hold of yourself," she hissed under her breath. But in her head, crisply commanding, it was Annie's voice she heard.

Laurel, taking slow sliding steps, forced herself to keep moving. She saw something up ahead, a long pane of glass set into the corridor wall, almost like a brightly lit shop window. That had to be the nursery. She made herself go faster, despite the stinging, throbbing pain between her legs.

And then she was peering through the glass at rows and rows of spotless white bassinets, in each one a tiny, precious baby. And one of those was hers. Her baby. Her son.

She tried the door, marked in large red letters: STAFF ONLY, and found it unlocked. She pulled it open and walked in. To her surprise, no one tried to stop her.

There appeared to be only one nurse on duty, a tall black woman. She was diapering a red-faced infant on the changing table against the far wall. Looking up and seeing Laurel, she was so startled that her eyes actually bugged out a little, the way they did in cartoons. Laurel nearly giggled.

"This area is restricted to hospital personnel," she informed Laurel in a clipped, West-Indian-accented voice. "I'm afraid I am going to have to ask you to leave." She straightened, holding the freshly diapered baby in front of her like a shield, as regal as a Masai princess.

Laurel, feeling intimidated, began to plead, "Please, I just want . . ." Her mouth snapped shut as if a powerful lever now controlled her jaw. Scanning the rows of babies bundled in their Plexiglas bassinets, she squared her shoulders and said, "I've come for my baby. Cobb . . . Adam Cobb."

She was embarrassed to admit she didn't know what her own son looked like. She'd only had that one, fractured glimpse. God, why didn't the woman *hurry?*

"This is completely irregular," the nurse snapped. "The babies are not scheduled for feeding for another hour. Please return to your room, Mrs.—"

"*Miss* Cobb," Laurel interrupted, sticking her chin out. "And I'm not going anywhere until you let me have him."

"You will have to speak to your doctor."

"He's not here."

"Then I'm afraid I will have to call Dr. Taubman . . . he's the intern on duty. If you have a problem—"

"I don't have a problem. I just want my baby."

The nurse's brown eyes sparked. "We have *rules* around here, young lady. And they are not for no reason. We cannot have just anyone marching in here, no proper scrubbing, no mask, with Lord knows what kind of germs—"

"I'm not just anyone . . . I'm his mother." Saying it aloud caused something to crumple inside her chest; she could feel it as distinctly as if her lungs or her heart had suddenly collapsed. Her eyes filled with tears. She felt so tired. Her legs were trembling with the effort to remain standing, and there seemed to be an enormous amount of blood seeping from her. "I'm his mother," she repeated. "Please, I only want to hold him. Just for a few minutes."

The nurse stared hard at her, then relented. "All right. But you will have to stay here. I cannot let you take him back to your room."

"I don't care about that," Laurel told her, nearly swooning with relief. "Can I sit down?"

The nurse pointed to a rocking chair in the corner. Laurel sank into it gratefully, closing her eyes for a moment. When she opened them, she saw a pair of slender black arms extending a fleecy white bundle. Tightly wrapped folds of flannel, with a squashed red face peering from an opening at the top. Her heart turned over.

"Oh," she breathed.

"We wrap them tight like that the first day or two," the nurse explained. "It makes them feel more secure."

Laurel held her arms out. Where she had felt unsteady before, her muscles now seemed springy with new strength. With the warm weight of her child, something dropped into place inside her. Tears slid from her chin, and splashed against the blanket, forming gray circles on the white flannel.

He was looking at her. Round blue eyes fixed on her with an intentness that caused her full breasts to prickle. A nose no bigger than a thimble, and a tiny mouth that seemed pursed in contemplation, as if he were sizing her up somehow. And so much hair! When she pulled the blanket away from his head, a tuft of black hair stood up like the fur on a kitten.

"Adam," she whispered.

She tried to imagine handing him over to some stranger, and then walking away, going back to school, forgetting about him. But she couldn't see herself doing those things.

If she gave him up, then her arms wouldn't feel right. Without the weight of her son, they'd be too light, awkward and unbalanced. She imagined that if she left him her blood would keep draining between her legs until she was hollow as a reed. She had thought that not having Joe's love was bad . . . but this would be much, much worse. It would kill her.

But how will I support him? And what about Annie? I'd have to find somewhere else to live. A place where Annie wouldn't be able to run my life and Adam's, too.

She looked down at him. He was still staring at her, *scrutinizing* her actually. *It's as if he's trying to memorize my face,* she thought, another piece of her heart breaking off at the thought that this might be the last time he'd see her, except maybe in his dreams. She *couldn't* give him up. Not now. Not ever.

She didn't care what she had to do . . . what sacrifices she'd have to make. He'd be worth it.

My son. Mine.

Adam had turned his downy head into her chest and was rooting against the front of her gown. Laurel lifted it, and felt his mouth instantly fasten onto her nipple and begin to suck. A sharp pain as his gums clamped about her tender nipple, then she sat back and closed her eyes, feeling a strong pull in her breast, and in her groin too, as the milk let go and flowed into him.

She began to understand it . . . this mother-love that made fools out of sensible people, and tyrants of the timid. If she could paint it, she would need a canvas bigger than the Milky Way. And Adam would be right in the middle of it, like the first star of the evening, the one you wish on.

CHAPTER 25

Even before she could hear a voice on the phone, Dolly, listening to the humming and crackling of the transatlantic line, felt her heart leap. "Henri?" she cried. "That you?"

It had been so long . . . weeks since he'd last called; months since she'd seen him . . . months that seemed like a hundred years. "Dog years," Mama-Jo used to call it when time crawled so you could swear you'd aged a dog's seven years in the space of just one.

Not that she'd spent all those months doing nothing but mooning over Henri. Why, last Christmas had been her most profitable so far, and business had hardly slowed down since. And just this month she'd been to *Tosca* and a *Kiss Me Kate* revival with Bill Newcombe, who'd finally stopped trying to sell her insurance and who couldn't have been more charming. She'd been a fund-raiser for the Bangladesh Drive. And on the committee for the sold-out ball for which they'd raised four hundred thousand dollars. And then, last month, at the annual chocolate fair at the Plaza, the display she had helped Pompeau put together had taken the second prize for Girod's.

Oh, yeah, she'd been one busy girl, all right.

So busy that when she crawled into bed each night, she felt lonesome as a pup locked out in the cold . . . even on the rare nights when she wasn't alone.

"*Ma poupée,* did I wake you?" came his voice, faint and crinkly with static. Yet so dear. All at once, it seemed as if no time at all had passed.

"Not a chance," she told him, though a glance at the faintly glowing malachite face of the clock on the mantel told her it was half past one in the morning. "I couldn't sleep to save my life. Must be something I ate." Only the second part was a lie.

Actually, she was sitting here in the dark, curled up in the

Eames chair, looking out her big window at the million fairylike lights of Tavern on the Green far away across Central Park, and sipping a cognac that she knew would probably make her feel worse later on. How appropriate, fateful too, that Henri should call just when she was wearing his favorite nightgown, a peachy iridescent satin, the color of a Singapore sling, with spaghetti straps and a plunging neckline guaranteed to cause pneumonia . . . or cure impotence, depending on whether you were wearing it or looking at it. Her skin tingled where its cool, slippery creases touched her.

"As a matter of fact, I'm having myself a pity party," she told him.

"Pardon?"

"A pity party. It's like this . . . you sit around feeling real sorry for yourself, preferably when there's nobody 'round to slap you on the back and say, Hey, lady, snap out of it."

"I wish I were there," he said, sounding amused.

"Then it wouldn't be a pity party. It'd be a . . . well, I'm too much of a lady to say what it'd be. At least, not over the phone." She smiled, and cupped the receiver against her mouth, kissing it almost. The cognac was taking effect, warming her insides—or was it just hearing Henri's voice?

She prayed it was good news he was calling with; for one week, she'd had just about all the upheaval she could take.

The baby—Laurel deciding to keep him—was a blessing, Lord knows, but it sure had knocked her for a loop. And Val Carrera turning up like a bad penny after all these years, pouncing on Laurel when she was at her lowest, probably looking for ways to rake up all kinds of trouble—why, it gave her chills just thinking about it.

"And the fair? You were pleased with how it went?"

For a confused moment, Dolly had no idea what Henri was asking. Then she remembered that he didn't know a thing about Laurel . . . or little Adam . . . or Val. In the old days, she'd have rushed to call him; practically every little thing seemed important enough to tell him then. Had they drifted as far apart as all that?

"The fair," she said, rousing herself. "Oh, you should've come. It was the best ever!"

"I was very much wishing I could go. But with you making the display, and Pompeau making certain there was not one crumb of the *gâteau* that was not perfect, we did not do so badly, no?" She could almost see him shrugging his Gallic shrug. "Besides, I could not leave my daughter. The babies were so ill, and Gabrielle was beside herself . . ."

"I know." Henri a grandfather—she still couldn't quite get used to the idea. "Heck, it wasn't your fault. Are they better now?"

"Little Philippe is gaining weight, but Bruno . . . Gaby worries about him; he has always been the sickly one. I think he will outgrow it in time, but . . . she is a mother, and mothers worry, no?"

"Yeah, I guess so," she told him. *She* would never be a mother, but with this baby of Laurel's, wouldn't she be sort of a grandmother? Dolly couldn't wait to get her arms around little Adam, soggy diapers, spit-up, and all. But for that, she'd have to wait at least until tomorrow, when she brought Laurel and Adam home from the hospital. Right now, Henri was waiting. "Well, anyway . . . the fair. Clarisse Hopkins was one of the judges this year, though that old biddy couldn't know a *thing* about chocolate. I do believe all she ever eats is sour lemons. And Roger Dillon—you remember Roger?— he said Girod's would've taken first, instead of second, if it hadn't been for Clarisse being averse to chestnuts. And brilliant me, of course I used the *marrons glacés* as the centerpiece for our display."

Henri chuckled, and Dolly felt relieved he didn't seem to mind about second place when, for three out of the last five fairs, Girod's had placed first in the overall category of general excellence. To some, especially the smaller chocolatiers struggling simply to survive, the *Gourmand* magazine awards were springboards to acceptance and bigger sales, and they meant everything in the world. But Henri seemed to have other things on his mind.

"*C'est ça.* But I did not call you at seven-thirty in the morning—for you, I know, it is the middle of the night—to talk about the business," he told her. He sounded tense. "*Alors,* where to begin?"

"Why not skip over the beginning," she told him, feeling herself begin to tense. "We've been through that part a few times already. I know it by heart."

"Well, then—how do you say it—the happy finishings?"

Inside her chest, Dolly's heart did a crazy bump-and-grind.

"Henri, what exactly are you trying to tell me?"

There was a pause, and she could hear his unsteady breathing. Finally, he said: "Dolly, come to Paris."

"Henri, we have been through this again and—"

"No, no, this time, it is different. Francine and I, we have now separated."

Dolly felt as if a thousand volts of electricity had just come zizzing down the line. She nearly dropped the receiver.

"What did you say?" she gasped.

"Francine, she has shown me the door," he said softly, but with a small note of triumph. "It was all so very civilized. She even packed the valises for me. Though I believe she was doing this only to make certain that I was not taking anything that belongs to her."

For once, Dolly couldn't speak. She placed her balloon glass of cognac on the end table beside her, where it chattered against the glass top before coming to a standstill, then stood up, taking the cream-colored princess phone with her, and paced across the deep pile in front of the fireplace, her satin nightgown twitching coolly against her calves.

"Henri, no fooling? You're really serious?"

"I assure you, *ma poupée,* I have never been more serious. It appears that my wife has taken a lover." He sounded fully as gleeful as he had a few months ago when he'd told her about the birth of his twin grandsons. "As one might expect, she is very discreet about who this man is. I would not be extremely surprised if he should be her priest."

"No!" Dolly was surprised, shocked even.

He chuckled. "Well, perhaps I exaggerate. *Qui sait?* For all I care, she could seduce the pope." His voice grew serious. "I must be honest with you, though. There will be no divorce. Francine will not accept that. In that way, I imagine, she is the *true* mistress of the church."

Henri's voice seemed to be fading, and then she realized it was her pulse pounding in her ears, not the long-distance connection, that was making it hard to hear. "Henri, what exactly are you proposing?"

"That you and I . . . that we live together. It is the modern way, no? After that . . ." His voice trailed off. He didn't have to say what they both knew: that he would marry her in a minute if there should ever come a time when he could.

"What about your father-in-law, does he know?"

"He is old, yes, but he is not yet blind. Without question, he would do everything within his power to reunite Francine and me . . . but he recognizes that there are limits even to his power. All this has indisposed him. He worries about the firm, and he is feeling his years, so we now have a new agreement."

"What kind? What do you mean?"

"I am to receive his controlling interest upon his death. I, of course, am obligated to continue supporting Francine. But it is all completed with witnesses, signatures, and the notary. This is for me a great contract, a deliverance even."

"Oh, Henri!" Tears of happiness filled her eyes. No one could deserve it more. How he must have had to battle old Girod for this guarantee.

"*Chérie,*" Henri continued soberly, "you have not answered my question."

Dolly sank back into the chair, the phone on her lap. Her head was spinning. She didn't know *what* to think. The chance to be with him all the time, to live with him! Isn't that what she'd yearned for, dreamt about, for almost as long as she could remember? Marriage was nice, but as long as she had Henri, she could do without a ring.

But she would have to move to Paris.

Paris was beautiful, and she loved it, but New York was her *home.* How could she leave—especially now? Laurel was going to need all kinds of help. And—okay, if she was going to be selfish about it—how, if she were three thousand miles away, could she be a proper granny to that precious little baby?

For as much as she longed for Henri, she also longed for a real family; this baby would bond her to Annie and Laurel in a way that nothing else had. And her business? She'd killed herself to build it up, and now it had become more than just a means of making money—it was a cozy place where she, and the people who came there, felt right at home. Her regulars came for their bittersweet bark or their Bouchons, then stayed to chat and somehow ended up spilling their hearts out. Nora Mulgrew, whose dentist husband was having an affair with his hygienist—she couldn't make up her mind whether to leave him or not. Ramsey Burke, the ball-breaking litigator, who stopped in every morning on his way to work for a single bourbon truffle, and was constantly debating about quitting his shrink, since he was making no progress whatsoever in dealing with his awful fear of heights, airplanes, and elevators.

Oh, they'd survive without her, they all would. But that wasn't the point, really. The thing was, she *enjoyed* all these people; she loved feeling as if she was making a difference in their lives, even a slight one. Who would she talk to in Paris? Her French wouldn't get her past the first stop on the Métro. And, besides, if she worked for Henri, it wouldn't be her shop; it would be just a job, a way to be near Henri.

She loved Henri; she was *nuts* about him. But had she ever *really* considered what a move to Paris might mean? She thought of the old Chinese saying, *Be careful what you wish for, you might get it.*

She'd been wishing for this for so long, that now that it was within her reach she felt, well, sort of cheated, as if she'd suddenly learned that she'd been wishing for the wrong thing all along. Or maybe it was just that she wanted to have her cake and eat it too: Henri *and* her life here.

"Where are you now?" she asked.

"I have a room at the Lancaster. In a week or two, perhaps, I was hoping you and I could look for an apartment together."

"Henri, look, I—"

"Is there someone . . . a man?"

"No, no . . . believe me, that's not it."

"You have not stopped caring for me, then?"

"Lord, no."

"Then what more is there to discuss? Dolly, I speak to you lightly about leaving my home . . . but I must tell you that after so many years in one place, it is a hard thing. I need you, *ma poupée,* more than I ever have. I need *us* . . . the two of us."

"But, Henri," she tried to explain, "don't you see? You're asking me to do the very same thing . . . leave my home and my family, even my *country*. Why, I'll bet you a pair of snakeskin cowboy boots there isn't an American alive who doesn't get the teeniest bit choked up when he hears 'The Star-Spangled Banner.' "

"Perhaps you could get used to the 'Marseillaise' . . . it is not so sad," he teased, but she could hear the weary desperation in his voice, and it caught at her heart.

Dolly felt herself wavering. Years ago, even when Henri had had little more to offer her than the shadowy half-life of a mistress, she had agonized over what to do. Now he was offering so much more, and yet she was holding back. Had her feelings for Henri

changed so much . . . or was it that her life here in New York had
grown that much more dear?

Either way, she owed him and *herself* a decision with the full
light of day shining on it, and a head unclouded with cognac.

"Henri, I've got to sleep on this," she said firmly. "Now don't
you go thinking I'm just too chicken to say what's on my mind. The
fact is, I don't know *what* is on my mind, exactly. All I know is,
anything comes out of my mouth now isn't gonna make an anthill
of sense. Can you wait until tomorrow?"

He sighed. "Do I have a choice?"

"Nope."

"In that case, sleep well, *chérie,* and I love you."

As Dolly hung up, her head pounding, she thought there was
about as much chance of her sleeping well now as there was of her
walking on the moon.

"He reminds me a little of Uncle Herbie."

Annie, gazing through the viewing window of the hospital
nursery, turned to find her aunt, brilliant in an emerald bouclé wool
suit with a gold-and-navy Hermès scarf knotted about her throat,
dabbing at her eyes with a lipstick-stained handkerchief. A gold
charm bracelet jingled at her wrist, and amid the miniaturized
clutter—tennis racket, Scottie dog, turtle, whistle, padlock—Annie
recognized the charm she and Laurel had given Dolly last Christmas:
a tiny gold candy box in the shape of a heart.

She remembered that Dolly had gone all weepy when she
opened it, and that she herself had felt pleased but also embarrassed
by the fuss her aunt had been making.

Uh-oh, here she goes again, Annie thought uneasily. This time it
was going to be the most darling, precious baby in the whole world
she would be getting all choked up about; and knowing Dolly, she
would be hovering over them, and the baby, twenty-four hours
a day.

"Eve ever tell you about Uncle Herbie? He was our mother's
brother," Dolly rattled on. "He had this thatch of black hair and a
red nose that kept getting redder over the years. Mama said it was
white lightning that caused it. I didn't know what she meant . . . but
after she told me, I used to hide under my bed whenever there was

an electrical storm." She chuckled. "Lord, what a character. He kept his kitchen door wide open, and let his filthy chickens have the run of the place, and fed them scraps right off the table like they were dogs."

"I think he looks like Dearie," Annie said, turning her attention back to the nursery. "Look at his chin, the way it's rounded, with that little crease in the middle." All the other babies were asleep, but Adam was wide awake. He waved his fists, and a tiny pink foot kicked loose from his blanket.

She felt Dolly stiffen beside her, then give a small sigh. "Why, maybe so . . . I guess it's tough to tell at this age, isn't it?"

"I wish Dearie were here. I wish she could have seen her grandson."

Her own sudden longing for her mother came unexpectedly. It had been a long time since she'd felt even a distant ache at the thought of her mother. But now she couldn't help thinking, *It should be Dearie standing here beside me, not Dolly.*

At once, she scolded herself. Poor Dolly . . . she tried so hard. And it couldn't be easy for her, with no husband or children of her own. Did she still see Henri . . . or was it over for good? Was there even such a thing as "for good" when you were crazy in love, the way Dolly was with Henri?

Annie thought of Joe, and she felt the tight grip she'd been keeping on her own her emotions slip a little. It was as if Joe were her center, her core, the axle around which she turned, and without him she could go flying off in a million directions.

And what about Emmett . . . where did he fit in? That night at his apartment . . . in the shower . . . and later in bed. . . . God, it had been so good. How could anything that good be just a fling? She'd been avoiding Emmett for the past week or so, but she couldn't put him off forever. She knew she didn't love him the way she loved Joe, but what she *did* feel was certainly more than mere fondness.

Annie nibbled on her thumbnail. She felt so confused. Then Adam raised a clenched fist over his head, looking so much like a hammy politician railing about tax increases that she couldn't help but smile. *Maybe, just maybe, it's still not too late for me and Joe,* she thought.

Everything would be different from now on. With Adam to mother, Laurel wouldn't have time to hang around Joe so much. She had even talked about moving out, finding a place of her own. At first, Annie had been against it, but now she was starting to think it really might not be such a bad thing. Maybe the time had come for Laurel to go out on her own.

"Carnations," Dolly said. "I remember when you were born, your father filled Evie's room with pink carnations, whole fields of them. Why, he must've cleaned out every florist from Bel Air to Westwood. Evie said she felt halfway between a corpse at a Mafia funeral and the winner of the Kentucky Derby."

Annie smiled. Then she thought of the huge bouquet of pink roses and baby's breath that Joe had sent Laurel. Her smile faded, and she felt something pinch at her heart.

"I think it's feeding time," she said, watching a nurse bend over Adam's bassinet and lift him out. She couldn't wait until it was *her* turn to hold him.

Dolly turned to Annie, her blue eyes bright and a high flush making her rouged cheeks even pinker. "Do you think they'd let me hold him? Just for a minute. I wouldn't get in the way."

Annie fought back her annoyance. What she felt like saying was, *Why should you be the first to hold him?*

Then, feeling selfish, she said quickly, "Why don't you tell the nurse you're his grandmother? You practically are, anyway."

Dolly looked as if she were going to kiss her, and Annie instinctively found herself sidling away.

"I'll go see how Laurey's doing," she told Dolly. "Give Adam a kiss for me."

Laurel was up and dressed in the clothes Annie had brought her the day before—turtleneck, and a loose-fitting blue maternity jumper that hung on her like a collapsed tent. She looked thin and tired, violet smudges under her eyes, but radiant nonetheless. She smiled as Annie walked in.

"Look who the cat dragged in," Laurel quipped. "I thought *I* was supposed to be the one recuperating here. You look even worse today than you did yesterday."

"For someone who's practically had a heart attack, I think I'm holding up pretty well." She crossed the room, and sat on the bed beside Laurel.

"That reminds me, you never *did* tell me where Louise finally tracked you down."

"For your information, I was in the offices of the venerable Kendall, Davis, and Jenkins. And when I got the call about you, I nearly plotzed right then and there."

"In your lawyer's office?" Laurel's eyes sparkled. "What were you doing there?"

"I was going to tell you—Tout de Suite's about to become a corporation. They're drawing up the papers. Can you believe it?"

"Actually, yes. What I can't believe is that I'm a mother." Laurel beamed, and her expression grew misty. "I could look at him for hours and hours and never get tired of him. Have you seen him today? Isn't he the most beautiful baby you ever laid eyes on?"

"By far! But I think you've got a ladies' man on your hands— I caught him making eyes at one of the nurses."

"Oh, he'll go for anything with boobs. You should see how he mauls mine." She touched the front of her dress and winced.

Annie looked at her sister, so pretty, so happy. For the first time since she came to the hospital, Annie saw, she'd washed her hair. Caught at the nape of her neck with a thick silver barrette, it hung down her back in a gleaming sheaf, catching the light that streamed in through the window. She smelled nice, too, like soap and rosewater. Annie felt the seed of resentment she'd harbored inside her for so many months begin to dissolve.

But then the vase of pink roses on the small table next to the bed caught her eye. They'd passed their peak, blowsy and beginning to droop, but the overheated room was drenched with their fragrance.

Annie thought of Joe and looked down, unable to meet Laurel's eyes. She felt the warmth inside her abruptly cool. After a moment of silence, she took a deep breath, and stood up. "Ready to go? Shall I tell the nurse to bring Adam?"

"In a minute."

"I have everything ready at the apartment," Annie told her. "Even the crib . . . Emmett helped me set it up last night."

"I know. Emmett dropped by this morning and told me. What a guy—he always comes up with the perfect thing. Remember when I complained about my feet always being cold, and he got me those extra-thick Alpine socks? Well, look what he brought me this time." From her overnight bag, propped against the foot of the bed, she fished out a T-shirt. When she held it up, Annie saw that it had a picture of a cow on it, and she smiled. "Don't laugh," Laurel told her. "The nurses around here have been calling me 'Elsie.' Even with Adam guzzling like there's no tomorrow, I've gone through so many nursing pads, they're threatening to hook me up to one of those electric pumps."

"You don't look as if you're suffering *too* much."

"I'm not. I'm just scared." Laurel flopped back on the bed, staring up at the ceiling, her hands crossed behind her head. "Annie, this morning when I was nursing him, I looked down at him and thought, 'What if I make a horrible mess of his life?' I mean, he's so . . . so trusting. He doesn't know any better, does he? If I'm doing everything all wrong, who's going to stop me? How will I know?"

Annie thought of all the wrong turns she'd probably taken with Laurel. Where would they be now if she'd done things differently, acted less impulsively? Still in California with Val?

Thinking of her stepfather, she felt her stomach knot. Yesterday, Laurel had told her about his visit. It had been a full five minutes before Annie's shock had worn off, and before she could remind herself that there was no legal way Val could harm either of them now. But would he try to see Laurel again? And Laurel . . . did she want him in her life even now that she didn't have to be afraid of him?

"I think the main thing is just to love him," Annie told her. "Then if you make a few mistakes, it won't matter as much."

"Annie?" Laurel appeared to hesitate, chewing on her bottom lip.

"Yeah?"

"Look, I know you've always done your best as far as I was concerned . . . and . . . and that most of the time it wasn't so easy." She sat up, the sudden movement bringing a rush of color to her face. "I just wanted you to know that . . . that even though I don't always show it, I'm . . . well, I didn't mean any of those awful things I said to you that night after . . . well, when we had that fight." Her eyes turned bright, and she wiped them with a sheepish little laugh. "Will you look at me? Leaking from every orifice. In Lamaze, they forgot to warn me about turning into a human fountain."

Annie felt tears in her own eyes, as well. Could they get beyond this jealousy that had sprung up between them? Would they someday, years and years from now, when they were two married ladies, each with a family of her own, look back on this and wonder how they could have let a man who, by then, neither of them might have thought of in ages, come between them?

Annie didn't know; right now, all she knew was that she loved her sister.

"Don't worry," she told Laurel briskly. "I packed plenty of Kleenex, just in case."

"Hey there, short stuff, you don't know me yet, but you just wait," Dolly cooed to the infant nestled in her arms. "I'm gonna spoil you so rotten you'll think you got born straight into heaven."

The baby's eyes fixed on her, squinting a little as if he were trying to bring her into focus. So much hair! And look at that scowl . . . when it was his turn, she thought, he surely wouldn't be shy about speaking up.

Under the watchful eye of the nurse standing just outside the door to the nursery, Dolly gently prodded the baby's curled red fist with her finger, and felt him grasp it tightly. Her heart caught, and her diaphragm seemed to swell upwards, making it hard for her to breathe.

Then, without warning, Adam's face puckered and he began to yowl. Dolly jostled him, but that only made him cry harder.

Her gaze darted in panic to the pie-faced nurse who stood with her arms folded across her flat chest, appearing not the least bit concerned. "Do you think he's hungry?"

"Gas, probably," the nurse said. "He just had his two o'clock feeding. Put him over your shoulder, and give him a pat or two. That should bring up the bubble."

Gingerly hoisting him to her shoulder, Dolly felt suddenly awkward, certain that she was holding him all wrong. What did she know about babies? The closest she'd ever come to being a mother was baby-sitting for Annie when she was little. But when Annie was this small, she'd had a baby nurse—a stout German lady named Mrs. Hildebrand, who had stood guard over Annie's crib like a Nazi storm trooper, not letting anyone within six feet.

Adam was really screaming now, jerking his legs and flailing his fists. Dolly felt like crying herself. Dogs were supposed to sense it if you were scared of them . . . was that true for babies, too? Could this little bitty thing be picking up on her inexperience? And if so, maybe he was smarter than forty-two years of living had made her. If he could talk, he might even tell her she was wasting her time with him, when she could be kicking up her heels in Paris with Henri.

Struggling to quiet him, and feeling woefully inadequate, Dolly had to fight to keep from handing her great-nephew back to the nurse and hightailing it out of there, straight to the nearest phone, where she'd call Henri and tell him she was on her way.

But something was making her stay put. Pacing back and forth along the corridor outside the nursery, Dolly kept cooing and jostling, talking to Adam as if he really could understand her.

"Oh, I know, I know . . . you don't like it one bit, being handed around to this person and the next like a sack of grain. But your mama's right down the hall, and you'll be on your way home before you know it. In a chauffeured limousine, no less. How's that for a red carpet send-off? You're gonna feel like Elvis Presley. Fact is, you look a little like him . . . all that black hair. Bet if we had some hair grease, we could make a cute little pompadour out of it." Softly, she began to hum "Love Me Tender."

Gradually, Adam stopped wailing. And just as Dolly was beginning to feel confident, and actually proud of herself, she heard the baby grunt . . . and felt something warm and foul-smelling splatter the front of her blouse. She looked down in dismay at a runny mustard-colored bowel movement dribbling from one leg of his loosely-fitted diaper.

The nurse bustled over. "Oops," she said. "Guess it was more than just gas. Stay right there . . . I'll get a washcloth."

Dolly stood rooted to the spot, feeling like a dog that's rolled in manure—and probably smelling like one, too. Then she began to chuckle. Staring down into Adam's dark blue eyes, she whispered, "Okay, short stuff, you've shown me your worst, and I'm still crazy about you. So what now? Can you tell me that? What do I tell Henri?"

Annie was on her way back to the nursery when she saw a green light flash on over one of the elevators. A chime sounded, doors slid open, and two nursing students stepped out, followed by a tall, spectacled man wearing faded jeans and a navy wool pullover, his head bent low as he if were used to ducking through doorways. His streaky brown hair was tousled and his face stamped with color, as if he'd run up the stairs instead of taking the elevator. She felt her heart leap.

"Joe," she called softly.

"Hey, Annie."

He looks tired, she thought. Even with his glasses partially hiding his eyes, she could see his dark circles.

She wanted to hug him . . . but she didn't feel she could. And, dammit, wasn't she hurting, too?

"How's Laurey?" he asked.

"Fine. I was on my way to the nursery to ask one of the nurses to bring Adam to her. She's taking him home."

"I know. That's why I'm here. I was in the neighborhood, and I thought maybe you guys could use a ride."

"Thanks," she told him, "But Dolly's taking us. Joe, I . . ." She swallowed hard and felt her throat clench, as if she were trying to force down something bitter. "I guess I ought to thank you. For getting Laurey safely through this. If you hadn't been there . . ." She couldn't bring herself to imagine what might have happened. "Anyway, I'm glad you were there."

He shrugged as if it were no big deal. "Any kid in that big a rush to get born doesn't need much of a hand. One look at him, and you can see he's a fighter. Cute, too, isn't he?"

"He doesn't look a thing like Laurey."

"The eyes," he said, solemnly touching the corner of his own eye with his index finger. "They remind me of yours."

Annie felt herself grow warm. Oh God, did he know what he was doing to her? Why, if he was going to keep his distance, did he have to remind her of what they'd come so close to sharing? She wanted to shout, throw herself at him, *force* him out of that polite foxhole of his. Even hitting him or having him knock another hole in the wall would be better than this.

But all she could do was smile. "His father is Puerto Rican. Laurey actually knew him in sixth grade back in Brooklyn, it turns out. He was in that school play you once rushed out to pick her up from. Then they met up again at Syracuse. Quite a coincidence, huh?"

Joe flushed, and he looked away, his gaze following a laundry cart piled high with sheets as it was trundled into an elevator by a dark-skinned orderly. But at the same time she thought she had seen something in his eyes . . . a flash of emotion that came and went so quickly she wasn't sure whether she'd imagined it or not.

Jealous? Could he be jealous that he's not the father?

She noticed he was carrying a gift-wrapped package under one arm. "Something for Laurey?" she asked as nonchalantly as she could.

He retrieved it from under his arm as if he'd forgotten it was there. "Dr. Spock," he said. "Everything you ever wanted to know about babies but were afraid to ask."

Annie didn't tell him that Laurel already had been given two copies, one from Rivka and one from Dolly.

A strained silence settled between them like a slowly sinking boat. Finally, he gestured toward the dreary-looking lounge with its plastic furniture and vending machines. "Can I buy you a cup of coffee?"

Annie thought that if she drank a cup of coffee right now, she could well burn a hole right through her stomach. Nevertheless, she found herself nodding. "Just a quick one. I promised Laurey I'd be right back."

The visitors' lounge was empty except for a man with a yarmulke who sat hunched over, forearms resting against his knees. After he'd fished out change for the coffee, Joe led her over to a pair of molded plastic chairs where they sat side by side, knees barely touching, hands folded about the steaming Styrofoam cups. Annie felt like a statue carved out of ice, yet her heart was racing, and she felt out of breath.

Do you know how often I've picked up the phone to call you? Do you know that once in the middle of the night I even went to your apartment? I got as far as your door before I turned around.

Annie stared down at Joe's scuffed Dock-Siders, their leather ringed with stains. Joe had long feet—not big, just long and narrow—with knobby ankles. For some reason she found herself remembering Emmett, that first night in Paris when he'd shucked his boots off before climbing into bed. How odd that, instead of being repulsed, she'd felt such tenderness.

But now it was Joe's long legs she imagined tangled about hers in bed, his breath in her hair, his hands . . .

"How's it going?" he asked. "The business, I mean."

"Too good," she told him, imagining him reading her thoughts, and feeling a hot prickle of discomfort. "I hired a new girl to help Louise in the kitchen. If it keeps up like this, I'll have to put on a swing shift. We can barely keep up with all the orders."

"If you need anything," he told her, "just let me know. I could spare a couple of the guys for a few days if you're ever in a real pinch."

"Thanks. I'll keep that in mind." She stared down at her coffee, which had an iridescence to it that made her think of machine oil; then she set her cup down on the small table, its surface charred with cigarette burns. "How are things at the restaurant? I mean, with the new addition and all."

"Bursting at the seams already." He smiled. "Thanks, in part, to my parents. Would you believe they eat dinner there at least once a week? And sometimes Dad shows up for lunch with a bunch of his cronies. I think he's mellowing with age. Miracles never cease, huh? Actually, I'm sort of getting used to them being around. I like it—a sort of reversal of my childhood, where I get to be the provider."

She found herself smiling, in spite of her tenseness. "I'm glad."

Silence fell again, deeper this time. Annie watched a young nun—one of those modern sisters in a knee-length powder-blue habit, with dark hair crinkling out untidily from under her cropped wimple—slide into the empty chair next to the apathetic man in the yarmulke. She was saying something to him, but Annie couldn't hear the words. They seemed to be an attempt at comforting him.

"Annie." She felt Joe's eyes on her, but she didn't look at him. She didn't know why, but she sensed he was going to say something she didn't want to hear.

She concentrated on holding herself very steady, like a too-full vase of water that might tip over.

If I don't answer, if I pretend I don't hear, then he won't say the terrible thing.

"There's something you should know," he went on in a quiet, almost hushed voice. "I'm glad I ran into you, but I just want you to know I would have called you anyway. I haven't said anything to Laurey. I wanted to talk to you first."

She tugged her gaze upward, forcing herself to meet his eyes. And what she saw in them *was* terrible. Pity. He was *sorry* for her. God, oh God.

"What is it, Joe?" she demanded. "For God's sake, what *is* it?"

"I'm going to ask Laurey to marry me."

Her mind seemed to separate from the rest of her, and float over her body like some bizarre version of the Holy Spirit. Everything looked strangely distorted; carts and gurneys seemed to rush past like cars on a freeway while a man creeping by on crutches seemed not to move at all. The overhead fluorescents suddenly seemed to be baking the top of her head until she thought her skull might just explode.

She began thinking of this game she and Laurel used to play when they were younger. "What if?" Simple, but gruesome: "If you had to die, how would you want to go?" Usually, she'd pick freezing over fire, because she'd heard it was less painful. But Laurey thought being guillotined like Marie Antoinette, or burned at the stake like Joan of Arc, would be more romantic. Now Annie realized that all those tortures combined couldn't seem worse than the agonizing pain she felt right now.

"What?" she heard herself say, but the words seemed not to be connected to her; they might have been flies buzzing against a windowpane.

"Annie . . ." He tried to take her hand, but she whipped back so violently she banged her elbow against the back of her chair. Pain shot up her arm, bright-hot, bracing.

"I don't want to hear it," she said. "Please, don't make me listen to this." She had an intense desire to cover her ears, the way a child would have.

Carefully, he removed his glasses and took the bridge of his nose, rubbing it between his thumb and forefinger. In spite of herself, she marvelled at his lashes, how long and thick they were. His green-brown eyes were bloodshot, as if he hadn't slept in days. He had to be suffering too.

She hated him for that; she hated him for making her feel sorry for him when what she really wanted to do was hurt him as much as he was hurting her.

"Are you in love with her?" she forced herself to ask. "Is that what this is all about?"

He paused.

She felt a piece of her injured heart rejoice. How much could he love her if he had to stop and think about it?

"You could say that," he responded, seeming to choose his words carefully. "I'll spare you the two-dollar speech. Annie, I don't want to hurt you, or insult you. But let me say this: There really *are* more than one or two kinds of loving, and there's a whole lot of gray shading in between."

"I hope you're not planning to put it to Laurey that way," she said bitterly. "And I hope you're not asking me to give you my *Good Housekeeping* seal of approval. You're not doing Laurey any favors, you know."

"It's more complicated than that, don't you see? Damn it, I wish it weren't!" He crumpled his empty cup, and flung it against the wall. "I wish I could say I was just being Joe Samaritan, and then let you talk me out of it."

"Do you *want* me to talk you out of it?" She stared at him.

He didn't answer. "I don't know," he said. "What I *do* know is that what I feel for you hasn't changed."

Annie struggled against the tears swelling at the back of her throat. She should tell him how she felt, she thought. She should beg him not to do this thing. But something was holding her back. It was as if her mouth was sealed tight. No, she couldn't do it . . . she couldn't.

Pride? She didn't know. All she knew at this moment was that she hated the man sitting beside her, hated him and loved him with all her heart and soul.

Annie saw that the man in the yarmulke had begun to weep, and now the young sister was putting her arms around him, rocking him a little. Had his wife died? God, what an awful thought. She watched the nun help the sobbing man to his feet. He stumbled a little, and his yarmulke fell askew, dangling from a bobby pin clipped to his thinning gray hair, so that when he reached up to straighten it, he looked, comically, as if he were tipping his hat at her. She imagined the poor man eating alone tonight, leftovers from a meal prepared by his dead wife.

Annie's heart ached for him, and for herself. But she knew that she'd reached a point where if she tried to cry, no tears would come. They were frozen inside her. And if she touched herself, her skin would feel cold. She'd felt this way once before, the gray afternoon she'd stood in the cemetery, watching Dearie's coffin being lowered into the ground. Except that this time, it was worse. The person who had died was herself.

"Go," she told him, her voice flat. "Go to Laurey."

Later that day, Dolly dialled the Lancaster Hotel, and waited patiently while the line beeped and buzzed its way to Paris. It was four in the afternoon, ten in France, and Henri should have had his dinner by now. She was in her office, upstairs at Girod's, where she felt more in control, more in charge of herself than at home. Even so, she felt sick at the thought of what lay ahead.

Finally it began to ring, and was answered by a *téléphoniste* who put her through to Henri's room. She prayed he wouldn't be in; suddenly, she wanted to put this off.

But tomorrow, and the next day, she knew that her decision would be the same. She *had* to do this now.

"Henri?"

"Ah! *Chérie,* you must have been reading into my thoughts. I could not wait any longer. I was just now going to call you."

The sound of his voice caused her to grow light-headed, as if she'd drunk champagne on an empty stomach. How, in the few hours since they'd spoken, could she have forgotten the effect his voice had on her?

Dolly faltered. But then she remembered how that little baby had felt in her arms. She could feel the warm imprint of his body against her bosom still, the firm pressure of his tiny fist wrapped about her finger. Adam was just a part of it, she knew . . . but he seemed to embody it all, everything she stood to lose.

"Henri, I can't, I just can't do it," she told him, a great aching hollow opening inside her. Tears streamed down her cheeks faster than she could mop them up with her handkerchief. "I'm a great-aunt now. Laurel's had a darling baby. Makes me more like a grand-mother really." *Even Annie had said so, hadn't she?* "His name's Adam . . . and he's beautiful, just the most beautiful child this side of heaven. And Laurel needs me, and the baby does, too. And I guess I need him. Besides, I'd just about die of homesickness, and don't you dare tell me otherwise. And don't tell me I could visit, or my girls could, because it's not the same thing and you know it. And, another thing, would you tell me where in the whole of Paris on Sunday morning I could buy a warm bagel?" She stopped, not because she'd run out of arguments, but she'd run out of breath.

For the longest time, except for the rustling of long-distance static, the line was silent.

Finally Henri spoke.

"Just now, I was remembering our last few moments together in Grenada, before our planes . . . how we never said good-bye, not the words. Perhaps we knew one day there would come a time for speaking them."

She smiled through her tears, surprised at the keenness of the hurt she felt. Her heart had been broken so many times, she'd have thought there'd be nothing left of it. But thank heaven he understood; he wasn't going to fight it. In fact, he must have known since last night, when she seemed hesitant in the first place, and had been preparing for this ever since. Gloom welled up in her like a creek threatening to overflow its banks. What could be more wonderful than the joy of spending the rest of her life with Henri?

"I love you," she told him.

"Even if I cannot give you bagels?" he teased, but she could hear the heartbreak in his voice, and how he was struggling to keep it light.

"*Mais oui, chéri,*" she ventured in her atrocious French. "Oh, Henri, what do I say now?"

There was a long silence, in which Henri seemed to be losing his struggle. Finally, he spoke, but his voice had the choked, tinny sound of a man close to tears.

"Just say '*Au revoir.*' After all these years who can tell what tomorrow will bring us?"

Dolly knew it was time to hang up, but she clung to the receiver. If she let go, she felt she'd be severing something, some vital artery that could never be made whole again. But even as she held on, she could feel it all unravelling, everything they'd shared, her hopes and dreams, even her memories of Henri, the solidness of him in bed beside her, his hand steadying her elbow as she tottered across the street in her impossible heels. Lord, was this really happening?

"*Au revoir*," she spoke softly into the receiver. A tear dripped from her chin onto the coiled phone cord, shimmering there like a raindrop on a spiderweb before dropping off.

"*Au revoir, ma poupée.*"

Dolly placed the receiver gently, gently in its cradle, as if the slightest pressure might shatter it. Then, sitting as tall and erect as Clint Eastwood on his saddle, she began straightening the clutter of order forms, invoice and phone slips scattered over her desk. A food editor from *Newsday* was interviewing her at four, then afterwards she had a meeting scheduled with Helmut Knudsen to see the new boxes he was designing for Valentine's Day. And tomorrow, the Children's Aid luncheon, then . . .

She stopped, her hands fluttering to rest on a stack of five-by-seven index cards on which she kept names, addresses, and birthdates of her regular customers, to whom she always sent a small box of truffles on their birthdays.

She let out a small, choked cry, then sucked in her breath, and thought, *If I keep moving, keep busy, then I won't have to think about it. Not ever. And anyhow, I'm no worse off than I was yesterday, so what's the big deal?*

When her desk was in order, Dolly reached for the mirrored compact and array of lipsticks she kept in the top right-hand drawer, next to a box of tissues. Bill Newcombe was picking her up at seven-thirty. This time he had tickets to *Grease*, and she couldn't exactly go looking like a rabid raccoon, now could she? Peering into the compact's mirror, she wiped at the mascara under her eyes with a tissue. She'd wear her red Halston with the sequined straps; if she got real lucky, he'd take her dancing afterwards, and she'd be so wiped out when she got home she'd fall asleep before she'd even slipped out of her spike heels.

She wouldn't let him stay over, though, no matter how much he might want to, because, Lord, there was nothing worse than crying into a pillow over a man who ain't there . . . and praying the one lying next to you won't hear.

CHAPTER 26

"It's not much of a honeymoon," Joe said, smiling at the sight of his wife curled in the platform rocker by the radiator with Adam, dead asleep, draped over her shoulder like a sack of flour. "I wish it could be Bermuda, or even the Poconos."

"I like it just fine right where I am," she replied, cupping a hand about the baby's head while she rose, carefully, her upper body held erect, looking like a golden-haired geisha in her silk kimono. The front of her robe, where she'd been nursing Adam, had fallen open, Joe saw. He glimpsed the curve of her breast, creamy-white, with just a touch of rosiness—the color of a Babcock peach. He felt oddly stirred by this, the sight of her with her robe innocently open, and his son asleep on her shoulder. His son! He could hardly believe it, but, yes, the adoption papers had been filed, and in six months or so Adam would be legally his. A minor technicality. He couldn't have loved Adam any more than if the boy had been his own flesh and blood.

But Laurel . . . what he felt for her was different, more complicated. Yet here they were, newlyweds. Christ. What was he doing? How could he possibly hope to make a go of this when not once in the four weeks they'd been married had he been able to look her in the eye and honestly say, "I love you"? He felt a swell of guilt break inside him.

"Need any help with him?" Joe asked, following her as she padded barefoot into the bedroom, where Adam's crib was set up next to their double bed. Looking around him, he still felt a mild shock at the transformation of his spare bachelor's quarters into this jumbled nest of baby furniture, crib quilts, diapers, tiny stretchy sleepers, and assorted jars and containers. Not to mention Laurel's strew of painting supplies, drafting board, canvases stacked against the wall, and clothes—a welter of slips, bras, lacy underpants, night-

gowns, leotards, tights, T-shirts, which seemed to have sprouted up
overnight, like some mysterious jungle.

"Hand me a clean diaper," she whispered. "For under his head."

Joe handed her a flannel diaper from the stack folded on the
changing table by the crib, and she spread it on the mattress before
lowering Adam onto it, facedown. Adam, six weeks old, with vaguely
Chinese eyes and a thatch of black hair that made him look like a
miniature sumo wrestler, grunted in his sleep, and jerked his knees
under him. In his yellow-terry stretch sleeper, with his padded bottom
hiked up in the air, he looked so comical that Joe chuckled softly.
He felt pierced by a shaft of love so intense that it seemed to radiate
out into the darkened room, making everything around him glow.
His eyes on Adam, he groped for Laurel's hand and squeezed it.

"Look at him, with his little butt in the air," she said, smiling.
"He looks like a Beatrix Potter hedgehog."

"Why does he do that?"

"Fetal position. Makes him feel more secure."

"How do you know so much? For a novice, you seem to be
awfully good at this."

"You forget. I got plenty of practice when I was living at
Rivka's." She laughed softly. "Rivka used to call me her little *ma-
maleh*. Now I know what she meant."

Joe pulled the knitted blanket with bunny rabbits embroidered
around its edges—a gift from Dolly—up around Adam's hunched
shoulders. The baby squirmed a bit, making faces in his sleep, then
was still. Joe never got tired of watching Adam.

"It'll be nice when he has his own room," she sighed. "But I'll
kind of miss this . . . the three of us, all together."

Joe thought of the ten-year-old Cape Cod–style house in Bayside they were trying to buy. They'd made a low, but fair, offer. He
hoped the owners were as eager to sell as Jack Neidick, the realtor,
had led them to believe.

"I talked to Jack this afternoon," Joe told her, keeping his voice
low, though Adam could have slept soundly in an IRT tunnel at
rush hour. "He said they're still thinking it over. They're supposed
to let us know by the end of the week."

"That's nice." Laurel's mind, he could see, wasn't on the house
in Bayside, or on any house. She stared down at her son, clearly
besotted.

Then she looked up, and Joe saw that he, too, was part of her enchantment. He felt a rush of pleasure mixed with shame. Why couldn't his love for her be as unclouded?

You married her, didn't you?

But a marriage license was no guarantee of love. Laurel deserved better than a halfhearted commitment. He remembered Annie's bitter words, how she'd reminded him that he wasn't doing Laurel any favors. But, no, it wasn't a question of rescuing her—Laurel, he knew, could manage just fine on her own. If anyone was being rescued, Joe reflected, it was him. He needed this . . . Laurel . . . Adam. A wife, a family. He hadn't known how much until now . . . or maybe he'd always known, deep down, and hadn't wanted to face it. The rest—the deep emotion, like what he felt for Annie —would follow, wouldn't it? What was standing in his way?

Annie.

Joe felt his heart catch.

Yes, dammit, he loved her. There was no question. But was she ready to settle down and be a wife? He wasn't so sure. He believed in her dream, applauded her for going after it, but the fact remained that she was totally absorbed in Tout de Suite. She didn't want children until she was more settled, she'd once told him, and knowing Annie, Joe guessed that that wouldn't be for a very long time. She thought she loved him, wanted him, and maybe she did . . . but trying to pin down Annie would be like laying bets on blackjack—sooner or later, you were bound to come up shortchanged.

But in spite of all that, he knew he *would* have married Annie anyway. If Laurel hadn't needed him more. If the thought of sharing with Laurel this new life he'd helped bring into this world, his son, hadn't suddenly seemed more urgent than anything else. And Laurel herself—she was so *there,* so immediate, he couldn't help feeling— after an age of running to keep up with Annie, running toward her the way you would toward a snowcapped mountain that always seems close enough to touch but which you never seem able to reach—that he had at last arrived somewhere warm and safe.

Joe gazed at Laurel, and saw in his mind a different Laurel, the young girl who'd looked up at him with such trusting eyes. Would he be able to keep from disappointing her? Would he grow to love her the way he loved Annie?

Right now, there was only one thing he felt sure of: He wanted her. With her hair scrambled about her shoulders, her eyes a little puffy from lack of sleep, her kimono half open, she looked so sweetly desirable, he ached to take her in his arms.

But he held back. In the month since they'd gotten married—a short, almost businesslike ceremony at City Hall, attended only by Dolly and a stone-faced Annie—he had not made love to her. Her body needed time to heal. Six weeks, the doctor had said. He hadn't minded, really. With Adam laying claim to her body, and noisily demanding nearly every minute of her attention, theirs was far from the romantic honeymoon newlyweds were supposed to have.

It wasn't just Adam coming between you. It was Annie, too. Admit it, buddy-boy. You wished it was her wearing your ring.

Joe felt something in his gut wrench. Maybe. Okay, yeah, he *did* think about Annie a lot. He wondered if she missed her old apartment upstairs, if her new place down on West Tenth was as comfortable. He wondered if she missed him.

But here, now, this minute, it was Laurel who was causing his pulse to race. Maybe it wasn't love, strictly speaking. Maybe it was just that old black magic, desire. But there it was.

In the baby-smelling silence, Joe captured a strand of her hair and twisted it about his forefinger. She smiled, and drew closer, letting him reel her in until their foreheads were almost touching. Her face seemed to grow misty, as if wreathed in fog, her hair a golden blur . . . and he realized her breath was steaming his lenses.

Joe, his heart beating much too quickly, stepped back and took off his glasses, laying them down on the changing table next to the crib. When he looked back, he saw that Laurel had let her kimono slip to the floor.

He'd watched her undress before, but this time it was different. He felt something cut through him, a shock of delight, as if he'd been swimming in a cold lake and had hit a patch of warmth.

Naked, she seemed to shimmer in the light filtering in from outside, her skin the silvery white of a moth's wings. Christ, she was beautiful. Even with her belly softly rounded and shot with fading purple stretch marks, and her breasts like heavy fruit ready to drop. Those things, in his eyes, made her even more beautiful. Almost a stranger to the Laurel he remembered from not so long ago—a tall stalk of a girl dashing about in blue jeans and baggy T-shirts.

He came to her then and kissed her, aware of a trembling that seemed to emanate from deep within his gut.

She tasted sweet, and smelled even sweeter . . . like Adam. Joe stroked the small of her back, marvelling at its delicate, shell-like curve and the cool silk of her skin. He felt a delicious, tantalizing ache spread through him. This time he knew he could let himself go. He'd given her body time to heal. Given himself time, too . . . time he'd needed to let it sink in that he was truly married to her.

Still, he hesitated, his hand resting against her spine, his face now buried against the side of her neck. Was it Annie holding him back? Or Laurel—the fact that he didn't love her the way he knew she loved him? He felt vaguely as if he were cheating her somehow.

"Joe." Laurel slowly slid her hands down the length of his arms, her thumbs briefly caressing the insides of his elbows before continuing on. Now her fingers were forming cool bracelets about his wrists. She brought one of his hands up, and held it to her breast. He could feel its fullness, the tiny indented stretch marks along its underside. Her heat seemed to fill his hand and spill between his fingers.

Joe moaned and pulled her to him, this time not so gently. Together, as if in a choreographed pas de deux, they sank to their knees on the carpet. The bed was only a few feet away, but Joe couldn't stop kissing her and touching her long enough to make his way over to it. He somehow managed to shuck off his pullover and undershirt, but each second that his skin was not touching hers seemed an agony.

"Oh, my God, Joe . . . *look*." Laurel giggled breathlessly.

Joe felt something warm and wet sprinkle his chest. He looked down and saw tiny streams of milk arcing from her nipples. Without stopping to think, he bent and drank from her, letting her warm, sweet milk fill his mouth. It seemed almost a forbidden act, what he was doing, and yet at the same time perfectly natural. He felt her nipple tighten and grown hard against his tongue. She arched back, and made a sound in her throat halfway between a sigh and a moan. Her knees parted, allowing him to slip his hand between her thighs and feel a different, silkier wetness. Below the waistband of his dungarees, Joe felt almost painfully tight. He wanted her badly . . .

badly enough to take her right here on the carpet, beside his son's crib.

"Are you sure it's okay?" he asked. He didn't want to hurt her. Laurel nodded. "Just go slow."

He rose and peeled off his dungarees, then drew her to her feet. Laurel seemed to unfold from her kneeling position on the floor like one of those timelapse sequences of a flower blossoming, her graceful limbs stippled with the shadows cast by the bars of Adam's crib.

Together, they sank down on the bed. He'd expected Laurel to seem shy and inexperienced . . . after all, he was only her second lover . . . but she surprised him by reaching out at once, and stroking him with knowing hands and fingers that needed no invitation. As he knelt over her, she guided him into her.

He entered her carefully, quivering with the effort to hold himself in check. She tensed a bit, then whispered, "It's okay. Yes, Joe. Yes. I love you. God, I love you."

Joe thought he might explode, but he forced himself to move slowly, precisely, each stroke an agony of pleasure. A pulse throbbed in the hollow of his stomach, another in his groin, and the roof of his mouth.

When he felt he could hold back no longer, he gripped her tightly. Burying his face in her hair, which smelled of milk and baby powder, he felt her hips arch up to meet his.

Joe came with a burst that seemed to go right through his skull.

She shuddered, and he thought she was coming, too. Then he realized she was weeping. She clung to him, her chest hitching with soundless sobs.

"Laurey . . . what is it?" he cried, panicked. Had he hurt her? Had he disappointed her? Had she suddenly realized that marrying him had been an awful mistake?

"Oh, Joe . . . I'm just so h-happy."

Joe felt himself relax a bit. While he held her and soothed her, her tears wetting his neck, her milk growing sticky on his chest, he told himself, *It'll be good between us. I'll make it good. I'll love her. I will.*

Laurel, lying beside Joe in the dark and listening to his breathing deepen, thought, *He's mine.* It seemed a miracle almost as great as giving birth to Adam, that Joe should love her, that he'd chosen her.

And now they were truly man and wife. Everything was perfect. Perfect.

Except for Annie. But Annie would get over Joe. After all, she had Emmett. He was a good man, and he loved her. She'd seen it in his eyes, that first day she'd met him, months ago, when Emmett had taken Annie and her to a Mets game at Shea Stadium; while everyone in the stadium was on their feet, wildly cheering a tie-breaking home run, Emmett's eyes had been on Annie. Why couldn't Annie, for once, stop wanting what was out of reach . . . and see what was right in front of her?

Laurel wanted her sister to be happy, but she felt glad that for once in her life she, Laurel, had something wonderful that Annie had no share in. Not that she meant to shut Annie out. No, no, that would be terrible. It was just that . . . well, now everything would be on her terms. Annie would visit, of course. But it would be *her* house, *her* husband, *her* baby.

Laurel felt a pang, and wondered if she was being selfish. Probably. But right now she didn't care. At this moment, all she wanted, needed, was right here in this room.

Part Three

1980

A garden inclosed is my sister, my spouse; a spring shut up, a fountain sealed. Song of Solomon 4:12

The maître d' led Annie to a window table in the Grill Room. Slipping into her seat, she breathed a sigh of relief that she'd gotten here ahead of Felder. The Four Seasons was too grand and austere a place to dash into with your hem flapping and your hair mussed, which she knew was how she arrived at most places these days. So although she didn't usually care much about being seen in the right places, or about what she looked like, today it might make a difference—because today, somehow, she had to get this man to save her.

She probably ought to have brought a lawyer with her, or one of Emmett's Wall Street buddies. What did she know about making major financial deals? If she hadn't been such an overconfident idiot in that department, she wouldn't even be here now.

Her heart was beginning to pound, and she found herself nibbling on her thumbnail, which she'd finally succeeded in growing to a respectable length. Annoyed with herself, she jerked her hand away and tucked it underneath her so that she actually was sitting on it.

She looked around her. The place was filling up with men and women in lookalike business suits, sober gray, navy, pin stripes, with only one woman brave enough to flaunt a huge broad-brimmed black hat and flamboyant pink scarf about her shoulders. Annie wondered if she were a movie star or maybe a designer. But where was Felder? She should have called to confirm their date. God, what if he wasn't coming?

Dumb. Of course he was. *He'd* made the reservation, after all. Nevertheless, her armpits felt damp, and she had to resist mopping her forehead with the elegant linen napkin arranged on her plate in a crisp white cone.

"Shall I bring you something from the bar while you're waiting?" the maître d' inquired.

405

"Perrier," she told him. It would help settle her stomach.

She glanced at her watch, a slender gold Piaget, a present from Emmett a month ago on her thirty-second birthday. Felder would be arriving at any moment; should she have waited until he got here before ordering her drink?

Watching her waiter thread his way among the well-spaced tables, Annie grew disgusted with herself. Dammit, if she couldn't do a simple little thing like ordering a drink without worrying, how on earth could she expect Felder to make a million-dollar deal with her?

While she waited, Annie withstood the temptation to dip into her purse for her pocket mirror and lipstick. She wanted to appear cool and sophisticated, not some little Nellie primping nervously. And, besides, hadn't she already done enough of that at home? This morning, she'd found herself buried in a heap of discarded skirts and blouses and sweaters. Finally she'd settled on this suit, a pumpkin-and-gold weave, with a purple silk turtleneck underneath, an antique gold watch chain that she wore as a necklace, and a pair of huge dangly gold earrings, which, coincidentally, she'd bought at Felder's. The overall effect, she thought, was businesslike, but also a bit dramatic.

Her Perrier arrived in a frosted glass with a lime wedge, and she sat sipping it, watching the four men at the table opposite hers. They were all laughing loudly. One of them looked vaguely familiar. She thought he might be a television actor. Hadn't she seen him on *Dallas?*

"Miss Cobb?"

Annie looked up at the stocky middle-aged man with bristling gray hair who stood over her. Felder? How had he managed to get all the way to this table without her noticing him? Probably, she thought, because he didn't look at all the way she'd imagined. From what she'd read in newspapers and magazines, she'd expected someone more . . . well, imposing; someone exuding the raw power and charisma of the great old-time Hollywood movie moguls. All those stories about Felder's surviving the Holocaust, arriving here from a D.P. camp, and how as a youth he'd made the rounds of the Garment District sweatshops each day, buying up remnants and selling them in his uncle's fabric shop, eventually building his way up to a hugely successful chain of discount department stores.

Except for the beautifully fitted muted-plaid suit he was wearing, the man standing before her might have been a plumber, or a butcher, or a house painter. A bit jowly, with a shave that had missed a few spots, a nose that reminded her of the drawing of Julius Caesar in her high-school Shakespeare book. His gray crewcut was strictly army issue, and his face was as deeply grooved as a woodcut.

"Annie. Please, call me Annie."

She started to get up, meaning to shake his hand, then discovered to her dismay that her hand, wedged under her thigh all this time, had gone to sleep. Attaining a sort of half-crouched position, she held it out like a wet rag, smiling brightly while cringing inwardly. He didn't smile back. She hadn't said anything but her name, and already she felt she was blowing it.

Oh, but she *needed* this to work. Emmett had warned her to slow down—Dolly too—but she'd gotten too caught up in her own hype, letting herself get seduced by the waterfalls and marble walkways of Glen Harbor's new, elegant Paradise Mall.

On top of the absurd rents she was already paying on her shops on Madison Avenue and Christopher Street, and now in Southampton, she'd known she was sticking her neck out by leasing at Paradise Mall, but she was on a roll, right? Tout de Suite, expanding faster than a supernova, could do no wrong.

Or so she'd thought.

To date, less than half of the mall's pricey, pickled-oak panelled stores had been leased. And despite the monumental hype, on any given Saturday only a trickle of customers graced the marble walkways and the glass elevators, or the skylit atrium with its cute ice-cream-parlor tables and chairs. Her ground level shop was *bleeding* money.

The mall business would eventually go up, she was sure, but it was taking longer than she'd anticipated. And that was just the tip of the iceberg. With the new plant in Tribeca, along with equipment and staff to run the production, accounting, shipping, and purchasing departments, she had to admit she'd overreached herself. Financially, she was perched atop a precarious sand castle that could be about to cave in.

How much longer could she go on—on top of her already hefty operating costs—paying sky-high rents, plus meeting her bank notes? Her usually mild accountant, Jackson Weathers, just last week had laid it out, pulling no punches. If she couldn't restructure her finances, and do it fast, Tout de Suite might be going down the tubes *tout de suite.*

That very same day she'd read in the *Wall Street Journal* that Felder's was planning to revamp by restyling some of its departments into small, intimate boutiques—including a gourmet-food section—and she'd called Hyman Felder immediately. His secretary had suggested she send samples and literature, if she had any. And then, just a week later, Felder himself had called and invited her to lunch.

"Hy," he greeted her in a deep, almost gruff voice.

"Hi!" she answered.

"No, I meant *Hy*," he corrected. "Everybody, even my stockroom boys, calls me Hy." His voice instantly brought to mind a flood of Brooklyn memories: cab drivers and Coney Island hot-dog vendors, mustard and sauerkraut.

He eased his bulk into the chair opposite her. A waiter materialized out of nowhere. Felder ordered a Dewar's with soda and a lemon twist.

"You're younger than I expected," he began. "You mind my asking how old you are?"

"I'm thirty-two," she told him, adding with a laugh: "But it's not the age itself I mind. What bothers me is not knowing how I got from twenty-five to thirty-two in what feels like about two weeks."

He chuckled. "Please, I got *daughters* older than you. I was around when they built the Brooklyn Battery Tunnel." He glanced at her mineral water. "You sure you don't want a real drink?"

"Another Perrier maybe. It can wait."

"The food here is good. Ever eaten in this place?"

"Once or twice. But I rarely get to restaurants at lunch. Usually, I just catch a sandwich or a yogurt. I'm pretty busy, Mr.—uh, Hy. If you catch me off my feet on a Sunday, it's usually because I'm underneath some machine or other, trying to get the damn thing to work."

He grinned. "Yeah? You good with machines? That's kind of unusual for a nice-looking lady. Me, I'm lousy with machines. But I probably know everything there is to know about working eight or nine days a week." He fished a mini ice cube from his drink and popped it into his mouth, sucking noisily. "You were smart to call me."

Annie felt as if the room's temperature had just been turned up fifty degrees. Did that mean he might seriously consider making a deal? God, east of the Mississippi alone, Felder's had forty-two huge stores. Her plant would have to gear up to running twenty-four hours a day just to try and supply them all, but she'd be able to cover all her payments and then some.

"I read that you were doing a major redesign of your stores, which are already the hottest thing around," she told him.

"You're good with flattery. I like that. But one thing you learn after a lotta years in business is what's successful today usually ain't successful tomorrow. I opened my first store after the war, when discount was the name of the game. Now times are better, and suddenly everything is designer . . . designer clothes, designer pillowcases, designer chocolate-chip cookies. Hey, if someone's gonna pay a hundred bucks for a pair of jeans, what's so terrible about offering him a cup of coffee or a glass of papaya juice? It's a whole different ball game."

Annie didn't know whether she liked him or not. He seemed warm, but underneath she sensed he could be tougher than nails.

"Did you like the samples I sent you?" she asked.

"Wish I could say I did. Truth is, I can't touch the stuff." He pressed a hand to his bulging midsection. "Some fancy doctors tell me that if I don't take some of this off, I'm gonna make Mrs. Felder a very rich widow in the near future."

"But . . ."

He held up a hand. "Hey, what I like is that you called. And the same day it all hit the press. You got moxie, and you're quick on the draw. But you see, for Felder's Pantry—you like that name? It has a nice ring to it, don't you think?—I was thinking, well, smelly French cheeses, high-end Colombian coffee beans, that kind of thing. Candies, too, but they'd have to be in boxes, like in the supermarket, only better quality."

"It's a wonderful idea . . . but in terms of chocolates, what I had in mind for you is a whole separate boutique," she told him, swallowing hard against the panic rising up in her throat. "Sort of a . . . a miniature version of Tout de Suite. Here, I've brought pictures." She pulled a back issue of *New York* magazine from the briefcase by her chair and spread it open before Felder. "This is an article they did on me last September."

"Hey, I like the chandelier. Where'd you ever find a chandelier made outa twigs and bird's nests?"

"I know a florist who makes them. Each one is a little different. He makes all my baskets, too. He decorates them with stencils and with different-colored ribbons, depending on the time of year, or for particular holidays."

"What's this?" He jabbed a meaty finger at a stone pedestal pictured in the corner of the spread.

"A birdbath. I rescued it from a house that was being torn down." She didn't mention that it was Emmett who'd found the house . . . and the birdbath.

"Nice touch. You like birds? They got chicken here like you wouldn't believe. Nice duck, too . . . made with cranberries. No kidding. You hungry? You want to order?"

No, what I want is for you to say that you'd love having such a charming boutique filled with my sensational chocolates in every one of your stores. But, of course, she couldn't say that. She had to smile and nod, and at the same time resist with all her might the force field that seemed to be drawing, no, *magnetizing* her thumb toward her mouth.

She leaned forward, locking her gaze on him, mentally demanding his attention. Then, certain that his gaze was not in danger of dropping to the menu, she said in an easy voice, "You're a very smart man, and you're right—we all do have to change with the times. And these days people want quality, and they're willing to pay more for it. They're buying Häagen-Dazs in pint containers. And David's Cookies at practically a dollar a cookie." She sipped in a long, slow breath, willing the throbbing pulse in her neck to subside. "Last year, Tout de Suite grossed three million. This year, it looks like we'll be up forty percent over that."

"With half a million plus in unsecured debt, a maybe sixty percent jump in your payroll with a union breathing down your neck, mortgage payments on your new plant, and a lease commitment in that new ghost town of a mall in Glen Harbor. But, hey, it could be worse." Jovial, avuncular call-me-Hy of a minute ago was now transformed into the flint-eyed Hyman Felder of legend.

Annie sat back, stunned . . . feeling violated somehow, as if he'd tried to slip his hand under her skirt. "How . . . how do you know all that?"

"I'm like you, Annie." He smiled, and it was the smile of every kid's favorite uncle—good old Uncle Hy, who never visited without a pocket full of candy. "I don't have time to horse around. If I hadn't gone and done my homework first, we wouldn't be sitting here."

"But—"

He held up his hand like a traffic cop. "But you shouldn't get the wrong idea. I'm not knocking you. You think I built Felder's with a triple-A bank account and solid-gold bricks? There was a time I had three mortgages on my house, and I was finagling to get a fourth. So be thankful at least you haven't gone public, or you'd *really* have problems."

"People have approached me about selling my company, but so far I'm not really considering it."

"Felder will not be one of those people." He laughed, and grabbed a braided poppy-seed roll from the basket their waiter had just placed on the table. "I got more headaches than a busload of frigid wives. Yours I can live without."

"Then what sort of arrangement did *you* think we might make?" She'd already more than broken the ice, she thought, so why hold back now?

"Look, we just met. We gotta feel our way."

"You do understand that I don't feel I'm asking for any favors. Felder's could do very well from what I'm proposing."

"You might be right. Eventually. But to begin with, who's gonna put up all the dough for those twiggy chandeliers and the birdbaths? My guess is they don't come cheap." He leaned forward, so close that she could see the hairs sprouting from his nose. "And your chocolate stuff has got to be expensive just to make. So how much can you mark it up? So how much upside could there be?"

"Well, what about gold jewelry?" she countered. "You sell that, don't you? Expensive, but probably marked up plenty. But the thing is, we're both aiming at the same customer, the kind who's more interested in how good it is than in what it costs—within reason, of course. Tout de Suite's chocolates are one of the ultimate luxuries. My customers feel as if they're indulging themselves . . . the same as if they're buying silk underwear or an ounce of Chanel No. 5— they want it because it's the best."

"I like your chutzpah. 'The best.' Sounds great, but says who? You? How do *I* know you're the best?" He stared at her, challenging her with an expression halfway between a smile and a shrug.

Annie had observed that slyly innocent look before, on cabbies who took you the long way around and butchers who said, "It's just a little over." So he was a chiseler. But then, who in his position wasn't? And despite his blunt, streetwise manner, he did seem genuinely interested. So now, how could she push him over the edge, convince him to let her open up in his stores?

He wants me to push him. He's testing me. Backing down wasn't Felder's style. Well, it wasn't hers either.

If only it weren't so *hot* in here, like a sauna . . . but Felder didn't seem uncomfortable at all.

Her mind was racing. *Come on, Annie, you've been in tight spots before.* An idea came to her. *Gourmand*'s annual chocolate fair at the Plaza was a week from Saturday. Chocolatiers were coming from the world over, the biggest names—Godiva, Kron, Tobler-Suchard, Perugina, Gianduja—and all the tiny great ones like Manon from Belgium and Teuscher from Switzerland. And, of course, Girod's. As always, there'd be a banquet, dancing, speeches . . . and . . . and . . . yes, prizes. Going up against those heavy hitters would be a bit like David versus Goliath, but for a fairly new operation like hers to win the general excellence award would mean manna from heaven: great free advertising, a tremendous boost in retail, and lots of new contracts, with hotels and gourmet outlets.

Annie remembered the excitement she'd felt the year Girod's had won first place. Other years, they'd placed second, and once third. Dolly, she knew, was counting on taking home one of the prizes again this year, but she had unofficially given Annie her blessing as well. "The only thing better than Girod's coming in first would be to see you walk off with that trophy," she'd said.

This would be Tout de Suite's first competition. Until this year, she hadn't felt confident enough about presenting the new line of small, exquisite tortes and éclairs she had only recently introduced in her shops, and was still experimenting with. But now Annie was determined that Tout de Suite should win. For months now, she'd virtually given up going home at night, experimenting endlessly with new flavors, shapes, new displays. There was not a detail she was going to overlook . . . even her dress, which Laurel was sewing for her. Tomorrow afternoon, in fact, she was driving out to Laurel and Joe's in Bayside, where Laurel was giving her a final fitting.

Was it the thought of her gown, with its sleek lines and plunging back, she wondered, that made her feel so daring now?

"I'm competing in the *Gourmand* chocolate fair a week from Saturday—in my business, that's the equivalent of the Academy Awards," she told him. She unfolded her napkin and smoothed it across her lap. *Keep your eyes down and your hands busy . . . don't let him see how much you want this.* Casually, she added, "If I take one of the prizes, will that be enough to convince you?"

"First prize?"

"You're really pushing me."

"*You* said you were the best."

Annie hesitated. A huge gamble, she knew, but she'd been pushed to the wall. How could she back down? If she couldn't convince Felder that she believed wholeheartedly in Tout de Suite, why should he have confidence in her?

Annie swallowed hard against the knot in her throat, and said, "All right. First prize. But what then?"

"You want me to sign a contract on an empty stomach?"

"As a matter of fact, I do. Otherwise, I'm not sure I'll be able to swallow a bite."

"Well, I guess I can't let such an attractive, determined lady like you go hungry." He winked, and with a corner of his napkin brushed poppy seeds from his lips.

"Then do we have a deal?"

He laughed, shaking his head as he picked up his menu. "Sure, why not? You bring home the trophy, and we'll talk turkey."

Annie wanted to jump up and kiss him, but she held her menu up over her face, so he wouldn't see what had to be a very stupid grin. Besides, it was too soon to get excited. Suppose she *didn't* win? Or they couldn't agree on the terms?

No what ifs . . . I have to win, she told herself.

For a moment, she felt sure she *would* win. Then her glow of confidence faded, and her stomach began to churn. For one indulgent moment, while Felder was studying the menu, she allowed herself a nibble of her newly grown-out and perfectly manicured thumbnail.

Less than an hour after her lunch with Hyman Felder, Annie stood in the small test kitchen off the main work area in Tout de Suite's Washington Street factory, peering over Louise's shoulder while she put the finishing touches on a cinnamon-truffle cake—a confection that consisted of four layers of rum-soaked chocolate génoise filled with alternating layers of cinnamon-chocolate ganache and praline buttercream, the whole thing frosted with ganache, then coated in a bittersweet glaze and ringed with toasted hazelnuts. Annie herself had devised the recipe one afternoon in the kitchen of her house on West Tenth Street, and had served it at a dinner party that same night.

She smiled at the memory of Trine Devereaux—the aged, rail-thin former ballerina who lived next door to Annie in the secluded mews she shared with three other houses—clearing her flamingolike throat as the dessert dishes were being taken away, and in her piping, girlish voice asking, "Please, if it's not too much trouble, may I have another sliver of that heavenly cake?"

Several other guests, including Hubert Dickson, her buyer friend from the Westin Hotel chain, had taken Trine's cue and asked for seconds as well. The cake was loaded with enough calories to sink a freighter, but no one had seemed to care. She hoped it would have a similar effect on the *Gourmand* judges.

"What about the Turkish délice?" she asked Louise, who, even after years of nibbling on chocolate all day long, still looked as waiflike as the Little Match Girl.

Louise blew her wispy strawberry-blond bangs out of her eyes. "Would you like to try it? I finished it while you were out for lunch." She nipped off a sliver of the Turkish délice, which was sitting on the marble slab that dominated the center of the kitchen.

Annie bit into a piece no bigger than her thumb. Wonderfully diverse textures and flavors swam excitingly in her mouth—layers of crisp phyllo and a brandy-laced, not-too-sweet syrup, ground pistachios mixed with a spicy, cardamom-tinged ganache, all of it covered in a brittle chocolate glaze dusted with ground pistachios and bits of crystallized ginger. She'd gotten the idea for the délice after a dinner out at a Turkish restaurant on Third Avenue, where she'd had the most divine baklava.

"Mmm . . . perfect," she told Louise. "Maybe a *touch* more cardamom?"

"Come on. You said it was perfect." Louise stopped frosting her cake and looked at Annie, again blowing up a stream of air that set her bangs fluttering. She wore a huge white apron with a hem that came down almost to her ankles, and ties that wrapped several times around her sliver-thin waist. The front right now looked like a child's finger painting done in chocolate.

"Well . . . *practically* perfect."

Louise laughed. "That line probably ought to go on your tombstone: 'HERE LIES ANNIE COBB, PRACTICALLY PERFECT.' " She licked a dab of frosting from the back of her thumb. "Oh, that reminds me, your brother-in-law called. No rush, he said. Just call him back when you get a free moment."

"You mean sometime in 1993?"

Annie laughed at her own joke, but inside, she felt a tug. Six years, and still, when she heard his name—or worse, when she saw him—a sudden lick of heat, followed by light-headed panic, like a child who accidentally starts a fire and must quickly stamp it out. Sure, everything was fine these days. Good friends, just as they'd always been, nothing more. Now and then, Joe stopped by for coffee on his way to the meat market, or sometimes called just to schmooze. Mostly, though, she saw him on family occasions—Thanksgiving and Christmas, the Fourth of July picnic Laurel held every year in her lush garden, Adam's birthday parties.

But, still, whenever he greeted her with a hug, or touched the back of her hand to make a point, something inside her stirred. Did Joe feel it too? If so, he kept it hidden. He was careful—too careful, maybe?—always greeting her with a kiss—as a brother-in-law would, and a lover would not. They kept it light, affectionate, jokey, especially in front of Laurel, and sometimes the whole thing *seemed* real even to Annie. But she knew it wasn't; it was an act, with its own unique rituals, as elaborate as Kabuki theatre.

If only . . .

Annie resolutely shut her mind against the thought that seemed always to be crouching there. She could not, *would* not, let herself imagine what her life would be like now if *she* had been the one to marry Joe. He was her sister's husband . . . end of story. If she let herself venture off that narrow, stony path, *even for one second,* they could all be lost.

I should call Emmett instead, she thought. *Remind him to pick up his new suit at the tailor's so he'll have it for tonight.* The party they were going to was to celebrate the publication of Tansy Boone's newest dessert cookbook, which included several of Tout de Suite's recipes. Tansy, of course, would be there, along with media types, publishing people . . . and, most important, food critics from *Gourmand* and *Cuisine* and *Connoisseur.* Tansy had even persuaded Stanley Zabar, an old friend, to let her hold the party in his store.

Annie, determined to get maximum mileage out of this for Tout de Suite, had offered to supply her desserts for the occasion. She made a mental note to check with Tansy to see if any last-minute guests had been added to the list, and also to have an advance copy of *And Then There Was Chocolate,* along with an invitation to the party, messengered over to Hyman Felder.

Yes, that was it, she'd focus on Felder, on pulling out of the red, no looking to the right or the left, no distractions, no way she could go astray with Joe, even by accident.

Annie left Louise, and briskly made her rounds about the factory, taking in the cluttered workstations with butcher-block counters and shelving underneath, which were set catty-corner to one another like walls in a maze. Workers in white aprons and white elasticized caps scurried from one to the next, whisking trays of paper-thin chocolate dessert cups, pistachio toffee, chocolate-dipped orange crescents, praline fondant, finished truffles ready to be boxed. Along one wall stood a row of stainless ovens, cooktops, deep sinks, tempering melters, with her old enrober and two newer ones taking up one end of the large space—which, Emmett had told her when he first showed her the place, had originally held a good-sized millinery factory.

She saw plump, coffee-skinned Netta carrying a tray of ladyfingers. Had Netta remembered to spread cardboard over the baking sheets before putting the ladyfingers in the oven? The last few batches had been a little dry, but the cardboard would keep the moisture in. Her gaze fell on a stack of wooden crates. Those grapefruits . . . they would have to be thrown out if they weren't used soon. Even candied, the peel had to be fresh . . . when you bit into it, it had to bite back.

Annie walked over to the counter at which Doug stood, a frown bringing his heavy black brows together in a single bushy hedge. He was having trouble with one of the conveyor belts—a traffic jam of empty cast-iron molds stood at one end, waiting to be passed under jets that would spray them with liquid chocolate. After these molded "tops" were cooled and dried, they would be filled with various liqueur-based cream fillings, and chocolate bottoms then slipped on. But there would be no bonbons if they couldn't get the belt working. Damn. She'd better call the manufacturer, and have them send someone.

She told Doug to keep tinkering with it, and moved on to the worktable where Lise was busy melting sugar in a large copper pot for the chocolate-pecan brittle. Had the Christmas molds been unpacked? Lise, wearing a white net cap and baker's apron, said something, but the hum of machinery and clattering of trays and pans drowned out her words. Holding out a hand smeared with chocolate, Lise pointed toward the industrial shelving lining the east wall.

In a box, on a high shelf, Annie found what she was looking for—a set of Victorian cast-iron molds, quaint and priceless: a Santa Claus straight out of Clement Moore, an elf wearing knickers and a stocking cap, an angel with a pouty Burne-Jones face, a pair of intertwined cats. She'd discovered them two years ago, in an antique store on Portobello Road in London, and had fallen instantly in love. That first Christmas, she'd made a hundred solid chocolate molds of each, and had sold every one the very first day. Now they were her great holiday staple. It was early in the season still, but wouldn't they make a charming addition to her display at the fair?

Annie closed her eyes for a moment, and tried to picture where in the display she'd fit these holiday treats. Lost in her thoughts, she didn't hear the footsteps behind her.

"Annie?"

She turned, startled. "Joe!"

"Sorry, I didn't mean to sneak up on you." Smiling that slip-sliding smile of his, he put out a hand, palm up, in a conciliatory gesture. He was wearing faded jeans and a flannel-lined denim jacket over a navy fisherman's sweater. Even through the perfume of cocoa and vanilla beans that filled the air, she could smell him; he smelled of blood and sawdust—he'd been to the meat market. "You have a minute? You feel like taking a walk?"

Annie had about nine hundred things to do, but she found herself nodding. "Sure, why not?"

Once she got outside, she was glad she'd said yes. Fall was here, really here, and until now she'd hardly noticed. Leaves from the catalpa tree outside her building littered the sidewalk, and the sky was the crisp menthol-blue of aftershave. The sun, setting into Jersey, still shone brightly, gilding these old warehouses and factory buildings with shafts of glorious light. Joe turned his face up to sample the breeze, his glasses catching the light, and she saw a wisp of cloud reflected on the twin mirrors of his lenses. In his taffy-colored hair, she was startled to see glints of silver.

They walked side by side down Washington Street without talking. Joe was so quiet that Annie began to worry. He obviously hadn't asked her to take a walk with him just for the pleasure of her company. No, there had to be something wrong . . . something he wanted to tell her.

Was it about Laurel? Annie suspected that Laurel and Joe were having problems. Though her sister had never confided anything in particular to her, whenever she talked about Joe in general a kind of overbrightness crept into her voice, as if she needed to make Annie believe everything was wonderful with her marriage, couldn't be better, in fact.

Maybe I'm imagining problems where there aren't any, Annie thought. Maybe, deep down, she *wanted* to believe things weren't a hundred percent marvelous with Mr. and Mrs. Joe Daugherty. Could that be why Laurel seemed so reluctant to confide in her? And why, despite how close they now were, how they teased each other and gossiped endlessly over the phone, she and her sister still held each other a bit at arm's length?

They reached Morton Street and turned the corner toward the sun and the Hudson. This part of town had once been storehouses for ocean freighters and huge printing plants. But here and there, Annie now saw scaffolding erected outside of sooty buildings, and workmen scurrying in and out of them, with lumber, Sheetrock, wheelbarrows of cement. These places would be converted into living lofts and apartments, filled with the children and maybe even the grandchildren of those who had once labored fourteen hours a day in these very spaces. And, God, it was happening so *fast*. Why did it sometimes seem as if everything was moving forward except her?

Finally, Joe turned to her and said, "It's my father. He's getting worse."

"Joe . . . I'm sorry." Annie badly wanted to take his hand, but she resisted.

Marcus *had* gone downhill since Joe's mother died last May; Annie had seen that much herself. Another minor heart attack . . . then he'd started having those weird mood swings, and memory lapses. The doctors called it Alzheimer's, but to Joe it was his father's way of coping with an orderly life that somehow had jumped its rails. Since he couldn't bring back either his health or his wife, the old man was simply, as Joe had put it, "locking the door and pulling down the shade."

"Even with half his mind gone, he's an impossible bastard." He sounded angry, but she could see the lines of weariness in his face . . . and, yes, the caring. "I've had three nurses quit on me in the last month and a half. The last one showed me her arms—bruises all the way to the elbows—and said she hoped I wasn't thinking she was the sort who'd *sue* as some would . . . no, what she needed was a good rest, but who could afford to take that kind of time off with bills to pay?" Joe shoved a hand through his hair, and gave a short, incredulous laugh. "Christ, do you believe it?"

"What are you going to do?"

"It's not the money," he went on. "She can sue me all she wants. It's *him,* my father. He's . . . falling apart." He took a deep breath. "Last week, I made an appointment with Naomi Jenkins . . . she's that counselor I told you about. She assesses people . . . families, really . . . in this kind of situation. You know, helps you decide if it's . . . well, *time.* She visited Dad the other day, and then she came to see me today at the restaurant."

"And?"

"She's recommending that he be placed in a home. There's really no other way."

"Joe, I'm sorry . . ." Before she had time to think what she was doing, she grabbed his hand and squeezed it hard. She stood that way for a long moment, linked to him in sympathy and in longing . . . afraid to let go for fear of what it might imply, and even more afraid of hanging on.

It was Joe who drew away first, bending to retrieve a penny on the sidewalk. An old penny, blackened and half hidden among a drift of fallen leaves; how had he managed to spot it? He stared at it for a second, then tossed it out over the pavement, his long body arching back, a small *whuff* of breath escaping him.

He turned to Annie, a sad smile surfacing on his beautiful, sensitive face. "The other night when I was tucking Adam in, he looked up at me and said, 'You know, Dad, sometimes second grade sucks.' " Joe laughed, this time with genuine amusement. "That about sums it up, don't you think? Sometimes life sucks. I think my father would agree."

So would I, Annie thought, but she wasn't thinking of old age or nursing homes. Just how unfair it was that you could love two people as much as she loved Joe and Laurel, and know that one love must cancel the other.

Unfair to Emmett, too. They'd been together so long, sometimes it felt like they were married . . . but she hadn't ever been able to take that final step. Maybe she never would. Not until she believed, truly believed, that Joe wouldn't care . . . or, even if he did mind, that she wouldn't.

Damn, why did she have to feel all this now, when Tout de Suite needed everything she could give it? Why couldn't she let it just ride?

It's been six years, so isn't it about time you accepted reality?

Okay, yes. But what exactly *is* going on here?

"I'm sorry," she told him, not sure who exactly she was sorry for. "It *isn't* fair."

"I haven't told Laurey. It'll really upset her. You know, it's funny, because they're about as opposite as two people can be, but from the very start she and Dad really got along. She's really crazy about him. She knew how to get around him in all kinds of little ways. Me, I'd always go head to head . . . and end up losing my temper."

"You'll have to tell her."

"I know." He looked down, but not fast enough. She had seen something in his eyes . . . something dark and unsettling.

"Joe . . . is . . . is everything okay between you and Laurey?"

He paused a beat too long, then shrugged. "Sure. Why do you ask?"

"I don't know. Forget it. It's none of my business anyway."

He smiled. "Well, well, you *have* changed."

Annie, relieved by his change in tone, eased gratefully into their old teasing routine. "Only during business hours," she quipped. "Evenings I turn back into a *yenta*. Rivka says I'm so good at it, I could give lessons."

He touched her arm. "How is Rivka these days?"

"Still counting heads . . . only this time it's grandchildren. She's up to nine, I think, with two more on the way. I'm embarrassed to say I can't keep all their names straight." She paused. "Joe, about your father. If there's anything I can do . . ."

He shrugged. "Thanks. I'm okay . . . just needed to unload on someone, I guess. I got Emma to promise she'd stay until the end of the month, bruises and all."

"God, Joe, what did you have to bribe her with?"

"A cruise to the Bahamas. Believe me, by the time she climbs on board, she'll have earned it."

Annie laughed. "I'll bet."

"You know something?" he said, staring off into the distance. "Sometimes I think it'd be easier on all of us if the old man would just die." He stopped, and scrubbed his jaw, looking rueful. "Jesus, I've never admitted that to anyone."

"It's okay," she told him. "I'm not shocked. In fact, I think your father would prefer it that way, too."

He touched her arm, and said softly, "Thanks."

"For what?"

"For listening. For not telling me what a heartless bastard Marcus Daugherty has for a son."

She stared at him. "I think," she said slowly, "I think what you're doing takes a lot of guts . . . and a lot of love."

"Funny." He squinted up at the sky, as if looking for confirmation of this. She watched his Adam's apple work. Tears stood in his eyes, making them glitter. Finally, in a strained voice, he said, "I never thought of him that way. In terms of love. He was just . . . my father."

This time, it was Joe who took her hand, and they walked that way, back to Washington Street, under the golden, biblical sun, as if they had been doing it all their lives.

For the first time in years, she felt relaxed with him, and oddly content. But at the same time something dark stirred inside her. An expression of Dearie's nibbled at her mind: *Let sleeping dogs lie.* But how were you supposed to do that once they woke up?

In Zabar's mezzanine, under a ceiling hung with colanders and bright enamel kettles and triple-tiered wire baskets filled with tea towels and potholders, and surrounded by walls crammed with everything from food processors to flatware, Annie sipped champagne and worked the room. Kissing a cheek here, shaking a hand there, stopping to chat with those she knew—Avery Suffolk, who had once interviewed her for an article in *Cuisine;* Tansy Boone, in a floral chiffon dress that made her look like a float in the Rose Bowl parade, holding court beside a pyramid of her books; and Lydia Scher, Tansy's editor at Speedwell Press, to whom Annie introduced her idea of a cookbook devoted entirely to truffles.

By nine, most of the bagels, whitefish, Nova Scotia salmon, lobster salad, pesto gnocchi, and pasta primavera from downstairs had been devoured. Now waiters dressed in crisp chef's whites were setting out coffee urns and cups and trays laden with Annie's desserts. And lots of people, she saw, despite the hefty amount of food they'd just eaten, seemed to be snatching them up.

But something wasn't right. Suddenly, she didn't feel on. Worse, as the raves for her truffle cake and her tiny white-chocolate dessert cups filled with brandied mousse came at her with enthusiastic handshakes, gushing declarations, and blown kisses, she wasn't getting her usual surge of triumph. All she was getting was a headache.

She was making her way over to the dessert table, hoping that a dose of caffeine would help, when Emmett came over and slipped his arm through hers.

Drawing her aside, he asked, "Having a good time?"

"Sure," she tossed back lightly, "why wouldn't I be?" She gestured about the room where they stood, at the shelves crammed with pots and pans and skillets in every size. She *did* feel at home, too, in a way—though she doubted whether her celadon silk dress and opal earrings were what she'd wear to whip up a batch of Kahlúa-hazelnut brownies.

"You've got that look," he said affectionately, smoothing back her short, dark hair from her temple.

"What look is that?"

His blue eyes sparkled. "Like General MacArthur storming Corregidor. Relax, Cobb, it's just a party. You don't have to conquer everyone here with your charm."

Annie stared at him, and felt a mixture of affection and exasperation rising in her. He could be such a pain sometimes . . . mostly when she knew he was right. Forever teasing her, needling her, challenging her, making her see things from every angle even when she didn't want to—like when she'd been considering that proposal from General Foods to back her own line of fancy frozen desserts. When she told him she was thinking of going ahead with it, Emmett—they'd been lying in bed, she remembered—had locked his hands behind his head and stared up at the ceiling, his good foot propped on the lowest rung of her brass bed. In his thoughtful, measured way that sometimes irked her, but never failed to draw her attention, he'd said, "The way I look at it, those who want fancy desserts made by Tout de Suite know where to find you. Kind of makes it a little more special if they have to go a bit out of their way, though, doesn't it? I mean, throwing it into your shopping cart . . . it just wouldn't be the same somehow."

Annie had argued that with the money she would make off this deal she'd be able to pay off her bank loans, and maybe even have some left over. But deep down, she'd known he was right. Something would have to give . . . and that something would be Tout de Suite's quality and cachet. Besides, did she really want to be Sara Lee? Two days later, she'd called General Foods and told them no thanks.

No, Emmett—despite his rolling gait and easy smile—was not the easiest person. Whenever she pushed to get her way with him, he pushed right back. They could never agree on which movie to see, or which restaurant to eat at. And he could be incredibly tactless. Like when he'd told her last week, just as she was shipping out a special order for a big wedding, that the elaborate mousse she'd labored over for hours tasted like chocolate pudding, she could've killed him.

But one thing about Emmett—in six years he'd never bored her. There were plenty of times when he got her so mad she felt like smacking him . . . but she never grew tired of him.

Right now, in his new suit—a soft charcoal-gray with faint burgundy stripes—he looked quite distinguished, as befitted a new partner in a major real-estate firm. Except for his boots, new ones that after only a few weeks looked as lived-in as his old pair, no one would have guessed that the man standing in front of her had once racked drill pipe on an oil derrick, or hauled nets aboard a shrimp boat. His rusty hair, too, though beautifully cut, wasn't altogether tamed—a few rogue wisps stood up in front, and in back, along the collar of his Brooks Brothers shirt, it had separated into wiry tufts.

"I wouldn't *be* here if it wasn't good for the business," she told him. "Just now, when I was talking to Ed Sanderson about his reviewing the book for *Chocolatier* magazine, do you know what he told me? He said he'd like to do a whole spread on me."

"I'll bet he would." Emmett winked lasciviously, coaxing a smile from Annie. "Stapled navel and all."

"I'm serious, Em, and if you don't stop making fun of me, I'll . . . I'll . . ."

He caught her upper arm, drawing her close, so close she could feel his sideburns tickling her cheek, his breath warm and smelling faintly of cloves. "You'll what? Kick me out of bed?"

"Just the opposite. I'll keep you there until you beg for mercy."

"That might take a while."

"I can wait."

He rubbed his lips lightly against her temple, and whispered, "What do you say we make a quick getaway now, and head off to my place so we can get started?"

Annie felt herself grow warm. Damn him, why did he *do* this to her . . . tempt her when she least wanted to be? Tonight, after the party, she'd wanted to be alone, to sort out her thoughts, replay her conversation with Joe.

She shook her head. "In a little while. There're a few people I want to talk to that I haven't gotten to yet."

A dark expression flitted across Emmett's square, seasoned face, but he merely released her and gave a light shrug. Annie felt a dart of worry. She was putting him off . . . and he knew it. What worried her was that he wasn't saying anything. Emmett, she knew, was quietest when he was the most troubled.

How much longer will he stick around this time?

Her mind flew back to last October, a year ago this month; Emmett suggesting—not for the first time—that they move in together, find an apartment big enough for both of them . . . and her telling him in the nicest way possible, no, she couldn't, she wasn't ready. She would never forget the look on his face, not angry or bitter, more like a door quietly clicking shut. They'd been at her place, just finishing dinner. Politely excusing himself, Emmett had stood, hooked his jacket from the back of his chair, slung it over his shoulder . . . and walked out.

She'd thought he would come back . . . but he hadn't. For eight whole months, he'd stayed away, no dropping in, no phone calls, no visits to the shop. She'd missed him more than she would've thought possible. Not like the bittersweet ache she felt for Joe. More like being kicked in the belly—stung, not quite believing it, and mad. Mad at herself, mostly, for caring as much as she did. And then, hearing that he'd become engaged to a woman he'd met through one of his real-estate deals, Annie had been plunged into a depression that had left her, for weeks and weeks, even on the mildest of days, feeling chilled and headachy, as if she were on the verge of coming down with a nasty flu.

She remembered clearly the day in early June when Emmett appeared without warning at her door, dressed in jeans and a Henley shirt, holding a wrinkled paper sack. "I was visiting some friends upstate over the weekend, and I came across these in their backyard," he'd said without any preamble, handing her the sack. "I thought you might like some."

Annie, peering into the sack, had felt her heart leap. Fiddleheads! He'd remembered how much she liked them, and how she'd complained she could never find them in grocery stores. All at once, she began to weep, tears dropping from her chin onto the sack of slightly wilted fiddleheads.

"Can you stay?" she quavered. "I could fry them up right now, if you have the time."

"I can stay," he said quietly, and in his blue eyes she had seen that he planned to stay not just for fifteen minutes or an hour, but for a good long while.

He'd never told her about the woman he had planned to marry, or why he'd broken off their engagement. And Annie never asked. She'd been content to have Emmett back in her life, and in her bed. Why rock the boat? And Emmett, since then, hadn't brought up the subject of their moving in together. It was on his mind, she knew, and she often sensed it was on the tip of his tongue. But he'd wisely kept it to himself.

But would he keep silent indefinitely? Knowing Emmett, she doubted it.

At this moment, as she stood facing him, wedged between a wall lined with copper skillets in every size, and a display of enamel pots arranged atop a stack of boxes, Annie felt suddenly lost and alone, as if she were stranded on an iceberg in the middle of a vast ocean. *I don't want to lose him,* she thought. Yet how could she tell him that she loved him, *adored* him . . . but not enough to marry him?

Sell her beloved mews house, and move in with him? She'd thought about it, and several times she'd even come close to taking that leap . . . but then something had held her back.

Joe? Maybe. Or maybe she just wasn't cut out for marriage . . . to anyone. She thought of her sister, to whom being a wife and mother came as naturally as building a nest did to a bird. Laurel's house was more than just a place where she slept and ate and entertained friends—it was a home, a haven, filled with old furniture Laurel had refinished herself, knickknacks she had collected over the years, books she had read and reread, quilts she'd stitched, baby toys of Adam's she couldn't bear to throw away. Annie loved her own place and what she was doing, and didn't wish for Laurel's life at all . . . but right now she felt strangely empty. "Em, I'm sorry . . ."

"No big deal." He glanced at her, a sharp, assessing gaze, then cut his eyes away. "But, look, if it's all the same to you, I'm kind of beat. After spending the past five hours showing lofts, I don't know if my feet can hold me up any longer. Mind if I cut out on my own?"

"Only if you promise to have dinner with me tomorrow night."

He winked. "You got yourself a deal."

Watching his broad back as he wound his way toward the stairs—catching admiring looks from several women as he passed them—Annie felt her gloom deepen. How long, she wondered, would it be this time? How long before he walked away . . . this time for good?

She felt suddenly tired. She wanted to run after Emmett, tell him she'd changed her mind, but her feet seemed bolted to the floor.

She found herself thinking of all the movies she'd seen with people running alongside trains they had no hope of catching, music swelling, engine chuffing, steam billowing, the teary-eyed love object of all their frenzy peering anxiously, fruitlessly, from the window of his or her car.

Though she hadn't moved an inch, or even called out to Emmett to wait for her, Annie felt short of breath, and there was a throbbing in her temples, as if she, too, had been running to catch a train she'd already missed.

CHAPTER 28

Laurel caught the softball and tossed it back to Adam. She watched him jump for it, arms straining skyward, standing almost on tiptoe, his Big Bird T-shirt pulling away from his grass-stained Toughskins to show a belly just starting to lose its baby roundness. The ball grazed the top of his glove, but he couldn't hold on to it, and it careened off, landing with a thump against the back of the house and scattering small flakes of paint like confetti over the grass below.

The place could use a new paint job, Laurel thought. God, it seemed just months ago that she and Joe had had the whole exterior thoroughly primed and painted. But that hadn't been since they'd first moved in, and Adam was just starting to crawl then. Six years . . . could it really be six years? Her gaze scanned upward, taking in the two-story Cape Cod with its charming blue shutters and big, screened sun porch. For almost a year, she and Joe had knocked themselves out fixing it up—stripping off layers and layers of paint dating back to the Depression from fireplace mantels and door frames, sanding and refinishing the flooring, replacing the original windows with new double-glazed ones, painting and spackling until their necks were cricked and their arms about ready to drop off. But it was a good place; it had been worth all the sweat and hassle. Bayside was only a half an hour's train ride to the city, and yet they had the advantages of suburban living too. Little Neck Bay was a five-minute walk from here; Adam's school, too. And in the warm months, there were her flowers and vegetable garden, and this good-sized grassy backyard for Adam to play in.

"Mo-o-o-ommm."

Laurel saw him standing by the line of tall hydrangeas dividing their yard from the Hessels'. He was holding the ball and jigging from one foot to the other as if he had to go the bathroom. Now he threw the ball to her, and this time she tossed it back underhanded, low enough so that he was able to catch it without having to jump up. Still, he fumbled a bit, and she thought he might drop it. But after a second, he scooped it into his glove and looked up at her, beaming as if he'd just intercepted a potential home run in the World Series. She felt a rush of pride and love.

"Good catch!" she cried. "Now you. Show me how Reggie Jackson does it."

"Watch out, Mom, this'll burn a hole right through your glove!"

"But I'm not wearing a—"

Laurel was so struck by the look of manlike determination on his small, amber-skinned face that the words died on her lips. She watched Adam swing his wiry arm around and around in an exaggerated windup, and pitch the ball with such force that he lost his balance and toppled onto his knees on the grass. The ball flew upward, and seemed to hang in the air, defying gravity, a perfect white hole punched in the glowing autumn sky. Then it crashed down through the branches of the old apple tree under which she stood, shaking loose a few wizened Gravensteins and landing with a *thwup* several yards from her in the crusty dirt of last summer's vegetable patch. She could see the ball, dirty white, half under a bug-eaten leaf near where a few stunted zucchinis clung to the vine. But the last of the squashes and cranberry beans and cukes had been harvested weeks ago, and now, with Indian summer turning to autumn, she was glad that, despite all the bother and heat she'd had to endure for canning, she'd put up enough pickles, preserves, and jams to fill two whole shelves in the kitchen's old-fashioned walk-in pantry.

Bending to retrieve the ball, Laurel thought how much like his real father Adam had looked just a second ago, his small fist thrust up in triumph, his dark eyes glittering. All of a sudden, she was seeing Jess Gordon standing on the steps of Schine Student Center speaking to a small crowd of mesmerized students, his fist punching the air above him. Adam had his father's crow-black hair and sharply angled features, and his egalitarian spirit too—at school, Adam's teacher had told her Adam would share his sandwich and cookies with any kid who asked . . . even if it meant leaving himself without a lunch.

Laurel remembered the blue airmail letter that she'd gotten from

Jess the year Adam turned three. He'd joined the Peace Corps and was living in Mexico, a funky Yucatán village where he was helping local farmers, who had been nearly wiped out by a terrible drought, dig irrigation canals. Having diarrhea most of the time was a bummer, he wrote, but he was happier than he'd ever been. He'd met a girl, a local girl named Rosa Torrentes, and they were going to be married . . .

The memory of her own hasty marriage at City Hall came flooding back. No white dress or veil, no bouquet, no rice even. But she'd been so over the moon she hadn't cared one bit about missing out on any big wedding. She had everything she wanted, standing right next to her.

But Joe, had he felt such happiness? And would she, off floating on her own cloud of bliss, even have noticed if he had seemed less than ecstatic? Kneeling on the grass that bordered the vegetable patch, she froze, her fingers clenched about the ball, ignoring the dampness seeping into the knees of her Levi's.

Don't cry. You mustn't. Not in front of Adam. But the tears were already starting, stinging her, and with them came the image her mind had been replaying, over and over since yesterday: Joe and that woman at the restaurant. She'd dropped off the finished drawings for *Sally, the Silly Goose* at Viking and then had stopped by the restaurant, thinking she'd pop in and surprise Joe. Coming up into the dining room, she'd spotted him with his back to her, in a booth with a pretty auburn-haired woman whom Laurel didn't recognize. They were both bent forward, so absorbed in each other that neither one noticed her standing there, motionless at the top of the stairs. The woman, Laurel could see clearly, was holding Joe's hand tightly between both of hers. Joe's face was hidden so Laurel couldn't see his expression, but she could tell he was upset. An apology? A lover's quarrel? A farewell?

And now, all over again, she was feeling the shock and horror she'd felt then. In her mind, disconnected images overlapped in some bizarre collage—the woman's square gold earrings catching the overhead light as she reached to stroke Joe's cheek; the curve of Joe's shoulder as he leaned toward her; a napkin beside him folded into a droopy peak that had made her think of an Easter lily. Gene Pitney's "Town Without Pity" playing on the old Wurlitzer stocked with top-forty hits from the early sixties. And Laurel standing there like a ghost, invisible to both of them.

All last night, and all day today, she'd been trying hard not to imagine the two of them together, naked bodies entwined, telling each other little jokes, kissing, making love. What if there was some other, innocent explanation for what she'd seen?

Okay. Maybe there was. But it wasn't just the woman in the restaurant. Lately, Joe had seemed so distant and preoccupied. He hadn't made love to her in more than two weeks. And this distance of his wasn't something that had just cropped up in the last month or so.

You knew. Even when he said the words, you knew when he married you that he didn't love you, not passionately, totally, the way you *love him . . . and you took him anyway. So if he's having an affair, why should it be such a shock? At least it's not An—*

"Did you see that? Wow-ee, Mom, did you see how high it gotted? Right up to *space* prac'ly!"

Adam's voice yanked her back to him. Raking her knuckles across her wet eyes, she stood and went over to her son.

"If I were a talent scout," she said, hugging him, "I'd sign you up for the Yankees . . . or maybe NASA. The way you snagged that ball, I'll bet you'd be good with rockets too." Though the day was cool, Adam felt damp with perspiration.

Adam pulled away from her, scooping his silky black hair off his forehead, and saying soberly, "Kids can't be scien-tises." His big dark-blue eyes regarded her with cool intelligence.

Her heart caught. *His world is so orderly—color inside the lines and you can't go wrong . . .*

Laurel wished life *were* that easy. She wished that love was like money in the bank—the more you put in, the more you got back. Joe's love, all the years she'd struggled to win it, she'd been so sure it was only a matter of time. But now . . . well, she wasn't at all certain.

There had been passion. Oh, yes. She remembered how it had been in the beginning, Joe's hands on her body, so knowing, so gentle. But always, in the back of her mind, she had wondered if it was Annie he would rather be making love to, Annie's body he imagined while he was stroking hers.

She'd told herself it was only natural for married couples to become less interested in one another after a while. Why, then, was she more in love with Joe now than she'd been on her wedding day? Why did she ache for him each night when he rolled onto his side, leaving her only the curved wall of his back?

"Mommy?"

Laurel, jerked from her thoughts, saw Adam's worried face and felt a tug of guilt. She mustn't let him know how scared she felt. She wanted her son to feel safe and secure—things *she* hadn't known at his age.

She reached again for Adam, hugging him so fiercely that this time he wriggled in protest. She loved his little-boy smell, so different from the way girls smelled. Grass cuttings, and sweaty socks, and the faint vanilla fragrance of Play-Doh. She kissed him and let him go, feeling him shoot from her embrace like a pebble from a slingshot. Now he was running in crazed circles about the leaf-strewn lawn, flapping his arms against his sides.

"Brrrrrrrrrrrr . . . I'm a rocket! Watch me go!"

"Where are you going?" she asked him.

"Mars!"

"Oh, that's too bad. I live on Jupiter. I was hoping you could drop me off on your way back."

Adam stopped running, and flopped down on the grass, giggling. "Mommy, you're silly."

"Look who's talking."

"What if you *really* lived on Joop-der? Who would tuck me in at night?"

"Daddy, of course." A tight, hot band formed about her heart.

"Annie too!"

"Oh, I don't know . . . your aunt Annie is pretty busy."

"But not too busy for *me*." He spoke with the imperiousness of a seven-year-old who, since the day he was born, had been incessantly catered to by not only Annie, but Aunt Dolly and Rivka, too.

"Of course not." Annie, though frantic with her chocolate business, always managed to find time to come visit Adam, or take him to a puppet show, or the zoo, or to miniature golf.

"She's coming today, isn't she? Isn't she?" Adam demanded.

"Later," Laurel told him. "After your nap."

"Ahhhhh . . . only babies take naps." He rose with a sigh of injured dignity, then added slyly, "I bet Annie wouldn't make me take a nap."

"You want to get over your cold, don't you? And Annie isn't here, so you'll have to do what your mean old mommy says." Laurel cupped a hand about the back of his neck, and steered him in the direction of the house. "Anyway, I have a surprise for you, but you won't know until you get in bed."

He tipped an excited face up at her. "You got them!"

"I'm not saying."

"The Luke Skywalker sheets! You got them! You got them!" He launched into a frenzied little dance, then stopped, casting a doubtful look at her. "Did you get them?"

Laurel had wanted it to be a surprise, but, oh, that look—the look she also saw on Joe's face when he got something wonderful that he hadn't been expecting, like that time she'd done a sketch of him asleep on the couch, and had had it framed for his birthday. She nodded, the band around her heart growing tighter, hurting.

"Can I stay up and show Annie?"

"*After* your nap."

When she had Adam settled upstairs in his room, which took a while—he was so excited about his new *Star Wars* sheets—Laurel made herself a cup of tea and carried it down the hall to the extra bedroom she'd turned into her studio. She loved this room, the smallest in the house. It had a window facing east, which gave her wonderful morning sun to paint by. And in the late afternoon, she sewed on the old Singer in the corner—right now, she was working on Annie's fancy dress for next weekend's chocolate fair. Her sister could afford to wear Halstons and Valentinos, but she'd spotted this particular dress in an Italian *Vogue* and had fallen in love with it. And naturally, big-mouth Laurel had to offer to make it for her . . . though finding the time had been a bigger challenge than the dress itself.

Laurel looked over to the wall on her right, which she'd covered from floor to ceiling with corkboard. Dozens of sketches were stuck up with pushpins, some curling in at the corners, giving the room a slightly off-kilter look. By the window stood her drawing board, with a clip holding several half-finished drawings. Next to it, her easel with a decrepit cocktail cart parked alongside that served as a stand for her paints and brushes. The rest of her stuff—large sheets of cardboard, drawing paper, canvases, paintbrushes, cans of gesso and turpentine and fixative spray, boxes of fabric scraps, big plastic jars of powdered paint and a coffee can full of crayons for Adam—were fairly neatly arranged on the shelves she and Joe had hung on the south wall. The woodsy smell of linseed oil and turpentine hung in the air—a smell she seemed to carry with her everywhere, on her clothes, in her hair, like her own perfume.

Laurel slid onto the high stool that faced her drawing board, and stared at her drawing of a unicorn that shimmered ghostlike under its sheet of protective tissue.

She had several ideas for the next drawing in the story, and she wanted to sketch them while they were still fresh in her mind. She tore a fresh sheet from her sketch pad, looked at it, but then her mind went blank. After a few minutes, she folded her arms and leaned onto the table's slanted surface. Gazing out the window at the backyard below, with its gnarled apple tree, and raspberry vines growing rusty with autumn, she felt a wave of tiredness sweep over her. Like all the times she'd been pregnant: drowsy, drugged almost.

Laurel felt her chest squeeze tight. Those babies . . . three of them. No bigger than the heads of pins, but they hadn't seemed small and insignificant. Not to her. She'd imagined each one a rosy-cheeked child. And losing each one had been terrible, almost as terrible as if she had lost Adam.

Joe's babies, his sons and daughters.

If she'd carried even one of them to term, would things be different now between her and Joe?

No, not fair, he loved Adam as much as he could love any child, even his own flesh and blood. She couldn't blame this distance on her miscarriages.

Inside, Laurel felt herself spiraling downward, and took a deep breath, steadying herself. Was she maybe blowing this out of proportion? What about the good times?

The trip to Barbados, when it had rained the entire time and they hadn't minded one bit. They'd stayed inside, drinking rum punches and making love, and eating tiny sweet bananas scarcely bigger than her thumb.

Another memory came to Laurel—the day a pipe had broken in the upstairs bathroom, and water had leaked down through the ceiling . . . all over her final drawings for *Jabberwocky*. Drawings she'd spent weeks and weeks slaving over. Every one, ruined beyond fixing. Even with Joe trying his hardest to make her feel better, she'd been inconsolable. Nothing could cheer her, she'd thought. Not even dinner at Rivka's, which she'd been looking forward to. It was Friday night, Shabbat, a night for restfulness and rejoicing . . . and she didn't feel at all like rejoicing. Even so, she'd put on a nice dress, and had gotten Adam suited up, and they had gone. She'd sat at Rivka's table, surrounded by Rivka's children and grandchildren, listening to Rivka's husband joke that if their family didn't stop growing, by this time next year, they'd have to rent Yankee Stadium for their Shabbat dinners.

And then, after the blessings, a wonderful thing had happened. Joe, beside her, had cleared his throat, and said, "There's one prayer I'd like to read in English. May I?"

Mr. Gruberman, in his richly embroidered yarmulke and severe black suit, looked a bit surprised, but had nodded. "Sure, sure, go ahead."

"It's from Proverbs." Joe found the place in the small prayer book Rivka had provided for them, which included English translations along with the Hebrew text. In a voice full of feeling, he began to read, " 'A good wife, who can find? Her worth is far above rubies. The heart of her husband trusts in her and nothing shall he lack. She renders him good and not evil all the days of her life . . .' "

As she listened, Laurel felt her heart catch, and her eyes begin to sting. The ruined drawings faded. All that mattered was this man beside her, his fine profile limned against the soft glow of the Shabbat candles, his gentle voice filling the room like music. *He loves me,* she had thought, rejoicing inside. *He loves me. . . .*

Now, years later, in her studio with its ceiling that had been replastered and painted so that not even the faintest watermark showed, Laurel was no longer sure of Joe's love.

She dropped her head onto her arms and closed her eyes.

She felt so tired. The truth was, she needed Adam's nap times more than he did. He was always complaining that naps were for babies, and that he was way too big for them . . . and probably he was right. But except on weekdays, when Adam was in school, these were the only quiet times when she could work. There was so much—two more illustrations for Mimi's book, *by next week* . . . and she hadn't even begun the cover painting. And Georgia Millburn at Little, Brown had called *twice* yesterday to ask if she'd done those trial sketches for *Beggar Bones* . . . or was it *Bag o' Bones?* She'd promised to get to it before the weekend, but how?

Oh, *why* had she volunteered to make that dress for Annie? Why was she always trying so hard to please her sister? Sometimes it felt as if . . . well, as if she were struggling to make amends for some terrible injustice she'd inflicted on Annie. But what? Not Joe. Not really. He had come to her willingly. Hadn't he?

And it wasn't Annie who was making her feel this way, either. Annie was terrific. And so great with Adam. It was just that she could be so . . . so *overwhelming* at times. Like a tornado—blowing in through the front door, high heels clacking, gold earrings flashing, leaving a trail of her musky perfume like a slipstream as she travelled from one room to the next, doling out hugs, kisses, gifts, compliments, advice. With Annie around, Adam became wild, hectic, uncontrollable even . . . then a half-hour or so after she'd gone, he'd simply collapse. She'd find him curled up on his bedroom carpet amid the wreckage of his Legos, or burrowed into a corner of the living-room couch. Then when he woke up he'd be whiny and impossible, asking over and over when Annie was coming back, until Laurel wanted to scream.

But she knew how he felt. After Annie's visits, things *did* seem duller somehow. This house, with its bright quilts and woven wall hangings, its stripped-pine furniture and pewter bowls filled with pine cones and cedar shavings, seemed to lose its color, bleached like curtains exposed to the sun for too long. Stirred up by Annie, even the air seemed to sparkle like champagne—just *breathing* it made you feel a little tipsy—but once she closed the door behind her, it settled into flatness.

Did Joe feel it too? He must . . . and sometimes it drove Laurel crazy with jealousy, thinking how Joe must be longing for Annie. At times, seeing the high color Annie brought to his face, how happy and . . . well, *charged* he was around her, Laurel would feel as if she were fading right into the walls. She had to remind herself that she, too, was an interesting and active person. Besides taking care of Adam and this house with its big garden, two of the books she'd illustrated had been nominated for the Caldecott. Her show at the

Robson Gallery on Spring Street had gotten two respectful notices and one glowing one, and she'd even sold six of those paintings, at those outrageous gallery prices, one to a small museum outside of Philadelphia. She sewed most of her clothes, baked her own bread, and was a pretty good cook. So why on earth should she feel second-rate?

No reason . . . no reason at all. Unless it was because her husband seemed *mesmerized* by Annie . . . while with her he was, well, affectionate.

Thank God it's not Annie he's having an affair with. The thought clung to the back of her mind. Another woman she might be able to handle . . . but Annie? God, no.

An image of Joe and the pretty auburn-haired woman—who from a distance *had* actually looked a bit like Annie—stole into Laurel's mind. Pain surged low in her belly, knifing, like the cramps before her miscarriages.

She had to stop this. She had to stop torturing herself, and simply ask Joe. There had to be some perfectly innocent explanation, and when she heard it, wouldn't she feel silly?

But, still, would it make up for everything else? For the million times she'd spied him staring off into space with that weighed-down look, like he was carrying the world on his shoulders and had no one to confide in when, dammit, *she* was supposed to be his best friend, wasn't she? And the nights she lay on her side of the bed, rigid with longing, *praying* he would make love to her. Once, nearly choking with embarrassment, she'd asked him if there was something wrong with her. Did he want someone more glamorous, instead of a wife who bummed around the house in jeans and T-shirts most of the time, who couldn't remember the last time she'd bothered with makeup? And Joe . . . God, he'd been so stricken that he'd taken her into his arms right then and made love to her so tenderly that afterwards she'd wept, but not with joy. No, for that one moment she'd had a taste of what they'd had in the beginning, of what had almost been hers, and it had pierced her heart.

No, even if he wasn't having an affair with that woman, in a way he had already left her. Though how could you be left by someone who was never wholly yours in the first place?

God, what could she do? What *should* she do? Stand by her man, like her life was some country-and-western song, and hope that one day he'd come around? Was she that pathetic, that needy?

But losing Joe . . . what could be more awful? She'd loved him as long as she could remember. She'd *grown up* loving him. How could she give that up? Would her feelings for him ever fade the way *she* seemed to have faded for Joe?

Annie. What would she do if she were in my place?

Oh, why did it always have to come back to Annie, Annie, Annie? This was *her* life. She didn't need Annie, or her butting in. *Remember how she hit the ceiling when you told her about Val?*

Casually, one day over lunch at a little Indian restaurant on Third Avenue, Laurel had told her sister that Val had written that he wanted to see her and get to know his grandson—Adam was two at the time—and that she'd agreed to having him come for a short visit.

"How *can* you?" Annie stared at her, dropping her fork onto her plate with a loud clink. "How can you even *consider* it?"

"Adam has a right to know his grandfather," Laurel had told her quietly, but firmly. "Even if Val *is* a little flaky."

"Flaky? You think that's all he is? My God, Laurey, I wouldn't put anything past that man. How do you know he won't pull something?"

"Like what? You make him sound like some sort of hardened criminal. He's not like that, Annie. In fact, I sort of feel sorry for him. He's got nothing much going for him. And nobody but Adam and me, really."

"And so you're going to fill in the blanks?"

Laurel had stared at her, seeing something in Annie's eyes that made her realize that Annie, under her steely surface, could be insecure, too. "This isn't a contest," she told her. "I'm not putting him over you . . . or saying you didn't do the right thing taking me away from him."

That had silenced Annie, but from the tight look on her face, Laurel knew Annie was far from convinced.

But it wasn't as if Val visited all that often; since that first time, he'd only flown out here twice. The truth—and this Laurel hadn't admitted to her sister—was that Val couldn't afford the plane fare.

Laurel now imagined how outraged Annie would be if she knew about the money she'd been sending her father. Not much, just small checks here and there—never enough so that Joe would miss it and maybe question her. It had started years ago, Val phoning and explaining sheepishly about this bind he was in, just temporary, but could he "borrow" enough to tide him over until the deal he was putting together came through?

Somehow, though, Val's "deals" never seemed to come through, and the loans were never repaid. Laurel didn't really mind. She felt sorry for Val . . . and guilty in a way. As if she were partly responsible for the way he'd ended up, though she knew she wasn't.

Oddly, it was Rudy she missed. Though she hadn't answered any of the dozens of letters he'd sent, and when he called her she always hung up immediately, the thought of her uncle always brought a lump to her throat. She knew she ought to really hate him for what he'd done . . . but she sensed that his lying to her—about Val, and later about that couple wanting to adopt Adam—wasn't born of malice. He couldn't have meant to hurt her. And in a way he'd done her a favor, hadn't he? If it hadn't been for Uncle Rudy, she might actually have given Adam up for adoption. Imagining what her life would be like without Adam, she felt sick.

Laurel needed badly to talk to someone. Should she tell Annie about this thing with Joe? If she didn't talk to somebody, anybody, she felt as if it was going to burn a hole right through her.

Maybe somehow she'll be able to help.

Thinking of how good it would feel just to unburden herself, Laurel straightened up and, with pieces of masking tape, began fixing a clean sheet of thick drawing paper to the table's tilted surface. With a charcoal pencil, she roughed out a sketch of a unicorn. Not an ordinary unicorn—this one had wings, iridescent wings like rainbows—and it was flying, soaring among the stars.

"A little higher, I think," Annie told her. "Just above the ankle."

Laurel, on her knees on the living room's braided rug, removed the quiver of pins clamped between her lips.

"I could make it really short, if you like," Laurel teased. "Mini-skirts, I hear, are coming back."

"In *Vogue*, maybe . . . but not on me. Isn't it enough that practically my entire backside will be showing? Anyway, this isn't a swimsuit competition. I want the judges to concentrate on my truffles, not my thighs."

Laurel peered up at Annie. "They'll love your stuff. What are you so worried about?"

"Everything." She put on a confident smile, but Laurel didn't miss how her hand fluttered up toward her mouth before she forced it down against her side. She was biting her nails again . . . a bad sign. But if not for that, who would guess Annie ever suffered a moment of worry?

Laurel rocked back on her haunches, and gazed up at her sister, glorious in the gown that until a few minutes ago had been just a hank of fabric sagging from its hanger. On Annie, it rippled, it glowed, it *danced*, rubbed velvet the pinkish-gold of hammered copper, supple as silk. Scoop-necked, with a subtle drape that softened her angular shoulders and emphasized her small breasts. The back, as Annie had joked, dipped way down past the Mason-Dixon line, but Laurel thought it looked spectacular. Annie's back, as she turned to let Laurel pin the hem, was fascinating to watch, the way her muscles, beneath her smooth olive skin, seemed to flex and ripple. And how smart of her to keep her hair short—Annie's hair was like Annie herself . . . sleek, practical, to the point.

Somewhere along the way, Laurel realized, Annie had become a real beauty. Not a Grace Kelly kind of beauty . . . more like Sophia Loren—exotic, her huge eyes made even bigger with eyeliner and mascara, and her wide lips colored unfashionably in deep plum that on her looked exactly right.

Laurel, dressed in old jeans and a checked cotton shirt washed to the softness of flannel, felt mousy in comparison. When was the last time she'd had her hair styled . . . or her nails manicured? She wore her hair exactly as she had in high school and college, parted in the center, hanging down to the small of her back. Now it was pulled back in a messy ponytail fastened with the rubber band from this morning's *Times*. She looked down at her hands. Her nails were rimmed with red and green and yellow from the poster paints she'd mixed for Adam, who'd been given special permission to paint at her easel while she measured the hem on Annie's dress. Manicure? Forget it.

Annie, like the fairy godmother in "Cinderella," bent to touch Laurel's shoulder. "You should come," she said. "Really. You'd have fun. Plenty of people you know will be there."

She shrugged. "Oh, I don't know."

This wasn't the first time Annie had asked her. Laurel felt torn, wanting to please Annie, to support her at such a big event, but she was so uncomfortable at parties.

She remembered the last fancy party she and Joe had gone to, his wine supplier's twentieth-anniversary bash. All those people, total strangers, laughing loudly, shouting to be heard over the thumping of the band, their wet glasses brushing her bare arm as they shoul-dered past. She hated having to think up things to say, trying to be witty or even interesting to people who wouldn't even remember her name the minute her back was turned, when all she wanted was to be home, in her old bathrobe, curled up with a book or watching an old movie on TV.

"Joe would love it," Annie said.

Laurel felt a dart of resentment. *What makes you such an expert on Joe?* she felt like snapping.

But she knew Annie meant well. And in all these years, honestly, had she ever, ever done or said—in even the smallest way—anything to imply she was more than a friend and sister-in-law to Joe?

"I'm sure he would," Laurel replied evenly. Actually, she'd already suggested he go by himself, or maybe escort Aunt Dolly.

"Then you'll think about it?"

"Okay, I'll think about it." Easier this way. Arguing with Annie was like trying to get out of one of those Chinese finger puzzles—the harder you pulled, the more stuck you got. "Now stand straight so I can get this even."

She stuck a few more pins in, and stood up. "There. Go take a look. Try the mirror in the bedroom, only promise not to look at anything else. The room's a mess. I haven't even made the bed."

The whole house, in fact, was a mess. Laurel looked about her, at Adam's Legos and Lincoln Logs strewn across the unvacuumed rug, the cushions scattered with crumbled saltines, and the sticky ring a juice glass had left on the drop-leaf table. Since she'd gotten back from Joe's restaurant yesterday, she hadn't wanted to do a thing except sleep.

Then Laurel realized that Annie had made no move to leave, and was staring at her with her I-know-something-is-wrong look.

"I don't give a shit about the bed," she said sternly. "It's *you* I'm worried about. Laurey, you look like hell. What's wrong?"

Laurel felt as if there were sandbags tied to her arms and legs.

She was so tired. How could she ever have thought talking things over with Annie would be a good idea?

"Nothing," she said, trying to make herself sound brisk. "I took a nap before you came. That's why the bed isn't made."

Annie peered at her with new sharpness. "You're not sick . . . or anything?"

"You mean am I pregnant?" Laurel snapped.

"*Are* you?"

Laurel sucked her breath in and blew it out. "God! Does everything have to mean I'm pregnant?" She thought of Joe sleeping beside her, not touching her, night after night. "If you want to know the truth, it'd be quite a miracle."

For a small moment Annie stood silent. She looked shocked.

Then she said, "Is something going on between you and Joe?"

"Nothing a good faith healer couldn't fix." Laurel gave a short, dry laugh. "Listen, do you want some coffee or something? I made some banana bread the other day . . . there's still some left, I think."

Ignoring the offer, Annie sank onto the maple rocker by the fireplace, her dress settling into shimmery little pools around her, pins sticking up from the fabric like tiny antennae. Her eyes never left Laurel's face.

"Do you want to talk about it?"

"No, not really."

"Have you and Joe been fighting?"

"No . . . nothing like that. Look, can we talk about something else? I'm really not in the mood to be cross-examined."

"You look tired."

"I *told* you I was."

"Is it something he did?"

Laurel felt as if she were clinging to a narrow precipice, and she was slowly losing her grip. It would be easy, so easy, just to let go. To let herself fall right into Annie's lap, and have Annie comfort her. But no, better not . . .

"I'm glad you like the dress," she said brightly. "I wasn't sure how it would turn out. Velvet is harder than silk to work with. You have to match up the nap, and then it slides all over the place so the seams come out puckered. I don't know how many times I had to rip out that left seam and do it over. And forget about the zipper . . . that's—"

"Joe loves you," Annie persisted. "You have to know that."

"—why I scooped the back. But I like it better this way, don't you?" But then her control broke, and a sob slipped out. "Oh, Annie, he's having an affair."

She told Annie about the woman at the restaurant, how awful it had been . . . and how she'd wanted to die. Even now, just talking about it, with each word she felt some little piece of her shrivel up. She looked down at the pincushion she was holding; it was in the shape of a heart, stuck full of pins and needles, and when she realized how maudlin she must look—like a bad metaphor—she began to giggle, tears rolling down her cheeks.

Stop it, she commanded herself. But she couldn't. She began to feel panicky. Any second now Annie would come rushing over to her. God, she didn't want that. Annie would take what little bit of dignity she had left and smother it.

But Annie wasn't moving. She was just sitting there. Frozen. And then she started to laugh. She was *laughing.*

Laurel's face stung as if she'd been slapped.

But then Annie *was* coming over to comfort her.

"God, you had me worried there. I thought—" She grabbed Laurel's hand and wrung it, still laughing, sounding relieved, breathless almost. "Laurey, oh sweetie, you've got it all *wrong.* Joe isn't having an affair. That woman you saw, she had to be the same one Joe told me about—she's some kind of counselor. He told me the whole story, about his father not being able to manage any more with just a nurse . . . about Naomi—I think that's her name— recommending a nursing home. Well, it *is* awful for Marcus to have to be put in a home. So you can imagine how upset Joe must have been. Naomi had to have been *comforting* him, don't you see? *Don't you see?"*

Oh, yes . . . Laurel saw. Everything, clear as day.

No affair with a stranger . . . something worse in a way. More of a betrayal. Joe . . . Joe had made this momentous decision about his father . . . *and he hadn't once mentioned it to her.* And it was Annie he'd confided in, not her, his wife. Annie.

Joe and Annie, all along, from the very start.

Now it was Annie who looked ill, the color draining from her face, her olive skin a pasty yellow. She grabbed Laurel and shook her, her fingers digging into Laurel's arms.

"Laurey? What's wrong? You're white as a sheet! My God, you don't think I'd lie about something like this, do you? Is that it? Do you think I'm making this up just so you'll feel better?"

"No, of course not."

Laurel's voice seemed to come from far away, a distant mountaintop, while little background noises became sharply focused—the sound of Adam singing in the next room, his clear, high-pitched voice wandering in and out of key. *Oh, can you tell meeeee . . . can you tell me how to get tooooo Sesame Streeeeet.* The rat-tat-tat of a woodpecker in the mulberry tree just outside the front window. The slow, ponderous ticking of the old regulator clock on the mantel.

"Laurey . . . what *is* it?" Annie sounded frantic.

Laurel turned, her movements jerky, as if she were held together with hinges and springs, like those ventriloquists' puppets she used to watch when she was little, on the *Ed Sullivan Show*. Charlie McCarthy, or was it Edgar Bergen? No, Bergen had been the ventriloquist. He—

She stared at Annie as if she'd never seen her before, feeling as if all her insides were flowing downhill, an avalanche of love, grief, sorrow, resentment.

"You," she said, the rushing in her ears so great she had to shout to be heard over it. "*You're* what's wrong."

Annie jerked, a hand flying to her mouth. "What?"

"You sit there smiling as if I should be *glad.*" She took a blind step backwards, the sole of her Weejun coming down on a Lincoln Log, her ankle turning with a painful wrench. She glared at Annie. "How can you? How can you pretend when we both know it's *you* he wants? At least have the decency to admit it. And you want him, too. Isn't that why you've been stringing Emmett along all these years? Stop being so goddamn noble, and *admit it.*" She felt herself unravelling. "Admit you want him for yourself!"

A thundering silence filled the room. Laurel stood trembling on the edge of the precipice. Annie stared, her huge dark eyes like two charcoal smudges on a blank sheet of drawing paper.

"Mommy?"

Laurel jumped as if she'd been struck. She looked over at Adam, standing frozen at the bottom of the stairs, wearing an old button-down shirt of Joe's with the arms rolled up and the tail dragging on the floor. The front of it was streaked with paint, and he held a fat paintbrush in one fist. His eyes were huge and scared. *God, oh God.* How long had he been standing there? How much had he heard?

She wanted to run to him, cover him with kisses, fill him with reassurances, but she couldn't seem to move. She stood glued to the floor, while Annie, in her shimmery velvet dress, its unfinished hem fluttering about her ankles, pins winking in the fading light, swooped across the room like a brilliant bird and took Adam by the hand.

"My goodness, look at you! I think more paint must've gotten on that shirt than on the paper. Do you want to show me what you've done? I'd love to see it." She was upset too, her voice ragged, but she was hiding it well. She was protecting Adam, just as she'd once protected little Laurey.

With a quick, sharp glance over her shoulder at Laurel, Annie steered Adam up the stairs. Laurel stared after them for a moment, then sank down on the sofa, wanting desperately to cry, but determined not to.

CHAPTER 29

J oe swung his Volvo into the driveway, crunching over a blanket of fallen leaves, his headlights cutting a swath of green through the privet hedge alongside the garage. The house was dark, he saw, except for a light in the upstairs hall. Nearly midnight. Laurel and Adam were probably fast asleep by now. And that's where he longed to be. Jesus, what a night. With orders stacking up, and everyone working double-time, the dishwasher had to go hinky, flooding the kitchen floor. And at the same time, twenty-eight bachelor-party Yalies were upstairs, drunk and pitching dinner rolls at each other. He'd had to post two waiters he couldn't spare from downstairs to keep them from destroying the place . . . and then, at dessert, eight more of the groom's good buddies showed up, demanding to be fed.

And every day this week, chasing back and forth from Morton Street to the new Joe's Place he was building at Third Avenue and Eighty-second. The December first opening, even with the menus now printed and the waiters hired, would never happen. The more he busted his ass, the bigger the delays. Not a single piece of the kitchen equipment had come when it was promised. The plumber had performed a vanishing act. And then Jorge, his head chef, had to go mouth off in Spanish to that city inspector, never suspecting that a paunchy Brooklyn type with a name like Jaretsky would understand him. So, bingo, three big code violations.

But none of the restaurant headaches compared with what he had tomorrow—a two o'clock meeting with the director of the St. Francis Center. And then he'd have to do what he'd been putting off for days: break the rotten news about Dad to Laurel. She was crazy about Marcus. She'd probably insist they take the old man in, and he'd end up sounding like a grade-A bastard for saying no. Christ, what a mess.

But as he got out of the car, and started along the little concrete path by the side of the house, Joe began to feel calmer, less dragged down. He could feel the night air against his cheeks, cool and tartly crisp, and he could see his breath puffing out in wispy plumes. He found his way easily in the dark to the side door that opened into the kitchen. And then looking up, he saw why everything was so clearly visible—a full moon, huge and orange, perched atop his roof like an enormous pumpkin awaiting Halloween. Breathing in, he caught the sharp, smoky scent of someone's fire, and the faint smell of cooked food that made him think of a foil-wrapped plate left warming in the oven.

But at the back of his mind something was tugging . . . something he sensed was out of place. Then it hit him. On nights when she knew he'd be getting home late, Laurel always left on the light over the little wooden porch he was now standing on. The light wasn't on.

Could she have forgotten? Not likely. She was sometimes distracted, but never about that damn light. And if she'd gone and taken Adam to Burger King, say, or to see *The Muppet Movie* for the umpteenth time, they wouldn't have stayed out this late.

Had something happened to her? He remembered last year around this time, getting up early one morning and finding Laurel, four months pregnant, passed out on the bathroom floor, her nightgown soaked with blood. Their *daughter's* blood. At the hospital, they'd told him it was a girl. Those other babies . . . lost before he'd fully gotten used to the idea of Laurel being pregnant. But this one . . . Laurel had been showing . . . a girl. Now, as he had then, Joe felt tears well up in him. Sadness, but relief too. Because what if he hadn't found Laurel in time? What if she'd bled to death before he could get her to the hospital?

She could have died.

But Laurel wasn't pregnant now. Even so, as he turned his key in the lock and stepped inside, he could feel his stomach tightening, a vague unease seeping through him. In the dark of the tiny laundry porch just off the kitchen, he breathed in the reassuring smells of detergent and clean clothes. He had an urge to call out to Laurel, but he held back. She and Adam had to be fast asleep.

But something *was* wrong; he could feel it. He could feel the hairs on the back of his neck stiffening, and there was that queer tightness in his gut.

He cut through the kitchen, which, with the moonlight washing in, he could see hadn't been cleaned up. Dishes piled on the counter, toast scraps and crumpled napkins scattered over the pine table in the breakfast nook. Even the African violets lining the windowsill looked neglected, droopy. And that wasn't like Laurel . . . usually when he got home this place was spotless. She was so proud of this house, saying she liked doing even the stupid little jobs most women hated: polishing furniture, vacuuming, dusting every little knick-knack; she refused to let him hire her even a part-time cleaning lady. She liked having her privacy. And besides, she claimed that house-work helped clear her mind so she could think up ideas for illustrations.

Joe made his way through the dining room with its round oak table and carved breakfront filled, not with fine bone china, but with Mexican pottery in bright, primary colors, and Laurel's precious knick-knacks, what Rivka called *chachkes*—brass elephants, each one smaller than the next, arranged trunk-to-tail as if they were all walk-ing in a line; lopsided clay animals Adam had made; an intricately painted Russian box; a pair of pewter candlesticks; a bank in the shape of a dog whose tail wagged when you dropped in a penny; a small basket heaped with bright marbles. On the narrow wall space to the left of the doorway, framed in a square of moonlight, he could see clearly the fans Laurel had arranged there—delicately painted Japanese fans, an antique one made of lace and bone, and some that were shaped like inverted teardrops.

Laurel's house, he thought. He lived here, but it was really hers, her creation. It struck him that he'd never fully appreciated how restful it was. When he arrived home each night, all wound up, the muscles in his neck aching, just walking in through the door he felt soothed, like crawling into a warm bed.

Laurel. All around him, he was seeing her reflection.

Something tugged at his mind . . . something he'd forgotten to do. Then he remembered how withdrawn she'd seemed last night —just tired, she'd claimed, but he had sensed she was holding back. Yet he hadn't pressed her.

Now, he was climbing the stairs, quietly and quickly taking them two at a time. Reaching the second floor, he popped his head through the open door to Adam's room. In the faint yellow glow of his Donald Duck night-light, Adam lay curled on his side, fast asleep, most of the covers kicked off, his thumb corked securely in his mouth. Joe felt his tension ease a bit. *You see?* If anything had happened to Laurel, would Adam be here in his pajamas, sleeping so peacefully?

He tiptoed over, and out of long habit, felt the front of Adam's Spiderman PJ's. Dry. Thank God for small favors. For a while, a year or so back, it seemed as if Adam was wetting every night. But lately he'd been getting up on his own at night to pee. Laurel, he remembered, had taken the brunt of it—Adam's misery, all that extra laundry—and almost never a complaint from her.

Joe kissed his son's damp, toothpaste-smelling cheek, and was gripped by an odd memory. All of a sudden he was back in the ninth grade, Mr. Dunratty's drama class, acting out a scene from *Our Town*, which at the time, with his stampeding hormones and his rush to get outside and play ball, hadn't made much sense to him. But now he knew exactly how the ghost-Emily must have felt as she stood by and watched the precious, precious minutes of her former life tick past, how frustrated and overcome with longing she must have been. He felt that way now, with Adam . . . just as he often had with Laurel. As if he were somehow hoarding these moments with his son and his wife, storing them up against the day when they'd be gone and he'd be left only with memories.

Which might not be so far off.

Joe felt the stitch in his gut tighten once more. Jesus, how had it come to this? With Laurel, he tried so damn *hard* to keep things together. But it was like running in sand, he always seemed to be going too slowly. Could he be trying *too* hard?

True, he hadn't been *in* love with Laurel when he married her. Bewitched, bothered, and bewildered, yes, but the deep love he felt for her now, that had needed time to grow.

Joe, in his mind, was seeing Laurel, how she'd looked that day in the hospital, just after Adam was born, when he'd asked her to marry him. How she'd seemed to see straight through him with her clear blue eyes when she asked, "Joe, do you love me?"

"Of course I do," he'd said, fighting to keep from cutting his eyes away from the frightful urgency of her sky-blue gaze.

"Not like that," she told him, almost angrily. "Not like you loved me when I was a kid. I mean *now*. Apart from Adam . . . and from"—he watched her throat clench as she swallowed—"from Annie. Do you love me?"

Joe, caught between the truth and a lie that was only half a lie, really, had taken her hand, and told her what she wanted to hear.

"I love you. Apart from Adam. Apart from anyone. And I want to marry you."

Then he'd *had* to look away, because if he hadn't, the heat of the joy pouring out of her would have scorched him. He'd thought: *How can I tell her that I love Annie, too . . . and that if things had been different, it'd be Annie I'd be proposing to?*

But deep down, she had to have suspected. Wasn't that the root of their problem now? Wasn't that why he couldn't touch her in bed anymore without feeling guilty somehow? It wasn't that he didn't love her or want her . . . it was that he loved and wanted Annie, too. Worse, Laurel knew it. She knew it, and it was killing her. He couldn't even talk to her about it, because if he did that, then he'd have to say it out loud, admit that she wasn't just imagining it. And if he did that, wouldn't he be hurting her even more?

But he didn't want to lose her.

When he looked at her, what he saw was a beautiful, smart, talented woman, a ferociously devoted wife and mother. Maybe she wasn't as outgoing or as outspoken as Annie, but in her own low-key way, Laurel could be just as strong and determined. Where Annie could be fire and lightning, he thought, Laurel was bedrock.

Another memory came to him, stealing up on him in the close-smelling darkness of his son's room. That summer he'd been tearing out rotten boards in the porch . . . and suddenly there were wasps swarming everywhere, stinging him, crawling down the back of his shirt. He must have knocked loose a whole nest of them. In an electric fog of agony, he remembered yelling to Laurel, on her knees in the garden, planting seedling tomatoes. She'd looked up, frozen for a second, then had reached automatically for the garden hose that lay snaked across the dirt beside her. Then he'd felt the cold spray hitting him, and there was Laurel, standing fearlessly in the path of the fleeing wasps, wielding the hose nozzle's spring-loaded grip as if it were a machine gun. He saw several wasps land on her arms, and another on her neck. She flinched when they stung, but didn't stop spraying until he'd run far enough to get free of them.

"Run!" he yelled, and then she was dropping the hose and pelting after him, the brim of her floppy straw hat bouncing, her sunburned arms and legs flashing.

"Take off your clothes," Laurel commanded as she caught up with him near the hedge that marked their property line. Frantically, she began shucking off her shorts and T-shirt.

"Christ, what are you doing?" He stared at her, not understanding, while the stings on his arms and legs began to throb and burn. He felt as if he were on fire.

"Just take them off!"

When they were both stripped down to their underwear, she began scooping up handfuls of mud where it had collected around the marigolds she'd watered earlier. She smeared herself, and him, until they both were nearly covered with mud. Joe, as he felt the fieriness begin to ease, suddenly realized how ridiculous they had to look, standing out here in broad daylight in their underwear, covered in mud, in full sight of the neighbors.

He began to laugh, holding his stomach, bowed by hilarity.

"What's so funny?" she demanded, hands on hips, her hair speckled with mud, and a muddy stripe along one cheek like a muttonchop sideburn.

"I was just wondering what Mr. Hessel next door would say if you walked over right now and asked to borrow his pruning shears."

Laurel bent down; then Joe felt something wet and sloppy hit his forehead, just above his eyebrow. Mud running down his face, he watched Laurel, giggling, dart for cover behind the chinaberry tree. Scooping up a handful of mud, he slung it, missing her by a hair. She squealed, and waggled her rear end at him, leaving him no choice but to chase her. Catching her easily—she was laughing too hard to run fast—he tackled her.

That was when he'd looked up, and caught sight of their elderly neighbor, Gus Hessel, staring over the fence, his jaw slack with astonishment.

Laurel spotted him, too. Springing to her feet, she had run for the back door, leaving Joe to offer his neighbor a sickly smile before making his own hasty retreat. Inside, they crowded into the shower, holding on to one another and laughing like a pair of lunatics until the muddy water swirling down the drain turned clear.

"How will I ever be able to look Mr. Hessel in the eye after this?" she'd groaned, laughing.

"You won't have to—he'll be too busy eyeballing the rest of you."

She hit him with a wet washcloth, and by the time they got out of the shower, their stings had stopped burning, and they finished in the bedroom what they'd started in the yard.

Now, Joe felt a deep longing for those carefree days. Lately, with all the pressure at the restaurant, and his father's increasing senility, he felt sometimes as if he were looking at Laurel through the wrong end of a telescope, seeing her—even when she was close enough to touch—as if from a distance. And then, God, yes, there was Annie . . .

Walking with her yesterday afternoon, he'd felt like a kid playing hooky, stealing a sweet piece of freedom away from all the pressures. Annie somehow had made him lighten up. Afterwards, he'd felt really terrific . . . for about an hour.

Joe gently pulled the kicked-off covers over Adam, and slipped out. His and Laurel's bedroom was next to Adam's, but when he peeked in, it was dark. At first, he thought it was because she was asleep. But the bed, though its covers were rumpled, was empty.

Slipping back downstairs, he headed for Laurel's studio, and as he approached he saw the sliver of light under its closed door. She was probably so caught up in her drawing that she'd lost all track of time. That had to be why she'd let the kitchen get so messy, and hadn't remembered to switch on the porch light. He felt himself relax.

Standing outside her door, he knocked softly. "Laurey?"

No answer.

He eased open the door and saw her perched on the high stool before her drawing table, hunched over its tilted surface, her long hair pooled on either side of her; at her elbow, a jumble of pencils, erasers, chalk stubs, charcoal sticks. In the white cone of light cast by the Tensor lamp clamped to the side of the table, her hand, madly sketching, seemed to glow with a light of its own.

"Laurey?" he called again, stepping inside.

Her head jerked up, her shoulders snapped back. She swivelled to face him, her elbow bumping the lamp's hood, making the room's shadows jump. Her face, half cloaked in that jittery darkness, looked oddly disjointed—huge eyes staring out from an array of overlapping angles and planes. She was wearing a loose silk robe, jaybird-blue, the color of her eyes. Its shimmering folds hung on her, and it struck him how thin she'd gotten seemingly overnight, her arms sticking out from her sleeves like pale reeds. She looked sick, frighteningly ill.

Joe felt his heart turn over. Jesus, what was going on?

"Hi. Sorry if I scared you," he said. *Keep it cool,* he warned himself. *She'll tell you when she's ready.* "Deadline?" He gestured toward the slew of crumpled papers littering the carpet at her feet.

She nodded. "They need it by Monday." Her voice sounded flat, toneless. "I'm trying something different, pastels and charcoal." She looked down at her hands, curled limply in her lap, her fingers black with charcoal. "It's not working, though. It's the unicorn. He's not—" She swallowed, her eyes cutting away from him.

Joe stepped closer, peering over her shoulder. The nearly finished drawing of a winged unicorn seemed to leap out at him, all fluid lines and supple movement. Extraordinary. She was so damn talented. The only talent she didn't seem to have was believing in herself.

"—what I wanted," she finished.

"What do you mean?"

Laurel shrugged, her hand flying up to her cheek, leaving a trail of black smudge marks.

Joe felt a prick of frustration. Why did he always have to pry things out of her? She was so wonderfully expressive with her artwork, but when it came to conversation, she could be about as open as a brick wall.

"It's good," he said softly, his gaze shifting back to the drawing. The unicorn, done in lilac pastel shaded subtly with charcoal, seemed almost three-dimensional, as if it were hovering above the paper. "Really good. Maybe the best you've ever done." He meant it, too.

Laurel frowned, and stared down at the floor. "No," she said in that awful, flat voice. "He's just a horse with wings and a horn."

"Is there a difference?"

She looked up at him, as if surprised that he couldn't see what to her was so clear. "He has to be . . . magical. The children who read this story should *believe* in him."

"Laurey," Joe gently reminded her, "it *is* just a story."

Now he could see tears shining in her eyes, hard and bright as chips of ice. "Don't you *see?* If you believe, it *is* real. Like Santa Claus and the Tooth Fairy. When I draw, no matter how fantastic the thing is, I believe in it. That's what makes it work."

"And you don't believe in unicorns? Or is it just this unicorn?" He smiled, hoping intensely to lighten her mood.

She stared at him, an expression of terrible sadness passing over her delicate face. Joe felt suddenly as though he were skidding, skidding all out of control, into the lonely future he'd feared.

"I can't seem to believe in it either." A shudder passed through her, and she hugged herself, hooking her bare feet through the rungs of her stool, pressing her knees together tightly. Softly, so softly it could have been the hiss of rain against the window, or leaves scudding along the rain gutters, she said, "Joe, I want us to . . . to be apart for a while. Please don't argue. Please. I don't think I could stand even talking about it right now. It'd be different if I didn't love you. I'd be stronger, I know. But . . . God, this is so hard." She took a deep, gasping breath.

Joe stared at her, not believing what he was hearing, yet at the same time feeling curiously relieved—as if he'd known this was going to happen, and had been waiting for it. "Laurey, what is it? What's going on?" He took a step toward her, but she held out her hand to stop him.

"Look," she told him when it seemed as if she'd regained some control, "it wouldn't do any good to start throwing around accusations. When Annie told me about . . . about your father, I felt so . . . so . . . well, but then I thought it over and I realized it wasn't anything new . . . my feeling left out. What's new is that I . . . I don't believe in us anymore. All the things I wanted, hoped for . . . they just aren't going to happen, are they? My own believing in them isn't enough."

Joe had known this moment would come for so long it half seemed as if he'd lived it already. Even so, a great, drowning sorrow flooded through him. With every fiber of his being he wished that he could convey somehow to Laurel how desperately he loved her, needed her.

"I'm sorry I didn't tell you about Dad. I was going to—" He broke off with a shrug. "But I guess that's not really what this is about, is it?"

"No."

The look on her face told him what she was thinking, and before Joe could stop himself he was saying it: "Annie?"

Laurel looked straight at him. "Yes."

Christ, she had it all wrong. He had to convince her . . . some-how. He couldn't deny what he felt for Annie. But what *was* the truth? There were no lines marking off his feelings, only the dismal knowledge that he loved two women, two sisters, who were as different from one another as night and day . . . and that the two halves of his divided heart could never equal a whole.

"Laurey, I—"

"Joe, will you just *go.*" She gave him a hot, furious look . . . then abruptly she put out a hand to stop him. "Wait—your father . . . does he know yet what you're planning to do?"

"Even if I told him, he wouldn't understand. He's way past that. You remember when we visited him last week, and he told us Hitler had just invaded Poland? Well, yesterday he didn't even know who I was. But then, I guess that's nothing new." He smiled thinly. "That's what makes this so damn hard. All my life, I've been wanting more from the old guy than he was willing . . . or able . . . to give me. And now it's too late."

"He loves you, Joe. Maybe he didn't always let it show, but I know it's true."

Even if it wasn't entirely true, he felt grateful to her for saying it. "Maybe. All I know right now is that I hate what I have to do. He may not have been the world's greatest father, but he had grit and style. Have you ever watched one of those five-hundred-year-old sequoias being felled? That's what it feels like to me, watching the old man go downhill." And Joe felt as if he, too, were losing his bearings, and might soon be crashing down.

He didn't want to go away. If he insisted on hashing it out right here and now, Laurel, he knew, would probably give in. Things would be smoothed over, for a few days, anyway.

But in the end, nothing would change. Maybe in some way she was being wise. And didn't he owe her this, honoring her wish? And who knew . . . maybe doing this would somehow help them.

God, but if this was the right thing, why did it have to *hurt* so damn much?

"I'll pack a few things," he said, his words thudding dully in his ears.

"Will you be staying at the apartment?" She cast him a forlorn glance, then quickly added, "Adam will want to know."

"Yeah, sure." Apartment? For a second he had to think, to clear the fuzziness in his brain. Then he remembered, the old place on Twenty-first Street, he'd hung onto it because his rent was so cheap, and he could crash there when, after a rough night, he was too bushed to drive home. But to live there again? Have Adam visit him there as if he were some nice uncle instead of the daddy who was supposed to tuck him in at night?

Joe felt a pressure in the bridge of his nose, and behind his eyes. No, he wouldn't think about Adam now. Later, when his heart wasn't racing like an overheated engine, he'd let himself think about Adam. "I'll call him sometime tomorrow," he told her.

"What do you want me to tell him at breakfast?"

Joe hesitated. It occurred to him that much more than Adam's security might be at stake. Maybe his and Laurel's whole future.

Christ, they had so much. Not just Adam, but years of sharing. Some of it great, and some of it funny—like that party they'd thrown for a book Laurel had illustrated, *The Boy Who Hated Baths,* while at the same time sewage was backing up in the basement. And some of it sad, like each time she'd lost a baby. There were jokes that only Laurel would know to laugh at. Memories. Albums full of snapshots that would bore anyone but them.

No, he did not want to lose all that. Not even one bit of it.

An image crystallized in Joe's mind: Laurel in a pretty flowered dress, getting ready for a Carnegie Hall piano recital they had tickets for. She was sitting at her dressing table, her head cocked to one side as she fastened a pearl earring, and he could see her reflection in the mirror; she seemed to be smiling at him, her eyebrows slightly raised. And without a word passing between them, he'd known that she needed help fitting the tiny clasp over the stud of her earring.

Why was he thinking of that now? Such a little thing. But maybe, he thought, that was the true essence of marriage, not wild passion, but the simple unspoken language shared by husbands and wives. Not the great highs and lows, but the small quiet moments that, strung together, were like the molecules that form a universe.

Joe did then what he'd wanted to do the minute he saw her. He crossed the room in two long strides, catching her in a hard embrace. Her perfume, like wildflowers crushed under a careless boot, enveloped him with a sudden, dizzying sweetness.

"Tell him I'll be back," he murmured, then quickly let go.

CHAPTER 30

enri, seated in the somber rue St-Lazare law office of Amadou et Fourcheville, felt as if he were trapped inside a stifling attic full of musty antiques. He noted the wormy wainscoting, and saw that around the fan-shaped *cosse d'orange* window that overlooked the rue de Caumartin, the ancient flocked wallpaper was peeling. In the anemic morning light that seeped in through the ratty swagged-velvet drapes, the room's massive brass-mounted Empire furniture seemed funereal. And, *mon Dieu,* when was the last time old Amadou had opened a window? The room stank of dust and stale pipe smoke. And the hoary advocate himself, seated behind a Louis Quinze bureau plat clumsily tamping his pipe, seemed almost more ancient than the furniture. And yet he fit the occasion. Old Girod had outlived all his friends; why shouldn't his last will and testament be read by a fellow ghost?

Henri caught Francine's eye. She was sitting with military erectness in a gilt-wood *fauteuil,* half facing him, her black hair drawn back in a seamless chignon that emphasized the sharp angles of her features. Elegantly dressed in an off-white wool crepe suit trimmed in navy grosgrain, she sat with one silk-stockinged leg draped casually over the other, a black patent-leather high heel carving little circles in the sluggish air. That smug look . . . he knew it well. The same expression she'd worn after she'd gotten Jean-Paul's last lover discharged from his teaching position and sent back to Algeria. Francine, of course, would never admit their son was a homosexual, but she spared nothing to sabotage his amours.

Could she know something about Papa Girod's testament that he did not? Henri felt a tickle of anxiety, like a feather brushing against the inner walls of his stomach.

It's only a pose, he told himself. *Once Girod's is mine, officially, legally, she'll have no further power over me and she knows it. At last, finally,*

*the divorce. No more strutting her false piety before the old man. I'll be
free. . . .*

Free to marry again if he so wished. But whom? Dolly? No,
no, he was foolish to indulge in such a hope.

*Dolly of course has put me into her past, and that is as it should be.
Six years is a long time.*

But simply thinking about her lifted his spirits. In two days he
would be in New York at the chocolate fair. He would see her, and
then he would know if still he had a chance.

Looking over at his children, seated next to him on a carved-
wood sofa beneath a framed photograph of Wilson and Clemenceau,
Henri wondered how his son and daughter would react to Dolly.
Jean-Paul, with his prematurely receding hairline, buried in his books
all the time, probably wouldn't notice her unless Dolly sat right on
top of him. And dear, plump, distracted Gabrielle, wearing that hid-
eous brown suit that made her seem part of the furniture; so busy
with her little ones she probably had given not a bit of attention to
how she had let herself go. He imagined Dolly taking Gaby shopping,
to Cacharel or Kenzo, buying her a closetful of bright, flowered
dresses, rainbow-colored scarves, wildly impractical shoes . . .

He stopped. No. Too much still was unsettled. But he couldn't
turn off the surge of blood to his head.

Henri shifted in his chair, making a small creaking noise that
sounded loud as fireworks in the stifling silence. *Get on with it,* he
silently urged the fumbling old lawyer.

He'd waited an eternity for this—finally, to be able to call
Girod's his own—yet, oddly, he missed the old man. Henri imagined
him enthroned on the straight-backed chair next to Amadou's desk,
bird-claw hands folded over the top of his cane as he leaned forward,
head cocked, eyes bright with glee. *How he would have smiled to see
me now, squirming in my seat like a four-year-old who feels the call of
nature.*

Yet why should he be nervous? Girod had kept his promise,
and signed the document right in front of him. He even had a copy
at home. Though Augustin might well have changed his testament
more than once in the last six years, the part concerning the firm
would of course remain untouched. Augustin, despite his pig-head-
edness, was a man of honor.

So why are you are so nervous?

Henri was conscious of Francine's eyes on him, as hard and sharp as the diamonds in her ears—a present from her lover, no doubt. Strange, the way she kept that part of her life so hidden—*mon Dieu,* anyone would think he must be an agent of the KGB. Six years since Henri had moved out of their Marais apartment, and the only change she had made was to turn his former study into a small chapel. Yet all her additional praying seemed to have done nothing to diminish her resentment of him. Everything was and would always be his fault, from her own headaches and liver pains to Jean-Paul's "bent" nature, and even the miserable death of their spaniel who, shortly after Henri's moving out, had ambled into the path of a speeding taxi.

She could bend them all, friends, lovers, children, even her stubborn old father, make them do her bidding, all except him, her husband . . . and *that,* he realized, had to be the root of her anger, her hatred even.

She would prefer, probably, that he hate her too—*that* she could understand and make peace with. His pity, he knew, was what cut her most. But how could he help pitying her? As hard and bitter as she'd become, the memory still lingered of the young woman with whom he had once—an aeon ago—strolled along a beach in La Trinité sur Mer—a girl, really, not yet nineteen, who had waded waist-deep into the icy water to rescue a pair of spectacles that had slipped off the nose of an elderly woman in a rowboat.

That girl reminded him of the impulsive, generous-hearted woman he longed for today. Dolly. *Dieu,* how he missed her.

Henri fixed his gaze on Amadou, who was lighting his pipe, puffing a cloud of foul-smelling smoke into the already thick air. Now, pipe stem clenched between his teeth, half-moon glasses resting against the hump on his nose, he rattled through the papers on his blotter.

"Now, where were we? . . . ah yes . . . here . . ."

He finished reading aloud the small bequests, to nieces and nephews, a favorite cousin, an elderly sister, and to Augustin's valet and driver, Mohammed Al-Taib, who for more than twenty years had served the old man faithfully.

"*Pardon,* Monsieur Amadou," Francine broke in. "But what my father left to his valet has absolutely no interest to us." She waved an imperious hand ridged with purple veins. A pity, Henri thought.

At fifty, her face was still remarkably smooth, but her hands were those of an eighty-year-old. "Please move on to what concerns us."

Cut to the chase, Henri heard Dolly quip in his mind. Pretending to scratch his chin, he cupped a hand over his mouth to hide his smile.

Amadou broke off, clearly flustered.

"Ah, yes . . . well, I was only . . . hmmmm . . . but of course, Madame Baptiste, if you wish. . . ."

Amadou began fussing once more with his pipe, tamping it, relighting it, scattering shreds of tobacco over the document before him, until Henri wanted to snatch it out of his liver-spotted hands. Then Amadou cleared his throat and again began to read in a ponderous tone that made Henri think of a provincial actor reciting Racine.

"Ah . . . here we are . . . 'To my grandson, Jean-Paul, I bequeath my library of rare books, excluding my first edition of Hugo's *Cromwell,* which I . . . leave to my esteemed friend, Professor Cottard of the Bibliothèque Nationale . . .'"

Books? Perfect. He observed how Jean-Paul's narrow shoulders straightened, how his hooded eyes lit up. He recalled how as a boy, his son had loved to bury himself among those finely bound volumes, not wanting to come out of that library even to eat. And now, too, Jean-Paul still preferred books to people, and certainly to the sticky pleasures of Girod's. Chocolate caused him to break out in nasty hives.

He studied his son, a tweedy, hook-shouldered man with large, damp hands, thinning dark hair, and a forehead as pale and shiny as porcelain. How strange that his loins should have produced such a son. Jean-Paul looked nothing like either him or Francine. And when Gaby introduced him as her brother, people smiled in disbelief. Only Jean-Paul's nose, narrow and straight, its flared nostrils chafed an asthmatic red, was Francine's. The rest of him seemed to have been assembled from a distant cousin's ears, an uncle's mouth, a great-grandmother's chin.

Yet Henri loved his son, the professor, the entomologist who lived and breathed beetles, who preferred other men to women. Was that why he loved him so, because of his strangeness? He remembered Dolly once looking at a truffle and saying, "I like the lumpy ones best, 'cause they remind me of people, how we oughta care about each other, warts and all." If only Jean-Paul could stand up to his mother, instead of sneaking off to meet with his lovers like a truant schoolboy.

But who am I to encourage him? What kind of an example have I been? He should have divorced Francine years ago, no matter what the consequences. Then he and Dolly could have married.

"Papa, are you okay? You look pale. Would you like me to get you some brandy?" Gabrielle, leaning over, whispered in his ear. "I know where he keeps it . . . over behind those maroon books." She gave him a conspiratorial smile.

Henri groped for his daughter's hand and squeezed it. Dear Gabrielle, the child of his heart. Dark and smooth like her mother, but with none of Francine's coldness. Still plump from the birth of her fourth child, a little girl, Gaby made him think of peaches and sunshine, the orchard behind the country house near Deauville, where a century ago he'd chased a fat, laughing toddler under the sun-dappled trees.

"I was thinking of peaches," he whispered back.

Gaby shot him a puzzled look, and smoothed a crease in his jacket. Henri had a sudden image of himself as an old man, living alone in his small rue Murillo apartment, looked in on by his daughter from time to time, Gaby making sure he was eating enough, getting out for walks, taking his medicines. He shuddered, and thought how different it would be if he were with Dolly.

Henri focused on Amadou's chapped lips, willing them to impart the words he so needed to hear.

" '. . . In the matter of Girod's,' " the old man droned on. " 'To my grandson, Jean-Paul Baptiste, and my granddaughter, Gabrielle Baptiste Rameau, I bequeath to each respectively ten percent of my stock. And to a trust for the benefit of my devoted son-in-law, Henri Baptiste, thirty-five percent . . .' "

Henri's heart lurched, and joy spread through him like a gasoline fire. He wanted to leap from his chair, hug Gaby, dance about the room. The old man had kept his promise! Thirty-five percent, in addition to the twenty he already owned, gave him an uncontested controlling interest. Now he could buy new machinery, hire more staff, upgrade the packaging, really run the place with no Augustin to pester him. And best of all, he could divorce Francine with nothing to fear.

But wait, more . . . Amadou was still reading.

" '. . . to be administered by the trustees on behalf of Henri and my daughter, Francine Girod Baptiste. In the event of either Francine or Henri's death, said interest will revert to the surviving spouse, and the trust will be dissolved. However, if for any reason, Henri and Francine should divorce, said interest will revert in its entirety to Francine.' "

Henri felt as if a brick had crashed down on his head. Had he heard correctly? He forced himself to look at Francine, saw her smug, self-satisfied expression, and knew then that it was true. They had planned it, the two of them; fashioned it link by link, like Marley's chain—to shackle him to Francine for the rest of his life. For the Church, and for appearances. Stupid, insane. *Merde!*

How could he have *allowed* himself to be made such a fool of! He should have made the old conniver turn the stock over to him before he died. Girod *had* liked and trusted him, more than anyone. Augustin was no actor. He could not have been pretending, but the ties of blood to his daughter meant more. *Sacré Dieu,* he should have known!

Henri, his head hurting, his gut knotted with anger, fought to keep from jumping to his feet and shouting that he would not accept this—it was monstrous! He wanted to strangle Francine, feel that skinny neck of hers snap between his hands.

I'll fight it! he raged. He would find a lawyer, a ferocious lawyer, not like this bumbling dotard. He'd go to court. Show the original testament as evidence of how Girod, in his senility, had been manipulated by his viper of a daughter.

Then, feeling Gaby's hand on his arm, the rage in him began to cool and die down, like a fierce wind quickly blowing itself out. No, he could not, would not, subject his children, his grandchildren, to such ugliness. A quiet divorce was one thing, but to battle in court, make a public spectacle, squabble like stupid peasants in the marketplace . . . the thought of it disgusted him. And, even if he were to fight this, there was always the chance he might lose.

"I believe that is all," Amadou ended, peering over his half-rim spectacles like a Daumier caricature. "If you . . . ahem . . . have any questions . . . please—"

Henri rose to his feet and strolled over to the large rubber plant by the window. He fingered one of its good-sized leaves, and asked,

"Tell me . . . what kind of fertilizer do you use to keep it so green? Some say horse manure is best, but others swear by guano . . . or bird shit, as we know it." He glanced over at Francine, and saw her eyes narrow, her tight smile falter. "Which do you prefer, Monsieur Amadou?"

The aged lawyer colored and sputtered, "I have never given it much thought . . . horticulture is not one of my . . . ahem . . ." He cleared his throat with a phlegmy rattle. "Actually, I believe your father-in-law would have been the one to ask . . ."

"Of course," Henri replied, nodding. "Augustin, I'm sure, will keep heaven exceptionally green."

A flush rose up the sides of Francine's neck, turning her ears pink. She shot him a murderous look. His barb clearly had struck home. But Henri felt little satisfaction. He was still too numb. His heart was racing. He needed to go somewhere quiet, and lie down.

"Monsieur, you must excuse me," Henri said, "but I have an urgent appointment." He turned to his son. "Jean-Paul, would you mind dropping me off on your way back to the Sorbonne?"

Jean-Paul shot him a startled look, then quickly cut his eyes away. "I . . . uh . . . actually, Papa, I'm going the other way . . ." he stammered.

No doubt yet another assignation, he thought sadly. But he merely nodded, and said, "Never mind. I can easily get a taxi."

Gaby stood up, clearly distressed, and looking more disheveled than before; tendrils of dark hair trailing from the pins holding them up, a stain on the shoulder of her lumpy brown suit that he hadn't noticed before—baby spit-up, from the looks of it. Francine, he saw, was frowning at Gaby with undisguised disapproval.

"I'll drive you, Papa," she offered timidly. "I'm going that way . . . I promised Marie I'd buy her a pair of ballet slippers. Did I tell you her ballet school is doing *Giselle?* Well, parts of it, anyway." Outside on the street, as he was folding himself into her tiny Citroën, she asked, "Is your appointment a long one? I thought maybe . . . if you have time . . . afterwards, we could take a coffee, or something to eat. My errand won't be more than half an hour. And my *au pair* is with the baby until two." He saw the tears shining in her eyes before she quickly looked down, digging in her purse for her keys.

"You don't need to console me," he told her gently.

"Oh, Papa." With a sob, Gaby buried her face in her hands. "It's so awful. I know how much you wanted . . . well, it's not *fair*. Maman doesn't know a *thing* about running Girod's. She only wants it so she can use it against you." She threw her arms about Henri, and sniffed into his shoulder. "What are you going to do?"

"First, I am going to keep my appointment. Then"—he stroked the untidy bundle of hair at the nape of her pink neck—"I am going to take you to lunch at Fouquet's."

"You can have my shares," she said fiercely. "I don't want them."

Henri hugged her and held her. A lovely gesture, but still not enough to make him the controlling shareholder.

He kissed his daughter's damp cheek. "*Merci, ma petite,* but you have just given me something more precious than all the shares in the world."

"Papa . . ."

"Hurry, or we'll both be late."

"Where?"

"The shop. Someone is meeting me there."

There was no appointment; he just needed to get away, to be alone, to think.

Wiping her nose on her sleeve, Gaby started the car, and pulled away from the curb, bumping over a small branch that had fallen from one of the plane trees lining the avenue.

She drove carefully, but Henri felt as if he were speeding, about to be hurled off some steep precipice. Could he walk away now, at his age, and start over from nothing?

But I don't live with Francine. And I won't even have to see her.

But without a divorce he would never be a truly free man. And he'd have no hope of winning Dolly back. He felt a sliver of ice wedge itself into his heart. As Gabrielle wove her way with surprising skill through the swarming madness of the place de la Concorde, Henri imagined Dolly's soft, powdery flesh pressed against him, her mouth . . . oh God . . .

It might already be too late. But his dreams, his hopes, how could he give those up? How could he face himself in the mirror each morning, knowing he had *chosen* to be chained to Francine forever?

Two days, he thought. *In two days, I will see Dolly. I will know then.*

With a sigh, Henri eased back in his seat and tried to stretch his legs among the clutter of plastic toys and baby bottles at his feet. Bracing himself as the tiny car lurched and swayed, he closed his eyes and held tight to his last image of Dolly—boarding her plane in a polka-dot dress and big straw hat, her tears almost, but not quite, disguised by a pair of huge sunglasses studded with rhinestones.

Dolly rang the doorbell and waited. No answer. But she sensed Laurel was home. She didn't know how she knew . . . she just did. Was it the petunias and sweet william along the walkway looking so fresh, as if they'd just been watered? Or the drapes in the front window—open just a smidgen, as if Laurel wanted to be able to peep out and see who was at the door?

She rang the bell again, but this time didn't wait for an answer. Stepping off the porch, she walked around the side of the house, her high heels sinking into grass still wet with morning dew, the hem of her full-skirted paisley dress snagging on a rosebush. In back, she tried the glass door to the sun porch. It wasn't locked. Stepping inside, she tip-tapped her way over to the partially open sliding door that gave onto the living room.

"Laurel?" she called. "Honey, it's me . . . Dolly."

No answer. Could she still be in bed? Not likely. It was only a quarter to nine, but Dolly knew her niece got up early on weekdays to get Adam off to school. More than likely, she just didn't *want* anyone to know she was here. After all, she wasn't even answering her phone.

It wasn't Laurel who'd told her about Joe—Dolly had had to hear the sorry news from Joe himself. After two days of calling their house and not getting any answer, she'd finally reached Joe at the restaurant. In a strained voice, he told her he'd moved out, but that he hoped it was just temporary. He hadn't gone into any explanations, but for the one who had done the walking, he'd seemed pretty broken up.

Dolly had not been able to keep from driving over. Invitation or no, she had to see if she could somehow console her niece. "Honey . . . you there?" In the weak light trickling through the slightly parted drapes, she noted the clutter of toys strewn about the living room's big braided rug, and felt oddly reassured. As long as she had Adam, Laurel would get through this okay.

"Hi, Aunt Dolly." Laurel's soft voice, seeming to come out of nowhere, startled Dolly into nearly dropping the large black patent-leather purse she carried.

She turned and found Laurel standing in the doorway to the kitchen, wearing a rumpled chenille robe that looked as if it had been slept in. Her long hair was bound in a messy braid that also looked as if it had just come off a pillow, and even in this puny light Dolly could see how red and puffy her face was. She felt her heart swell in sympathy.

Don't I know what it feels like . . . aching for a man who's not there? Haven't there been plenty of mornings I've woken up to a damp pillow and a load of heartache?

"I knocked, but I guess you didn't hear," Dolly said, not wanting to embarrass her niece any more than she probably already had, barging in here like the FBI.

"I . . . I must've been in the bathroom," Laurel told her with a feeble wave of her hand toward the back of the house.

"Well, right now you look as if you could use some coffee," Dolly said, briskly walking over to her. "Why don't you sit tight while I make you some?"

In the kitchen, Dolly yanked open the curtains, letting in a flood of sunlight. Laurel squinted and shrank down into one of the bentwood chairs scattered around the breakfast table. Dolly found coffee in the cupboard by the stove, and while it was brewing she went about hunting up eggs, bread, butter. She sniffed a carton of milk that smelled a tad sour but would do.

"When was the last time you had a decent meal?" Dolly asked.

"You don't have to go to so much trouble," Laurel told her in a stuffed-up voice that sounded as if she had a head cold. "Really, I'm not hungry."

"That's not what I asked, is it?" Hands on hips, Dolly directed a stern look at her niece. "Bet you haven't eaten a thing this morning . . . or the night before. Why, just look at you. You look like something the mailman stuck under the door."

Laurel sighed. "I haven't been feeling very good."

"Well, I can *see* that." Dolly sank into the chair opposite her niece. Gently, she asked, "You want to talk about it, sugar?"

Laurel shook her head, her eyes bright, her lips pinched tightly together, as if she feared that opening them would let loose a flood of tears. In the good sunlight pouring in thick as honey through the windows, Dolly could see the unkempt wisps standing up all over her head. Her slept-in braid had the look of a frayed rope.

"Joe told me he'd moved out." Dolly spoke gently, taking Laurel's limp hand and pressing it flat between both of hers.

She seemed to grow even paler, if that were possible. "What . . . what did he say?"

"Nothing much. All I know is, he seemed pretty miserable about the whole thing. Not like a man who'd walk out on his wife and son without some pretty strong reasons."

"I asked him to leave." Laurel's voice caught, and she gulped in a deep breath, clearly fighting for control.

"I know you have your reasons, and I'm not gonna pry into them," Dolly said, rubbing Laurel's fingers between hers as if she could somehow warm them. "But you better be sure this is what you want, because a thing like this . . . well, it might just push you further apart. Troubles in a marriage need sorting out, and there's not much sorting gets done between two people miles apart from one another."

"I . . . I don't know if it's possible to sort this out."

"Think. I want you to think now . . . are you and Adam really gonna be better off on your own?"

Laurel withdrew her hand, lowering her head and pressing the heels of her palms into her temples, as if she had a headache. Dolly waited, tense, forcing herself to remain silent when she wanted to cry out, *You don't know how bad it can be, sleeping in an empty bed, night after night. You don't know the loneliness.* What could be worse than what she'd suffered in the years since Henri?

"It's Annie," Laurel said, so softly that at first Dolly had trouble hearing her. "She's the one he wants. It's always been Annie."

Dolly felt her arms tighten with gooseflesh, but she wasn't shocked, not really. Hadn't she always known? "Did he tell you that?"

"No. I just know. Believe me, I'm not imagining it."

"Are you sure?"

"I'm sure."

"Okay, suppose it *is* true. What are you going to do about it?"

Laurel lifted her head, blinking in surprise. "What do you mean? I *am* doing something. I asked him to leave."

"Well, if it's a divorce you're looking for, then I'd say you're on the right track. But if you think this marriage is worth fighting for, then I suggest you *do* something about it."

"Like what?"

"For starters, letting me put some food in you. Then how about changing out of that awful robe into something nice? Fix your hair, put on some lipstick. A dab of perfume wouldn't hurt, either."

"Perfume? Oh, Aunt Dolly, I know you mean well . . . but lipstick and perfume aren't going to fix what's wrong between Joe and me."

"I didn't say they would. But you have to start somewhere, don't you? And if you don't feel good about yourself, how can you feel good about anything else?" Dolly pushed away from the table, and rose to finish making breakfast. "Now . . . you want jam with that toast, or just plain butter?"

"Jam, please. There's some in the fridge." Laurel looked as miserable as ever, but it was a start.

Minutes later, when Dolly put a plate in front of her, Laurel even managed a wan smile. Looking down at the eggs fried to crispy brown lace around the edges, and toast that was more black than brown, she said, "It looks delicious."

Dolly felt herself blushing. Laurel was just being polite, and they both knew it. "Well, I never said I was Julia Child. But it's nice and hot."

"Thanks, Aunt Dolly." Laurel touched Dolly's hand. "Can I ask you something? About you and Henri?"

"Sure, go ahead." She smiled, even though she didn't feel like smiling, and nibbled at a strip of soggy bacon.

"Why didn't the two of you ever get married?"

"Well, that's easy enough. You know the answer yourself— how could I marry Henri when he's already got a wife?" She kept her voice light, but inside her heart was thudding heavily.

"I know. But if he loved you so much, why didn't he get a divorce?"

She sighed. "A lot of reasons, sugar."

"Do you ever see him anymore?"

"Only once in a while. Business, mostly. Conventions, fairs, that sort of thing. We talk on the phone now and then." It was an effort to keep smiling, but she'd been hiding her heartache for so long she was good at it.

"But you just said that people have to stay together to work things out. Why didn't you and Henri stay together?"

For a long moment, Dolly sat still, nursing her coffee and staring out at a red squirrel cadging some seed from the bird feeder that hung from a low branch of the maple tree outside the window. How do you learn to stop missing someone, she wondered, when he's always there—peeking out from behind every thought, crouched at the back of every smile?

"It wasn't for lack of loving," she said, choosing her words carefully. "Maybe we were just too far apart to begin with. I know this much—if it'd been *me* Henri was married to, I'd never have let him get away. Not a chance."

"This is probably going to sound silly—I mean, I know it's been years and years—but do you think you and he might get back together someday?"

"I think about it," Dolly answered honestly. God, did she think about it. But wishing wasn't going to make it so. She'd faced that long ago. "You want some more toast?"

Laurel shook her head, but Dolly noticed she'd eaten most of what was on her plate. There was a smear of raspberry jam on her upper lip. Dolly reached out and dabbed it off with her napkin. As she was drawing back, Laurel captured her hand and give it a hard squeeze.

At this moment, Dolly wasn't sorry for what she'd given up . . . because what she'd gotten in return made her feel so blessed—a family to love, who loved her in return.

"I'll clean up here while you go get yourself dressed," she told Laurel. "And then after that, we're going shopping."

"Shopping?" Laurel stared at her. "What for?"

"A dress, that's what. The prettiest evening gown in Bendel's, for you to wear tomorrow night at the chocolate fair."

"But, I'm not—"

"Well, of course you're going." Dolly cut Laurel off with a wave of her hand that set her charm bracelet tinkling. "Do you a world of good. And who knows what'll come of it?"

CHAPTER 3 1

Emmett, standing in a large workstation near the second-floor entrance of the Tout de Suite factory, breathed in the rich, dense aroma of chocolate. Funny thing, he thought, how a certain smell could trigger a memory. It was that way with him—one whiff of a breeze blowing in off the ocean and he'd feel a rolling deck under his boots, and the rough weave of a shrimp trawler cutting into his palms. Or driving through a field of corn at the height of summer, he'd be seventeen again, making love to Cora Bigsby under a canopy of rustling green, with the sun slatting through, warming his backside.

But years from now, when he smelled chocolate, what memory would it bring? Would he remember Annie, at one in the morning, tumbling into his bed after a long night at the factory, the scent of chocolate on her skin, her hair, her lips? Or would it bring a lump to his throat? Would it make him think of this night . . . of having to tell her good-bye?

Don't, he told himself sharply. *You haven't left yet . . . you haven't given her a chance to change your mind.* He'd tell her about the offer he'd gotten—sales manager at Fountain Valley, ninety million dollars' worth of beautifully-designed luxury houses just outside of La Jolla. An opportunity he might never see again. He'd tell her the time had come for her to fish or cut bait. He needed her. But he needed her once and for all to commit—to become his wife. Or he'd best forget about her, and move on.

He watched her now, working alongside Doug and Louise, her hair damp and spiky from the steamy heat that pervaded the factory, her hands and the front of her apron covered with chocolate. They were dipping plastic leaves into melted couverture for the tree—made entirely from chocolate—that would be the centerpiece of Tout de Suite's display at tomorrow's fair. The counter at which Annie stood, he saw, was covered with pans of melted chocolate, marble slabs smeared with chocolate for dipping, and metal trays on which finished leaves were drying. He watched Louise, with the back of her wrist—the only part of her hand not coated in chocolate—push her flyaway blond bangs out of her eyes, and dip again into the brown goo in front of her. When the couverture on the leaf was dry, he knew, it could be peeled off and, using a warm chocolate paste, "glued" to a branch of the tree he could see standing half assembled on a butcher-block table in the middle of the room. Four feet high, its trunk and branches carved from solid chocolate, it was more than ambitious—it was a masterpiece.

"I've never heard of anyone being able to make a whole tree from scratch . . . except maybe God," Emmett joked, aware of a dull ache low in his belly. *What can I say to convince a woman who thinks she can play God that she'd be better off with me?*

"Yeah," Annie sighed, wiping her hands on her apron. "Except God created the whole world in six days, and we'll be lucky if we can get this display together in the next twenty-four hours. If I stopped to think about how long I've been at this, I'd probably pass out."

"Maybe it's time you *did* pass out," Doug volunteered with a smirk, looking up from painting a veneer of chocolate glaze onto a branch.

Emmett shot him a grateful look. Doug, a short squat fellow with a thatch of dark hair and heavy eyebrows, was good for Annie—his constant ribbing keeping her from taking herself, and Tout de Suite, too seriously. Now Doug was consulting the diver's watch strapped to his hairy wrist. "We started at six-thirty this morning, and it's now a quarter past midnight. When do we get to turn into pumpkins?"

"Thanks so much, Douglas." Annie shot a withering glance in his direction, a smile nonetheless tugging at her lips. "How would I ever keep track without you?"

Emmett, looking past her smile at her drooping shoulders and the purplish smudges under her eyes, felt a longing to rescue her somehow, scoop her up in his arms like some heart-of-gold lawman in an old Western, and carry her off into the sunset . . .

Wise up, he reminded himself. *She won't marry you . . . she won't even move in with you. . . . As far as you're concerned, bucko, the sun has done set.*

Not now, Em, please can we talk about this some other time? How many times had he heard that from her? And, shoot, between her crazy schedule and his, when was there *ever* a good time? Just this week, he'd been holed up in a lawyer's office for three whole days, trying to be the fair-and-square go-between on a sales contract, for a gutted brownstone, he thought would never get signed. And he'd had two closings, three evening meetings with out-of-town investors looking to buy second-class office buildings, and in between a conference with an accountant on a tax-shelter deal.

And tonight, lonely old Haberman stretching out their dinner with coffees and double brandies, so he could pontificate on how what America and the New York real-estate market needed was to have Ronald Reagan in the White House cutting taxes. What did some Georgia cracker peanut-farmer know about running a nation? All evening, Emmett had been itching to get away. He hadn't seen Annie in days, and now, *tonight,* he had to talk to her.

But here, watching her knock herself out to get her display ready in time for tomorrow, he was having second thoughts. She looked really frazzled.

Still, he was here, so he might as well lend a hand.

"Anything I can do to help?" he asked, shrugging off his jacket.

"Yeah, stay out of our way," quipped Louise, tossing him a smile to show she was just joking. "No, seriously, there *is* something you could do . . ." She shot a worried glance at Annie. "Get her out of here. Please. Just for an hour. Take her out and feed her. She's been here longer than any of us, and won't take even a five-minute coffee break."

"Fat chance!" Annie yelled over the hum of the tempering machine as she was carrying a tray of finished leaves over to Doug. Then her foot must have caught on something, for she lurched forward, staggering, the tray nearly sliding from her grasp.

Doug caught the tray, and Annie, with a loud exhalation of breath, rocked back on her heels. Placing her hands on her hips, she glared at Louise. "If I don't get this display finished by tomorrow and looking good enough to win first prize, I might as well take off for Tahiti . . . or, hell, just retire for good. Because, trust me, unless

I make that deal with Felder, there may not *be* any excuse left for busting my buns."

In her jeans and chocolate-smeared apron, her forehead shiny with sweat, she looked ready to collapse.

"Hell, Cobb, it *is* tomorrow," Emmett pointed out. He wanted to wrap his arms around her, chocolate smudges and all, and at the same time he wanted to kick her in the butt for being so damn stubborn.

"There really isn't that much more to do," Doug told her. "Lou and I, we can handle the rest on our own . . . trust us."

"I don't know . . ." Annie was weakening, he could see, but she still resisted. "We haven't even started on those marzipan pears."

"Lise is coming in at the crack of dawn to do them," Doug argued. "The dough's all ready in the refrigerator."

"But . . ."

"Either you go . . . or we go on strike," Louise threatened.

"You wouldn't!" Annie gasped.

"Try me," Louise replied, her usually pixieish face now plainly in earnest.

Then Emmett, surprising himself almost as much as her, grabbed Annie around the waist, lifting her off her feet and hoisting her over his shoulder. For a fairly tall woman, she felt surprisingly light; it was like hefting a day-old calf.

"Em . . . stop it . . . put me down!" He felt her weakly struggling to free herself as he carried her toward the door.

"Sorry, Miss Kitty, but it's for your own good," he drawled, clumping his way around counters, carts, stacked boards of cooled ganache. Glancing back over his shoulder, he saw Louise gaping at them.

"Em, I mean it, you're really pissing me off. This . . . this . . . is ridiculous! I won't be carried out of here like a sack of potatoes! Put me down! I mean it! I have to . . ." Annie stopped struggling, and started to giggle. "God, if Hy Felder were to walk in right now . . ."

"Screw 'im." He rounded a bank of free-standing metal shelving stacked with shipping cartons. Reaching the door, Emmett tried to kick it open . . . but his boot only clunked hollowly against the metal. The door didn't budge. Why was it that in Westerns little things like turning doorknobs never seemed to enter the picture?

With a grunt, Emmett set her down in front of the door, using his body to hold her pressed against it. "Can I trust you? Or do I have to tie you up?"

"Em . . . you're crazy." She clapped her hand over her mouth to stop herself from laughing.

"Crazy about you." He pulled her hand away, and kissed her mouth, feeling her resist, then grow still and soft, the tip of her tongue lightly teasing him. She smelled good, and tasted even better, buttery and irresistible. He felt the ache in his belly deepen. She was the damndest woman . . . but he loved her. How could he walk away from her?

She drew back. "Doug and Louise . . ." she started to protest.

"They can't see us back here, and so what if they could? We're no big secret, you know."

"Okay, okay, you win." She sighed, and let her head rest against his shoulder. "But if I agree, will you promise me one thing?"

"Anything."

"That you'll stop talking like Matt Dillon. It's starting to make me nervous."

"Why's that?"

" 'Cause at the end of every *Gunsmoke* episode, there was always a showdown."

Was she worrying about the stiff competition she'd face at tomorrow's fair, or was she maybe sensing that the time had come for a showdown with him?

Minutes later, they were strolling up Washington Street toward an all-night pizzeria on West Houston. Hell, Emmett thought, maybe I should get this thing off my chest here and now, before it burns a hole right through me.

I'm thirty-six, Annie, and sick of waiting. Tired of being on hold. I make a damn nice living selling apartments and houses, and I still don't own one of my own. Like a half-ass drifter with more dreams than brains, I've been waiting for when we could buy one together. . . .

He remembered that Turtle Bay brownstone he'd had his eye on and probably could've stolen—a real wreck, but he'd imagined them fixing it up, together. And Annie had blasted it right out of the water. She wasn't ready. She loved him, she said, but if she moved in with him, she didn't know whether she could stick it out. And wouldn't moving out on him after they'd been living together for a while be worse than her not moving in in the first place? Dammit, she was right, that *would* be worse. But, Christ Almighty, couldn't she let herself believe there might be a chance of them sticking it out?

That time, a year ago now, he *had* washed his hands of her. If she couldn't make up her mind about him, he'd thought, then he'd find somebody who could.

He remembered those months without her, hardly sleeping, pains in his stomach half the time. He'd been determined to get Annie out of his system—not calling her, not seeing her, even going out of his way to avoid places where he might run into her. And then, like spring appearing suddenly one day after a winter you'd thought would never end, he'd met Elaine. As different from Annie as a wide-open daisy from a tightly furled rosebud. Softly rounded, always wearing a pretty dress and often a ribbon in her curly hair. She taught sixth grade at St. Luke's in the Village. But she wasn't driven like Annie—not consumed with her work. A real homebody, and so sweet on him, too. When he asked her to marry him, it'd taken her less than a second to say yes.

So why hadn't he gone ahead and tied the knot?

Now, looking at Annie trudging beside him, wearing a yellow raincoat tightly belted against the evening's chill, her cropped hair bristling up where the wind was blowing it, he knew why he hadn't married Elaine.

Because she wasn't Annie.

Simple as that. Elaine was good, smart, pretty, fun . . . but she wasn't the woman he wanted. So, yeah, he could kind of understand how Annie might feel about Joe Daugherty. For half her life, she'd been in love with the guy, and as far as Emmett knew, Joe and Annie had never even had the chance to give it a tumble. Emmett kind of wished they had. The great obsessed lovers, the Romeos and Juliets, were always the ones who could never quite get it together. And how the hell could he—with his gimpy foot, his snoring, his hogging the covers at night—compete with an obsession?

He'd tried. He'd tried like hell. Hoping that one day all on her own she'd come to her senses, realize that all the dumb little things they did together—reading the Sunday *Times* in bed at his place or hers, soaping each other down in the shower, then fighting over who got the last dry towel, coming home late from a movie, half-starved, and scrounging up leftovers from the refrigerator, listening to Doctor Ruth on the radio and laughing their heads off—*that* was loving, the best kind, the only kind that mattered.

But Annie, well, she was good at seeing things about other people, and business-wise, she was smart as a whip . . . but when it came to knowing what the right thing for herself was, she was as shortsighted as a cross-eyed mule.

Emmett touched her elbow. "You still nervous about to-morrow?"

"Better now." She smiled at him. "Just don't get any ideas about trying anything like that stunt again." In the glow of a street lamp, he caught the stern look she was trying to give him.

"Cross my heart."

"How come I never know if you're teasing me?"

"If I were serious right now, I'd say you belong in bed . . . preferably mine." Crossing over to Houston, he grabbed her hand and held it tightly, hoping she couldn't feel the pulse that was making his whole arm throb.

"I'm sorry, Em . . . I know I haven't been around much lately. There's just been so much going on . . . getting ready for this fair, and keeping up with all my orders, and . . ." She let out a breath that left a faint wisp of smoke in the chilly air. Then, with what appeared to be an immense effort, she squared her shoulders. "Anyway, look who's talking. You haven't exactly been lounging around these past few weeks. Did you close on that building on Mercer?"

"Not yet, but it's going to go. Just tonight, as a matter of fact, I had dinner with Haberman, the guy who's organizing the limited partnership. He's got six investors, and they're going ahead, even if they can't buy out those last few tenants."

Annie, caught in the midst of yawning, shot Emmett an apologetic look. "Sorry. I didn't get much sleep last night either."

"Working?"

"No, as a matter of fact, I was on the phone with my aunt. She's really worried about my sister."

"Laurel? She sick?"

Annie shook her head, and she looked away from him, watching a taxi that had stopped on the corner and was letting out three crewcut guys in identical black leather jackets. "Not exactly. But Dolly says she's really broken up. Joe . . . well, he's moved out . . . back to his old apartment. Laurey asked him to."

Emmett slowed his steps, feeling a need to move cautiously all of a sudden, as if he were picking his way down a stony incline.

"Didn't know they were having problems. They always seemed to get along." Emmett liked Laurel . . . and Joe, too, for that matter. And they *had* seemed pretty happy . . . so why wasn't he all that surprised to hear they might be breaking up? "I suppose it must have been building up for a while."

Emmett sensed there was more to it than what she was telling him, but he didn't press her. When it came to Joe Daugherty, he steered clear of asking too many questions.

"You think they'll work it out?"

"I don't know."

Did she mean she hadn't a clue . . . or was she hoping they *wouldn't* get back together? Emmett, thinking of Joe and Annie having a clear shot at what he, Emmett, had wanted for so long, felt his stomach wrench, sending a taste of his dinner backfiring up his throat.

"Something else is bothering you," he probed, the sound of his boots clopping against the pavement suddenly making him think of a hitchhiker heading off down some lonely highway. "Want to tell me about it?"

"The other day when I was out at Laurey's house, she was pretty upset. She seemed to think Joe was having some kind of an affair. I tried to talk her out of it, and she blew up at me. She said . . . well, she . . . she blames me for . . ." Annie's voice caught. "For a lot of things . . . and, God, I don't know, maybe she's partly right."

"Annie, whatever went wrong between them . . . that's between *them.*"

"It's not . . ." She shoved her hands deep in her pockets, and hunched forward a little. "Not as simple as you think."

"Nothing ever is."

He was thinking of Annie, how even though she sometimes held him at arm's length, her affection, her love, if you could call it that, was more solid, more sustaining to him than Elaine's utter devotion had been. And that's what had kept him going, wasn't it? What had stopped him from calling it quits, time and again. But now . . . now he was worn down.

"Annie, there's something . . ."

But before he could get the words out, before he could tell her about California, about the development in Fountain Valley, about the incredible job he'd been offered, Emmett saw that they were nearing Arturo's. A garishly-lit sign over the steamy window advertising calzones, pizza, falafel.

"What?" She half turned toward him with an expectant smile.

No, he thought, better wait. Right now, she needed to relax, and eat something—and Arturo's, in his opinion, served the best calzones in New York.

"It'll keep," he told her. "I'll tell you later."

After the fair, he thought. Tomorrow, or the next day, when she wasn't feeling so pressured. He'd explain how New York was making him feel hemmed in, and in a weird way, shut out, too—as if, in the highest-stakes real-estate game on earth, he could never be more than a bit player. And that unless she gave him the reason to do so, he couldn't see himself sticking around. Because this time, after he asked her to marry him, and she said no again, he knew he'd need to be miles and miles away from her. Or how else would he keep from turning right back around and making a damn fool of himself all over again?

C H A P T E R   3 2

Rudy pushed his way in through the plate-glass door of the Venice health club where Val worked. Glancing around the dingy reception area with its trampled puke-green pile and mildewed walls, he wondered if Val was still here, or if he'd already split for the day. Christ, what a dump. And this was what his handsome brother had sunk to, the best job he could get, teaching karate to fags in some crummy Washington Boulevard club?

It'd been six years since he'd seen or talked to Val. *Some things never change,* Rudy thought. What if Val still held a grudge against him? What if—even when he told Val why he'd come—Val just told him to fuck off?

Rudy began to feel queasy, beads of sweat pricking his forehead. It *was* a little steamy in here, but he knew that wasn't why he was sweating . . . or why his stomach was pitching. Steeling himself against a wave of dizziness that threatened to swamp him, he forced himself to concentrate on the kid behind the reception desk.

"Yeah, what can I do for you?"

Rudy stared at the pimply, overdeveloped young man sitting at a wood-grain metal desk, holding open in front of him a well-thumbed copy of *Ring* magazine.

"I'm looking for somebody," Rudy said.

"You a member?"

"Naw."

"Didn't think so."

Smart-aleck kid, needling him for his shortness, for his bulging gut that the expensive jacket he was wearing couldn't quite hide. "What the fuck makes you so sure?"

"It's just . . . I haven't seen you around before." The meatball blinked and tilted back in his chair, clearly taken aback by Rudy's acid response.

Take it easy, don't blow this before you've even gotten your foot in the door. Rudy took a deep breath, and forced a grin that felt like he was trying to wrap his lips around the grille of a Greyhound bus.

"Like I said, I'm looking for someone." He kept his voice even, smooth. "Val Carrera, I heard he works here."

"Val? Yeah, sure, he's around. I don't think he's teaching a class right now. He might be in the weight room."

Rudy started toward the doorway leading to the exercise area.

"Hey, you can't go in there 'less you're a member!" The kid was getting up. He was big . . . sucker had to be at least six-five. "I'll have to see if I can find him for you." He sounded resentful, as if Rudy was pulling him away from his real job of loafing around.

Rudy's head began to hurt. He'd wanted to just pop in on Val, get him cornered before Val knew what was coming down. Rudy suspected that if he'd gone to Val's apartment, Val would've slammed the door in his face. So he'd come here. And now this pizza-face joker could be messing up his plan.

Rudy pulled out his wallet—a lizard-skin Mark Cross with gold corners; cost almost as much as the bills inside it. Fishing out a twenty, he slipped it to the hulky kid.

"Here's a nice bookmark for you. It'll keep the pages of your magazine from getting stuck together."

Hercules had to arch backwards to cram the bill into the front pocket of his skin-tight jeans. Now, amid the raw hamburger of his face, his small dark eyes were lighting up with interest. "Val in some kinda trouble?"

Kid watched too many cop shows, so maybe slipping him that bill hadn't been such a good idea. "Naw, nothing like that. I'm just a . . . friend. I heard he might be here. Thought I'd stop by and say hi."

"Well, I'm not s'posed to let you if you don't have a card . . ." His eyes shifted nervously toward a door labelled "OFFICE." "But I guess it'd be okay this one time. Exercise room's down the hall, you can't miss it."

Rudy strolled down a dreary, mildew-smelling hallway, its green walls and ceiling a mass of cracks from the clammy moisture he could feel swamping the air about him. Poking his head into the first door on his right—a good-sized space filled with exercise bikes, rowing machines, slant-boards, Nautilus equipment—he saw half a dozen men, most of them young and muscle-bound. But no Val. Could he have slipped out without the hulk out front noticing?

"Any you guys seen Carrera?" he yelled into the whir of bicycle wheels and grunting of weight lifters.

"Try . . . steam . . . room . . ." panted a crewcut behemoth who was bench pressing what looked like about a thousand pounds. He pointed toward a doorway just beyond a row of stationary bikes.

Rudy, walking through the doorway, found himself in a small-ish, sour-smelling locker room. Rows of scarred, battleship-gray lockers with slatted wood benches between them filled the place. A dozen or so guys were dressing or undressing, some naked or with towels wrapped around their waists, others shaving or blow-drying their hair in front of a row of sinks and mirrors. On the wall to his right, Rudy could see a slab of metal with a big pull handle that looked like the door to a meat locker. A sign above it read: STEAM ROOM. He was about to make his way inside when he realized he was still fully dressed. He'd look pretty funny, wouldn't he, going in there with all his clothes on?

But, slipping down his trousers, he began to feel like may-be this wasn't such a great idea. He didn't mind so much being naked . . . but next to Val, he'd feel like a slug crawling in there, just looking to get squashed.

His heart began to hammer.

Then he reminded himself, hey, they wouldn't be alone in there. With other guys around, Val wouldn't risk getting vicious. Besides, when you got right down to it, what did he have to lose?

Grabbing a damp towel from the bench by the door, Rudy wrapped it around his pudgy waist. He hadn't put even one foot inside the steam room, and he could feel sweat rolling off him. Christ, he hated feeling so . . . so exposed.

But everything . . . Laurel . . . little Nicky . . . hinged on Val. Rudy *had* to see her, and Val was his ticket. If he could get Val to give him this one break . . . get him to talk to Laurel, just *talk* to her, for Chrissakes, that's all he was asking. Get her to see that he, Rudy, hadn't meant to hurt her. She hadn't answered any of his letters, and the dozens of times he'd called her, she'd hung up as soon as she realized it was him. He'd waited and waited . . . hoping she'd come around. But now he couldn't wait any more. If he didn't do something, then soon it might be too late. . . .

A locker door clanged shut. Rudy glanced at the big clock on the wall, and saw that it was almost three-thirty. Jesus, he'd better get moving. He had to be at the doctor's in an hour.

Pulling open the door to the steam room, Rudy was half blinded by billowing clouds. He glimpsed the edge of a bench, then a ghost-like foot, a hand. Val? He took a deep breath to calm his pounding heart, and a gout of steam clogged his lungs. He coughed, feeling as if he were choking. The heat, already almost unbearable, seemed to be growing hotter. Jesus Christ, did people do this for *fun*? He'd never before been in a steam bath, and after this hoped he'd never have to set foot inside one again.

"That you, O'Donnell?"

Val's deep voice drifted toward him, strangely muted. Rudy stiffened. Jesus, were he and Val the *only* ones in here?

Now his eyes were adjusting. Through the mist, he made out a single figure draped across the lower bench. A muscular, white-haired man, stark naked, reclining on one elbow, with one leg stretched out and the other flexed, resting on the wooden slats. Rudy's stomach lurched, and he had an urge to duck out, now, before Val recognized him.

But then his mind was filled with his last image of Laurel—standing on a freezing sidewalk, big with child, waving a mittened hand good-bye. He *had* to see her . . . just one more time. And the little boy who'd come so close, so very close to being his.

Rudy walked over to where Val was lounging.

"Hiya, Val."

Val stared, shock dawning on his sweat-sheened face. His cold black eyes fixed on Rudy like a snake's.

"Jesus Christ . . . how did you . . . what the fuck do *you* want?"

Rudy, swallowing his own anger, studied his brother. At fifty-two, an age when most men were losing their hair and letting out their suits, Val only seemed to have grown fitter, harder, more chiselled. Seeing him lounging there, wreathed in mist, tanned muscles glistening, Rudy felt smaller and uglier than he had walking in. Even Val's *dick*—for Chrissakes—it was the size of a fucking fire hose.

"I want to talk to you," he said, struggling to keep the bitterness from his voice. "Just talk, that's all."

"Yeah? Well, why is it that whenever you talk, I seem to get fucked over?"

Val sat up, planting his feet on the floor tiles, the muscles in his arms coiling, fists clenched. He was getting that *look* in his eye. Trouble.

"For Chrissakes, Val, it's been years. Haven't you punished me enough?"

"Enough? You?" Val roared. He shot to his feet, towering over Rudy like a mountain, his snowy head obscured in a cloud of mist. "You call this *punishment*? After what you did? Jesus, I oughta wring your fat little neck!" With his index finger, he jabbed Rudy in the chest.

Rudy backed up a step, dull pain burgeoning where he'd been poked, and he felt the warm kiss of tile against his backside. "Listen, I . . ."

"*You* listen to *this*."

Val's hand raked through the mist, catching Rudy across his face, a sharp open-handed blow that knocked him into the wall. As his head struck the tiles, Rudy heard a crack like an icicle snapping in two. A white flash exploded behind his eyes. A hot, coppery taste flooded his mouth, and he realized he was bleeding.

Hatred rose in Rudy, black, choking. A slap, a lousy slap. Had Val used his fist on him, Rudy could have taken that, could have written it off. A fist showed respect, at least. A slap was how you hit a woman.

Rudy let out a high, braying laugh. "Go ahead, beat the shit out of me, wring my neck. You'd be doing me a favor."

That stopped him. "What the fuck you talking about?"

"I mean I'm gonna die anyway. Might as well kick off in a steam room with my loving brother's hands wrapped around my neck." He chortled, feeling himself seized by a sort of semi-hysteria. "Hey, sounds kinda of cozy, don't you think?"

"What kinda shit are you pulling, Rudy?"

"Just the truth, which, come to think of it, *is* pretty shitty." He tapped his gut. "Cancer. The kind you don't talk about in polite company."

"You don't look sick to me."

But Rudy could see from Val's suddenly less-than-sure expression that a worm of doubt was wiggling into his pea-sized brain.

"I feel okay most of the time. Doctor gave me this stuff to

drink, radioactive Maalox or something. And pills. Painkillers. I take so many pills, I'm gonna turn into Elvis Presley."

"Well, Christ, you don't *look* like him."

They both snickered that time.

Then Val caught himself, his eyes narrowing with menace.

"I swear, Rudy, if you *are* shitting me, I'll kill you. I'll fucking wipe the floor with you."

"Okay, go ahead. But don't you want to hear what I have to say first?"

"You mean there's *more?* Jesus!"

"I didn't come here to tell you I was sick, if that's what you mean." Rudy spoke carefully, not wanting this to turn into some kind of tear-jerking reunion. "You coulda found that out reading my obituary. Hey, mind if I sit down?" With the back of his hand, he wiped away the blood that had mixed with his sweat and was running off his chin. He felt shaky. And scared. Not of Val . . . but of what lay ahead.

Val gestured toward the bench, but he remained standing.

"It's funny," Rudy began, keeping his voice light, even semi-amused, "the things that go through your head when you know you're dying. Like I was remembering the time Shirley had an attack of motherhood and took us out to Coney Island, and on the way back you got sick on the subway from all the hot dogs you ate."

"I don't remember that."

"Sure, because *I* was the one who got clobbered for it."

"How do you mean? Why you?"

"I shoulda kept a better eye on you, Shirley said, made sure you didn't eat so many. But you always were cramming too much stuff into you." He chuckled, the effort sending a thread of bile up his throat. "When it came to goodies, you could never get enough."

"Yeah? Well, what's that got to do with anything?"

"Nothing. Except, I've been thinking, I was just a kid myself, see, and there I was, supposed to be looking after you. It kinda gets to be a habit after a while, you know?" He licked his lips, which, oddly, felt dry as cardboard. "You see, when I first located Annie and Laurel, I was gonna tell you. Honest to Christ, that was my first thought. 'Cause you know I always looked out for you." He paused to let this sink in before launching into the second half of his lie. "But then Laurel told me if I ever let on to you, and you tried to get near her, Annie was going to find a way to kill you. The way she said it, well, I believed her. 'Cause I knew what she did to your head. She's one tough little piece, let me tell you."

"That bitch. I wish I'd kicked the shit out of her when I had the chance." Val lashed out with his hand, which landed this time with a wet splat against the tiles inches from Rudy's throbbing head.

"So you see, I was kinda stuck. I was looking out for you, just like I always have. Okay, so maybe I didn't handle it so perfectly. Maybe I shoulda told you. But you know how things get, they just sort of snowball, and then *wham*. Look, Val, I guess what I'm trying to say is I'm sorry."

"How come you never told me this before?"

"You wouldn't let me!"

A tug of war seemed to be taking place right on Val's face, his ingrained suspicion straining against wanting to have his smarter, richer older brother back on his side. Finally, he sank onto the bench beside Rudy. Rudy felt a bright bead of triumph rise in him.

"Yeah, well . . ." He glanced wearily at Rudy. "You really that sick, huh?"

Rudy shrugged. "I'll spare you the gory details."

"They got these clinics in Mexico . . ."

"Laetrile. Yeah, I've heard. Maybe I'll give it a shot. Anything's worth a try, I guess." He touched Val's arm. "Look, they say when you're dying your life passes before your eyes, sort of like instant replay. Only if you're jumping off a cliff, or getting knifed in the gut, there's no time to do very much, is there? So I figure I'm lucky that way . . . I've got some time to make amends. Starting with you."

"I'm touched."

The way he said it, Rudy couldn't tell whether he meant it or not. He felt himself getting faint; Rudy looked down, and saw that his legs had grown as shiny and pink as boiled shrimps. Christ, if he didn't get out of here pretty soon, he'd pass out.

"Laurel," he said, and stopped. Even saying her name, he was getting choked up. He tried to swallow, but his throat felt as if it were clamped shut. Finally, he got the words out. "I need to see her. But I don't want her to know . . . about this." He touched his stomach.

But Val, dammit, was shaking his head.

"Forget it. She'd never go for it. Why don't you just tell her you're sick? She's a soft touch . . . I mean, if she knew you were about to croak and all, she'd probably feel sorry for you and decide to let bygones be bygones."

Jesus Christ, didn't Val get it? Rudy didn't want Laurel's *pity,* for Chrissakes. What he wanted was . . . just to see her one last time, to explain.

"I've got my reasons," he said.

"Yeah, I know, you've always got your *reasons.*" Bitterness crept into Val's voice. So much for giving his dying brother a break. *Fuck you, Val, and the ass you rode in on.* But then, when had Val ever cared about anybody but himself?

"Will you do it? Talk to her?" He tried not to sound as if he were begging, but he wanted this so badly.

"I don't know," Val hedged. "Listen, I got a good thing going now, and I don't want to mess it up. She could take it the wrong way if I was to start dragging you into her life."

In other words, you don't want the well to dry up. Rudy knew that shifty-eyed look . . . goddammit, Val had been hitting Laurel up for money. He didn't have to look in Val's wallet to know that's why he was so hesitant.

Suddenly, Rudy saw the future as clearly as if it were a billboard right out there in front of him. While Val slowly dug himself deeper and deeper into a hole, he would go on borrowing money from her. And then one day, years from now, when he was a pathetic old man, broke, and too feeble or too sick to do any kind of work, then he'd *really* start sucking up. He'd push all the right buttons, get her to feel sorry for him, to take care of him. Jesus. And, he, Rudy, wouldn't be around to do a damn thing about it.

Rudy suppressed a shudder. "How much?" he growled. "How much would it take? I'll pay you."

"Jesus. What do you think? I'm some kind of lowlife what'd try and put the squeeze on his sick brother?" Val tried to look offended, but Rudy could almost smell the circuits in his brain sizzling away.

"I'm not saying that," Rudy said, suddenly tired, too tired to call him on his bullshit. "Look, think of it as . . . well, an inheritance, sort of. After I die, everything goes to Laurel and the boy. But this way, you'll be taken care of, too."

And Laurel, I hope, will be off the hook as far as you're concerned.

"Jesus, Rudy . . ."

"How does three hundred thousand sound?"

Val looked as if he was going to fall right off that bench. "You shitting me? Three hundred grand?" Through the cloud of steam, Rudy saw his brother's eyes grow wide with greedy incredulity.

" 'Course you wouldn't be getting it all in one lump. It's locked up in investments, but they throw off a nice income."

"How much?"

"Roughly? Around three thousand a month. Not a fortune, but if you stay away from the tracks and the tables, you could live pretty comfortably."

Val stood and began pacing, his soles making soft slapping sounds against the wet tiles . . . but it was clear he'd already made up his mind.

"I don't think she'd agree to see you at her house . . . she'd be nervous about you being around the boy. But when I called the other day, she told me she's going to some big shindig at the Plaza Hotel this weekend. I could call her back . . . sort of soften her up . . . then ask her to meet you in the lobby or for a drink in the bar, maybe."

"Yeah, okay. Thanks, Val." Saying the words was like spitting glass, but Rudy knew that without her father's help he'd get nowhere with Laurel.

Anyway, what did Val matter? Already, Rudy's mind was racing ahead. He was thinking about Laurel, imagining what he would say to her . . . and praying that this time she would listen. She had to. He *needed* this so much.

"You had enough?" Rudy, through the mist that now seemed to have seeped into his skull, became aware that Val was getting up and heading for the door, a towel now tucked about his waist.

He forced a chuckle that seemed to rattle in his chest like loose gravel. But he couldn't let his brother see how ill and desperate he felt. He'd rather kick the bucket right here on this floor than give Val the satisfaction.

"Yeah, let's go. Any more of this," he cracked, rising on legs as wobbly as a pair of rubber chickens, "and I'll be donating my organs to a dim sum joint instead of to science."

CHAPTER 33

Annie came to a halt in front of the building where she and Laurel had once lived. She'd been walking, lost in thought, and had no idea how she'd ended up here. The sidewalk was deserted; it had to be three or four in the morning. She stared up at the building's grimy brick façade, feeling like a sleepwalker or someone under deep hypnosis who's just been finger-snapped awake.

She remembered going to Arturo's, wolfing down two slices of pizza and half a spinach calzone, then Emmett forcing her into a cab, ordering her to go home and get some sleep. Exhausted, she'd let the cabbie take her to West Tenth, to her homey but messy apartment. She had a foggy memory of unlocking the wrought-iron gate facing the street, and making her way across the private drive shared by her carriage house and four others, nearly stumbling several times on old frost-heaved cobblestones. Then fiddling for what seemed like hours with the three keys to her door. Finally, inside, feeling her way through darkened rooms. Too tired even to switch on any lights, she must have fallen onto her bed, clothes and all. Vaguely, she recalled waking up hours later, her mouth dry, her heart pounding, feeling hot and closed in, trapped even. Dying to get out . . . get some fresh air.

Then, as if in a fog, not seeing really where she was going, walking . . . walking . . . walking.

It occurred to Annie, standing on the sidewalk in front of her old building, shivering in the too-thin suede jacket she'd absent-mindedly thrown on, that in some deep part of her she must have known all along that this was where she'd been heading.

To Joe.

She saw the lights blazing on the second floor, and somehow she wasn't surprised.

She had to see him, had to find out if Laurel was right . . . if *she* had something to do with Joe and Laurel splitting apart. God, what if it was true? Did she *want* it to be true? She brought a hand to her mouth, and before she was aware of it she was nibbling off a carefully cultivated fingernail.

She thought of Emmett, picking her up and carrying her out of the factory. That was how she felt now, as if she were being swept along by something outside herself. Now she was mounting the building's cracked stone outside step, pushing open the heavy glass door to the narrow lobby with its wainscoting of grimy tiles. Her hand went almost automatically to the button for Joe's apartment, and she jammed her thumb against it.

The intercom crackled; a distorted voice echoed in the cold stillness. Joe, but not groggy or sleep-thick. He sounded almost as if he'd been expecting her . . . or somebody.

Annie, as she climbed the stairs lit only by dim naked bulbs, felt her head begin to clear. *This is crazy,* she thought, *I shouldn't be here. I'll probably only make things worse for Laurel.*

She thought of Emmett, of how she had felt last year when they'd been apart—not devastated to the point where she couldn't get up out of bed, but . . . empty, like a house of bare rooms, its furniture gone, its busy, noisy family moved away. Until he'd gone off, she hadn't quite known how intensely she cared for him, how entwined their lives had become. But that final step—a ring, a lifetime commitment—she just hadn't been able to. She'd wanted to . . . she still did . . . but something was holding her back. Some maze inside herself she had to find her way through first. Was she here because it was Joe who could show her the way?

Nearing the top of the stairs, she saw him waiting on the landing, standing in front of his open door, the light at his back. A tall man with rumpled brown hair, his long shadow angling across the landing and halfway up the wall across from him. He was wearing a pair of faded chinos, and an old crewneck sweater, its sleeves pushed up over his elbows. His feet were bare, as if he hadn't noticed how cold it was, or didn't care.

She kissed his cheek, which felt like ice. She felt as if she were under water moving very slowly, yet her heart was beating fast. Now she was swimming past him, through his open door and down his narrow, dimly lit vestibule, into the bright living room.

Turning, she saw Joe standing in front of her, looking mildly baffled, as if he hadn't quite decided whether she was real, or if he was *dreaming* that she had just floated in.

"Annie. Jesus. What the hell are you doing here?" He rubbed his face with his hand. The skin along his jaw looked raw and blotchy.

"Would you believe I just happened to be in the neighborhood? I saw your lights, and thought you could use some company."

"At four in the morning?"

"I couldn't sleep."

"Yeah . . . me too."

"Can I sit down?"

"Oh . . . sure." He blinked, shaking his head as if to clear it. "Coffee? I made enough to keep the whole city wired."

"No thanks." She looked around. Years since she'd been here, but it was exactly the way she remembered it—the polyurethaned wood floor with its lone Navajo rug, whitewashed brick walls, the monkish Stickley couch and chairs. On the coffee table, she spotted an old *Newsweek* with Elvis on its cover—three or four years since Elvis's death, and Joe hadn't thrown it out. God, this place was a museum . . . like going back into history, *her* history; everything she looked at held a memory, a dozen memories.

"It's strange," she said, "being here again. Seeing you in this place. It's like you never moved out."

"It doesn't feel that way." He looked about him, as if he half expected to discover he'd wandered into the wrong place by mistake. "Somehow, living here again, it just doesn't fit. It feels like I'm trying to cram myself into something I've outgrown."

Annie touched his forearm. "Joe . . . what's going on with you and Laurey? The other day when I was out there, she seemed pretty upset. But I never thought . . ."

"What did she say?"

"She seemed to think . . . well, that maybe you were having an affair. She'd seen you with that woman at the restaurant—that counselor. But when I told her she had it all wrong, she . . . she got really angry. Said a lot of crazy things I'm sure she couldn't have meant. About me . . . and you."

"Maybe they're not so crazy. Maybe *we're* the ones who are."

He was looking at their reflections in the darkened window, wearing an odd, distant expression. He wasn't wearing his glasses, she saw. Without them, he looked somehow naked, vulnerable as a little boy. The skin around his eyes was pink as if he'd been rubbing there. Heartbreaker eyes. "Ever listened to silence?" he went on in a soft voice, almost as if he were talking to himself. "I mean *really* listened? No music, no TV, no white noise even. You can hear your heart beating. It's scary. You start thinking it could just . . . stop. Like a watch winding down to nothing." He stopped, half turning, for the first time seeming really to see her. And she, too, was seeing him more clearly than she had in years and years. He looked haggard, yes, but his face, those features that when he was younger hadn't appear to mesh, now had grown into one another, seams connecting, angles not so sharp.

Laurel had done that for him, Annie thought. Maybe those first few years Joe hadn't been wildly in love with her . . . but Laurel had given him something that maybe she couldn't have. A home, a family, a place safe from the pressures and turmoil of running a business. So why, now, was it all falling apart?

"Jesus, listen to me," Joe said, shaking his head as if to clear it. "I must be getting morbid in my old age. Either that, or I've had one too many coffees."

"Have you talked to Laurel? I've been trying to reach her, but I keep getting a busy signal. I think she's leaving the phone off the hook."

He sighed. "She won't talk to me, either. Just gets Adam to call." He pushed his palms over his forehead, flattening his hair against his skull then releasing it. "Christ. You don't know what that's like, telling your kid you don't know when you're coming home."

Suddenly, Annie felt weak, as if she couldn't trust her legs to support her. She sank onto the hard leather sofa, her heart leaping with shallow bounds inside her.

"Joe, are you saying that . . . You and Laurey aren't thinking of . . ."

"Divorce?" He stared at her, his eyes bleak and raw-looking, his jaw clenching. "Jesus, no, not that. Laurey just wants some time. Alone. To think. See where we're headed." His mouth twisted in a bitter smile. "Euphemisms. What she's really saying is, 'You let me down, you son of a bitch.'"

Maybe you did. But I'm partly to blame, too.

Outwardly, she had let go of Joe, but not in her heart. There, she had held fast to her love, secretly tending it, shielding it like a flickering candle that might otherwise blow out. Using it to keep Emmett at arm's length . . . and maybe using it, too, to punish Laurel for taking Joe away from her.

But if that were true, she hadn't meant to.

"Laurel's just hurt. She'll get over it." Annie spoke rapidly, wanting to get the words out so she could hear them and maybe even believe them.

"No . . . it's more than that." Joe sank onto the sofa beside her, his forearms resting on his knees, his head drooping forward. She could see the soft hairs on the nape of his neck, like Adam's baby hair. She fought the impulse to reach out and stroke him there. "She's . . . different. I married a kid. Now that kid is grown up. She loves me, but she doesn't really *need* me anymore, not the way she used to. And that's okay . . . but, you see, the thing is . . . *I need her.*" His voice choked on the last words.

"What are you going to do?"

"Thought I'd write her a letter." He gestured toward a legal pad with some words scribbled on it and a few wads of balled-up paper littering the coffee table.

"What are you going to write?"

"That I love her."

"She must know that."

"She does. At least, I hope she does."

"Then *why?* Why all this?"

"Because she knows she's not the only one. She knows how I feel about you."

Annie heard the creak of footsteps from the floor above. Outside, on the windowsill, a pigeon cooed, making her wonder if morning was near. She felt cold deep in her bones. And her own heart —what if, like a watch, it slowly ran down?

"We haven't done anything wrong," she said, feeling like a stupid child in school not knowing what to say, how to answer.

Joe let his breath out between his teeth with a whistling noise.

"Christ, sometimes I think *everything* we've done was wrong. All our pretending."

She wanted to cover her ears, shut out his voice. At the same time, she felt a quickening inside her, a spreading warmth.

"No!" she cried. "It wasn't like that. I wanted . . . *honestly* wanted you and Laurey to be happy."

In her mind now she was stepping back, examining her words like a careful shopper inspecting an item of clothing for stains and snags, a loose button, a torn seam. She relaxed a little. Yes, she'd told the truth. Of course, she'd wanted her sister to be happy, for her marriage to be good. Of course.

"So did I." Joe pressed his thumbs against his closed eyelids. "So did I."

"Tell her that. Tell her . . ."

Joe looked up at her, the pain in his eyes unbearable. God, how could he stand it? And she, could *she*?

"Sometimes I think," he began slowly, his eyes fixed on her face, "that if we'd only made love, you and I. Just once. Then I wouldn't have felt so . . . cheated."

Silence seemed to be swallowing them. There was only the throaty murmuring of a pigeon outside the window. The steady ticking of the radiator as it cooled.

"Do you want to make love with me now?" The question slipped out of her before she realized she was saying it. She sat back, shocked, breathless, her heart galloping.

Yet she also felt strangely calm, as if she were dipping into a wooded pond, deep and cool, shimmering darkly with her reflection. She'd travelled forever to get here, and maybe now the journey would be over. Wasn't this what she'd come here for? To quench a desire so old it had become part of her, her bones, her flesh? When she was with Joe, her desire for him was at the edge of every sentence, at the heart of every thought. And yet always she was holding herself back, taking care to fashion each word, each touch, each public kiss, in exquisite miniature. Always circumspect, within the bounds of sisterliness.

Joe stared at her, his eyes holding her with the tenderness of an embrace. His eyes in this light more brown than green. What a lovely color. How could anyone think brown was dull? Joe's eyes were the color of the earth, of the ages. Even the tiny fretwork of lines fanning out from the corners of his eyes—they moved her, made her want to hold him.

With a jerking motion that startled her, he stood up, not touching her, not even looking back at her as he walked out of the room.

Annie, as if in a trance, followed him.

Joe's bedroom was smaller than she remembered it, with one tall window looking out over a tiny yard, lit by a yellow bulb that spilled a waxy light over low evergreens and a patch of half-dead impatiens left from summer. The room was dark except for the glow from the yard, giving everything an oddly stark look, as if this were a black-and-white movie. One that had no beginning or ending . . . only what was here, now.

Joe said nothing while she undressed, his dark eyes fixed on her, unreadable. Then he pulled off his sweater, and stood before her wearing only his chinos, his long torso stippled by the shadow of an ailanthus tree that was moving so that it seemed to be breathing along with him.

An image of Laurel edged its way into her mind, but she blocked it out. *This belongs to me,* she told herself fiercely. *To us. Laurey will never know.*

She watched him take off the rest of his clothes.

Annie was shivering, but not from cold. It was the sight of Joe, naked and beautiful—a tall, gleaming blade of a man. His face seemingly composed of nothing more than shadow and light.

They stood before one another, naked, not touching. Yet Annie felt as if she were gripped in an electrical field, the air around her charged with static, sparking against her bare skin, down into the roots of her hair. She half-saw tiny faraway stars glimmering just at the edge of her field of vision. There was a high humming inside her head. She felt scared, weak and trembly, barely able to stand.

If she didn't back away from him now . . . quickly . . . she'd be swept away. She might never stop.

But if a speeding train had been thundering right at her, Annie could not have moved.

Joe began to touch her. Her hair, her face, his fingertips brushing lightly over eyelids, nose, lips, ears. Gentle strokes that soothed and excited her at the same time. It was as if he were mapping her out, memorizing her. They were joined at so many points, it was strange to realize how much there was still to discover. A universe.

Smooth palms cool one instant, almost fiery the next, sliding, sliding down neck, shoulders, arms. Now cupping her breasts, him leaning down to kiss each one. She grew faint, pinpricks of blue light dancing behind her eyelids.

"Oh, God . . . Joe."

He shuddered, making a noise low in his throat, halfway between a sigh and a moan. He drew her to him, letting her feel his own excitement, his heat. Finally, he kissed her. No, not just a kiss . . . it was more, oh, so much more. Had he entered her at that moment, she didn't think she could have felt more exhilaration than she did now. Bright heat filled her, made her feel that she glowed and shimmered. God, how could she have denied this for so long? How could he?

She touched him. There . . . and there. Oh, he was beautiful. She loved the economy of him—there was nothing extra, nothing that didn't fit perfectly with the rest of him. Long bones, muscles like a cat's. Hard shanks shaped like shallow spoons. And here, where she was touching him now . . . narrow and smooth . . . a bead of moisture at the tip, warm and sticky.

The room swayed, tilted. Now she was lying on the bed, Joe kneeling over her. He kissed her breasts, her navel . . . and below. Annie cried out, the tender shock of his mouth taking away her breath, so acute it was almost agonizing. She grasped his head, the heels of her hands pressing against his temples, where she could feel a pulse jumping.

She began to cry, silently, tears running from the corners of her eyes into her hair. She wanted him . . . oh, she wanted him . . . but she didn't want this to end, either. She longed for this to go on forever.

But at the same time she was straining toward some higher, finer point. She could hear it in the quickening of her breath and Joe's. She could feel it intensifying, blossoming at every pulse point—wrists, throat, temples. She was swollen with it, and wet.

Now.

"In you," he gasped. "Feel it. Feel me. So good. Annie. Your name. God, I love your name. Annie, Annie, Annie. Oh, Jesus, I'm coming . . ."

"Yes," she cried.

There was a searing rush, white, blinding, sweeter than anything she had ever felt. *Yes . . . oh yes . . .*

Lying there afterwards, both exhausted and exquisitely sensitized, Annie thought, *Can I let go of this? Is it possible to let go and still go on living?*

Yet even if she did let go of him, Annie had a feeling that she would not walk away unchanged. She felt as if, yes, a circle inside her had finally closed. Though imagining a life without Joe had always been an agony to her, she felt strangely at peace.

The world began to trickle in. Muted voices drifting up from below, a toilet flushing in the apartment overhead. Outside, the plaintive mewing of a cat, the rattle of a garbage can. In the distance, a siren wailed.

Morning.

She turned to Joe, who lay curled by her side, one long leg hooked over hers, an arm looped about her middle.

"I love you." The words came easily, like a line she'd rehearsed countless times inside her head.

Joe brushed a tendril of hair from her cheek—she'd cut her hair just last week, shorter than before, a shiny dark-brown wedge that fit her head like a cloche. Now she wished she'd let it grow long, that she had wavy waist-length tresses Joe could wind about his fingers and bury his face in.

But he wasn't looking at her hair; his soft brown eyes were fixed on her face. "Thank you," he murmured. "For that. For you."

"It was easier than it ought to have been."

"Don't say that." He placed a finger lightly against her lips. "I can't feel guilty. Maybe I should . . . I don't know. But it seems like in trying to be honorable and upright we've both done more harm than good."

"Joe . . . do you think if we had . . ." She tried to sit up, but Joe held her gently pinned.

"Annie, it's just us . . . the two of us here right now in this bed. I don't know what's going to happen tomorrow or the next day, or next year. But right now, I know one thing—I love you."

The image of Laurel flickered, then died. Tomorrow, she would face it. The guilt, too. Couldn't this one moment be hers?

"Again, Joe," she whispered, holding him tightly. "Make love to me again."

But even when he was once more inside her, she could feel it —the moment passing, far too quickly, falling away from her even as she clutched it to her, as if she were drinking from a cup with a hole in the bottom, trying desperately to quench her thirst before all the water trickled away.

CHAPTER 34

D olly swept into the reception area outside the ballroom, and was enveloped at once in a haze of cigarette smoke. So many people! The narrow, high-ceilinged room was jammed—tuxedoed men, gowned women in fluttery silk, stiff brocade, glittering sequins, all standing together in clusters, arms now and then reaching out to lift a glass of champagne or a canapé from silver trays proffered by maroon-jacketed waiters. Every crimson-upholstered chair, she saw, was occupied, and the potted palms and tables with their shirred, rose-shaded lamps had been pushed against the wall to make more room.

A chamber quartet, only barely audible, was fiddling away in a corner under a gilt sconce. They made her think of mechanical figures atop an elaborate music box. Looking at the lovely mirrored doors, the gilt moldings along the ceiling and on the walls, she found herself remembering other years, other chocolate fairs, when she and Henri had held hands under the dinner table, almost counting the minutes until they could go back to her apartment and snuggle up.

She felt an ache in her chest, and brought her hand to her bosom above the scooped neck of her emerald satin gown. A little dizzy, too, she felt herself teeter on her five-inch heels as if she were attempting to balance on a precarious ledge. She grabbed hold of the large sapphire pendant nestled in the cleft of her bosom as if to steady herself.

Henri. Damn it, where was he? He *had* said he'd be here, hadn't he? But the message on her answering machine had been so garbled, so much background noise. He'd been calling from Charles de Gaulle, that part was clear . . . his plane leaving in minutes . . . and he'd said he'd be in New York for the fair. And—at this point, her heart had taken a plunge into ice water—he'd said he needed to speak with her about something very important. . . .

She'd made herself wait until late this afternoon before trying to reach him at the Regency, where he always stayed. Yes, Mr. Baptiste had reserved, she was told; but, no, not checked in yet. She'd left a message, but he hadn't called. Could something have happened to his plane? And, what, dear Lord, could his cryptic message have meant?

Dolly closed her eyes. *Am I losing my marbles? . . . Or maybe it's the change I'm going through, and it's getting me all muddled. But I just can't stop imagining that Henri's needing to talk to me is more than just business. And if I don't get that dumb notion right out of my head, before he walks in, I just know I'm gonna make an awful fool of myself. . . .*

She thought back. It had been four years since Henri had come to New York for the *Gourmand* fair—usually he sent Pompeau, along with Maurice or Thierry. So why was he coming this year?

Funeral, was that a word she'd really heard in all that static? Could old Girod have died? And if he had, did that mean Henri finally was free?

No, more likely Henri had come with bad news. What if Francine had won—and she was going to force Dolly out? Yeah, that'd be big enough for Henri to fly here to tell her himself. Dolly felt a shortness of breath.

She *had* to find Henri. She had to *know*.

Dolly brushed past a waiter extending toward her a tray of tulip glasses fizzing with champagne. Rocking onto the toes of her emerald-satin pumps, she strained to see above the sea of heads. But no Henri. Her eyes blurred with tears.

She blinked, her vision clearing. Now she began to spot familiar faces. Over by the bar, chatting it up like the dearest of chums, were the heads of the two biggest Belgian chocolate houses—Kron and Neuhaus. Rivals, each probably wished a chandelier would fall on the other's display. On the other side of the room, Dolly spied a tall, well-built man with curly graying hair, Teddy McCloud, an old friend from Perugina. She blew him a kiss, and he tipped her a wink. And near the table where dinner seat assignments were being handed out, that slim bespectacled man nibbling on a prawn, wasn't that Robert Linxe from La Maison du Chocolat? She recognized, too, Maurice Bernachon and Maurice's son, Jean-Jacques, and Marie Biard of Debauve & Gallais.

There were others whose faces she recognized, but whose

names had slipped her mind. That heavyset fellow from Charleston
Chocolates, supposedly Elizabeth Taylor's favorites. The blond lady
from Li-Lac. A handsome, florid-faced man from Leonides.

But where in blazes was Henri?

The thought struck her: Maybe he was inside, checking on
Girod's display.

Dolly was making her way toward the mirrored doors that
opened onto the ballroom, when she saw someone trying to wave
her over. An imposing blond fellow straight out of a Wagner opera,
smoking a thin brown cigarette—she'd forgotten his name, recalling
only that he was somehow connected with Tobler-Suchard. She
waved back, but kept moving.

Entering the ballroom, which was quiet and devoid of people
except for hotel staff putting finishing touches on the tables and
Gourmand judges scribbling notes about the displays. Later, while
dinner was being served, the judges would sample and evaluate the
edible entries. In the truffle and bonbon category, flair and flavor
counted heavily, she knew, but the quality of the chocolate itself
was equally, if not more, important. Chocolate was judged on various
criteria—"presentation," which meant the chocolate should have an
even, glossy surface; "snap," or in other words, whether it broke
apart easily, without splintering or folding down into waxy sludge;
"mouth feel," or texture . . . not gritty or overly moist; "taste," to
determine sweetness, percentage of chocolate liquor, and bouquet.

Dolly, satisfied that Girod's chocolates were up to snuff, paused
under the long marble-columned arcade that bordered the dining
area. Waiters swept past her along the passageway, holding empty
canapé trays, disappearing through double doors to the kitchen, and
reappearing minutes later with freshly laden ones.

Beyond the marble pillars, she could see the main ballroom, lit
by two enormous crystal chandeliers—its cream-colored walls edged
in gold, and its vaulted ceiling adorned with cameo-like oval paintings
of pastoral scenes surrounded by filigreelike moldings. At one end,
there was a stage framed in great swags of rose-colored velvet; and
along the wall opposite her, four raised, arched coves resembling
small opera boxes. Clusters of tables, each with a pale-pink damask
cloth and an arrangement of freesias and baby pink roses, were
arranged about the main floor.

She thought back to this morning when she'd been helping

Pompeau set up their display. The whole place a buzzing beehive, Teamsters lugging in cartons of all sizes, hotel staff arranging the dinner tables, chocolatiers in chef's whites carefully uncrating their fragile creations, putting together their displays on the long white-clothed tables set in front of the stage, applying the finishing touches to their chocolate masterpieces.

Now everything was complete and in place, and it all looked so exquisite, such a triumph of human ingenuity and artistry, that Dolly could only stare, spellbound.

Each display was set slightly apart, and on a small gold card was the name of the chocolatier it represented. Silver trays with elaborate arrangements of truffles and chocolate creams; luscious cakes and tortes and cookies displayed as if they were jewels in Cartier's window; an enormous Georgian-style punch bowl made of chocolate and piled with strawberries, each of which had been dipped half in white chocolate, half in dark.

She saw a chess set—its board and carved pieces made entirely of dark and white chocolate. Next to it, a chocolate replica of a Spanish galleon, complete with a life-sized ship's log, spyglass, and bag of gold-foil-wrapped "doubloons." She smiled at the sight of a toy train set made of chocolate, each open car piled with molded chocolate creams in the shapes of toy soldiers, dolls, alphabet blocks. Propped on an easel behind it, a jigsaw puzzle of a village scene, dark chocolate painted on white. Beside it, an amazing copy of the Mona Lisa, on a white chocolate "canvas," done with paint that, she knew, was made from cocoa powder mixed with coffee extract. Its elaborately carved frame was also made of chocolate, and decorated with bits of gold leaf.

There was a miniature log cabin, rough-hewn logs dusted with cocoa powder, a tiny stone well in front fashioned from chunks of broken chocolate. An eagle carved from a huge block of dark chocolate, delicately scored, its face and leg feathers painted with white chocolate, so lifelike that it appeared on the verge of taking flight.

In the center of the big table, she saw something that made her clap her hands and laugh out loud—a dollhouse-sized fairy castle made out of chocolate puff pastry, crenellated walls, towers, turrets and all, surrounded by a moat of whipped cream. A man holding a camera stood nearby, and she watched a white-jacketed chef carefully lift the roof off the castle keep so the photographer could snap the inside—a silken cloud of coffee-colored cream studded with fresh raspberries and toasted hazelnuts. Dolly's mouth watered.

Then she saw the tree.

It was the centerpiece of Tout de Suite's display, set atop a low pedestal on one of the long tables, ringed by exquisite-looking cakes on rustic wooden plates, and truffles spilling from baskets made of chocolate twigs. A "picnic"—how clever of Annie! Walking over for a closer look, she saw that the trunk and branches of the tree were molded from the darkest bittersweet, studded with crushed nuts and feathered with a sharp knife to give it the look of rough bark. The leaves were so delicate they almost seemed to rustle in the drafts from the air-conditioner vents. And, suspended from its branches on slender gold threads, dozens of small, exquisite marzipan pears.

A triumph—and Annie, her own Annie, had made it. Dolly felt pride welling up in her. She remembered her niece calling her the other day, and telling her about the tree, how complicated it was to make. But this . . . why, it was beyond anything Dolly had imagined. And sure to knock the socks off the judges.

First prize. Annie had said she had to win, and Dolly now felt sure she'd get it. That girl had her mother's fire, all right, but none of Evie's fragility. If only she could see her way to marrying that darling man of hers. Emmett was pure gold, and Annie just couldn't see it. Dolly itched to grab her and tell her, Get him, tie him down, before it's too late, before he gets away.

But who am I to be handing out advice about men?

Her mind turning back to Henri, she inspected Girod's display, an array of small tortes, bonbons and truffles, set at varying heights like a garden in bloom. Would Henri approve? It certainly wasn't the most eye-catching display, but then Girod's could afford the quiet confidence that came with being at the top. Still, Dolly fretted. Had the chocolate marquise risen enough? And could Pompeau have possibly missed that tiny crack in the *boule de neige*'s bittersweet glaze? Oh, but the St. Honoré au chocolat, how perfect! A ring of caramel-glazed puffs filled with chocolate pastry cream, floating on a cloud of mocha whipped cream set in a crisp pâté brisée shell. *Henri will be pleased.* . . .

Then she saw that in the middle of their display an area the size of a serving platter had been cleared—as if at the last minute

Pompeau had decided to make room for an addition. But what? She'd gone over and over each item with him, down to the last sliver of candied ginger, and if he'd wanted to include something else, wouldn't he have said so? Unless. . . .

Dolly buttonholed a judge she knew, Clark Nevelson, who was busy jotting notes on a steno pad. "Do you know Monsieur Baptiste from Girod's? Have you seen him?"

Nevelson, tall, thin, but with a sagging paunch that gave him the shape of a kangaroo, was editor-in-chief of *Gourmand* and probably knew everyone here. "Henri? Sure, saw him just a few minutes ago. He's in the kitchen working on something or other."

He's here. Dolly's heart was thumping, and all of a sudden the room turned warm. What could he be up to?

Nevelson, she could see, was staring at her cleavage, almost like someone poised on the edge of a pool contemplating diving in.

Dolly, secretly pleased that The Knockers That Ate Cleveland still had what it took, pretended she didn't notice.

"Thanks," she told him, hurrying off toward the kitchen.

But at that moment, the doors to the reception area were thrown open, and the crowd began pouring in. Dolly found her path blocked by three tuxedoed men and a fat woman in a brocade gown. Swearing under her breath, she circled around them. But now it was getting to be like rush hour in the Times Square subway station.

Edging past a man who'd clearly drunk more than his share (why was it, she wondered, that a man in a tuxedo could get stinko and still seem as elegant as Cary Grant, while a boozer in blue jeans and a John Deere cap just wound up looking disgusting?), she spotted Annie by one of the red marble pillars.

Her niece was deep in conversation with an older man, stocky, florid-faced, gray crewcut. Hyman Felder—Dolly recognized him from either *BusinessWeek* or *Forbes*. Annie was wearing a full-length velvet dress the color of hammered copper, and cut like something Marlene Dietrich might have worn in *Blue Angel*. Each time she gestured, or leaned forward to make a point, the dress subtly shifted in hue, shimmering like something on fire. Her olive skin glowed, and her smooth wedge of brown hair gave off winking highlights. Long dagger-shaped earrings, made of gold, swung from her ears.

Yet Dolly could see the tension knotting Annie's shoulders, the sharp tilt of her head as she listened to something Felder was saying. Winning first prize—and getting that contract from Felder—meant so much to her. *Please, let her win.* . . .

For Girod's, coming in second, or even fifth, wouldn't be the end of the world. Their reputation was firmly established, and nothing would be lost if they didn't win first prize. But Tout de Suite, Dolly knew, needed it merely to stay afloat.

If only there was some way I could convince Felder myself. She was angling her way over, fixing to give old Felder a dose of charm, and maybe a good look at her cleavage, when a tuxedoed man up on stage spoke into the microphone, "Please . . . everyone find your seats. Dinner is being served."

Dolly felt a rush of dismay. Now she'd have to wait, and just hope that Henri was going to be at her table. . . .

Then it struck her that she hadn't seen Laurel, either. Her niece had said she might be a little late, but here it was, after eight, and still no sign of her. Had she changed her mind about coming? Could the prospect of seeing Joe here have scared her off? If so, it'd be ironic, since as far as Dolly knew, Joe hadn't showed up either.

Dolly felt an arm slip about her waist, and she whirled about, her heart bumping up into her throat. Henri? But, no, it was only her old friend, Seth Hathaway, president of the Confectioners' Association.

"Dolly!" he cried, his Staffordshire-mug face with its network of ruddy veins swimming into focus. "Where have you been hiding yourself?"

"Right in front of your nose," she parried.

He peered at the seating card she was holding. "Just my luck, we're at the same table." With courtly solemnity and a twinkle in his eye, he offered her his arm. "May I have the honor of escorting the prettiest lady in this room to her seat?"

Dolly allowed him to lead her over to their table, smiling broadly to keep from gritting her teeth in frustration, her heart hammering like a steam-driven piston.

Henri . . . where the devil are you?

"You've got guts," Felder said. "Taking a chance on something so risky, a chocolate tree, who would have thought?" He shook his head admiringly.

"Taking chances is what it's all about, right?" She sipped her champagne, sneaking glances at Felder while trying to look relaxed. Inside, she felt as nervous as a caged cat. *What if he thinks I'm too showy, that I'm pushing too hard?*

But her display was more than just show—her stuff, she knew, tasted heavenly, especially the *aveline* torte, her favorite. She could see it out of the corner of her eye, incongruously elegant against the backdrop of checked picnic blanket—layers of rum-soaked chocolate génoise and chocolate-hazelnut cream, covered in a bittersweet glaze thin as ice on a windowpane, flecked with gold leaf and tied with a crimson "satin" ribbon made of candied raspberry syrup. One bite, and any normal person was hooked.

But what if the five judges—among them Nan Weatherby from *Metropolitan* and that new dessert columnist for *Gourmand*—didn't like rum or hazelnut cream? Where did she get off thinking she could win over Manon, or Teuscher, or Neuchatel? Just coming in second or third would be a triumph of sorts, except that would leave her exactly where she was at this minute with Felder: nowhere.

I *have* to make this work, she thought. Somehow, I have to convince him that even if I don't win, he should make this deal with me. Maybe if I turn on the charm over dinner, before the prizes are announced.

Then if she *did* take first, he'd think he was a genius for sewing her up before anyone else did.

Suddenly Annie felt she didn't want to smile any more, talk any more, be here in this crowd. She hadn't slept at all last night, and felt as if she were running on empty. Part of her was listening to what Felder was saying, another part of her was drifting.

Images of last night with Joe flitted through her head like grainy frames from a worn-out movie print. Joe's face poised over hers in the milky early morning light; their bodies a fretwork of tangled arms, legs, sheets. As if it had happened years and years ago. Not the beginning of a love affair, she realized. More like something remote, from another era.

Was that what it had been . . . a good-bye?

She felt a sweet sorrow rinse through her.

They probably had both known it was the end, which had to be why they'd felt no need even to say the words. Now, no matter what happened with Laurel, she and Joe would never be to each other more than what they'd always been—friends who had loved one another; lovers who loved others better.

She felt sad, but somehow complete . . . as if she'd come to the end of a long journey, and had found, if not what she was looking for, then at least a place where she could rest.

Across the crowded esplanade, she caught sight of Emmett— he was standing near the mirrored doors, talking to a group of Belgians. She felt a wobbling sensation inside her chest, like a top running down. She ought to be with Emmett right now, working things out with him, not Felder. She remembered arriving home from Joe's early this morning, and finding that strange note Emmett had left on her kitchen table: "Hope you found what you're looking for."

What did that mean? Had he guessed, or found out somehow, that she was with Joe last night? She'd been frantically busy all day, and had gotten here early tonight—more than an hour ahead of Emmett—to check on her display, so she hadn't yet had a chance to talk to him. Now, she felt a sudden intense need to be with him, to find out what he'd meant.

He hadn't approached her in the reception area. But now, catching her eye, he began working his way over to her. And he wasn't smiling.

With great effort, Annie pulled her attention back to Felder.

". . . California, that'll be a first for me," he was saying. "Upscale malls, one in Pasadena, and one in Century City, each one built around a Felder's, real class—you know the kind, with indoor waterfalls and a lot of ferns and music piped in. And none of that Muzak crap, I'm talking Mose-art . . ."

Annie, straining to appear interested, started to ask what kind of financing he'd assembled for these malls. But all of a sudden she felt Emmett's solid presence at her back.

"Promise you'll sit next to me during dinner so I can hear every detail," she said, touching his arm lightly and giving him her brightest smile. "Would you excuse me a moment? I see someone I must talk to."

Felder bobbed his head, dismissing her with a genial wave of his blunt hand, which sported a diamond pinkie ring. "Sure, sure. You go ahead."

Annie turned, and was treated to a close-up view of Emmett

in a dark blue tuxedo with a shirred-silk shirt, and a bolo tie fastened
with a polished agate. His blue eyes fastened on her with an odd
intensity.

"Annie," he said, still not smiling. "May I talk to you? Alone?"

She nodded, her heart plunging with a sharp, downward twist.
Something is wrong. Very wrong.

Now Emmett was guiding her swiftly through the mirrored
double doors into the reception area, where only a few stragglers
lingered. He moved with long, loping strides, hardly limping at all.
Just beyond the coatroom, where the corridor branched off into a
small waiting area outside the restrooms, he stopped.

As he turned to face her, his blue eyes fixed on her, as cool and
flat as two stones at the bottom of a creekbed. Why was he looking
at her that way? And why was it suddenly so cold in here?

Annie felt scared. She longed desperately for Emmett to put
his arms around her, hug her, love her, tease her, even scold her.
Anything but that hard, determined look on his face—the look of a
man whose mind is made up.

He knows, she thought. *Somehow he knows where I was last night . . .
and how can I tell him it's all over between Joe and me without telling him
everything that happened?*

There was so much she wanted to tell him . . . things that
should have been said years ago . . . but, oh God, that look . . .

*Em . . . I've been so stupid not to see what I had in front of me all
this time. I took you for granted. I thought you'd always be there. I didn't
know how much you meant to me any more than I thought about breathing
or eating or sleeping. . . .*

*But I see it now . . . and if you'll give me just one more chance, I'll
make it all up to you. . . .*

"Annie—"

"Em, I know what you're going to say," she broke in, as breathless almost as if she'd run a mile to catch up with him, her heart
banging against her rib cage. "Please, don't say it. Not yet. We'll
talk later, when we get home . . . when all this is over."

"It *is* over. This. Us. I've had enough." She heard no anger in
his voice, only sorrow and regret. "Look, I'm not blaming you. I
knew what I was getting into, and like a dumb rodeo cowboy I
figured the guy who stays on the bronco's back longer than anyone
is the one who wins. In life, though, I guess nothing's that simple."

She watched his lips move, and remembered when she had found his freckled lips fascinating and strange. But sexy, too. She wanted Emmett. She wanted him as eagerly and hungrily now as she had wanted Joe the night before.

"I love you," she told him, and for the first time she knew that she meant it.

His blue eyes, flickering like neon, cut into her. "I was worried about you last night after I left you . . . you looked so damn beat. I didn't want to wake you by calling, so this morning I stopped by to check up on you. Five o'clock, and you weren't home . . . so I called the factory, I even called Louise at home, woke her up. She said you weren't due to get there until six-thirty. And then I remembered about Joe. Is that where you went last night . . . to him?" His big hands, she saw, were clenching and unclenching at his sides. "No . . . don't answer that. I don't want to know. Or let's just say I don't want to hear it." He brought a fist up in a swift, furious arc that stopped short of her. Tenderly, with his knotted white knuckles, he brushed her cheek.

Annie wanted to tell him he was wrong, that she loved *him* . . . but how could she explain?

Emmett shook his head, spreading his big hands in a gesture of hopelessness. "I realized something last night. I always thought of love as something infinite, like the stars, or God. But it's not, you know. You can run out of love just like a car running out of gas. Or a tire that just gets worn out after so many miles of bumpy roads. I'm tired, Annie. I've got nothing left."

Annie felt stunned, as if she'd taken a dive into water that was too shallow. She hurt everywhere, her chest, her head, her stomach. Tears rose in her eyes, and began spilling down her cheeks. She had to make him understand. She had to make him *know* how much she wanted him . . . now . . . and tomorrow . . . and forever.

"Em . . ." Her voice cracked, and then faded on her lips. She wanted to beg him, but something held her back. She realized that if only she could, maybe her whole life would've turned out differently . . . but she was stuck with her stiff spine just as Emmett was with his crippled foot.

"Anyway," he went on, "I wanted to let you know I'm not sticking around for the banquet. I really just came to say good-bye."

"Dressed in a tux?" She managed a wobbly smile through her tears.

One corner of his wide, freckled mouth tipped up in a smile. "Couldn't ride off into the sunset looking like a deadbeat, now could I?"

Ride off? "Are you going somewhere?"

He shrugged. "I'm pulling up stakes here. Moving out west." He grinned, a flash of white against the freckled brown of his broad face. "Jesus, there I go sounding like Matt Dillon again."

"Matt Dillon didn't make a living selling real estate." She sniffed hard, and pushed her tears away with the heel of her hand, angry at herself, angry at him. It was wrong. He had no right to go. It wasn't fair, everyone she loved leaving her. "I don't want you to go . . . you know that, don't you?"

Emmett looked at her a long time, and for a moment—a flicker of his eye, a shadow passing over his face—she thought he just might change his mind. Then he kissed her lightly and said, "There's a difference between not wanting someone to go, and wanting them to stay."

For a long moment, he lingered, and his gaze held hers—his blue, blue eyes squinting ever so slightly, as if he were looking toward some distant horizon. Or maybe trying hard not to cry. She felt a sudden longing to touch him, reassure him somehow . . . though, God knew, right now, she was the one who felt as if her whole life was falling apart. Tentatively, she reached up and felt the wetness at the corner of his eye, smoothing it away with her thumb. His mouth hooked up in a sardonic smile, and Annie felt a tearing pain inside her.

He touched her cheek, briefly, sadly, and turned away.

Annie watched him go, a big rusty-haired man with one crippled foot and one good one, and more heart than she'd ever deserved. She felt like crumpling onto the carpet, under the gilded ceiling of the Plaza Hotel, and crying until she had no more tears.

But, no, she couldn't. Not now. Later, when she was alone.

Feeling cold and numb, Annie turned and started back toward the ballroom.

There was still Tout de Suite, she told herself. And though she yearned to chase after Emmett, she knew that if she didn't stay here and win Felder over, she might lose not only Emmett, but her business as well.

She'd have nothing.

Annie, straightening her shoulders and blinking away her tears, swept in through the mirrored doors, holding her head up, like a queen proceeding to her coronation.

"*Merde!*" Henri swore as the sheet of chocolate he was cutting with his knife broke in two.

He'd just removed this one from the refrigerator, and the cold had made it too brittle; he should have let it sit at room temperature a few minutes more. But here in the Plaza kitchen, where he stood hunched over a small corner table, the air felt warm enough to melt butter. And if the chocolate became too warm, he knew, his nearly finished three-dimensional model—made entirely from chocolate—would grow soft and begin to collapse where he had "glued" its pieces together.

His hands were shaky, but he forced himself to work slowly. No more mistakes. He placed a piece of heavy paper in the shape of a swan's wing over the rectangle of couverture in front of him, and with several deft slashes cut through the half-inch-thick sheet. The thing had to be perfect, flawless . . . a way of showing her how much he still loved her.

Just a few more pieces to fit in, and it would be finished—the lake in the Bois de Boulogne, where all those years ago, on their first outing in Paris, he'd taken Dolly.

The lake itself he'd fashioned from a thin oval of chocolate brushed here and there with white chocolate to give it the look of a rippled surface. Around the edges of the lake, slender, dagger-shaped wedges, set perpendicularly atop it, formed tall reeds, some dusted with cocoa to give them a textured look. There were lily pads made of milk chocolate, blooming with white-chocolate flowers, their curved petals thin as eggshells. And in the center, a rowboat molded from chocolate "plastic"—a pliable mixture of couverture and glucose—with two figurines in it, a man and a woman. Around the rowboat, swans and geese, and raised at one end, even a small waterfall fashioned from shavings of milk, white, and dark chocolate.

Would she recognize it? Would she remember? Even if she did, she might not want him anymore. . . .

So many years wasted.

Why had he been so pigheaded, insisting that she come to Paris?

Non. If she would have him, they would begin again. Here. Together. He had some money put aside, thank heaven, and there were his shares of Girod's, for which Francine, if she wished to keep them in the family, would have no choice but to pay a good price.

Girod's. The thought of never again stepping into his beautiful, beloved shop, tasting Pompeau's latest creation, joking with the apprentices and sales clerks, was almost unthinkable.

But he could do it. Those people would go on without him, and he without them. He had entered his father-in-law's small business, and through his hard work, his skill with chocolate, and his choice of the right people to help him, had built an enterprise of great prestige. And those abilities he could take with him anywhere. Even if he were to start again from nothing, at the absurd age of sixty-two.

So, yes, this replica of a lake, like Girod's, was more than just pieces of chocolate cut out and glued together. It represented all he knew, the skill his hands possessed. And what better way of expressing his feelings to Dolly? With words, he would no doubt appear foolish. Let her see this . . . and know that his heart had gone into every lily, every reed.

Henri dipped the broadest end of the swan's wing into a bowl of melted chocolate, kept warm in a bain-marie, and gently pressed the wing onto the body of the swan, holding it there until it had hardened.

But this was taking so long! Henri burned to go out and find Dolly, but he forced himself to move slowly. Everything had to be exactly right. Around him in the kitchen, chefs were barking orders, whipping sauté skillets on and off hot flames. Doors endlessly swinging open and shut, waiters with trays hurrying in and out. Clouds of steam rising from a long hooded row of steam trays.

Mon Dieu, if he could only keep his hand steady! Not for years—not since his days as pastry chef at Fouquet's—had he sculpted anything in chocolate. He did not seem to have lost his touch, but he had to go slowly where once he'd wielded his knife and brush with skilled abandon. He felt a queer tightness in his chest, and wondered if he might be having heart trouble. No, he was afraid, that was all. Afraid that he would find that he was too late.

After applying the last of the leaves, and spraying the entire model with confectioner's glaze, Henri tore off his apron and stood back to admire his creation. Yes, she would recognize it, she would know it was the Bois—the waterfall, the swans, even that toy sailboat he remembered her exclaiming over.

Henri checked his watch. *Mon Dieu,* already half past eight! No time to go back and change. He had on the gray suit he'd worn on the plane coming over, but wrinkled or not, it would have to do.

Carefully, carefully, Henri lifted his masterpiece, which sat on an acrylic board like some magical, storybook island. Slowly, bearing his precious offering, Henri made his way toward the double doors.

Weaving to avoid a waiter bearing an enormous tray laden with steaming soup bowls, Henri felt panic rise in him.

Look, already the first course! If I don't find Dolly now, now, before she is seated . . . before the interminable speeches begin . . . I will have to wait until after the entire dinner. . . .

Why hadn't he thought to call someone about being seated at her table? At least then he could have been near her, breathing in her perfume, touching her.

Henri found himself remembering the first time he'd laid eyes on her, coming into his basement kitchen at Girod's wearing a red dress with a bright, diamond-patterned scarf tied about her hair. She'd caught him at a bad moment—something about the ganache had put him in a foul temper—but she had merely laughed at his grumblings. "Oh, don't mind me," chirped this lovely woman he did not know, who nevertheless intrigued him with her boldness, and her easy familiarity. "You just go on ahead . . . I won't take it personal."

After all these years, would she still want him? After all, as Dolly would say, his foot-dragging?

Henri, his throat thick with longing, balanced his great gift to her with one hand while he pushed open the kitchen's padded door.

Rudy sat in the Oak Bar on the main floor of the Plaza Hotel and sipped his tonic. No gin, not these days . . . doctor's orders. Then why did he feel as if he'd socked away half a dozen martinis? The somber room with its dark oak walls and carved plaster ceiling seemed to be rocking to and fro, making his head spin and his stomach heave. There was a thick, nasty taste in his mouth like sour milk. From his table, set back against the wall, he watched the entrance, rolling his sweating glass back and forth between his palms while he forced himself to remain in his seat.

Eight-thirty, and still no Laurel. Jesus. She was supposed to have been here half an hour ago. Val had said so. He'd *promised.* But suppose Val had been bullshitting him? Or maybe Laurel had changed her mind. Suppose she'd thought it over, and realized she didn't owe him a damn thing, not even a few minutes of her time?

But he *had* to see her. This might be his last chance.

Only yesterday, they'd nearly shanghaied him into the hospital. Exploratory surgery, yeah sure . . . but Rudy knew damn well what they'd find. He could *feel* it . . . almost *taste* it—his insides rotting. Cancer of the colon. Christ. No dignity to it. But then when had he ever been anything more to God—if there even was a God—than some kind of practical joke?

Okay, he'd go with it. But not just yet. Not until after this trip, after he'd seen Laurel. Not until he'd told her what had been eating away at him for years and years. Cancer? What a fucking joke. It wasn't the cancer that was killing him . . . it was Laurel.

Absentmindedly, Rudy reached into the bowl in front of him and popped a peanut into his mouth. As he swallowed it, a bolt of acid shot through his stomach, causing him to double over, pain hammering at his gut. Out of the corner of his eye, he caught the bartender shooting him a curious look, and willed himself to straighten.

Concentrate. Concentrate. Don't let it show that you're sick.

"Uncle Rudy?"

The pain in his gut was nothing compared to the blast that went shearing up Rudy's spine at the sound of Laurel's voice. He jerked upright, nearly knocking his drink over and then catching it just in time.

She was only a few feet away, swaying toward him on high heels to which she was obviously unaccustomed, wearing a high-necked chiffon dress the pale ivory of Easter lilies, which floated about her ankles as if buoyed by some invisible updraft. Her hair was pulled up into a loose knot atop her head, leaving long wisps trailing about her neck. Pearl studs in her ears and an antique cameo brooch at her neck; she looked like a cameo herself.

Christ . . . so beautiful . . .

Rudy was gripped by an odd sense of distortion that made it appear as if each step she took, instead of bringing her nearer, was somehow taking her farther from him. He wanted to jump up and catch hold of her, but he was certain that if he tried to stand up now his legs wouldn't support him.

"Laur . . ." Her name grated to a halt in his throat, which felt as if it were clotted with rust.

Now she was standing directly in front of him, on the opposite side of the table, holding on to the back of the chair nearest her as if to protect herself. She looked nervous, her eyes darting off to the bar, over which was hung a large painting of the Plaza fountain. But, Christ, she was *here* . . . that was the important thing, wasn't it?

Rudy forgot his pain, and found his voice.

"You came," he said. The words came out flat, dull, not at all as he'd intended them. Inside, he felt ready to burst.

"I almost didn't."

"Well, now that you're here, why don't you sit down?" He gestured toward the chair she was holding on to. He was scared that if he stood up she would bolt. "This place, it's something else, isn't it? You ever see so much carving? I feel like I'm in the Vatican or something. Hey, you want something to drink?"

"Nothing. Thanks. I can only stay a minute. I'm already late —the L.I.E. was backed up for miles."

"This won't take long. I promise." He sucked in a deep breath. "So . . . how've you been?"

"Fine. Working hard." She spoke in the automated voice of a grocery clerk or a bank teller wishing him a nice day.

"Yeah, I've seen your books. They look great." He didn't tell her that he had all seven, that he kept them on a special shelf in his den. "You working on something right now?"

"A couple of things, actually." She shifted in her chair, looking uncomfortable, and made an attempt to smile that fell short. "I love my work. The trouble is, the money comes and goes. It's not like having a steady paycheck. But Joe, my husband—" She stopped, but not before he heard the slight catch in her voice.

"Yeah, I heard you got married."

"Joe and I are separated." She raised her eyes, and in that millisecond before she recovered herself, he saw something dark and raw in them. Rudy longed to know more, but he didn't dare ask, because now Laurel was tapping her fingernails impatiently against the polished table top. "Val said you had something you wanted to tell me." She stared at him, her lovely eyes narrowing the tiniest bit. "I'll be honest with you. I wouldn't have come if he hadn't talked me into it. Obviously, he's decided to let bygones be bygones."

"And you?"

"I don't know what to think. All I know is I trusted you . . . and you . . ." She sighed. "Oh, what's the point in raking it all up again?"

Rudy felt the dull thud of her words as they dropped like stones into the pit of his stomach. He'd known. Christ Almighty, he'd *known* she hadn't forgiven him. So why did it hurt so much?

"I didn't ask you here to let me off the hook," he told her, speaking quietly, even smiling a bit, though he could feel his smooth mask beginning to crack a little around the edges. "I figure you have a right to feel the way you do. So I'm not asking you for anything. I just wanted to see you."

Laurel wasn't smiling . . . but she wasn't getting up and walking away, either. Thank God. Rudy felt the room settle about him, and his dizziness begin to fade.

He watched Laurel fiddle with the mother-of-pearl clasp on her evening bag. "Look," she told him, "I'm not mad at you anymore. I mean, I don't go around thinking about you all the time, or anything, if that's what you're worried about." Rudy knew she wasn't trying to hurt him, but her words cut him deeply. Not to *matter* . . . that was as bad, maybe even worse somehow, than her hating him. "So if it'll make you feel any better," she went on, "I really don't need to hear any big explanations."

"No big explanations. I promise." He opened his hands, grinning like a magician showing he's got no tricks up his sleeve. Laurel didn't have to know what it was costing him to keep from breaking apart into a million tiny pieces. "Just one thing—I still care about you. I always have. You gotta know that."

"Then why did you do it?" She propped her elbows on the

table and rested her chin on her clasped hands, looking honestly bewildered.

Rudy felt himself starting to shake, and he had to lean forward and grip the backs of his knees to steady his arms. *You really want to know? You want to hear that you're the only person in my whole life I ever loved who loved me back . . . even a little?*

No, he didn't want her feeling sorry for him. He'd rather have her hate him. Rudy toyed with a napkin, shredding it into tiny bits as he spoke.

"I had this case once . . . client of mine loses his custody battle, and he's so desperate that one day he takes his little girl and splits. Kid's five years old—never been away from home longer than overnight. Lucky for everybody, the police nab my client before he's over the state line. 'So why'd you do it?' I ask him. Intelligent guy, mind you, a CPA. And he just looks at me with these big sheep eyes and says, 'I had to.' " Rudy paused, scooping his shredded napkin into a little snowdrift about the base of his glass. "I guess I know now how that guy must've felt. Doing something you know is wrong, just because you have to."

He looked up, searching her blue eyes for some hint that she understood. But she wasn't looking at him. Her gaze was on the carved head of a maiden decorating one of the oak pillars.

"I'm sorry." Rudy pushed the words out. "Jesus, you don't know how sorry I am. Everytime I think of you and the boy . . ." He stopped, his throat growing tight.

Laurel sat motionless, staring off into the distance for what seemed like an eternity. Finally, she brought her eyes back to him, and he thought he saw a flicker of understanding in them. But was he only imagining it?

"His name is Adam," she said softly. "Would you like to see a picture of him?"

Rudy nodded. He watched her pull a slim wallet from her evening bag, from which she withdrew a small photo—a three-by-five taken by some school photographer. It showed a little boy in a striped T-shirt with a huge, gap-toothed grin, and dark bangs falling in his eyes. Rudy felt his heart squeeze. He stared at the picture for a long time before he could bring himself to hand it back.

"You can keep it," she said. "I have copies at home."

"Thanks," he said, gruffly, too gruffly maybe. But he couldn't

let her see how deeply her gesture had affected him. There were so
many things he wanted to know. Was she going to be okay living
on her own? Did she need anything? Did the boy . . . Adam . . .
miss his father? But already it was too late . . . she was rising, her
dress rippling about her in soft little waves.

"I'd better be going," she said. She didn't say it had been nice
talking to him, or any of those pleasant, phony things people say.
She just put out her hand, and briefly—so briefly, Rudy was scared
he'd imagined it—touched the back of his wrist. " 'Bye."

She started toward the door, then abruptly wheeled. So abruptly,
Rudy felt as if the walls around him had come unhinged and were
toppling in on him. When he saw the tears shining in her eyes, he
felt as if she'd given him some priceless gift.

"You did me a favor, you know," she told him. "Adam turned
out to be the best thing that ever happened to me." She smiled this
time as she turned to go, even waving a little, the small gesture that
caused his heart to break.

Watching her walk away, Rudy held his palm, with the photo
of her son tucked inside it, pressed against his solar plexus. He felt
its heat warming him, soothing the dark ache in his gut.

Laurel edged her way into the ballroom, and saw at once that she'd
come too late to be able to slip in unnoticed. Dinner was in progress,
everyone sitting around pink-draped tables, eating, laughing, talking.
Waiters bearing huge serving platters were setting out laden plates;
others were pouring wine, refilling bread baskets. She hung back in
the shadowy recesses of the Romanesque arcade, feeling sorry she'd
agreed to come, wanting only to turn around and go home.

I don't belong here.

She felt shaken, too, by her meeting with Uncle Rudy. In spite
of her not wanting to, she'd found herself feeling sorry for him.
She'd sensed there'd been more to his wanting to see her than he
was telling her, and it tugged at her conscience . . . the feeling that
she'd let him down somehow. But that was ridiculous, wasn't it? She
didn't owe him anything.

Anyway, Rudy wasn't why her heart was racing now. Or why,
instead of slipping away before anyone spotted her, she continued
to scan the faces in the huge room, searching for just one. Joe. Was

he here? Annie had invited him—well, the two of them, actually—but would he have come on his own? *Dolly had to have told him I'd be here.* Given Dolly's big mouth and her even bigger heart, she'd probably engineered the whole thing to try and get them back together. She more than likely had even arranged for them to be seated at the same table.

Laurel felt a moment of dizzying weightlessness, as if she were being plucked up and lifted high. How would he act when he saw her? Had he missed her as much as she'd missed him? Did he want to come home as badly as she wanted him home?

But Joe, she realized with a sinking heart, was not among those seated at the tables. *He hadn't come.* He didn't want to see her. He didn't miss her at all.

A waiter raced past her with a little rush of warm air. Laurel stepped back, hugging one of the mirror-panelled columns. Up on the velvet-curtained stage at one end of the ballroom, a portly man in a tuxedo was making an announcement. In a few moments, he said, the prizes would be announced and then everyone was invited to help themselves to dessert.

"And if you think the judges had a tough time picking a winner," his jokey, talk-show-host voice boomed out over the room, "just wait until you come up and try choosing something from among that mouth-watering array. . . ."

Scattered applause and a few affable groans.

Laurel caught sight of her sister, at a table near the stage, seated between Aunt Dolly and a coarse-looking man with a stubbly gray crewcut. She was holding court, telling some story or joke that had everyone at her table leaning forward, their eyes fixed on her, their faces glowing. Annie, as usual, was absolutely in charge, on top, handling everything and everyone as she always did—perfectly. Even wearing the dress Laurel had worked so hard on—which, despite how upset she'd been, Laurel had finished and sent to her sister—Annie managed to look as if she didn't need anyone's help, as if she could take on the whole world all on her own.

Laurel felt suddenly, achingly, out of place, as if she could never, ever fit into Annie's world—the world Joe loved and was comfortable in. Was that maybe why he hadn't come tonight . . . because he knew that it wouldn't work? That she could never, ever be what he wanted?

It's Annie he wants. And I can never be like her.

But did she even want to be? Was it fair of Joe to have married her, expecting her to fit some ideal that wasn't her at all?

I don't want her world, Laurel thought now as she watched her sister deliver the punch line of her story with a flourish of her slim olive-skinned arms that was sending her audience into gales of laughter. Right now, Laurel longed to be home, tucking Adam into bed, reading him a story that would put him to sleep halfway through. She didn't want crowds of people admiring her; she just wanted a husband who loved her, a little boy who still crept into her bed at night sometimes when he was scared and needed a hug.

And if Joe can't see that . . . then I don't want him, either.

She could survive without him.

But right now, at this moment, it was all Laurel could do to pull herself free of the invisible weights dragging her down, and slip quietly out the door.

Annie, holding her knotted fists in her lap where no one could see them, watched Seth Hathaway lean into the microphone. "I'm delighted to announce the judges' number one choice in the category of general excellence . . ."

She held her breath. *Please, please . . . let it be me . . . I need this so much.*

". . . Le Chocolatier Manon."

Annie felt as if she'd been slapped, a rush of heat to her cheeks, followed by a sharp stinging sensation at the back of her nose.

Applause filled the room, nearly drowning his next words, "And in second place . . . let me tell you, folks, it was a close call . . . let's give a nice hand to Tout de Suite."

Dolly saw the look on Annie's face, and her heart sank. *Nothing but the best is ever gonna satisfy that girl. Nothing.* It wasn't enough that Tout de Suite was the envy of chocolatiers all over America, all over the world. Or that in six years Annie had accomplished more than plenty who'd been around for decades.

No. As Annie rose to her feet on a nice round of applause, the strained look on her face seemed to say *I want more.* That girl wanted . . . no, *needed* . . . to be first. Not just on account of Felder, either. Anything less, and she'd go around feeling she was a failure.

Eve had been the same way, Dolly recalled. So much more than just talented, she'd had fire in her belly. When Eve walked into a room, people sat up and took notice. She *made* them notice. Rehearsals to which hardly anyone paid attention, she treated like command performances, throwing herself into her parts as if she'd been born for the sole purpose of playing them; and then, even off the set, *becoming* that character. As Billy in *Storm Alley*, dyeing her hair red, taking up smoking and listening to country-and-western music—which Eve had always hated, because it used to remind her too much of Clemscott.

It struck Dolly then, a kind of epiphany: *I could have been a star, too . . . I just didn't want it bad enough.* All those years, resenting her sister, and it hadn't really been Eve's talent, or her own lack of it, that had stood in her way. Syd, the bastard, had been right about that all those years ago—she'd had drive, but no unquenchable, insatiable hunger. She'd wanted top billing the way a thirsty kid wants a popsicle on a hot day; Eve had needed it the way a drowning person needs air.

Listening to the applause, seeing her sister's daughter start toward the stage, Dolly felt a sudden longing.

By rights, it oughta be Eve sitting here, not me. She would've been so proud of Annie. . . .

Dolly's eyes filled with tears. Like a movie fade, the room blurred, and Annie seemed to take on a starry corona, red sparks glinting in her hair, the folds of her dress spilling pockets of light as she moved forward, chin high, to claim her prize.

Then, across the room, seated at the table nearest the stage, Dolly spotted Henri. He'd come. He was here! She wanted to jump up on her chair and wave at him. Even from a distance, she could see that he'd aged—his hair, even his mustache, more gray than she remembered—but, Lord, how good to see him! She felt her whole being lift up, like in a dream when you feel yourself flying like a bird. Except this was the real thing.

Their eyes met. Henri didn't smile, or wave. He just stared, and though he hadn't moved a muscle, she felt as if he were rushing toward her. Then she saw he was pointing at the Girod display table right near her. Why? And she saw . . . an elaborate model of some sort she hadn't noticed before. She half rose to get a better look . . . and, oh, blessed Lord . . . reeds, lilies, a lake, a boat, a waterfall cascading down . . . why, it had to be . . .

The Bois de Boulogne. That first day they'd spent rowing. He'd remembered!

Dolly felt an exquisite heat spread through her.

He still loves me.

Then Dolly turned and saw that Felder had gotten up and was heading toward the exit. A short while ago she'd seen him duck out to the men's room, so this time he had to be leaving. Annie would be devastated!

He doesn't know me from a hole in the ground, but maybe if I sweet-talk him . . . tell him how terrific she is . . . he'll see what an advantage she'd be for Felder's. . . .

Dolly, torn between Henri and wanting to help her niece, hesitated only a moment before leaping from her chair and following Felder into the lobby. Luckily, she caught sight of him as he was disappearing down the wide marble staircase that led to the main floor below.

Anxious now, Dolly dashed after him, holding onto the white marble banister as she lurched down the stairs, cursing herself for having worn such high heels. She imagined herself catching up with Felder . . . and then what? What exactly was she going to say?

Oh, she'd think of something. Some way of convincing him he'd be making a huge mistake if he passed up this deal.

Dolly was nearly out of breath by the time she reached the ornate lobby with its cascading chandelier and huge Chinese tub bursting with tiger lilies, gladiolus, delphiniums. But where had Felder gotten to?

Not waiting for the doorman, she pushed open the heavy glass door and ducked outside. Once again, she caught sight of Felder . . . he was crossing the street toward a stretch limousine idling at the opposite curb. With scarcely a glance in either direction, Dolly dashed after him.

"Mr. Felder!"

Too late, she heard the squeal of brakes, and saw glaring head-lights looming before her.

Something was slamming into her; she felt herself crumpling, the sky tipping over onto her head like a bucket of dirty water—a film of gray through which just a few faint stars poked through.

Disjointedly, she thought, *How silly of me.*

Jaywalking. How many times had both her driver and Henri warned her?

Lord, but it hurt . . . hurt so bad.

But now a bright white light was seeping into her head, making everything look fuzzy, blocking out her pain, making even the rumble and screech of traffic fade. And, oddly, Dolly wasn't scared anymore. She felt as if here, now, this, was where she'd been heading all along . . . ever since the moment she'd let that hateful letter slip from her fingers into that mailbox.

But she so wished that she'd been able to tell Henri how much she still loved him . . . and always would. . . .

Lying on the pavement, her legs bent at odd angles she seemed unable to set right, Dolly peered up at the blurry sea of faces that had appeared above her. Some seemed to be shouting for help, but she couldn't hear their words. She could only see their mouths flapping open and shut amid the cacophony of police whistles, traffic noises, the shrieking of sirens.

A chill sank into her bones like silt settling along the bottom of a creekbed. She felt herself slipping . . . slipping away from the jangling noises . . . her gaze was drawn upward by a peculiar light that had appeared in the buzzing darkness.

The sun glinting on a wave as it combed toward shore.

The wave broke. A young girl's delighted laughter rang in her ears. She could smell salt air, hear seagulls.

Dolly saw her sister: running along the beach at Santa Monica, her lithe body outlined in gold by the setting sun, her hair fluttering, the water rushing in, swirling about her long slender legs.

Evie . . . you dope . . . you forgot to take your stockings off!

I don't care! Oh, Dor, stop being such a stick-in-the-mud. Look, we made it! We're here! Cali-for-ni-yay. Can you believe it? Oh, God, I think I up and died in my sleep last night. Is this heaven?

They're your last pair. If you ruin them, you can't have mine.

Doris Burdock, you sound just like Mama-Jo. Look around you! Look at this! Sand! Have you ever seen so much sand? I feel like taking off all my clothes and digging myself a great big hole.

Well, just don't expect me to dig you out of it. I didn't ride a bus all the way from Kentucky just to build sand castles. Will you just look at that . . . you've got a run already. Eighty-nine cents a pair. Now just how do you plan on getting to be a movie star looking like something the cat dragged in?

Oh, Dor, stop fussing. We're here! Can't you just taste it on the tip of your tongue? Can't you feel it? All that other stuff, it's all in the past. Clemscott's just a bad dream. And I'm not ever goin' back, hear? Not ever. Not even in my mind. From here on, I'm somebody. I'm a . . .

"Star," Dolly whispered, and felt herself sink down, the warm sand closing over her head.

Lilies? An enormous bouquet of them, stiff and white as candles, swam into her view. In the light seeping through the shuttered blinds, they now seemed to glow. Sweet . . . they smelled too sweet . . . artificial somehow, like candy roses on a wedding cake. But lilies were for funerals. . . .

Dolly tried to press her eyes open more widely, but it felt as if sandbags were sitting on her eyelids. She couldn't manage more than thin slits. Her whole body, in fact, felt like after a day at the beach, hot and itchy all over, sand gritting in every crevice.

"I'm not . . ." She started to say she wasn't dead, not yet, that the lilies didn't belong here, but the only sound she could make was a gargled croak.

Out of one slitted eye, she saw a shadowy form unfold itself from a darkened corner. Then arms were encircling her, lips pressing against her cheek, her forehead. She closed her eyes; the effort of keeping them open was too great, and anyway, she didn't need eyes to know it was Henri. She could feel him, his warmth, his solidness, the roughness of his cheek, the prickling of his mustache. His clothes stank of being slept in, and of too many Gauloises—but, Lord Almighty, when had she ever smelled anything so wonderful?

Maybe she *had* died . . . and this was heaven.

"Henri?" she croaked.

"Dolly . . . oh, *ma poupée* . . ." His voice, too, sounded hoarse.

Dolly tried to lift her arms—one of them appeared to be hooked up to an IV line—to embrace him, but the effort sent a rocket of pain exploding through her ribcage. She could manage only the smallest of movements. Even so, a dull hammering moved up from her wrists, spreading through her.

"*Non . . .*" She could feel Henri lightly pressing her shoulders into the mattress. "You must not move. It is better if you remain still."

"Where . . . ?" She opened her eyes, and he came into focus. She looked into a pair of slate-colored eyes red-rimmed with tiredness, and bright with tears.

"Lenox Hill. It is a good hospital, they tell me. Now, you must not worry yourself."

"How long have I been here?"

"Since yesterday night."

"And now? What time's it now?"

She saw him glance at his watch. "Half past five. The sun is nearly setting."

"You mean all this time I've been out like a light?"

"You do not remember last night, your niece being here?"

"Annie?"

"Yes. And Laurel, too . . . she telephoned last night two times, and came to see you this morning. You opened your eyes, but we could not know if you saw her. I had so much fear, enormous . . . but now, the doctors, they have reassured me. They can repair you."

"Seeing those flowers, I thought at first maybe I'd died." Dolly forced a weak smile. "But nobody dead could hurt this much."

"You have good fortune. Four broken ribs and a bad concussion, very bad, but you are strong. You will get better."

"Then how come I feel like fifty miles of bad road?"

Henri chuckled. "It's good. If you can joke, that is the best sign."

"Oh, forget it. Oooh!" Her legs, as she tried to shift them, ached something fierce.

She clutched hold of Henri's hand as wave after wave of dizziness spiraled through her. The flowers on the table beside her bed appeared now to be swaying, as if blown by a strong breeze.

"Lilies," she slurred, knowing it had to be sedatives making her act and feel this woozy—as if her head had come unpinned from the rest of her. "They've got no color. I can't abide lilies. . . ."

"*Oui, ma poupée,* Mr. Felder does not know you as I do. When we are married you shall have roses, bright red and yellow ones . . . and you shall wear red . . ." His voice caught, and his eyes brimmed. "A red dress, like the one you were wearing that first day you came into my shop."

What was he saying? Was it the drugs and her pain making her head so foggy she couldn't hear straight? Was he really asking her to marry him?

"Henri . . . are you . . . ?"

"No, please . . . let me say it. I know I have waited much too long for this . . . and you may no longer wish to hear it. But, yes, I wish you to become my wife. I have quit Girod's . . . and that means you must quit it also. Do you think we two could ever start again, from the beginning?"

His face was grim, the lines about his eyes and mouth more pronounced than she remembered from years ago. He looked weary . . . and more than a little scared. As if he couldn't bring himself to trust in the preciousness of this great gift he was holding out to her.

Dolly now was struggling against the tide of wooziness threatening to swamp her . . . struggling to tell Henri what she'd been waiting six years to say. So much. She wanted to tell him how no other man—and she'd tried a few on for size—had ever measured up to him. And how it didn't matter that they'd have to start over from scratch; she'd love every minute of it. And, yes, she wanted him . . . in her apartment, in her bed, his toothbrush parked next to hers in the medicine chest, his robe hanging on the back of the bathroom door, even the acrid smell of his Gauloises.

Her heart was thumping like crazy, each thump bringing with it a wallop of pain, but that didn't matter. Her old body would heal. Her head would eventually stop spinning. What mattered now was getting it straight, getting the words out . . .

But all Dolly could say was, "Try me."

Three days later, Dolly was sitting up in bed, sipping a ginger ale and wondering if her being impatient as hell to get out of this depressing place meant she was getting better, when Annie walked in.

"Hi," her niece greeted her, depositing several glossy magazines on the table beside Dolly's bed before dropping a kiss onto her forehead. She wore cream-colored gabardine slacks and a turquoise sweater. "I thought you'd like something to read besides the tabloids I saw a candy striper passing out next door. Anything has to be better than 'MOM RAPED BY ALIENS GIVES BIRTH TO TWO-HEADED BABY.' "

"You know the old saying . . . two heads are better than one," Dolly quipped.

Annie groaned, a smile crinkling her eyes. "You sound as if you're feeling better."

"Heaps," Dolly told her. Annie had visited her every day, sometimes twice a day, always bringing her some little thing to brighten her up—a bouquet of yellow chrysanthemums, a basket of raspberries from Balducci's, a tube of her favorite Jungle Fever lipstick. If there was a silver lining to this whole ordeal, it was being able to spend these precious hours with her niece.

But, still, something inside Dolly twisted and turned like a restless sleeper seeking a comfortable spot on the mattress. She knew what it was, and she dreaded it. But now with Henri at her side, she could dare to risk it—say the words, and maybe put an end to this eternal gnawing inside her, this guilt. Yes, the time felt right somehow to finally come clean with Annie . . . tell her the truth, let her know what had come between her and Eve. Being given a fresh start with Henri—it was like a miracle. She imagined herself, her life, like an old house that had to be cleared of cobwebs and filth to make way for its new occupants. She wanted, *needed* to begin her new life scrubbed clean.

Even so, she fretted, *What if, once she knows the truth, she never wants anything more to do with me?*

Her heart lurching, Dolly sidled onto a safer topic. "How did your talk with Felder go?" she asked.

Annie, who had met with the department-store tycoon this morning, brightened, seeming almost to glow. "He says he's still interested in making a deal with me . . . that if my aunt thinks highly enough of me to go dashing out in front of a taxi in order to convince him how good I'd be for him, I must be something pretty special." She grinned. "But you know what I think?"

"What's that?"

"That you're the special one." Her eyes turned suddenly bright. "I don't know if I should be thanking you for almost getting yourself killed on account of me, but would it help just to tell you I love you?"

Dolly felt a jolt, as if she were being hit by that cab all over again. Had Annie really said that? Not in all the years she'd known her, had Dolly ever heard Annie say those words to her. *I love you.* Her eyes filled with tears, which she quickly blotted with a corner of her sheet before they could smear her mascara.

"Oh, sugar, it does me a world of good, your saying that. But . . ."

Now was the time. Before the moment slipped past. The truth about dear, self-sacrificing Aunt Dolly.

"Speaking of love, I was expecting to find Henri camped out here as usual," Annie interrupted. Clearly uncomfortable with a large dose of sentiment, she was already backing off from a scene that could turn maudlin. She laughed lightly and added, "Don't tell me. He's off ordering the wedding invitations, right?"

"Not so fast. He won't get his divorce for another six months, maybe longer." Dolly tried to pull herself up a bit, but the effort sent pain stabbing through her rib cage. She grimaced. Then there was Annie, reaching behind her to rearrange her pillows. "But," she added, "I've waited so long, what's another few months?"

"You're right. Henri's definitely worth the wait." Annie's dark-blue eyes seemed to cloud over then, and Dolly wondered if she was thinking about Emmett. Annie had told her about his moving to California. What Dolly itched to tell her was, *Go after him . . . don't let him get away.*

But look what had happened the last time she'd tried to straighten out Annie's affairs—she'd nearly gotten herself killed.

"Annie," she began, capturing her niece's moist hand and tugging her gently down onto the bed beside her. "There's something that's been on my mind for a long time. I've been meaning to tell you, and if I don't get it off my chest now, while I'm lying here with all my defenses down, I don't know when I'll ever again get up the nerve."

"It's about Dearie, isn't it?"

Dolly nodded, her throat suddenly thick.

"Your mama was a good person," she began. "And I don't want you thinking what happened to her was her fault . . . because it wasn't. I know. It was me that brought all that misery down on her . . . and on you and your sister, too. Lord knows I'm not asking your forgiveness. Not when I can hardly forgive myself. You see, I did a terrible thing . . . the thing that ruined your mother's career, and broke her heart. I just want you to know—"

"You don't have to say it," Annie broke in, squeezing Dolly's hand hard enough to send darts of pain shooting up into her wrists. "For a long, long time I wondered what had happened between you and Dearie—what could have been so terrible that it made her stop speaking to you for all those years. And now . . ." She paused, looking as though she wanted to choose her words carefully. ". . . I know that whatever it was, nothing can change how I feel about you. I'm not my mother," she added softly. "What came between you and her . . . well, I'm not the one to judge. And whatever it was that made you think you're responsible for the way things turned out . . . well, she made her own choices, too. I loved her. She was my mother. But she wasn't perfect."

Dolly felt relief, like a vast ocean wave, sweep through her. It was as if for years and years she'd been scrubbing at a stain that wouldn't come out, and now suddenly it was gone.

"I loved her, too," she said. Oh, how good it felt to be able to say those words aloud without feeling like the worst sort of hypocrite!

"I know," Annie said. "Why else would I be here?"

CHAPTER 36

Laurel eyed the flowers Dolly was clutching as the older woman, resplendent in crimson, made her way up the aisle of the sedate Church of the Resurrection on East Seventy-fourth Street.

No traditional bridal bouquet for her aunt . . . just a single spray of orchids, deep purple ones striped with yellow. Her dress, too . . . not white lace, but a red silk suit with a flaring peplum jacket edged in cream silk twist. A huge cartwheel hat with a cream-colored ribbon was tilted at a jaunty angle atop her piled-up platinum hair, its pearl-studded netting dipping down over her eyes, giving her the look of a forties movie siren. Dolly's gaze was fixed on the altar, decked with a profusion of lush roses, just ahead of her, where Henri, solid and sober-looking in a pearl-gray cutaway and vest, stood waiting.

But it wasn't, Laurel realized, the bright dress or the extravagant hat or the orchids that were making such a glow. It was that look on Dolly's face, her smile that lit the somber sanctuary—as if she'd swallowed the sun whole for breakfast.

Sitting on her hard pew right up in front, just a few feet from the altar, Laurel felt her throat tighten. She was happy for Dolly. She *was*. No one deserved this happiness more. But Dolly was not the reason she was choked up right now.

She glanced over at Joe, seated directly across the aisle. Beside her, Adam squirmed and whispered, "Why can't Daddy sit with *us?*"

"Because," she whispered back.

This was hardly the time to go over it again with Adam, and besides she was too upset. Seeing Joe, here, of all places, was hard enough. Maybe that was why Dolly had chosen not to have any attendants—she'd have known how torn up Laurel would have felt, taking part in a wedding when her own marriage was in shambles.

Looking at Joe out of the corner of her eye, she felt her heart catch, and thought, *He cut his hair.* It was always some little thing, knocking her off balance. Days or weeks would go by when she didn't see him, and then instead of just pulling into the driveway and honking his horn for Adam, he'd show up at the door . . . and she'd be overwhelmed by even the smallest changes—one sideburn cut slightly shorter than the other, a button missing from his favorite shearling jacket, a shirt or a pair of pants she hadn't seen on him before.

Eleven and a half months and I still break out in goose bumps whenever I see you . . . or hear your voice over the phone. I'll catch myself daydreaming, and find I've set an extra place for you at the table . . . or I'll be calling Annie or Dolly, and realize I've dialled your number by mistake. And that old Yankees sweatshirt of yours that I told you I couldn't find . . . well, I have it. I keep it in my closet, and sometimes at night when I can't sleep, I get up and find it, keep it next to me to breathe in your smell. . . .

Stop it. Forget that stuff. She mustn't keep thinking of him. Or she'd never be able to get through the rest of this day.

Laurel felt her eyes begin to sting. She willed herself not to cry. God, if she started, she might never stop. It might look as if she was crying out of happiness for Aunt Dolly; but it'd be for herself, grieving for her husband who sat across the aisle, a stranger in a navy suit and striped tie. Close enough for her to reach across and almost touch . . . but so far away they might have been on separate continents.

Can I go on like this? Can I keep on living without him?

Well, you have, for almost a whole year, she told herself.

Those first weeks of misery—she'd gotten through them by imagining her life as a painting she was gessoing over, preparing a blank white canvas on which she would paint something new, maybe something better. It would be a lot of work, exhausting, having to start from scratch, but she would do it. Others did. Besides, she wanted to. She had to prove to herself that she could stand on her own two feet.

And she'd managed to pull it off, hadn't she? More commissions than she could handle. And now a book she'd both written and illustrated on the *Publishers Weekly* young reader's best-seller list. Since its June publication, *Patches for Penelope*—about a little girl, who, by helping her grandmother make a patchwork quilt, learns to cope with her parents' divorce—had gone back to press three times. Lovely reviews. But best of all, the kids liked it. She'd seen them entranced, sitting around in a circle being read to in the Bayside library.

Like Penelope, she, too, was somehow coping. Mostly, she'd found, it was a matter of finding little ways of tricking herself into not feeling so lonely. Making a lunch or dinner date with one of her publishing pals on birthdays and anniversaries, to avoid sitting home and pining. Staying Busy—in the evenings forcing herself to go to a PTA meeting or a gallery opening . . . even when she'd rather curl up in bed with a good book. Making Time for Herself—fixing her hair and putting on a little makeup, even when she was sure no one but Adam and possibly the mailman was going to see her.

But if she'd grown so strong, how was it that all her carefully cultivated independence crumbled the second she laid eyes on Joe?

Laurel, swallowing hard against the tightness in her throat, focused on Annie, seated on her left next to Adam, wearing a black-and-white houndstooth skirt and fitted red jacket. *Please, God, give me some of Annie's strength.*

But Annie, she saw, was weeping. She didn't seem to notice or care that it was ruining her makeup. Mascara was smudged under her eyes, and inky tears dropped from her jaw onto her folded hands. She'd been chewing her fingernails again too, Laurel noticed. Was she thinking about Emmett, missing him . . . or was it Joe?

Laurel could see Adam staring quizzically at Annie, and it struck Laurel: *He's never seen her cry.* Mom's crying, on the other hand, was old hat—Laurel had about as much control in that department as a leaky faucet. Now she watched her eight-year-old son tug on Annie's sleeve, and offer her the small, plastic Mighty Mite model clutched in his sweaty fist. Annie, accepting his gift with reverence, slipped her arm about his small shoulders and gave him a squeeze.

Laurel, feeling her own tears begin to well up, tried to concentrate on what the bald-headed, hawk-nosed minister was saying. But his words, though they had a hearty, uplifting ring to them, were just sounds. Was she being terribly selfish, with Dolly getting married, to be feeling so heartsick about Joe?

Laurel suddenly became acutely aware of the space separating her from Joe, a few feet that seemed to bristle, making her whole right side feel tight and tingly. She ached to have him beside her, his arm around her, his hand in hers . . . but she knew that if she made one move toward him, afterwards she wouldn't be able to stop herself from begging him to come home with her.

No, she told herself. *No, I've fought too hard for this. I won't let him take all that away from me.*

He wouldn't *mean* to, of course. But he would, just the same. With just a gesture, a touch, a stray kiss, he'd destroy her newfound self-reliance as easily as a child kicking over a sand castle. By loving her—but not enough. By making her need *him* more than she needed herself.

A bell was tinkling, part of the service, and now she found herself thinking of Uncle Rudy, remembering that L.A. lawyer phoning. "Your uncle has died," he'd said. Three months ago. How sad she'd felt, then how shocked. He'd left a fortune—the house in Malibu and the one in Brentwood, not to mention checks every month from partnerships in shopping malls and office buildings—to her and to Adam. And he'd given her something more precious even than the money itself—financial security. Now, she would never need Joe's money, or any man's.

But this isn't about money, is it?

Oh, she so envied Dolly. Even from this distance, there was no mistaking that Henri's eyes and heart were for Dolly, and Dolly alone.

Laurel looked about, recognizing a number of the guests, most of them Dolly's friends. Colleagues from the Confectioners Association, her housekeeper, her driver. Gloria De Witt, who'd once managed Dolly's shop, wearing an oversize jacket embroidered with sequins over a slinky purple dress. And wasn't that old guy in back the one Dolly had lent money to so he could start his own florist business? The heavyset black lady next to her doorman friend, Bill, she was the founder of the Harlem Coalition—Laurel recognized her from news photos. Dolly had helped her raise money for scholarships for ghetto kids. The woman, Laurel saw, was sniffling into a handkerchief.

And Rivka, wearing a modest blue sweater-dress and her best *shaitel*—she had come, too. Religious Jews, Laurel knew, weren't supposed to enter churches—but for Dolly, Rivka had made an exception. Laurel recalled how when Channa, Rivka's youngest grandchild, was in the hospital recuperating from meningitis, Dolly had hired a clown, who arrived at Kings County with balloons and a bag full of magic tricks. Rivka had scolded Dolly. It was too extravagant, not in the least necessary. But then she'd hugged Dolly and confessed that she'd never seen Channa look so happy.

Laurel had promised herself while Dolly and Henri were exchanging their vows that she would not look at Joe. But now, like an alcoholic too weak to resist that one little drink, she sneaked a sidelong glance.

But Joe's gaze, she saw, also wasn't on the altar—he was looking straight at her. Laurel felt guilty, as if she'd been caught cheating on an exam. She could feel blood rushing up into her face.

And he wasn't just looking; it was the *way* he was looking at her: puzzled, bemused maybe, as if she were a stranger he thought he might have met and was trying to place.

Excuse me, madam, but you look awfully familiar. Are you sure we weren't married at one time?

Laurel, feeling a hysterical giggle about to erupt, had to clamp the tip of her tongue between her teeth. Tears leaked from the corners of her eyes. *You don't need him,* she reminded herself. *You only think you do.*

She remembered the big rainstorm the first week after Joe moved out. It had knocked a branch from the sycamore tree onto the roof over the garage—the kind of thing Joe would have taken care of, but now *she* was in charge. Yet in a way, it had been good for her, forcing her out of her bleary, apathetic state, getting her to change out of the old flannel robe and sheepskin slippers she'd been hibernating in for days. Outside, ankle-deep in mud, struggling to get the aluminum extension ladder propped against the tree, she had slipped and fallen on her rear. Shocked, her bottom smarting, she'd started sobbing. But then after a while she began to see how ridiculous she had to look, lying there in the mud, crying like a big overgrown baby.

God, how pathetic! No wonder Joe had had enough of her.

Braced by her self-contempt, she'd forced herself to stand, and clamber up the ladder. With an ax, she'd somehow managed to chop enough small branches off the torn tree limb to be able to drag it off the roof. Then, exhausted, she'd staggered inside and taken a long hot shower—the first in days—and afterwards fixed herself and

Adam breakfast, fresh-squeezed orange juice, scrambled eggs with mushrooms, toasted English muffins.

She realized that she would live after all. No matter how bad things got, she had Adam . . . and she had herself. And Annie, too. Yes, Annie. No matter how mad at Annie she sometimes got . . . they were joined forever. Sisters.

Even so, thinking ahead to when Joe would be free to marry someone else, Laurel felt gripped by a queasy weakness. That had to be why she'd put off discussing their getting divorced. Was it because she was afraid that if he was free, he'd marry Annie?

And, if he did, then what?

No, he couldn't. She'd give anything for another chance with Joe. But Joe had to want it, too. She couldn't make him want her. She'd already tried that, and look where it had gotten her.

Arriving at Dolly's apartment, a bit late after being stuck behind a double-parked delivery truck, Laurel found the wedding reception in full swing. Bill Watley, a long-time member of his Chelsea AA chapter, was toasting the bride and groom with Pepsi, telling about the time he'd roared into Dolly's shop dressed as Santa Claus, high as a kite, and instead of throwing him out on his ear she'd given him a bottle of Cherry Heering "to keep the chill off." He ended up not drinking it, he said, and the very next day had gone straight to AA. He'd been dry ever since. And to this day, he kept that bottle in his kitchen cupboard as a reminder.

"Better watch out, Henri," Bill bellowed, "or she'll reform you, too."

"*Mais oui,*" Henri replied with a chuckle. "But she already has done this."

Laurel, depositing Adam with Henri's eight-year-old twin grandsons, watched Adam immediately drag the pair off to the guest bedroom where Dolly kept a box of toys and games. Then, after dredging up enough of her high-school French to exchange pleasantries with Henri's daughter—a pretty, plump woman in a fluffy pink dress that was all wrong for her—she walked over to the bar, and poured herself a drink. Stolichnaya. Neat. She wanted to be happy for Dolly . . . but right now, even more, she wanted to be numb.

"Laurey."

At the sound of his familiar voice, she turned too quickly, vodka splashing over the rim of her glass, stinging her knuckles. She looked up into a pair of round steel-rimmed glasses, at reflected images of herself flickering in his lenses.

It was as if it had been a hundred years since they'd spoken. Yet he called at least once a day, to speak to Adam. But now his voice sounded different, softer. Or was she just imagining that?

"We need to talk," he said in a low voice. "The terrace. We'll have some privacy out there. I'll get your coat. It's a little chilly."

Chilly? Did he know about cold—the bone-deep cold of waking up to find yourself reaching for your husband in bed and not finding him there? What it's like when you can't stop shivering, even with the thermostat pushed up to eighty and with three heavy blankets over you?

But now she felt too warm, her heart swollen, knocking against her ribs, a haziness clouding her thoughts, her carefully built-up rationalizations. Damn him. Why was he doing this to her?

But she didn't argue. Just nodded, and waited quietly while he got their coats.

He's going to tell me he's seen a lawyer, that it's time we got divorced. Oh, he's right, of course . . . but, God, can I bear it?

Outside, she didn't bother to button her coat. The October wind was whipping at her hem, but she wasn't cold. She wondered if she might be running a fever. Her face felt hot and tight, her throat achy.

Standing on the wide rear terrace, looking west over the fall hues of Central Park, Laurel imagined she and Joe were alone on a raft together, sailing on a blue ocean. She wanted them to stay like this forever, never reaching shore, together, just the two of them. The Owl and the Pussycat, in their beautiful pea-green boat.

I hate endings, she thought. Even in books, I hate turning the last pages. It's as if the characters you loved had died. Or abandoned you.

Don't wait for him to say it. Get this over with while you still have a shred of dignity left.

"I think I know what this is all about, Joe, and I don't . . ." She stopped, her throat tightening. She cleared it and began again. "I don't want it to be any harder than it already is. You know, the way couples end up fighting over dumb things like who gets the martini pitcher."

Joe smiled at her. Over his good blue suit, he wore an old but beautifully kept navy greatcoat that had been his father's, its collar pulled up around his ears, its brass buttons twinkling. "We don't have a martini pitcher," he pointed out.

"Well . . . you know what I mean."

"Yeah, I think I do."

"I mean, things aren't the issue here, are they? Oh, I suppose we'll have to do some . . . sorting out. You know, like with Adam. He still asks me every night when you're coming home. It'll be hard enough on him as it is without us fighting." She took a deep breath, and felt as if instead of air she was pulling salty water into her lungs. "It's just as well, I guess, I never had those other babies."

"Don't say that." Joe grabbed her by the shoulders, turning her to face him. In the sunset's glare, she couldn't see his eyes, but she could feel his powerful fingers through her thick coat, gripping her tightly. "Don't ever say that." He sounded angry.

"Why not?" She felt herself glare at him, her own hurt welling to the surface. "It's true, isn't it? Another child would've been just one more thing standing between you and . . . and what you really wanted."

The heat inside her was galvanizing her. She wasn't going to be afraid. Because that was what it all boiled down to, wasn't it? Adam. The reason Joe hadn't asked for a divorce before this.

"What makes you so sure you know what I want?"

"How can I know when you never tell me anything! Dammit, Joe, you should have told me. About your father. About Annie. Everything. You should have told me in the very beginning that you were only marrying me because of Adam!"

"That isn't true."

"Why are you doing this to me? Of course it's true. I knew it then, deep down, and I wanted you badly enough to marry you anyway. I thought I could make you love me. But you can't make a person love you, can you?"

"I know I should have been more honest with you. I'm sorry."

"I used to have this fantasy . . . oh, I know it was child-ish! . . . but I used to imagine you'd wake up one morning, and just like a fairy tale, you'd see me lying there . . . and it would be as if an evil enchantment had been lifted, and you were seeing me for the very first time. Falling in love with me. As if you had never loved"—her voice broke with a tiny gasping cry, and she felt the sting of hot tears against her icy cheeks—"my sister."

"It wasn't a competition. Believe me, it was never anything like that."

"I know."

How could I even come close to Annie's charm and her brilliance?

The sun's glare abruptly dimmed, a passing cloud probably, and she could once again see his eyes, soft in contrast to the planes and angles of his face, and filled with tenderness. He didn't let go of her, but his hands relaxed their grip. "Laurey . . ."

Say it, she pleaded silently. *Please just say it and get it over with.*

"I love you."

God, he was killing her. Damn him!

She pulled away, and stepped back, trembling. "That's not fair!"

"Laurey, wait. I know it hasn't always been—"

"No!" she broke in. "I don't want to hear it! Just pretend I'm dead! Because that's how I want to feel about you, dead inside me." Tears were running down her cheeks. "Joe, please, if you love me at all, even a little, then stop this. Just *stop.*"

Laurel, feeling desperate, walked away from him, going all the way around the terrace to the Park Avenue side. She needed to find a way . . . something . . . anything to save herself from this new, futile hope quickening inside her. Blindly, savagely, she wrenched the gold wedding band from her finger, and flung it over the wrought-iron railing. She watched it arc toward the street twelve stories below, becoming smaller and smaller, falling as if in slow motion, like a coin tossed into a wishing well. She imagined it simply dissolving into the air, a sorcerer's spell, which she now had broken forever.

Looking back at Joe, she saw that the blood had drained from his face, leaving blotchy red smudges where the wind had scoured his cheeks. She expected him now to say how sorry he was, how he hoped they could stay friends . . . for Adam's sake, if for no other reason.

Instead, he bolted across the terrace, flung open the sliding glass door, and disappeared inside the apartment.

Stunned, she stood there for a moment, puzzled, disoriented, as if now, working the very last piece of a jigsaw puzzle, she'd found it didn't fit. Where had he gone? What did it mean?

Then, in a dizzying rush, it struck her. Her ring. He had gone after it. Like Jason charging after the Golden Fleece.

The air seemed to be sucked from her lungs, and she felt her legs wobble. She leaned over the wrought-iron railing, peering down. At first, she saw only the dizzying drop . . . then sidewalks the width of snail tracks, vehicles the size of Adam's Matchbox cars, streaming in opposite directions along Park Avenue. Waiting, she began to feel chilled, then she spotted him, a tiny figure darting out from under the apartment building's green-and-white canopy. At the curb, he appeared to be hesitating; then he was plunging headlong into the ongoing traffic. Laurel, terrified for him, felt as if she were falling, down, down all those stories toward the gray pavement, the traffic sounds swelling in her ears.

She blinked, and was back on the terrace.

Her blood drumming in her ears, she watched the tiny figure that was Joe stride before the oncoming cars, arms extended like a cop's, bringing some to shrieking, squealing halts, while others swerved and fishtailed around him. A cacophony of angry horns blasted at her ears all the way up here.

Joe, like a man obsessed, ignoring them all, hunkered down— right there in the middle of the chaotic avenue.

"Joe! Come back! Come back here!" She knew he couldn't hear her, but she couldn't stop herself from screaming.

Watching a taxi come straight at him, and then at the last second swerve to avoid him, Laurel gripped the railing so hard she could feel its rough edges pricking her.

With the traffic now surging around him, she lost sight of him. It couldn't have been more than seconds, but it felt like hours. Then at last she spotted him—he was standing in the middle of Park Avenue on the dividing strip, legs apart, arms held high, his navy coat flapping out behind him, holding what had to be that damn ring up to the sky like it was an Olympic gold medal.

"Joe . . . you idiot," she choked.

Minutes later, when he'd returned to her side, the ring clenched in his fist, his face red with cold and his eyes bright with triumph, she told him to his face exactly what she thought of him.

"You could have been killed! And for nothing!"

"No, not for nothing," he panted, his breath blowing out in white plumes. "Laurey, I can't change what happened. Back when we got married, maybe I wasn't feeling everything you were. Jesus, who even remembers? All I know is how I feel now. I love you. I can't fall asleep at night without you next to me. I can't get through a single hour without thinking of you, missing you. I've tried . . . believe me, I have. All these months I've been waiting for you to tell me you missed me, that you wanted me back, and when you didn't . . ." He stopped, took her hand. "Oh, what difference does it make who started what? All I know is what I want . . . and it's you. Laurel Daugherty, will you marry me?"

She stared at him, too stunned, too overflowing with happiness to know quite what he meant, or what she should say.

"Now. Say yes."

"Joe . . ."

"We'll start over, from here, from this second."

"Are you sure it's me you want . . . not Annie?"

"You, my sweet Laurey." He touched her cheek. "Only you."

Joe, breathing hard, his hair whipping about his cold-bitten face, snatched up her left hand, and eased the ring back onto her finger. She felt its coldness encircling her . . . then he was kissing her hand . . . holding it to his lips . . . and she could feel his breath against her palm, warming her.

"Say 'I do'," he murmured, pulling her into his arms, his lips curving up in a teasing smile. "Say it quick before I do something really nuts like throwing myself over this balcony."

Laurel pulled in a deep breath, frosty air that tasted of smoke and soot and exhaust fumes. Tiny cinders blew against her cheeks, stinging them. But inside, she felt new and clean and shining. As if she'd just now, this very minute, been born.

"I do!" she cried, loud enough for all of Park Avenue to hear her.

Back inside, she found people clustered around the piano, where one of the neighbors was playing "Some Enchanted Evening," one of Dolly's favorites. A chesty lady from the Metropolitan Opera chorus, wearing a cream wool suit trimmed in mink, put her drink down on the piano's ebony surface, and began to sing the words in a rich, boozy voice.

"Where's Adam?" Joe asked, his eyes sparkling. "I want to tell him I'll be home for dinner."

"Playing the diplomat with Henri's grandkids," she told him.

While Joe went off to look for Adam, Dolly came over and slipped an arm about Laurel's shoulders. "That song . . . it gets me every time."

Laurel nodded, too filled with emotion to speak.

"But anyone with eyes can see that's not why *you're* so misty."

"I'm just so happy."

"Well, I guess I don't have the market cornered on happiness . . . though Lord knows it sure feels that way."

"Joe and I . . ."

"You don't have to say it. It's written all over your face." Dolly hugged Laurel, her flowery perfume floating up around her. "Oh, sugar, you've just given me the best wedding present I can think of."

"I honestly didn't expect it to turn out this way—for either of us."

"Funny thing about love," Dolly observed with a wry grin. "It's like a mule that way . . . just when you get tired of pushing it, and sit back to take a breather, it goes off and kicks you right in the gut." Dolly gave her a little shove. "Now go on, get out of here. Get on home, where you can celebrate properly."

"But you haven't even cut the cake!"

"Sweetie, I wasn't talking about you toasting me and Henri. You and that good-looking husband of yours . . . you two have your own toasts to make." She winked, and gave Laurel another little push. "Don't worry about Adam. I just looked in on him—he and the twins are having a grand old time. I'll have Felipe take him home later on . . . after you and Joe have had a chance to get reacquainted."

"But what about you . . . your honeymoon? Isn't Felipe driving you to the airport?"

Dolly smiled and smoothed a wisp of hair from Laurel's cheek. "Henri and I . . . we changed our mind about St. Bart's. We're spending our honeymoon right here. After all the backing and forthing we've done, isn't it about time we stayed put?"

Laurel kissed her aunt, and said good-bye to Henri and the

others she knew, but she didn't see Annie. Probably she was in the bathroom, or in the dining room checking on the triple-layer white-chocolate cake she'd made for the occasion. Laurel felt the tiniest bit relieved. She didn't really feel like talking to Annie right now. Since Joe had moved out, things had been sort of strained between her and her sister. On the surface, of course, they acted as if nothing was wrong . . . but underneath, every time she spoke with Annie, Laurel could feel the tip of something sharp and jagged buried underneath. She'd find herself wondering, *Is she just biding her time until she thinks I'm over him?*

Joe had gone to get his Volvo, parked a few blocks away, and would meet her in Bayside. She could hardly wait to get home.

Outside, walking briskly east toward the garage near Third Avenue where her own car was parked, Laurel became aware of the staccato tapping of heels coming up rapidly behind her.

She turned, and saw Annie, hurrying to catch up with her. She had on a saffron-colored raincoat made of some silky fabric, and in the dusky light, she seemed to glow, the scissoring of her long legs sending the coat's hem billowing, causing Laurel to think of a sky-diver parachuting to earth. And now Annie was waving at her to wait, waving so energetically that a passing cabbie, thinking he was being hailed, lurched to a stop.

Laurel waited. Seeing her sister, as always, brought forth a grab bag of feelings. Love, affection, resentment, guilt. *What now?* she wondered. Laurel felt herself holding tight to her joy, hogging it the way a kid might have kept a special toy all to herself. Why did she feel worried, as if Annie might somehow try and take this from her?

Laurel only wished that whatever Annie was rushing to tell her could have waited just a little while longer. If only she could just leave now, and float home on this heavenly cloud of hers.

But she couldn't put Annie off. She owed her that much at least.

"Dolly told me," Annie panted when she'd caught up, "about you and Joe. I wanted to tell you . . . well, really just to say how happy I am for you . . ." Laurel searched her face, but Annie's expression was sincere.

"Thanks," Laurel told her, feeling suddenly awkward, not knowing what else to say except, "You're not leaving, too, are you?"

"No. I just wanted to catch you before you took off. I'm going back now to help serve the cake."

"I saw it. It's beautiful. It looks like the ceiling of a Victorian parlor . . . all those rosettes and swags and curlicues."

"That's where I got the idea, actually." Annie laughed. "From a mansion in Newport. You want to hear something really funny? I showed a picture of a cake just like Dolly's to Hy Felder . . . and he ordered one for his daughter's wedding. I'm charging him a small fortune."

"How's it going with Felder's?"

"Looks like it'll be another few months before the grand opening, but I'm beginning to gear up to go into production."

"The rate you're going, you'll need a factory the size of Brooklyn before too long." Laurel felt impatient, wanting to stop chattering, be off.

"It's true what they say about number two—we try harder."

"You'll never be second at anything," Laurel observed with a little laugh. She glanced over at Annie, who now appeared lost in her thoughts. "By the way, have you heard anything from Emmett?"

Annie looked away, but not before Laurel had seen the hurt in her eyes. "Not a thing. You know what they say, a clean break heals the quickest."

"I figured maybe you two would . . ." *Admit it, you were hoping they'd get back together so Annie would be out of the running as far as Joe was concerned.*

No, it was more than that. Laurel had genuinely liked Emmett . . . and she missed having him around. His sense of humor, the way he kept Annie . . . well, *centered,* sort of.

"Well, we're not," Annie spoke a bit too sharply. Then, catching herself, she added lightly, "I guess I'm just not cut out for marriage. Or maybe I'll end up like Dolly, marching down the aisle when all my friends are having grandchildren."

"What about kids?" Laurel asked. "Don't you want at least one?"

Annie was silent for several long minutes while she contemplated the progress of a tour bus trundling slowly past.

"I was just remembering," Annie said at last, softly, "those first weeks in New York when you used to cry all the time. I felt so bad, like I'd done this terrible thing that you'd hate me for. I guess that's how mothers must feel a lot of the time."

"I didn't hate you," Laurel said. "I just felt so . . . well, uprooted. Like Dorothy in *The Wizard of Oz*. As if I'd been picked up by a cyclone, and carried off to this strange land where I didn't know anyone, and all the time I was scared."

"Say it, why don't you?" Annie brought her head up, and gave Laurel a sharp, wounded look. "You blame me for taking you away. It's all my fault, isn't it? Everything."

A deep calm flowed through Laurel. For maybe the first time ever, she felt as if she were in charge, as if it were her role, her duty, to protect and comfort her sister. "No, Annie, I don't blame you. You did what you had to do. And I followed . . . like I always did."

"You could have stayed behind."

"What choice did I have? Without you there, it would have been awful. No. If I blame anyone, it's Dearie. She just checked out on us. You know, you loved her more than she deserved."

"She was the best mother she knew how to be."

"To you, maybe. But you're the one who really mattered to me."

"We're sisters," Annie stated matter-of-factly. "Sisters look out for each other."

"But don't you see? It was always you looking out for me. Never the other way around." She stopped. "It was partly my fault, too. I let you take over." She touched Annie's arm. "Look, I'm sorry about the way things have been. It's just that with Joe gone . . ." She let her voice trail off, not sure what, exactly, she wanted to say.

"I know." Annie's eyes, shining with emotion, met Laurel's, and Laurel felt as if they'd just made an unspoken pact.

Laurel watched a woman in a plaid coat up ahead, waiting for her little dog to lower its uplifted leg. The sidewalk, she saw, had a scattering of leaves—as if, without her ever noticing, winter had sneaked up and stripped the trees.

"You'll come for Thanksgiving, won't you?" Laurel asked gently.

"I wouldn't miss it."

"You can carve the turkey."

Laurel was remembering their first Thanksgiving in New York, when all they had was frozen turkey TV dinners. Annie, peeling back the foil on hers, had quipped, "I don't know why everyone makes such a big deal about carving the turkey. Look how easy it is." Since then, it had become an annual joke with them.

Annie rolled her eyes. "It wasn't all so terrible back then, was it?"

"No," Laurel said softly. "It wasn't."

"There's one thing I've always wondered about, though. Remember when Joe and I used to tease you about your mystery boyfriend? Just what *were* you being so secretive about?"

Laurel thought about Uncle Rudy, and wondered if the time had come for Annie to know that she wasn't the only one who'd been brave in order to protect someone she loved. But what was the use? She didn't need to prove herself. Not anymore.

"You know something," Laurel said, her lie coming easily, "I don't even remember anymore. I was probably just playing hooky."

Annie shrugged, as if she weren't completely convinced but had decided it was so long ago it no longer mattered much.

"Well, I guess I'd better get going," Laurel told her. "Joe'll be wondering what's kept me."

"Joe? Oh, yeah . . . sure. Well . . ."

Laurel watched her sister start to step back, looking suddenly awkward and slightly forlorn, as if she were a teenager again, only this time there was no one for her to take care of . . . and maybe no one to watch out for her, either. Not looking where she was going, Annie caught the side of her heel in a deeply indented crack in the sidewalk. Thrown off balance, she lurched forward.

Laurel started to catch her, and even managed to grab hold of Annie, but her stance was somehow wrong, and she went sprawling onto the sidewalk with Annie on top of her.

After the first shocked moment, Laurel was able to sit up, pushing Annie up with her. As they sat there with Annie's yellow parachute of a raincoat puddled about them, Laurel felt overcome, realizing how much she loved her sister. How much she still needed her in all sorts of little ways.

Suddenly, she found herself giggling.

Annie, laughing a little, too, and wiping her eyes on her sleeve, said under her breath, "Don't look now, but that woman with the dog . . . she's looking at us like she thinks one of us is getting mugged."

Pulling herself up, Laurel helped Annie to her feet, brushing off the wet leaves that clung to Annie's saffron coat.

To the woman with the Yorkie, staring at them openmouthed, Laurel called: "It's okay . . . we're sisters!"

Epilogue

Annie handed her car keys to the parking valet, and started up the canopied walkway leading into the Beverly Hills Hotel. Driving in from LAX, stalled in traffic much of the way, she'd felt tense and wound-up. But here, in this lovely shade, tubs of pink azaleas and ruby rhododendrons flanking her on both sides, she felt herself begin to unwind. She glanced at her watch. Twelve-forty—she had hours until her meeting. Time for a short nap, and maybe afterwards a swim.

Then, nodding to the green-and-gold-uniformed doorman as he held open the heavy glass door to the lobby, she thought of *who* she was meeting, and why, and she felt her stomach tighten.

Emmett.

More than a year and a half since she'd seen him, and in all that time no letters, phone calls, not even one postcard. Then last week, the shock of his voice over the phone drawling, "Hey, there," as if it had been merely days, not ages, since they'd last spoken. He had his own real-estate agency now, he told her, in Westwood. He was "doin' okay," which, given Emmett's laid-back way of putting things, could have meant anything from a hole-in-the-wall with an answering machine to some swank address with a dozen employees. But he hadn't just called to shoot the bull. He had something he thought she might be interested in.

Bel Jardin. It was on the market, and he had an exclusive listing.

Annie, so close now to seeing her childhood home, felt her heart begin to race.

That she might once again actually live in Bel Jardin seemed like a fairy tale too good to be true. . . .

Suppose it's way more than you could possibly afford. Why didn't you at least ask him the price over the phone? What was the point of flying out here half-cocked just to take a stroll down Memory Lane?

549

Because, face it, Bel Jardin was not the only reason she'd come.

She imagined Emmett's sharp blue eyes taking in her telltale bitten nails, and then crinkling in amusement. Could he want her out here just for herself? Could he possibly know how, after he'd called, she'd felt as if she were going to jump right out of her skin . . . and how, in the heat of July, she'd had to soak in a hot bath to stop her shivering?

No, no way. He couldn't be thinking of her *that* way. By now, he was probably married, might even have a child. He hadn't mentioned a wife, but then why should he? It was just a business call.

She tried imagining how his wife might look—all arms and legs and sun-streaked blond hair, sleek and tanned, Colgate smile. She probably played volleyball on the beach in her string bikini like in those Pepsi commercials. Malibu Barbie.

Except Emmett was no Ken doll. Not by a long shot. Did he still wear those old cowboy boots? Or had he switched over to huaraches? Did he still get that funny cowlick when his hair was damp? Had he forgotten he ever loved her?

"May I help you, ma'am?"

Someone was speaking to her, Annie realized, a white-jacketed young man behind the desk.

"A reservation for Annie Cobb," she told him, her voice crisp, businesslike.

"Do you have any luggage?" he asked after she'd signed in. *He* looked like a Ken doll, she thought: blond crewcut, great tan, even white teeth.

"Just this." Annie, who always made it a point to travel light, hefted her single suitcase—a Mark Cross shoe bag, cinnamon calfskin with chocolate-colored straps, monogrammed with her initials: AMC. The size and shape of a carpet bag, it was big enough for short trips, and sewn into the lining were eight elasticized pouches for shoes, into which she could also tuck toothpaste, hand lotion, shampoo.

"And I can take it myself," she told him.

But the bellhop, who looked like a former Olympic athlete, deftly took it from her and led her across the wide lobby, a sea of pink and green, gleaming white latticework, moss-green diamond-patterned carpet. To Annie, it looked unreal, an old-fashioned Hollywood designer's vision of tropical opulence, a mix of *Casablanca* and *Road to Rio.*

Upstairs, a pink corridor splashed with a trompe l'oeil of banana leaves led to her room, which overlooked a winding pebble path verged by islands of emerald grass, creeping philodendron, slender stalks of bird of paradise. Her bed, she saw, was the size of a small tropical atoll. And—God forbid she go hungry here—atop a reproduction Queen Anne writing desk sat a cellophane-wrapped basket of fruit.

Annie kicked off her pumps, and sank down on the bed. Despite the air-conditioning, in her silk-and-linen suit she felt as uncomfortable as if she were swaddled in thick wool. Well, if she ever moved out here, she'd have to buy a whole new wardrobe.

But who said anything about moving? Sure, she'd been toying with the idea, and not just since hearing about Bel Jardin. She could still keep her apartment in New York, and live in L.A. part of the year. And with the Rodeo Drive Tout de Suite opening next month, that would keep her hopping out here for a while anyway. And now, with Dolly and Henri supervising the manufacturing, her stores, and Felder's boutiques, she could scout out some other West Coast locations as well. Why not a Tout de Suite in La Jolla, Sausalito, Carmel . . . ?

But business, she knew, would not be why she moved out here . . . if she did.

It was weird, but Annie couldn't help feeling that coming out here permanently would somehow be running away. But not from Tout de Suite. She would work just as hard here as anywhere else, even though the business was now even more successful than she could ever have dreamed.

And not from Laurel . . . she felt closer to her sister than she ever had. And Laurel, in her sixth month and already big as a house, radiant, bubbling over, didn't need her next door.

Was it that she'd be running from herself?

Or might the running be not away, but *toward* something . . . peace, contentment, the happiness that was always just beyond her reach? How many times did Rivka keep telling her, she ought to be married . . . have a family of her own? Thirty-four. In Rivka's world, she was an old maid.

But the men since Emmett—tied to their mothers, their therapists, their jobs, their hobbies (Russ, with his passion for collecting antiques), their allergies (David, with a humidifier and a Dustbuster in every room) or simply their own egos. Most of them nice men, some of them amusing, fun for an evening or a weekend. But for a lifetime?

Why, when she had him, hadn't she valued Emmett more? Why hadn't she begged him to stay, to give her another chance?

And how would it be, seeing him after a year and a half? Would she feel only some pleasant nostalgia, like meeting up with a school chum? Or would she get all sweaty, heart racing, palms itching, as she had when he'd called? It seemed so damn unlikely, but could it be that she was still in love with Emmett?

Forget it.

Think about Bel Jardin, she told herself. How perfect if it were to be hers. Even if she lived in it only part of the year. Laurel and Joe could use it, too. And Adam and his little brother or sister would play on the same lawn where she and Laurel had played Mother-May-I and Hide-and-Go-Seek. And so what if the place turned out to be all run down? She'd do whatever it took to restore it to the way it had been before Dearie got sick.

Now, in her mind, she was ambling up the long curving drive, the petticoat palms rustling overhead, shadows from their long ragged fronds rippling out over the grass. And then the house coming into view, the color of a peeled grapefruit, all creamy yellow and white, with its curved terra-cotta roof tiles, and its windows and balconies adorned with filigreed wrought iron. Bordering the lawn in front, roses bloomed, and along the wide front porch, stone jardinieres held miniature kumquat and red-pepper bushes. And bougainvillea vines were growing up around the mullioned windows, displaying cascades of purple flowers. . . .

Oh, boy, there she went . . . getting ahead of herself again. Already living in Bel Jardin, and she hadn't even seen it yet!

Soon, she thought, her heart again beginning to race.

Annie, seated at a redwood patio table on the deck of the Crow's Nest in Santa Monica, overlooking the Pacific, sipped her white Zinfandel and waited for Emmett. A Cinzano umbrella shaded her from the intense sun. Drifting out from the indoor dining area she could hear a guitar playing blues riffs; it sounded like Muddy Waters. Yet—despite the laid-back-sounding chatter, mellow laughter, the tinkle of ice in tall drinks speared with big chunks of unpeeled pineapple—she felt tense.

The tables around her, she noticed, were filled mostly with people even younger than she. Hip Californians. She eyed a pony-tailed blond girl wearing a Hawaiian-print sarong, a white blouse knotted beneath her breasts that showed off a midriff so smooth and flat and uniformly tanned it looked unreal, like a doll's. Her companion, a guy in wraparound sunglasses, baggy shorts, and tank top, looked as if he could pose for a Coppertone commercial. They were leaning across the table and staring into each other's eyes—or maybe it was just their reflections in each other's sunglasses.

Annie, in her perfectly pressed slacks, gold silk blouse, high heels, and pearls, felt overdressed, out of place. Then she remembered arriving in New York all those years ago, how out of place she'd felt . . . and now look what a city slicker she'd become!

Would Emmett, too, take one look at her, and notice how she didn't belong? God, what was taking him so long? It felt like hours since her Hawaiian-shirted waiter had brought her wine. But glancing at her watch, she saw that it wasn't even three, which was when Emmett had said he'd get here. As usual, she'd gotten ahead of herself.

A shadow fell across her, and she looked up, shading her eyes. He stood with his back to the light, a stockily built man, his face hidden in shadow. But his hair . . . she'd have known him anywhere from that hair. Lit by the sun, its wiry ends glowed, the color of dying embers. Then he was bending down, warm, dry lips brushing her cheek. His smell—the familiar smell of kicked-around leather—cutting through the Sea & Ski and piña colada smells around her.

"Hey, there, Good-looking." Emmett dropped into the redwood chair opposite hers. "You beat me to it. I was gonna have vintage champagne on ice when you got here."

"I don't think anyone here is interested in anything more vintage than today's weather report." She smiled, willing herself to remain calm, but she was feeling all wrong, her heartbeat picking up, her breath in this sparkling-clean sea air growing suddenly, alarmingly short. She folded her hands about the stem of her wineglass. "Hi, Em. It's good to see you."

"You're looking prettier than ever. Success agrees with you, I can see. I read that piece on Tout de Suite in the *Times* magazine last week . . . it made you sound like a cross between Horatio Alger and Gloria Steinem. Photo didn't do you justice, though." He leaned back, hooking one leg over the other. "Congratulations, anyway. I didn't know you were opening up a store out here."

"Is that why you thought I'd be interested in Bel Jardin?"

"Naw. I'd have called if I'd heard you were moving to Borneo. I know how much that old place meant to you."

"Who said anything about moving?" She heard the defensive edge in her voice, and immediately wanted to kick herself.

Emmett seemed to stiffen, his easy smile now a degree less warm. Why had she said that? Was she trying to convince Emmett . . . or herself? But then, what if he guessed that the real reason she was sitting here might have more to do with *him* than with Bel Jardin? God, she'd die.

"Well, then, let's just say that for whatever reason, I figured you'd be interested." Emmett now was squinting out at the Santa Monica pier.

His blue eyes seemed lighter, as if in the year or so since she'd seen him they'd been bleached by constant exposure to the sun. She noticed little sun-lines radiating from their corners.

But otherwise, the same old Emmett. He hadn't gone native, thank God. In his sporty-looking blazer, he looked plain relaxed. But then, hadn't he always? She looked down, and saw those same old cowboy boots of his. More weatherbeaten, maybe, but obviously cared for, too, their old, stitched leather freshly saddle-soaped, heels newly shod. Seeing them, Annie felt an absurd happiness steal through her.

Before he could see the goofy smile she could feel imprinted on her face, she quickly bent her head, searching inside her handbag for her sunglasses. Slipping them on, she glanced at his broad, freckled hand. No wedding band. Well, that at least was something. But what did it prove? Not every married man wore a ring. And, besides, he could be engaged, or living with someone.

"I guess I ought to be congratulating you, too." She had to change the subject. "I called your office, to confirm our appointment. A very nice lady told me you were out showing a house, but would I like to speak to one of the other salespeople? God, Em, how many do you have?"

"Just two full-time," he said. "But they're on commission only, so it's not as if I have a huge overhead." He nodded. "But, yeah, I'm doing okay. I like it out here. It ain't Paris"—he gave her the full warmth of his grin. The back of her neck tightened with goose bumps—"but it sure beats El Paso."

And you . . . how are you? she longed to ask. *In love?*

But all she said was, "Well, I'm not surprised."

A waiter, she saw, was approaching.

Emmett pointed at her glass. "You want another wine?"

"No . . . thanks. I'd probably fall asleep on you. What about you—aren't you having anything?" She prayed he wouldn't order one of those California-tropical monstrosities.

"Löwenbräu," he told the ponytailed young man.

Same old Emmett. Annie felt disportionately relieved, and oddly excited.

"You're probably wondering why I dragged you all the way out to Santa Monica," Emmett said, "when Bel Jardin would've been a hop, skip, and a jump from your hotel."

"Yeah, it crossed my mind." Down on the sand, she saw, a volleyball game was in progress, teenagers in shorts and bathing suits batting a ball over a sagging net suspended between iron pipes. Mostly, what they appeared to be doing was kicking up a lot of sand. "But I don't mind. It's nice here. I'd forgotten what the sun feels like."

"My place isn't far from here," he said. "It's just down the road, as a matter of fact. I thought maybe we could stop there first. Would you like to see it?"

Annie felt something inside her catch, like a fishing line, after a long, hot morning of just trolling, suddenly pulling taut. She sipped her wine, which had grown warm. Anything, anything to make this stretched, strumming feeling go away.

"Sure," she said.

"Well, okay, then." He pulled himself to his feet. "Let's roll."

"What about your beer?"

"Forget it. Anyway, I'm driving." She watched the volleyball shoot into the air and over the deck railing, Emmett catching it easily and tossing it back, as if he were one of the players.

Right now, if he'd asked her to, Annie would've gone with him to the moon.

"It's kind of small," he said. "I've got something else lined up . . . something a lot bigger. But"—he shrugged—"it's not definite yet."

Annie stepped over the threshold into a house that somehow appeared even brighter and sunnier than the outdoors. Glass, everywhere, as if the whole house were nothing more than panes of glass held together by a few sticks of wood. Walking over to look out the floor-to-ceiling window that spanned the entire rear wall, she felt an odd, almost dizzying sensation. The house, set a bit higher than those nearby, overlooked a beach and the ocean beyond. Small? Maybe so. But with this house, it seemed like Emmett had managed to wrangle hold, not just of land, but of the sky, the sun, the sea.

"Hi, you must be Annie."

Annie turned and saw a barefooted woman walking toward her, hand outstretched. She didn't look anything at all like the smooth-skinned blond Barbie Annie had imagined Emmett being married to. For one thing, she was no youngster; she looked about Annie's age. A nice roundish face with brown eyes that crinkled up at the corners; not beautiful, but her smile was so warmly inviting she made you think she was. Her hair, the color of maple syrup, was a tousled mass of curls. She wasn't especially tanned either. She was wearing dungarees cut off at the knees, and an old shirt streaked with different colors of paint. An artist? Yes, that would fit. Come on, hadn't she known Emmett would never go for some brainless young pinup? And how good, how perfect, that he'd found a woman who looked so obviously right for him.

But her arm, as she reached out to shake the woman's hand, felt as if it weighed a ton. She could feel her heart sinking, her limbs growing heavy as if she'd suddenly found herself on a planet where the force of gravity was far stronger than the earth's.

"Hello."

Was that *her* voice, so normal-sounding, so businesslike? She forced a smile that felt stretched, insincere.

"I'm Phoebe." Annie saw her shoot a mock dirty look at Emmett. "You could have at least warned me. Gosh, will you look at me? Standing here in my scuzziest clothes." With the back of her paint-spattered hand, she pushed a stray lock of hair off her forehead, and laughed. "Oh, well, even if you *had* called I probably wouldn't have changed. When I'm in the middle of painting, I sort of lose track of everything. Including myself."

So natural, so down-to-earth. *Oh, why couldn't you be Malibu Barbie?* A bimbo Annie could have disdained and felt superior to.

"Look, can I get you something, some tea maybe?" Phoebe was looking around distractedly, as if hoping a tea tray would magically appear.

Annie looked around at the couches and chairs covered in Haitian cotton and scattered with pillows, no two alike. A Franklin stove with split logs stacked haphazardly beside it, and a big basket overflowing with pinecones. And sprouting up in the midst of it all, like some fantastic-looking piece of driftwood, an enormous burl table piled with old issues of *National Geographic* and *Architectural Digest,* seashells sugary with sand, a pair of swimming goggles, some unopened mail, a coffee mug. Yes, just the kind of place Emmett would be comfortable in.

She spotted a rather good seascape on the far wall, surf crashing against rocks. The artist—Phoebe?—had nicely caught the violence of the ocean. And right now, Annie too wanted to lunge forward and hit something, or somebody, and at the same time, wanted to melt into the floor. She had no real business being here.

Eighteen months, no letter, no call, no nothing . . . what kind of an idiot could I have been to think there might still be a chance? What on God's green earth could I have been thinking?

"I'd love to, but I'm afraid I didn't plan on staying. Maybe another time?" Annie glanced pointedly at her watch. "Emmett, I forgot to mention, I have a meeting at five-thirty . . . so we probably should get going." She actually was having dinner, but quite a bit later, with an old chum of Dolly's who used to run a designer boutique, and who might soon be managing Annie's Rodeo Drive Tout de Suite.

Phoebe shrugged—easy come, easy go.

"Ready when you are." Emmett was now digging into his pocket, jingling his keys. "Anyway, you've seen the best part—the view. Isn't it an eyeful?"

"It's fantastic." Annie again took in the view of the ocean, twinkling off in the distance, and the beach scattered with loungers and bathers. "I envy you." She realized, as she was speaking, that she was looking not at Emmett, but at Phoebe.

Yes, that's right, I want what you have. I wish more than anything that I had grabbed my chance when I had it. . . .

"Well, I *do* hope I'll see you again." Phoebe was padding alongside her as Annie walked back to the door. "Honestly, Emmett's told me so much about you. Annie, Annie, Annie, that's all I ever used to hear."

I'll just bet he has. Annie, who took him for granted and gave back only little bits and pieces. Annie, who used him as a stand-in for another man. Annie, who cheated on him.

"That would be nice," she told Phoebe at the door. "Anyway, it was nice meeting you."

"Take it easy, Bee, don't OD on turpentine," Emmett called to her, the voice of a contentedly married man.

Annie climbed back into her rented Ford. She'd know the way to Bel Jardin blindfolded, and had insisted on Emmett's leaving his BMW here. Starting the engine, she felt as if she were on fire. Face blistering, heat waves licking along her scalp, her hair crackling. She imagined herself racing along the Pacific Coast Highway—it didn't matter in which direction—windows rolled down, the wind rushing at her, cooling her. How could she pretend to be calm, to drive with Emmett only an arm's length away? Make small talk when she felt like crying out, *I was a fool not to love you, blind not to see how wonderful you are. . . .*

"You still haven't told me a thing." She was turning off Sunset Boulevard onto Bellagio, a narrower tree-lined road leading up into Bel Air. Almost there now, only minutes away. She could feel her stomach fluttering. "I mean, if they're asking the moon, I have no business even looking at it. Even if it's reasonably priced, by Bel Air standards, I probably can't afford it."

"It won't cost you a thing," Emmett said.

Annie, gliding past the gentle green swells of the Bel Air golf course, nearly slammed on her brakes. "What?"

"Just what I said."

"Em, if this is some kind of joke . . ."

"It's no joke."

"What are you saying, then?"

"Annie, I didn't want to say anything before . . . but Bel Jardin's been sold."

Now she *was* slamming on the brakes, hard enough to fishtail off the road onto the shoulder, the side of the car scraping some low shrubbery. What kind of cruel joke was this? First Emmett, now Bel Jardin . . . both of them dangled in front of her, then snatched away. She felt like screaming.

Annie's chest felt tight from holding herself in. She turned to Emmett, sitting there calmly beside her, as if this was just some minor inconvenience. And to him, of course, that's all it probably was.

"Do you mean to tell me I came all the way out here for you to tell me it's been *sold?*"

"I'm sorry, Annie." She felt his hand on her arm, and jerked away. "It just came up. This morning, as a matter of fact."

"I thought you said you had an exclusive listing?"

"I did . . . I do. But a friend of the couple who owns it made a good offer. I didn't even know about it until after the fact. Sometimes it happens that way. Listen, if it makes you feel any better, you were probably right about not being able to afford it. It went for over three million."

"Emmett"—she twisted around so she was almost facing him —"would you mind telling me what the hell we're doing here? I mean, if Bel Jardin's been sold, what's the point of me looking at it?"

"You're here, aren't you? What's the harm? Like I said, the looking's for free, and when I explained to the owners that you used to live there, they were all for letting you have a stroll around the old place. Now, are you planning on driving the rest of the way . . . or should we get out and walk?"

Emmett grinned, and she felt herself growing angry. How could you go from one minute wanting to kiss a man . . . to the next minute wanting to sock him?

"I ought to let *you* walk . . . all the way back to Santa Monica."

"I nearly forgot . . . that temper of yours." Emmett grinned. "Hell, Cobb, once you got a notion into your head, you always did like to hang on to it."

"As if I'd have gotten anywhere in this world if I hadn't!"

Annie, oddly, was starting to feel better, her chest opening up, letting air into her lungs. Stronger, too, as if she were actually climbing up to Bel Jardin on foot, blood pumping, heart racing.

"Who says," he asked gently, "there's anything wrong with the way you are?"

"*I* do! Maybe I just should've been happy with what I had. Maybe I was a damned idiot not to see what was right in front of me the whole time." A pressure was building behind her eyes, in her nose. "Look where it's gotten me!"

"Are we still talking about Bel Jardin here?" He spoke quietly, yet his voice seemed to echo inside her head.

"No," she said sharply, "we're not." With a wrench of the steering wheel, she turned the car back onto the road, knowing that if she didn't get going, get *moving,* she'd probably do something dumb like telling a married man she was in love with him.

Then she was winding her way up Chantilly Drive, and there, gliding out from behind a tall oleander hedge, was Bel Jardin. Its curved iron gates wide open, the house's pink façade, at the end of the long crushed-shell drive lined with steeple-high palms, glowing in the setting sun. Pink? Had they really painted Bel Jardin pink? Oh dear, maybe coming here wasn't such a good idea.

But, oh, how good to see it! She could feel her annoyance at Emmett fading, and she was gripped by an excitement that had nothing to do with whether or not she could *buy* Bel Jardin. It was, she realized, hers already. In her heart, Bel Jardin would always be hers.

Pulling to a stop in the turnabout at the end of the drive, Annie got out and pulled in a deep breath. Lemon blossoms, oh yes, she could smell them. And jasmine. And look how the bougainvillea had climbed up around the porch, right up to the roof almost. In front, along the flagstone path leading to the porch, no roses . . . peonies, with blossoms the size of small cabbages, pink, crimson, white. And low clumps of alyssum and violets. She stared at the heavy, carved Spanish-looking door beckoning to her from under the porch eaves, and felt her heart turn over in her chest.

Home. She was home.

All she had to do was walk up and pull the iron latch . . . and then she would be inside.

Annie turned to Emmett, who stood alongside her, asking, "Are they home? The . . . what did you say their name was . . . Baxters?"

"No. But I have the keys. Want to go in?"

"You make it sound so easy . . . just walking in . . . just like that. Oh, Em, I don't know, it feels sort of . . . well, like cheating."

"You mean because they aren't here?"

"No, it's me. Maybe I'd be cheating myself. Seeing it the way it is instead of the way I remember it."

"Why don't you describe it to me, while we take a look around? Who knows, maybe the new owner would like a few decorating suggestions."

"Why should he?"

"I don't know . . . why don't you ask him?" Emmett draped his arm about her shoulders. "He's standing right here."

Annie stepped away, her knees buckling a little, staring at him as if she were seeing something that was, well, maybe not quite real. A dream. Or maybe a nightmare. She wasn't sure which. Was Emmett doing this to taunt her . . . to get back at her for how she'd treated him before? Or was he saying that . . . that . . . oh, no, but that couldn't be . . .

"You?" she gasped. "*You* bought Bel Jardin. But why? Why bring me all the way out here?"

Emmett's blue eyes, in the fading light, seemed to blaze with an almost unnatural brightness, as ageless somehow as stars in the heavens. A mild breeze was blowing his hair up in front into that funny cowlick, which she had a strong urge to smooth down.

"Because I'm not doing as well as you think I am. Oh yeah, businesswise things are going okay. It's *you* I'm talking about, Annie Cobb, your own sweet, stubborn self. For almost two years I've been trying to get you out from under my skin, and I haven't had a helluva lot of luck. When this listing more or less fell into my lap, I sort of figured it was some kind of fate . . . like maybe if I bought it, owning Bel Jardin would be like having a part of you. And then, after I talked with Laurey—"

"You called Laurey? Why?"

"Gun-shy, I guess." He shrugged. "I just didn't want to be hurt again, not a direct hit anyway. It was your own loving sister who gave me the scoop on you."

"What did she say?"

"That you weren't married. And that you'd once told her, not too long ago, that not marrying me was the biggest mistake you ever made. So I figured, well, maybe, you'd be interested in sharing Bel Jardin with a reformed drifter like me."

"What about your wife?" she asked.

His forehead crinkled in confusion, then a slow, amused smile spread across his face. "Phoebe? Well, I don't blame you for thinking that. In fact, there was a time . . ." He shrugged. "But that was a while back. Now we're just friends. I let her use the extra bedroom as a studio." He stepped forward and cupped Annie's chin in his big, warm hand. "It's the light. She says the light's better for her painting. All those windows." He was bending to kiss her, but she drew back slightly.

"You're not still . . ."

"Sleeping with her?" He laughed. "Naw, we're too good of friends now to mess around with that. 'Sides, she's got a boyfriend now. Nice fella. We hang out together sometimes, shoot a little pool down at Charlie's, play cards."

"That's about the nicest thing you've ever said to me." Tears filled her eyes, and her vision blurred. Her relief and joy were so vast she could not have put them into words. "Now, will you shut up and kiss me."

He did. A kiss that made her remember everything good she had ever longed for in her entire life.

A sweet, golden warmth filled her. Rapture. Just a word until now . . . a thing she'd heard about, but never experienced. A state of ecstasy enjoyed by religious zealots, drunken poets, and heroines in romance novels. But . . . there could be no other way to describe this feeling . . . this dazed lightness, this heart-struck bliss. Yes, rapture.

In her mind, she heard Dearie say, *Grab it, kiddo . . . a second chance like this one may never come your way again. . . .*

"Let's go inside," Annie said, pulling back and taking Emmett's hand. "And I'll show you where we'll put my mother's Oscar."